# Wavecrest

It's more than just a coming of age story

## John B. Nelson

# Copyright

--------------------------------------------------

Publisher: John B. Nelson, P.O. Box 69, Bradford, PA, 16701
ISBN: 979-8-218-52109-7
Library of Congress Control Number: 2024921699

# Acknowledgement

----------------------------------------------------------------

To my wife, Sandra. Words cannot fully express the depth of my gratitude for your unwavering support throughout this novel-writing journey. You have been my rock, my confidante, and my most ardent supporter.

Your emotional investment in this story matched my own, as you became just as attached to the characters as I did. Our countless discussions and brainstorming sessions breathed life into the narrative, making each character as real and vibrant as they are today.

Your dedication to this project went far beyond emotional support. Your meticulous proofreading and insightful feedback were invaluable, shaping and refining the story in ways I could never have achieved alone. You didn't just help me write a book; you helped me create a world.

Sandra, you've been more than a partner in this process—you've been a collaborator, a muse, and an inspiration. This novel is as much a product of your love and support as it is of my writing. Thank you for believing in me, for pushing me forward, and for being an integral part of this incredible journey.

# Prologue

The picturesque coastal town of Wavecrest, California, perched on the edge of the Pacific Ocean, stirred with electrifying energy as the summer months arrived. It transformed into a vibrant paradise where sun-drenched days and moonlit nights became the backdrop for unforgettable adventures and cherished memories. This was where dreams took shape, and the promise of love hung in the air like a sweet, intoxicating fragrance.

The boardwalk, a bustling hub of activity, stretched along the coastline, creating a colorful tapestry of sights and sounds. Young adults and teenagers flocked to this beach town, seeking summer freedom and yearning for exhilarating experiences. Laughter, music, and animated chatter filled the air, infusing every moment with an infectious spirit.

The beaches became a spectacle to behold, adorned with lively beach umbrellas, vibrant towels, and an array of beach toys and equipment. The crystal clear waters of the Pacific enticed both locals and tourists, inviting them to dive into the joys of swimming, surfing, and paddleboarding. It was a playground where the rhythmic symphony of crashing waves intertwined with the laughter and excitement of beachgoers.

As the sun reached its peak, the boardwalk transformed into a culinary paradise. Aromatic scents of grilled seafood, freshly churned ice cream, and sizzling street food wafted through the air, tantalizing the senses of passersby. Crowds gathered around food vendors, savoring delectable treats while relishing the warmth of the summer breeze.

The fashion of the season was on full display as well. Girls sauntered along the boardwalk in stylish bikinis, their sun-kissed skin radiating under the summer sun. Boys sported vibrant bathing shorts, injecting splashes of color and playfulness into the town's lively ambiance. Everywhere one looked, there was a mesmerizing kaleidoscope of beach fashion and summer styles.

As the day gracefully transitioned into evening, a new enchantment descended upon the town. The boardwalk was adorned with twinkling lights, casting a magical glow illuminating the surroundings. Music permeated the air as street performers captivated audiences with their talents, drawing crowds to their awe-inspiring performances. The night became an invitation to dance, revel in the sand's warmth beneath bare feet, and create indelible memories that would endure a lifetime.

In the heart of this summer paradise, two teenage girls, Jessica Reese and Fawn Gaddesden, stood on the precipice of a thrilling summer. Best friends since kindergarten, they had woven a bond of friendship that had withstood the test of time, growing stronger with each passing year. Having just tossed their graduation caps into the air, they eagerly embraced the world with open arms, their dreams shimmering like sunlit waves.

# Chapter 1

-------------------------------------------------------

Just four blocks from the lively atmosphere of Wavecrest's boardwalk, eighteen-year-old Fawn Gaddesden lounged on her black leather sofa in the living room of her home at 501 Oceanside Ave. She wore a heather gray crop top and frayed denim shorts that hugged her frame. Her long blonde hair cascaded over her shoulders and shimmered in the sunlight streaming through the picture window, illuminating the essence of a young woman on the cusp of adulthood.

Across from her, seventeen-year-old Jessica Reese perched herself on the coffee table, her petite frame adorned in a white tank top tucked into cuffed shorts. Her long brown hair flowed around her shoulders, adding to the vibrancy of her youthful appearance. She watched as Fawn painted delicate butterflies on her nails, her admiration for her friend's artistry evident in her expressive eyes.

Framed memories graced the living room's walls, capturing Fawn's journey from a toothy-grinned child to a confident artist. Among these were snapshots of her with Jessica, whose smaller stature sharply contrasted with Fawn's taller frame. Despite her size, Jessica truly embodied the adage 'good things come in small packages' with her formidable presence. Their closeness was evident, their contrasting heights symbolizing the milestones of a friendship deep in strength and rich in history.

As Jessica watched the meticulous strokes of Fawn's brush, she couldn't help but marvel at her friend's talent for painting tiny objects with such precision.

"Fawn, your nail art is amazing," she expressed, her voice imbued with awe. Fawn's ability to transform a simple blank nail into a vibrant canvas was her signature, her passion for each nuanced detail evident in every delicate wing she painted.

With a soft, lighthearted laugh, Fawn replied, "Aw, Jess, that's so sweet of you to say." Her fingers moved with the precision of an artist, the joy in her craft reflected in the curve of her smile. "But honestly, your nails are naturally pretty. I just enjoy painting them."

Their laughter and conversations filled the room, echoing the lively buzz from the streets of Wavecrest. With each brushstroke, Fawn transferred a piece of her soul onto Jessica's nails—a ritual that underscored their deep connection. The air, laden with the scent of the ocean and the promise of summer adventures, enveloped them, a testament to their shared history and the freedom that lay just beyond Fawn's front door.

Gazing at the butterflies on her nails, a poignant and bittersweet wave of nostalgia struck Jessica. "I can't believe how fast time has gone by," she mused, memories vivid as if from yesterday. "It doesn't seem that long ago when we were little and playing dress-up."

Fawn paused, allowing the nail brush to hover mid-air as she contemplated Jessica's words. "I know what you mean," she agreed, her smile softening into a reflective gaze. "It's crazy, but I'm grateful for all the memories we made together."

The room seemed to pause, absorbing the weight of their reminiscence. Jessica's eyes glittered with playful mischief, a stark contrast to the poignancy of the moment.

"Remember when we hid that tiny speaker in Mr. Clark's bookshelf?" she began, her voice bridging the gap to their youthful pranks. "The look on his face when we played those cat meows was priceless. He must have checked every corner of the room for that cat."

Laughter erupted between them, dissolving any lingering tension. Fawn's glee was infectious as she continued the trip down memory lane. "And how we all tried to keep a straight face, only to burst out laughing when he called out, 'Here, Kitty Kitty.'"

"Oh my God, that was so funny," Jessica agreed, her laughter a testament to the joy of those moments.

As Fawn resumed her meticulous work, a smirk played on her lips at another memory. "How about the time we hid Marty Cosser's backpack under Mr. Bennett's desk? The whole time, Marty didn't even know it was missing, and then, right as the bell was about to ring, Mr. Bennett pulled it out with this puzzled expression, asking the class whose it was."

Once again, their laughter filled the room, a sweet sound that echoed off the walls. But as the laughter died down, an encompassing silence took its place, marking the journey from their playful childhood to the cusp of adulthood.

"We sure had our moments of mischief, didn't we?" Fawn mused, her smile a tender homage to their days of innocent rebellion.

The mirth of shared stories faded as a shadow of realization passed over Jessica's face, a subtle shift Fawn caught with an artist's keen perception. "You know, once college starts, everything will change," Jessica's voice wavered, laden with the weight of a future fast approaching. "We'll be in different cities, starting a new life." There was a pause, a beat of silence that seemed to stretch on, filled with the significance of her admission. "Everything is going to be so different, Fawn." The air between them was charged with the truth of her words, and time stood still for a moment.

Jessica's eyes, usually mirroring a quiet reserve, now flickered with doubt and fear. She was the quieter one, the thinker, Fawn the doer, the painter of their duo's bold strokes. They were a complementary pair, and the possibility of distance was an unwelcome intrusion into the sanctity of their friendship.

Fawn set the nail polish aside, a gesture that said she was there, fully present for her best friend. "I know, Jess," she replied, her voice a mirror of Jessica's concerns, yet steady and reassuring. They had been each other's constants in a constantly changing world.

The fear of starting in a new school, once just whispered shadows in the back of Jessica's mind, now took form in her words. "Just thinking about walking into my classes and not knowing anyone, freaks me out. And what if my classes are total nightmares? Or even worse, what if I don't fit in?" Her fingers nervously played with the hem of her top, betraying her anxiety.

Fawn reached out, her hand clasping Jessica's in a gesture that conveyed her support. "Jess," she said gently, "you're way tougher than you give yourself credit for. Remember all those times you were like, 'No way, I can't do this,' and then you totally did? You're stronger than any challenge you face." She paused for a second, her gaze softening with a reassuring smile. "And hey, I'll only be a phone call away if you need a little bit of encouragement."

Fawn's attempt at comfort was sincere, although her heart mirrored Jessica's fears. She let out a heavy sigh, one that seemed to carry all her own doubts. "But you know what? I'm nervous, too. I've never been to Boston, and I worry about getting lost or not finding my way to my classes." For a moment, the vulnerability she usually masked with her confident persona was visible.

Jessica's raw emotions and shimmering eyes spoke to the dread that had taken root in their conversation. "You know what scares me the most? Us being apart for the first time. What if we lose touch or drift apart?" The fear of change, of losing each other to the inexorable march of time, loomed over her like an unspoken prophecy.

Yet, Fawn's response was quick and tender. "Aw, don't be silly, Jess. That will never happen. You're my rock, my soul sister. That will never change." Her words were a soft caress, meant to heal and reassure as much as words could. She paused, her emotions steadying before she added with conviction. "We'll keep in touch and see each other during our breaks." It was a promise, spoken with the sincerity that only true friendship can muster.

Jessica managed a small, brave smile, though the sadness still lingered. "I know. I'm just going to miss seeing you every day. I wish we were going to UCSB like we originally planned," she confessed, the dream of their shared future at their neighboring college a bittersweet tang amidst the excitement of new beginnings.

The silence returned, a specter of the future they had once envisioned together. UCSB had been the dream, the shared goal etched into their upbringing blueprint. Through countless conversations and detailed plans, the girls had painted a picture of college days spent under the familiar California sun, a continuation of their inseparable journey.

Fawn's voice, tinged with the wistfulness of abandoned plans, broke through their reflections. "I remember how we talked about going to UCSB. It was the perfect choice at the time," she reminisced, the memory hanging between them like a soft echo. Then, with a shift in her tone, she bridged the gap between past aspirations and present realities. "But when I heard about the opportunities in Boston, it felt like destiny calling, you know?"

Jessica's response was of quiet support, a mirror to their years of unwavering friendship. "I know. You've always been the brave one, Fawn. Always looking for new adventures. I've always admired that about you," she said, her pride in Fawn's courage shining through the mist in her eyes.

Fawn offered a gentle smile, touched by Jessica's words. "Aw, hearing you say that makes me feel even more certain about Boston," she said, her eyes gleaming with a mixture of gratitude and renewed conviction.

She paused for a moment, lost in the memory of the excitement that coursed through her when she received her acceptance at the art school. "You know, when I got that letter—it was like a sign. Like it was meant to be," she affirmed, her voice carrying a mix of excitement and certainty about her future in the arts, a future that now beckoned her onward with irresistible allure.

Jessica voiced her uncertainty with a frustrated edge, familiar to those facing life's crossroads. "Well, unlike you or Michelle or Krista," she began, an edge of irritation creeping into her tone. "I don't have a clue as to what I want to do with my life. If it were up to me, I wouldn't even be going to college." Her words fell, exposing the turmoil within, the pressure of looming decisions she felt unprepared to make.

With a hint of defiance that spoke of her struggle against the expectations of others, she continued, "Yet everyone is telling me I've got to spread my wings and give college a try." Jessica's annoyance stood in sharp contrast to Fawn's gentle optimism, underscoring the starkly different paths they found themselves on as they looked toward their futures.

Fawn considered Jessica's words; her dreams had always had a direction, unlike Jessica's undetermined path. "Jess, college is an opportunity. Trust me, you'll figure it out. Just like I will. We'll both find our way," she said, her optimism a steady flame in the dimming light of their teenage certainty.

Jessica's reply carried a whisper of hope through the fear of the unknown. "I know," she admitted. "That's why I chose Austin when you decided on Boston. That way, I would still be close to my family because Aunt Veronica and Uncle Gary live not too far." It was a decision made with both heart and head, a compromise between new horizons and the comfort of family proximity.

In that shared space, as sunlight waned into the warmth of the afternoon, the two friends sat, enveloped by the earnestness of their conversation. Their future was uncertain, with untraveled paths ahead, yet their friendship stood firm, a guiding light into the next chapters of their lives.

Fawn's sigh was deep and full of contemplation as her eyes settled on her graduation photo on the wall. It served as a fresh reminder that just two days ago, they had been clad in their caps and gowns, with their futures as wide open as the ocean beside their town. She mused aloud, "It's crazy how quickly things change. One moment, we're planning our future together; the next, we're each headed in different directions."

Absorbing the weight of her own words, she paused, momentarily overwhelmed by the swift pace of change. Then, turning back to Jessica, she found resolve in her friend's familiar gaze.

"But Jess," she said, her voice soft but filled with conviction. "When we do go off to college, just know we'll be carrying a part of each other with us. No matter where we end up, that connection... it stays."

Jessica managed to smile, though it didn't quite reach her eyes. "I know. It's just going to be hard to say goodbye," she admitted, the notion of parting clearly weighing on her.

Fawn leaned toward her best friend, her expression etched with determination. "We're not going to say goodbye," she said, her voice carrying the strength of their years of friendship. "We won't be apart for that long. Christmas break will be here before you know it, and we'll both be home, catching up and sharing college stories."

The hint of hope that sparked in Jessica's eyes was enough to bolster Fawn's own spirits. She took a moment to gather her thoughts, then spoke with renewed vigor. "And next summer? We'll be right back here after finishing our first year in college, just like always."

Their eyes met, silently conveying a mutual understanding of their shared fears and unspoken courage. Recognizing the gratitude and lingering anxiety in Jessica's innocent blue eyes, Fawn leaned in, resting her hands on her shoulders. Drawing a quiet breath, she offered the familiar words that had always been Jessica's beacon through uncertain times.

"You got this, Jess," Fawn whispered, infusing the words with the strength and conviction that had become their shared anthem. Those words, simple yet profound, had been a source of encouragement for her, a reminder of her inherent bravery in the face of adversity.

Jessica's breath trembled as she spoke of her own fears. "Okay. Just promise you won't find a new BFF and forget about me." Her plea echoed the vulnerability of every friendship tested by distance.

Fawn's reply was immediate, her assurance unwavering. "I promise! We'll always be besties, Jess. Forever and ever." The words were a gentle vow, a reaffirmation of their enduring connection.

"Forever and ever," Jessica echoed, allowing the promise to soothe her uneasy heart.

With a playful glint returning to her eyes, Fawn then sparked a new idea that spoke of adventures yet to come. "Hey, Jess. Let's make a pact. Let's make this summer unforgettable. A summer we'll always look back on, no matter where we are."

Jessica's voice rose with excitement, her earlier apprehensions giving way to the thrill of plans being made. "Absolutely! Let's make this the best summer ever!"

Fawn's enthusiasm matched Jessica's as she suggested, "Exactly! And what better way to start our summer than going to the beach party Sunday night." The future was uncertain, but the promise of shared joy was a solid anchor.

Their conversation turned to summer plans, each idea another brushstroke on their canvas of adventures. Fawn resumed the delicate task of painting Jessica's nails, the butterflies taking wing as if to celebrate the pact they'd just made.

And so, in that cozy living room, with painted nails and hearts full of summer dreams, they basked in the glow of their last carefree summer, cherishing the beauty of this bitter-sweet moment. With each butterfly that emerged on Jessica's nails, a testament to their enduring friendship was sealed, an unspoken agreement that no distance would diminish their bond.

# Chapter 2

----------------------------------------------------------

Under the broad expanse of the Sunday afternoon sky, the beach stretched before Jessica and Fawn. It had been six days since the caps had flown and tassels turned at their high school graduation, marking both an end and a beginning. The sun warmed their backs, its steadfast glow acknowledging time's passage. As they laid their blankets upon the fine sun-bleached sand, the soft rhythmic symphony of the waves provided a soothing backdrop, punctuated by the occasional cry of seagulls and the murmur of distant laughter, framing their newfound freedom in a serene, rhythmic cadence.

Jessica's blue and flowered swimsuit was a splash of vibrancy against the sandy hues, its petals, and patterns a testament to her bright, lively spirit. Beside her, Fawn's sleek black bikini made a bold statement amidst the color of the beach, complementing her free-spirited boldness. Lying on her stomach, Fawn was the picture of relaxation, her sun-kissed skin glistening under the summer sun, while Jessica sat upright, her legs crossed, gazing over the beach as an amused observer in search of intriguing distractions.

The silver anklet on Fawn's ankle sparkled in the sunlight, its history a sharp contrast to the beach's carefree vibe. Noticing the gleam of silver on Fawn's ankle, Jessica's expression shifted to one of recognition and bewilderment.

"Isn't that the bracelet Jerry gave you?" she asked, her tone rising with surprise at seeing the token from a romance that had blossomed in innocence but ended in heartbreak.

Fawn glanced at the anklet, each charm whispering memories of Jerry Cranmer. Their relationship, once a vivid tapestry of youthful passion and pain, had softened in her memory.

"No real reason," she said with a dismissive shrug, downplaying the weight of their past like a wave receding from the shore. "I just like how it looks." Her voice carried a faint echo of a time when Jerry's name held meaning, but now, it merely served as a footnote to an accessory worn without the burden of sentiment.

Jessica laughed, the sound light and melodious, her amusement and admiration mingling at Fawn's dismissive shrug. She knew the sting of betrayal Fawn had endured, yet here she was, looking at the anklet with detached appreciation. "You always were the strongest of us," Jessica thought, her heart swelling with pride at Fawn's resilience, her spirit unburdened despite the shadows of the past.

She turned her attention back to the ocean, where boys frolicking in the surf mirrored the summer's carefree laughter, blending with the steady roar of the waves. It was a moment that captured the fleeting joy summer promised, a pleasure they intended to grasp in the dwindling days before adulthood claimed them.

Her eyes meandered along the shoreline until it settled on a figure standing next to a lifeguard stand. Dressed in a white muscle shirt that hugged his solid athletic build and colorful shorts, he stood out against the backdrop of sunbathers and swimmers. His surfboard, a silent testament to his love for the waves, leaned against the stand as if taking a brief respite under his watchful eye.

The boy's tanned skin glowed under the afternoon sun, a stark canvas for his wavy blonde hair, which seemed to capture the golden hues of the beach. Even behind the dark shades that shielded his eyes, an unmistakable sense of a warm, genuine spirit emanated from him. Jessica could almost see the kindness in his eyes, a reflection of the soul of someone who cared deeply and lived fiercely—a traveler, perhaps, who had found his way to the shores of Wavecrest.

"God, Fawn, just look at him," Jessica whispered, her voice heavy with awe. Her excitement was infectious, drawing Fawn in as she leaned closer.

Fawn's eyes fluttered open, drawn by the urgency in Jessica's voice. "What? Who?" The question was out before her eyes found the answer, focusing on the boy with the surfboard.

A spark of recognition lit her eyes, a playful amusement dancing in them as she noticed the direction of Jessica's captivated stare. "Oh, Jessica!" she teased, her words tinged with the warmth of their history of similar moments.

A playful flush rose on Jessica's cheeks as she stood her ground. "Oh, forget it. You're just jealous I found him first," she shot back, the words a playful joust in their ongoing game of friendly rivalry.

Fawn playfully replied, "Jealous? Really? Who's the one drooling over some random surfer?" Her tone might have been teasing, but the look she shot back at the boy was tinged with genuine curiosity.

Jessica's laughter was clear and bright as she shook her head with playful frustration. "Hey, he's not random," she defended. "He's hot!" Her voice lowered, taking on a conspiratorial tone. "I bet you anything he surfs really well."

Fawn's roll of the eyes was affectionate, her smile unwavering. Jessica's penchant for attractive boys was familiar, but it always brought a sense of fresh delight to their interactions.

As the laughter and light-hearted jibes danced between them, Jessica's attention remained focused on the lone figure by the lifeguard stand while Fawn, ever content in the here and now, reclined once more on her beach blanket. Together, they savored the simple joy of their friendship and the endless potential of a summer's day.

The mid-June sun blazed over Wavecrest, a scorching presence in the seaside sky. Below, Jessica felt its weight as a tangible reminder of the day's unspoken promise, the heat amplifying the magnetic pull of the mysterious boy by the lifeguard stand. His blonde, wavy hair was tousled by the sea breeze, and his athletic frame, poised for action, exuded an adventurous spirit that tugged at Jessica's curiosity.

Charged with 'what ifs,' her fascination was a live wire of possibility, yet hesitation wrapped around her like a familiar shroud. It was an internal tug-of-war between her desire to reach out and her instinctive retreat into her safe shell.

"Oh, Fawn," Jessica murmured, her voice heavy with wistful yearning. Her longing to bridge the gap was palpable, yet she remained tethered to her spot, a silent bystander to her own wishes.

Fawn, ever observant, detected the longing in Jessica's voice. Turning with a knowing gleam in her eyes, she teased, "Oh no, you don't! You don't get to just sit here and pine! Not this time. You need to go over there and talk to him."

Jessica's reaction was an immediate protest, a reflex to protect herself from Fawn's bold suggestion. "What?! No, I can't," she stammered, her eyes darting away as if to escape the idea.

But Fawn was steadfast, her encouragement a solid anchor like the sand beneath them. "Jess, you'll never know if you don't try," she coaxed, her voice a lighthouse guiding Jessica through the fog of her doubts.

She then painted memories with her words, drawing from a well of past triumphs they shared: the art gallery where Jessica's admiration for someone led to a new friendship, and the Halloween dance where she'd confronted her shyness and turned it into conversation.

With each memory Fawn recounted, Jessica's posture straightened, her smile became less tentative, and the edges of her reserve softened by the reminder of previous bravery.

"You're right," she admitted, her voice steadier now, the glimmer in her eyes reflecting a growing resolve.

Jessica stood, a mix of hesitation and hope painting her movements. A last glance at Fawn brought a wave of silent encouragement, visible in the expectant light of her friend's eyes. With each step toward the lifeguard stand, her heart played a tense yet excited rhythm, a symphony of possibilities set in motion.

The rich tapestry of their shared history lifted her spirit, transforming each step into a stride closer to the unknown. The gap between her and the boy visibly narrowed, diminishing the distance not only on the sand beneath her feet but also in the journey from the girl she was to the woman she was becoming. It was their friendship—a dynamic dance of encouragement and daring—that nudged her forward, inching her toward the brink of a new connection.

Jessica's heart raced as she neared the figure by the lifeguard stand, each step a battle between her innate shyness and the pull of her burgeoning curiosity. Leaning against the wooden post, the surfboard provided an ideal starting point for dialogue—a conversation waiting to happen.

Immersed in the sea's rhythm, the boy felt her presence and turned, his smile unfurling like a sail in the wind. The warmth in his expression was a beacon, transforming Jessica's hesitant steps into a walk of emerging confidence.

"Nice surfboard," Jessica said, her voice carrying across the conversational gap with a nervous yet sincere note in her tone.

"Thanks," he replied, his smile a clear reflection of his friendly demeanor. "Do you surf?" His voice had a genuine lilt of interest that invited conversation, not just a polite exchange.

Jessica's laugh was light, a clear chime amidst the ambient sounds of the beach. "I tried once, but it didn't go well," she admitted, a hint of self-deprecation in her humor.

He chuckled and slid his shades off, revealing his eyes with the theatrical flair of uncovering art. "Maybe you didn't have the right teacher." His words were playful, edged with a challenge.

His bright blue eyes sparked an exhilarating thrill in Jessica, as though her heart had stumbled upon a new beat within his gaze. She responded with a nervous giggle, her eyes alight with amusement and a touch of shyness. "Nah, I'm just a hopeless case. I think I'll just stick to the beach," she quipped, raising her sunglasses in a playful admission of her aquatic shortcomings.

As their eyes locked, the world around them seemed to pause, the air charged with an electric anticipation. A ripple of awareness spread outward, as if the very fabric of the beach itself responded to their gaze. Between them, an unspoken connection took form, visible in the lingering hold of their eyes, the slight parting of lips, and the almost imperceptible lean forward. They stood there, enveloped in a silence that was anything but empty.

As thoughts of the evening's festivities sparked in Jessica's mind, she found the courage to speak again. "Do you know about the beach party tonight?" she asked, her voice a soft blend of hope and hesitation.

"Sure do. Are you going?" he asked, his tone light, friendly, maybe even hopeful.

"Uh-huh. Maybe I'll see you there," Jessica said, her shyness making a comeback, a subtle undertone in the melody of their conversation.

"I hope so," he said, his grin taking on a flirtatious quality, affirming the impact of their brief encounter.

Not wanting to tarnish the moment with more awkwardness, Jessica decided to retreat.

"Well, I gotta go."

"Yeah, me too," he replied, his grin lingering, though shadowed by the surf's sullen mood. "The ocean doesn't seem to be in a playful mood today."

With a parting wave, Jessica began her retreat, the soft sand a witness to the tentative dance they had just shared. Carrying the imprint of his smile and their unspoken connection, she started her walk back to where Fawn waited, the magic of the moment enveloping her, undeniable and vivid.

As she continued her way back, a victorious spring buoyed each step, weaving through the beach's laughter and languor. From a distance, Fawn's eyes found Jessica, magnetized by the silent currents of their deep-seated friendship. The anticipation in her eyes served as a beacon, guiding Jessica the rest of the way.

As she settled back onto the blanket, a blush of excitement painted Jessica's cheeks. Fawn propped herself up, her eyes alight with anticipation. "Well? Did you talk to him?" Her question crackled in the air, charged with the thrill of imminent confessions.

The words tumbled from Jessica in a vivacious stream. "I did—and I think I'm in love!" The words sparkled in Jessica's eyes, her smile radiating the dreamy glow of newfound affection.

Fawn's reaction was immediate, her laughter a mixture of disbelief and delight. "Seriously, Jess? Love at first chat?" Fawn teased, her affection for Jessica audible beneath her playful skepticism.

But Jessica stood firm, her resolve ricocheting back to Fawn. "I'm serious, Fawn," she insisted, fervor in her tone. "I never felt this way before." The sincerity of her declaration was undeniable, as clear as the bright day surrounding them.

Fawn's heart swelled at Jessica's earnestness; such an admission was rare for her usually reserved friend. She couldn't resist prodding further. "So, what's his name?"

The question loomed, and Jessica's bubble of infatuation popped at that moment. A look of dismay painted her face as she realized her oversight. "I... I don't know," Jessica confessed, the tune of her voice tinged with annoyance. "I forgot to ask."

Fawn laughed again, her voice rich with empathy for Jessica's nervous bravery. "Aw, Jess, you silly girl," she chided gently, her amusement mingling with pride.

Jessica's playful slap on Fawn's arm was light, but underscored by her attempt to shrug off the embarrassment with humor. "Well, I was too captivated by his eyes, so give me a break."

Fawn's response was a bubbly giggle. "Okay, okay. Just don't forget to ask him his name if you see him at the party tonight," she teased.

Jessica's smile was a promise. "Oh, don't worry. I won't forget this time."

Lounging on their blankets, the girls engaged in a conversation that flowed as naturally as the tide, brimming with excitement for the evening ahead. They laughed and spoke with anticipation, enveloped in the freedom and sweet promise of the coming night—a night aglow with the mystery of the unknown and the unbridled joy of summer's youthful chapter.

As the afternoon waned into the late hours of daylight, the girls decided to call it a day at the beach. They shook out their blankets, folding them in a practiced rhythm, and stuffed them into their bag with the efficiency of seasoned beachgoers. With the weight of the bag slung over her shoulder, Jessica led the way to the boardwalk, leaving a trail of footprints in the sand behind them.

The boardwalk hummed with the activity of the post-beach crowd. Cyclists whizzed past, their tires buzzing against the wooden planks, while street musicians filled the air with the strumming of guitars and the soulful licks of harmonicas. Saltwater mingled with the sweet scents from ice cream parlors and the savory aroma of grilled seafood from open restaurants and food stands. The girls moved through this tapestry of sensations; their bare feet comfortable on the warm boards that had absorbed the sun's heat throughout the day.

"Can you believe we've been coming here since we were no higher than this railing?" Fawn mused aloud, her hand grazing the sun-warmed wood as they walked.

Jessica laughed, "And yet, we still find a new adventure every time." Her eyes twinkled with the reflection of the sun's golden light, mirroring the ocean's sparkle.

As they approached the ramp leading to the street, they were well aware of their home's proximity to this slice of paradise. "Two blocks to my house, two more to yours," Jessica said, her voice tinged with appreciation. "We're pretty lucky, aren't we?"

"The luckiest," Fawn agreed with a grin as she waved to a group of friends passing by.

They continued their stroll, the familiarity of the route grounding them in a shared history that was soon to branch into separate journeys. For now, they cherished their close-knit world: the beach, home, and the heart of Wavecrest's social buzz—the simple comforts they held dear.

Fawn nudged Jessica with her shoulder, a teasing sparkle in her eyes. "Think you'll talk to beach boy at the party?"

Jessica's response was a mix of nerves and excitement. "I'll need a pep talk first," she admitted, already dreading and anticipating the evening's possibilities.

"Don't worry, I've got your back. Let's get some dinner in you, and you'll be ready to charm the entire beach," Fawn declared with the confidence of a general rallying her troops. With that, they stepped off the ramp and onto the street leading them home, their laughter echoing behind them.

As they stepped through the front door of 827 Driftwood Drive, the warmth of the Reese household enveloped Jessica and Fawn. In the kitchen, Teresa Reese gracefully tossed a salad at the counter. Sunlight spilled through the window, catching her brown hair in a soft glow that echoed the warmth in her gray-blue eyes. Her slender figure moved with refined elegance, each motion a testament to her career as a seasoned beautician, as evidenced by her manicured nails catching the ambient light.

"Did you have a nice time at the beach?" Teresa's voice was the auditory equivalent of a warm embrace, inviting the girls to share the joys of their day.

"It was alright," Jessica replied, striving for an even tone and a calm demeanor to hide the day's heart-fluttering adventures.

Fawn, leaning against the kitchen counter with an eyebrow raised in playful collusion, countered, "It was more than okay from what I saw." Her tone was laced with mischief. "Jess here definitely caught some attention at the beach today."

Jessica playfully swatted at Fawn, their familiar banter resounding through the kitchen as she protested, "Shut up, Fawn!"

Teresa giggled, well-acquainted with the bickering that brought life and love to the room. She watched the girls with a lightness in her heart, knowing their banter was a melody of a long-standing friendship.

As the laughter subsided, Jessica's thoughts turned to her father. "Where's Daddy?" she asked, placing the beach bag on a chair.

As if on cue, Tom Reese strode through the back door. He entered the kitchen with a posture softened from military to domestic, his broad shoulders relaxed. His bright blue eyes, a family trait passed to Jessica, scanned the room with a fondness reserved for family.

"Here I am," he announced, his voice carrying the resonant timbre of home and the comfort of years.

Tom washed his hands at the kitchen sink, his every movement speaking of a disciplined life while his gentle manner unveiled the warmth underneath. Teresa turned to Fawn with a mother's consideration. "Are you staying for dinner, sweetie?"

Fawn shook her head, her blonde hair catching the light like spun gold. "No thanks, Mama," she said with a warmth that echoed years of shared meals and memories. "I've got to get ready for the party tonight."

As he dried his hands, Tom looked at the girls with a mock sternness that belied the sparkle in his eyes. "What? Another party? Isn't this a school night?" he teased, a playful challenge in his voice.

Laughter filled the room again, a testament to their shared humor and comfort. "Uh, no, Dad. We graduated almost a week ago. Duh!" Jessica said, rolling her eyes in the affectionate way one does with loved ones who've missed the memo.

"Oh, that's right," Tom chuckled, playing along with the charade, scratching his head in a show of forgetfulness that only drew more giggles from the girls.

As he moved toward the living room, Tom rested his hands on each girl's shoulder, a silent language of love and jest. "You two better behave yourselves tonight," he said, his words tender but firm.

Fawn's grin was all the answer he needed, her voice ripe with feigned innocence. "Of course, Papa."

"Whatever, Dad," Jessica replied, her sarcasm as affectionate as the squeeze of her father's hand.

In this household, laughter and playful exchanges were the norm, weaving a fabric of comfort and closeness around them all. To Teresa and Tom, Fawn was like a second daughter; her presence in their home was as natural as the ocean's tide. And just two blocks away, Fawn's family shared the same fondness for Jessica, a testament to the enduring connection the two families had formed through the friendship of two inseparable girls.

Fawn stood at the front door, ready to leave for home, still in her sleek black bikini. Teresa paused, her gaze lingering on the young woman. Her eyes narrowed in a mix of contemplation and concern before a decision took hold.

"Just a minute, dear," Teresa said, her voice trailing off as she disappeared into her bedroom. Moments later, she reemerged holding a colorful kaftan, a riot of patterns that spoke of carefree summer days. She handed it to Fawn with a knowing look, her smile light and playful. "Put this on, sweetheart. You teased enough boys today," she added with a wink.

Fawn's laughter was a melody that filled the room as she accepted the kaftan, draping the fabric over her shoulders. "Thanks, Mama," she said, the term affectionate and fitting, like the kaftan—a perfect blend of comfort and style.

With the kaftan fluttering around her, Fawn turned to Jessica and promised, "I'll be back after dinner."

"Okay," Jessica replied, her voice soft and her hug gentler.

With a farewell wave, Fawn receded down the familiar path, the colorful garment flowing behind her like a walking artwork against the quiet suburb of Wavecrest. The kaftan, a thoughtful offering from Teresa, was more than just a piece of clothing; it represented the warmth and affection she received from Jessica's family.

As Jessica retreated to her room, anticipation swelled within her. The murmur of her parents in the background contrasted with the excitement bubbling inside her. She thought about the beach party, feeling a mixture of nervousness and excitement at the possibility of seeing the boy again. With each thought of the evening ahead, her heart raced faster, drawn to the allure and possibilities that awaited her under Wavecrest's starlit sky.

# Chapter 3

------------------------------------------------------

As daylight surrendered to dusk on the boardwalk, Wavecrest marked time as faithfully as the tides obeyed the moon's silent command. The final hues of sunset succumbed to a soft, purple twilight, draping the bustling boardwalk in a tender glow. Stars winked into existence above, mirroring the arcade and shopfront lights now sparking to life. The air, heavy with the tang of salt and the sizzle of frying treats, carried the symphony of laughter and the ocean's distant serenade.

Jessica and Fawn, the epitome of effortless summer elegance, strolled side by side. Jessica's airy white top danced in the evening breeze, paired with denim shorts that flattered her petite frame. Fawn echoed her friend's relaxed grace in a sunflower-yellow crop top that hugged her torso and high-waisted shorts that showed off her long legs. Their outfits, a testament to their intimate understanding of each other's tastes and personalities, told a story of shared adventures and a comfortable friendship that had weathered many a summer.

"You think there'll be a lot of people tonight?" Jessica asked, her voice full of excitement.

Fawn looked at her with mischievous eyes. "With summer kicking off? It's going to be teeming. Just the way we like it."

Standing in front of Arnold's Arcade's flashing lights and catchy tunes, Krista Anderson caught sight of her approaching friends. Her lively and unmistakable shout sliced through the atmosphere. "There they are! Fashionably late as always!"

At eighteen, Krista stood out with her red pixie haircut against the arcade's neon glow. Outfitted in a graphic tank top and black shorts, her vibrancy was infectious, her laughter setting the evening's lively pace.

Beside her, Michelle Parker, also eighteen, presented a stark contrast in both energy and appearance. Her auburn hair flowed in soft waves around her contemplative hazel eyes, which seemed to soak in the boardwalk's vibrancy. Dressed in a teal sundress with a lightweight cardigan, her outfit was the epitome of comfort, enabling her to glide with effortless elegance. Together, they formed an eclectic duo: one a blaze of energy, the other a serene stream, yet each carried an undeniable spark of youth.

Michelle's face brightened with a smile as Jessica and Fawn approached. "We were just about to start a game of Skee-Ball without you," she teased, her eyes warm and inviting.

"You wouldn't dare," Fawn shot back, her voice light and teasing. They embraced in a group hug, a comfortable tradition forged from years of friendship.

"Seriously, though," Krista added, her eyes alight with excitement. "How about a midnight swim after the party? Who's with me?"

Jessica's laughter rang out, any hint of shyness melting away among friends. "You're just looking for an excuse to flaunt your new bikini," she quipped, sparking laughter among the group.

"I'm more interested in the food," Michelle admitted, her tone momentarily serious.

"Alright, guys, whether you're after food or a swim, let's get going," Fawn announced, gesturing towards the beach. Together, they moved as one, their anticipation for the night's adventures lifting their spirits.

As they transitioned from the boardwalk to the natural path to Callahan Cove, the vibrant atmosphere of Wavecrest's center began to fade. The aroma of popcorn and fried dough gave way to the fresh, salty embrace of the ocean. The arcade noise and crowd chatter gave way to the rhythmic whisper of the ocean and the soft crunch of sand underfoot. Yet, the girls' laughter and chatter shone brightly, undimmed, as the lively energy of the boardwalk dissolved into the peacefulness of the night.

As they neared the end of the walkway, the silhouettes of people gathering in casual groups heralded the evening's festivities. Among them was eighteen-year-old Heather Marino, who seemed to personify a summer night's dream. Her thick, black hair cascaded in waves over her shoulders, setting off a boldly cut red tank top that flattered her curvy figure. A pair of worn denim shorts and strappy sandals completed her look, showcasing her painted toenails. Heather's makeup, applied with meticulous skill, highlighted her eyes with her trademark eyeliner, enhancing the beauty of her Italian features. Her laughter, a distinct melody of untamed joy, floated above the playful exchanges of the college guys drawn to her dynamic presence.

"There she is, the queen of the cove," Krista remarked, her voice laced with admiration.

Michelle smiled. "She sure loves the attention, doesn't she."

Leading the way, Fawn advanced with assured steps. "Heather!" she called, her voice cutting through the twilight.

At the sound of her name, Heather's vivacious demeanor softened, her face lighting up at the sight of her friends. "My girls!" she beamed, arms wide open. The men around her faded into the background, their attention unnoticed as Heather enveloped Jessica and

Fawn in a hug that testified to a friendship rooted since fourth grade.

"You guys made it!" Heather exclaimed, stepping back to look them over with a gleam of joy. "I've missed my partners in crime!"

Michelle and Krista then received their hugs, a little less fervent but equally heartfelt, affirming their deep-seated friendship.

"Look at us all together again," Heather said, her eyes dancing from one friend to another. "It's been way too long."

Jessica chuckled, her eyes twinkling with playful disbelief. "Heather, it's only been a week."

"A week too long," Heather countered with a cheerful smile

Their reunion buzzed with the warmth of hugs, laughter, and the rapid exchange of stories unique to those with a rich tapestry of shared experiences. Approaching the end of the boardwalk, Callahan Cove's lights twinkled in the distance.

"Let's see what the night has in store for us," Krista declared, her smile wide as they stepped off the wooden planks.

Away from the cadence of the boardwalk, the vibrant essence of Callahan Cove enveloped them like a warm summer embrace. Bonfires dotted the beach, casting a golden glow across the sand, while tiki torches flickered, their dancing shadows mingling with the night's festivities. The air thrummed with a vibrant mix of summer anthems and classic tunes, syncing with the soothing rhythm of waves breaking on the shore.

Moonlight draped the scene in a silver radiance, its light dancing on the ocean's surface, transforming the waters into a mosaic of shimmering diamonds. The cool sand underfoot provided a soothing relief from the day's warmth, its softness a testament to the ocean's eternal embrace.

As they wove through the crowd, the girls encountered familiar faces—classmates and neighborhood friends welcoming them with enthusiastic cheers and smiles.

"Hey, volleyball stars!" Derek, a towering presence from their school's basketball team, called out, waving in friendly recognition.

"Hey, Derek! Keeping busy this summer?" Jessica's greeting carried the warmth of their longstanding friendship.

Approaching with a jog, Derek's height made him a noticeable figure. "For sure. Just trying to get a head start before college tryouts," he replied, his voice casual, yet underscored by a hint of determination for the upcoming season. "Heard you guys aced the finals. What's the plan now after ruling the school?"

Jessica mirrored his smile, her response as light as the summer breeze. "Just soaking up some freedom before life gets crazy again. Tonight's about having fun—everything else can wait," she said, her excitement for the moment shining through.

Nearby, another group of classmates relaxed, one holding a volleyball under her arm. She effortlessly tossed and caught it, her skill honed from many a day spent spiking and serving on the beach. "How about a friendly game for old times?" she proposed, her smile broad. "Think you still got your mojo, ladies?"

Fawn responded with a mischievous grin. "Lose our mojo? No way," she replied, her eyes sparkling with the anticipation of a friendly match. Then, with a laugh as warm and inviting as the summer night, she looped her arm through Jessica's. "But sure, we'll give you a chance to try to take it from us—only if you're ready to lose again!"

Heather's hearty laughter blended with Michelle and Krista's lighter chuckles, all entertained by the playful exchange. This moment of jovial rivalry was one of many that wove the rich tapestry of their friendship.

The strong connection between the girls was evident, creating an atmosphere of camaraderie that naturally attracted others as they moved through the celebration. Their kindness and warmth had earned them a special place in the hearts of many, making them popular not just for their athletic achievements but for their genuine connections.

The strains of a guitar floated through the air, a melodious interlude amidst the lively bustle of the beach party. Krista, always attuned to the call of music, paused. "Do you hear that?" she asked, her attention captured by the musical whisper, her posture reflecting her intrigue.

The group halted, letting the guitar's melodious strumming wash over them. The chords, though simple, carried the essence of the summer night—intimate and captivating.

"It sounds incredible." Krista remarked, her expression dreamy, as if the music spoke directly to her soul.

"Not bad," Heather conceded, scanning the area for the musician.

Jessica, always drawn to life's hidden gems, felt an itch of curiosity. "Let's go check it out," she suggested, her eyes alight with the bonfire's glow.

"Sounds like a plan," Fawn agreed, her adventurous spirit undimmed.

Eager for new experiences, Heather took the lead. "Let's go," she declared, guiding them toward the music.

Absorbed in her phone, Michelle glanced up to see her friends moving toward the sound. "Hey, wait up!" she called, half in jest. Her smile broadened as she hurried to catch up, slipping her phone away into her pocket.

With Heather leading, they weaved through the partygoers, drawn to the guitar's enchanting melody. They soon spotted a young man, his long dark hair moving with the sea breeze, his fingers weaving a fervent passion into the guitar strings, mirroring the intensity of the nearby bonfire.

Transfixed by the serene strums of the guitar, they settled into the sand's welcoming warmth. Jessica and Fawn perched on a nearby rock, Heather lounged close by on the sand, while Krista and Michelle sat closer to the musician, captivated by the charm of the music.

"Wow, he's really good," Jessica murmured, cautious not to shatter the enchanting

18

atmosphere.

"He sure knows how to play the guitar," Fawn remarked, her eyes locked on the boy as she watched his fingers glide over the strings.

Seated cross-legged, Heather mused. "We should ask him to play at one of our parties. Imagine this vibe on our own terrace."

Krista and Michelle nodded in agreement, the former already lost in the music, the latter just happy to be a part of the moment.

In the midst of their lighthearted exchange, Jessica found herself adrift in thought, replaying the afternoon's encounter with vivid clarity, as bright as the bonfire's blaze. Her eyes scanned the crowd, searching for a face she'd only met but couldn't forget.

"Earth to Jessica," Heather's gentle jest coaxed her friend from her reverie.

Caught off guard, Jessica turned, managing a smile that didn't quite mask her inner turmoil.

"You okay, girl?" Heather's tone shifted from teasing to concern, noting the faraway look in Jessica's eyes.

"Yep, I'm good," Jessica assured, her smile genuine yet tinged with a hint of melancholy.

As Jessica resumed her quiet search, her eyes flitted across the crowd. Heather exchanged a concerned look with Fawn, her whisper blending jest with worry. "What's the matter with Jess?"

Aware of the cause, but respecting her friend's privacy, Fawn chose to keep it a secret. Casting a nonchalant glance at Jessica and then back to Heather, Fawn reassured, "Nothing. It's been a long day; she's probably just tired."

Heather accepted the explanation and allowed her focus to drift back to the evening's potential adventures. Yet Fawn stayed observant, her supportive hand on Jessica's shoulder conveying unspoken solidarity.

Beside the fading glow of the fire, a new intensity ignited within Jessica. Time seemed to stretch, drawing her attention irresistibly to a figure with sandy blond hair standing alone in the distance. Illuminated from behind by another bonfire, his silhouette was in shadow, yet the way he stood, the ease of his posture, struck a chord of deep familiarity within her.

"Oh my God," Jessica exhaled, her tone blending with wonder and thrill, her hand trembling as she pointed. "There he is!"

Fawn quickly turned, her gaze sharp, following Jessica's direction to the lone figure. Driven by a mix of intrigue and concern, Heather, Michelle, and Krista also shifted their attention.

Jessica's heart fluttered with excitement, even as a shadow of doubt edged in. "At least I think that's him," she confessed, her voice tinted with uncertainty.

With a focused vision from years of tracking volleyballs across the courts, Fawn scrutinized the figure before turning back to Jessica with a broad, affirming smile. "It sure is," she confirmed. "That is definitely your beach boy."

"Beach boy?" Heather's laughter wove around the nickname, her amusement evident.

"Uh-huh," Fawn affirmed, her smile unwavering. "Jessica met him on the beach earlier today."

"Aw, Jess," Heather's tone was warm, her affection for Jessica evident in her gentle teasing. The thought of her friend, always so caring and reserved, taking an interest in someone, brought a soft happiness to Heather.

Jessica's cheeks flushed a deep shade of red, the spotlight on her burgeoning feelings.

"He's pretty cute," Michelle chimed in, her eyes focused on the boy.

With her heart pounding, Jessica looked at Fawn, seeking reassurance in the familiar steadiness of her best friend's gaze.

Heather, always one to spur others into action, gently prodded Jessica. "You go, girl. Savor the moment."

Jessica's smile flickered, her nerves palpable but eased by Heather's support. She turned to Fawn, her eyes conveying a wordless plea for further encouragement.

Fawn, as dependable as ever, delivered the reassurance Jessica needed. "You got this, Jess," she affirmed, her voice a steady presence. Those words had long been a source of comfort and strength for Jessica, urging her to tap into her courage.

Buoyed by Fawn's unwavering confidence, Jessica rose, her friends' faces an array of supportive smiles. "Okay," she murmured, her resolve firming in her quiet tone. "I'll catch up with you all later."

Jessica turned away from the safety of her friends and stepped into the enveloping night. Her figure blended into the shifting shadows as she ventured towards the unknown, toward the boy who had become the focus of her daydreams. Her friends looked on, their breaths held in silent testimony to their support and admiration for her bravery.

As Jessica disappeared into the crowd, drawn by the threads of a possible romance, Heather felt a familiar thrill of adventure. The comfort of soft sand and the hypnotic dance of flames no longer held her attention. Eager for action, she sprang to her feet, her eyes bright with the anticipation of new exploits.

"Come on, girls," she said, brushing the sand off her shorts. "Let's see what kind of trouble we can get into."

In tune with Heather's adventurous zeal, Fawn rose, her enthusiasm mirroring Heather's. Together, they prepared to dive into the night's possibilities, their spirits in perfect harmony with the adventurous pulse of the evening.

Michelle and Krista glanced at each other, their expressions revealing a hunger for more than adventure. "Go ahead," Michelle suggested. "We're hungry, so we're going back on the boards to get something to eat."

Fawn's response was a playful pout, a teasing expression of disappointment at the thought of splitting up. Yet, they embraced each other in a group hug, enveloping themselves in warmth and softening any sense of parting with their camaraderie.

"See you later, peeps," Heather said, her farewell infused with the comfort of enduring friendship.

Fawn tightened her embrace, her arms weaving a tapestry of countless shared moments. "Love you, girls. We'll meet up later," she promised, their bond as tangible in that hug as the promise of their hopeful reunion.

As they diverged, Michelle and Krista's figures gravitated toward the inviting lights of the boardwalk, while Heather and Fawn ventured further along the beach, their forms casting long shadows in the moonlight.

Ahead lay the thrill of the unforeseen, a blank slate ripe for the creation of memories on this spontaneous summer night. The sounds of laughter and conversation from the party dwindled, becoming a faint echo, the perfect underscore of their forthcoming escapades. The expansive beach beckoned with the promise of untold adventures, whispering secrets only Wavecrest could hold. Embracing the call, Heather and Fawn stepped forward, eager to unravel the adventures that awaited them under the starlit sky.

# Chapter 4

-------------------------------------------------------------

As Jessica moved closer to the boy, each step felt guided by an unseen force, a pull as natural as the tide drawn to the moon. A familiar warmth enveloped her, like invisible arms offering a comforting embrace. This sensation wasn't new to Jessica; it had been a subtle yet constant presence since she was six years old. It was a comfort she had grown to accept and cherish, as integral to her being as the very air she breathed.

The gentle breeze of the ocean, carrying the scent of salt and adventure, seemed to whisper directly to her heart. Its wordless murmurs sang a song of encouragement, assuring her she was exactly where she was meant to be. At that moment, under the blanket of the night sky, everything felt aligned, as if the universe itself had orchestrated this meeting on the moonlit shores of Wavecrest.

Unbeknownst to Jessica, the boy felt a similar pull. A shared destiny seemed to guide him as he turned, his eyes locking with hers. In the moonlight, her eyes sparkled, embodying a sweet innocence that touched his heart, a feeling profound yet inexplicable. To him, she was a vision of pure beauty, her serene presence almost ethereal. A warm smile spread across his face, drawing him to her like a moth to a flame.

In this destined moment, a benevolent presence, unnamed yet deeply felt, watched over Jessica. Its nurturing touch, a constant in her life, acted like an unspoken guardian, offering reassurance in moments of uncertainty. As Jessica and the boy's paths converged under the moonlit sky, this silent protector remained in the shadows. Once a guiding force, its role subtly shifted, empowering her to embrace life's new chapter with strength drawn from years of silent companionship.

Under the moon and stars' vigilant gaze, Jessica approached the boy, drawn by an unfathomable force. She stopped before him, summoning her bravery. "Hi. Remember me?" she asked, her voice tinged with nervous hope.

His eyes lit up with a warm smile. "Of course I do. I was looking for you," he replied, his smile genuine, reaching his eyes and making them sparkle.

"You were?" Jessica asked, her surprise evident, heart fluttering at the realization that he had been looking for her as well.

The boy's amused grin widened in response to her astonishment, filling the air between them with a palpable connection.

After an awkward yet charged silence, Jessica said, "I forgot to ask your name," her cheeks pink with embarrassment, which she tried to disguise with a giggle.

His laughter mingled with hers, lightening his heart. "Don't feel embarrassed. I forgot, too," he admitted, his cheeks taking on a hint of color.

"I'm Jessica," she introduced herself, her nervousness easing just a bit.

"I'm Ethan. Ethan Harris," he offered, his warm gaze appreciating her, finding her name as enchanting as her presence.

Silence enveloped them once more, yet Jessica, armed with newfound courage, shattered it. "Do you live around here?" she asked, her voice laced with hope that he wasn't too distant.

His smile faded as his eyes locked onto the distant glow of a bonfire. "No, I'm from Pine Haven. My brother and I recently discovered this place and thought it would be a good spot to spend our summer."

"Pine Haven? Where's that?" Jessica's interest spiked, eager to learn more about the boy who had wandered into her life.

"It's up north, about four hundred and fifty miles from here," Ethan explained, his words introducing a sobering distance into their nascent connection.

Jessica's face betrayed disappointment at the revelation of their significant separation, but she cast aside her dismay and beamed, "I've lived here my whole life."

"Oh, really? How old are you?" Ethan's tone carried a genuine curiosity.

"Seventeen," Jessica began, quickly adding, "But I'll be eighteen at the end of the month." She hoped her soon-to-be age would ease any concerns about her youth.

Ethan's response was a mix of surprise and acceptance. "Nice. I just turned twenty-one last month."

The revelation momentarily widened Jessica's eyes, but it didn't dampen her interest. "Does my age bother you?" she ventured, a hint of uncertainty in her voice.

Ethan's soft chuckle was reassuring. "Of course not. I'm not that much older than you." His words eased her concerns, acting as a comforting reassurance.

In the moment that followed, Jessica and Ethan's connection deepened, moving beyond the mundane. An invisible thread, woven from the essence of their souls, connected them in a silent dance. The air pulsed with their shared rhythm, echoing unvoiced emotions and desires. This wasn't mere attraction; it felt like an ancient awakening, a profound resonance within them. Amidst this anticipation, Ethan's voice emerged, both gentle and

23

significant. "Would you like to hang out for a while?"

As Ethan's invitation hung in the air, Jessica's cheeks bloomed with a soft pink blush. Her heart, already dancing to a new and enchanting beat, seemed to flutter, captivated by the moment. "Yes, I would love to," she answered, her voice carrying a melodious tone of excitement. The authenticity in her voice was undeniable, mirroring the joy and anticipation she felt about spending more time with Ethan.

Ethan's fingers grazed Jessica's, a deliberate yet tender gesture that seemed to draw the night closer around them. His touch, slight yet charged, sent ripples through the space between them, as if the air itself whispered of possibilities. In that instant, Jessica's world narrowed to the warmth spreading from their intertwined fingers, a tangible echo of the connection they were beginning to forge. The night was only beginning to unveil its enchantment, and Jessica was more than ready to explore the journey ahead.

The rhythm of the beach party enveloped Fawn and Heather, its flickering bonfires like beacons in the night, alive with laughter and music. They walked along the beach, leaving soft impressions in the cool sand, each step drawing them closer to the heart of the celebration.

Approaching a small bonfire, its warm glow revealed a group of friends from school. Heather's restlessness shimmered. They paused, the circle of light and warmth pulling them in.

"Hey, Fawn, Heather!" a voice from their volleyball team called out. "Join us!"

Fawn's smile lit up her face. "Hey, everyone!" Her enthusiasm bubbled over as she settled among them. But Heather lingered at the edge, her gaze stretching over the horizon. "Hey, guys," she said, her voice tinged with impatience.

As laughter and memories wove through the group, Heather's attention wandered. She nudged Fawn, whispering, "Let's keep moving. I'm in the mood for something more... exciting."

Fawn caught the sparkle in Heather's eye and laughed. "Lead the way, wild child."

Their visit was brief, just enough for pleasantries and a few laughs before Heather's restless spirit pulled them onward. The night air buzzed with possibilities, and Heather was determined to find a group that matched her vibrant energy.

As they wandered, they encountered various gatherings—some singing to guitar tunes, others just soaking in the night sky. They engaged in light conversations at each stop, yet Heather's eyes remained restless, always on the lookout for the thrill the night promised.

"Looking for some fun, huh?" Fawn teased as they moved on from another group.

Heather's grin spoke volumes. "You know me—I can't stay in one place too long."

Finally, they found a group of college guys, their laughter echoing above the waves. Their energy was magnetic, exactly what Heather sought. She turned to Fawn, her eyes sparkling with mischief.

"Hey, Fawn, I know these guys!" Her voice brimmed with anticipation, the excitement of the upcoming interaction evident in her tone. Knowing Fawn's reservations about rowdy groups, she warned, "They can be a bit wild, but I want to hang out with them for a while. Are you okay with that?"

Familiar with Heather's love for lively social settings, Fawn nodded understandingly. Though she preferred quieter, more tranquil gatherings, she recognized the appeal of such vibrancy to Heather. With a smile that spoke of years of friendship and understanding, she said, "Sure, Heather. Go ahead. I'll catch up with you later."

Heather's face brightened with appreciation, her smile reflecting the freedom Fawn's acceptance provided. She gave her a quick hug, a gesture of their close bond. Then, with an enthusiastic wave, she approached the group, eager to immerse herself in the dynamic atmosphere that beckoned her.

Fawn watched her friend merge into the crowd, a contented smile gracing her lips. She understood these moments were vital for Heather, energizing her vibrant spirit. As for herself, she felt drawn to the beach party's quieter corners, where she could embrace the night at her own pace.

As she wandered along the sandy shoreline, the symphony of crashing waves and the gentle touch of the sea breeze provided a serene retreat from the party's vibrant chaos. Her explorer's heart led her to secluded stretches along the water, where the party's lively energy became a distant hum. In these tranquil spots, she discovered a peace that resonated within her.

In the calm of the moment, Fawn felt enfolded in a familiar, comforting presence, the night air around her imbued with secrets that only her heart could hear. As her eyes settled on the vast, moonlit ocean, her eyes became mirrors to its shimmering surface, reflecting the deep, unspoken bond she shared with the mystical essence of Wavecrest. This connection, an invisible embrace that had cradled her since childhood, offered not just serenity but also a profound understanding, serving as both a beacon and a nurturing spirit guiding her journey of growth.

Fawn couldn't help but return a smile into the darkness, her eyes lingering on the horizon where the moonlight danced upon the waves. This smile was more than an expression of joy; it was recognition, a silent acknowledgment between her heart and the soul of the world around her, marking the enduring companionship that had guided her through life's ebbs and flows.

Walking away from the tranquil embrace of the ocean's edge, Fawn re-entered the beach party's lively thrum. The stark contrast of energy enveloped her, a wave of sound, movement, and color that swept her from reflective solitude into the heart of communal celebration. Navigating through a sea of revelers, she felt the rhythmic pulse of music and voices wash over her, grounding her in the present's vibrant energy.

Amid the blur of faces and laughter, she spotted a familiar figure—Tommy Reynolds, a peer from her academic circles. Even in the dim light, his silhouette was unmistakable: oversized glasses on the brink of sliding off his nose, a wild mop of dark hair that seemed to follow its own rules and clothing that prioritized practicality over style.

"Hey, Fawn!" Tommy's voice cut through, a blend of enthusiasm and intellectual curiosity. His broad and genuine smile illuminated his face with excitement. "How's the summer going for you?"

Knowing Tommy's knack for diving into deep, conceptual discussions—although impressive, but often exhausting for those around him—Fawn braced herself for the inevitable. "I'm just going with the flow. Taking each day as it comes," she answered, her tone polite but cautious, aiming to avoid a lengthy conversation.

Unfazed by Fawn's concise response, Tommy ventured into a wide range of topics, from philosophical thoughts to daily observations, his eagerness unflagging. Ever the gracious listener, Fawn nodded along, her attention drifting between the conversation and the party's vibrant backdrop. She appreciated Tommy's intellect, yet her thoughts lingered on the evening's festivities, yearning to immerse herself once more in the celebration.

But when Tommy touched on a topic dear to Fawn's heart, her focus instantly sharpened. "Have you heard about the art contest at our school this summer?" he asked, his interest evident. He knew of Fawn's passion for art, often observing her more absorbed in her sketchbooks than in her textbooks.

Fawn's response was a blend of surprise and curiosity. She shook her head, eager to learn more.

As Tommy detailed the contest, his excitement grew, his voice taking on a rhythmic quality. "It's open to all students in our area. They even have art professors from UCSB to judge the contest. And here's the best part, Fawn!"

He paused, heightening the anticipation. Caught between impatience and eagerness, Fawn encouraged him, "Yeah, go on!"

With a proud smile, Tommy announced, "The grand prize is two thousand dollars!"

Fawn felt a surge of excitement. Two thousand dollars meant more than just money to her; it symbolized freedom, opportunity, and a way to ease her family's financial strain. It was a platform for her dreams, a tangible aim for her artistic pursuits. Her eyes shone with ambition and gratitude. "Thanks, Tommy. That's... that's an incredible opportunity," she said, her voice laced with a fresh resolve.

"Don't mention it," Tommy replied, his voice carrying a hint of pride. "I knew you would be interested."

As their conversation ended and they went their separate ways, both retreated into their own thoughts. Fawn's mind buzzed with creative possibilities, igniting a renewed sense of purpose as she merged back into the party's flow. Meanwhile, Tommy adjusted his glasses, his lips curving into a content smile, pleased to have shared something meaningful with a classmate. As they disappeared into the night, their paths diverged. Yet, the imprint of their brief interaction lingered, a testament to the unexpected connections and opportunities that can emerge from a single conversation.

As the night continued to whisper its secrets, Fawn navigated the nocturnal canvas. With her heart ablaze with inspiration and ambition, she moved with a lightness, her steps almost floating as she wove through the sandy gatherings, each one radiating the warmth of friendship that welcomed her.

For Fawn, the beach party transformed from a mere social event into a fountain of artistic inspiration. The prospect of winning the contest and unveiling her talent to the world infused her with purpose and exhilaration. This opportunity was more than just a competition; it was a gateway to her dreams, a chance to mold her future with determination and skill. Strolling under the starry expanse, her imagination took flight, envisioning canvases yet to be created and stories yet to be told through her beloved brushes and colors.

Beneath the moon's silver gaze, Jessica and Ethan drifted from the lively echoes of the beach party, hands entwined as if they were pieces of a long-lost puzzle now complete. The world around them quieted, transforming into a more intimate landscape under the moon's celestial lantern, which cast a soft, ethereal glow over the dark beach.

As they walked, freedom enveloped them, the cool sand beneath their feet and the gentle rhythm of the waves creating a symphony of serenity. Drawn to a large rock near the water's edge, they found an ancient sentinel weathered by time and the elements, its presence both commanding and welcoming. This guardian of the shore, with its surface smoothed by countless years of wind and waves, curved invitingly, offering the perfect perch for the couple.

As they approached, the rock seemed to extend a silent invitation, its rough, pock-marked face resembling a kindly old man smiling in the moonlight. The rock and the sea whispered together, their age-old dialogue a lullaby for the young hearts seeking solace in each other's presence.

Perched side by side, a blossoming surge of joy enveloped Jessica. Ethan's nearness, tangible and warm, served as a comforting balm against the cool night air. The slightest touch of their shoulders sent a thrill through her, a connection extending beyond the physical, reaching deep within.

In their secluded sanctuary by the sea, the moment belonged solely to them, timeless and suspended. The rhythmic crashing of waves against the shore provided a soothing soundtrack to their shared daydream. For Jessica, it was like stepping into a dream where their reality was the only one that mattered. Her happiness felt like basking in a sunlit pool, a warmth radiating from within, fueled by Ethan's presence, which ignited a unique light in her heart.

In the quiet comfort of their moonlit niche, Jessica listened to Ethan with rapt attention, captivated by the stories he wove. His voice, a mix of excitement and reflection, painted a vivid picture of his life's journey and the crossroads ahead.

Jessica leaned closer, her curiosity sparked as she asked, "So what brought you all the way from Pine Haven to here?" Her question invited him to share more of his story.

"This summer, like every summer, my brother and I set out to explore new places," Ethan began, his eyes reflecting the moon's glow. "We're adventurers at heart, you know? That's how we ended up in Wavecrest."

Jessica nodded, her eyes fixed on his, eager to hear more. The idea of summers dedicated to discovering unknown places sparked wanderlust within her.

Ethan continued, "I'm almost done with college. I just have one more semester to go. Then, I'll have my bachelor's degree." His voice carried a mix of pride and wistfulness as he faced the close of a significant chapter in his life.

"That's impressive," Jessica said, her admiration clear. "What do you plan to do afterward?"

Ethan paused, his eyes shifting to the ocean, reflecting on his internal debate. "That's the big question," he admitted. "I haven't decided yet whether to join the Army or work in our family business." A sigh escaped him, betraying a hint of weariness. "My dad has been pushing me to go to work with him, so it's complicated." The pressure from his father was clearly a source of tension, pulling him away from a path he might have chosen on his own.

Jessica found herself moved by Ethan's openness and vulnerability. His determination to make a meaningful choice for his future revealed a depth and drive that surpassed the carefree adventurer image she initially perceived.

"It sounds like you've got some big decisions to make," Jessica remarked, her voice filled with empathy.

"Yeah, it can be overwhelming at times," Ethan admitted, turning to face her. "But I suppose that's a part of life, right?" Feeling a sense of mutual openness, he asked, "How about you? What's your story?"

Jessica's eyes lit up, mirroring her recent accomplishments. "I just graduated from high school," she said, her voice carrying a note of joy.

Ethan encouraged her with a nod. "That's awesome. Are you going to college?"

Looking up at the star-filled sky, Jessica's expression mixed hope with contemplation. "Yeah, I'm going to the University of Texas," she disclosed, her voice blending pride with a hint of uncertainty. "I'm kinda excited about it, but I'm also unsure about what I want to do with my life."

Ethan offered an understanding look, his face showing empathy. "I know what you mean. It's a big step, that's for sure."

"It really is," Jessica agreed, her tone capturing the weight of the transition.

Their honesty connected them, bridging their experiences of anticipation and uncertainty. Beneath the night sky, their conversation wove a tapestry of dreams and aspirations under the gentle illumination of the moon and the stars.

Ethan's gaze, alive with curiosity, ventured into the delicate realm of personal life. "Do you have a boyfriend?" he asked, his voice hesitating, hinting at how much her answer meant to him.

A soft blush colored Jessica's cheek, a tender reaction to the intimate question. She slowly shook her head, her gesture conveying her single status. Her response silently confirmed her heart was unclaimed.

Encouraged by Ethan's openness, Jessica echoed his inquiry, her voice tinged with cautious hope. "Do you have a girlfriend?" she asked, her heart fluttering with the hope that his answer would align with her wishes.

Ethan replied with a playful smile. "No, I don't. I haven't met a girl I want to be in a serious relationship with."

A wave of surprise swept through Jessica, her mind wrestling with the idea of him being single. The initial shock quickly transitioned into a budding sense of elation. They were both free, unbound by romantic commitments, sailing similar seas of solitude. This mutual understanding sparked a warmth between them, a shared acknowledgment that they were each navigating life's journey on their own. It was a comforting and exhilarating realization, igniting the possibility of a summer romance filled with sweet moments and tender discoveries.

As they sat together and listened to the ocean's soothing murmurs, a tender connection began to unfold between them, a connection that only the vast, star-filled skies of a summer night could foster.

As the hours melted away beneath the enchanting night sky, Jessica and Ethan's connection deepened. Their conversation flowed as naturally as the waves caressing the shore. Eventually, a comfortable silence enveloped them, and Jessica, feeling a surge of affection, leaned in to rest her head on his solid shoulder. Ethan instinctively wrapped his arm around her, drawing her into a warm embrace. Together, they created an intimate world, a stark contrast to the distant buzz of the beach party.

Captivated by the moonlight reflecting off the ocean waves, they found solace in the sea's symphony, its rhythmic pulse echoing their silence. Within this intimate space, Jessica's heart opened, each breath and touch pulling them closer in a dance of discovery.

Yet, a flicker of concern pierced Jessica's contentment. Thoughts of her friends—Fawn, Heather, Michelle, and Krista—surfaced, reminding her they were waiting amidst the party's revelry. Acknowledging the need to return, she whispered, her voice tinged with sadness. "I should go now. My friends might be looking for me." Her eyes met Ethan's, finding understanding reflected in his eyes.

Ethan responded with tenderness, his fingertips brushing her face, tucking a stray curl behind her ear in a moment that seemed to pause time. Their hearts beat in unison, hesitant to disrupt the magic of their newfound connection.

Understanding her dilemma, Ethan offered comfort and reassurance. "It's okay. We'll see each other tomorrow, right?" His words were a promise, a beacon of hope in the night.

Joy surged within Jessica, her eyes gleaming with anticipation. "Yes! Tomorrow! I'll see you tomorrow!" she confirmed, her excitement evident in her voice.

With a reluctant sigh, Jessica pulled away, her gaze lingering on Ethan as she started back. With each step, the invisible thread connecting them tugged at her heart, a bond as tangible as the sea breeze caressing her skin. She glanced back repeatedly, holding onto Ethan's image until he blended into the shadows of the night.

Navigating through the crowd, a whirlwind of emotions enveloped her. The anticipation of tomorrow and the thrill of a budding romance swirled within her, mixing excitement with nervousness. As she sought her friends among the partygoers, her thoughts were awash with memories of Ethan, their shared moments, and the promise of tomorrow, coloring her night with the hues of a summer romance just beginning to unfold.

As the first blush of dawn began to paint the sky with hues of pink and orange, Fawn felt an irresistible pull toward Jessica, her lifelong friend and confidante. Their shared history and unbreakable bond drew them together as they weaved their way through the dwindling crowd of the beach party.

"There you are!" Fawn's voice rang out, her excitement palpable in the air as she caught sight of Jessica. Her joy shone like a lighthouse in the darkness, unmistakable and radiant, cutting through the dim light.

Still basking in the evening's glow, Jessica cast a curious glance around. "Where is everybody?" Her smile remained steadfast as she surveyed the thinning crowd for their friends.

"They all took off. It's just you and me now," Fawn said, wrapping her arm around Jessica in a comforting embrace.

Illuminated by the moon's gentle light, Jessica's face was alight with happiness as she shared her encounter with Ethan. Her words, infused with the thrill of new romance, painted a vivid picture of her emotions and the connection she had experienced.

Captivated by Jessica's tale of budding romance, Fawn's heart swelled with joy for her best friend. She felt thrilled to witness this new chapter in Jessica's life, a story as fresh and exhilarating as the first breath of spring after a long winter's nap.

In turn, Fawn couldn't resist sharing her own adventures from the night. She spoke about the people she met, the conversations she had, and the laughter that filled her evening. And then her excitement soared, her eyes twinkling as she mentioned the Summer Art Contest, describing the opportunities with a voice brimming with the passion of her dreams and ambitions.

Together, they strolled back to the familiar boardwalk, their voices mingling in the soft glow of dawn, recounting the night's adventures and dreaming aloud of the summer days yet to come. As they moved through the quiet of the early morning, each step carried them closer, not just to home but to the countless possibilities that lay ahead. Though the night was drawing to a close, a new day was dawning for Jessica and Fawn, full of potential, simmering excitement, and dreams on the cusp of exploration. Side by side, Jessica and Fawn stepped into the burgeoning day, their hearts buoyed by the shared joy of anticipation and the solid ground of their enduring friendship.

# Chapter 5

As the early Monday morning light washed over Wavecrest, the small seaside town came alive, signaling the beginning of a new week. In that moment, a clear contrast emerged between the lives of the younger residents and the adults. As the town awoke to the soft hues of dawn, it was the interplay of seasonal excitement and daily responsibilities that defined the day ahead.

For the youth of Wavecrest, Monday mornings in the summer were a continuation of their sun-drenched escapades. Freed from the confines of school, they enjoyed the freedom that only summer could provide. The beaches, once their weekend playground, now welcomed them daily, promising new adventures and endless possibilities.

Groups of teenagers, energized by the prospect of another day without schedules or textbooks, gathered on the sandy shores, their laughter mingling with the rhythmic crash of the waves. Their days stretched out before them, brimming with the promise of impromptu volleyball games, sunbathing, and spontaneous trips to the boardwalk for ice cream and amusement.

Adults, on the other hand, faced a different rhythm. The serenity of Wavecrest's mornings was a brief respite before they embarked on their daily commutes. In this seaside community, many worked in cities beyond its tranquil borders, with some traveling as far as Santa Barbara. Cars lined up on sun-dappled streets, ferrying diligent workers across scenic routes that bridged their quiet seaside life with bustling urban centers. Their days were dictated by office hours and professional obligations, a stark contrast to the youth's carefree days.

In this small town, the divide between the carefree enthusiasm of youth and the steady diligence of adulthood was never more apparent than on those summer Mondays. While teenagers reveled in their seasonal freedom, their parents and guardians upheld the routine of work and responsibility. The morning sun, rising with impartial warmth over Wavecrest, illuminated a community living in parallel yet divergent worlds, united only by the shared backdrop of their picturesque coastal retreat.

Early Monday morning unfolded in the Gaddesden kitchen with an air unlike any other day. Brian, Fawn's father, dressed in a blue and white gingham check shirt paired with charcoal gray dress pants, sat at the kitchen table, his posture rigid. His fingers wrapped around a cup of coffee, a silent testament to his contemplative mood. Morning light streamed through the window, accentuating the lines of concern on his face, a departure from his usual calm demeanor.

Across from him, Anna, Fawn's mother, presented a soft contrast. Dressed in an elegant ankle-length nightgown of a soft pink, she usually brought warmth to the room. This morning, however, her grace was overshadowed by palpable tension. Her eyes, once aglow with maternal love and refinement, now reflected the deep worry that consumed her.

Upstairs, Fawn was asleep in her bedroom, blissfully unaware of the tension below. Dreams of the upcoming Art Contest, which had filled her with excitement the night before, likely played through her mind. Her room, a haven of creativity and youthful spirit, stood in sharp contrast to the somber mood downstairs.

The silence in the Gaddesden kitchen was a far cry from its usual vibrancy. The atmosphere was heavy, charged with an unspoken dread. On this Monday morning, Anna and Brian were not just parents preparing for the day ahead; they were confronting a dreadful reality, a challenge that threatened to disrupt the harmony of their family life.

Brian's voice, heavy with a rare ominous tone, shattered the morning silence. "I think it's time to tell Fawn, Anna. Today. We can't put it off any longer."

Anna's reply reflected her hope against hope. "Are you sure there are no other options?"

"I don't know what else we can do at this point. I've tried everything," Brian admitted, his shoulders slumping under the burden of hopelessness. His urgency intensified as he added, "We only have until September, you know."

"You do know this is going to devastate Fawn," Anna said, her voice a whisper of despair.

"I know, I know. But I don't know what else to do," Brian replied, the sadness in his voice painting a somber picture.

"How do we approach this? Do I tell her everything? Do I tell her the reasons behind our decision?" Anna asked, navigating the sensitive conversation.

"No. Just tell her what she needs to know. I don't want her carrying the burden with us," Brian answered, his tone protective.

Anna's disagreement was palpable. "She's not a little girl, Brian. She should know the whole story."

However, Brian stood firm, his voice gaining an authoritative edge. "No! She might feel responsible in some way. I don't want her to think that. It's not her fault that we're in this predicament."

"Well, I think we should at least tell Tom and Teresa," Anna suggested, offering a compromise.

"No, Anna. Just tell them the same thing. I don't want anyone's pity or help. This is a family matter, and we'll get through it," Brian declared definitively.

"But they are family, Brian," Anna argued, her voice rising with emotion. "You know, Jessica is as much a daughter to us as Fawn."

"Which is all the more reason not to tell them. I'm thinking about Jessica, too," Brian reasoned.

As Anna sought alternatives, her voice carried a tinge of desperation. "There must be another solution, Brian."

Brian retorted sharply, "Well if you know of one, tell me because I don't. We both know how expensive it is to live in Wavecrest."

Anna looked like she was already grieving for an impending loss. "I know. I just wish there was another option."

"So do I, Anna. So do I. But we have no choice. Believe me, this isn't something I want either," Brian replied, his voice heavy with regret.

"Alright. I'll have a talk with her this morning," Anna conceded, worry coloring her tone.

Brian attempted to lighten their somber dialogue. "She'll be okay. After all, she'll be leaving for Boston at the end of summer and starting a new life."

"I hope you're right, Brian. I really do," Anna replied, clinging to a sliver of hope.

As they reached a fragile agreement amidst their troubles, Brian rose from the kitchen table, straightening his shirt in preparation for his day at Atlas Manufacturing. Anna stood beside him and was quickly pulled into a loving embrace—a brief escape from their shared anxieties.

"It's going to be okay, honey," he whispered reassuringly, before letting her go. "I have to go. I'll call you later." His attempt at normalcy sounded almost alien against the backdrop of their difficult situation.

Anna accompanied him to the front door, watching as he blended into the early morning light. As she listened to the car engine fade into silence, she turned back into the house, her eyes drifting upward toward Fawn's bedroom door. A heavy sigh escaped her, dreading the impending conversation that would forever change their family's dynamic, a weight of unspeakable heaviness pressing on her heart.

Later that morning, as Jessica stirred from a dream-filled sleep, the echo of Ethan's name lingered on her lips, forming a smile that seemed to draw its warmth from the previous night's memories. Her bright blue eyes fluttered open, casting away the delicate haze of sleep. The memory of their seaside encounter danced in her mind, stirring a blend of anticipation and a faint whisper of nervousness that made her heart flutter.

Rubbing the sleep from her eyes, Jessica slid off her plush queen-size bed, the centerpiece of her bedroom that whispered of comfort and relaxation. She slipped into her bathrobe, its fabric soft against her skin, a familiar comfort. Her room, a haven of youthful dreams and cherished memories, glowed with the gentle light of the mid-morning sun.

Around her, the room was a living collage of her journey from childhood to the cusp of adulthood. The sturdy dresser, adorned with a collection of photographs and mementos, told the story of Jessica's life. Her desk, a witness to nights of study and flashes of creativity, stood as a testament to her dedication and passion. Beside it, a mirrored vanity cradled her beauty essentials, silent witnesses to her morning rituals and nightly reflections.

A shelf adorned with an array of trinkets served as a visual diary, chronicling her evolving interests and escapades. Below it, a TV and a PlayStation console hinted at evenings spent in entertainment and relaxation, often in the company of Fawn. The adjacent walk-in closet, a kaleidoscope of styles, bore testimony to Jessica's maturing fashion sense, each piece a symbol of her self-expression.

But it was the ceiling that cradled the true enchantment of her room. Adorned with a scattering of glowing adhesive stars, each luminescent point, a gift from her father, had been a constant presence since she was five. By day, these stars lay dormant, blending into the plain backdrop. But as night fell, they ignited, transforming her room into a private galaxy. This celestial canvas had watched over countless sleepovers with Fawn, nights filled with whispered secrets, shared dreams, and the unbreakable bonds of friendship.

Among the constellation of stars adorning her ceiling, there was one star that held a special place in Fawn's heart. Unlike the others, with their sharp, uniform points, this star boasted a rounded edge, its one point softer and a little shorter than its companions. It was during her first sleepover, at the tender age of six, that Fawn's eyes were drawn to this peculiar star. Its uniqueness captivated her young mind, fostering a narrative that this star, with its slight flaw, was precious and deserved special tenderness and care. It became a beacon of Fawn's empathy and kindness, reminding her of the beauty in imperfection and the power of caring for those who seem a little different.

Jessica's bare feet padded across the carpeted hallway, each step grounding her in the home's tangible warmth. Moving toward the kitchen, her heart thrummed with anticipation for the new day and summer's endless possibilities.

Entering the kitchen, she found it buzzing with the morning's routines—the soft clink of porcelain, the sizzle of the pan on the stove, all enveloped in the comforting aroma of homemade oatmeal. Sunlight streamed through the window, bathing the terracotta tiles in a cheerful glow and illuminating the center of the Reese household.

"Good morning, sweetheart," Teresa said, placing her hand on Jessica's shoulder. "Did you sleep well?"

Jessica nodded, her gesture conveying more than mere contentment; it was an acknowledgment of a night that had painted her dreams with vibrant strokes.

"I had the most incredible time last night, Mom," she shared, settling into her chair. "I met this amazing guy named Ethan at the beach party. He was charming and funny, and he invited me to hang out with him today. I can't stop thinking about him."

The spark of excitement in Jessica's eyes, reflecting the night's magic and a budding connection, was unmistakable. It ignited a warm surge of maternal pride within Teresa.

"Oh, sweetheart, that's wonderful," she replied, her actions punctuating her words as she placed a bowl of oatmeal before her daughter. "It sounds like you had quite a memorable evening. I'm glad you had a great time."

The warmth from her first spoonful of cereal mirrored the wave of comfort Jessica felt. Her mother's acceptance sweetened the moment more than any sugar could. It bolstered her spirits, infusing her with the happiness that came from seeing her mother share in her joy.

"I wanted to tell you before Dad comes home," she shared between bites, mindful of her father's protective streak and uncertain about his reaction to Ethan. "You know how he gets sometimes, but I have a good feeling about Ethan. I want to see where this goes."

Teresa took her seat across from Jessica, their hands clasping over the table, a steady presence amidst uncertainty.

"Your father only wants what's best for you," she reassured, her grip firm and comforting. "But I trust your judgment, Jessica. You're growing into a remarkable young woman, and I have faith in your ability to make wise decisions."

"Thanks, Mom," Jessica replied, her heart warmed by her mother's support.

As they sat together at the kitchen table, Teresa's eyes held not only faith but an implicit promise—a commitment to support whatever tides Jessica would sail on her journey to adulthood. The vibrant atmosphere of the kitchen paused for a moment, marking a moment of change. For Jessica Reese, this day was more than a transition into summer; it was a step into a world full of new possibilities.

As Jessica finished the last of her oatmeal, Teresa glanced at the clock and rose from her seat. "Well, I have to get going. I'm working at Brenda's shop, so I'll be gone for most of the day," she said, her voice a mixture of routine and warmth.

Dressed in her beautician's smock, Teresa stood ready for the day. She bent down and kissed Jessica's head, her gesture a silent testament to her maternal affection. "Have a nice time with your new friend," she said, her eyes alight with the thrill of her daughter's budding romance.

With a final glance, Teresa turned and moved toward the front door, her soft clicks on the tile marking her departure. Soon, the familiar hum of Teresa's car faded away, leaving Jessica in a home now vibrant with the promise of a new day.

With a dreamy smile lingering on her lips, she gathered her empty bowl and spoon and placed them in the dishwasher. As she made her way down the hallway, each step felt like a stride toward the thrilling unknown, a new chapter poised just beyond the threshold, ready to unfold.

Stepping into the bathroom, Jessica peeled off her robe and stepped into the shower, turning on the faucet. Warm water cascaded down, gently kissing her skin before enveloping her completely. Each droplet, sparkling like a tiny diamond in the soft light, sent a cascade of warm tingles across her skin. Her worries about college and leaving Wavecrest dissolved, spiraling away with the suds down the drain, as if the water cleansed not just her body but the weight of her concerns, rendering her lighter, almost buoyant.

Emerging from the shower, she wrapped herself in a fluffy towel, the warmth clinging to her skin. Steam curled around her like ethereal wisps, the perfect aftermath of her soothing shower. The thought of seeing Ethan again sent a flutter through her heart, a joy so profound it seemed to radiate from her, untouched by the water's embrace.

In the silence, punctuated only by the drip of water, Jessica grasped a profound realization. Today marked not just another chapter in her summer story but a step toward an exciting, unknown future—a future she hoped would cast Ethan Harris in a role beyond a fleeting summer memory.

Stepping out from the steam, Jessica returned to the comforting familiarity of her bedroom. She approached her vanity and sat on the embroidered stool. The mirror reflected her anticipation, her eyes sparkling, her smile revealing the excitement within. She studied her face, noting the natural flush that tinted her cheeks.

With skilled hands, Jessica applied her makeup with practiced ease. A hint of mascara brushed against her long lashes, framing her large, expressive blue eyes. She dabbed a soft peach blush onto the apples of her cheeks, giving her a radiant glow. A light pink gloss on her lips completed the look, her smile reflecting her satisfaction with the subtle enhancements.

She brushed her wet hair, encouraging the natural waves to form around her shoulders. Opting against a hairdryer, she decided to let her hair air dry into beachy curls, embracing a carefree summer style.

Next came the choice of outfit—a statement of self and intention for the day ahead. After browsing through her closet, she made her choice and donned the chosen garment, assessing her appearance in the mirror.

In the reflection, Jessica saw how the cobalt blue of her crocheted poncho enveloped her, its hue vibrant against her skin. The poncho, an intricate tapestry of lace-like patterns, allowed glimpses of the white t-shirt beneath, its simplicity cradled by the elaborate weave. As she moved, even with the slightest twirl, the scalloped edges of her poncho danced lightly, giving her an effortless bohemian elegance that seemed to whisper of distant shores and sunlit afternoons.

As Jessica's eyes drifted downward, they paused on the denim shorts hugging her hips, their snug fit complementing the intricate weave of the poncho above. A small, satisfied smile played on her lips, a silent testament to the outfit's blend of elegance and ease that mirrored her own spirit. The way the fabric moved with her, the colors against her skin in the mirror—they all whispered of open skies and adventures waiting just outside her door.

As she slipped her feet into sandals, she couldn't help but smile as she gazed at the tiny butterflies adorning her toes, compliments of Fawn's artistic touch. These whimsical designs were more than mere decoration; they were a bridge to the previous night's laughter and dreams, a reminder of the joy in shared moments and the anticipation of today's adventure with Ethan.

This was Jessica in all her exuberant charm—a medley of carefree spirit, youthful beauty, and an infectious anticipation that glowed from within. Facing the mirror one last time, she nodded at her reflection, a silent pact made with the image that beamed back happiness and confidence. She was ready.

As Jessica stepped out of her house, she felt the thrum of excitement pulsating within her heart, a beat that matched her steps toward her destination. The sun's warmth wrapped around her as she walked the familiar path, her mind a blend of last night's conversations and today's possibilities. Each thought accelerated her heartbeat, drawing her closer not only to new experiences but also to a deeper understanding of the woman she was meant to be.

Just ahead, the boardwalk stretched out before her, a blank canvas eager for the day's colors—unpainted but vivid with potential in her imagination. Today marked not just another page in her summer story but perhaps the beginning of an entirely new chapter in which Ethan would play a starring role. With each step toward their meeting place, Jessica's smile widened—a beacon that spoke not only of joy but also of an open heart, ready to explore the path ahead with Ethan by her side.

The mid-morning sunlight streamed through the window, coaxing Fawn from her dreams. She savored a moment in bed, allowing the last night's festivities to blend with today's bright, warm hues. The Art Contest, a thrilling spark of anticipation, had jolted her awake, filling her with a surge of excitement.

Stretching, Fawn sat up, her eyes adjusting to the daylight that washed over the familiar chaos of her bedroom. This room, a living canvas of her vibrant artistry, had witnessed her transformation from a child to a budding artist. The walls, a patchwork tapestry of paintings and sketches, were the silent storytellers of her journey. Each stroke and color on canvas and paper revealed a fragment of her soul.

Swinging her legs over the edge of the bed, a spot shared with Jessica during countless sleepovers, Fawn took in the scene. The throw pillows scattered around the room weren't just splashes of color; they cushioned whispered secrets and laughter that once filled the nights. She could almost hear Jessica's laughter echoing in the room as she glanced at a photograph pinned to the corkboard above her desk—a snapshot of one such sleepover where they had dressed up in boas and oversized sunglasses, striking dramatic poses for an imaginary audience.

Against one wall stood her dresser, its surface a testament to their sisterly bond. Framed photos capturing moments frozen in time: her and Jessica at school dances, on beach outings, their arms around each other's shoulders, always together. It was more than a piece of furniture; it was a keeper of memories.

Fawn anxiously slid into a pair of vibrant red shorts trimmed with white—a favorite for its comfort and flair—and paired them with a relaxed white t-shirt tied at the waist. The sequined detail on her shirt caught the light as she moved, reflecting her artistic spirit even in her choice of clothing.

As she opened the bedroom door, she paused, casting a glance over her room. Her eyes settled on the mural covering an entire wall—a vast depiction that brought Wavecrest's shoreline into her home. This was more than just a painting; it was a tribute to countless sunsets enjoyed with her best friend, each wave a testament to their shared moments.

Descending from her personal gallery of memories and dreams, Fawn followed the comforting scent of coffee wafting from below. Each step down the stairs brought her closer to the day's promise—the high school and Art Contest loomed like a blank canvas eager for its first brushstroke.

"Good morning, Mom," she called out upon entering the kitchen, her voice still husky from a night filled with laughter and conversation. The room, awash in the gentle light of morning, wrapped around her like a well-worn sweater.

Anna glanced up from the stove, where she was stirring a pot of simmering oatmeal. Her short, dark blonde hair, cut in a lively pixie style, caught the kitchen lights with a subtle shimmer.

"Morning, sweetheart," she responded, her stirring pausing as she smiled. "Did you and Jessica have a good time last night?"

Bubbling with excitement, Fawn pulled out a stool from under the kitchen island and sat down. The sturdy surface, cluttered with a scattering of her art supplies, was a testament to its versatility as it changed roles from a culinary workspace to an artist's corner at her whim.

"We had an amazing time," she began, her hands moving as though she could paint the scenes in the air for her mother. "The beach party was awesome. It was so much fun dancing and hanging out. Jessica met this hot-looking guy named Ethan, who is visiting for the summer. They really hit it off."

Anna leaned against the polished granite countertop as she gave Fawn her undivided attention. The oatmeal simmered behind her, the kitchen surrounding them in warmth. This space was more than a place to eat; it was a haven for family bonding and storytelling.

Fawn shared tales of dancing under the stars, her eyes glittering like the sequins on her shirt. She described an impromptu volleyball game among new friends, her enthusiasm painting the scene with her hands.

When Fawn's account of Tommy Reynolds and the Art Contest came up, it sparked a subtle shift in Anna's expression—a mix of concern and happiness flickered in her eyes. With breakfast ready, she and Fawn moved to the rectangular kitchen table, a silent witness to quieter conversations and family gatherings. Anna placed a bowl in front of her daughter and sat across from her, their morning ritual unfolding in the quiet of the kitchen.

As Fawn's animated tales dwindled, a contemplative silence enveloped the room, heavy with unspoken words. Across the table, she noticed her mother's smile dim, replaced by a crease of contemplation between her brows. The usual light in her eyes seemed to fade, a shadow of worry overtaking her features. Sensing the change, Fawn paused, her spoon in mid-air, her expression mirroring the concern that had quietly taken hold of her mother.

"What's the matter, Mom?" Fawn's voice softened, tinged with concern. "You seem troubled."

Anna's grip tightened on her spoon, betraying a moment of hesitation that charged the room with tension. Taking a deep breath, she braced herself for the conversation ahead. Reaching across the table, she sought Fawn's hand, longing for the comfort of her touch.

"Sweetheart," Anna began, her voice heavy and somber. "There's something important your father and I need to discuss with you."

Fawn's eyes locked onto her mother's, reflecting the seriousness of the moment. A mix of curiosity and concern flickered in her eyes. "What is it, Mom?"

Anna's voice softened. "Honey, we've been contemplating the changes that life some-times necessitates." She paused, gathering her thoughts. "I know this may be hard for you to understand, but living in Wavecrest has become very difficult for us financially." Struggling to keep her voice steady, she continued, "Because of this, your father and I have had to make some difficult decisions."

Fawn's spoon clattered against her bowl, a silent echo of her growing confusion. "What do you mean by 'difficult decisions?'" she asked, her voice quivering with uncertainty.

"With you leaving for Boston at the end of the summer, your father and I have decided it's time for us to make a change in our lives, too."

"And what change is that?" Anxiety edged Fawn's words.

With a look of sorrow, Anna disclosed, "We're going to move, honey. We're going to sell the house and move to Montana."

At that moment, the room seemed to sway under Fawn's feet, the once comforting walls now distant and cold. Her heart raced as she struggled with the implications of her mother's words—not only for her, but also for Jessica.

"Sell the house? But Mom…" Fawn's voice broke. "Wavecrest is our home. It's where all my memories are—with Dad, with you, and with Jess." Her voice dwindled to a whisper, emotions welling up.

Anna nodded sympathetically. "I know how much this place means to you." She tightened her grip on Fawn's hand, offering a tender reassurance. "Believe me. This wasn't an easy decision for us either."

Suddenly, the kitchen was no longer a place of meals and memories. It had become a poignant crossroads between the cherished past and the uncertain future—a junction where childhood ended, and adulthood loomed with all its complexities.

"I don't believe this," Fawn murmured, her voice strained with emotion. "This can't be happening." A pang of realization gripped her, signaling a tidal wave of change.

Tears welled in Anna's eyes, a testament to the struggle to hold back her sorrow. "Sweetheart, I'm so sorry. Your father and I agonized over this. It was not an easy choice. But we must think about our future and do what's best for our family. We just can't afford to live here anymore."

The sensation of the earth crumbling under Fawn's feet overwhelmed her. "So, when are we moving?" she asked, her voice barely audible.

Anna's reply was tender. "We're planning to move at the end of August. This will give us enough time to pack and make arrangements for the move."

A numbness enveloped Fawn, making it seem as if she were watching the conversation unfold from outside her body. "The end of August? But that's when I'll be leaving for college," she protested, her voice thick with emotion.

Anna met her gaze, mirroring the pain she saw. "I know, honey. We thought if we left at the same time, it would be less difficult for you."

With a heavy heart reflected in her eyes, Anna reached for Fawn's bowl and returned to the stove. As she scraped the uneaten oatmeal back into the bubbling pot, a torrent of thoughts overwhelmed Fawn: Jessica, Wavecrest, and Montana, of all places. Everything was changing too fast, leaving her feeling utterly powerless to stem the tide.

Turning to face Fawn again, Anna's voice carried a note of maternal reassurance. "Look, honey, moving to Montana is going to be a big adjustment for all of us, but we'll be okay. Your father and I will do everything we can to make this transition as smooth as possible."

Rising from her seat, Fawn struggled to articulate her feelings. "I just can't believe this is happening, Mom. Wavecrest has always been our home. It's where Jess and I grew up."

Bridging the gap between them, Anna wrapped her daughter in a warm embrace, offering a beacon of comfort in the tumult of change. "I know, baby. Change is never easy, but your father and I will do everything we can to help you get through this."

In her mother's embrace, Fawn sought comfort, a safe haven from her swelling grief. A spark of hope flickered in the tight embrace, igniting an inner strength that, until now, lay dormant within her. But beneath that comfort, a sense of betrayal nagged at her—the stark realization that her parents did not include her in this monumental decision. She was their daughter, after all, molded by their love and dreams, yet excluded from a conversation that would change her life forever. Wavecrest, the setting of her childhood stories, was destined to become a mere memory, sacrificed to the demands of financial necessity and adult decisions.

Needing time alone to process this upheaval, she retreated to the familiarity of her bedroom, a sanctuary where thoughts and emotions roamed wild and untamed. She sought comfort among the whispers of the past and the echoes of laughter that had once filled the room. Taking her seat at the vanity, she confronted her reflection in the mirror—a tableau of her youth, now showing a pivotal transformation. Her reflection wasn't just that of an aspiring artist, but a young woman on the brink of irrevocable change.

With purposeful movements, Fawn applied her makeup, her hands steady despite the turmoil within. The makeup served as both a façade for the world and a shield for her grief. As she applied mascara, a determination solidified within her. The Summer Art Contest emerged in her mind, transforming from a mere local event into a beacon of hope, a chance to regain control of a life spiraling from her grasp.

The reflection in the mirror held a promise—a vow to seize this opportunity and craft it into something beautiful. She drew strength from the thought of standing before her peers and judges, expressing her soul through her art.

She stood, slinging her purse over her shoulder. Lingering at her room's doorway, she took in every corner filled with cherished memories, knowing her safe harbor would soon be left behind.

Yet, every goodbye brings a new greeting. The sun outside beckoned, inviting her into its embrace. It whispered promises of possibility and new beginnings, even as it acknowledged the pain of leaving behind what once was.

With a deep breath, almost ceremonial in its intent to prepare for the journey ahead, Fawn crossed the threshold of her home into a realm filled with both uncertainty and opportunities. The high school awaited like an old friend, ready to welcome her back one last time before ushering her off into the vast world of adulthood.

The path to school stretched out before her, weaving her past and future together like strands of a ribbon. Each step she took was a delicate balance between the weight of sadness and the lightness of hope. With every step, Fawn felt driven forward by the excitement of the contest—a chance to paint the first brushstroke on the canvas of her future and blend it with the rich colors of her life in Wavecrest.

# Chapter 6

-------------------------------------------------------------------

Filled with eager anticipation, Jessica made her way to the bustling epicenter of the board-walk, her footsteps in harmony with the rhythmic serenade of the waves, a melody that had lulled her to sleep more nights than she could count. With each step, the air enveloped her in its salty embrace, a gentle gesture from the sea, brought ashore by the soft caress of the wind. It seemed as though the sea itself extended an invisible hand, drawing patterns of mist in the air as an invitation to her.

As Jessica arrived at the boardwalk, a breathtaking view unfolded before her. The waves, majestic in their fury, rose from the ocean's depths like ancient titans, their power undisputed. They crashed against the shore, morphing into delicate veils of foam that shimmered in the sunlight, performing a dance of shadows and light across the beach.

At that moment, amidst nature's grandeur, Jessica felt an unseen presence envelop her, a tender cocoon of warmth and comfort that felt as real as a gentle hug. This unseen guardian, an essence interlaced with the very soul of Wavecrest, seemed to close the distance, its silent vigil encircling her with parental care.

She felt the embrace deepen, a comforting presence shaped by a childhood filled with its constant companionship and silent whispers of guidance. It was a poignant reminder of their intertwined lives, a subtle acknowledgment of the love and warmth that formed the foundation of this personal bond, a testament to connections deeply rooted in the fabric of her being.

Perched on the edge of the sea's timeless melody, Jessica immersed herself in the comforting presence of the town's protective spirit. It was a quiet recognition that even as the tides of life ebbed and flowed, the core of Wavecrest—its unseen heart, its love—would remain a steadfast anchor in her soul.

Her lips curved into a hopeful smile as she stepped onto the weathered planks, her eyes bright with expectation as she scanned the golden stretch of beach. The morning's peace enveloped her, punctuated by the few birds that dotted the landscape, a contrast to its usual bustle. Each beat of her heart mirrored her desire to spot one individual among the calm. Ethan!

Suddenly, she saw him against the backdrop of the ocean's rhythm, his form blending with the spray of the waves—a mesmerizing sight. His dark hair, wet from his encounter with the ocean, lay against his forehead, a silent witness to his aquatic adventure. The sun's rays enveloped him, turning the droplets on his skin into glistening jewels and casting an almost otherworldly glow around him.

His swim trunks, vibrant against the muted tones of the beach, seemed to shout his love for life, mirroring his energetic soul. Beside him, his surfboard hinted at his passion for the sea, for the exhilaration found in conquering its waves.

Jessica was struck by the realization of Ethan's deep connection with the ocean, a revelation that added depth to his already intriguing character. Fueled by this discovery, she hastened her approach, the beach's warm sand welcoming her steps, each grain weaving a tapestry of sensations underfoot.

With each step that brought them closer, Jessica's heart matched the waves' rhythm, creating a harmonious blend of nature's grandeur and their budding connection. Ahead lay a day full of exploration, unguarded laughter, and the possibility of a deeper connection taking root.

As she approached, Ethan's face broke into a wide, welcoming smile, and he quickly bridged the gap between them. Their greeting, a warm hug, mirrored the joy of their reunion.

"Wow. You were already surfing this morning!" Jessica exclaimed, her voice a mixture of admiration and playfulness, her eyes sparkling with mirth. "You really do love to surf, huh?"

"Oh, yeah. I've been riding those waves since I could walk. I'm practically part fish," Ethan joked, miming swimming motions that added a light-hearted flair to their conversation.

A laugh bubbled up from Jessica at his theatrics. "A surfing fish? Now, that's a sight I'd pay to see! Do you have any secret moves, like the 'Flippity-Flop' or the 'Tidal Twirl'?"

Ethan adopted a mock-serious tone. "Ah, the legendary 'Flippity-Flop.' Only the bravest dare to attempt it. And as for the 'Tidal Twirl,' it requires years of intense training."

"Well, I hope you'll give me a private lesson someday. Maybe you can teach me the 'Splash-and-Spin' maneuver," Jessica teased, playfully elbowing him.

"Hmm, the 'Splash-and-Spin' is quite advanced. But for you, I could make an exception. Just be prepared for the waves of laughter that will follow!" Ethan's playful warning sparked more laughter, their voices rising above the crashing waves.

As their banter and laughter filled the salty sea air, a seagull squawked overhead, almost as though joining in their amusement. Arm in arm, they sauntered back toward the boardwalk, their easy camaraderie painting an atmosphere of joy and affection that promised to color the rest of their day together.

Bathed in the glow of their laughter, Jessica and Ethan strolled along the boardwalk, their hands intertwined as the ocean breeze flirted with their hair. The peaceful harmony of their walk was interrupted by the sound of Ethan's stomach, a comical interruption to their tranquil melody. His eyes scanned the lively scene, embarking on a mission for food. Jessica, still full from breakfast, watched his quest with a quiet chuckle of amusement.

The air around them hummed, vibrant with the chatter of vendors heralding their culinary delights. The rich and inviting scent of buttered rolls ensnared Ethan's senses, drawing him irresistibly toward a bustling stand. His eyes lit up with the thrill of discovery as he glanced back at Jessica, a gleam of excitement dancing in his eyes.

"I found the ultimate snack," he proclaimed, gesturing toward the source of the enticing aroma. "I can never resist buttered rolls. Would you like one?"

Jessica's smile spread, as radiant as the sun. "I'm good, thanks," she replied, her tone light and satisfied. "But a bottle of water would be great."

Leaving her at a table, Ethan ventured into the line at the roll stand, surrounded by the rich scent of butter and bread that heightened his hunger. After a brief wait, he was rewarded with a warm buttery roll that promised sheer joy.

Returning to Jessica, roll in hand, Ethan took his seat and savored his snack. Each bite was a testament to the simple pleasures in life, and Jessica observed him with a heart growing fonder by the moment. His every contented murmur and the joy in his features deepened her affection for him. Sipping her water, she reveled in the beauty of the moment and the soft feelings for Ethan that blossomed in her heart.

As Ethan savored the last bite of his roll, they turned their gaze to the day stretching before them, a pristine canvas eager for the strokes of adventure that awaited. Their conversation, alive with anticipation, felt like selecting colors for the masterpiece of memories they were about to create.

Jessica's eyes glimmered with a hint of playfulness, her suggestion carrying the thrill of discovery. "You know, we could spend the day exploring the hidden coves. The coves only us locals know about."

Ethan leaned forward, captivated by the idea, his interest reflecting the adventurous gleam in Jessica's eyes. "Hidden coves, you say? I'm intrigued. Go on."

Her grin widened, as inviting as the call of an unseen oasis. "I've been to a few of them with my friends. They're tucked away in secluded spots, away from everything. It's like stepping into a hidden paradise."

Ethan's excitement was palpable. "Wow. Let's do that. I'm all for discovering these hidden gems. Lead the way, Jessica."

Leaving behind the quaint nook and the fading aroma of buttered rolls, they set out, their fingers laced together in silent promise. Jessica's heart thrummed in harmony with the ocean's call, pulsing with excitement for the day that lay unfolded before them.

Together, they delved into their adventure, guided by Jessica's intimate knowledge of the hidden coves. The sun blanketed their path with its warm, golden light, blessing their journey as they left the familiar comfort of the boardwalk. As they embraced the thrill of exploration, the rest of the world seemed to dissolve, leaving only the magnetic pull of their growing connection.

As Fawn meandered through the well-trodden streets of Wavecrest, a flood of nostalgia washed over her. The very paths she walked on, the landmarks they led to, all whispered tales of her youth, painting a vivid tapestry of friendships and moments that had woven her into the fabric of this close-knit community.

Passing an empty playground that had once been a repository of her youthful energy, Fawn's memories took flight, returning to the sunny days spent in the company of her and Jessica's closest friend, Lily Green, a girl whose quiet demeanor was magnified by the large glasses that framed her doe-like eyes. Their laughter, once unrestrained in this playground, echoed in Fawn's heart, bringing back the pure joy and innocence of those days. A shadow of sadness crossed her thoughts as she recalled the day Lily moved away, taking a piece of their childhood with her.

As she walked toward the high school, Fawn's eyes were drawn to a house that had once pulsed with the life of Laura Perkins. Overwhelmed with memories of birthday parties filled with laughter and the warmth of friendship, Fawn felt a comforting sense of gratitude for those moments. She paused to pay a silent tribute to the now-hushed house, acknowledging Laura's absence, her relocation leaving a space that teemed with their shared past.

Further on, a picturesque avenue guarded by towering trees brought back memories of adventures with Mark Santiago. The thrill of their bike rides along this tree-shaded street lingered with her: the wind's playful tug at her hair, their laughter cutting through the air, and the exhilarating sense of freedom. Yet another friend who had stepped beyond Wavecrest's boundaries, leaving an enduring impression on Fawn's heart.

As she navigated the landscapes so deeply imprinted with the essence of her childhood, Fawn was bathed in the poignant memories that painted the rich canvas of her life in Wavecrest. Each vivid memory brought a bittersweet smile across her face, igniting a profound sense of gratitude for the bonds forged and moments spent within this treasured coastal enclave.

With the high school looming ahead, Fawn paused her journey for a moment as her eyes instinctively veered toward Jessica's house, though it was out of sight from her current vantage. This place, a significant marker in her life's narrative, unleashed a torrent of cherished memories. The thought of that familiar home sent waves of warmth cascading through her, vibrating with deep affection and nostalgia.

Memories of moonlit confessions from countless sleepovers came flooding back. Beneath the Reeses' welcoming eaves, they had nestled into cozy blankets, their hushed mirth blossoming into heartfelt revelations about young love as the night gradually yielded to the morning sun. Jessica's home had been a quiet observer to their lively chatter, their hopes and dreams, and the trials and triumphs of their journey through adolescence together.

Fawn's mind danced to the memories of the innocent pranks they had orchestrated against their unwitting teachers, the sweetness of their laughter still resonating within her. Their shared sense of humor fueled their connection, transforming even the simplest moments into fond memories and cementing their reputation as partners in crime.

In moments of despair, Fawn always found comfort in the sanctuary of Jessica's unwavering support. She had been her beacon, a guiding light through the stormiest seas, offering a comforting hug and soothing words in times of heartache or academic stress. Their lives, so deeply intertwined, had found solace and resilience against life's adversities. This unity had fortified their friendship, molding it with the resilience of tempered steel.

These vibrant echoes of shared joy, camaraderie, and steadfast companionship attested to the profound connection between Fawn and Jessica. Through life's rhythmic dance of highs and lows, they twirled in the radiant days and held firm in the storm-tossed nights, akin to sisters bound not by blood but by the powerful chords of their hearts.

As Fawn's journey down memory lane neared its end, a veil of sadness enveloped her. The poignant realization that these memories, though securely lodged within her heart, would soon fade into distant echoes from a bygone era. The looming move of her family and the sale of their home in Wavecrest weighed heavily on her heart.

As she approached the entrance to her high school, a spark of determination kindled within her. Drawing a deep, fortifying breath, she embraced the resolve to live in the now and chase the promise of new beginnings. The vibrant energy of the school coursed through her, nudging her to realize that this was her chance to write the final chapter of her Wavecrest story, to inscribe her legacy within these hallowed halls, a testament to her passage through its doors.

Stepping inside, Fawn entered a realm where light and shadow played across the walls, bringing to life the sketches that adorned the lobby. Ink and pencil masterpieces revealed the heartfelt expressions of her peers, each piece a narrative that tugged at her soul. The atmosphere, enriched by this visual chorus of black-and-white creations, ignited a spark of eager anticipation in her.

In this gallery of youthful expressions, she noticed a group of teachers engaged in lively discussion, their words mingling with the backdrop of contest forms and artistic endeavors. Among them was Mrs. Gwendolyn Sprite, her art teacher, whose eyes met hers with a greeting as warm as the morning sun.

"Fawn, dear!" exclaimed Mrs. Sprite, her voice bubbling with genuine excitement. "How wonderful to see you! Have you come to enter the contest?"

Affirming with a nod, Fawn felt a mix of nerves and excitement churn within her. "Yes, Mrs. Sprite, that's why I'm here."

Mrs. Sprite's eyes sparkled with encouragement, her belief in Fawn's talent clear. "Your art has always stood out to me, Fawn. You have a distinct flair that could very well take you to the top in this competition." She leaned in, emphasizing her following words. "Just be mindful of the guidelines. Your piece needs to be on a canvas no larger than 11 x 14, and it must be a sketch in ink or pencil. It's important that you stick to these requirements; they're quite strict about them."

Her cheeks warmed by the praise, Fawn offered her gratitude, "Thank you, Mrs. Sprite. I'll do my best."

Clutching the contest form, Fawn penned down her information, her commitment etched with each stroke of ink. After handing the completed form back to Mrs. Sprite, a sense of accomplishment filled her with every breath.

"Now it's official," Mrs. Sprite announced, her voice laced with eager anticipation. "I look forward to seeing what you create. All the best, dear."

Overwhelmed with appreciation and a renewed sense of purpose, Fawn replied, "Thank you, Mrs. Sprite."

As she started to leave, the Art Contest loomed in her mind as a beacon of challenge and potential triumph. But her attention was captured by a familiar figure sitting quietly in a corner: Felix Copeland, a classmate she had recognized but never truly known. Driven by a budding curiosity, Fawn decided to bridge the gap and approached him for a friendly introduction.

Felix stood somewhat apart from the flurry of school life, his slender frame and unassuming presence merging with the vibrant hues of the surrounding art, rendering him almost invisible. A cloak of self-doubt hung around him, the product of years of mockery for his geeky persona, the glasses resting on his nose, and his less-than-fashionable clothes. The constant barbs, aimed at his unique name and lack of interest in sports, had whittled away at his self-confidence. Once swept up in the currents of her peers' behavior, Fawn had silently participated in the teasing, a memory she now looked back on with regret.

As the sands of time sculpted her journey through high school, Fawn's blossoming maturity significantly shifted her perspective. A sprout of genuine remorse took root in her heart for her insensitivity toward Felix. Though she made no effort to understand the layers beneath his bespectacled gaze, witnessing him bear the relentless bullying stirred a wellspring of empathy within her.

Moved by this newfound understanding, she felt an undeniable pull to reach out to him.

As she approached, a firm resolve took shape within her, shedding the layers of apathy that had kept them apart. She was determined to bridge the gap of misunderstanding that had separated them for so long.

"Hey Felix!" she called out with a warm smile.

Caught off guard, Felix looked up to meet her gaze, his eyes—magnified behind his glasses—widening in surprise. The recognition set off a flurry of emotions within him. Fawn, the girl who had haunted the corners of his heart since the innocent days of seventh grade, was now speaking to him.

Gathering his courage, he managed to reply, albeit with a slight tremor in his voice, "Hey, Fawn. What brings you here?"

Fawn's answer was calm and filled with sincere interest. "I've just signed up for the art contest. What about you?"

Hearing the genuine curiosity in Fawn's voice, Felix relaxed, making a habitual gesture of adjusting his glasses. His excitement caused him to become more animated. "Oh, cool. I've already turned in my drawing. Do you want to see it?"

Fawn's smile widened, warmth and eagerness evident. "Yes, I'd love to." She followed Felix, intrigued by the prospect of seeing the world from his perspective, ready to appreciate his artistic expression.

When she reached the easel where Felix's artwork was displayed, her eyes were drawn to the sketch depicting a stately home nestled between two majestic trees. Although the drawing lacked refined detail, she chose not to critique it, wary of dampening Felix's budding confidence. With a casual curiosity, she inquired, "Interesting. Can you tell me more about it?"

Felix's expression brightened with pride and eager anticipation, bolstered by Fawn's interest. He eagerly shared, "It's Lipton Manor. You know, that big house on Washington Street?"

Understanding dawned on Fawn, and she masked her thoughts behind a veil of encouragement. "Oh, right. I can see what you were aiming for. You've really managed to capture its spirit," she replied.

Acknowledging the potential in Felix's work, Fawn chose to focus on his dedication and passion. Her encouragement aimed to build his confidence, ensuring their interaction remained uplifting and supportive.

As she engaged in conversation with Felix, a resonant, authoritative voice cut through the air, instantly commanding her attention. It was Mr. Morrison, the principal, whose presence seemed to loom large—not just in stature, but in the sense of order he imposed. His silver hair and sharp features had always marked him as a figure of authority, inspiring both respect and nervousness in even the unruliest students.

Although her days as a student were behind her, the sound of Mr. Morrison's voice still conjured a familiar unease, a reminder of the times his stern gaze had unsettled her. Facing him, Fawn managed to put on a polite smile, the respect ingrained from her high school days lingering.

"Hello, Mr. Morrison. I was just leaving," she offered, her voice carrying a hint of the deference she felt.

Mr. Morrison, with his commanding aura, eyed Fawn, his presence filling the space. "Where is Ms. Reese? Why isn't she with you? You know that trouble always comes in pairs," he remarked, nodding to their notorious reputation for pranks.

Fawn, suppressing a chuckle at his observation, replied, "She's doing her own thing today. I'm just here to sign up for the Art Contest."

With his arms folded behind his back, Mr. Morrison issued a firm reminder. "Make sure you behave yourself while you're here, Ms. Gaddesden. I'm in no mood for your silly pranks today."

With that, he turned to leave, his departure as commanding as his entrance. Fawn watched him go, reflecting on the countless times she and Jessica were summoned to his office. Yet, as he paused at the edge of the corridor, a subtle change in his demeanor caught her off guard.

In a moment of unexpected vulnerability, Mr. Morrison looked back at Fawn, his usual sternness giving way to a softer, more thoughtful tone.

"I'm going to miss you, Fawn. Good luck out there," he said, a farewell that revealed a rare glimpse into the depth of his character.

Stunned by this softer side of Mr. Morrison, Fawn remained still, his parting words echoing in her mind, a poignant reminder of the complexities hidden within those they presume to fully understand.

As she prepared to leave, Fawn offered Felix a soft, nurturing farewell smile. The familiar scent of aged paper and graphite filled the air as she made her way to the exit. However, just before her hand reached the cool handle of the door, an impulsive thought stopped her, drawing her back towards Felix.

Turning on her heel, her eyes gleaming with anticipation, she called across the lobby. "Hey, Jerry Cranmer is having a graduation party at his house on Saturday. Would you like to come?"

Felix's reaction was one of sheer surprise, his eyes widening at the thought of attending a gathering with his peers. He purposely avoided these encounters due to his shyness and the scars from being bullied. A tsunami of self-doubt threatened to sweep him away, causing him to stammer, "Oh, I don't know."

Yet, Fawn remained unaffected by his hesitation. Her enthusiasm was infectious, her eyes shining with the promise of inclusion and celebration.

"Come on, Felix. It'll be fun. We've all worked hard to get through high school, and we deserve to celebrate. That includes you, too!" she encouraged, her voice rich with conviction.

Moved by Fawn's sincere invitation, Felix felt a surge of courage and a newfound willingness to step beyond his usual confines. He found himself agreeing, albeit with a hint of nervous excitement, "Alright. I'll go."

Fawn's smile broadened, a reflection of her delight, as she confirmed, "Great! See you there, Felix."

Buoyed by this positive exchange, she pushed through the glass barrier and stepped back into the town's vibrant hum and comforting scent. Her heart pulsed with the rhythm of exhilaration—for the Art Contest and the upcoming graduation party, where she and her fellow graduates would toast to their shared journey and to the dreams they dared to dream.

# Chapter 7

-------------------------------------------------------

Under the caress of the afternoon sun, Wavecrest revealed itself as a serene canvas paint-ed in soft hues, exuding tranquility. Hand in hand, Jessica and Ethan ventured into the enclaves of the town's lesser-known sanctuaries, where the whispers of the landscape spoke volumes to Jessica. These secluded retreats, guarded by the intimacy of local lore, beckoned with a mysterious allure. For Jessica, unveiling these treasured spots to Ethan was akin to sharing the sacred secrets of her coastal haven, with Ethan assuming the role of an awe-struck voyager, navigated by her guidance.

Their exploration began in a cove shielded by lofty cliffs and ancient sentinels watching over the meeting of land and sea. Here, the ocean's waves crashed against the unyielding shore in a relentless dance, creating a melody unique to the seascape. Seagulls danced above, their calls interweaving with the ocean's rhythm, orchestrating a symphony of the wild. This peaceful alcove, nestled in nature's splendor, captured Ethan's wonder. The sparkle in Jessica's eyes, lit with the thrill of sharing this realm, only enriched his fascination. Each spark in her eyes cast the surroundings in a new light, unveiling the marvels that lay before them.

Their next escapade brought them to a cove with a hidden beach, its entrance obscured by lush foliage that shaded a winding path. The beach's sands, warm and inviting, caressed their feet, while the soft whispers of waves serenaded them with nature's lullaby. Jessica, with her talent for storytelling, brought the tide pools to life, narrating the tales of the creatures dwelling within. Ethan, drawn into her world, knelt beside her, their shoulders brushing as they explored the microcosm of marine life. Jessica's passion and insight turned a simple observation into an immersive journey.

With each mystery they unraveled, Jessica's knowledge of these secret coves painted their journey with the vivid hues of nature's hidden wonders. Ethan, being more of a participant than a spectator, was mesmerized by the glow and eagerness that Jessica radiated. These coves became more than just places; they were glimpses into the essence of Jessica's soul, portals to the enchantment that wove her reality. Every speck of sand, every caress of a wave, and every shimmering pool was a tribute to that enchantment, drawing Ethan deeper into the tapestry of Jessica's world.

As the sun embarked on its gradual descent, the sky transformed into a canvas streaked with shades of molten gold and fiery amber. Jessica led Ethan to their final stop—a cove that held a special place in her heart. This secluded treasure, saved for the last of their day's exploration, was embraced by the serene arms of nature, untouched by the chaos outside. Though the day's adventures had lent a touch of fatigue, Jessica's steps were buoyed by an infectious enthusiasm reflected in the gleam of her eyes. The anticipation of unveiling this sacred space to Ethan filled her with vibrant energy, an emotion too profound to articulate.

An awe-inspiring sight greeted them as they approached the entrance to the cove. Giant trees, guardians of the forest, reached skyward, their branches interlocking to form a canopy that scattered light and shadow below. This leafy dome created an atmosphere of twilight serenity, a sanctuary bathed in sunlight, suggesting a collusion of the elements to create a peaceful haven. She closed her eyes for a moment, taking a deep breath that filled her with a profound sense of peace that seemed to lift the weight of the world from her shoulders.

This cove, situated further from the bustling shoreline, shielded itself from the full fury of the ocean. Yet, the melody of the sea reached their ears, a tender lullaby that spoke of waves embracing the distant shore. This gentle harmony between water and land whispered mysteries just out of reach, inviting the soul to wander into realms of wonder. It was in this space that an indescribable resonance to something greater enveloped them, weaving a spell of enchantment around their experience.

At the heart of the cove, a stream flowed over smooth stones that cascaded into delicate waterfalls. This lively brook, clear and vibrant, reflected the pristine beauty of their hidden retreat and nurtured a lush array of flora along its banks. Flowers in a variety of colors and shapes adorned the edges of the cove, their petals reaching upward as though seeking to hold the very essence of beauty. The air was alive with the scent of the flowers, which mingled with the earthy perfume, creating an aromatic symphony that filled the cove with a palpable sense of magic and vitality.

For Jessica, this place was more than a mere retreat; it cradled her in the town's essence, a gentle whisper that danced through the air, wrapping her in a comfort that seeped deep into her bones. Amid the beauty and serenity, she didn't just find peace; she melded with something beyond the tangible, a nurturing presence that seemed to echo the spirit of Wavecrest itself. The leaves rustled as if in greeting, the waves whispered secrets only her heart could hear, and the sunlight bathed her in a warmth that felt like a personal embrace from the very soul of the town.

As the day's light softened into golden hues, Jessica and Ethan found their place in the center of the cove, their final refuge. Nature seemed to have carved a seat just for them, a log that embraced their figures with gentle precision. They fit together as if designed to complement each other against the backdrop of the cove's dance of light and shadow, reflecting the growing affection between them.

Overwhelmed by the beauty surrounding them, Ethan broke the comfortable silence. "This place... it feels like we've stepped into another world. It's incredible, Jessica."

Her eyes lit up with shared wonder. "I know. It's amazing, right?"

Ethan's gaze became introspective. "All of Wavecrest is amazing," he mused, his voice filled with awe. "There's something mystical about this place. I've felt it since the first day I got here. It's like..." He paused, struggling to encapsulate the feeling, then shrugged, resigned to the mystery. "Well, I can't really explain it."

Jessica nodded, her smile soft and knowing. "Well, I've always had that feeling, ever since I was little. It's comforting, you know?" she confided, her tone revealing deep affection for her hometown. Gazing around their serene surroundings, her eyes reflected its beauty. "I've only been to this cove a few times," she continued, her voice tinged with shyness. Then, casting a sheepish glance, she added, "You know, you're the only person I've ever brought here."

His response was one of humble surprise. "Really?" he asked, touched by the gesture. "That means a lot to me, Jess. I'm honored." His sincerity underscored the depth of the moment, acknowledging the trust Jessica had placed in him by sharing her most treasured retreat.

In this secluded haven, something unspoken yet brimming with significance passed between them, highlighted by Jessica's act of sharing her most sacred place with Ethan. The air seemed charged with a new understanding, a mutual recognition of something precious blossoming in the silence that enveloped their shared solitude.

Seated beside Ethan on the log, Jessica found herself captivated by the unique looking cross that hung from his neck. Its intricate craftsmanship, echoing tales of ancient lore, seemed to call out to her. With a tenderness akin to reverence, she reached out, her fingers delicately tracing its contours, a gesture that stirred a deep emotion in Ethan.

"It's beautiful," she whispered, the quiet admiration in her voice mingling with the serene whispers of the cove.

Ethan nodded, a prelude to sharing the cross's story. "My grandfather gave this to me when I was twelve," he shared, his voice a soft echo in the tranquil air. "It was more than just a gift. He described it as a guardian."

He paused, his eyes resting on the cross, now glowing softly in the dim light. "He said it was made by a monk centuries ago in a monastery nestled among the Tibetan peaks," Ethan recounted, his fingertips gently following the patterns etched into the metal. "The design, he told me, was inspired by mandalas—sacred symbols that, in a way, map the cosmos."

Jessica's curiosity piqued, and she leaned closer, locking her eyes on the intricate design. "Mandalas? What are they exactly?" she asked, her voice laced with fascination.

Ethan looked thoughtful. "Mandalas serve as spiritual guides, in a sense. Each detail within the pattern symbolizes a step on the path to greater understanding, to something beyond our immediate grasp."

Jessica's fingers grazed the cross, her touch gentle. "It's beautiful," she remarked, her eyes never leaving the detailed craftsmanship. "It must mean a lot to you, knowing its history and all."

His smile broadened, a soft glow of appreciation lighting up his features as he caught her gaze. "It does. And these stones," he explained, his fingers touching the embedded obsidian alongside hers. "They're said to act as protectors, keeping harm at bay."

Jessica's eyes lifted to meet Ethan's, her look one of deep interest and respect. "I've never seen anything quite like it. It's like you're wearing a piece of history," she said, her tone imbued with wonder.

As the late afternoon sun draped them in its golden hue, the story of the cross deepened its significance. For Jessica, it opened a window into the realm of ancient traditions and spiritual beliefs, an exhilarating discovery. Ethan, on the other hand, treasured it as a tangible connection to his grandfather, a symbol of the wisdom that had been passed down to him.

He then drew Jessica's attention to the delicate details adorning the edge of the cross. "See these tiny marks here?" he showed, guiding her fingers to feel the miniature engravings where each indentation held an obsidian stone. "This material, called obsidian, is actually volcanic glass."

As Jessica's fingertips explored the texture of the cross, her face lit up with curiosity. "Obsidian?" she echoed, intrigued by the unfamiliar word.

"Yeah," Ethan confirmed, pleased by her interest. "It's known for its protective properties. It is believed that these stones will protect the wearer from harm."

Her eyes remained fixed on the cross, absorbing this newfound knowledge. "So, each of these stones are like little guardians?" she mused, visibly fascinated by the thought. "That's really fascinating. I never knew jewelry could have such meaning."

A tender smile graced Ethan's lips as he met her gaze. "This isn't just a piece of jewelry; it's a legacy, a safeguard handed down through my family." His voice was laced with respect, bringing the history of the cross to life for Jessica in a new and meaningful way.

As he went on, his expression grew thoughtful. "My grandfather believed this cross would keep me safe, that it would act as my shield when he was no longer here to protect me." His sincere and heartfelt words mingled with the soft murmur of the waves, entwining the tale of his grandfather and the cross with the tranquil atmosphere of the cove.

Listening with unwavering attention, Jessica was moved by the depth of Ethan's connection to his grandfather. The emotion in his eyes and the weight of his words painted a vivid picture of an enduring legacy.

"It's as though he's still looking out for you," she said softly.

Ethan nodded, a warm acknowledgment in his eyes. "I know. I feel his presence all the time, like he's still guiding me." His eyes lingered on the cross before drifting toward the vast expanse where the ocean kissed the sky, lost in reflection.

In the serene embrace of the cove, Ethan's story became an integral part of their deepening bond, enriching it with a level of understanding and intimacy that went beyond mere words.

Touched by the depth of his tale, Jessica brushed her thumb across the surface of the cross. As she did, she felt a faint pulse emanate from the artifact, startling her with its unexpected warmth. The sensation was unlike anything she had ever felt, touching her heart in a way that words could never capture. This experience was as mysterious to her as it was comforting, hinting at a profound connection that went beyond the ordinary. Her eyes widened in shock, the warmth from the cross suffusing her. Almost instinctively, she released the cross from her grasp, a reflex to the unexpected yet intimate contact with the unknown.

Ethan's eyes met hers, wide with a mix of astonishment and recognition, silently acknowledging the mysterious energy pulsing between them. It was a look that said he, too, had felt that unique vibration, a secret he thought was his alone until now. In the space between their locked gazes, an unspoken realization bloomed, a realization that what bound them together was far from ordinary, enveloping them in a bubble of shared wonder. The cove around them, with its serene beauty and whispering winds, seemed to echo the rhythm of their synchronized heartbeats, their connection growing deeper, vibrating with the same intensity that thrummed through the earth beneath their feet.

As the day waned, the quiet growl of their stomachs prompted a return to reality. "We should probably head back," Jessica suggested, her words tinged with a hint of reluctance, hesitant to break the spell of the cove's tranquil atmosphere.

Ethan's agreement came silent, his hand finding Jessica's in a seamless gesture of unity. With their fingers entwined, they stood together, a silent pledge of the deep connection they had forged in the magical landscape of Wavecrest.

Together, they strolled along the cove's winding path, now bathed in the soft glow of the waning sun, their steps weaving a rhythm that echoed the harmony of their hearts. The cove, with its tranquil embrace, seemed to bid them a tender farewell, the very air around them pulsing with the vibrant essence of the connection they had nurtured. Even as they moved away from its sheltering bounds, the cove's serene farewell lingered, a reminder of the sanctuary they were leaving behind yet carrying within.

As the distance between them and the cove grew, Jessica and Ethan's footsteps found harmony with the vibrant pulse of Wavecrest. The bond they had nurtured dispelled any shadows of doubt, guiding them forward with a renewed sense of purpose. Hand in hand, their hearts found a rhythm in harmony with the bustling energy that welcomed them back. Against the canvas of the late afternoon's hues, the promise of a burgeoning romance unfolded, glowing with the warmth of newfound love, illuminating their path like the first stars adorning the twilight sky.

As the evening sky donned its dusky cloak, Fawn perched on the edge of her bed, a sanctuary as familiar as a childhood confidante. Her hands, operating on autopilot, wove the brush through her cascading blonde locks, her thoughts a whirlwind. Her room, a tangible expression of her vibrant creativity, was alive with colors and a mural that encapsulated the spirit of Wavecrest. Amid this burst of artistic fervor, she pondered her strategy for the forthcoming art contest. The choice between the meticulous precision of pencil lines and the bold dynamism of ink sketches fluttered through her mind, an artistic conundrum yet to find its resolution.

However, beneath this layer of creative contemplation, a deeper, more personal turmoil took root. Fawn faced the devastating prospect of sharing life-altering news with Jessica—that her home, a repository of their laughter and countless memories, would soon be on the market. Each nook and cranny of this haven was steeped in their collective history, and the shadow of this imminent change loomed over their last summer of unfettered youth before the diverging paths of college life beckoned.

The phone on her bedside table seemed almost to pulse with urgency, a silent call to action in the cozy warmth of her art-adorned bedroom. Fawn grappled with the weight of her decision. Would revealing this truth tonight cast a pall over Jessica's blossoming happiness with Ethan? This dilemma, a delicate balance between the candor their friendship warranted and the instinct to shield Jessica from sorrow, tugged at her heart.

Yet, deep down, Fawn knew what she had to do. The cornerstone of their friendship, cemented by unwavering trust and shared experiences, demanded openness. She could not withhold such a pivotal revelation from Jessica, her ally, through good times and bad. Although the future promised a maelstrom of change and looming goodbyes, their friendship stood as a beacon of hope, guiding them through the tempestuous seas of life's uncertainties.

Drawn by a need for clarity, Fawn rose and drifted toward the bedroom window. Before her, the sky unfurled a masterpiece, with sunset hues of gold and blush pink that mirrored the turmoil within. The shadows in the room grew long and bold, reaching across the walls to caress the artwork—each piece a reflection of her soul.

Surrounded by the evidence of her artistic journey and the tools that brought her visions to life, Fawn's determination solidified. She whispered a pledge into the gathering dusk, "Tonight, I'll tell her. Tonight, we'll face this together." It was a promise made in the sanctuary of her own space, a space vibrant, with a testament to the enduring connection she shared with Jessica.

As daylight surrendered to the night's embrace, Fawn prepared herself for the crucial conversation ahead. Standing before the mirror, she searched her reflection for a calm to steady her racing heart. With each breath, she reaffirmed her belief in the strength of their friendship, silently trusting in its ability to withstand the challenges to come.

She hesitated, her fingers hovering over her phone. Taking a deep breath, she finally tapped out her message: "Hey, r u busy? I need to talk to u." She released the words into the digital void, her heart hitching as she waited for a reply.

Moments that felt like hours later, her phone lit up with Jessica's response, a simple but solid: "ok. meet me at our rock at 9," accompanied by a heart emoji. Relief washed over Fawn, unwinding the tight coil of tension in her chest.

Despite the weight of the conversation that awaited them, Fawn allowed a smile to grace her lips. For a moment, she pictured Jessica in her mind, her fingers quickly typing, her eyes bright with excitement from the day. A surge of curiosity welled within her, eager to hear the latest about Jessica's adventures with Ethan. However, her smile vanished as quickly as it had appeared, immediately overshadowed by the dread of sharing the unsettling news.

As the time of their meeting drew nearer, a sense of urgency nudged Fawn from the stillness of her room toward the bustling boardwalk. Stepping out into the dusk, its light fading yet inviting, she found herself enveloped by the vibrant life of Wavecrest in the evening. The world ahead, pulsing with energy, seemed to echo the boardwalk's symphony of laughter and sea-sprayed melodies, offering her a momentary reprieve as she moved toward her destination.

Walking the familiar path, the flood of cherished memories was unmistakable. The night air, mingled with the salted whisper of the sea, transported her back to countless evenings spent on their sacred rock. This secluded spot had been their private haven, where laughter and confessions mingled freely under the stars' watchful gaze. With each step towards the boardwalk, the anticipation of seeing Jessica and the rock's significance grew. It had transformed from a mere piece of the landscape into a monument of their friendship, a silent witness to their whispered promises of 'forever' amidst the ceaseless sound of the waves.

As she stepped onto the wooden planks, the salty air and the rhythmic serenade of the ocean comforted her. Laughter and voices mingled around her, creating a melody of shared joy that, for a moment, illuminated her heart. Her eyes caught snapshots of intimacy in the crowd—couples sharing tender moments, their happiness a bright spark in the twilight.

As she passed the familiar facade of Hal's ice cream shop, a wave of nostalgia washed over her, igniting memories of summers past spent with Jessica. Their youth unfolded as a vibrant tapestry of fun-filled adventures, all painted against the backdrop of endless, sun-soaked days.

But time, ever relentless, propelled her forward, shortening the distance to her best friend. The sunset painted the world in golden hues, a natural beacon guiding her away from the lively boardwalk to their chosen meeting spot.

Leaving the vibrant life of the boardwalk behind, Fawn moved toward the beach, her heart a mix of heaviness and hope. As she neared their familiar meeting spot, she caught sight of Jessica, her presence a comforting silhouette against the vast, calm ocean. This sight sparked a surge of gratitude, grounding her amidst the swirling uncertainty of change.

As Fawn neared, Jessica immediately sensed something was amiss. The usual spark in Fawn's eyes was noticeably absent, even from a distance. Watching her best friend approach, a wave of worry washed over her. "What's going on?" she asked, her voice laced with concern as she reached out to Fawn.

Meeting Jessica's gaze, Fawn's voice carried a gentle encouragement. "Forget about that for now. I want to hear all about your day with Ethan. Tell me everything!"

Jessica's face brightened as she recounted the day's escapades with Ethan, her enthusiasm infectious. Fawn's response was a smile that belied the inner turmoil she felt, reveling in Jessica's happiness. Yet, beneath the surface, a tempest loomed, the reality of her news casting a long shadow on this serene interlude.

As the final echoes of Jessica's tale dissipated, a tangible silence enveloped them, heavy with unspoken fears and looming goodbyes. Fawn's eyes, clouded with the agony of impending loss, locked with Jessica's. A solitary tear escaped, carving a path down her cheek, foretelling the emotional storm on the horizon.

"There's something I need to tell you, Jess," Fawn murmured, her voice a fragile thread of sound amidst the brewing storm.

Apprehension deepened in Jessica's eyes, the gravity of Fawn's words pulling at her heart. "What's the matter, Fawn? You're scaring me," she said, her voice laced with concern.

Drawing a deep breath, Fawn braced herself against the crushing weight of her news. "My parents are selling the house. We're moving to Montana," she revealed, her voice laden with the burden of this new reality.

"What???" Jessica gasped, struck silent, her world suspended in disbelief. Fawn's announcement felt like a physical blow, shaking the foundation of their world. Her eyes, wide and searching, sought understanding in Fawn's tear-streaked face, as if trying to piece together the fractured image of their future.

"Montana, Jess! Can you believe it? Fucking Montana!" The desperation in Fawn's voice was evident, her heart breaking with each syllable. Tears cascaded down her cheeks, mirroring the depth of her anguish, the profound sense of displacement overwhelming her.

Her sobs tore through the silence, an unfiltered expression of grief, leaving her trembling in its aftermath.

Instinctively, Jessica drew Fawn into her arms, embracing her against the storm of emotions that swirled around them. She cradled her friend's grief, her own heart aching in resonance, yet steadfast in her resolve to be the support Fawn so desperately needed. Amid the upheaval, Jessica was determined to be Fawn's lighthouse, an unwavering beacon through the tumult of change and sorrow.

This poignant moment stood in sharp contrast to the carefree adventures they had envisioned for their summer, a harsh deviation from the joyous memories they had created in Wavecrest. The news of Fawn's impending move clouded their future, casting long shadows over their dreams of endless days filled with laughter and youth.

As the moon rose, casting a soft glow over them, Fawn's sobs gradually subsided, leaving a heavy weariness in their place. The quiet of the night seemed to hold them in a gentle embrace, a silent witness to the turmoil within.

With her vision blurred by tears, Jessica desperately searched for the right words to ease Fawn's pain. Yet, the right words remained elusive, the shock of the revelation binding her own thoughts. In this moment of unbearable sorrow, they found themselves adrift in a sudden sea of change, grappling for something solid to cling to.

"I can't believe this is happening, Jess," Fawn managed, her voice hoarse from crying.

Jessica tightened her hug, her voice steady yet thick with emotion. "I know. Neither can I. But you're not alone in this, Fawn. Whatever happens, we'll face it together—like we always have."

At Jessica's words, a fragile smile touched Fawn's lips, a testament to the solace she found in their unbreakable bond. Together, they brushed away their tears, a silent pledge to navigate the uncertainty ahead with shared strength.

As the ocean continued its eternal dance with the shore, Jessica and Fawn clung to one another, their hearts forged by the power of friendship. In their embrace, against the backdrop of an infinite sea, they found a beacon of hope—a light guiding them through the uncharted journey ahead. Together, they stood resilient, a testament to their unbreakable solidarity amidst life's relentless waves.

# Chapter 8

----------------------------------------------------------------

As the morning sun slipped through the curtains, it painted Jessica's room in hues of tender gold and shadow, gently coaxing her from a night restless with the echoes of Fawn's heartbreaking revelation. Her eyes fluttered open reluctantly, her heart heavy. Drawing a deep breath, she felt the chill of the air against her skin as she swung her legs from the warmth of her bed into the silent room—a stark contrast to the turmoil within. Dressed in a worn black tee that hung loosely over her frame, paired with blue sweatpants, she ventured down the hallway, her every step echoing the silent anguish she carried.

In the kitchen, Teresa moved with the practiced ease of someone well-acquainted with her surroundings, though her expression showed concern. At the sight of Jessica entering the room, she instantly discerned the depth of her daughter's grief—a sight she had mentally prepared for. The night before, when Jessica had returned, looking diminished and withdrawn, she had retreated to her room without uttering a single word. Teresa and Tom were already grappling with their own shock over Brian and Anna's abrupt decision to leave Wavecrest. The heavy silence that filled the room was a tacit recognition of how deeply this news had affected everyone involved.

Jessica moved closer to the table where Teresa waited. She collapsed into the chair, shrouded in a silence that Teresa delicately pierced. "Do you want to talk about it, sweetheart?" Her voice, tender and empathetic, aimed to close the distance created by Jessica's turmoil.

Overwhelmed by a flood of emotions, Jessica didn't lift her gaze. Her eyes, usually clear and calm, now reflected the chaos of a stormy sea, swirling with anger and grief. She breathed out a bitter, "I hate them," her voice heavy with pain, slicing through the calm of the morning.

Teresa absorbed the outburst with the calmness of understanding, knowing well the heart from which these words poured.

"Who do you hate, sweetheart?" she asked, though she already knew. She recognized the anguish in Jessica's words, not as actual malice but as a visceral response to her world turning upside down. Fawn's parents, who had always enveloped Jessica in the same kindness as their own child, now unwittingly became the focal point of her anger.

Tears brimming, Jessica's voice broke as she said again, "Mama and Papa! I hate them!" It was a cry from the depths of despair, a voice grappling with the harsh reality of loss and the fear of a future without her best friend by her side.

Teresa remained silent for a beat, feeling a twinge of pain that mirrored the anguish in Jessica's voice. She knew her daughter's wrath wasn't genuinely aimed at Fawn's parents, but at the relentless tide of sorrow and the gaping void of uncertainty that threatened to engulf her. With patience, Teresa gave Jessica the room she needed to disentangle her emotions.

"Sweetheart, I know it hurts right now," she began, grasping Jessica's hand to offer a tangible sense of comfort. "The unexpected news of Fawn's family moving is hard to swallow, and it's okay to be angry and sad. But deep down, you know that Fawn's parents love you and consider you part of their family. This decision must not have been easy for them, either."

Caught in the compassionate gaze of her mother, Jessica discovered a glimmer of comfort. The storm inside her calmed, unmasking a strand of understanding.

"I know, Mom," she whispered, her voice a tender thread stretching across her inner chaos. "I don't really hate them. It's just that Fawn and I had so many plans for the summer, and now, it seems like everything is falling apart." Her admission lingered, a poignant reminder of how fragile hopes can be when confronted with the relentless march of change.

The silence that followed was charged, a blank canvas awaiting Teresa's insightful guidance. Seizing the moment, she revealed a truth hidden beneath Wavecrest's idyllic surface.

"You know, honey, I can understand why Fawn's parents want to move. Living in Wavecrest is becoming increasingly difficult for families like ours. The taxes, the mortgage, and the rising cost of necessities can be overwhelming." Her words painted a stark picture of the realities many families face as she sought to guide Jessica through the complexities of adulthood.

Jessica's face paled, the weight of her mother's words sinking in. Wide-eyed, she met Teresa's gaze, her vulnerability laid bare. "You mean for us, too?"

"Yes, for us too, sweetheart. But don't worry, we're doing just fine," Teresa reassured, her voice a steady light amidst the shadows of doubt.

Confusion furrowed Jessica's brow. Her town had always shimmered with the magic of endless possibilities, where joy sprang up as naturally as the tide. It was a place defined by carefree days, each moment brimming with laughter and adventure. This sudden clash between her cherished memories and the stark reality presented by her mother was deeply unsettling.

Teresa's tone softened, closing the gap between illusion and the harshness of life. "Brian and Anna have been struggling with mounting debts and financial pressures for some time. It seems that moving might be their only way to a better future."

At Teresa's words, a veil lifted from Jessica's eyes, revealing a stark new aspect of Wavecrest—a reality marred by the same struggles and hardships that touch lives everywhere. The revelation pierced the bubble of her once carefree life, injecting a dose of harsh truth into her world of endless summers that were imbued with unbridled joy.

With the warmth and care that only a mother's love can weave, Teresa's words flowed softly, striking a delicate balance between tenderness and the stark realities of life. "You know, Jessica," she began, her voice tender and reassuring, "we've always tried to protect you from the challenges we face."

She paused, allowing her words to sink in, a testament to her efforts to shield Jessica from adult burdens. "We wanted you to grow up in a loving and happy environment, to experience the joys of childhood without the concerns that weigh on us adults."

Their eyes met in a moment filled with deep understanding and silent empathy. Teresa continued, her tone gentle yet earnest. "In your eyes, Wavecrest has always been this enchanting place, free from the cares and challenges of life. But for us adults, the picture is quite different."

She gave a slight nod, acknowledging the dual reality of their beloved town. "Despite its allure, Wavecrest has its own set of obstacles," she revealed, giving Jessica the space to absorb this new perspective. "Wavecrest is truly a world better suited for the young and those who revel in the freedom it offers."

As Teresa's revelations took shape, Jessica was thrust into a broader, more complex worldview. Fawn's impending departure, coupled with the looming specter of her own family facing a similar dilemma, sharpened the focus of the dialogue into a revealing clarity.

A storm of insight swirled within her, mixing a tumultuous array of emotions. Standing on the brink of adulthood, she peered into the dense maze of responsibilities and choices that had always seemed a world away. The idyllic existence in Wavecrest, once thought immune to such complexities, was now showing its delicate balance. This realization forced Jessica to confront not only the impending changes in her beloved town, but also her own journey into the multifaceted truths of life.

In the quiet that enveloped them, the thoughts and feelings swirling between Jessica and Teresa felt almost palpable. Caught in a whirlwind of curiosity and fear, Jessica found herself on the brink of voicing a question that had sparked deep within her. Gathering her bravery, she asked the question that had been haunting her thoughts.

"Does this mean that you and Daddy are thinking about selling our house, too?" Her voice shook, each word fragile and laden with vulnerability.

Teresa looked at her daughter, her expression reflecting the emotional turmoil Jessica's question stirred. She paused, a furrow of concern crossing her brow as she weighed her words, understanding Jessica's need for reassurance more than anything else at that moment.

With eyes filled with compassion and a voice infused with soothing reassurance, Teresa answered, "No, sweetheart, not now. While your father and I have considered various options, actively planning to sell our home is not something we're pursuing at this time. We have a lot to think about, and any decisions we make will be in the best interest of our family's well-being." She paused to let her words sink in, maintaining a steady and loving gaze.

Leaning in, Teresa took Jessica's hands in hers, her eyes unwavering in their conviction and love. "I want you to understand, Jessica, that we love you, and your happiness and security are our greatest concerns."

Jessica felt a rush of relief as the tight bands of worry that had formed around her heart began to loosen. Though her mother's words hinted at underlying challenges, they served as a soothing salve to her fears, affirming that her parents were carefully considering her well-being amidst their own personal challenges.

Surrounded by the warmth of the kitchen, mother and daughter found a moment of solace. It served as a brief respite amidst life's swirling uncertainties, a testament to the enduring strength of family. Their shared resolve, rooted in love and unity, promised to weather the tremors of change.

Teresa's voice, blending care with concern, pierced the reflective quiet. "How about we start the day with something nice? Breakfast, maybe? How does a stack of your favorite pancakes sound?" Her smile, both gentle and hopeful, shone like a lighthouse, guiding Jessica toward a semblance of normalcy, her eyes sparkling with the desire to lift her daughter's spirits.

A faint smile brushed Jessica's lips, a silent acknowledgment of the comfort found in her mother's words. She nodded, a subtle yet meaningful affirmation, gravitating back toward the familiar comfort that had always framed their lives.

As Teresa turned to the stove, the kitchen became a place of healing. The simple act of making pancakes filled the space with a warm glow, intertwining the threads of care that fortified them against life's complexities.

As Jessica's eyes wandered to the kitchen window, the world outside seemed to echo the turmoil within. The luminous glow that had once filled her room now gave way to a brooding canvas of clouds, their heavy presence dimming the morning's earlier brightness. The air, thick with the promise of rain, seemed to press against the glass, infusing the day with an unspoken melancholy. This change in the weather, in stark contrast to her inner longing for light, echoed Jessica's feelings, as if the sky itself shared in her grief, shrouding her world in shades of gray.

Sitting at the table, Jessica found the promise of her mother's pancakes knitting a strand of solace into her whirlwind of thoughts. Memories—a mosaic of joy and sorrow—flitted through her consciousness, each a marker of paths walked and those yet to be tread. The day lay ahead, a canvas of shadow and brightness, challenging her to find her way through its intricacies.

In the kitchen's embrace, Jessica found herself at a juncture between reflection and the unforeseen. Each moment wove itself into the vibrant tapestry of her life, with her spirit swinging like a pendulum between the warmth of cherished memories and the cold uncertainty of what lies ahead.

As the day unfolded, the morning's brooding clouds dissipated, revealing the rich, golden hues of late afternoon. Bathed in this revitalizing sunshine, Jessica and Fawn found themselves sitting on a well-worn bench along the boardwalk, a familiar spot that held countless memories. Together, they watched the endless Pacific, its waves keeping time with their own heartbeats. In a wordless pact, they chose to set aside the impending reality of Fawn's imminent departure, focusing instead on making this summer an indelible chapter in their lives.

With a playful glint lighting up her bright blue eyes, Jessica gently elbowed Fawn, her lips curling with a hint of sly amusement. "You know that it snows in Montana, right?" she quipped, her tone dripping with feigned solemnity.

Fawn met her friend's jest with a growing grin, her eyes gleaming with shared mischief. She shot back with equal playfulness, "Oh, sure, but don't forget. Texas has lots of snakes and big, ugly spiders."

At this, Jessica's face mixed amusement with exaggerated disgust as she shuddered for effect. "Ew!" she burst out, her laughter joining Fawn's in a harmonious symphony that danced in the summer air.

With their worries momentarily set aside, the girls reveled in the comfort of each other's company. The ease of their banter and the sound of their laughter illuminated the depth of their connection, unshakeable even amidst life's uncertainties.

The tranquil silence that settled around them was broken only by the soft murmurs of the sea breeze teasing their hair. Turning to Fawn, Jessica's words were filled with genuine warmth. "You know, Boston gets snow, too," she reminded her, nodding towards the city that awaited Fawn's artistic pursuits.

Fawn's eyes sparkled with curiosity and anticipation. "I've never seen snow... only in pictures and movies," she admitted.

Sharing in Fawn's sense of wonder for the unknown, Jessica echoed, "Yeah, me neither." Her tone carried an undercurrent of excitement. "But it sounds like it could be fun, doesn't it?" Her encouragement was a gentle push for Fawn to look forward to the adventures that awaited.

Their eyes locked, sharing a silent understanding of the exhilaration and endless possibilities that lay ahead, their imaginations drifting to snowy landscapes and playful snowball fights.

"Yeah, maybe," Fawn conceded, her voice tinged with a hint of hesitation. The concept of cold, snowy winters was foreign to her, far removed from the sun-kissed shores of Wavecrest they both cherished.

Jessica glanced at Fawn, a nostalgic smile playing on her lips. "Do you remember when we were little and how we wished it would snow here in Wavecrest?"

Fawn laughed, the sound mingling with the breeze. "Yeah, I remember. Every year at Christmas time, we'd wish for it to snow, and..." Her voice faded into a thoughtful pause, prompting Jessica to continue.

"Yeah," Jessica sighed, the corner of her mouth lifting in amusement. "It was a silly dream, wasn't it? But part of me always hoped it would happen."

Fawn nodded, her eyes lingering on the horizon. "Me too. But I guess some dreams were never meant to come true."

She let her thoughts drift out, a tender confession in her voice. "You know, Jess, I think I'd prefer sand over snow." Her words revealed a preference for the warm, familiar embrace of their beachside upbringing over the stark, cold unknown of snow-covered landscapes. The thought of facing harsh winters seemed suddenly less appealing.

Jessica met her friend's confession with a nod full of understanding, her voice tinged with a sweet ache of nostalgia. "Me too, honestly," she admitted, her heart in each word. "That's what I'll miss the most—the ocean, the sand, the beach. It's going to be a big adjustment." Her words hung in the air, a silent recognition of the significant changes looming on their horizon.

The girls then cast their eyes back to the vast ocean stretching before them. In its ceaseless ebb and flow, they found a solace echoing the constant in their lives—their friendship. As the waves hummed their timeless melody, they sat immersed in serene silence, comforted by the knowledge that, though their paths might diverge, the depth of their connection would remain unchanging, as enduring and reliable as the sea itself.

As the minutes ticked by, Jessica's anticipation grew, each second stretching longer than the last. Then her eyes landed on a familiar figure in the distance, sparking an instant surge of happiness within her. Ethan's approach, casual yet unmistakable, sent her heart into an ecstatic flip. Overcome with joy, she nudged Fawn, her eyes alight with pure delight.

Fawn turned, following Jessica's gaze. Her face lit up as she recognized Ethan against the golden hue of the afternoon sun. His arrival seemed to weave another thread of magic into their seaside tableau.

Unable to contain her excitement, Jessica sprang from the bench, her heart swelling with affection. She closed the distance between them with a few quick steps, folding herself into Ethan's open arms. Their hug was a silent testament to her feelings, deep and unspoken.

Turning to Fawn, Jessica introduced them with a bright smile. "Ethan, you remember Fawn, right?"

Ethan's smile widened, his eyes meeting Fawn's with genuine warmth. "Of course I do. Hi, Fawn," he greeted her, his voice carrying a mix of sincerity and pleasure. "Jessica's been filling me in on all your adventures—and, well, your misadventures too," he added, his laughter ringing true and hearty.

A soft blush tinted Fawn's cheeks as she smiled back, a mix of amusement and shyness dancing in her eyes. "Don't believe everything she says," she shot back playfully. "Jessica is the real mastermind here."

Their laughter melded in the air, resonant and joyful. "Oh no, it's definitely you who gets us into trouble!" Jessica countered with a grin.

Fawn's reply was quick, her tone teasingly sarcastic, "Sure, sure, you keep telling yourself that, silly girl!"

Their laughter, joined by Ethan's amused chuckles, painted the afternoon with vibrant strokes of joy and camaraderie. As it faded, Fawn rose from the bench, her movement as if lifting a spell from the air around them.

"I think I'll head back now," Fawn announced, her voice tinged with reluctance.

Jessica reached out, grabbing Fawn's hand with a gentle but earnest grip. "No. Stay a little longer," she pleaded, her voice laden with a mix of hope and quiet desperation.

Understanding the unique bond between Jessica and Ethan, Fawn gave Jessica's hand a reassuring squeeze, her smile gentle yet apologetic.

"No, you guys go ahead," she urged them, her expression supportive as she acknowledged their need for solitude. "I've got an art project that needs my attention. We'll catch up later, okay?"

Jessica's eyes shone with gratitude as she embraced Fawn, whispering softly, "Okay, see you later."

With a clear purpose, Fawn walked away, leaving behind her dear friend and moving toward the creative call of her art. Jessica watched Fawn's figure recede along the boardwalk, her heart swelling with both longing and deep appreciation for their friendship.

Observing the emotional exchange, Ethan gently cupped Jessica's face in his hands, his blue eyes filled with concern. "You okay, babe?" he asked, his voice brimming with tenderness.

A smile slowly spread across Jessica's face in response, her words a soft murmur. "I am now."

Wrapped in Ethan's embrace, she found a place of comfort and warmth, the strength of their connection serving as her anchor amidst life's uncertainties. Though tinged with the bittersweet reality of change, the summer ahead promised a tapestry of cherished moments and unforgettable experiences, a journey they would embark on together.

# Chapter 9

The first day of summer cast its radiant glow over Wavecrest, transforming the seaside town into a hub of vibrancy and activity, just as lively as when summer break had first begun. As June prepared to give way to the vibrant month of July, the last nine days brimmed with artistic promise for Fawn and the sweet lure of summer romance for Jessica. Standing at this pivotal moment, every tick of the clock carried the potential for new adventures and treasured moments, framing the threshold of a summer destined to be remembered.

On this Saturday, anticipation swelled for a grand graduation party, a festive marker of the close of their high school chapter. The event, hosted by their classmate Jerry Cranmer—Fawn's ex—promised an evening awash with laughter, celebratory toasts, and reflections on the transformative journey through the hallowed halls that had seen them grow.

However, the party wasn't the only milestone on Jessica's horizon. Her eighteenth birthday was swiftly approaching. The twenty-sixth of June promised to unfold as a grand celebration, a gathering steeped in affection and cheer, to honor her passage into adulthood and the remarkable young woman she had evolved into. Ethan, her first real love, would be by her side, his pride for her adding an additional sparkle to the joyous occasion.

She found herself caught in a whirl of anticipation and excitement. The merging of her academic achievements and the approaching threshold of adulthood painted a vivid tapestry of moments to come, uniting friends and family in a jubilant celebration of love and new beginnings.

As Jessica emerged from her dreams, her heart thrummed with vibrant anticipation. The long-awaited graduation party had arrived, a day imbued with deep significance. This day was not just a farewell to cherished friendships, but also a stage for an important introduction. She was eager to introduce Ethan to her friends, to show off the boy who had etched himself into her heart. With this thought fueling her spirit, she sprang from her bed, wrapping herself in a bright pink silk bathrobe, its radiance echoing her mood.

With quiet joy, she walked down the familiar hallway to the kitchen, where the rich scent of brewed coffee greeted her, enveloping her in its warm embrace. There, the comforting presence of her parents further warmed the room.

"Good morning, Daddy. Good morning, Mommy," she chimed, her smile as bright and promising as the day ahead.

Standing tall in his crisp blue button-down shirt and sleek black slacks, Jessica's father embodied a refined presence. His broad shoulders and quiet authority were softened by the kindness in his eyes and his ever-present, comforting smile. He approached Jessica, placing a tender kiss on top of her head. "Good morning, baby girl," he greeted, his voice a soft echo of deep affection.

Teresa watched her daughter with the adoring gaze only a mother could have, noticing the radiant change as Jessica settled at the table. "You're practically glowing this morning," she noted, her voice carrying a hint of relief. The usual cheerfulness that had been missing from Jessica's demeanor in recent days had made a welcome return, easing Teresa's concerns.

Unable to contain her excitement, Jessica turned to her parents, her eyes sparkling. "Today's the graduation party," she announced, her voice bubbling with eagerness. "Ethan will be driving Fawn and me to Jerry's. I can't wait for everyone to meet him," she added, her excitement evident in her words.

Teresa's smile grew, moved by the sparkle in Jessica's bright blue eyes. "Ah yes, the party at the Cranmers'," she recalled, aligning her thoughts with the day's events. After a moment's reflection, she continued, "It was very generous of them to host such an event."

Amid a symphony of familial harmony, Teresa rose to dive into the familiar comfort of preparing breakfast. The kitchen came alive with the sounds of sizzling bacon, the hiss of cooking eggs, and the gentle flip of fluffy pancakes. As Jessica cradled her hot coffee, her anticipation for the day's events coursed through her veins. The air, thick with the rich aroma of coffee, grounded her in the serene scene, each sip a moment to savor, quietly acknowledging the excitement building inside her.

The sound of the front door swinging open abruptly broke this peaceful moment. Jessica's face lit up with a smile as she saw Fawn enter the house. As Fawn made her way into the kitchen, Teresa greeted her with a warmth that radiated maternal affection.

"You're just in time, honey. Take a seat, and I'll fix you some breakfast," she offered, her voice enveloping her in the warmth of familial love.

"Thanks, Mama," Fawn replied, her smile wide with heartfelt gratitude and fondness. She settled beside Jessica with the familiarity of countless mornings shared in this very kitchen.

Each time Fawn called her 'Mama,' Teresa felt overwhelmed with affection. This simple act was a profound indicator of the deep connection between Jessica and Fawn—a relationship that had evolved far beyond mere friendship. To the outside observer, they were best friends, yet in reality, their friendship had deepened into a kinship so significant that both families embraced them as beloved members of their own.

"You're up bright and early," Jessica remarked, her admiration evident as she took in Fawn's chosen ensemble for the day. Dressed in a floral crop top paired with white shorts and her blonde hair styled to perfection, Fawn radiated an effortless elegance. To Jessica, her friend's glowing appearance only deepened the affection she harbored for her.

With a beaming smile and a mischievous glint in her eyes, Fawn replied, "I had to make sure I looked my best for today, right?" She playfully flipped her hair, adding, "We can't have the graduation party start without us making a grand entrance!" Her enthusiasm was contagious, mirroring the anticipation and joy she felt towards the day's festivities.

Caught in the wave of Fawn's exuberance, Jessica chuckled. "Well, you're definitely rocking it today! That top is my absolute favorite on you," she said, remembering the day they had discovered it during a shopping adventure. Despite her disheveled, just-out-of-bed look, Jessica graciously offered, "I just woke up, so I'm a mess. You can hang out here while I shower and get dressed."

Fawn retorted with a mischievous twinkle. "Well, it's a good thing one of us is ready for the camera this morning."

Jessica rolled her eyes and replied with a lighthearted jab, "Oh, please, Miss, 'I woke up like this.'" Their playful exchange was a testament to the ease and familiarity of their friendship, a gentle ribbing that came as naturally as breathing.

Following a fulfilling breakfast, they made their way to Jessica's bedroom, where Fawn took her usual spot on the welcoming bed, fitting into the space as if it were her own. As Jessica grappled with a stubborn knot in her hair, Fawn stepped in, her fingers working through the snarl with ease.

With her hair now lying smooth over her shoulders, Jessica turned to Fawn with a sincere smile. "Thanks!" she said before heading into the bathroom for a shower.

As the soothing sound of running water filled the room, Fawn sank deeper into the softness of Jessica's bed, her eyes wandering around the room she knew so well. Despite countless hours spent in this space, each visit offered a chance to rediscover the room's intimate details—with each object and keepsake telling a story of their shared journey.

Her eyes settled on a shelf brimming with various knick-knacks, among them a tiny glass giraffe. The sight of this delicate figurine whisked her back to a trip to the zoo they had taken in the fifth grade. A gentle smile of reminiscence spread across her face as she embraced the memory.

Continuing her visual journey, Fawn's eyes landed on a seemingly forgotten pile of stuffed animals nestled in a corner. These colorful mementos conjured up vivid memories of happy days spent on the boardwalk, where Jessica had skillfully won these fluffy prizes. She reached out, touching the worn fabric of a teddy bear, its frayed edges speaking volumes of time's passage and the depth of the moments they had shared.

In the quietude of Jessica's room, Fawn took a mental inventory of her surround-ings—the shelves, the cozy corners, each precious keepsake—knowing that these images would be a source of comfort in times when she longed for her best friend's company.

Minutes later, Jessica emerged back into her room, wearing a bath towel of soft blush shades, with her damp hair neatly bundled into a fluffy white towel atop her head. She moved with an ease that filled the space with a sense of renewal, her presence infusing the room with the crisp aroma of cleanliness. Catching the sight of Fawn comfortably settled on her bed, Jessica greeted her with a hearty, inviting smile.

Taking a seat at her vanity, Jessica embarked on her morning skincare routine, her fingers wrapping around a bottle of moisturizer. She applied it in gentle, careful strokes, followed by her favorite brand of face cream, each action a part of a familiar and comforting ritual.

Fawn observed her for a moment before breaking the silence with a question. "Do you remember Felix Copeland?" Her voice was light, tinged with a hint of curiosity.

Jessica paused as she delved into her memories. "You mean the kid who got picked on at school?" she replied, a spark of recognition lighting up her features.

Fawn nodded. "Yeah. I ran into him at school when I signed up for the Art Contest."

The mention of Felix took Jessica by surprise, stirring her innate compassion. "Really? I remember Felix. He was in a few of my classes. I always felt bad for him," she confessed.

Fawn's voice echoed the sentiment. "Me too," she agreed, then revealed her unexpected move. "That's why I asked him to come to our graduation party."

Jessica's reaction was immediate, her face registering stark surprise. "You invited Felix to the party?" she asked, a note of disbelief coloring her voice.

With an almost regretful smile, Fawn elaborated. "I did. It always bothered me to see how everyone was so mean to him, so I thought this would be a kind gesture."

Reflecting on Fawn's rationale, Jessica's heart warmed to the idea. "Yeah, he did get picked on a lot. I could never understand why." Her words resonated with a deep under-standing and appreciation of Fawn's kind-hearted action.

In that moment of mutual understanding, Jessica and Fawn recognized their personal growth. Jessica's voice carried a tone imbued with newfound maturity. "But we're not like that now, right? We're adults now."

Fawn's reply came with unwavering certainty. "Yep. Those days of childish behavior are behind us. It's time we start acting like the grown-ups we are."

Jessica nodded, her voice reflecting Fawn's determination. "Exactly! From now on, I'm going to embrace the new me." Then, with a sudden burst of playful energy, she spun her chair around to face Fawn and dramatically freed her hair from its towel. Her hair spilled out wildly, framing her face in a whimsical mess.

"Look at me, Fawn! I am pretty!" she declared, her face contorted in mock vanity.

Fawn burst out into laughter at Jessica's antics, their mirth mingling in a perfect symphony of glee. In the midst of her giggles, she jested, "You're crazy, girl, you know that?"

As their laughter subsided, the warm afterglow of shared amusement enveloped the room. Jessica, with her chuckles fading into a contented smile, turned back to her vanity. She picked up her brush and smoothed out her hair, the strokes rhythmic and thoughtful.

In this quiet moment, as the brush glided through her locks, Jessica thought about Fawn's compassionate act. It was a gesture that spoke volumes about her character, highlighting a depth of kindness she had always admired. She paused as she looked at her friend in the mirror.

"You know, inviting Felix to the party was really kind of you, Fawn. I'm proud of you," she declared, her admiration clear.

Fawn smiled warmly in response to Jessica's words as she watched her friend move through her morning routine. These simple moments mirrored their journey from innocent little girls to thoughtful, compassionate young women. Surrounded by the familiarity of her surroundings, Fawn recognized how profoundly their friendship had influenced each other; it was a relationship that had not only endured but also nurtured personal growth and mutual understanding.

With their preparations complete, Jessica and Fawn stepped out of the comforting embrace of the bedroom, ready to face the exciting day ahead. Walking side by side, their laughter echoed through the hallway, filling the home with vibrancy and eager anticipation. Together, they were about to celebrate a significant chapter in their lives, each moment enriched by the memories they had created together. As they ventured forward, they carried with them not only their treasured past but also the hopeful expectations of this summer's final chapter, a beloved interlude before stepping into the world of adulthood.

As the midday sun filled the sky with its golden glow, Wavecrest transformed under a radiant light. Its beaches and boardwalk, pulsing with life, echoed with the vibrant energy of a community indulging in the leisure of a Saturday afternoon. In the midst of this dynamic scene, Jessica and Fawn meandered along the lively boardwalk. Their eyes flitted across the vivid tapestry of sights, their spirits lifted by the eager anticipation of meeting Ethan. With time smiling upon them, they veered towards their beloved ice cream shop, a haven of nostalgia and the perfect escape from the summer's warm embrace.

Dressed in a red crinkled chest top and light sky-blue shorts, Jessica slipped into her sandals. Together, she and Fawn crossed the threshold of Hal's Ice Cream Shop, a place as integral to her history as her own home.

Hal, the proprietor, whose gentle presence had become a fixture in their lives, greeted the girls with a warm smile. Since her youth, when her parents first introduced her to the joys of ice cream delights, Jessica had captured the hearts of both Hal and his wife. Each visit, marked by her bright blue eyes, infectious charm, and tiny stature, endeared her even more to them. In those early days, Hal and his wife would often gift her with cones of her favorite flavor, a sweet testament to the enduring bond that had blossomed over scoops and smiles.

It didn't take long for Fawn to join Jessica on their visits to the ice cream shop, becoming an equally cherished figure in Hal and his wife's eyes. As the girls grew, their continued visits to the shop only deepened Hal's affection for them. Their presence had woven itself into the fabric of the shop's daily rhythm, standing as a heartwarming testament to the lasting relationships forged through years of affectionate smiles and countless ice cream cones.

Sitting at their usual spot, Jessica and Fawn soaked in the welcoming atmosphere of their favorite ice cream shop. Behind the counter, Hal's warm smile, framed by wavy silver hair and a neatly trimmed mustache, asked, "The usual?"

The girls' response was an enthusiastic nod and smile, giving him the go-ahead to whip up their beloved concoctions.

As they waited, the lively scene outside the large window captured their attention. Families strolled past, seagulls pirouetted against the sky, and the harmonious lull of waves underscored their growing excitement.

Soon enough, Hal approached, each step reflecting the timeless grace his attire of a crisp white shirt and pants suggested. In his hands, he balanced two towering ice cream cones, each generously crowned with an extra scoop. The sight lit up Jessica and Fawn's faces with sheer delight.

As Fawn extended her hand for the cones, Jessica reached into her purse for payment. However, Hal, with a light-hearted chuckle and eyes twinkling with mischief, gestured dismissively. "No, these are on the house today," he whispered, as if sharing a secret between old friends. "Well, just for you two. Let's keep it between us, shall we? Wouldn't want the missus to find out."

With a wink and his ever-present warm smile, he sauntered back to the counter, leaving Jessica and Fawn to revel in the sweetness of his gesture, both the ice cream and his enduring generosity.

As the girls savored the exquisite flavors of their ice cream, they exchanged a glance that spoke volumes, a silent acknowledgment of their unique relationship with Hal and his wife. These visits to the ice cream shop had become more than just moments of indulgence; they were treasured interactions that punctuated the story of their friendship.

With each delightful lick, they took in the lively scene beyond the glass: the uninhibited joy of children playing and the soft sea breeze that seemed to whisper tales of distant shores. In these moments, cradled between the sweetness of youth and the depth of their friendship, they recognized they were more than just patrons in this cozy little ice cream shop; they were valued friends.

Amid their sweet reminiscences and the bustling world outside, a pressing concern quietly wove its way into their conversation. Jessica looked at Fawn, her eyes brimming with empathy. "Are you going to be okay seeing Jerry at the party? It's going to be hard to avoid him there," she voiced, her concern evident.

Fawn hesitated, a shadow of uncertainty crossing her features. "To be honest, I'm not sure. I'm looking forward to the party, but being at Jerry's... It's going to bring back a lot of memories," she confided, the joy momentarily dimmed by the past.

Jessica reached across the table, offering her hand in a gesture of support. "I can only imagine. But remember. I'll be right there with you. We'll face it together, okay?" she offered reassuringly, anchoring Fawn with her steadfast presence.

A small smile broke through Fawn's apprehension, illuminating her gratitude. "Yeah, that will help. I guess it just feels weird thinking about being back there after everything that happened," she said, her confidence blossoming with Jessica's encouragement.

Jessica's nod conveyed her deep understanding. "I know, Fawn. But this day is about us—it's about our friends—our graduation. It's our moment to celebrate. We won't let anything, or anyone, spoil that—not even Jerry," she stated firmly, embodying their collective strength.

Fawn inhaled deeply, her determination visibly taking root. "You're right. It's our day to celebrate. And I'm not going to let old ghosts ruin it. We've come too far for that," she asserted, her voice regaining its vigor.

The warmth of Jessica's smile bridged the space between them. "Exactly. And who knows? This might be a chance for you to get some closure, to finally put the past where it belongs," she hinted, optimism dancing in her eyes.

With a firm nod, Fawn embraced the thought. "Closure... Yeah, I think I'm ready for that. Today's going to be a memorable one, Jess, and in a good way," she proclaimed, her resolve clear and unwavering.

Bolstered by their profound exchange, Jessica and Fawn savored the last bites of their ice cream cones. After thanking Hal, whose kind presence had added warmth to their day, they stepped out from the cool air-conditioned comfort into the lively atmosphere of the sunlit boardwalk, ready to embrace the vibrant pulse of Wavecrest once again.

As the girls emerged onto the crowded boardwalk, the sun's rays greeted them like an old friend, its warmth a contrast to the shop's cool interior. The rhythmic tapping of their sandals on the aged planks blended seamlessly with the symphony of seaside sounds, guiding them toward Ethan.

Arriving at their chosen spot, Jessica and Fawn found themselves under the watchful gaze of a majestic palm tree, a landmark that felt like an old friend. This small parking lot wasn't just any place; it was where Jessica and Ethan had agreed to meet time and time again, the starting point of countless escapades that had deepened their connection. The distant, rhythmic crashing of waves lent a tranquil backdrop, each surge a whisper of the adventures that lay ahead.

Before long, Ethan's distinctive army-green Jeep came into view, its approach marked by the dust of travels past. The vehicle, like Ethan, seemed imbued with a sense of adventure, eager for the day's journey. As he pulled into the lot, his bright and genuine smile greeted the girls the instant he saw them.

Joy sparkled in Jessica's eyes as she rushed into Ethan's arms, their hug a vivid display of their deep connection. After a moment, they reluctantly pulled away, their eyes still locked on each other as if holding onto the moment just a bit longer.

Ever the gentleman, Ethan quickly moved to open the passenger door. Jessica took her place in the front seat while Fawn settled in the back. The sound of the door closing marked the beginning of yet another shared adventure.

Once the girls were seated, Ethan took his place behind the wheel. With a gentle touch and an affectionate smile, he ran his fingers through Jessica's hair. Their connection was palpable, each look and touch reinforcing the depth of their relationship.

Turning his attention to Fawn, he met her gaze in the rearview mirror with a warmth that felt like sunshine. "Hi, Fawn," he said, his voice as welcoming as the open road ahead. Fawn returned his greeting with a smile that lit up the Jeep, her excitement and camaraderie shining through.

Jessica gazed at Ethan, her eyes glowing with affection at his cool demeanor. His sleeveless black shirt showcased his toned physique, while his tan shorts lent him an air of laid-back allure. She felt a surge of pride and happiness at being by his side.

"You look beautiful, babe," Ethan said, expressing genuine admiration, causing Jessica's cheeks to tint with a warm glow.

"Thank you," she murmured, her voice carrying the soft warmth of her feelings.

Turning his attention back to Fawn's reflection in the rearview mirror, Ethan said, "And you, Fawn, you look very pretty today." His compliment, genuine and kind, contributed to the day's light-hearted mood.

"Aw, thanks!" Fawn beamed, her happiness evident.

After sharing a few light-hearted exchanges and settling into their seats, Ethan started the Jeep, its engine humming to life. Jessica, with a familiarity born of many trips together, tuned the radio to their favorite station. The Jeep was soon filled with familiar tunes, setting the perfect soundtrack for their journey ahead.

As they drove away from the coast, the scenery shifted from the breezy beachfront to the manicured elegance of Wavecrest's residential areas. They passed rows of colorful houses, each boasting meticulously groomed lawns that sparkled under the sun. Vibrant flower beds and ornate garden decorations caught their eye, while residents of all ages enjoyed the outdoors, some tending to gardens, others jogging or walking their dogs. Each home they passed framed their drive with a slice of local charm and vibrant community life, painting a picture of idyllic suburban bliss on their brief journey to the graduation party.

As they approached Jerry Cranmer's house, they were greeted by a surprising sight—a line of cars parked along the curb, far more than they had expected. Jessica and Fawn exchanged a glance, their eyes wide as they took in the crowd. A shared sense of relief washed over them at not being the first to arrive, easing the flutter of nervousness in their stomachs.

Ethan, ever adept, found a spot to park the Jeep. Although their drive had ended, another chapter was just beginning at Jerry's house, promising an afternoon filled with new memories and joyful reunions.

# Chapter 10

---

Jerry's residence stood as a grand spectacle, its towering presence casting long shadows across the neighboring homes. The lush green of its expansive lawns, both in the front and back, set the perfect backdrop for a memorable celebration. Hand in hand with Ethan and Fawn walking beside them, Jessica led the way along the neatly paved path to the heart of the festivities. Their eyes widened, absorbing the grandeur of the scene before them, a veritable feast for the senses.

Stepping into the backyard, they found themselves amidst a vibrant array of balloons, each one bobbing in the breeze. These colorful spheres of various shapes and sizes bore cheerful messages such as "Congratulations" and "Good Luck, Graduates," adding to the festive atmosphere. The space buzzed with new and familiar faces, each playing a role in the rich tapestry of their school years, now gathered to celebrate this significant milestone. Tables lined the perimeter, laden with an assortment of snacks and refreshments. Near the large grill on the deck, raw burgers and hot dogs waited their turns to sizzle on the grill, promising a delicious feast.

A tantalizing mix of scents filled the air—the mouthwatering aroma of grilling food mingled with the subtle hint of coconut oil. This aromatic blend played with their senses, enhancing the joyous mood. Laughter and spirited shouts echoed from the large in-ground pool, weaving through the air and leaving an imprint on this memorable day.

Jessica, nestled on Ethan's arm, had eyes that sparkled with excitement and wonder. Their brightness mirrored the lively scene around them as the trio stood at the edge of the party, taking in the vibrant atmosphere. Their arrival sent a subtle wave of recognition through the crowd, marking their presence in this vibrant tableau of celebration.

Heather, embodying the fiery spirit of her Italian heritage, emerged from the lively crowd with the grace of a sunbeam. As one of Jessica and Fawn's dearest friends, her presence radiated warmth and vivacity. Her greeting rang out like a melodious bell.

"Hey, guys!" Her eyes, alight with playful mischief, landed on Ethan, and her lips curled into a teasing smile. "And who might this be?" she asked, her voice tinged with a flirtatious undertone.

In response, a rosy blush painted Jessica's cheeks, her grip on Ethan's arm tightening. Swelling with pride, she introduced him: "This is Ethan... my boyfriend."

Heather's reaction was a broad, joyful smile, her expression reflecting genuine happiness. "Aw, I'm so happy for you, Jess," she exclaimed, her attention shifting to Ethan. "I'm happy for both of you." Jessica felt a wave of contentment at this acknowledgment, capturing this moment as a treasured snapshot in her heart.

With a flourish of her hand, Heather gestured toward the bustling party. "Well, go on, guys. There's plenty of food and drinks and lots of friends waiting to see you." With these words, she gracefully retreated into the sea of celebration, her spirit undeniably drawn to the joy of the occasion.

As they stepped into the heart of the party, Jessica squeezed Fawn's hand, her eyes sparkling with excitement. "Can you believe it, Fawn? It seems like just yesterday we were freshmen—wide-eyed and clueless!"

Fawn laughed as she scanned the familiar faces around them. "I know. It's crazy how time flies," she mused, her tone tinged with a touch of wistfulness. Jessica nodded, her gaze sweeping across the landscape, absorbing every detail.

Around them, the party buzzed with energy. Old classmates shared laughs and told tales of high school escapades, their voices a symphony of joy and nostalgia. In one area, a group discussed their college plans and dreams, their faces aglow with the promise of new adventures. In another, a couple slowly danced to a song from their first school dance, lost in their own world.

Jessica leaned closer to Fawn, her voice dropping to a whisper. "It's strange, isn't it? How we're all moving on, leaving all this behind." She let her eyes sweep over the crowd, a soft sigh escaping her lips.

Fawn followed her gaze, her heart swelling with a bittersweet ache. "I know. We finally figured out high school, and now we have to start all over again," she agreed.

As the girls stood together, immersed in their shared nostalgia and anticipation, they noticed a group of friends waving them over nearby. Their faces were full of curiosity and eagerness for reconnection.

"Hey, Fawn, Jessica! Over here!" one of them called out, her voice rising above the lively chatter of the party.

Fawn exchanged a knowing glance with Jessica, a silent agreement between them. They made their way toward the group, each step taking them further into the heart of the celebration. As they approached, the group's attention turned to Fawn, their expressions a mixture of excitement and genuine interest.

"So, Fawn," one of them began, leaning in with a smile, "we've all been talking about our plans for the future. What about you? What plans do you have?" Their eyes shone with anticipation, eager for her answer.

Fawn felt a surge of joy and pride swell within her as she looked around at her peers, gathering her thoughts. "I'm heading to Boston to study art," she declared, her eyes sparkling with the fervor of her dreams.

The group expressed genuine enthusiasm and congratulated Fawn on heading to Boston. Their expressions filled with admiration as they took turns hugging her, their gestures conveying their support for her artistic journey.

As the warm congratulations for Fawn simmered down, Jessica tugged on Ethan's arm, guiding him through the crowd to join another group of friends. "Everyone, this is my boyfriend, Ethan," she announced with a reassuring squeeze of his hand. Smiles and handshakes followed, each greeting enveloping her in a comforting embrace.

When asked about her plans for college, Jessica hesitated, then took a deep breath before answering. "I'm going to the University of Texas," she revealed, her voice tinged with nervousness. "I'm still figuring out what I want to do, career-wise."

Her friends immediately rallied around her, their smiles encouraging and their nods affirming. "That's the best part of college, Jessica," one of them exclaimed, her eyes shining with optimism. "You're going to have the time of your life discovering what you love."

"Exactly! Don't worry about deciding everything now," another added, his voice brimming with assurance. "Just have fun. You'll figure it out along the way."

Jessica felt a wave of relief wash over her, their words a soothing balm on her anxieties. The atmosphere buzzed with understanding, carrying the excitement of new beginnings and the promise of self-discovery in the transformative years ahead.

Meanwhile, Fawn made her way through the lively crowd and rejoined Jessica and Ethan. As the trio mingled with their classmates, a familiar, exuberant voice cut through the hum of the party.

"Hey, Jess! Hey Fawn!" called Krista, her vibrant red hair a fiery beacon in the crowd.

Standing next to her was Donny Richardson, her nineteen-year-old boyfriend. Modest in height, his round build and neatly combed brown hair gave him an endearing, unpretentious air. He comfortably draped his arm around Krista's shoulders, a gesture that spoke of their close bond and easy affection for each other.

Fawn's face lit up with delight. "Hey, guys!" she exclaimed, moving toward them with open arms. She and Jessica greeted Krista and Donny with the effortless camaraderie of longtime friends, their smiles blending into the festive atmosphere.

Krista's eyes sparkled with excitement. "This party is epic, isn't it?" she beamed, squeezing Donny's hand.

Donny nodded in agreement, his eyes scanning the crowd. "It's awesome to see everyone together like this," he added, his voice warm and genuine.

Feeling a surge of happiness at being surrounded by her closest friends, Jessica turned towards Ethan. "Guys, I want you to meet someone special." With a friendly smile, she gestured to Ethan, who had been observing the warmth and camaraderie of the group. "This is Ethan, my boyfriend," Jessica introduced with a touch of pride in her voice.

Ethan extended his hand, offering Krista and Donny a friendly handshake. "Nice to meet you both," he said, returning the smile. "I've heard a lot about you guys."

Krista's response was a playful grin. "All good things, I hope!" she joked, giving Ethan a firm handshake.

Donny's handshake followed, equally warm. "Good to meet you, dude. Any friend of Jessica's is a friend of ours," he said, his tone reflecting the inclusive nature of their circle.

The group shared a moment of easy conversation, the bonds of friendship evident in their relaxed stances and laughter. It was a scene that captured the essence of their years together—a mixture of joy, nostalgia, and anticipation of what lay ahead.

As the laughter from their recent exchange subsided, a new wave of excitement bubbled up within the group. From the corner of her eye, Fawn spotted Michelle weaving through the crowd, her auburn hair shimmering in the warm glow of the afternoon sun. Her effortlessly chic style, accented with a light cardigan that fluttered with each step, caught the light beautifully.

"There's Michelle!" Fawn exclaimed, her voice brimming with happiness.

Krista turned, her eyes lighting up. "Michelle! Over here!"

With a graceful stride, Michelle approached, her hazel eyes sparkling with delight as she took in the sight of her friends gathered. "Hey, everyone!" she greeted, her voice carrying a melodious joy.

Jessica beamed at Michelle, her heart swelling with warmth at having all her close friends around her. "Michelle, there's someone I'd like you to meet." She gestured toward Ethan, who had been observing the cheerful reunion. "This is Ethan, my boyfriend."

Ethan stepped forward with a welcoming smile and extended his hand. "Hi, Michelle. It's nice to meet you."

Michelle's response was a mix of warmth and enthusiasm. "Nice to meet you too, Ethan! Jess has told us so much about you." Her words were genuine, welcoming Ethan into the fold.

With the group now complete, the air around them vibrated with the energy of their friendship. They shared stories, reminisced about past adventures, and laughed over inside jokes. The music from the party blended with their voices, creating a symphony of celebration.

At one point, Krista's eyes twinkled with a mischievous idea. "Hey, guys! Let's take a group photo! We need to capture this moment," she exclaimed, already assuming her favorite pose.

The girls quickly gathered, each adopting their signature stances with playful enthusiasm. Michelle tilted her head, her smile soft yet radiant. At the same time, Krista struck a dramatic pose with her hand on her hip, her red hair catching the brilliant hues of the afternoon sun.

Fawn leaned in, her smile bright and genuine, as she playfully threw up a peace sign. Jessica, true to her spirited nature, opted for a goofy face, sticking out her tongue and bringing a ripple of laughter from the group. Ethan, somewhat bemused but enjoying the moment, stood behind Jessica, his hand on her shoulder, smiling at her antics.

With a practiced hand, Donny positioned his phone to capture the group. "Alright, everyone! Say 'Wavecrest!'" he called out.

At his cue, they all chorused the name of their beloved town. The camera clicked, capturing their beaming faces—a tableau of joy, playful spirits, and the bond of deep friendship. It was a snapshot that encapsulated the essence of their camaraderie and the excitement of their journey into new beginnings.

As the party progressed, their laughter mingled with the rhythm of the music, their movements a testament to their carefree spirits. They danced, sang along to their favorite songs, and made the most of their time together, each moment a treasured memory in the making.

After excusing herself from the group to grab something to eat, Fawn navigated through the clusters of chatting classmates. As she reached the food table, her heart skipped a beat as she unexpectedly found herself face-to-face with Jerry Cranmer. Her breath hitched at the sight of her ex, stirring a whirlwind of emotions she thought she had long since managed to contain.

Towering at 6'1", Jerry's athletic build was a testament to his dedication to sports. His sandy-brown hair shimmered in the light, framing deep-set brown eyes that exuded quiet confidence. Jerry's charisma—a seamless mix of social charm and affluence—stood out even among the diverse personalities of their high school. His presence carried an air of relaxed sophistication, reflective of his life in one of Wavecrest's most opulent homes. Yet, beneath his charming exterior, lay a complex depth shaped by his history with Fawn.

In the buoyant days of their junior year, Jerry and Fawn's love had blossomed in the stormy sea of adolescence. Their world was awash with the fervor of new emotions, the dizzying rush of first love weaving its magic around them. Enveloped in this whirlwind, Fawn treasured the tapestry of moments they wove together, nurturing a deep, emotional connection that seemed to transcend the ordinary.

Yet, over time, the shimmering veil of young love dimmed. The fabric of their relationship, once seamless, frayed under the strain of petty arguments and creeping doubts. These small but persistent rifts began to crumble the foundation they had built.

The turning point came when Fawn discovered Jerry's unfaithfulness. This painful truth shattered their bond, scattering the fragments of their shared dreams and leaving them adrift in the aftermath of heartbreak.

In the days that followed the breakup, Fawn navigated her world with renewed caution, intentionally avoiding Jerry. The hallways of their school transformed into a labyrinth, each turn carefully calculated to dodge the ghost of their past. Social gatherings, once joyous shared spaces, became tactical maneuvers to keep their paths separate, each finding solace in the growing distance between them.

Now, as Jerry approached, a tumult of emotions surged within Fawn. Memories, both sweet and bitter, flashed through her mind, each a stark reminder of what they had lost. Taking a deep, steadying breath, she consciously allowed their history to recede into a distant corner of her past, steeling herself for the inevitable exchange.

Jerry closed the distance between them with measured steps, each one seeming to bridge the chasm of their estranged past. Now standing in front of her, his eyes met Fawn's, locking in a gaze that carried the weight of unspoken words and lingering feelings.

"It's been a while, hasn't it?" he said, his voice mixing wistfulness with subtle apprehension and a trace of awkwardness.

Unsettled by the resurgence of old emotions, Fawn managed a nod. "It has. Isn't it crazy how fast everything changes?" Her voice held a tinge of melancholy she did not try to hide.

Jerry pondered her words as if piecing together a long-lost puzzle. "Yeah, I've noticed that, too. How have you been?"

"I've been okay. Just finding my way," Fawn replied, maintaining a composed facade that masked the complexities of her emotions. "And you? What's next for Wavecrest's star athlete?"

His laughter, now a softer echo of his once boisterous nature, lightened the air. "Well, I'm off to Caltech at the end of August. Engineering, surprisingly enough."

"Caltech? That's impressive," Fawn acknowledged, her smile genuine. "Looks like we'll both be starting a new life soon, huh?"

As Fawn spoke, Jerry looked at her with a new understanding, seeing her not just as a figure from his past but as the person she was becoming. "We are at that," he agreed, his voice carrying a mix of trepidation and excitement.

Their gazes remained locked, each recognizing traces of their younger selves but also something more profound—a maturity shaped by life's experiences. In the fleeting silence of their exchange, against the party's vibrant backdrop, Fawn and Jerry shared a moment of mutual understanding, a serene acknowledgment of their individual paths, each as vibrant and promising as water lilies on a tranquil pond.

Jerry's expression, tinged with sadness and regret, lingered for a moment before he parted. "You take care of yourself, Fawn," he murmured, his voice laden with sorrow for the pain he had caused.

Fawn felt a familiar ache as she replied, "You too, Jerry." Her words were simple, yet they carried the weight of unspoken feelings and a lingering affection that hadn't completely faded.

As Fawn watched Jerry walk away, a cascade of emotions washed over her. There was relief, sadness, and a faint glimmer of hope—not for what could have been, but for what lay ahead for them both. She took a deep breath, allowing the moment and Jerry, a bittersweet part of her history, to drift away.

As the afternoon wore on, Jessica became increasingly aware of Fawn's restless glances, each sweeping across the throng of partygoers with a sense of searching. These looks carried a silent plea, as if Fawn was scanning the crowd for a specific face. With each passing hour, concern furrowed Fawn's brow, her anxiety tangible over Felix's notable absence. As the party's energy waned and friends began to disperse, Jessica and Ethan found themselves drawn to Fawn's side, feeling a shared sense of worry.

"I don't get it. Why didn't Felix come to the party?" Fawn mused aloud, her voice tinged with worry. "He said he would come. I hope he's okay."

Sensing her friend's distress, Jessica suggested, "Well... maybe we could drive to Felix's house and see if he's alright."

Relief washed over Fawn's face, breaking through her concern like a ray of light. "That's a good idea, Jess. At least I can find out why he didn't show up."

Turning to Ethan, Jessica's voice was warm and affectionate. "Are you okay with that, babe?"

Empathetic to Fawn's concern and recognizing the deep bond she shared with Jessica, Ethan readily agreed. "Sure! I'm a little concerned, too. Let's go to his house and make sure he's okay."

Jessica replied with a beaming smile, her arms wrapping around him in a heartfelt embrace.

Fawn watched this affectionate exchange, her eyes glistening with appreciation for Ethan's genuine concern and readiness to support their friendship. "I know the way," she announced with renewed determination. "Someone here knows where he lives, so I asked him for his address."

Ethan nodded, his expression resolute. "Well, okay then. Let's get going," he said, signaling a readiness to embark on their mission to check on Felix.

As the late afternoon sun played peek-a-boo behind the clouds, offering a brief respite from the day's heat, the trio returned to the Jeep. Their departure was marked by poignant goodbyes to friends lingering at the edges of the dwindling party, each farewell a somber reminder that this may be the last time they see each other.

Settled inside the Jeep, Ethan brought the engine to life, its gentle rumble marking the start of their mission to Felix's house. The atmosphere inside the vehicle was tinged with both anticipation and concern as they embarked on this unexpected detour.

A heavy silence soon enveloped the space, thick and palpable. Fawn found herself lost in a maze of contemplation, her eyes fixated on the ever-shifting scenery outside the window. Jessica, lost in her own introspective world, played absentmindedly with her hair. Ethan, their steadfast guide, kept his eyes on the road, navigating the intricate network of streets.

After enduring several minutes cloaked in quiet, Jessica broke the silence, her voice weaving a thread of empathy. "You know, Fawn... considering how everyone treated him in school, I can understand why he didn't come to the party. Can you blame him?" she ventured with a soft tone.

Fawn, her gaze still locked on the changing view outside, replied with gentle intensity, her words teetering on the edge of thoughtful introspection. "I know. People were so cruel to him, but people can change. I've changed, and I wanted Felix to see that."

Jessica absorbed the weight of Fawn's words, their significance resonating in the silent space between them. She considered turning on the radio to lighten the mood, but quickly dismissed the idea. The somber reality of their discussion made even the music seem inadequate, an intrusive disruption to the contemplative atmosphere within the Jeep.

As their vehicle navigated away from the familiar confines of their neighborhood, the environment began to transform. The sun, once a cheerful constant in Wavecrest, now hid behind a dense canopy of wild foliage that cast a gloomy twilight over everything. The scenery shifted, the landscape appearing almost hostile, as if silently rejecting their intrusion. Houses they passed bore signs of neglect, with overgrown lawns and peeling paint contributing to a general air of desolation. This stark contrast to their vibrant community sent an unsettling shiver through the girls, underscoring the deep divide within their small town.

Amid this eerie setting, Jessica voiced her discomfort. "Oh my God, this place is so depressing," she remarked, her voice tinged with disbelief.

"Creepy, if you ask me," Fawn added, her tone laced with unease.

Jessica continued, her eyes wide as they scanned the unfamiliar territory. "I've never been to this part of town."

"Me neither," Fawn agreed, her relief palpable. "I'm glad we don't live out here."

Catching Fawn's reflection in his rearview mirror and glancing at Jessica beside him, Ethan smiled, amused by their apparent uneasiness. Having traveled extensively, scenes like this were not unfamiliar to him, and their reactions added a touch of light-heartedness to the otherwise heavy atmosphere.

As they drew closer to their destination, Fawn assumed the role of navigator, directing Ethan with precise instructions toward Felix's elusive address. As the Jeep turned onto Felix's street, Fawn urgently reminded Ethan to look for house number 142.

Ethan, with the focus of an explorer, scanned the numbers on each house. Jessica, equally attentive, peered through her window, attempting to decipher the fading numerals on the houses they passed. Fawn's anxiety was palpable; her eyes darted from side to side as she searched for any sign of Felix's house.

The road's rough texture rattled the Jeep, each jolt a stark reminder of the area's neglect. Ethan navigated the uneven terrain with ease, driving as carefully as a pathfinder, charting unexplored territory. Then, as if emerging from a shroud of obscurity, they spotted Felix's house. Ethan brought the Jeep to a stop at the curb, aligning them perfectly with their intended location.

In the silence that followed, the three remained motionless, caught in a moment of silent anticipation. They fixed their eyes on the house before them, each person absorbed in their thoughts about what awaited them inside. Felix's residence stood as a stark reminder of the contrasting realities within Wavecrest, and for a moment, they were united in a shared sense of purpose and concern.

The house that Felix called home seemed to embody the same quietude as its neighbors, blending into the somber atmosphere of the area. Its facade, cloaked in faded gray, told a story of time's unyielding passage, evidenced by the flaking paint that adorned its walls.

The house was modest in size, starkly contrasting with the grandeur of the houses Jessica and Fawn were accustomed to. A screened porch stood sentinel at the entrance, flanked by three concrete steps that descended to the barren yard. This landscape, devoid of life, was a sharp departure from the pristine beaches of Wavecrest they knew so well. A narrow path led from the steps to an aged gate that stood between sections of a rusty fence.

Inside the Jeep, heavy with unspoken thoughts, Fawn reached for the door latch, ready to face the unknown that awaited her.

Feeling a surge of protective instinct, Jessica offered her support. "Would you like me to go with you?" Her voice was filled with genuine concern.

"No, I have to do this alone. It won't take long," Fawn answered, her expression resolute.

With a determined step, she exited the Jeep and ventured toward the dreary gate. Ethan and Jessica watched her intently, their eyes sharp and alert. They were united in their silent vigil, a tacit agreement hanging in the air between them. They were there for Fawn, unwavering and prepared to face whatever challenges might arise, a testament to the strength and solidarity of their friendship.

With unwavering determination, Fawn pushed open the stubborn gate, forging her way through the desolate yard toward the porch. As she approached, a figure emerged from the house's interior, materializing on the porch like an apparition. Fawn's steps faltered momentarily as her heart raced at the sight of Felix. Composing herself, she continued forward until she stood at the base of the steps, her eyes fixed on him.

Dressed in clothes reminiscent of their high school days, Felix met her gaze with a mixture of nervousness, awkwardness, and a hint of embarrassment. With his hands buried deep in his pockets, Felix broke the silence, his voice tinged with unease.

"I know. I'm sorry I didn't go to the graduation party," he admitted, pausing briefly as if gathering his thoughts. "I know I said I would go... but when it came down to it, I just couldn't. The thought of being there—it just felt overwhelming."

Driven by a mix of concern and curiosity, Fawn pressed for an answer. "Why?" Her eyes searched his, seeking the truth behind his guarded exterior.

Felix replied with a mixture of sadness and regret. "Nobody at the party likes me. I have no friends there. I have no friends at all." His candid admission resonated deeply with Fawn, awakening a profound sense of empathy within her.

In a gentle, reassuring tone, she replied, "Felix, that was back in school. We were all so immature and quick to judge then. But we've grown up; we've changed. We've learned to understand and respect each other." Her voice grew stronger with conviction. "That's exactly why I wanted you at the graduation party. I wanted you to see for yourself that people can change. You would have been welcomed and accepted by me and my friends."

Felix's eyes met Fawn's, a part of him longing to believe in the solace of her words. Yet, the scars from years of being bullied and mistreated formed a barrier against trusting others, even Fawn—the girl who had unknowingly won his heart. He retreated into silence, his hands delving deeper into his pockets, his eyes casting down to the ground, a silent testament to his internal struggle.

Realizing that her words alone might not penetrate Felix's guarded skepticism, Fawn decided on a different approach. She contemplated her next move, a nuanced dance of emotions playing out in this delicate interaction. Feeling a mix of frustration and urgency, she glanced back at the Jeep, where Jessica and Ethan waited.

"Hey, guys?" Fawn called out, her voice tinged with urgency.

Turning back to Felix, she took his hand in a gentle, reassuring grasp and led him toward her friends, signaling their involvement with a determined gesture. "Come on!" she encouraged, her tone carrying a slight edge of impatience. "I want you to meet a couple of my friends." She walked toward the Jeep, where Jessica and Ethan stood like loyal guardians.

Upon reaching them, Fawn began the introductions, first to Jessica. "You already know Jess, right? She's been in a few of your classes."

Felix acknowledged Jessica with a timid nod, met by her warm, inviting smile.

Fawn then gestured towards Ethan. "And this is Ethan, Jessica's boyfriend." Ethan met Felix's gaze with an easy, welcoming smile and a nod of recognition.

Felix looked into Ethan's eyes, feeling a twinge of anxiety. His past experiences with school athletes, often the perpetrators of his torment, had left him wary. However, he noticed something different about him. His eyes conveyed kindness instead of malice, a contrast that eased Felix's apprehension, subtly shifting his perception.

As they all interacted, Fawn guided the conversation, skillfully drawing each person into the exchange. Jessica's laughter filled the air, punctuating the dialogue with her bright energy, while Ethan shared stories that captivated their attention, his anecdotes sprinkling warmth into the atmosphere. Felix, initially hanging back, began to interject his own thoughts, his contributions tentative but gradually growing more confident.

With each word and smile, Felix's posture relaxed, and his eyes brightened as the weight of isolation seemed to lift from his shoulders. Watching the easy banter and the laughter shared among new friends, Felix felt a stir of hope. Perhaps, just perhaps, there was space in his life for these genuine connections. This burgeoning sense of belonging, delicate yet palpable, was like a light piercing through the long shadows of his past.

The tranquility of the moment shattered as the porch door creaked open, revealing a tall, slender figure. The man moved with measured, cautious steps, his age betrayed by silver streaks in his hair and his reliance on a trusty cane.

Jessica, Ethan, and Fawn watched his slow progress across the yard, their faces etched with growing concern. Felix, noticing their attention had shifted, turned to see his father. A complex mix of recognition and deep-seated emotion flashed across his face as he beheld the familiar, weathered features of the man who had raised him.

"That's my dad," Felix said, his voice tinged with sadness. "He got hurt on the job a couple of years ago." His words fell, each syllable heavy with the weight of private struggles and quiet suffering. In that moment, he gave his newfound friends a glimpse into the challenges of his life.

A wave of empathy swept over Jessica and Fawn, their hearts heavy as they deepened their understanding of Felix's circumstances. They realized that Felix's existence, once perceived as that of a quiet, bookish boy at school, was marked by trials far more significant than they had imagined. The depth of his experiences, hidden within both the halls of their school and the confines of his home, now lay bare before them, forging a new layer of connection between them.

Grateful for Jessica and Ethan's support in reaching out to Felix, Fawn felt the tug of departure. With a hint of regret in her voice, she turned to him. "We have to go now, Felix. But maybe I'll come back one day, and we can talk some more."

Casting a lingering, poignant gaze back toward Felix, they each carried the weight of the day's revelations in their hearts. With slow, almost reluctant steps, they made their way back to the Jeep, the gravity of the moment grounding their movements.

Ethan steered the vehicle homeward, pulling away with deliberate slowness. Inside the Jeep, the mood was somber and reflective; each person lost in thought about the visit and its profound impact. As they drove off, Fawn turned in her seat, locking eyes with Felix. She raised her hand in a hesitant wave, a silent gesture of farewell mixed with a promise of return. Her gaze lingered until Felix became just a speck in the distance, the connection fading but the emotional imprint remaining vivid in her heart.

Standing beside the rusted gate, Felix watched the Jeep disappear, a faint smile touching his lips. The encounter had enveloped him in a cocoon of unfamiliar emotions—a mixture of gratitude and surprise at the genuine kindness he had experienced. As the sound of the Jeep faded into the distance, he remained alone with his thoughts and the memory of their visit, a rare moment of connection in his solitary world.

# Chapter 11

-------------------------------------------------------

Jessica's eyes fluttered open, welcoming the morning light that danced through her curtains. The remnants of a dream, sweetened with Ethan's laughter and the sea's soothing pulse, lingered in her mind. Wrapped in the comfort of her bed, she savored the echoes of the previous night's warmth. But her tranquility shattered as she settled her eyes on the clock beside her bed—10:50 a.m., and she realized with a jolt that she had overslept.

With a swift movement, Jessica slipped from her bed's embrace, the cozy blanket trailing behind her as a barrier against the cool morning air. She wrapped herself in the soft folds of her bathrobe and then walked down the hallway toward the kitchen. Along the path, she encountered her mother, poised by the front door in her Sunday best, embodying grace and elegance.

Teresa's warm and reassuring smile brushed against Jessica's forehead in a tender kiss. "We're a bit late, sweetheart. You'll need to fix your breakfast this morning," Teresa informed her before disappearing through the doorway.

Tom, with his comforting smile and paternal charm, echoed Teresa's sentiment, playfully reminding Jessica, "You behave yourself." His voice trailed off as he followed Teresa out the door, leaving Jessica standing in the foyer, a wave and a smile lighting up her face. The house, now quiet, held the promise of a peaceful morning, a small yet cherished gift of solitude.

In the kitchen, Jessica poured herself a cup of coffee, the aroma of freshly brewed beans enveloping her. The warmth from the mug seeped into her hands, each sip a crescendo of anticipation. Despite a mild grumble from her stomach, she chose a simple breakfast of toast, the crunch and warmth of each bite comforting her. The modest meal and the invigorating caffeine worked in harmony to awaken her fully, attuning her to the day's rhythm.

Returning to her bedroom, Jessica paused before her vanity, her reflection staring back at her with a mischievous twinkle in her eyes. She examined her tousled hair, deciding it was perfectly imperfect for the day. Her gaze shifted to her face, contemplating a stroke of eyeliner, but she chose to embrace her natural appearance instead. With a playful smirk, she made faces at her reflection, her giggles filling the room, a private performance of lighthearted jest. "I'm so pathetic," she whispered with a mock sigh, relishing her playful self-mockery.

With a sense of leisurely anticipation for her visit to Fawn's house, Jessica decided against further adornment. She chose comfort, opting for an old cropped black tank top and snug denim shorts that flattered her petite figure. Slipping into her sandals, she was ready to embrace the day's offerings, her heart alight with the promise of sharing adventures with Fawn.

As she locked the front door behind her, excitement rippled through the air. The day beckoned with the sweet allure of friendship, of stories yet to be discovered at Fawn's house. Wearing a smile as radiant as the morning sun and feeling its warmth bathe her skin, Jessica stepped out onto the sidewalk, ready to weave herself into the day's unfolding tapestry of experiences.

In the warm embrace of late morning, Jessica neared Fawn's house, a haven rich with echoes of laughter and childhood memories. As she approached, her eyes instinctively found a cherished scene as familiar as it was poignant. There, under the sheltering arms of an old palm tree, Fawn sat on the old white bench swing, sketchpad in hand—a sacred nook that had cradled their childhood adventures.

The swing, weathered yet resilient, bore the marks of their enduring friendship. It had silently observed their joy and comforted their sorrows, its green cushions imprinted with the passage of time. Each scar on the swing told a story of giggles that sparkled like stars and tears that glistened like moonbeams.

Jessica couldn't help but smile as she absorbed the familiar scene, a reminder that this sight was the heart of their shared youth. The air around her vibrated with an unseen, calming rhythm, harmonizing with the gentle sway of the swing and the whispering of the palm leaves above it.

With fluid grace, she approached the swing, the familiar creak of its ropes blending with the soft rustling of the palm leaves above. She took her seat beside Fawn, their sides touching lightly, a silent acknowledgment of their shared space. As Jessica settled in, the swing responded with a comforting sway, mirroring the rhythm of their longtime friendship.

"Hey," she greeted, her voice wrapping around Fawn like a melodic hug.

Fawn looked up from her sketchpad, her features marred by frustration. "Hey," she echoed, her voice threaded with a subtle strain.

Sensing her friend's unrest, Jessica asked, "What's wrong?"

Fawn let out a frustrated sigh, her eyes scanning her sketches. "I just... can't figure out what to draw for the art contest," she admitted, her voice tinged with disappointment. "Everything I come up with feels wrong."

Jessica's curiosity sparked as she observed a collage of intricate flowers. "Are you thinking of doing a flower piece?" she asked, her eyes tracing the delicate lines of the drawings.

Fawn set the sketchpad aside, resting her head in her hands, her voice shadowed with defeat. "I'm not sure," she confessed, her usual vibrancy dimmed by creative block.

Jessica closed the gap between them, wrapping an arm around Fawn in a gesture of solidarity and comfort. "You'll figure it out, Fawn. You always do," she reassured, giving a gentle squeeze. "Besides, you have until August. You still have plenty of time to find inspiration."

Fawn ran her fingers through her hair, exposing her face from beneath its strands. Looking into Jessica's eyes, she admitted, "I don't know, Jess. With everything that's happening right now, I just can't seem to focus, especially after our visit to Felix's house yesterday."

Jessica felt the weight of Fawn's words, the heaviness of her frustration and concern. She rested her head on Fawn's shoulder and murmured, "I know," sharing in the depth of emotions that swirled between them. The silence that followed spoke volumes, Jessica's steady presence offering comfort and reassurance.

As if ignited by a sudden burst of inspiration, Fawn's demeanor transformed, her face alighting with enthusiasm. She turned to Jessica, her eyes gleaming with an idea. "What if you invite Felix to your birthday party? It could be a chance for him to be around some friendly faces, don't you think?"

Jessica's face brightened at the suggestion, a knowing smile spreading across her features. "That's a great idea. I can't believe I didn't think of that. But do you think he'll come?"

Fawn's gaze held a spark of determination, her voice brimming with confidence. "Oh, he'll definitely come because I'll go to his house and take him there myself."

At Fawn's resolute spirit, Jessica let out a cheerful giggle, her support clear in her leaning gesture. "You go, girl!"

The familiar vivacity returned to Fawn's eyes, her signature playful grin firmly in place. Jessica felt a wave of comfort wash over her, seeing her friend's spirits lifted. As they sat together on the bench swing, she watched as Fawn's hand returned to her sketchpad, her doodles punctuating their dialogue while she shared tales of her moonlit escapades with Ethan.

Their lively conversation abruptly ceased as the gravelly sound of a car pulling up disrupted the peaceful morning. Jessica and Fawn turned, their curiosity tinged with an undercurrent of unease. The sight of the "Anderson Realtor Agency" car sent an icy shiver down their spines, heralding unwelcome news.

A man emerged and pulled a sign and a hammer from the trunk. His actions, performed with disconcerting ease, cast a shadow over the girls' spirits. He walked to Fawn's front yard and planted the sign into the ground. The rhythmic tapping of the hammer seemed to echo their anxious hearts. When he was done, the man offered the girls a brief, almost regretful smile before he drove away.

As if drawn by a magnetic force, Jessica and Fawn slowly approached the newly placed sign. The stark words "For Sale" stared back at them, a harsh wave of realization sweeping over them. They exchanged a look of bitter acceptance; Fawn's cherished childhood home, a treasure trove of memories, was on the cusp of being relinquished. They stood motionless, the grim message of the sign casting a long shadow over them.

Fawn's expression twisted in distress as she turned to Jessica. "Whatever. Let's get out of here," she said, her voice tinged with bitterness.

They walked away from the house in silence, each step echoing their sadness. Jessica felt the melancholy emanating from Fawn, understanding her friend's desire to escape the place that was no longer just a home. Side by side, they moved through the somber morning, their hearts heavy with the weight of change and loss.

The streets they passed were nearly empty, dotted only with a few late risers. As if in tune with their mood, the sun cast a gentle light over their path, its rays offering to comfort the turmoil within them. They walked side by side in reflective silence, exchanging glances that conveyed unspoken support.

Their steps eventually brought them to a serene park, a haven of green stillness that whispered with the gentle sway of leaves. Fawn led them to a bench nestled under the sheltering arms of an ancient oak, its branches forming a protective dome overhead. They settled into its wooden embrace, the quiet rhythm of the morning cocooning them in comfort.

There, in the peaceful solitude, Jessica reached out, her fingers intertwining with Fawn's in a gesture of support. Fawn's eyes, a blend of gratitude and sorrow, met Jessica's. In a voice as soft as the breeze, she admitted, "I don't know what I'd do without you, Jess."

A tender smile graced Jessica's lips, her heart swelling with love for her lifelong friend. "You'll never have to find out, Fawn. I'll always be here for you."

Together, they remained on the bench, immersed in the park's tranquil beauty, finding refuge in each other's company. The world around them faded into the background, leaving only the profound strength of their friendship, ready to face life's challenges together.

As the day unfolded from its morning cradle, Jessica and Fawn agreed it was time to leave. Despite the emotional whirlwinds of the day, their shared strength comforted them. They rose from the bench, their hands still linked, and walked back, their steps lighter than before.

Standing at the entrance to Fawn's home, they paused. With a voice tinged with a hint of sadness, Fawn said, "I think I want to be alone for now."

Jessica met her gaze, her eyes a deep well of steadfast support and care. "Okay, Fawn.

Just remember, no matter what happens, we're in this together."

Fawn nodded, a faint smile touching her lips. "Thanks, Jess. I'm so lucky to have you." Their goodbye was a hug filled with the strength of their connection, a silent promise of enduring support.

Jessica watched as Fawn walked to her front door, her steps symbolizing her readiness to face what lay ahead. As Jessica headed home, she carried the comforting truth that their friendship was a beacon, guiding them through life's perilous storms.

Throughout the afternoon, Jessica paced restlessly between her bedroom and the living room, unable to shake the uneasiness of Fawn's house being up for sale. The news cast a pall over her thoughts, its weight invading the once peaceful ambiance of her home. Though she respected Fawn's desire for solitude, Jessica couldn't help but feel a sense of helplessness. Their intermittent text exchanges offered a faint thread of comfort amidst her anxiety.

In the Reese household, Sundays were traditionally a time for leisure, a practice that now felt distant under the current circumstances. After church, Tom and Teresa would typically sink into the comforting embrace of the living room to escape the day's heat. The living room, with its plush sofa and a soft, inviting blanket draped over it, beckoned them to rest and enjoy familial warmth. The walls, painted in soothing hues, maintained the room's harmony, while the large woven area rug added a touch of homeliness underfoot.

Spotting an opportunity to unburden her heart, Jessica entered the living room where her mother sat reading a book. The sun streamed through the curtains, casting a gentle glow around her. Sensing her daughter's troubled demeanor, Teresa looked up with a warm, inquiring gaze.

"Mom," Jessica began, her voice tinged with concern. "Something happened this morning at Fawn's house."

Teresa set her book aside, giving her daughter her full attention. "What happened, honey?"

"A realtor came to the house and put up a 'For Sale' sign," Jessica said, her words heavy with the weight of her friend's predicament.

Teresa's expression softened as she understood the depth of what this meant for both Jessica and Fawn. "Oh, sweetheart," she replied, her voice a soothing balm. "That must have been quite a shock for both of you."

Jessica nodded, sinking into the sofa, the comforting familiarity of the living room wrapping around her. "Yeah, it's just... she's so sad, Mom, and I don't know how to help her."

Teresa reached out, her hand resting reassuringly on Jessica's. "You're already doing so much just by being there for her. These things... they're never easy. But remember, we're here for you and for Fawn."

In that moment, surrounded by the quiet comfort of the living room, Jessica felt a measure of solace. Her mother's empathy, as steady and reassuring as the sturdy oak furniture around them, reminded her that she wasn't alone in navigating these turbulent times.

As the afternoon unfolded across Wavecrest, Ethan was immersed in the unique cama-raderie only siblings share, planning an outing with his older brother. Before setting off, he texted Jessica, arranging to meet her on the boardwalk at seven. His message, brimming with excitement for the evening's promise, reassured her. Although Jessica longed for Ethan's physical presence, their frequent texts served as a comforting lighthouse, keeping their connection vibrant and close despite the distance.

The kitchen, with its terracotta tiled floor and the warm glow from the hanging pot racks, was a hive of activity as four o'clock approached. The air was rich with the mouthwatering aroma of roast beef, and the comforting scent of mashed potatoes wafting through the room. Teresa, the master of this culinary domain, moved with practiced grace, her hands weaving through the ingredients with an artist's touch.

Drawn to the kitchen by the enticing smells, Jessica offered her help. "Mom, do you need a hand with the salad?" she asked, approaching the counter where a spread of colorful vegetables awaited.

Teresa smiled, welcoming her daughter's company. "That would be lovely, sweetheart. Could you slice the tomatoes?" she replied, handing Jessica a knife and a chopping board.

Together, they worked in a symphony of slicing and stirring, the kitchen humming with the sound of their collaboration. As they prepared dinner, Jessica shared her plans for the evening. "I'm meeting Ethan on the boardwalk later. He's going to introduce me to his brother," she said, her voice tinged with excitement.

Teresa's face brightened at her daughter's enthusiasm. "That sounds wonderful. It'll be good for you to have some fun after this morning," she said, her voice infused with a mother's love and understanding.

Jessica's smile widened, her thoughts adrift in the evening's anticipation. Teresa hoped this night would be a soothing diversion for her daughter, a momentary respite from the day's earlier turmoil, and a chance for her to revel in the delight of new experiences and young love.

As the final touches were added to the meal, the Reese family gathered around the dining room table. Teresa's feast was a symphony of flavors, each bite a testament to her culinary prowess. The air was rich with the aromas of roast beef, creamy mashed potatoes, and the fresh zest of salad.

As they savored the meal, Tom shared a lighthearted tale. "You should've seen me at the car wash today," he began with a chuckle. "I managed to get more soap on myself than on the truck!" Laughter filled the room, the story adding a joyful note to their dinner.

Teresa chimed in with her own update, her eyes gleaming with pride. "You should see my flower garden. The roses are blooming beautifully. It's like they're thanking me for all the pampering I give them." Her comment sparked smiles and nods, adding another layer of warmth to the family's evening.

Their conversation meandered, bringing a comforting rhythm to the meal. However, when the topic of Fawn's house came up, Tom's expression turned somber. "It's a shame about their house. I just don't understand why they're moving," he said, his voice tinged with subtle displeasure.

Teresa sighed, sharing in the sentiment. "I don't know why, either. Maybe they think they'll have a better life in Montana," she said, her tone a blend of understanding and sadness at the thought of their friends moving away.

Tom's frustration was palpable as he added, "What the hell is in Montana? Are they—"

"Tom!" Teresa cut in, her eyes flicking toward Jessica. She didn't want to delve deeper into the topic, wary of upsetting her daughter with their grown-up concerns.

Realizing the tone of his words and their potential impact, Tom paused, collecting his thoughts and emotions. He looked at Jessica and then back at Teresa, his expression softening.

"Sorry," he said, his voice tinged with regret. "I didn't mean to let my feelings get the better of me." His sincere and considerate apology acknowledged the sensitivity of the situation, especially in Jessica's presence.

Understanding her father's concern, Jessica replied, "It's okay, Daddy. I know you mean well." Her words, full of empathy and understanding, eased the tension, acknowledging her father's good intentions despite the sensitive nature of the topic.

As Jessica savored the last bites of her meal, she felt the familial warmth, yet a subtle undercurrent of melancholy lingered from their conversation.

"Thanks, Mommy. That was delicious," she said, her words imbued with gratitude.

Teresa smiled, her heart warmed by her daughter's thoughtful appreciation. "You're welcome, honey," she replied, her satisfaction radiating in her glowing expression.

As dinner wound down, Jessica excused herself, leaving her parents in the quiet comfort of the dining room. She retreated to her bedroom, her mind already adrift with thoughts of the evening ahead. With a sense of excitement, she began to prepare for her rendezvous with Ethan on the boardwalk, the night promising new memories to be made.

She stood before her walk-in closet, her eyes scanning the selection of clothes. She was on a quest for the perfect outfit that would effortlessly blend chic elegance with a subtle hint of the excitement bubbling inside her. Her fingers danced over the fabrics, each garment telling a story as she considered her options. She chose a sundress that hugged her figure, its fabric whispering against her skin with every movement. Complementing her elegant silhouette, she selected open-toed heels, their subtle sophistication perfect for the evening.

Her hair fell in silky waves, beautifully framing her face. The makeup she applied enhanced her natural features, striking a perfect balance between understated and captivating. As she stood before her mirror, she admired the reflection that captured her youthful exuberance and the excitement for the night ahead.

Satisfied with her appearance, Jessica grabbed her purse and headed towards the front door. "I'm off to see Ethan and meet his brother," she called out to her parents, her voice carrying the flutter of excitement in her heart.

Teresa's voice floated back from the living room, tinged with warmth and a hint of nostalgia. "Have a wonderful time, sweetheart. And remember, don't stay out too late."

Stepping out into the evening's embrace, Jessica felt the pulse of excitement quicken in her heart. The breeze seemed to tousle her hair playfully, as if it was encouraging her to look forward to the adventures of the night. She smiled, thinking of Ethan's embrace and the promise of a new experience waiting for her on the boardwalk.

As Ethan guided his Jeep into their designated meeting spot, it marked more than just the beginning of an evening. The small parking lot, imbued with memories of their previous encounters, hummed with the proximity of the ocean and the vibrant energy of the boardwalk. Spotting the familiar silhouette of Ethan's Jeep easing into its space, Jessica felt her excitement burgeon. Her steps quickened toward the passenger side, her grin beaming across her face as she opened the door and slid into its welcoming interior.

The excitement of seeing Ethan again washed over her in a euphoric wave, each sensation heightened at the moment of their reunion. Their greetings mingled joyously, the shared delight reflected in their eyes. A tender kiss marked the culmination of their exchange, sealing the moment before they set off toward Ethan's temporary home. Ethan and his brother had secured a place in the lively part of town, where the energy seemed to pulse through the streets. Hotels and storefronts, vibrant and varied, lined the roads, each alive with the buzz of vacationers.

As the Jeep wove through the animated streets, Jessica took a deep breath, bracing herself to share the disturbing events of the morning. She turned to Ethan, her voice full of emotion. "Something happened at Fawn's today," she began, her eyes reflecting the morning's turmoil. "A real estate agent put up a 'For Sale' sign in her yard. It was so sudden, so final."

Ethan's expression grew attentive and concerned as he navigated the Jeep through the vibrant neighborhood. "That must have been tough to see," he said, his voice a blend of sympathy and attentiveness.

"Yeah, it hit us hard," Jessica continued, her voice wavering slightly. "Fawn's been my rock, and seeing her house, our childhood hangout, up for sale... it's just a lot to take in."

Reaching over, Ethan took her hand, offering a silent show of support. "I'm here for you, babe," he assured her, his grasp warm and reassuring. "If there's anything I can do."

Jessica sighed, feeling a mix of gratitude and helplessness. "I don't think there's any-thing anyone can do now," she said, her words tinged with resignation. In Ethan's reas-suring grip, she felt a glimmer of comfort, a reminder that she had someone by her side through these difficult times.

A few minutes later, Ethan parked his Jeep in front of the aged, two-story apartment building. He gestured toward it with a casual sweep of his hand, his pride in the place evident. The old, weather-beaten building stood proudly, its gray exterior telling stories of enduring sea breezes and relentless coastal storms. With fluid ease, Jessica and Ethan exited the Jeep. He reached out to Jessica and guided her toward the staircase with a gentle grasp of her hand.

When they reached the top of the stairs, Ethan's older brother emerged from the back and greeted them as they entered the cozy apartment. Jessica instantly noticed the strik-ing resemblance between the siblings. Despite him being three years older, they shared an unmistakable likeness, their features mirroring each other as if reflected in water.

Ethan's brother's eyes widened as he took in Jessica's appearance. "Oh my God. Look at those beautiful blue eyes," he exclaimed, visibly struck by her captivating presence. A warm blush colored Jessica's cheek, her smile widening as she met Ethan's proud gaze.

"Jess, this is my brother, Jake," Ethan said.

Jake extended his hand with a friendly handshake, his voice welcoming. "It's so nice to meet you, Jessica. Ethan has told me all about you. In fact, that's ALL he ever talks about these days!" His laughter was infectious, his teasing light and jovial.

A mixture of delight and slight embarrassment washed over Jessica, prompting her to giggle as she glanced back at Ethan. Being the gracious host, Jake motioned them toward the couch and excused himself to get some refreshments.

Settling onto the couch, Ethan and Jessica exchanged a look of excitement and comfort. For Jessica, this moment marked the beginning of a deeper connection with Ethan's world, a step into the realm of his family and the warmth of their summer home.

Over the next half hour, Jessica and Jake engaged in a lively exchange of stories and laughter. Jessica shared vivid snapshots of her life in Wavecrest, her words painting color-ful scenes from her journey from childhood to the cusp of adulthood.

"There was this one time in high school when Fawn and I accidentally turned our chem-istry lab blue. It was hilarious!" she chuckled, recalling a particularly amusing escapade.

Jake listened intently, his interest clearly piqued. In turn, he shared tales of his and Ethan's adventures.

"Ethan's always been the daring one," he said with a fond smile. "Last summer, we went cliff diving. Scared the daylights out of me, but Ethan, not a care in the world."

As Jake spoke, Jessica sipped her lemonade, captivated by the tales of Ethan's past. The stories painted a picture of a young man with an explorer's heart, further deepening her affection for him. "He always had that adventurous streak, even as a kid," Jake added, his smile widening.

With each anecdote, Jessica felt she was peeling back layers, gaining insight into Ethan's true essence—a restless explorer, always seeking new horizons. This spirit, burning with a passion for adventure, had led Ethan to Wavecrest. It was his natural desire to explore that had fortuitously brought him to that lifeguard stand on the beach, where their paths had fatefully crossed.

As the conversation flowed, Jake's phone buzzed. He glanced at it, his expression shifting to one of mild regret. "Ah, I've got to step out for a bit. Meeting up with some folks from around here," he explained as he stood up.

Jessica felt a twinge of disappointment; she had enjoyed the warmth and vibrancy of Jake's stories. "It was really great hearing about all your adventures," she said, her smile genuine.

Jake grinned as he headed toward the door. "Make yourselves at home, guys. And Jessica," he paused, turning back to her with a warm look. "It was great to meet you. My brother is a lucky man."

With a final wave, he left, and the apartment settled into a comfortable silence. Ethan and Jessica, now alone, shared a look of contentment, their hearts filled with the excitement of the evening ahead.

As the door clicked shut, Ethan wrapped Jessica in a tender embrace, creating a moment of peaceful seclusion from the world. In this quiet space, they found comfort and warmth in each other's arms, their connection deepening as they relaxed on the couch, their heartbeats synchronizing in a silent, intimate rhythm.

Feeling a wave of emotional weariness wash over her, Jessica guided Ethan to one side of the couch. She grabbed a couch pillow, placed it on his lap, and curled beside him, her head resting peacefully on the cushion. Her eyes, tired yet filled with affection, met Ethan's in a silent exchange full of understanding and warmth.

Ethan responded by gently stroking her hair, their eyes locked in a silent expression of deep emotion. In this shared silence, they expressed their love for one another without uttering a single word.

After a moment of peaceful quiet, Jessica's curiosity flickered to life. "What's it like where you live?" she asked, her voice carrying a note of wonder.

Ethan's gaze momentarily wandered as if traversing the landscapes of his memory. When he looked back at Jessica, his eyes sparkled with the joy of sharing a piece of his world.

"It's not much different than here," he began, his voice tinged with a touch of nostalgia. "We don't have the ocean and beaches, but we have the mountains... and the trees."

His voice deepened with reverence, his tone revealing a profound appreciation for the natural beauty he had grown up with. "You should see the trees back home, Jess. They're huge, like giants standing guard over the mountains. In the morning fog, they look kind of mystical, you know? And when the sun hits them just right, the whole place lights up. It's pretty awesome," he continued, his words painting a picture of majestic forests that had captivated his heart.

He paused, his expression shifting to one of wistful reminiscence. "And the seasons? We get to experience them all—the sweltering heat of summer, the frosty touch of winter snow, and everything beautiful and breathtaking in between."

As he spoke, Jessica could almost see the vivid tapestry of Pine Haven through his words, each season unfolding with its own unique beauty, painting a world that was both familiar and new to her. A gentle smile spread across her face as she imagined the beauty of his hometown.

"It sounds wonderful," she whispered. "I'd love to visit Pine Haven with you someday."

Ethan's fingers continued their gentle journey through Jessica's hair, his eyes filled with pure adoration. "There are a lot more beautiful places to see than Pine Haven, babe," he murmured back.

Jessica's eyes sparkled with curiosity. "Of all the places you've been, which one is your favorite?" she asked, eager to know more.

Ethan's smile widened, and his answer was immediate and certain. "Wavecrest," he declared.

Jessica's expression fluttered with surprise and delight. "Wavecrest? Really? Why here?" she asked, her voice a blend of wonder and amusement.

Ethan's smile deepened as he leaned closer, his breath a warm whisper against her cheek.

"Because you're here," he answered, his words simple yet profound.

Overwhelmed by the sincerity in his words, joyful tears glistened in Jessica's eyes. She tenderly cradled his face in her hands, her touch conveying the depth of her feelings. Then she leaned upward, and their lips met in a kiss that was gentle yet brimming with emotion.

As the evening continued, the apartment became a haven for their growing love. Together, they basked in a night filled with peaceful togetherness, their connection deepening with each shared moment. In the quiet sanctuary of Ethan and Jake's apartment, they found a world of their own, where their love flourished in the gentle embrace of the night.

# Chapter 12

As the morning sun cast its golden hues across the sky, Jessica emerged from her shower, refreshed and eager for the day's adventure with Fawn—a visit to Felix's house. While adjusting her hair in the vanity mirror, Jessica recognized the familiar hum of an engine—it was Fawn arriving. She hastened to the door, opening it to reveal Fawn's figure, her usually mischievous eyes shadowed with unease.

Jessica instinctively wrapped her arms around her friend in a comforting embrace. "Are you okay? I was worried about you," she murmured, her voice laced with concern.

"It's cool," Fawn replied with a forced smile, trying to sound reassuring. "I'm here now, so all is good."

Leading Fawn into the kitchen, Jessica avoided discussing the sensitive topic of Fawn's house being up for sale. As she poured the coffee, she started discussing her upcoming birthday party.

"It's going to be a small gathering this year," she explained while handing Fawn a mug. "With family coming from Texas and both sets of grandparents visiting, I have to keep the guest list short."

Fawn's eyes lit up with interest amidst the steam of her coffee. "So, who made the cut this year?"

"Just our crew: Heather, Krista, and Michelle," Jessica listed. "I want to spend as much time with them as possible before everyone scatters."

A sigh escaped Fawn, a reminder of the changes to come. "Yeah, it won't be long before we all move on." Trying to change the subject, Fawn teased, "Ethan's coming, right?"

At Ethan's mention, joy bubbled up inside Jessica like champagne fizz. "Yeah, he'll be there," she confirmed with an infectious grin.

Fawn's smile grew as she playfully prodded further. "Oh boy, your dad meeting him will be interesting."

Jessica's grin wavered for a moment at the thought. "I know, right? I've never introduced a boyfriend to Mom and Dad." She pondered momentarily before adding, "Mom will be fine, but Dad..."

Seeking to ease Jessica's concerns, Fawn reached out across the table, her touch reassuring. "Papa is cool. I think he'll be okay with it."

Jessica exhaled, a mix of hope and apprehension in her eyes. "I hope so," she murmured, her thoughts adrift on the tide of her father's possible reaction to Ethan.

After finishing their coffee, Jessica and Fawn stepped out of the house and into Fawn's car, which she had borrowed from her mother. As they pulled out of the driveway, Fawn flashed a playful grin tinged with sarcasm. "Well, this is going to be interesting," she quipped.

Jessica responded with an eye roll, acknowledging the challenge of convincing Felix to come to the party.

Soon, they left the vibrant energy of their coastal town and ventured into less familiar territory. As they approached the town's outskirts, the change in their surroundings reminded them of their first unsettling visit to Felix's house.

"This place still freaks me out," Jessica admitted, her voice filled with unease as she scanned the dim landscape outside her window.

"Yeah," Fawn agreed, focusing on the dimly lit road.

Before long, Felix's street appeared, almost ghostly in the dusk. Fawn carefully maneuvered the car onto the uneven road, the memory of its rough texture making them cautious. They parked near a well-trodden path leading to a rusted iron gate that marked the entrance to Felix's front yard.

Stepping out of the car, they were immediately enveloped by a sweltering heat, a stark departure from the air-conditioned comfort they had just left. The air felt thick and heavy, bereft of any breeze to alleviate the oppressive warmth.

Standing on the threshold of Felix's home, they shared a look, their faces etched with uncertainty. With a hesitant pressure, Fawn nudged the gate open, clearing their path to Felix's world.

Entering the yard, the girls saw Felix's father sitting on a wooden chair inside the screened porch. His face, worn and etched with lines of discomfort and pain, spoke volumes about his struggles. His blank gaze was fixed on some unseen horizon, while the cane propped against his chair served as a stark reminder of the workplace accident Felix had once mentioned. A swell of empathy swept over them as they grasped the magnitude of the burden Felix bore on his youthful shoulders.

As the girls stood on the edge of the porch, they were momentarily frozen, their feet sinking into the grainy earth as they balanced a tightrope of concern and apprehension. They were acutely aware of the delicate balance in Felix's life and how their presence might disrupt it. Exchanging a glance that communicated their shared unease, they silently debated their next course of action, while the man seated inside remained blissfully unaware of their presence.

The creak of the screened porch door cut through the silence, echoing like a whisper from the past. Felix emerged from the shadows, visibly startled by their arrival. His cheeks flushed a soft pink, and he stood motionless, hands buried in the deep pockets of his baggy black shorts. His eyes, wide and a mix of anxiety and intrigue, flitted nervously under Fawn's gaze—the girl who had unknowingly captured his silent admiration during their high school years.

In the quiet that followed, Jessica's warm voice broke the stillness. "Hi, Felix," she said, her tone imbued with friendliness, offering solace to his apprehensive heart.

Felix managed a timid smile, his eyes darting between Jessica and Fawn, lingering a moment longer on Fawn.

The reason for their visit remained unspoken until Jessica wove it into words. "I'm here to invite you to my birthday party on Thursday. I would love for you to come and celebrate with me and Fawn."

Felix's eyes opened wide in astonishment as he processed the unexpected invitation. A storm of emotions churned within him—gratitude mixed with doubt.

"I don't know," he faltered, his voice quivering with uncertainty.

Sensing Felix's turmoil, Fawn moved closer, her voice a comforting blend of empathy and encouragement. "Come on, Felix. It'll be fun. It's just a small gathering with some really awesome people." Her genuine words suggested an acceptance of him as a friend, kindling a flicker of warmth within him. Yet, the grip of his deep-seated insecurities remained firm. He shrugged, his indecision mirroring the heavy, still air.

Undaunted, Jessica decided to play her strongest card: a heartfelt plea delivered with an innocent charm that was uniquely hers. "Please? Please? Please?" she urged, her voice dripping with a sweetness that was hard to resist.

Felix's expression softened, a fleeting smile breaking through as he absorbed Jessica's genuine warmth and acceptance. He contemplated the prospect of attending the party, imagining a taste of a life previously unknown to him. For a moment, the world beyond his fence seemed within reach.

But then, like a cloud passing before the sun, a shadow of worry darkened his brief glimmer of hope. His eyes turned to the porch, where his father remained anchored in his realm of pain and dependency. The weight of responsibility rested heavily on his shoulders once again, extinguishing the spark of excitement that had briefly ignited within him.

"I don't know," he murmured, his voice echoing his inner turmoil. "I'll need to get back because..." Felix paused, pointing toward the front porch where his father sat, a visible reminder of his responsibilities. "That's my dad, you know. He got hurt at his job a few years ago, and he needs me," he continued, his voice laden with duty.

In that instant, Jessica and Fawn exchanged a look of deep empathy, their hearts touched by Felix's unwavering commitment to his father. They understood that his dedication was more than mere duty; it was a testament to his profound loyalty and selflessness.

Recognizing his inner conflict, Fawn stepped in with a gentle reassurance. "Felix, I promise, if you come to the party, I'll make sure to get you back home in a couple of hours. It could be a nice break for you," she assured him, her voice soothing. "Your dad will be just fine for a little while," she added, offering a comforting smile to ease his worries.

Felix's eyes lingered on Fawn, a mix of gratitude and uncertainty flickering across his face. Slowly, a tentative smile began to form as he considered her words.

"Okay, I'll go to Jessica's party," he mumbled, the weight of his decision evident in his voice.

His glance returned to the porch, his concern never fully dissipating, but the gentle assurance from his friends lent him a newfound resolve. "Thank you, Fawn, Jessica," he added, his voice stronger, touched by a hopeful note as he embraced the possibility of a brief escape from his responsibilities.

With silent nods that expressed their satisfaction, Jessica and Fawn retraced their steps toward their car. As Fawn's hand brushed against the driver's side door, she paused and glanced back at Felix. Her voice was soft yet firm with a promise as she said, "Don't forget, Felix. I'll be here Thursday around two o'clock to pick you up."

With his hands still nestled in the comfort of his pockets, Felix watched them drive away. The familiar hum of their car engine faded into the silence as it disappeared into the morning haze. A maelstrom of anticipation and apprehension stirred within him as he lingered by the aging gate that whispered tales of rust and time.

Turning back toward the house that held both his heartache and heartstrings, Felix allowed himself to believe in the possibility—however uncertain—of joining them on Thursday. His eyes traced their vanished path one last time, clinging to the glimmering thread of hope and connection they had woven into his world.

Following their poignant visit with Felix, the girls sought solace in the rhythmic embrace of the ocean. It was an unspoken pact between them to fill the day with laughter and companionship, letting the complexities of their lives drift away, if only for a while. Though her heart longed to share these joyful moments with Ethan, Jessica chose to dedicate this time to Fawn, intuitively sensing her friend's need for support. Sitting in the car parked in Fawn's driveway, Jessica texted Ethan about her plans, promising to meet him on the boardwalk later that evening.

When they entered Fawn's house, they were greeted by Anna, whose eyes radiated maternal warmth. "How was your morning, girls?" she asked.

"It was alright, nothing special," Fawn replied with a casual shrug, masking the emotional weight of their morning.

Jessica offered a supportive smile to Anna, silently agreeing to keep the morning's true nature under wraps.

After returning the car keys to her mother, they headed upstairs to Fawn's bedroom—a vibrant testament to her artistic passion and a sanctuary from the outside world.

"Mind if I borrow one of your bikinis? I didn't think to bring mine," Jessica asked as they entered the room.

"Of course! Help yourself," Fawn said, opening a drawer brimming with colorful swimwear.

Jessica chose a brightly colored bikini that mirrored the lively spirit of summer. As they changed, their spirits lifted, enveloped by a light-heartedness in anticipation of the day ahead.

Once dressed, Jessica and Fawn admired their reflections in the full-length mirror. Their images radiated youthful energy and a carefree spirit, embodying the vibrant essence of summer.

"Ready for the beach?" Fawn asked, her voice teeming with excitement.

"Absolutely," Jessica replied, her smile wide with a sense of freedom and exhilaration.

Together, they left the room, their bare feet eager for the warm embrace of the sandy beach and the enchanting melody of the waves. The promise of a day filled with simple joys and the strength of their friendship lay ahead.

Just as Jessica and Fawn were about to head out for their beach adventure, Anna approached, her hands cradling a beach bag generously stocked with an assortment of snacks and chilled water bottles.

"Here you go, girls. I thought you might need these," Anna said, handing the bag to Fawn, her voice laced with the affectionate concern of a mother ensuring her children's comfort.

Fawn's eyes lit up with appreciation. "Thanks, Mom, but you didn't have to do this," she said.

Anna smiled, the corners of her eyes crinkling with affection. "I know how you girls get when you're out there in the sun all day. I just want to make sure you both stay hydrated and have something to eat," she replied.

"Thank you, Mama," Jessica added, her voice rich with appreciation. "You always think of everything."

With a final wave, the girls stepped out into the radiant afternoon sun. The boardwalk, alive with the vibrant pulse of Wavecrest, beckoned them from a distance. Their hearts beat in sync with the excitement of the moment, irresistibly drawn toward the ocean's call—a melody intertwined with the spirit of their beloved town.

Walking the four blocks from Fawn's house to the boardwalk, the girls strolled through the quaint streets of their neighborhood, each turn a familiar page in their storybook of memories. Homes adorned with climbing roses and windows gleaming in the afternoon sun greeted them. They chatted idly, their conversation ebbing and flowing like the distant ocean waves. The laughter of children playing nearby, and the occasional bark of a dog, enriched the symphony of small-town life, drawing them deeper into the comforting embrace of their surroundings.

As they reached the boardwalk, the soft creak of the wooden planks beneath their feet played a familiar melody. They strolled past vendors selling colorful trinkets and food stands wafting sweet, enticing aromas. Laughter from beachgoers and music from a nearby loudspeaker wove a vibrant tapestry of summer sounds.

As they descended the ramp to the beach, their pace slowed as their feet sank into the warm, golden sand. Breathing deeply, they filled their lungs with the salty air. They scanned the beach, their eyes wandering over the scattered groups of sunbathers and families, searching for a quiet spot. Finally, they found the perfect place at the water's edge, slightly apart from the others, offering them a serene slice of the shore.

After laying out their towels, the girls settled into the leisurely pace of beach life. The rhythmic crash of the waves and the caress of the sea breeze enveloped them in serenity. Jessica's bright blue eyes, once searching the beach for attractive boys, now reflected a contentment rooted in her deep connection with Ethan. She had found her soul mate, making other possibilities as fleeting as footprints washed away by the tide.

As they reclined on the warm sand, basking in the sun's embrace, their worries unraveled, replaced by a sense of peace and joy. Together, they reveled in companionable silence, punctuated by bursts of laughter that blended with the ocean's lulling cadence, creating perfect harmony on this tranquil afternoon.

The irresistible allure of the ocean's rhythm soon beckoned Jessica and Fawn, their eyes alight with a mischievous sparkle. As they lay on their beach towels, Jessica turned to Fawn with a playful grin, adventure twinkling in her bright blue eyes.

Are you thinking what I'm thinking?" she asked, her voice dancing with excitement.

Fawn responded with a mischievous grin, her eyes reflecting the same playful spirit. "Uh-huh," she replied, her tone brimming with anticipation.

In unison, they sprang to their feet, their smiles radiating playful delight as they made their way toward the water. Their laughter, a symphony of unbridled joy, mingled with the whispering sea breeze. An invisible force seemed to guide them, pulling them closer to the waves and granting them a moment to be carefree once more.

Plunging into the sea's foamy embrace, Jessica and Fawn surrendered to unbridled delight. They splashed and played tag, darting through the waves with youthful exuberance. Their laughter, pure and uninhibited, echoed over the water as they ducked and weaved, each trying to outmaneuver the other. With playful screams reminiscent of their childhood, they chased each other, hiding behind the rising crests of the waves, only to emerge with triumphant giggles.

The simplicity of this moment, immersed in the ocean's frothy dance, rekindled their spirits with pure joy. The water seemed to wash away any lingering shadows of worry, their laughter painting vibrant memories onto the canvas of the afternoon. For a brief spell, they were transported back to the golden days of youth, where each day was an adventure waiting to unfold, and their friendship was being cemented into something unbreakable.

For now, the uncertain paths of their futures, the impending divergence of their lives, and the distressing news of Fawn's family moving away were all forgotten. They were two friends, immersed in the present, their spirits intertwined with the joy and freedom of the moment. In the warm embrace of the sun and the playful touch of the waves, they found a temporary haven—a place to cherish the beauty of their friendship and the preciousness of their shared memories.

As the sun's intensity waned in the late afternoon sky, Jessica glanced upward and then at Fawn, a hint of reluctance in her expression. "Looks like it's getting late," she observed, her voice tinged with a touch of regret.

Fawn nodded, her eyes lingering on the horizon where the sun flirted with the sea. "I guess we should head back," she agreed, though her tone suggested she wished they could linger a little longer.

Together, they began gathering their belongings, shaking the sand from their towels, and packing up their beach bag. The playful sparkles of the ocean seemed to fade as they zipped up the bag, sealing away the remnants of their carefree day.

With one last look at the waves that had been their joyful refuge, they started their walk back, their hearts still echoing with the laughter and joy of their seaside play. The rhythmic comfort of the ocean waves followed them as they left their cherished beach behind, each step taking them a little further from their haven of sand and surf.

As she approached her house, Jessica noticed an unfamiliar car in the driveway. This strange presence amidst the familiar surroundings of her home sparked a flurry of questions in her mind. Who could be visiting? Her pace quickened, driven by a growing curiosity. The moment she spotted the distinctive "Texas" license plate on the car, a wave of excitement surged within her.

"Oh my God! It's Aunt Veronica and Uncle Gary! They're here already!" she exclaimed, her voice echoing with pure elation. "I thought they were coming tomorrow," she added, her surprise mixing seamlessly with the thrill of their early arrival.

Sharing Jessica's excitement, Fawn's smile widened. "It looks like your birthday celebration is starting early," she chimed in, her enthusiasm mirroring Jessica's.

Together, they hurried toward the house, their earlier fatigue forgotten. Replaced by eager anticipation, their spirits soared with the unexpected joy of greeting Jessica's beloved aunt and uncle. This surprise visit added a sprinkle of joy to an already memorable day, lifting their spirits even higher.

As they entered the house, the lively banter of Veronica, Gary, and Teresa filled the space, transforming the living room into a vibrant hub of family warmth and reunion.

"Aunt Veronica! Uncle Gary!" Jessica called out, her voice resonating throughout the house.

At the sound of Jessica's voice, Veronica's and Gary's faces lit up with radiant smiles, their excitement reflecting their deep affection for her. They rose from the sofa with the eagerness of a long-awaited reunion, their smiles lighting up the room like sunshine breaking through the clouds.

Veronica, tall and graceful, exuded an air of sophistication mingled with warmth. Her dark hair was styled in an elegant updo that framed her soft, caring eyes. She enveloped Jessica in a warm embrace, her touch gentle and reassuring, embodying the nurturing spirit she was known for.

Gary, robust in build and with a heart as big as Texas, hugged Jessica with affectionate strength. His deep-set blue eyes, framed by laugh lines and a well-maintained beard, sparkled with pride.

"Look at you, Jesse. You're all grown up now," he said, his voice a blend of pride and wonder. He placed his hands on her shoulders, his touch reassuring as he gazed at her with a fondness that spanned years. Turning to Teresa, he asked with light-hearted curiosity, "What's it been, three or four years?"

Teresa, glowing with maternal pride, paused to reflect. "Yes, something like that," she agreed, her voice laced with the warmth of shared memories.

Turning to Fawn, Veronica, and Gary welcomed her into the familial embrace with equal warmth. Gary's eyes, twinkling with mischief, rested on Fawn.

"I see you still have that mischievous spark in your eyes," he teased, his hands resting on her shoulders as he marveled at her growth.

Stepping back, Gary surveyed Jessica and Fawn, his voice tinged with nostalgia. "I remember watching you girls play in the backyard when you were just this big," he said, lowering his hand to his knee to indicate their height back then. "Even then, I could see how close you two were," he mused, his words thick with sentiment.

Turning to Veronica and Teresa, he added, "It's a rare sight these days, don't you think?" The women nodded in agreement, their expressions softened with pride and affection as they observed the two friends.

Caught in this moment of collective sentiment, Jessica and Fawn exchanged glances filled with the unspoken understanding of their unique friendship. Their smiles were silent acknowledgments of the rare and precious bond they shared, a treasure that had withstood the tests of time and emerged stronger. They stood together, surrounded by the loving gaze of family, a living testament to the enduring nature of their friendship.

Teresa, moving with effortless elegance, gracefully rose from her recliner. With purposeful steps, she disappeared into the kitchen, only to return with two chairs in hand. She positioned them in the living room, creating an inviting circle that beckoned Jessica and Fawn to join. The seating arrangement was a masterpiece of coziness, with Veronica and Gary seated on the sofa, their presence framing the conversation with comforting warmth.

Veronica, her face aglow with a gentle, maternal smile, turned toward Jessica. Her soft and melodious voice was laced with affectionate curiosity. "Are you excited about college, sweetheart?" she inquired.

Jessica felt a whirlwind of emotions stirring within her. The excitement that once sparkled at the thought of college had dimmed, now tinged with melancholy. The idea of leaving the familiar embrace of Wavecrest, the thought of parting ways with Ethan, and Fawn's impending move to Montana, ignited a flicker of sorrow in her heart.

With a calm exterior belying her inner turmoil, Jessica offered a subdued smile. "Yeah... I suppose so," she replied, her voice a quiet reflection of her mixed feelings.

Gary noticed the subtle undercurrents in Jessica's response. He leaned forward, his voice soft yet reassuring, trying to alleviate her concerns. "I know it might seem daunting, Jesse, but you're going to love it in Austin. The University of Texas is an excellent school, offering opportunities to make new friends and experience the thrill of college life."

Although Jessica appreciated his comforting words, the thought of a future without the nearness of her loved ones still weighed heavily on her. Sensing her unspoken fears, Gary continued with determined optimism. "And remember, we're only a hundred miles away from Austin. We'll always be there for you whenever you need us. You'll never be far from family."

Veronica's voice resonated with the same warmth and reassurance. "Absolutely, sweetheart. We'll be at the airport when you arrive, and we won't leave until you're settled in your dorm. We're here to support you every step of the way."

A surge of gratitude washed over Jessica as she absorbed their words. Their assurances rekindled a small flame of hope amidst her apprehensions, reminding her that this new chapter wasn't a solitary journey; her family's love and support would be with her, a guiding light in the distance. Her smile became genuine and heartfelt as she expressed her gratitude. "Thank you, Aunt Veronica and Uncle Gary. Knowing you'll be there if I need you means the world to me."

Veronica and Gary exchanged a look of shared pride and affection, understanding the significance of this moment for their niece. They believed in her strength and resilience, confident in her ability to navigate this new chapter of her life. Their faith in her was unwavering, a steadfast anchor as she prepared to set sail into her future.

"And Teresa, you'll be flying out a few days later, right?" Veronica turned to Jessica's mother.

"Absolutely. I wouldn't miss Jessica's orientation week for the world," Teresa confirmed, her voice rich with maternal pride. "This is a big moment, and I want to be there through it all," she added, her smile tinged with wistfulness.

Jessica, touched by her mother's commitment, felt a surge of warmth and gratitude welling up within her. She knew her mother's presence would be a comforting bridge between the familiarity of home and the newness of college life.

The sound of the back door swinging open interrupted the peaceful hum of family conversation. Emily, Jessica's sixteen-year-old cousin, stepped in, adding a new dynamic to the room. She paused at the doorway, her presence a blend of reticent shyness and unmistakably nonchalant charm. A cascade of tousled chestnut hair that fell over her shoulders highlighted her slender frame. Emily's striking, deep-blue eyes, mirroring Jessica's, were a vivid reminder of their shared Reese heritage.

Emily's presence surprised Jessica; her cousin's attendance at her birthday celebration was unexpected. The physical distance and infrequent visits had created a gap between them, preventing the development of a close relationship.

She stood in the room, seemingly oblivious to Jessica's presence until prodded by Veronica. "Emily, aren't you going to say hi to your cousin?" Turning toward Jessica and Fawn, Emily offered a half-hearted smile and a nod of recognition.

"Don't mind Emily," Veronica said to Jessica, her voice tinged with a hint of annoyance. "She's not thrilled about being here." She then turned to Teresa, switching the topic to her two older children. "James and Keith wanted to come, but they're busy working this summer."

Teresa nodded sympathetically. "It's understandable; they're at that age where they have their own responsibilities."

Seemingly irritated by the ongoing conversation, Emily directed her attention toward Jessica. "Do you still have your PlayStation?" she asked, her tone revealing a slight thaw in her otherwise aloof demeanor.

"Yes, it's in my room," Jessica replied, her voice calm as she tried to mask any irritation at Emily's distant approach.

"Can I play some of your games?" Emily's voice softened with the request.

"Sure," Jessica answered, maintaining a welcoming attitude despite her cousin's brusque manner.

As Emily headed toward Jessica's room, Veronica and Gary exchanged knowing looks, silently acknowledging Emily's typical attitude. Once she was out of earshot, Jessica and Fawn shared a knowing glance, their expressions conveying unspoken thoughts about Emily's behavior. With a wry smile, Fawn whispered, "She hasn't changed much, has she?" Their exchange was a quiet acknowledgment of Emily's bratty nature, an understanding shared between two friends who had witnessed it over the years.

As the evening unfurled its dusky veil, Fawn hinted to Jessica that it was time for her to head home. With a shared resolve, they both rose, preparing to depart.

"Fawn has to go home now, and I want to walk her back. Is that okay, Mom?" Jessica asked, seeking her mother's consent with hopeful eyes.

Teresa's eyes, warm and understanding, swept over the two girls. "Of course, it's okay. Just don't be gone too long. Dinner will be ready in about an hour," she replied with a gentle nod.

Turning to Veronica and Gary, Jessica and Fawn offered their goodbyes. Fawn expressed her gratitude. "It was nice to see you, Aunt Veronica, and Uncle Gary."

Veronica beamed at them, her affection evident. "Oh, it's always a pleasure, honey. We're looking forward to seeing you at Jessica's birthday party. Be safe on your walk home," she said, her voice carrying the comforting timbre of maternal care.

With his characteristic good-natured smile, Gary added, "You girls enjoy the rest of your evening. We'll see you at the party. Don't get into too much mischief on the way!" His voice held a teasing, jovial note, typical of his playful demeanor.

As the girls stepped out into the softening light, Gary turned to Teresa, admiration in his voice. "You've done a remarkable job raising that child, Terri," he said sincerely.

Feeling a surge of pride at his words, Teresa couldn't help but feel a twinge of unease at the thought of Jessica's impending move to Austin. The idea of her home without Jessica's vibrant presence, laughter, and energy was daunting. She accepted Gary's compliment with a small smile, but her mind still wandered to the upcoming changes and the silence that would soon fill her home. Despite this, she put aside her concerns, focusing on the present moment and the joy of having her family gathered around her.

# Chapter 13

--------------------------------------------------------------

*Twelve years ago, on a crisp Saturday morning in April, the sun painted golden hues across the quiet suburban neighborhood where six-year-old Fawn lived. Her bedroom window offered a perfect vantage point, a portal to the world outside, where a hint of mystery unfolded before her curious gaze.*

*Beside Fawn stood her faithful companion, five-year-old Jessica, a kindred spirit in youthful wonder. Together, they watched intently as Brian, Fawn's father, accompanied by a few of his friends, engaged in a secretive endeavor at the edge of the side yard. Their animated movements and the clanking of metal parts intrigued the young onlookers, piquing their curiosity like a dormant flame ignited by a gentle breeze.*

*With a small and curious voice, Jessica asked, "What is your daddy doing?" her eyes bright with inquisitiveness.*

*With an equal amount of confusion, Fawn furrowed her brow and replied, "I don't know," her sweet, childish voice carrying a hint of uncertainty.*

*Intrigued, the two girls left the comfort of Fawn's bedroom and ventured out onto the porch, eager to unravel the mystery that lay before them. But as they approached the front door, Anna, Fawn's mother, aware of their intentions, interjected with a gentle warning.*

*"Don't bother your father, Fawn. He's busy right now."*

*Pouting her lips in disappointment and anticipation, Fawn couldn't resist asking, "What's Daddy doing, Mommy?"*

*A playful smile graced Anna's lips as she replied, "Never mind, you'll see."*

*Fawn and Jessica, their curiosity now fueled with even greater intensity, settled into the inviting embrace of the front porch. From there, they had an unobstructed view of the scene unfolding in the yard—a theater of craftsmanship and ingenuity.*

*Like magicians wielding shiny metal tubes, the men orchestrated their movements with precision. Piece by piece, the white metallic puzzle took shape, each side resembling an elegant "A" standing tall on the ground below. Fawn's eyes were fixed on her father, her eyes widening with recognition as he positioned the crossbeam connecting the two A-frames. It became clear—this mysterious creation held the promise of something magical.*

*Then, as if in a moment of revelation, Jessica exclaimed, "Look, Fawn!" Her tiny finger excitedly pointed to two men emerging from the garage, carefully cradling a white bench in their arms.*

*Fawn and Jessica watched spellbound as Brian attached two ropes to the sides of the bench. With the measured care of a craftsman, he lifted the bench into position and secured the ropes to the waiting crossbeam. The shimmering white bench swing, now gracefully suspended, danced gently in the morning breeze.*

*Overwhelmed by the sight, Jessica's voice quivered with awe. "Wow, Fawn. It's a swing. You are so lucky," she said, her voice a sweet, breathless whisper of amazement.*

*Fawn beamed with joy, her heart filling with gratitude for this unexpected gift. She gazed at the shiny new swing, now an enchanting addition to her yard and a haven of dreams waiting to be explored.*

*As Fawn's father and his friends tidied up the area around the bench swing, his voice carried over to the girls, inviting them to experience the culmination of his labor. "Come on over and try it out," he called.*

*Fawn and Jessica leaped anxiously off the porch, their little legs propelling them toward the shining spectacle. Without hesitation, they landed on the welcoming bench and settled into the soft green cushions. As they leaned back, legs dangling in the air, the joy etched on their faces conveyed an unspoken appreciation, a testament to the worthiness of Brian's endeavor.*

*The rest of the spring morning unfolded in a symphony of laughter and playfulness. Fawn and Jessica reveled in their newfound toy, the swing carrying them to new heights of imagination and delight. Under the protective shade of a majestic palm tree, the white bench swing became their private sanctuary—a vessel for shared secrets, whispered dreams, and unbreakable bonds.*

*As they swung, a gentle breeze caressed their cheeks, carrying a hint of ocean salt and a touch as soft as a whisper. It left them with a fleeting sense of cozy warmth, as if the swing and the palm tree above were giving them a tender, loving embrace.*

*Little did Fawn and Jessica know that this humble swing, lovingly crafted and nestled under the watchful gaze of this ancient palm tree, would become a significant part of their childhood and shape the story of their friendship for years to come.*

On this Wednesday morning, eighteen-year-old Fawn sat on the old white bench swing, lost in thoughts about the upcoming art contest. This swing, a silent witness to her youthful adventures and a testament to the passage of time, now cradled her in its worn, sun-bleached cushions and rust-streaked frame. As it whispered secrets of times past, Fawn found solace and inspiration in this tranquil refuge, shared only with her dearest friend, Jessica.

As Fawn sat lost in thought, her tranquility was shattered by the arrival of a car marked with the "Anderson Realtor Agency" logo, igniting apprehension in her chest. Three figures stepped out, moving decisively toward what Fawn considered her personal domain. This intrusion, reminding her of the looming changes threatening her cherished memories, sparked a defiant resolve.

She rose from the swing, her voice piercing the morning calm. "My parents aren't home right now, so you'll have to leave!" The strength in her voice mirrored the fierce protectiveness she felt for her home.

The Realtor, a portly man with a gleaming scalp, countered her challenge with a disarming smile. "Well, you're here. You can let us in, can't you?"

His casual dismissal only intensified Fawn's determination. These strangers, poised to invade her sanctuary, felt like conquerors threatening her beloved home.

"I don't think so!" she retorted sharply, her stance as fiery as her gaze. The Realtor and the accompanying middle-aged couple found themselves stunned by the intensity of her defiance.

Attempting a more reasoned approach, the Realtor continued, "You don't understand, Miss. My clients have traveled a long way to see your home. They're very interested in buying it."

But Fawn's conviction held firm, her rejection unwavering. "I don't care! My parents aren't home, so you're not going inside!" Her words rang out decisively, leaving no room for argument.

Silenced by her steadfast opposition, the Realtor signaled to the bemused couple to return to their car. With a reluctant nod, he conceded, "Okay, Miss. We're leaving."

Fawn, hands in her shorts' pockets, watched them drive away. The storm of her anger slowly gave way to a quiet sense of triumph.

After the Realtor's car disappeared, Fawn returned to the old white bench swing and sank into its faded green cushions. As she settled, she felt the air shift around her, bringing a cool, soothing touch that eased the lingering tension in her shoulders. The swing, a silent witness to her life's journey, seemed to recognize her turmoil and offered a gentle caress.

Lulled by the swing's gentle sway, Fawn turned her attention upwards as the rustling leaves of the towering palm tree caught her ear. They whispered directly to her soul in an ancient, comforting language, a sensation as familiar and natural as breathing. This presence had been an integral part of her existence, akin to the dreams that greeted her each night.

113

The soothing motion of the swing brought a calmness that felt like an invisible, tender embrace, easing the knots of worry and uncertainty within her. This ethereal presence, a constant comfort, seemed to guide and support her in times of need.

As the sunlight filtered through the palm fronds, it cast dappled patterns of light and shadow around her, creating an almost otherworldly aura. In this moment, her concerns about the art contest, the Realtor, and the future seemed to lift from her shoulders, carried away like leaves on a gentle breeze.

Fawn closed her eyes, immersing herself in a tranquility that was both familiar and refreshing, like waking from a comforting dream to a reality just as serene. It was a silent reassurance that she was not alone—that this gentle, unseen presence, which had been with her since the first day she and Jessica claimed this swing as their own, continued to surround her.

Here, in the embrace of the old white bench swing and the whispered secrets of the wind, Fawn found a renewed sense of peace. Her spirit, once clouded with anxiety, now basked in a lightness, as if reminded of a truth she had always known. In this quiet corner of Wavecrest, amidst the sway of the swing and the whispers of the leaves, Fawn felt an unspoken promise: no matter the challenges ahead, she would never truly be alone.

Later that morning, a heartwarming surprise brightened Jessica's world as the gentle murmur of beloved voices danced through the corridors of her home. Wrapped in her cozy bathrobe, she left the comfort of her bedroom and followed the tender echoes to the kitchen, where she found her grandparents, Grandma Clara and Grandpa Robert Bowman, sitting at the table.

Grandma Clara's soft white hair was elegantly tied in a chignon, her once vivid green eyes now a muted shade, yet still sparkling with wisdom and mischief. She wore her signature knee-length floral dress paired with comfortable flats, creating a picture of classic grace. Grandpa Robert, with his neatly combed salt-and-pepper hair, stood next to her, his observant hazel eyes peering from behind square glasses. He wore a cardigan over a shirt with classic trousers, epitomizing neatness and a love for the old ways.

As Jessica approached, the kitchen seemed to come alive with their presence. It had been months since their last visit, and the joy of reunion filled the room. They rose together to envelop her in an embrace that was as solid as a mountain and as warm as the midday sun. Their faces lit up with affection and delight at seeing her.

"There's our sunshine," Grandma Clara exclaimed, her voice a soft tapestry of affection. "Growing more beautiful each day."

"Grandma, Grandpa, I've missed you so much!" Jessica's voice trembled with emotion.

Grandpa Robert's eyes crinkled with warmth. "We've missed you, too, bright eyes. It's still hard to believe you'll be eighteen tomorrow."

Sitting with them at the table, Jessica felt wrapped in the rich tapestry of memories and the intimate warmth of family. Their presence was a vivid reminder of the unconditional love they had woven into her life, a testament to the family bond that had always been her anchor.

The rich aroma of morning coffee filled the air as Teresa, her eyes alight with maternal pride and curiosity, handed Jessica a comforting mug. "How was your evening with Ethan, honey?" Teresa inquired.

Jessica responded with a soft, enigmatic smile. "It was good," she said, glancing towards her father, who was leaning against the counter, absorbed in his morning coffee ritual. An undercurrent of nervous anticipation about introducing Ethan to her family at her birthday party stirred within her.

"Who's Ethan?" Grandma Clara chimed in, her curiosity piqued.

"He's Jessica's boyfriend," Teresa answered, glancing at her mother. "They've been seeing quite a lot of each other lately."

Papa Robert's eyes lit up. "Is that so? Tell us about him, Jessica," he urged, his voice tinged with the gentle nosiness typical of grandparents.

Jessica squirmed slightly under their eager gazes. "We're just getting to know each other better," she said, her cheeks coloring.

"Nonsense, dear," Grandma Clara chuckled. "We can see there's more to it than that. What's he like?"

Tom, quietly observing from the sidelines, added to Jessica's sense of scrutiny. She fumbled for words, trying to divert their interest. "He's nice, kind... um, and he loves to surf," she offered.

"And does this Ethan have plans for college?" Papa Robert probed further, leaning forward with keen interest.

"Yes, he's working on getting his business degree," Jessica replied, her voice trailing off as she felt her father's gaze intensify.

Papa Robert nodded approvingly. "A businessman. That's impressive," he remarked.

Sensing her daughter's growing discomfort, Teresa quickly changed the subject. "Let's focus on breakfast, shall we? Who's hungry?"

Jessica breathed a silent sigh of relief, grateful for the diversion. However, her heart continued to flutter with mixed emotions of excitement and apprehension about the upcoming introduction, a significant step in her journey into the depths of love and commitment.

Time had slipped away in the comfort of shared stories and laughter. Finally, Grandma and Grandpa Bowman decided it was time to bid farewell, their hotel suite calling them back for some much-needed rest. The long journey from Pennsylvania to Wavecrest had left them visibly tired but still brimming with joy for the time spent with family.

"Well, darling, we better get going," Grandma Clara said to her daughter as she stood, smoothing her floral dress. "We need to catch up on some rest before the big party tomorrow."

Jessica, Teresa, and Tom accompanied them to their car parked in the driveway. "Thank you for coming all this way," Jessica said, wrapping her arms around each of them. "It means a lot to me that you're here."

"Wouldn't miss it for anything, bright eyes," Grandpa Robert replied, his voice warm with affection as he gave her a gentle squeeze. "We'll be back bright and early to celebrate your big day."

Then Teresa stepped forward, her eyes moist with the thought of parting. "Love you, Mom and Dad," she said, her voice thick with emotion as she hugged them both tightly. "We'll see you in the morning."

With final waves and smiles, the grandparents got into their car. The engine hummed to life, and they pulled away, leaving behind a trail of love and lingering affection in the air.

Jessica and Teresa turned back toward the house, but Jessica's eyes followed her father as he took a detour toward the backyard. Aware of the busy week ahead, filled with family reunions for her milestone eighteenth birthday, Tom had cleared his schedule to immerse himself in these cherished moments. Nervous about introducing Ethan to her father, Jessica followed him, seeking a quiet moment to discuss her concerns about Ethan.

Approaching the weathered storage shed where her father stood, Jessica wrestled with her thoughts, seeking the right words. Taking a deep breath for courage, she spoke in a voice laced with nervous determination. "Daddy, can we talk for a sec?"

Tom turned, his eyes reflecting a deep well of paternal love and concern. "Of course, baby girl. What's on your mind?" he replied, his tone inviting and open.

A whirlwind of emotions swirled within Jessica, threatening her calm facade. She gathered her resolve and spoke her truth. "It's about Ethan, Daddy. He'll be coming to my birthday party, and it would mean a lot to me if you could treat him nicely while he's here."

Tom listened in silence, his expression one of thoughtful consideration. Feeling a surge of nervous anticipation, Jessica continued, "I love Ethan, Daddy. I really do. It's important to me that I have your approval and that you accept him when you meet him." Her words hung in the air, a fragile plea for understanding and support.

In that hushed interlude, Jessica found comfort in her father's softened gaze, a gentle transformation from sternness to a rich tapestry of love and understanding. Tom drew her into a comforting embrace, his voice a soothing thread of reassurance and profound affection. "Sweetheart, I am so proud of the woman you have become. Your mother and I have always trusted your judgment, and you have never once let us down with your choices."

Tears, glistening like morning dew, brimmed in Jessica's eyes, a testament to the relief and love she felt. Her father's words were like a soothing balm, washing away her fears and doubts about Ethan's acceptance. He tenderly brushed a tear from her cheek, a gentle gesture that brought a smile through her emotional tumult.

"I promise you, baby girl, Ethan is welcome here, and I will treat him with respect and kindness," Tom said with heartfelt sincerity.

Jessica's heart swelled with gratitude, her embrace tightening around her father. In his arms, she found the strength and love that had always been her guiding force. This moment crystallized a deep-seated certainty in her heart, a promise that her birthday would be a celebration of love and acceptance.

"I love you, Daddy," she whispered, her voice thick with emotion. The weight of her worries seemed to dissolve in his embrace, replaced by a growing sense of peace and joy. In this moment, she was transported back to the early days of her youth, safe in her father's arms, fortified and ready to face any challenges ahead.

# Chapter 14

--------------------------------------------------------------

*Eighteen years ago, on the morning of June 26, Teresa Reese found herself in a state of pure awe and overwhelming joy. As she looked down at her beautiful baby girl cradled in her arms, she couldn't help but be consumed by a sense of wonder. Her husband, Tom, sat beside her, his eyes brimming with tears of happiness as he gazed upon the precious sight before him. It had been a long and arduous journey, filled with heartbreak and despair, but they had never lost hope. And now, their unwavering faith had brought them to this profound moment of bliss.*

*For years, Tom and Teresa had faced the heartache of miscarriages, their dreams of parenthood seemingly slipping away with each loss. But deep in their hearts, a glimmer of hope remained. When Teresa discovered she was pregnant again, a flicker of anticipation ignited within her. "This is it, honey," Teresa had whispered to Tom, her voice filled with conviction. "I really believe that this time, God will answer our prayers and bless us with a baby."*

*And so, with unwavering faith, they began a journey of prayer and unwavering devotion. Each day, Tom and Teresa poured their hearts out to the heavens for a healthy baby, for a smooth pregnancy that would bring their little one safely into their arms. Each month, their hope grew stronger as Teresa felt the gentle flutter of life in her womb.*

*When the moment of birth finally arrived, Teresa's labor was remarkably smooth, guided by the divine hand of fate. Tom stood by her side, his unwavering presence a source of strength and reassurance. Together, they witnessed the extraordinary miracle unfolding before their eyes, their hearts swelling with indescribable love.*

*Their precious baby girl, so delicate and petite, weighed only six pounds, but her arrival filled the room with an ethereal aura. The radiance of her sparkling blue eyes was captivating, hinting at a world of curiosity and wonder contained within her tiny frame. In that moment, as mother and daughter locked eyes, an unbreakable bond was forged that transcended time and space.*

*Tom and Teresa gazed upon this miracle, their hearts overflowing with gratitude. With every fiber of their being, they knew that their prayers had been answered, and that God had given them one of His angels. With this realization, a profound sense of purpose washed over them, and they made an unspoken vow to love and cherish their precious daughter for the rest of their lives.*

*Teresa held her baby girl close to her chest, feeling the gentle rise and fall of her breath, the tiny heartbeat that echoed the rhythm of their love. They knew without a shadow of a doubt that their baby was a miracle—an extraordinary gift from above. And with hearts overflowing with joy, they christened her with the name that had been destined for her since the beginning of time: Jessica, a name that would forever symbolize the boundless love and blessings that had graced their lives.*

*And so, on that remarkable day, as the sun bathed the world in its warm embrace, Tom and Teresa Reese welcomed their beloved Jessica into their arms and into a future filled with endless possibilities.*

On this morning of June twenty-sixth, Jessica awoke with her heart brimming with the same excitement that heralded the start of her summer break. It was a transition not just of seasons but of life itself as she teetered on the cusp of adulthood, supported steadfastly by her family's love. Sunlight streamed through her window, casting a golden glow that danced in tune with her buoyant mood. Slipping into her bathrobe, she felt enveloped in childlike wonder.

The house was alive with a symphony of celebration—happy chatter and the clinking of dishes creating a melody. Each step toward the kitchen pulsed with increasing excitement. As she stepped into the room, a chorus of warm greetings enveloped her.

"Happy Birthday, Jessica!" came the unified cheer, their smiles as bright as the morning sun.

Uncle Gary's laughter boomed through the room, his voice rich with affection. "Jesse! Look at you, all grown up," he exclaimed, lifting her off the ground in a bear hug.

Tom stepped forward with tenderness in his eyes, wrapping her in a hug that felt like a fortress of safety. "Happy Birthday, baby girl," he murmured, his voice a blend of love and pride.

Teresa, the heart of their home, fluttered about the kitchen alongside Aunt Veronica. Their movements were a graceful dance as they prepared a breakfast feast. The aroma of pancakes, eggs, and bacon filled the air, weaving a tapestry of happy summer mornings from years past.

Glancing toward the living room, Jessica's eyes lit up at the sight of a pile of gifts on the coffee table. Each package, wrapped with care, was a testament to her loved ones' thoughtfulness. The room seemed to thrum with excitement, echoing the closeness of their family bond.

Surrounded by the faces she cherished most, Jessica felt her family's joy resonate in her heart. Echoes of her childhood filled each corner of the room, reminding her of the love and laughter that had shaped her into the young woman she had become.

As she settled into her seat at the kitchen table, the weight of the day's significance washed over her. Today wasn't just another birthday; it was the start of a new chapter in her life. The excitement of introducing Ethan to her family added a unique layer to the occasion.

"I can't wait for you all to meet Ethan," she said eagerly, her voice tinged with affection.

Teresa, always nurturing, smiled warmly as she placed a generous helping of pancakes on Jessica's plate. "We're anxious to meet him too, sweetheart," she assured, her voice soothing any underlying nerves Jessica might have had.

Tom smiled and winked at his daughter, his gesture a silent promise of acceptance and a warm welcome for Ethan.

With his characteristic humor, Gary teased, "So, who is this mysterious boy we keep hearing about?"

Jessica laughed, responding playfully yet with genuine emotion. "Oh, you know who Ethan is, Uncle Gary. He's just the love of my life. No big deal." Her words mixed pride with tenderness, reflecting their close-knit bond.

Gary chuckled, glancing at Veronica with a shared look of affection and nostalgia. "Ah, young love," he mused, his voice wistful. "Oh, to be young again, eh, dear?"

Veronica, finishing the touches on Jessica's breakfast plate, smiled. "Ah, yes, to be young again," she echoed, her voice laced with a hint of longing.

As Teresa placed the breakfast plate filled with Jessica's favorites in front of her, the delicious aromas wafted through the air. Looking up at her mother, their eyes met in a deep, unspoken understanding. Teresa leaned in and kissed Jessica's forehead.

"Happy Birthday, sweetheart," she whispered, her voice imbued with years of love and care.

In that moment, surrounded by her family, Jessica felt a profound sense of love and gratitude. The room brimmed with not just the aromas of a lovingly prepared breakfast, but also the warmth and affection of her nearest and dearest. On this birthday, amidst the laughter and gentle teasing, Jessica realized that the presence and love of her family were the greatest gifts she could ever receive.

The sound of the front door opening reverberated through the house, catching Jessica's attention mid-chew. Cousin Emily shimmered into view, her steps tracing a rhythm toward the kitchen. Spotting Jessica sitting at the table, immersed in her birthday banquet, Emily moved toward her, her voice simmering with familial warmth. "Happy Birthday, Cuz!" she called out.

With her mouth full of pancakes, Jessica replied with a bright, appreciative smile.

Gary, his features a portrait of fatherly affection, rose from his chair and gestured to Emily with a warm smile. "Here, take my seat, honey," he said, his voice filled with welcoming warmth.

Emily nodded and sat down as Gary moved to join Veronica and Teresa standing at the counter. Veronica's soothing voice rang out, "Your breakfast is almost ready, dear." The kitchen hummed with family chatter as Emily idly scrolled through her phone.

Then, a sudden knock at the front door resounded through the house, cutting through the breakfast symphony with a surprising chord. Tom stirred, ready to uncover the identity of the unexpected visitor, but Gary intervened. "I'll see who it is. You finish your coffee," he assured, wanting his brother to enjoy his morning ritual.

Jessica, just finishing her birthday meal, observed the unfolding scene with a trace of intrigue as her uncle moved toward the door. A whirl of speculations spun in her mind, her curiosity piqued. It couldn't be Fawn, she thought; Fawn is family, and she doesn't need to knock.

In a blink of an eye, Gary reappeared, cradling a bouquet of vibrant spring flowers in his hands. His eyes twinkled with playful mischief as he posed, "I wonder who these could be for?" A grin danced on his lips, casting a teasing light on Jessica.

Recognizing that the extravagant bouquet was meant for her, Jessica felt a thrilling shiver of anticipation course through her. She sprung up from her chair and rushed toward her uncle, her heart drumming a rapid beat of exhilaration. Gary, basking in her enthusiasm, teasingly held the bouquet just out of Jessica's grasp, prolonging the playful suspense.

"Uncle Gary!" Jessica's laughter rippled through the kitchen, a playful reprimand for her uncle's antics. Her excitement bubbled over as she reached for the floral gift. Surrendering to her infectious joy, Gary finally handed the bouquet to Jessica.

Cradling the flowers in her arms, Jessica's heart urged her to find the accompanying card. Gently, she unfolded it and read the heartfelt message: "Happy birthday, my beautiful Jessica. Love, Ethan." A rush of warmth swept over her, and her lips curved into a bright smile. This bouquet, her very first floral gift, had the added significance of being from Ethan, the boy who had captured her heart.

Teresa and Veronica gathered around Jessica, their faces reflecting her joy as they admired the exquisite bouquet. "They're beautiful," Teresa marveled, draping her arm around Jessica in a protective maternal embrace. Veronica echoed the sentiment, her voice tinged with a mix of admiration and a hint of wistfulness. "That was very thoughtful of him. I like him already."

Filled with emotion, Jessica turned to her father, who remained seated at the table. His approving smile dissolved the last vestiges of anxiety she had about his acceptance of Ethan. At that moment, a surge of certainty washed over Jessica, assuring her that the day ahead would be filled with joy and free of worry. It was shaping up to be the most memorable birthday she had ever experienced.

Teresa moved gracefully across the kitchen to the counter where an empty crystal vase stood, catching the morning light in a prismatic dance. She picked it up and turned to Jessica, her eyes twinkling with affection. "Here you go, sweetheart," she said, offering the vase for the flowers.

Jessica accepted the vase with a gentle touch, as if it were as delicate as the emotions swirling within her. She filled it with just the right amount of water—clear and cool—and carefully arranged Ethan's bouquet within its crystalline embrace. The flowers seemed to come alive, their colors more vivid against the sparkling backdrop.

With a serene smile, Jessica carried the vase to her bedroom. The room welcomed her with its familiar comfort, each detail a testament to the years she had spent growing and dreaming within its walls. She placed the vase on her dresser, where morning light shined through the curtains, casting a soft glow on the petals and leaves.

Sitting on her bed, Jessica allowed herself a moment of quiet contemplation. She inhaled deeply, taking in the fresh scent of spring that now permeated her room—a fragrant reminder of Ethan's thoughtfulness. As she exhaled, her heart swelled with gratitude and love.

Her thoughts then drifted to her grandparents' upcoming visit, sparking a flutter of excitement in her chest. The day promised to unfold like the pages in a storybook, filled with laughter and cherished moments. It was a day to be savored—a collection of joyful experiences waiting to be embraced.

Rising from her bed after some time spent basking in quiet joy, Jessica felt an urge for renewal. She undressed and stepped into the shower, where water cascaded down like a gentle summer rain, washing away any remnants of sleepiness. It was rejuvenating, leaving her skin tingling with freshness and vigor.

Once dry and wrapped in the comfort of a plush towel, Jessica approached her closet with a sense of purpose. Her fingers danced along the hangers until they paused at a favorite summer dress—one that seemed to sing with color and exude lightness. It was a garment that captured the season's exuberance and mirrored Jessica's blossoming spirit.

Slipping into the dress, she felt the fabric kiss her skin—a perfect fit that flattered and comforted her. Looking at her reflection in the mirror, Jessica saw not just herself but also an embodiment of summer's promise—bright, bold, and beautiful.

She twirled once, allowing herself a moment of childlike delight before steadying herself with a deep breath. Clothed in happiness and wrapped in confidence as vibrant as her dress, Jessica was ready for whatever joys and surprises this birthday would bring.

The news of her grandparents' arrival swept through the house like a fresh summer breeze, prompting Jessica to hasten from her room, her hair still damp from the shower. The familiar timbre of their voices, seasoned with years and warmed by love, beckoned her to the living room. As she entered, a tableau of familial warmth enveloped her: both sets of grandparents were there, their faces alight with affection for their granddaughter.

Grandma and Grandpa Reese stood together, a testament to enduring love. Grandma Reese, petite and elegant with soft white hair framing her face like a halo, extended her arms with a grace that defied her years. Her pale hazel eyes sparkled with delight at seeing Jessica. Grandpa Reese, his silver hair closely cropped, smiled warmly, his bright blue eyes crinkling at the corners. His laughter, deep and resounding, filled the room as he shared tales with his wife by his side.

Without hesitation, Jessica rushed into their open arms, feeling the full measure of their love wrap around her. "Happy Birthday, beautiful princess," Grandma Reese cooed, embracing Jessica tenderly. Her eyes were pools of fondness, reflecting the joy of the moment.

"You're looking more and more like your father every day," she observed, her voice rich with pride as she smoothed back a strand of Jessica's damp hair.

Tom chuckled from where he leaned against the doorway, his bright blue eyes dancing with amusement—a clear mirror of his father's. "It's definitely a family trait," he said, winking at his daughter. His eyes shifted toward Emily, hoping to include his niece in the praise. However, Emily remained engrossed in her phone, oblivious to the compliment and the surrounding banter.

Laughter echoed through the room as Grandpa Reese and Grandpa Bowman swapped jokes and stories from days gone by, each anecdote seasoned with the humor that only years can bring. Uncle Gary's voice boomed alongside theirs, his Texas charm adding a vibrant splash to every word he spoke.

In another corner of the house, Veronica and Teresa orchestrated the decorations with meticulous care. Grandma Reese moved among them like an artist, tying ribbons and placing balloons with gentle precision, while Grandma Bowman hummed softly—a melody that seemed to weave itself into the fabric of the celebration.

The entire house was transformed under their collective efforts, each room blooming into a vibrant life in honor of Jessica's coming of age. The backyard became an oasis of color and light, ribbons fluttering in the breeze and balloons bobbing happily in anticipation.

Jessica watched as her family spun threads of happiness into every corner—a tapestry that told a story of love and kinship. A profound sense of gratitude swelled within her chest as she took it all in—the sights, sounds, and scents that would become treasured memories etched upon her heart. She knew that this birthday would be memorable for years to come—a beacon of joy that would continue to radiate long after the candles had been blown out.

As the clock struck noon, the sun shone high in a cloudless sky, illuminating Wavecrest with an effervescent glow that matched the festive atmosphere in the Reese household. The merriment paused momentarily as Fawn and her mother, Anna, walked through the doorway, completing the circle of family and friends.

Anna's approach was unhurried, her arms opening wide as she drew Jessica into an embrace that felt like home. "Happy Birthday, honey," she said, her voice soft yet rich with affection. Her smile was a portrait of maternal warmth, reflecting years of closeness with Jessica.

Gratitude rose inside Jessica as she pulled back to meet Anna's eyes. "Thank you, Mama," she replied, her voice threaded with sincere appreciation for the woman who had become her second mother.

Fawn stepped forward next, her embrace enveloping Jessica in familiarity and comfort. Her mischievous grin belied the tenderness in her eyes as she ribbed Jessica. "Finally caught up to us in age, huh?" Fawn's tease was light-hearted, but the depth of their friendship resonated in every word. "Happy Birthday, girl," she added, sealing her greeting with a smile that echoed years of shared secrets and dreams.

Inside the kitchen, where laughter and chatter blended into a symphony of joy, Teresa welcomed Anna with an open heart. "It's good to see you," Teresa said, her voice laced with genuine pleasure at their arrival.

Anna returned the greeting with equal warmth but couldn't hide her apologetic tone as she explained their tardiness. "I'm sorry we're late; we got held up because a Realtor was showing our house again." Teresa's nod conveyed understanding and empathy for Anna's predicament.

While the adults exchanged pleasantries, Jessica noticed Fawn's gaze flicker with annoyance when her mother mentioned the Realtor. Sensing an undercurrent of tension, Jessica leaned closer to Fawn and whispered a soft inquiry, "Everything okay?"

Fawn masked her irritation with practiced ease, offering Jessica a smile that didn't quite reach her eyes. "I'm fine," she replied, attempting to downplay her feelings.

"Are they still upset with you?" Jessica asked, referencing Fawn's recent confrontation with the Realtor and potential buyers.

Fawn rolled her eyes in her typical fashion, trying to brush it off. "I don't really care if they are or not," she declared.

Yet, Jessica sensed the deeper struggle within Fawn; she knew how much Fawn feared losing her childhood home—the backdrop to countless memories they had woven together over the years. Seeking to provide solace amid swirling worries, Jessica suggested a respite from the day's emotions.

"Come on, Fawn. Let's go for a walk before you have to go pick up Felix." Jessica's invitation hung between them like an unspoken promise of escape—a chance to let go for just a little while.

The suggestion seemed to bring Fawn a wave of relief. Together, they stepped out of the house, leaving the sanctuary of celebration behind. As they walked the two blocks to the familiar boardwalk, the noise from the party faded into the background, replaced by the rhythmic sound of their footsteps on the pavement.

"Are you really okay? I've been worried about you," Jessica asked, breaking the silence as they approached the sandy path that led to the beach.

Fawn sighed, her shoulders dropping slightly under the weight of her thoughts. "I'm okay. It's just a lot, you know? Seeing my room in the real estate listing photos made everything so real."

Jessica nodded, understanding her friend's turmoil. "I know how hard this must be, Fawn, but I'm here for you, no matter what."

Gratitude flickered in Fawn's eyes as they stepped onto the beach. The salty air seemed to wash over them, carrying away the remnants of their earlier tension. With each stride toward the rolling waves and sun-kissed sand, they shed layers of concern and unease until only friendship remained—two souls seeking refuge in each other's company against life's relentless tide.

As two o'clock approached, Jessica's birthday party was ready to start. Balloons in every shade of joy and streamers dancing in the breeze transformed the house into a canvas of merriment. A bold, bright banner stretched across the front yard, proclaiming, "Happy Birthday, Jessica."

In the backyard, Tom presided over the grill with the precision of a seasoned conductor. His spatula moved deftly, coaxing a chorus of sizzles from the burgers and hot dogs on the flames. The scent of grilling meat, mingling with the sea-salted air, served as an aromatic invitation that drew guests like moths to a flame.

Meanwhile, Teresa, alongside Anna and Veronica, laid out a feast fit for royalty. Each salad—a medley of potatoes, macaroni, and vibrant vegetables—was a testament to their culinary affection. Adding to the spread, Uncle Gary served his Texas-style baked beans with an entertainer's gusto. Each spoonful was a labor of love, and his broad smile was as infectious as it was proud.

A surge of laughter heralded the arrival of Krista and Michelle, integral threads in the fabric of Jessica's life. The backyard buzzed with new energy as they joined the celebration.

"Happy Birthday, Jess!" Krista exclaimed, pulling her friend into a tight hug. "We've put our gifts on the coffee table with the others," she added, gesturing toward the house.

"Thank you! It means a lot to have you both here," Jessica replied, her eyes shining with memories of their adventures.

Michelle followed with her own embrace, then stepped back with a playful grin. "Of course we're here. Wouldn't let you celebrate without us!"

With a playful pout, Krista added, "Donny sends his love, too. He's bummed he couldn't be here—he had to work today."

Jessica nodded sympathetically. "Aw, that's too bad, but hey—we're still going to have a great time, right?"

Looking around, Michelle asked in her gentle tone, "Where's Fawn? I thought she'd be here by now."

Jessica glanced at her phone before tucking it back into her pocket. "She's on her way to pick up Felix," she explained with a knowing smile. "She wanted to make sure he felt comfortable coming today."

Krista chuckled softly. "That sounds just like Fawn—always looking out for everyone."

"Yeah," Jessica agreed, a fond smile playing on her lips. "She has such a big heart."

They shared a collective nod, their expressions mingling warmth and admiration for their absent friend, who was as much a part of this day as the sun above them. After a moment, Krista glanced around the bustling backyard and then turned back to Jessica with a curious tilt of her head. "Hey, is Heather coming too?"

Jessica nodded, her expression a mix of anticipation and eagerness. "I invited her, so I hope she does," she replied, the thought of all her close friends at the party brightening her smile even more.

The minutes unfurled into an afternoon rich with warm embraces and heartfelt wishes. Birthday cards affectionately scripted were passed into Jessica's hands—one from Krista adorned with playful doodles and another from Michelle featuring elegant script—which celebrated not only the milestone of her eighteenth birthday but also the beautiful weave of friendship they had spun together over the years.

As the banquet table teemed with friends and family, their plates formed a vibrant mosaic of the afternoon's feast. Laughter and voices mingled into a jubilant symphony, echoing around plates piled high with vibrant salads, grilled meats, and Gary's signature baked beans. The air was rich with the scents of summer and celebration.

Amidst the revelry, Jessica's phone chimed—a digital herald of good news. Her bright blue eyes sparkled as she read the message from Ethan: "I'm on my way, babe. Be there in a few." Her pulse quickened at the thought of his arrival, sending a flutter of excitement through her. With a smile brightening her face, she glided toward the front door, her delight barely contained as she anticipated greeting him.

Moments later, after waiting with bated breath, the familiar crunch of gravel signaled his arrival. Ethan stepped out of his Jeep, the embodiment of casual elegance in a blue button-down shirt that matched his eyes, black shorts, and stylish sandals that epitomized summer ease.

As Jessica opened the door, Ethan greeted her with a smile that could outshine the sun. "Happy Birthday, Beautiful," he said, his voice enveloping her like a warm breeze.

Jessica melted into his embrace, their hug an intimate dance to which only they knew the steps. "Thank you," she murmured against his shoulder. "I love the flowers you sent—they're absolutely gorgeous."

Ethan pulled back just enough to look into her eyes, his fingers gently caressing her cheek. "I wanted to give you something just as beautiful as you are," he replied with heartfelt sincerity.

Their connection was palpable; an electric charge filled the space between them. Words were unnecessary when their hearts spoke so clearly through each tender touch and loving glance. They were content to be in each other's presence, celebrating Jessica's birthday and their remarkable journey together.

The moment that had been casting long, anticipatory shadows in the corridors of Jessica's thoughts had finally arrived—the threshold where her beloved Ethan would cross into her family's intimate realm. Clasping Ethan's sturdy arm, a blend of trepidation and exhilaration coursed through her as they walked through the kitchen, emerging into the backyard where her family awaited.

"He's here!" Jessica's voice rang out, shimmering with pride and happiness.

The river of conversation momentarily receded as all eyes pivoted toward the radiant couple, their joy spreading like ripples in a tranquil pond. Tom and Teresa, Jessica's anchors in her world, rose from their seats. Tom reached for his wife's hand, their fingers intertwining in a silent show of mutual support as they moved to greet their daughter's guest.

"Mom, Dad, this is Ethan," Jessica introduced, her voice tinged with nervous anticipation.

Teresa's eyes twinkled with warmth, the corners crinkling in a heartfelt smile. "It's a pleasure to finally meet you, Ethan. We're thrilled to have you here, celebrating our daughter's birthday with us," she said, her welcoming spirit woven into every syllable.

Tom extended his hand, a gesture met by Ethan's firm yet respectful grip. "Nice to meet you, sir," Ethan acknowledged, sincerity glistening in his gaze. "It's a pleasure to meet both of you," he added with a warm smile.

Jessica watched as her father, typically a figure of stoic authority, visibly softened under Ethan's respectful demeanor. The silent approval in Tom's nod and the firm handshake between the two men buoyed Jessica's spirits, infusing her with a profound sense of relief and contentment.

Tom took position between the young couple, his hands resting on their shoulders. His eyes locked with Ethan's in a moment of unspoken acceptance.

"Help yourself to the food and drinks. Make yourself at home," he invited, then guided Teresa back to their chairs, the warmth of their welcome still lingering in their smiles.

A swell of relief bathed Jessica and Ethan as the formalities of the introduction receded. Their eyes met in a shared glance, an unspoken dance of victory marking this significant milestone—the blossoming of their relationship and the merging of their worlds.

They plunged back into the swirling festivities, welcomed into the heart of Jessica's tribe. This day would be etched in their memories, a celebration of new connections that would live in their hearts forever.

The sun hung high in the sky, a silent observer of the events unfolding below. The backyard of the Reese family was alive with a symphony of voices, each carrying stories and laughter that fluttered on the breeze like butterflies in spring.

Uncle Gary's voice rose above the crowd, a hearty chuckle lacing his words as he told stories from Jessica's childhood. Each anecdote drew an affectionate groan from Jessica and a chuckle from the gathered relatives. Aunt Veronica and Grandma Bowman leaned in, their faces alight with mirth, hanging on his every word. The soft clatter of silverware against plates provided a steady rhythm to the afternoon's soundtrack.

Ethan, ever attentive, stayed close to Jessica's side as they navigated through clusters of family members. Approaching her teenage cousin Emily, who sat apart from the others, Jessica said, "Ethan, this is my cousin Emily. Emily, this is Ethan."

Her gaze was distant, but her lips curved into a small smile at their approach. Ethan offered a friendly wave, which Emily shyly returned.

With each introduction, Ethan's charm and genuine interest left a warm impression on Jessica's family members. Grandpa Bowman, after hearing about Ethan's adventurous spirit and love of surfing, gave him a hearty pat on the back.

"So, Ethan," he asked with a twinkle in his eye, "how do you keep yourself from taking a tumble when riding those waves?"

Ethan replied with a playful grin. "Lots of practice, sir. Lots of practice!" His light-hearted yet sincere answer resonated with a sense of shared adventure and camaraderie.

As they approached Grandma Reese and Aunt Veronica, Jessica felt a flutter in her stomach—these were the matriarchs whose opinions held weight like anchors in her family's sea. But as Ethan greeted them with his natural grace and respect, their initial appraisal softened into affectionate smiles.

"Look at you," Grandma Reese said, turning her gaze toward Ethan, her voice spiced with wisdom and experience. "You've got kind eyes. Jessica has always been one to trust her heart."

Ethan replied with humble sincerity. "Thank you, ma'am. Your granddaughter is very special to me."

The conversation flowed effortlessly, weaving Ethan into the family tapestry with every word exchanged. With a nostalgic glint in her eyes, Aunt Veronica turned to him with a smile, sharing a glimpse into Jessica's childhood.

"You know, when Jessica was just a little girl, she and I would spend hours with her

Barbie dolls. She had a knack for picking the prettiest outfits for them," she reminisced, her eyes twinkling with the joy of the memory.

Grandma Bowman turned toward Jessica, her eyes alight with fond memories. "Do you remember us baking Christmas cookies together? You were so adorable; even as a little girl, you were so careful not to make a mess," she reminisced in a warm and reflective tone.

Flushed with embarrassment and tenderness, Jessica admitted, "I remember, Grandma." Her voice was a whisper of nostalgia, carrying with it the blush of childhood memories revisited in the company of those she loved most.

As Jessica watched Ethan interact with her family—her world—her heart brimmed with gratitude. She had feared this moment but found herself enveloped in its perfection instead.

Amidst the family's warm reminiscing, with Veronica and Grandma Reese sharing cherished memories, the conversation paused as Tom stood and raised his glass, signaling a moment of significance. He waited for a brief hush to sweep over the gathering, then began with a clear, resonant voice that carried across the backyard.

"To Jessica, our shining star who brings light into our lives just by being who she is," he declared, his words filled with pride and affection.

The toast resonated deeply with everyone present. "To Jessica!" the assembly echoed, their voices mingling in the afternoon air as glasses clinked in unison. All eyes turned toward her, whose glow seemed to reflect the love and light of which her father had spoken.

As the echoes of the toast subsided, Jessica stood beside Ethan, feeling his hand squeezing hers—a silent message of support and love. Her eyes, glistening with tears, moved across all the faces she loved so dearly—the people who had helped shape her into the person she was today. In their smiles and in the warmth of their eyes, she saw the reflection of her journey, one marked by unconditional love and steadfast guidance.

Overwhelmed by a surge of emotion and buoyed by Ethan's reassuring presence, Jessica knew this birthday would remain etched within her heart forever. It wasn't just the celebration itself, but what it symbolized: a beautiful moment of new beginnings and enduring connections, of new love seamlessly woven with steadfast bonds and the harmonious merging of two worlds into one.

# Chapter 15

On this momentous day, another significant event was about to unfold—the long-awaited arrival of Felix Copeland at Jessica's birthday party. Burdened by a history of relentless ridicule, Felix had never experienced the warmth of genuine friendship or the comfort of unconditional acceptance.

Determined to guide him toward a brighter future, Fawn appreciated Jessica's thoughtful gesture of including Felix in the celebration. Together, they hoped to create an environment where Felix could shed his protective shell and reveal his authentic self, free from the shadows of mockery and isolation. This event offered a perfect opportunity for Felix to connect with those eager to welcome him, serving as a beacon in his quest for genuine friendship.

When Fawn arrived at Felix's house, she found him standing by the worn gate. He glanced through the car window with a timid smile, like the first light of daybreak, affirming Fawn's promise. As he settled into the passenger seat beside her, his smile deepened, reflecting not only his happiness but also a quiet thrill. Being this close to Fawn, the object of his secret affection, stirred a mix of exhilaration and subtle nervousness within him, feelings he carefully concealed.

"Hi, Felix. Ready to have some fun?" Fawn asked, her smile mirroring his.

Felix's eyes met hers, a mix of excitement and trepidation. "I guess so," he replied, his voice tinged with uncertainty.

"It's going to be great, Felix. Just relax," Fawn encouraged, her tone as calming as a gentle stream. She started the engine and steered their vehicle toward the lively ambiance of Jessica's home. "Jessica and Ethan are looking forward to seeing you," she continued, keeping her eyes focused on the road.

"Really?" Felix's question carried a tone of incredulous doubt, seeking affirmation.

"Absolutely. She invited you to her birthday party, didn't she?" Fawn's voice was firm, filled with conviction as she navigated through the darkened streets of the neighborhood.

A reflective silence fell over Felix as he pondered the genuine kindness in Jessica's invitation—an unprecedented sense of being valued that reached deep into his heart.

"Yes, she did," he acknowledged, his voice carrying an emotional weight. "And you said you'd pick me up at two."

Fawn turned toward him, her smile as bright as daylight. "And here we are," she declared, her enthusiasm unmistakable.

At that moment, Felix let out a sigh of relief and sank deeper into the seat. As he watched the landscape pass by, he was comforted by the thought that, for once, his presence was truly welcome. This new sense of belonging ignited a warmth within him that made him feel truly appreciated.

As Fawn and Felix drove away from the monochrome hues of his neighborhood, it felt as if they were peeling away a worn, gray layer to reveal the vibrant spectrum of Wavecrest. The transition was like passing through a gateway into another realm. Above, the sky stretched like a sprawling canvas of deep blue, dotted with billowing clouds. The gentle murmur of the sea, infused with the scent of salty freedom, carried on the breeze.

Mesmerized, Felix watched the changing scenery through the window, marveling at the transformation. The homes they passed radiated warmth and fulfillment, representing a life he had only dared to dream of. Pristine lawns speckled with vibrant blooms painted a tranquil scene, a stark contrast to the worn landscapes he knew so well.

As they drew closer to Jessica's house, the ocean's call grew louder, its rhythmic cadence swelling into an enchanting chorus that resonated deep within him. Fleeting images of his mother flickered in his mind—remnants of a time when her laughter mingled with the sea breeze during their boardwalk strolls, her smile a beacon in his turbulent youth.

When Fawn pulled into Jessica's driveway, those sweet memories faded as Felix braced himself for the reality ahead. He stepped into a world abuzz with festivity; Jessica's backyard was alive with jubilation. A current of nerves washed over him as he surveyed the bustling scene and unfamiliar faces. The sounds of laughter, spirited chatter, and festive energy enveloped him, both exhilarating and slightly daunting. Felix was not just entering a celebration but embarking on a voyage into unexplored territories of connection and acceptance.

After exiting the car, Felix followed Fawn as she navigated through the group of guests. Looking for Jessica and Ethan, Fawn spotted them near the food table, deep in conversation with Krista and Michelle. Her excitement was obvious as she called out, "Come on, Felix! There's Jessica!"

With Fawn leading the way, Felix's heart pounded with a mix of excitement and nervousness. As they approached, Jessica turned, her eyes lighting up as she saw them. With a warm, welcoming smile, she approached hand in hand with Ethan.

"Hey Felix!" she exclaimed, her voice rich with genuine pleasure. "I'm so glad you made it."

Feeling somewhat out of place, Felix replied with a timid smile, "Thank you for inviting me, Jessica. Happy Birthday."

Jessica, still holding Ethan's hand, introduced them. "Felix, this is Ethan. You remember him, right?"

Felix's eyes shifted to Ethan, his nervousness visible. Sensing this discomfort, Ethan smiled warmly and extended his hand. Felix's handshake was hesitant, almost delicate. Recognizing the need for a more relaxed approach, Ethan attempted to lighten the mood. "Hey, let me show you the 'bro' handshake. We can be on the same level, man."

In the moments that followed, Ethan patiently coached Felix through their unique 'bro' handshake. Though Felix stumbled at first, Ethan's supportive guidance and encouraging words helped him gain confidence. Jessica and Fawn watched with amused smiles as the two boys navigated this playful exchange.

Finally, Felix mastered the handshake, earning an enthusiastic pat on the back from Ethan, who cheered, "Now you got it, bro! Good job!"

The air around them seemed to sparkle with newfound energy as Felix was welcomed into the group. This moment marked a significant turning point, breaking down barriers and fostering a spirit of camaraderie. Riding this wave of unity, Jessica suggested they grab some refreshments.

Together, they moved toward the picnic table where the older members of the party congregated. As they approached, Jessica spotted her parents in conversation with Aunt Veronica and Uncle Gary. She coughed gently, a soft signal that drew their attention. They turned, their faces lighting up with welcoming smiles that radiated familial warmth and affection.

"Mom, Dad, this is our friend, Felix," Jessica introduced, gesturing in his direction. The group's attention shifted, enveloping him in a warm and inviting gaze.

With his characteristic jovial nature, Tom playfully remarked on Felix's lean appearance. "You better get something to eat, son. We need to put some meat on those bones," he joked, drawing a laugh from Jessica.

"Dad!" she exclaimed with mock exasperation, though the mirth in her eyes betrayed her amusement. Ethan's chuckle and Fawn's giggles joined in, creating a symphony of merriment around them.

Felix, momentarily self-conscious, glanced down at himself, then smiled as he looked back up at the group, swept up in the warmth of their laughter.

"Thank you, Mr. Reese. I will," Felix replied, his smile one of gratitude. He reveled in the warmth of their lighthearted teasing, feeling a sense of acceptance that enveloped him like a comforting blanket.

As laughter faded from the lively group around him, Felix's eyes drifted past the chatter, landing on a solitary figure on the back deck. There, Jessica's cousin Emily stood apart from the festivities, her eyes engrossed in her phone. Overcome with a rush of uncharacteristic impulsiveness and awe, Felix couldn't help but blurt out, "Wow, she's pretty."

Jessica and Fawn exchanged a quick glance, a silent conversation passing between them. They were well aware of Emily's prickly nature and her tendency to be standoffish, which made them hesitant to introduce her to Felix.

Unaware of their internal debate, Felix again voiced his admiration, this time in a soft murmur that floated toward them on the breeze. "She really is pretty."

Jessica sighed softly, a note of caution in her voice as she replied, "That's my cousin, Emily. She's here from Texas," she revealed, deliberately leaving the sentence hanging like an unfinished painting. By choosing not to elaborate, Jessica hoped to shield Felix from any potential cold shoulder due to Emily's unpredictable temperament.

As the group gathered around the table laden with food, Jessica suggested to Felix and Fawn to enjoy the spread first. They filled their plates with vibrant salads and hearty burgers and found a spot under a colorful umbrella at an unoccupied table. As they took their seats, the lively chatter of the party mingled with the clinking and clattering of dishes and silverware. Felix took a moment to savor the flavors, allowing the casual atmosphere to momentarily distract him from his thoughts of Emily.

Yet, as the meal came to an end and the last bites were taken, his curiosity began to resurface. Turning to Fawn, his eyes reflecting a mix of emotions, he asked, "Why didn't Jessica introduce me to her cousin?" His voice carried a hint of disappointment, stirring the air between them.

Choosing her words carefully, Fawn replied, "Well, Emily can be a bit difficult. She's not the easiest person to get along with. Jess and Emily aren't exactly close, and I can't say I'm particularly fond of her, either."

"Oh, I see," Felix murmured, his voice reflecting a note of sadness. He glanced at Emily, who sat alone on the deck, her isolation mirroring the loneliness he often felt.

Noticing Felix's thoughtful expression as he sipped his drink, Fawn felt a tug at her heartstrings. It was rare for Felix to show such interest in someone—especially someone like Emily. Moved by his vulnerability, Fawn made her way to Jessica, who was biting into a burger. The sight of Jessica trying to speak around a mouthful of food made Fawn giggle before she composed herself.

"Jess, maybe we should introduce Felix to Emily," she suggested, her eyes conveying understanding.

Surprised by the unexpected proposal, Jessica quickly swallowed her bite and said with a playful roll of her eyes, "Seriously?"

Fawn glanced over at Felix, catching him gazing longingly at Emily. Turning back to Jessica with a tender expression, she answered, "Seriously. I think Felix really likes her."

Seeing the sincerity in Fawn's eyes and trusting her friend's judgment in matters of the heart, Jessica nodded and replied, "Alright, let's give it a try."

After finishing their meal, Felix and Fawn set aside their plates, finding themselves in a momentary lull. Sensing the opportunity, Jessica turned to Felix to prepare him for meeting her cousin, her words carrying the gentle caution of a painter adding subtle shadows to a portrait.

"Don't take her seriously if she acts like a brat," Jessica advised, her tone infused with genuine care. "That's just Emily being Emily; it has nothing to do with you."

With an appreciative nod that masked his inner flurry of nerves, Felix took her advice to heart. Then, the trio walked toward the back deck, where Emily was still engrossed in her phone.

"Hey, Cuz!" Jessica called out cheerfully, drawing Emily's attention as they approached. "I'd like to introduce you to a friend of ours."

Emily's gaze lifted from her screen, her eyes sweeping over Felix with a mix of detachment and mild curiosity. Her posture was relaxed yet distant, her arms crossed as if to shield herself.

"Felix, this is my cousin, Emily. Emily, this is Felix," Jessica continued, bridging them with her words.

A tense silence hung in the air as Emily scrutinized Felix, her expression unreadable. Jessica and Fawn braced themselves for a sharp retort while Felix steeled himself for potential scorn. However, defying expectations, Emily's usual reserve gave way to a surprisingly genuine smile.

"Hi, Felix," she greeted him, her voice carrying an almost imperceptible softness. Her arms uncrossed, shifting towards a more open and inviting posture.

Jessica and Fawn were stunned by Emily's uncharacteristic warmth, their surprise evident. Felix, caught off-guard, hesitated, his pulse quickening as he grappled with this unexpected kindness. He managed a small, nervous smile, his own body relaxing as he responded to her greeting.

The silence stretched as they stood there—Emily and Felix unsure how to proceed, while Jessica and Fawn exchanged looks of astonishment. Jessica's lips formed the silent words to Fawn: "Oh. My. God." Neither could believe that the icy barriers surrounding Emily had seemingly vanished without warning.

Sensing the mounting tension like an actor aware of her cue, Fawn interjected. "Hey Felix, why don't you stay here with Emily? You two can talk and get to know each other," she suggested, cutting through the awkwardness.

Emily smiled at her suggestion, acknowledging Fawn's timely intervention. Though visibly concerned, Felix conveyed his thanks with a wide-eyed glance at Fawn.

As Jessica and Fawn retreated, leaving Felix to engage with Emily alone, they struggled to suppress their giggles, reminiscent of their own awkward social encounters. It seemed fate had humorously orchestrated the meeting of these two unlikely souls.

Just then, Ethan approached with playful curiosity, noticing the budding interaction on the deck. With a teasing nudge to Fawn, he joked, "I see you're a fast worker. I didn't know you were also a matchmaker."

The lighthearted banter sparked laughter in both girls—Fawn's eyes shining mischievously as she replied with playful bravado. "What can I say? When you got it, you got it."

Their shared amusement floated on the breeze as they turned back toward the party's hum and buzz. But before they were engulfed by the crowd, Fawn called out to Felix over her shoulder. "Have fun, Felix. We'll see you later."

As the afternoon wore on, Jessica and her friends basked in the warm cocoon of their companionship, immersing themselves in the serene harmony of the sunny day. In the familiar sanctuary of Jessica's home, they shared laughter and told stories, weaving a delicate tapestry of affection and camaraderie.

Ethan and Jessica found solace in each other's embrace, their fingers intertwined as if by fate, basking in the electric connection that hummed between them. Ethan's touch traced a gentle, wandering path across Jessica's back, each caress luxuriating in the softness of her sun-kissed skin. His tender gestures composed a silent ode to her heart, subtly detaching her from the surrounding bustle of conversation.

Nearby, Fawn reclined on the cool, comforting grass, allowing the earth to cradle her as she soaked in a moment of peace amid the day's celebrations.

Krista and Michelle settled on the lawn, with Krista's infectious energy enlivening their shared past. Michelle listened with sparkling eyes, drawn into Krista's spirited storytelling. Together, they completed the circle, each friend adding a unique hue to the vibrant mosaic of their shared history and enduring friendship.

Just then, Jessica spotted Heather approaching, a birthday card clasped in her hands. A spark of pure joy ignited in Jessica's eyes, warmly glowing at the sight of her friend.

"Heather! You made it!" Jessica's voice rose above the murmur of conversations, a melodious beacon welcoming her into their midst.

Heather's smile widened at Jessica's call. "Like I'd miss this, girlfriend," she replied spiritedly, presenting the card as a testament to their enduring bond.

Jessica accepted the card, her hands trembling with emotion. Unfolding it, she savored the words Heather had written:

*"Happy Birthday, Jessica!*

*From the fun times on the playground to those long summer days at the beach, every moment with you has been amazing. Your laugh always makes everything more fun, and your kindness keeps us all grounded. As you head into this next chapter, just remember you're not just turning a year older. You've got a whole lot of new adventures, love, and dreams waiting for you!*

*Here's to more midnight talks, spontaneous road trips, and the kind of laughter that leaves us breathless. May your 18th year be as bright and beautiful as you are.*

*Love, Heather"*

A wave of emotions crested within Jessica as she absorbed Heather's heartfelt senti-ments. She quickly whisked away a single tear, then, without a word, pulled Heather into a warm hug, the physical connection underscoring her emotional response. "Thank you, Heather," she murmured, her voice a whisper within their embrace.

Fawn leaned in, playful anticipation shimmering in her eyes. "Give me, give me!" she implored playfully, eager to share in Heather's endearing tribute.

With a tender smile lingering from Heather's touching words, Jessica handed the card to Fawn. Her finger brushed away another rogue tear as they all basked in the gratitude emanating from their circle, the admiration for Heather's thoughtfulness felt by all.

As Fawn relished the warmth of their gathering, her eyes occasionally drifted to the back deck, where Felix and Emily had begun to forge their own connection. She observed Felix, now at ease, and Emily, skimming her phone screen to share snippets of her world with him. Emily's lively manner and spirited gestures, a refreshing change, captivated Fawn's attention.

Meanwhile, the gentle lull of the afternoon enveloped the partygoers like a soft shawl. However, within Ethan, a spark of eagerness began to flicker. His eyes scanned the back-yard and settled on a weathered volleyball net, its sagging form a testament to past days filled with competitive spirits and laughter.

Turning to Jessica with excitement in his voice, Ethan asked, "Hey, babe, do you have a volleyball?"

Caught off guard but intrigued, Jessica replied, "Yeah, somewhere," her interest piqued by the idea.

Ethan's enthusiasm quickly spread like wildfire. "What do you say we get a game going?" he proposed, his anticipation palpable.

Looking around at her friends, Jessica saw smiles and nods of eager consent. Energized by their collective excitement, she agreed, "Sure. Let me go find it." With that, she headed toward the house, determined to find the volleyball for what promised to be an invigorat-ing and fun-filled game.

As Jessica left to retrieve the volleyball, Ethan, brimming with enthusiasm, called out to Felix and Emily from their spot on the deck. "Hey, guys! Come on down! We're about to play some volleyball, and I need Felix on my team!" His voice, clear and ebullient, cut through the lazy afternoon air, extending an invitation to the sunlit activity below.

Felix looked up at Ethan, his face a mixture of surprise and hesitation. Being chosen for a team was an unfamiliar experience for him, intriguing yet intimidating. "Uh, I don't know," he hesitated, his uncertainty evident in his voice. "I'm not good at sports."

Undeterred by Felix's reluctance, Ethan's confidence remained firm. "You'll be fine," he assured him with a nod. "I'll coach you, and by the end of the game, you'll be a volleyball champ." His words anchored Felix, instilling a sense of newfound courage.

Beside him, Emily's eyes twinkled with a mischievous challenge. "Come on, let's go. We'll show them what we're made of," she encouraged, her voice a mix of support and playful dare.

Encouraged by Emily's words, Felix allowed himself to be drawn into the welcoming circle of friends gathered on the grass. Their warm reception felt like sunlight piercing through clouds—unexpected yet profoundly welcoming.

At that moment, Jessica emerged from her house like a victorious explorer, holding the volleyball aloft like a prized discovery. Ethan's eyes lit up as he spotted her returning, his expression reflecting a mix of amusement and pride.

"We're going to pick teams now," he announced, his natural authority drawing everyone's attention.

Without hesitation, Jessica made her first pick. With an enthusiastic shout that echoed their deep friendship, she called out for Fawn. Fawn approached with a swagger that matched Jessica's excitement, their synergy as clear as the sun in the sky.

Ethan followed with equal confidence. "Well, I'll take Felix," he declared, placing an arm around Felix's shoulders in a silent but meaningful gesture that underscored his belief in his potential.

The air filled with good-natured banter as they sorted into teams, formed not just through strategy but through the weaving of new and old bonds. Ethan's team included Felix, Emily, and Heather. As Heather flashed a thrilled smile at being on Ethan's team, she shot a teasing look at Jessica. "Looks like I might be scoring points on and off the court today," she quipped, winking.

Jessica rolled her eyes playfully, retorting, "Yeah, right. Just focus on your game, superstar." Her tone was light, her smile genuine, signaling the deep trust and understanding that defined their friendship.

Michelle and Krista rounded out Jessica's team alongside Fawn, each member ready to face the net with camaraderie forged through countless shared experiences. Together with Heather, these five had built a reputation on the high school volleyball team for their seamless teamwork and formidable skills, often leading them to championship victories. Now, with Heather on the opposite side, Jessica couldn't resist ribbing her. "Bet you're going to miss our championship-winning spikes today!" she called across the net with a smirk.

Heather replied with a mock-serious tone, hands on hips. "Oh, I've been practicing, so you better watch out! I've got a few tricks up my sleeve!"

Fawn laughed and yelled back, "Just don't forget which side you're scoring for, traitor!"

Meanwhile, Krista bounced on the balls of her feet, clearly eager to start, while Michelle chimed in with a playful, "Hope those tricks aren't too rusty, Heather!" The group erupted into laughter, the playful jabs adding an extra layer of excitement to the game about to unfold.

As the playful banter continued, Ethan, Felix, and Emily couldn't help but join in the laughter, the warm camaraderie infectious. Ethan grinned, his eyes sweeping over the enthusiastic group, and then clapped his hands together, signaling a shift in focus.

"Alright, everyone, let's get this game going!" he declared, his voice brimming with excitement. His teammates rallied around him, their spirits high and ready for the challenge.

As the two teams approached the net, their laughter spread across the yard, reaching the ears of the adults watching. Teresa and Anna watched the lively preparations with smiles that crinkled their eyes, the scene evoking fond memories of cheering on their daughters at their high school volleyball games.

The stage was set for an afternoon filled with competition and camaraderie—a lively tableau echoing with laughter and life. As the two teams faced off across the net, it symbolized more than just a game; it was a testament to lasting friendships and memories in the making.

Under the cerulean expanse of the California sky, Fawn orchestrated the opening volley with the elegance of a seasoned athlete. Her serve sliced through the air, igniting the friendly competition on the lush lawn of Jessica's home. Ethan, moving with the grace of an athlete, responded by sending the ball back over the net with precision.

Jessica intercepted Ethan's return with the poise of a volleyball virtuoso. She leaped and struck the ball with finesse, directing it toward Felix. In a moment destined to be remembered with fond amusement, Felix's earnest attempt to return the volley took an unexpected detour, sending the ball spiraling toward Uncle Gary's head.

Laughter erupted in the yard as Uncle Gary theatrically clutched his head, feigning injury. He turned to Jessica with a mischievous glint in his eye and quipped, "Did you set me up for that?" His jovial accusation sparked more laughter among the onlookers.

With cheeks tinged red from the mishap, Felix approached Uncle Gary to retrieve the ball. Despite his embarrassment, a sense of camaraderie blossomed, fueled by everyone's lighthearted reactions. Uncle Gary, tossing the ball back with an exaggerated flourish, teased, "You know you don't get points for that, right?"

Heather quickly joined the jesting. "I think we should, Uncle Gary," she declared playfully. "That was an epic play! Way to go, Felix!" Her words, laced with playful sarcasm, were wrapped in a blanket of affection.

The laughter continued to ripple through the group as Felix chuckled, his initial embarrassment melting into the warmth of shared mirth. Uncle Gary returned to his post by his wife's side, their smiles reflecting their enjoyment of this lighthearted turn of events.

As the game unfolded under Wavecrest's idyllic summer charm, each participant showcased their unique style. On Jessica's team, Krista and Michelle formed a dynamic duo, while Heather's vivacity perfectly complemented Ethan's skillful maneuvers on the opposing side. Under Ethan's tactical guidance and with enthusiastic support from his teammates, Felix began to find his rhythm—his serves grew more confident, and his spikes gained momentum.

Yet, despite Felix's noticeable improvement and the determined efforts of Ethan's team, they found themselves consistently matched by the remarkable teamwork and skill of Jessica and Fawn—a testament to years of friendship solidified on countless courts.

The match became an epic battle, with the score now tied at 25-25. In this friendly match, the usual strict rules were relaxed, adding to the excitement with each point scored. Now, in a climactic moment, both teams, their gazes ignited by the fiery glow of competition, unleashed their sharpest strategies. Every move became crucial in their spirited quest for victory.

The defining moment came when Jessica stepped up to serve, a daunting challenge for Ethan and his team, given her legendary precision. The ball soared over the net in a perfect arc, and Felix, positioned like a knight ready for battle, felt an adrenaline rush. He charged the net, his body making an elegant curve in the air before unleashing a masterful spike. The ball crashed into the grass, triggering an explosion of elated cheers from Ethan's side.

"You did it, Felix! You won the game!" Emily's voice rose above the others, enveloping Felix in a cocoon of triumphant joy.

Heather approached with a radiant grin, her words a sunlit beam of camaraderie. "Not bad for a newbie," she commended, giving his shoulder an encouraging tap.

Ethan came next, their handshake a silent testament to their newfound friendship. "I knew you had it in you," he said with genuine respect. "You'd be surprised at what you can accomplish when you believe in yourself."

On the other side of the net, Jessica's team took their loss in stride. With playful defiance, Jessica stuck out her tongue at Ethan, her competitive spirit undimmed. Fawn teased the victors with a wry smirk, "You guys just got lucky."

Amidst the banter, Heather couldn't resist performing a little teasing victory dance in front of them, her movements exaggerated and playful, sparking laughter even from her former teammates. Michelle and Krista joined in the amusement, their laughter a testament to the rare defeat of Jessica and Fawn, the team's usually unbeatable duo.

In the whirlwind of accolades and brotherly back slaps, Felix felt dizzy with an unfamiliar elation—the intoxicating sweetness of victory and acceptance by his peers. Even Jessica and her teammates couldn't help but praise Felix's standout play, their voices adding to the symphony of admiration that washed over him.

Hand in hand with Emily, Felix returned to their spot on the deck, each step buoyed by his newfound sense of accomplishment. Watching them, Fawn's heart swelled with unspoken pride for Felix's breakthrough. Beside her, Jessica shared a serene smile, both basking in the glow of fulfillment at having played a role in Felix's discovery of life's rich possibilities.

As the volleyball game wrapped up and the excitement gradually waned, the group shifted their focus to the next celebration. Teresa, with practiced ease, emerged from the back door onto the deck, carefully balancing Jessica's birthday cake in her hands. The cake was a masterpiece of icing and fondant, each detail an edible testament to the love infused in its creation.

After setting the cake on the table, Teresa raised her voice to cut through the lively chatter. "Come on, everyone! Let's gather around for cake!" she called out, her eyes seeking Jessica and her friends lounging on the grass. Standing beside her, Anna lit the eighteen candles atop the cake, each flame marking a year of Jessica's life. The candles flickered like miniature stars, casting a soft glow on their faces.

The adults left their chairs, drawn to the deck by the promise of celebration. Fawn, Heather, Michelle, and Krista gathered close to Jessica, their proximity an unspoken vow of enduring friendship. Nearby, Felix and Emily, having formed a new connection earlier in the day, joined the group, enhancing the festive atmosphere. Ethan stood next to Jessica with his arms around her waist, underscoring their deepening bond.

Uncle Gary cleared his throat and began to sing "Happy Birthday," his baritone voice setting the tempo. Soon, others joined in, the chorus growing harmonious and full.

Under the adoring gazes of her loved ones, Jessica's face radiated joy as she listened to them serenade her. She took in the sight of her family and friends—faces both old and new—all there to celebrate this significant milestone in her life.

With all eyes on her, it was time for Jessica to make her birthday wish. The air thickened with anticipation as she closed her eyes, silently forming her wish.

"Make it a good one!" Ethan whispered into her ear, his words prompting Jessica to nod as she took a deep breath.

"Go on, Jess! Wish for something really awesome!" Fawn cheered from beside her.

With a puff that was more comical than graceful, Jessica blew out the candles, her breath extinguishing the flames one by one until all eighteen were out.

The crowd erupted into cheers and applause, celebrating not only the extinguished candles but also the eighteen years of joy Jessica had brought into their lives.

Laughter and cheerful chatter filled the air as Teresa began slicing the cake and serving generous portions. Each slice promised sweetness, not just on the palate but also in memory—a perfect endnote to an afternoon awash with sunlit affection and celebration.

As the sun traced its golden arc across the blue canvas of the sky, a sudden realization struck Fawn. Felix had only intended to stay at the party for a few hours, mindful of his responsibilities to his frail father. Glancing at her phone, she was startled to see that nearly four hours had slipped by unnoticed. Time had stealthily whirred past, capturing Felix and Fawn in the delightful whirl of the gathering. Now, with a sense of duty stirring within her, Fawn knew it was time to resume her role as Felix's chauffeur and ensure he faced no repercussions for his extended stay.

She approached Felix and Emily, who were comfortably seated on the back deck, and gently interrupted their conversation. "Hey Felix, I think it's time for us to get you home.

It's getting close to six o'clock."

A shadow of disappointment crossed Felix's face. He had been so absorbed in the blossoming friendship with Emily that the idea of leaving now felt particularly harsh. Aware of Emily's imminent departure from Wavecrest the following day, he wished for time to pause, allowing him a few more precious moments. However, the call of duty was too strong to ignore. Turning to face Emily, Felix's voice carried a whisper of regret as he said, "I have to go now. My dad needs me."

Emily's eyes reflected disappointment as she gave Felix a warm hug. When they parted, her voice was soft yet tinged with sadness. "It was nice getting to know you, Felix. You're a pretty cool guy," she said.

Felix responded with a shy, appreciative smile, the corners of his mouth lifting slightly in a sign of newfound confidence and gratitude. Then, turning away, he followed Fawn, leaving Emily in her solitude. Each step took him further from her, leaving behind a subtle connection—a thread of friendship woven into their brief but meaningful encounter.

They navigated through the jovial crowd, each farewell tinged with the sweet afterglow of a day rich in laughter and new memories. As they approached Jessica and Ethan, who were engaged in conversation with Heather, Krista, and Michelle, Felix felt reluctant to leave this sanctuary of friendship.

"Hey guys," Fawn called out, signaling their intent to depart. "We're heading out."

Heather was the first to respond, her smile as bright as the day. "Felix, you're leaving us already?" she teased, her tone playful yet tinged with genuine disappointment.

"Yeah," Felix replied, a shy grin emerging. "I need to get back. My dad needs me."

Krista jumped in with a quip that drew a chuckle from the group. "Well, make sure you come to the next one. We'll need a rematch!"

"And bring that spike game of yours," Michelle added, her eyes sparkling with mirth.

Standing before Jessica and Ethan, Felix's expression softened into a grateful smile. "Thank you for inviting me, Jessica. This has been the best day ever." His voice held a hint of embarrassment as he added, "I'm sorry I wasn't able to bring you a gift."

Jessica's reply was immediate and warm, her smile enveloping him like a sunbeam. "Oh, Felix, you didn't need to bring anything. Being here was the best gift you could have given me." Her gratitude was obvious in the affectionate hug she gave him, echoing the deep appreciation they all felt for his presence.

It was then Ethan's turn to bid Felix farewell. With an easygoing grin and their 'bro' handshake, Ethan offered words filled with genuine encouragement. "Keep your head up, dude," he said earnestly. "You've shown everyone here what you're made of. Remember, no one on this planet is better than you or me. We are who we are, and if anyone has a problem with that, it's their problem, not ours."

Felix absorbed Ethan's words like parched earth soaks up rain—nourishing and life-affirming. He nodded in silent acknowledgment, the gravity of the moment settling within him.

As Fawn leaned in for a quick goodbye hug with Jessica, she whispered conspiratorially, "I'll text you when I get home. Don't forget to stop by after Ethan leaves. I've got something special for you." Her eyes danced with mischief and promise.

With their farewells exchanged and hearts full from the day's events, Fawn led Felix away from the backyard that had witnessed an afternoon rich with laughter and joy. Watching them leave, Jessica let out a contented sigh, her thoughts already on Fawn's mysterious surprise and the unfolding summer adventures that awaited them all.

As Fawn drove toward Felix's home, a thick silence enveloped the car, heavy with the weight of unspoken thoughts. She glanced sideways at Felix, whose eyes were fixed on the passing scenery. The storm of emotions that played across his features betrayed his inner turmoil, his mind no doubt tangled with thoughts of his budding connection with Emily.

Fawn's heart ached in an echo of his silent struggle. Trying to lighten the mood, she asked, "So, did you have fun at the party?"

Felix turned to her, a fragile smile touching his lips as he replied, "Yes. It was the most fun I've ever had." The sincerity in his voice sent a wave of gratification over Fawn. However, as he returned his gaze to the window, a brief silence followed. Then Felix's voice carried a note of sorrow. "I'm never going to see Emily again, am I?"

The raw emotion in his words caught Fawn off guard, and she scrambled mentally for some form of reassurance. "Just because she lives in Texas doesn't mean you can't stay in touch. Don't you have a phone or internet at your house?"

Felix shook his head, his eyes lowering in discomfort. "I never had a reason to want a phone. I didn't have any friends to call," he admitted, his voice tinged with shame. "And we can't afford a phone or internet."

The revelation struck Fawn with the cold clarity of Felix's predicament. She had never considered life without such essentials—they were the invisible lifelines binding her to her friends when distance stretched between them. A desperate search for solutions whirled in her mind as she sought ways to bridge this unexpected gap for Felix and Emily. Despite her efforts, there was no immediate answer.

As they pulled up to Felix's house, Fawn noted his father's lonely figure sitting on the porch—a stark reminder of the burdens Felix carried. His voice cut through the silence again, heavy with unspoken resignation. "I guess I won't be seeing you again either, right?"

The question hung in the air like a delicate but unbreakable thread. Fawn felt a pang of sympathy stir within her. With gentle conviction, she replied, "I'll be back, Felix. I'll stop by to check up on you. I'll still be here for a couple more months."

A small, tentative smile tugged at Felix's lips as he nodded, finding solace in Fawn's promise—a lifeline amid the waves of change. He stepped out of the car and trudged toward the gate, which creaked open with a sound that seemed to echo his reluctance.

Slowly, he walked up to his father and disappeared behind the door of his home, pausing only to glance back at Fawn with a nod that spoke volumes—a silent thank you and a vow to cling to the hope she had kindled.

As the sky softened into the tender hues of the evening, Jessica and Ethan found solace on the front steps of her home, their presence a beacon in the dimming light. Jessica noticed the weary shadows beneath his eyes, prompting her to whisper with concern, "Hey, babe, you look exhausted. You should get some sleep."

Ethan initially resisted the idea, his reluctance to part from Jessica evident in his eyes. Yet, he conceded, recognizing the truth in her observation. "Yeah, you're right. I should head back and catch some shut-eye."

With a tender smile, Jessica acknowledged his decision as they walked to his Jeep. Pausing for a last embrace, their kiss held the promise of tomorrow. "I'll see you later, babe," Ethan murmured, his eyes locked with hers in a silent vow.

As he settled into his Jeep and started the engine, Ethan gave Jessica a parting glance. "Make sure you get some rest, too," he said affectionately.

"I will," she assured him, her voice playful. "But first, I've got to swing by Fawn's—she's got something for me."

Ethan's lips curled into a knowing smirk, his eyes sparkling with a shared secret. "You brat! She told you?" Jessica teased him with feigned indignation.

His triumphant grin was all the reply she needed as he blew her a mock kiss and drove off into the embrace of night, leaving Jessica's heart pulsing with love and eager expectation.

After Ethan's Jeep disappeared, she burst through her front door, calling out with a vivacious spirit, "I'm heading over to Fawn's! I'll be back later!" Her heart raced with curiosity as she began her walk towards Fawn's house, her mind alive with the possibilities of what awaited her there.

As her steps carried her across the well-trodden path to Fawn's property, her bright blue eyes caught sight of the stark "For Sale" sign standing like an unwelcome specter in the yard. The bold letters were a harsh reminder of the imminent rift that would stretch between their lives. The thought of distance diluting their cherished connection cast a somber veil over Jessica's eager spirit.

But when Fawn appeared in the doorway, her presence shone like a beacon, dispelling the shadows that had crept into Jessica's heart. With a smile that radiated the warmth of countless summers, Fawn beckoned, "Meet me by the swing." Her excited voice pulled Jessica out of her reverie.

The old white bench swing awaited them, a testament to their enduring friendship—a witness to countless giggles and heart-to-hearts. As Jessica approached, each step seemed to echo with the laughter and cheerful banter that had filled many sunny afternoons and starlit evenings. This was where their souls had been bared and fortified against life's trials and triumphs.

Settling onto the familiar weathered slats, Jessica was overwhelmed with gratitude for this sacred space. Here, amidst the gentle sway and creak of the ropes, they would celebrate yet another milestone—the gifting of a birthday present steeped in history and heart.

Soon enough, Fawn emerged, cradling a blush-colored gift bag with tender care. Her eyes shimmered with anticipation, a contagious spark of excitement. Settling into the swing beside Jessica, she handed over the gift bag.

"Happy Birthday, Jess," she smiled, her voice full of genuine affection.

Jessica's eyes sparkled with anticipation as she reached into the bag. She carefully pulled out a gleaming white miniature bench swing, gasping at the sight. It was a perfect replica of the swing they were sitting on, complete with two small figurines—one blonde, the other brunette—their arms wrapped around each other, their faces touching in a display of deep affection. The intricate details that so beautifully captured their friendship were a testament to Fawn's artistic talent. Jessica felt a surge of emotion, deeply moved by the thoughtfulness of the gift.

"That's you and me, right?" Jessica asked, her voice quivering as her fingertips gently caressed the small faces that mirrored their own.

Fawn's affirming smile was all the confirmation Jessica needed. She leaned her head against Jessica's shoulder, allowing the silence to speak for her, their heartbeats syncing in a silent symphony of their enduring friendship.

"It's beautiful, Fawn. Thank you," Jessica breathed out, each word imbued with love and gratitude that filled the space between them.

For the rest of the evening, Jessica and Fawn remained seated on the old white bench swing, savoring the waning moments of Jessica's birthday. It was a picture-perfect portrait of serene contentment, a moment steeped in the warm hues of love and friendship that defined their bond. As night's velvet shroud draped around them, a profound sense of joy and gratitude enveloped Jessica. This birthday, illuminated by friendship's glow, would forever be etched in her memory as an emblem of youth's fleeting yet enduring grace.

# Chapter 16

----------------------------------------------------------------

As June relinquished its hold on the calendar, July stepped forward with a flourish, heralding the peak of the summer season in Wavecrest. The town, adorned in its festive best, swelled with tourists flocking to its sun-kissed beaches, eager to immerse themselves in the warm embrace of the Pacific and the lively atmosphere of the boardwalk. The air buzzed with laughter and carefree spirits—a haven for those fleeing the mundane rhythms of everyday existence.

However, stormy skies overshadowed July's arrival. For three consecutive days, a relentless deluge drenched Wavecrest, muting the vibrant summer hues with sheets of rain and rolls of thunder. Confined to her home, Fawn found herself battling a creative block, desperately seeking the spark of inspiration she needed to fuel her artwork for the upcoming contest.

As strangers paraded through her home, each viewing felt like an invasion into her sacred space, a stark reminder that her world was on the brink of upheaval. In silent protest, Fawn allowed her room to spiral into a state of disarray. Clothing carpeted the floor in disorganized heaps, and her bed lay in a tangle of linens—her visual defiance against those who dared to disrupt her sanctuary.

Sensing her daughter's unrest, Anna took leave from her job at the clinic. She recognized that Fawn was in no state to present their home in an appealing light to potential buyers. Tension simmered beneath the surface of their daily interactions as Fawn's shock morphed into a bitter blend of anger and feelings of betrayal. She felt a deep sense of injustice, perceiving that they had not taken her voice into account and disregarded her emotions in the decision-making process—a verdict passed without considering its impact on her.

For Fawn, Wavecrest was more than just a house or a town—it was her safe harbor, a place imbued with acceptance and belonging. The thought of relocating to Boston had always unsettled her, yet Wavecrest remained her anchor amidst life's uncertainties—a tangible link to Jessica and their trove of cherished memories. However, the prospect of moving to Montana, a place she had never visited, felt alien and unwelcoming. The mere thought of this distant landscape, filled with strangers and unfamiliarity, was enough to incite a wave of revulsion within her.

On the fourth day of July, the persistent rain that had enshrouded Wavecrest in shades of gray finally ceased. The sun ascended majestically, scattering the clouds to unveil a sky of unblemished blue. A collective sigh of relief swept through the town as both residents and tourists basked in the resurgence of summer's luminous glory.

Confined to her room for days, Fawn sensed the change as beams of sunlight pirouetted through her window. The oppressive gloom that had weighed upon her heart began to dissipate, though a nagging unease about her home falling into the hands of strangers still lingered. Determined to cast aside her melancholy, Fawn embraced the invigorating warmth of a shower, letting each droplet wash away traces of her sorrow. Refreshed, she chose an ensemble that mirrored her liberated spirit—a white knit crop top paired with denim cutoffs, epitomizing the carefree essence of summer.

Before venturing outside, Fawn instinctively grabbed her phone to reach out for a connection. She texted Jessica, her constant in the chaos of life. "Are you up?" she sent into the digital void, hoping for a reprieve.

Jessica's reply was swift and carried with it a note of laughter. "Just got up. Mom is making breakfast. Get your butt here," followed by an emoji that winked mirth into Fawn's morning. A genuine giggle broke through the gloom that had enveloped her; Jessica's teasing was a beacon of normalcy in turbulent times.

With renewed vigor, Fawn brushed through her hair, leaving it in a tousled cascade as she descended the stairs and headed toward the front door. From the kitchen, Anna's voice carried a mix of hope and concern. "Would you like some breakfast, honey?" she called out.

Despite the gentle offer, Fawn declined with a polite detachment that belied her inner turmoil. "No, thanks, Mom. I'm going to Jess's," she declared with finality, eager for the comfort of escape.

As she stepped outside, a gentle breeze caressed her blonde locks, easing her worries. The sun, radiant and nurturing, enveloped her in a warm glow, lighting her path with golden hope. Breathing deeply, Fawn felt invigorated by the sweet scent of summer air, which carried the liberating essence of freedom. Each step lightened the weight of recent gloomy days, replacing it with a budding sense of optimism.

Convinced that Jessica's presence would shield her from lingering doubts, Fawn's heart quickened with the promise of a new beginning. She made her way to Jessica's house, each step drawing her closer to the solace only a lifelong friendship could provide.

The moment Fawn crossed into Jessica's home, she was met by the comforting aromas of eggs and bacon sizzling on the stove, the essence of domestic bliss surrounding her.

Teresa moved about with effortless grace, her smile brightening the room as she master-fully orchestrated breakfast in the morning light. As Fawn walked into the kitchen, Jessica leaped from her chair and wrapped her in an embrace filled with unspoken understanding.

Teresa's eyes were full of affection as she greeted Fawn. "Right on time, sweetheart." Although her words spoke of punctuality, her voice conveyed an open-hearted welcome.

Tom, leaning casually against the counter, chimed in with feigned admonishment. "No, she's not. She's late," he quipped, his mock sternness dissolving into a smile.

Jessica rolled her eyes playfully at her father's teasing and retorted with an endearing, "Whatever!"

The girls settled into their familiar spots at the table, where Teresa served up heaping plates of scrambled eggs and crisp bacon, setting the stage for what promised to be an eventful day.

After the morning's comforting feast had settled in their stomachs, the girls retreated to Jessica's bedroom. The walls offered Fawn a warm embrace, making the space feel like an extension of her own—a refuge in times of turmoil. Jessica, her hair still damp from the shower, sat at her vanity brushing her locks, each stroke an effort to smooth away the complexities of life.

Fawn claimed a spot on the plush bed, sighing as she sank into the familiar softness. Breaking the quiet that filled the room, she confessed, "It was the worst three days of my life."

Jessica's heart sank as she turned from the mirror to meet Fawn's eyes. "I'm sorry. I wish you had told me. You could have hung out with Ethan and me."

With a quick shake of her head, Fawn dismissed the notion, her voice thick with appre-ciation. "No way, Jess. You two need your time without me being in the way."

"You wouldn't have been in the way, Fawn," Jessica insisted, her tone tinged with frus-tration to emphasize her seriousness. "I want to spend as much time with you as possible before we leave for college. Ethan gets it—he knows what you're going through. We both want to be here for you."

Fawn sighed, the weight of her emotions evident. "I know," she murmured, conceding to the ripples that her situation had sent through Jessica's life as well. "This whole thing just... sucks." She lay back on the bed, letting her eyes drift up to the constellation of glow-in-the-dark stars above.

Jessica left her seat at the vanity and joined Fawn on the bed, their silence enveloping them like a blanket. They lay side by side under the artificial night sky that stretched across the ceiling.

Venturing into delicate territory, Jessica asked, "Did you get any work done on your art project?"

Fawn exhaled dramatically and rolled her eyes skyward—a silent dance of frustration. "I tried," she admitted, her voice tinged with defeat. "But it's impossible. I can't focus on that with everything that's happening. It feels like I wasted my time entering the contest."

Jessica turned sharply toward Fawn, her eyes wide with disbelief. "Seriously?" she gasped. "But you're so talented. You have to enter that contest!"

"Oh, I wouldn't have won anyway," Fawn replied with a shrug, unable to hide her sense of loss.

Refusing to let her friend sink into despair, Jessica countered strongly. "You know that's not true, Fawn. You have just as much of a chance, if not more, to win the contest. You're an amazing artist."

The kindness in Jessica's voice enveloped Fawn like a warm hug. She smiled and conceded with a hint of hopefulness. "Maybe." She paused before adding firmly, "But not today. I don't want to think about any of that right now."

After a few moments of silence, Jessica made another casual suggestion. "Ethan will be here soon. We're going to the mall. Why don't you come with us?"

Fawn grinned at the invitation. Though the allure of retail therapy was tempting, the vibrant atmosphere of the boardwalk on Independence Day appealed to her even more than air-conditioned stores.

"Nah," she decided aloud. "I think I'll just hang out on the boardwalk today, maybe meet up with some friends. You two have fun at the mall."

Jessica accepted her decision but couldn't resist reminding her of their Fourth of July tradition. "Alright. But we'll meet up later and watch the fireworks, right?"

Fawn's eyes lit up, her voice vibrant with certainty. "Absolutely!"

As Jessica and Fawn chatted idly, the distant rumble of an engine cut through the tranquility of the moment, signaling Ethan's arrival. Fawn glanced out the window, spotting his Jeep as it turned the corner. Jessica's face brightened with anticipation as she gathered her things with renewed energy.

"He's here!" she exclaimed, her eyes fixed on the Jeep as it pulled into the driveway.

Together, they hurried down the hallway to the front door. Stepping outside, Jessica gave Fawn a quick hug before eagerly climbing into Ethan's Jeep. Fawn waved goodbye to her best friend from the steps and watched them drive off, taking comfort in the thought of reuniting later under the bursts of color and light in the night sky.

The boardwalk buzzed with life, pulsing with eager souls drawn to the hum of vintage arcades and the thrill of gravity-defying rides. The impending dusk promised a burst of color in the sky, setting the stage for Wavecrest's famous Fourth of July fireworks display, which was poised to paint the night with splendor. The event's legendary status acted as a beacon, drawing a diverse crowd of locals and tourists alike, all lured by the promise of an unforgettable show.

Fawn wove through the lively throng, her senses alive with the boardwalk's vibrant offerings. Familiar laughter reached her ears, drawing her effortlessly into a group of familiar friends. Radiant as ever, Heather pulled Fawn into a comforting and exuberant hug. "Hey, girl, what's going on?"

"Not much. I'm just taking it all in," Fawn replied, her voice steady despite her inner turmoil.

Heather cocked her head, a playful gleam dancing in her eyes. "Where's Jessica?"

Gazing out at the sea's endless dance, Fawn replied with a smile that didn't quite reach her eyes. "Jess and Ethan are off to the mall today. But don't worry, they'll be back in time for the fireworks tonight."

The sparkle in Heather's eyes mirrored the twinkle of anticipation for the evening. Leaning in, she asked, "You excited for tonight? Rumor has it that this year's show will outshine all the others!"

Fawn's grin widened as she recalled a funny incident. "Do you remember that one year when a rocket went off and exploded right over our heads?"

Heather's laughter mingled with the surrounding merriment. "Who could forget? We were all covered with ashes!"

Their laughter faded into a moment of contemplation. Heather's expression softened. "You know, with you guys leaving for college, this might be our last Fourth of July together here. It kinda sucks, doesn't it?"

Fawn let her gaze linger on the horizon where the sky met the sea—a canvas soon to be streaked with fiery artistry. Her voice carried a mix of wistfulness and resolve. "Yeah, it sure does. But I don't want to think about that now. Let's just make the best of the time we have left."

With a firm nod, Heather's resolve shone brightly. "You're right! And tonight, we're going to make some unforgettable memories. Just wait and see!"

Laughter and chatter, the very essence of youth, reverberated through the boardwalk, weaving a symphony of exuberance as vibrant as the neon lights of the nearby arcade. In the thick of it all, Fawn and Heather were surrounded by the familiar faces of their classmates.

Lucas, a fellow graduate with an easy smile that never seemed to fade, called out to them. Raising his arm high in greeting, he beckoned them over to where he lounged with others near the cotton candy stand, its sugary scent wafting through the air.

"Hey, Fawn, Heather! Get over here!" His voice carried over the din of chattering tourists and playful screams from roller coaster riders.

Beside him, Tiffany, who still has one more year to go before graduating, was a whirlwind of motion with her camera, a fixture in her hands as she sought to capture every fleeting moment.

"This will be perfect for next year's yearbook," she declared, her eyes alight with the fervor of a dedicated archivist.

Fawn couldn't help but grin as she made her way over. "Hey, Tiff," she greeted warmly. "Make sure you get a good shot of the fireworks later!"

Tiffany turned toward her with a mischievous glint in her eye and retorted, "Only if you promise not to photobomb it like last time!" In a swift motion that was almost too quick to see, she lifted her camera and captured Fawn's surprised expression.

"You brat!" Fawn exclaimed, feigned shock written across her face. Her lighthearted words brought another round of laughter among their friends as Tiffany chuckled triumphantly. "Gotcha! This one's going in the yearbook for sure."

Tyler chimed in next, his reputation as the class clown, well earned. His grin spread across his face. "I hope the fireworks this year are as explosive as my last chemistry experiment!" he joked.

Instant laughter ignited within the group as each mind flashed back to the infamous day Tyler's experiment had gone spectacularly awry. Heather leaned in close to him, her features painted with an exaggerated look of mock horror. "Oh my God! Let's hope not, for everyone's sake!"

Their shared laughter rose above the cacophony of carnival games and seaside vendors, a chorus of friendship echoing off the wooden planks of Wavecrest's beloved boardwalk. Each peal of mirth added another thread to the rich tapestry of memories they had woven together throughout their high school years.

Amidst the banter and frenetic activity, an unexpected encounter loomed on Fawn's horizon. Among a gaggle of friends, Jerry Cranmer—the boy who broke her heart—caught sight of her. His face lit up with a familiar warmth as he called out her name, his voice cutting through the din to reach her ears.

Fawn turned, her expression shifting to surprise as she registered Jerry's presence. He wove through the cluster of friends, drawing Fawn to one side with gentle urgency. The revelry continued unabated around them, a stark contrast to the gravity that passed between the two.

There was a hint of concern in Jerry's eyes as he broached the subject. "I drove past your house the other day and saw the 'For Sale' sign. Is your family moving to Boston, too?"

Fawn's reply was tinged with bitterness, her voice sharp enough to slice through the festive air. "No!" she spat out. "They're moving to fucking Montana!"

Jerry's eyebrows shot up, a visible jolt at Fawn's choice of words and the venom behind them. "Montana? That's... crazy, man," he said. A spark of curiosity ignited in his eyes as he ventured further. "Why Montana?"

With a dismissive flick of her hand and a pronounced roll of her eyes, Fawn shrugged off the query. "I have no clue. They made their decision without including me," she vented, the sting of her resentment infusing her tone.

Jerry extended an arm, an instinctive gesture to comfort her in this moment of distress. "I'm sorry, Fawn. That's fucked up," he murmured, his voice a quiet echo of his intent to soothe.

Touched by Jerry's kindness, Fawn momentarily lowered her guard and offered a nod of thanks before quickly rebuilding her walls. "Whatever. It's the Fourth of July, so I don't want to think about that today."

Jerry seized the opportunity to steer them back toward lighter topics. "Well, it's a beautiful day. Would you like to hang out for a while?" The undercurrents of their past swirled around them as Jerry extended his olive branch—a plea for forgiveness wrapped in hope.

Fawn hesitated, a flicker of uncertainty crossing her face. "I don't know, Jerry," she murmured, her voice tinged with nervousness. "It's not that simple."

Seeing the reluctance in her expression, Jerry took a deep breath before continuing. "Fawn, what I did in the past was stupid," he confessed. "I know I hurt you, and I'm truly sorry. We had something good going, and I messed it up. But I still want us to be friends. You still mean a lot to me."

Fawn searched his face, finding traces of genuine remorse that softened her heart just enough. "You mean a lot to me, too," she admitted quietly. "But we can't change the past. I guess we can try moving forward as friends, though."

A bright smile chased away the shadows on Jerry's face as he teased, "How about we start with me winning you a prize from one of these games?"

Fawn's lips curled into a smile at his playful challenge, and together, they stepped away from their friends, promising to reunite later that evening.

The day unfolded like a vibrant tapestry as Fawn and Jerry made their way through the pulsating crowd of the boardwalk. Their laughter mingled with the lively buzz of the crowd, creating a harmonious soundtrack to their renewed camaraderie. Together, they braved dizzying rides that sliced through the sky, immersed themselves in the electronic symphony of arcade games, and succumbed to the siren call of sugary treats from boardwalk vendors.

Amidst the revelry, their conversation stitched a poignant bridge between their once entwined past and the tentative threads of a rekindled friendship. As they navigated this delicate dance against the backdrop of the Fourth of July festivities, each shared experience deepened their layered connection.

As shadows lengthened and the sun bathed Wavecrest in a golden glow, Fawn and Jerry retreated to a secluded enclave away from the festive fervor. There, Jerry's eyes lingered on Fawn with an intricate blend of affection and sorrow. With a gentle voice, Jerry confessed, "You know, Fawn, being here with you today... it's like we've stepped back in time."

Fawn felt her heart stir with a mix of nostalgia and caution as she met his gaze. "It does feel like old times, Jerry. But I can't ignore everything that's happened."

He nodded, his features etched with regret. "I know," he admitted. "I wish I could go back and make things right."

A wistful smile graced Fawn's lips as she contemplated his words. "Sometimes, I wish for that too. But we both know it's not that simple."

In that quiet corner of the world, unspoken words hung heavily between them—echoes of pain and possibility mixed in the air. Jerry reached out hesitantly, his fingers brushing hers in a gesture that once felt so natural, but now carried the weight of their history. Fawn allowed the contact, but her blue eyes were like stormy seas—churning with conflicting emotions.

"Jerry," she whispered with vulnerable strength, "there's still a part of me that cares for you—maybe even loves you. But I can't just forget... I can't let myself be hurt again."

Jerry's hand withdrew, the motion slow and full of care, respecting her unspoken boundaries.

"I understand," he replied. "Maybe someday we can find our way back to each other." His words carried a fragile hope—a seed of possibility that would require time, patience, and healing to bloom.

Fawn's eyes, shimmering with unshed tears, met Jerry's with a depth of emotion that words could not convey. Her heart ached, a tumultuous mixture of longing and the sharp sting of past hurts resonating within her. She wanted to say something, anything, to bridge the gap between their shared history and uncertain future. Yet, the words eluded her, caught in the maze of her conflicting emotions.

Finally, with a voice barely above a whisper, strained with the effort to maintain composure, Fawn said, "I think we should head back now. It's starting to get dark." It was a retreat, a step back from the precipice of their complicated past, a protective measure against the vulnerability that Jerry's presence stirred within her.

They rose together to rejoin the celebration as dusk settled in, just as a firework unfurled above them in a dazzling cascade of color—a mirror to their internal maelstrom of love and loss. They exchanged a glance charged with shared history before merging into the vibrant stream of boardwalk life, each carrying remnants of what had been and what could never be.

As dusk gave way to the evening's embrace, Fawn clutched the plush teddy bear she'd won, its softness contrasting with the electric thrill in her veins. She spotted Jessica and Ethan at the edge of the boardwalk, their figures outlined against the backdrop of an ocean kissed by lunar silver. A wave of elation swept over her.

"Look, there's Jess and Ethan," Fawn announced, her voice tinged with joy as she nudged Jerry's arm. "Let's go over there!" Together, they walked through the festive crowd toward their friends.

When Jessica saw Jerry and Fawn approaching arm in arm, her heart skipped a beat. The memory of their conversation at Jerry's graduation party—their first in over a year—flashed in her mind. This visual of unity was still startling against the backdrop of their stormy past, stirring a whirlwind of emotions that held remnants of bitterness and anger for the pain Jerry had inflicted on her best friend.

As they reunited, Jessica pulled Fawn aside, her voice a whisper against the gentle sea breeze. "You and Jerry?" she asked, incredulity threading her quiet question.

Fawn responded with a mix of tender humor and soothing reassurance, stifling a chuckle. "It's not what you think, silly girl," she whispered back, her voice a calming melody. "We're just friends."

Relief flickered across Jessica's face, her smile faint. "Okay," she murmured. "I just don't want to see you get hurt again. You know I don't trust him."

Fawn reached out, her fingers intertwining with Jessica's in a silent promise of solidarity. Her eyes shimmered with understanding as she nodded. "I know," she whispered, affirming their deep bond and shared trust.

As the night sky unfurled its velvety curtain, their intimate circle swelled with the arrival of Heather, Krista, and Michelle, each adding their own cadence to the growing chorus of joy and lively conversation.

The air thrummed with palpable anticipation for the impending pyrotechnic marvel, each pulse ticking down to the moment the sky would erupt in celebration. As the clock neared ten o'clock, an unspoken signal guided them to their traditional spot on the sandy shore—a hallowed gathering place under the celestial tapestry.

Jessica and Ethan found solace on a secluded rock, ensconced in the warm embrace of companionship. Amidst the buzz of excitement, Heather's voice, laced with the thrill of secrecy, cut through. "Guys, listen up! There's something incredible in the works, and if all goes according to plan, it will be epic."

Jessica's eyes sparked with intrigue, unleashing her insatiable curiosity. "What is it? What is it? Tell us!"

A sly grin played upon Heather's lips as she shook her head. "No can do—not yet. I don't want to jinx it. But trust me, if everything falls into place, you girls will be the first to know."

Jessica cocked her head in a mock sulk. "You're such a tease, Heather," she said in a playful tone.

Fawn's laughter rang true, echoing under the stars as she playfully elbowed Jessica. "She's just trying to be difficult. Classic Heather," she said with a smirk.

Krista chimed in with a playful wag of her finger. "If you keep this up, Heather, we might start hiding your makeup brushes as payback!"

Michelle giggled at Krista's suggestion, her laughter a light echo in the night air.

Heather's laugh joined theirs, her eyes sparkling with mischief. "Can't I ever have my moment of mystery and intrigue?"

Jessica shot back with a teasing glint, "Where's the fun in that? Besides, your mystery moments usually last about five seconds before you spill."

Heather feigned outrage, while Fawn, chuckling, gave her a gentle shove. "You know we can't let you sit on a secret for too long," she teased.

Their lighthearted ribbing mingled with the distant laughter of their peers and the soothing cadence of the sea. For an instant, time held its breath in anticipation of nature's own theater igniting above them.

The evening air, once a silent stage, now thundered with the sound of a rocket exploding overhead. Vibrations rippled through the crowd as a chorus of cheers and gasps rolled like waves along Wavecrest's beaches and boardwalk. The night came alive with vibrant bursts of light, painting the darkness with an artist's palette of colors, leaving the onlookers in a state of rapturous awe.

As the last light of day receded, an expectant silence fell over the crowd. They stood shoulder to shoulder, faces upturned in collective anticipation. Children, their eyes wide with excitement, perched on their parents' shoulders for a better view, while young couples scattered across the pristine beach, leaned into each other, whispering predictions of the show to come.

The first firework soared into the sky, erupting into a chandelier of glittering stars that hung suspended before gracefully cascading downward. Silver and gold streams reflected off the water's surface, eliciting a symphony of oohs and aahs from the crowd. The rhythmic crackle and pop of the fireworks melded with the lapping waves, creating an entrancing melody that captivated the onlookers.

On their secluded rock, Jessica and Ethan sat, wrapped in each other's presence. Jessica's bright blue eyes sparkled, mirroring the fiery dance above. She leaned into Ethan, her pulse synchronizing with each new explosion that lit up the sky.

A cascade of reds, blues, and yellows unfurled across the firmament, tracing trails of light that lingered before slowly fading away. The reverent whispers of the audience wove into a tapestry of shared wonder, as mesmerizing as the aerial ballet unfolding above them.

Anticipation built to a fever pitch as the finale approached, a display rumored to surpass all previous shows in grandeur. Then it came: a breathtaking eruption that filled the sky with churning colors and shapes, each more magnificent than the last. The ground beneath Jessica and Ethan vibrated with the concussive booms that thundered through Wavecrest, resonating with the night's energy.

As they held each other closer under the barrage of light and sound, Ethan was struck by a level of awe he'd never experienced before—a feeling born not only from the pyrotechnic majesty, but also from having Jessica by his side. Together, they watched as the final salvo painted a kaleidoscope across the night's canvas, their hearts alight with wonder.

Despite having witnessed many Fourth of July fireworks from Wavecrest's lively board-walk, this display held a unique charm for Jessica. The magic and shared wonder were amplified by Ethan's presence, which pulled irresistibly at her heart. Every delicate stroke of Ethan's fingers, each stolen glance brimming with awe, sent ripples through her heart. To her, this was a cosmic spectacle orchestrated solely for them—a radiant celebration of both their burgeoning love and Independence Day.

Amidst the brilliant spectacle and blossoming love, a whisper of sorrow tinged the moment with bittersweet poignancy. Their first Fourth of July together would forever be a cherished memory, yet an undercurrent of uncertainty loomed, casting a faint shadow over their future celebrations. A tender question mark punctuated their shared euphoria: would they be able to revel in this unity and celebration in the years to come? The fireworks offered no answer; they simply blazed on into infinity before fading into smoke against the vast ocean backdrop.

In the aftermath of the spectacular fireworks display, the group began to stir from their shared reverie. Jessica and Ethan climbed off their secluded rock while Heather, Krista, and Michelle stood, brushing the sand from their clothes with light, rhythmic strokes. As they all regrouped, Fawn and Jerry joined them, their expressions a mix of satisfaction and fatigue from the day's emotional rollercoaster. Together, they exchanged smiles and soft laughs, savoring the lingering echoes of the night's joy.

After a day of laughter, camaraderie, and tangled emotions, the lure of the sanctuary of home began to call to Fawn, despite the inevitable turmoil that awaited her there. Turning to Jerry, Fawn admitted, "I'm beat," her voice tinged with the weariness of the day. "I think I'm going to head home and try to get some sleep."

Jerry's response was a soft nod, a gentle ripple in the ocean of their shared understanding. His words, heavy with sincerity, served as a comforting balm. "Alright, Fawn. Just know that I'm here for you if you ever need a shoulder to lean on."

Against the backdrop of their chaotic past, Fawn felt a surge of self-pride. She had allowed herself to let go of the toxic bitterness that had once enveloped her heart and shut out Jerry. Though the once blazing embers of their romance had been reduced to a mere flicker, she found quiet joy in their renewed friendship. With a genuine smile that softened her features, she replied, "Thank you, Jerry. I appreciate that." At that moment, a warm glow filled her heart, his words providing the comfort she needed.

As Jessica and Ethan approached the tired couple, Jessica noticed the fatigue etched into Fawn's features. "You look exhausted, girl," she murmured, her voice heavy with concern.

A sigh escaped Fawn's lips, her voice a soft whisper reflecting the exhaustion that clung to her like a shadow. "Yeah, it's been a long day," she conceded, her words as spent as the light in her eyes. "I'm going home now. See you tomorrow."

In tune with Fawn's need for refuge, Jessica enveloped her friend in a comforting embrace, her arms a protective cocoon against the world. "Hang in there, girlfriend. Try to get some rest."

As their hug slowly dissipated, Fawn rewarded Jessica's empathetic gesture with a sincere smile. This simple act of kindness had lit a small beacon of warmth in her heart, reaffirming the irreplaceable strength of their friendship.

After Fawn bid a warm farewell to their group of friends, Jessica's gaze lingered on the receding figure of her dearest friend, concern simmering beneath her calm exterior. Her eyes, pools of deep concern, followed Fawn as she disappeared into the ink-black canvas of the night. Her heart ached with an unspoken understanding of the battles Fawn still had to face, even within the perceived safety of her own home.

With a heavy heart, Jessica turned to Ethan. Her eyes, the windows to her soul, were clouded with worry and sorrow. Reading the turmoil in her eyes, Ethan pulled her into his embrace, providing a sanctuary amid the emotional storm. He could feel the raw emotion emanating from her, palpable in the warm night air. He gently guided her head to rest on his shoulder, his fingers stroking her hair in an effort to calm her troubled spirit.

As they stood together, Ethan experienced a strange and comforting sensation. It was as though an unseen presence had enveloped them in its invisible arms, offering solace and warmth. This ethereal embrace felt ancient and nurturing, like a whisper from beyond the tangible world, imbuing their moment with a sense of deep ancestral comfort.

A moment later, Jessica lifted her head, and Ethan gazed into her eyes. The worry that had shadowed her was gone, replaced by the sweet, playful light he knew so well. Her beautiful blue eyes sparkled once again with the joy and resilience that defined her.

Ethan's heart lightened at this transformation, a smile spreading across his face. Together, they turned to look out into the vast, dark ocean, its endless depths mirroring the mysteries of life.

As they stood there, with the remnants of the night's celebrations echoing in the distance, a sense of peace enveloped them. It was a quiet assurance that no matter what the future held, they would face it together. Hand in hand, their silhouettes merged with the night sky, creating a serene tableau against the ocean's expanse. In this moment of quiet contemplation, their presence became a testament to the enduring power of love and the unseen forces that guide us through life's journey.

# Chapter 17

--------------------------------------------------------

The sultry summer night hummed with the distant echo of fireworks. Twinkling lights danced in the air, and the faint scent of gunpowder wafted lazily, a lingering memory of the evening's spectacle. As Fawn approached her home, the walls appeared almost spectral in the dwindling light, filling her with a sense of apprehension and uncertainty. The "For Sale" sign in her front yard stood like an unwelcome intruder, amplifying her discomfort—a stark reminder of the strangers who had invaded her home.

Each uninvited visitor who entered her bedroom stoked the embers of resentment within Fawn. Her home had been her fortress, her retreat from the world's clamor. Now, it was polluted by the intrusive scrutiny of these strangers, each invasion a wound that cut deep, leaving a raw scar on her peace.

Amidst her tumultuous emotions, Fawn found herself questioning her parents' motives. How could they decide to sell their family home so suddenly, without consulting her or considering her deep connection to it? This dismissal of her feelings felt like a bitter betrayal, adding to her already blazing emotions of hurt and abandonment.

The emotional cyclone raged within Fawn as she wrestled with the upcoming move to Boston, a city completely foreign to her. Adding to her anxiety was the daunting prospect of finding her place in a new school, surrounded by unfamiliar faces and routines.

Adding to her turmoil, Fawn felt the sharp sting of the impending end to her carefree youth. Wavecrest, her beloved town, was slipping through her fingers like sand. She recognized the profound weight of her approaching leap into adulthood and the reality that this was her last dance with the magic of a Wavecrest summer before diving into the uncharted waters of her future.

As she crossed the threshold of her home, the soft glow of the living room lamp cast a warm light, revealing her parents engrossed in the flickering images on the television screen. They briefly acknowledged her arrival with a wave of cheerfulness, but Fawn barely noticed, heading straight for her bedroom. As she approached, a wave of disbelief swept over her. The scene in her personal space ignited a flash of anger that crackled through her veins.

In a silent act of defiance, Fawn had turned her bedroom into a sprawling landscape of disorder, hoping that its wild state would repel potential buyers and hinder the sale. But the scene she was now confronted with was one of astonishing neatness and meticulous organization. From the doorway, her anger swelled like a storm-tossed sea as she took in the dramatic transformation of her space.

The clothes and towels she had strewn across the floor in calculated chaos were picked up and neatly put away. The sheets and blanket she had carelessly left strewn across her bed were now arranged with meticulous precision, their tidiness mocking the idea of welcoming coziness. Her intimate trinkets and keepsakes had been rearranged, their changed positions screaming the invasion of her personal domain.

Every meticulous detail that assaulted her vision fanned the flames of Fawn's rage, causing her to shake with a fury so intense, it seemed to ripple through the air around her. Unable to contain the torrent of frustration that had been simmering within her for weeks, her eyes sparkled with gleaming determination—a fiery declaration of battle. She spun around and stormed downstairs to the living room, where her parents remained engrossed in their television world. The time for quiet resistance had reached its tumultuous finale.

Witnessing their daughter's stormy march, Anna and Brian found themselves transfixed by the wildfire in her eyes and the anger etched into her expression. It was an alarming spectacle, one that was foreign to them, an aberration that pierced their hearts with shards of regret and concern.

"Who was in my room?" Fawn thundered, her voice heavy with indignation. "Don't I deserve any privacy in this house anymore!?"

Anna tried to speak, hoping to douse the flames of Fawn's anger, but the storm her daughter had unleashed stifled her efforts. Fawn, on the edge of her tolerance, was in no mood for feeble justifications. She demanded nothing less than the unadulterated truth from her parents.

"Obviously, this isn't my home anymore," she shouted, her eyes glistening with embryonic tears. "You obviously don't care what I think! You certainly didn't care about my feelings when you decided to sell the house! You didn't even bother to include me in the discussion!"

Brian held out his hands in a vain attempt to calm the brewing storm, but Fawn's anger refused to be tamed.

"No!" Her retort ricocheted through the room, her words a heartbreaking protest. Her eyes blazed with a mixture of rage and pain, a volcanic release of pent-up resentment toward her parents. Seeing their shell-shocked expressions, she felt her body shake, the tension building in her stomach.

"I deserve answers!" Fawn's voice wavered with raw emotion, her plea desperate. "I should have been involved in this decision! And why Montana, of all places?"

As Fawn unleashed her pent-up frustration, her body shook with a tumultuous release. "I don't even feel like a part of this family anymore! We used to make important decisions together!"

Anna tried to speak again, her voice filled with concern, but Fawn's anger rose, drowning out any attempt at reassurance.

"I have never felt so betrayed," Fawn declared, tears streaming down her cheeks. "Betrayed by my own parents!" Her words snapped, suggesting a rebellious alternative. "Maybe I should just forget about college and my dreams! Maybe I'll stay here in Wavecrest and let you go to Montana without me! I can find my own way, get a job, and rent an apartment!"

The threat of Fawn abandoning her dreams of attending Boston's prestigious art school struck her parents with a chilling realization. They exchanged glances, their expressions marked with stunned shock and deep regret.

"Fawn, you don't understand," Brian pleaded, his voice filled with desperation. "Please..."

But Fawn's heartache drowned out his words, her wounds too raw to be soothed. Tears streamed down her cheeks as her body shook with a whirlwind of grief and rage. She let out a wail, her voice stripped and bereft. "I don't care anymore. All I know is I can't stay in this house! It doesn't feel like home to me anymore!"

With her last words still echoing in the air, Fawn stormed out of the house, her steps heavy with anguish. She slammed the door behind her, cutting off any further pleas. Tears raced down her face as her sobs echoed into the night, and she walked down the familiar street feeling adrift and abandoned.

Her parents rushed onto the porch, their hearts pounding in sync with the rhythm of their growing fear as they watched Fawn disappear into the distance. Anna's voice, knotted with despair, cried, "Fawn, come back! Please! Let's talk about this!"

But Fawn remained steadfast, ignoring her mother's desperate pleas. Feeling neglected and abandoned, as if suddenly without a home, she wandered the darkened streets. Guided by intuition, her feet led her to the one place where she had always felt accepted and loved—a haven of comfort.

Minutes later, her body still convulsing with sobs, Fawn found herself standing on the familiar doorstep of her best friend's home, the only place she now recognized as safe.

In the comfort of Jessica's home, Teresa cleaned up the remains of an evening snack in the kitchen, leftovers from a meal enjoyed while watching the magnificent fireworks display from their front yard. In the adjoining living room, Tom was relaxing in his leather chair, engrossed in the news on the sleek flat-screen television.

The distinctive creak of the front door opening piqued Teresa's curiosity, and her heart fluttered in hopeful anticipation of Jessica's familiar laugh. Instead, haunting sobs filled the house, a heartbreaking sound that seeped into the foyer. A veil of worry covered her face as she quickened her pace toward the source of the distress, her mind filled with images of her daughter's potential despair.

Upon reaching the foyer, Teresa was confronted by the sight of Fawn, her face marred by a sea of grief, tears streaming down her cheeks, her posture burdened with the weight of unseen sorrow. Teresa's maternal instincts kicked in, her mind racing with alarming possibilities. What had happened to Fawn? Had she been injured? Had something spoiled her evening, or—chillingly—was it Jessica who was in trouble?

Driven by an irresistible maternal pull, Teresa wrapped her in a comforting embrace, offering her shoulder as a cushion for Fawn's trembling form. Though her voice wavered with concern, she reassured, "Honey, what's wrong?"

Overwhelmed by her intense sobs, Fawn clung to Teresa's maternal warmth, her raw emotions—anger, despair, heartbreak—pouring out unchecked.

Moments later, Tom rushed in from the living room, his face etched with surprise and concern. Upon seeing the harrowing scene, he stammered, "What the hell?" His concern for Fawn was palpable as he anxiously asked, "What's wrong with Fawn?"

Teresa cradled Fawn's head as if it were a precious gem and whispered, "I don't know." Her touch was light as a feather as she stroked Fawn's hair, her arms forming a protective fortress around the distraught girl.

With a gleam of concern in his eyes, Tom turned to Fawn. "Did someone hurt you, Fawn?" A spark of indignation flared within him at the mere thought of anyone harming his 'little girl'.

Struggling to speak through her sobs, Fawn tried to answer. Recognizing her difficulty, Teresa loosened her embrace, her hands resting on Fawn's shoulders, encouraging her to voice her distress.

"Honey, what happened? Did someone hurt you?" Her voice overflowed with genuine concern, her eyes searching Fawn's tear-filled eyes for answers.

Through her tears, Fawn managed a nod and a fragile "No."

"Okay, sweetheart," Teresa reassured, relief washing over her. She pulled Fawn back into her tender embrace, resuming the gentle strokes in her hair and soothing the tremors that shook her.

"Try to calm down. Everything will be okay," she whispered, wrapping Fawn in a blanket of comfort and love.

As she held Fawn in her nurturing embrace, rocking gently and whispering words of comfort, Teresa glanced at Tom, who stood nearby, his gaze reflecting their shared concern. Together, they stood as a beacon of support for Fawn, providing the strength and comfort she desperately sought in this storm of distress.

Slowly, the violent tremors that once shook Fawn's delicate frame began to subside, her anguished sobs giving way to a somber silence. The remnants of her trembling lingered like echoes of a tortured symphony as she pulled away from Teresa's enveloping warmth. Her arms hung at her sides, her pleading eyes—desperate and begging—sought refuge in Teresa's, her voice trembling with intermittent sobs.

"Can I... Can I..." Fawn trailed off, her words lost in the storm of emotions still swirling within her.

In response, Teresa's voice softened, as soothing as a lullaby. "Can you what, honey?"

Through a veil of tears, Fawn found the strength to utter her heartbreaking plea. "Can I... stay here?" Her words trembled under the weight of her despair. "I don't want to live at my house anymore," she confessed, her voice breaking in a cascade of renewed sobs.

Teresa's heart tightened at Fawn's tearful plea, her distress painfully visible. The impact of the unexpected sale of Fawn's home was evident in her words, adding to the strain already felt by Jessica. Teresa could only imagine the depth of the emotional storm Fawn was experiencing.

With eyes softened by empathy and a voice filled with sincere reassurance, she offered her comfort, and said, "Of course you can stay here, sweetheart. This is your home, too."

In Teresa's assurance, Fawn found the acceptance and love she desperately needed. Her eyes, a mirror of gratitude, met Teresa's; her tears, once symbols of despair, now mingled with relief. In Teresa's tender care and unequivocal affection, Fawn found her refuge, a place to call home amidst her chosen family.

As the storm of her emotions began to subside, Teresa led Fawn into the kitchen and helped her sit down at the kitchen table. Fawn sank into the chair like a ship trying to regain its course after a storm. Meanwhile, Tom entered the room, his fingers gently stroking Fawn's golden curls, a silent acknowledgment of her place in their family.

Armed with a comforting box of tissues, Teresa approached Fawn while Tom retrieved a bottle of beer from the refrigerator. Kneeling before the young woman slumped at the table, she dabbed away the tear streaks from Fawn's cheeks. As she saw the vulnerability on Fawn's tear-stained face, she was reminded of the countless times when Jessica and Fawn were little—the times when she tenderly nursed their wounds from their backyard adventures. These precious memories stirred within her and intertwined with the bittersweet emotions of the present, creating a mosaic of love, worry, and family ties.

In the span of a few precious moments, Fawn's emotional maelstrom subsided enough to allow words to form, no longer interrupted by her uncontrollable sobs. As Teresa's motherly ministrations ended, her gentle hands having wiped away the last of Fawn's

161

tears, Fawn lifted her gaze to meet Teresa's eyes, shining with heartfelt gratitude.

"Thank you, Mama," she whispered, her voice a rich tapestry of unspoken emotions.

Turning her back as she walked toward the counter, Teresa fought back her own tears, her heart aching at Fawn's dejected state. Over a dozen unforgettable years, Fawn had woven herself seamlessly into the intricate fabric of the Reese family. The friendship between Jessica and Fawn had blossomed, their bond evolving into something resilient and unbreakable. To Tom and Teresa, Fawn was like the sister they had always imagined for Jessica. Watching their little angels grow into striking young women had only deepened their love for both girls.

As she approached the counter, Teresa's eyes darted to Tom, who was sipping his beer nearby. She caught a brief flicker of anger in his eyes, fueled by his resentment toward Fawn's parents for their abrupt decision to uproot their lives. He was deeply troubled by the inevitable impact it would have on the girls, and his anger simmered beneath the surface, fueled by the escalating tension and grief he observed.

Though Tom often kept his emotions hidden, only revealing them to Teresa in quiet moments at night, she knew that his simmering anger was building to a boiling point—a testament to his deep-seated love for his daughter and Fawn.

Teresa always kept Fawn's favorite herbal tea in her kitchen, a small gesture that now took on profound meaning. Determined to calm Fawn's frayed nerves, she began to brew a soothing cup. As she filled the kettle, the creak of the front door reached her ears.

"Hey, I'm back!" Jessica's cheerful voice announced her return, quickly followed by the final click of the door closing.

With a gleam of joy in her eyes, she breezed into the kitchen and greeted her parents. However, the unexpected sight of Fawn sitting at the table, her eyes shadowed by emotional strain, immediately dampened Jessica's spirits.

"Oh, my God! Fawn!" Jessica's startled exclamation echoed through the room, her tone filled with shock at her best friend's distress.

Fawn managed a faint smile as she rose to meet Jessica, who stepped forward to give her a hug. The warmth and familiarity of her embrace anchored Fawn amidst the tumultuous sea of her emotions.

"What happened, Fawn?" Jessica asked, her voice thick with worry.

With a resigned nod, Fawn replied in a voice tinged with a bitter mixture of disgust and resentment. "It just became too much, Jess. I can't stand being home anymore."

Jessica's heart clenched as she saw Fawn's pain reflected in her haunted eyes, bringing a prickly sting to her own. She ached to share Fawn's tears, to let her own grief spill over, yet she summoned the strength to be a fortress, a beacon of unwavering support in this turbulent time.

The disturbing ordeal of strangers entering Fawn's home due to the realtor's visits had poisoned what had once been a place of love. Understanding that Fawn needed a refuge away from her own home, Jessica turned to her parents with a determined look, ready to use her most powerful weapon—her heartfelt plea.

"Can Fawn stay here? Please? Please? Please?" Jessica's question filled the room, her eyes wide and pleading, her voice saturated with heartfelt desire.

"Yes, sweetheart, she's staying here," Teresa confirmed, her lips curving into an indulgent smile. She was well aware of Jessica's ability to melt hearts with her bright blue eyes and innocent charm. "After I make Fawn's tea, I'll call her parents and let them know that she's safe and will be staying with us for the time being."

Jessica and Fawn exchanged silent glances, their eyes glistening with tears of relief. Armed with the knowledge that they would weather the storm ahead together under the same roof, they drew strength from each other as they prepared to face their uncertain future.

As the minutes ticked by, Tom found himself caught in a web of mounting irritation, a silent inferno burning within his usually calm demeanor. Each sip of bitter beer acted as a punctuation mark in his silent manifesto of resentment.

Fawn looked up, her eyes meeting those of Teresa and Tom. The sadness in her eyes was palpable, a reflection of the turmoil inside her. In a voice barely above a soft whisper, she murmured, "I'm sorry for being such a baby," her words tinged with embarrassment.

"It's okay, sweetheart. You have every right to feel overwhelmed," Teresa replied in her usual soothing tone, her words flowing naturally like the melody of a comforting lullaby.

However, Fawn's guilt-laden words proved to be the breaking point for Tom's fragile reserve. Like a volcanic eruption, the silent storm within him erupted, shattering the tranquility of the cozy kitchen.

"No... it's not okay," he growled, his voice like the rumble of an approaching storm. He slammed his beer bottle down on the counter, the sound echoing sharply, punctuating his declaration with force.

An electric wave of suspense swept through the room. Jessica and Fawn glanced at Tom in astonishment, their expressions reflecting the shock rippling through them. Teresa jerked, so surprised that her heart skipped a beat.

"What the hell were they thinking!?" Tom's words erupted, his frustration spilling over in an angry cascade. "Why are they selling the house now, of all times?"

He began to pace, each step echoing his escalating anger like a metronome ticking to the chaotic symphony of his emotions. "What made it so urgent that they didn't even consider Fawn's situation!? She's already struggling with the idea of leaving home for Boston! They could have at least waited until she was settled in school!"

Amid the storm of Tom's anger, Teresa tried to inject a thread of calm, her voice a velvet command. "Calm down, Tom," she pleaded.

"No, I'm not going to calm down, Terri," he retorted, his words bouncing defiantly off the kitchen walls. "I get it! Wavecrest is getting too expensive, and it's getting difficult for everyone! But why now?"

Teresa's features tensed, mirroring Tom's exasperation. "I don't know why," she confessed, her voice a mixture of irritation and disappointment.

Though filled with anger, Tom's words brought an odd comfort to Jessica and Fawn. It was a confirmation of their own frustrations, their shared outrage now expressed through Tom's tirade.

"All the time Brian and I went fishing, golfing, and bowling, he never once mentioned Montana!" Tom exploded, shaking his head as if to dispel his own disbelief. "What the hell is in Montana, anyway!?"

As Tom continued pacing, his footsteps a rhythm of anger, Teresa chose to silently affirm his sentiments. They both were painfully aware of how Fawn's ordeal was overshadowing the girls' precious last summer of unencumbered youth.

"I can't believe Brian would quit his job after twenty years and give up his pension! It just doesn't make sense!" Tom's incredulity reverberated throughout the room, his words tinged with an underlying layer of disbelief.

As his tempest began to die down, Tom leaned heavily against the counter. Sensing a moment of calm, Teresa spoke with a hint of determination. "I'll talk to them in the morning, honey. I'll find out what's going on."

Still seething from his outburst, Tom asked, "Do you want me to go with you?"

Teresa's eyes widened at the suggestion, aware of the potential for his emotions to reignite. In a cautious tone, she replied, "No, Tom. I'll go alone. I don't want any trouble with Brian and Anna."

The screech of the teapot, reminiscent of a miniature train pulling into the station, signaled the completion of a comforting ritual. Teresa attended to the call of the kettle, silencing it and allowing the warm bouquet of herbal essences to rise, enveloping the dimly lit kitchen in comfort.

Amidst the familiar furniture, Jessica and Fawn found solace in their old, well-worn seats, sinking into the cushions as if embracing a comforting memory. Jessica positioned herself next to Fawn, her presence a beacon of support as palpable as the warmth emanating from the tea.

"This should make you feel better, honey," Teresa crooned, placing the steaming cup in front of Fawn. Her voice wrapped around her like a warm blanket.

With a whisper of affection and a kiss on Fawn's head, Teresa retreated, her fingers gripping the cool edge of her phone. "I'm going to call your mom and let her know that you'll be staying with us for a while," she said, her tone calm and reassuring as she moved into the living room.

Leaning against the counter, Tom watched Fawn with gentle intensity. She seemed a subdued version of herself, her usual radiant energy tempered by a deep calm. Her golden hair lacked its usual luster, and her eyes, usually aglow with playful sparkle, appeared clouded and dull, the red rims silently testifying to her emotional turmoil.

His eyes lingered on her tear-stained face, stirring a paternal instinct within him. Noticing her slender shoulders sagging under the weight of her emotions, he watched as she cradled the warm teacup, seeking comfort in its warm embrace. His need to protect flared, forcing him to act.

Closing the distance, Tom lowered himself to her level and took her hands in his. "Fawn, I know you already know this, but I think it's worth repeating," he began, his voice enveloping her like an invisible hug. "This is your home, too. No matter where we are or where we live, our home will always be your home."

His heartfelt assurance hung in the air, as comforting as the smell of freshly baked bread. Fawn teetered on the brink of fresh tears, her heart pounding with the depth of love his words conveyed. He continued, "While you're in Boston, if you ever need us or want to come home, just let us know, and we'll make arrangements to get you here."

The resonance of his words washed over Fawn like warm summer waves, softening the sharp edges of her fears. Her heart swelled, a wellspring of love overflowing the rims of her eyes. Watching the tender scene, Jessica felt a familiar tug on her heartstrings.

"Do you understand what I'm saying, Fawn?" Tom nudged gently, his voice laced with playful sternness.

A glimmer of her characteristic sparkle returned to Fawn's eyes as she nodded.

Not content with a simple nod, Tom conjured up a playful game from their childhood. His fingers reached out to pinch Fawn's nose and joked, "I'm not giving your nose back until you tell me you understand."

Fawn's giggle bubbled up like a clear stream, an echo of innocent childhood memories that drew Jessica into its contagious joy. Amid the laughter that filled the kitchen, she managed to declare, "I understand, Papa," her voice drenched in appreciation and love.

"Okay, then," Tom replied playfully, pretending to straighten Fawn's nose before standing up, leaving a trail of giggles in his wake. He turned to Jessica with a wagging finger in mock warning. "You better watch out, too, or your nose is next," he said, barely suppressing a mischievous grin.

With Tom's departure, the kitchen was transformed into an intimate haven exclusively for Fawn and Jessica. A subtle sense of relief danced through the air, weaving tranquility into their surroundings. The enduring ties to Wavecrest now promised to cushion Fawn's spirit, assuring her that this cherished home would remain a constant anchor amid the shifting seas of her life, regardless of her journey to Boston.

For Jessica, the impending separation became more bearable, comforted by the knowledge that Fawn's return was only a matter of time. Their relationship, like an elastic band, would stretch and contract with the inevitable ebb and flow of life.

"That's good news, right?" Jessica's voice, tinged with optimism, broke the silence. Her words were like threads of hope, her smile a ray of sunshine piercing the clouds to illuminate Fawn's spirit. "Maybe next year, during our summer break, you can come here instead of going to Montana or staying in Boston."

But Fawn's answer was a heavy sigh, echoing from a darker place, burdened with the weight of her fatigue. "I'm not even sure I want to go to college anymore," she confessed, her vulnerability revealing the depth of her turmoil.

Jessica felt a cold wave of disbelief wash over her. Fawn's innate passion for art and her eager anticipation of Boston's prestigious art school made this sudden reluctance seem eerily out of character. She found herself adrift in her own sea of confusion, her expression reflecting her internal struggle as she grappled with Fawn's startling revelation.

Their conversation was interrupted by Teresa's return from the living room, her hand clutching the phone as she approached. Her eyes settled on Fawn, and seeing the girl's exhaustion, her voice softened. "I spoke to your mom, and she understands why you want to stay here. They want you to know that you have a home to return to whenever you're ready," she conveyed with reassuring assurance.

Fawn responded with a silent nod, her expression unreadable.

Noticing the weariness etched on Fawn's face, Teresa naturally slipped into her mother-ly role. "Why don't you take a nice, warm shower and try to get some sleep?" she suggested. "It'll help you feel better."

As Fawn looked up with gratitude in her eyes, Teresa continued with a nurturing touch, tucking a loose strand of hair behind Fawn's ear. "I'll find one of my nightgowns for you to wear to bed," she added, her tone combining practicality with warmth, a comforting presence in the swirl of emotions.

"Okay, Mama," Fawn replied, her voice filled with emotion as she rose wearily from the table.

Prompted by this, Jessica also stood up, a question on her lips. "Do you want to sleep in my room or in the guest room?"

Fawn offered Jessica a faint smile, a soft glow against her exhaustion, and said, "Your room, of course." The simple words carried the weight of treasured memories of their past sleepovers, echoing a safe haven from her churning emotions.

Jessica's smile mirrored Fawn's, nostalgic yet comforting. Despite the emotional up-heaval that had overtaken their Fourth of July, this moment felt like a lighthouse guiding them through the storm. As Fawn headed to Jessica's room, Jessica felt a poignant mixture of empathy and sadness fill her. Their sisterly bond, intertwined with friendship and shared memories, would serve as their compass through the difficult times ahead.

Leaving the kitchen, Jessica made her way to the living room, seeking solace in its cozy confines. She sank into the sofa, its familiar folds offering a temporary haven amidst the tumult of emotions swirling within her. Wrapped in the fabric's embrace, her heart felt heavy with the seismic reverberations of the night's events. In the silence, punctuated only by the subtle hum of her breathing, she awaited Fawn's return from the soothing comfort of the shower.

Meanwhile, Tom, the stoic beacon of her family, eased himself out of the leather chair. His face showed the fatigue of the night, a silent testament to the emotional storm that had swept through their lives. As he shuffled past Jessica, he leaned in to plant a soft, lingering kiss on the top of her head.

"Good night, baby girl. Try to get some sleep," he whispered, his words a soothing breeze in the tension of the summer night.

Jessica lifted her head to meet her father's gaze. Her eyes, bright with gratitude and love, reflected the warmth of his gesture. "Good night, Daddy," she replied, her voice carrying the tender intimacy of their shared moment.

In the quiet aftermath of Tom's departure, Teresa walked down the hallway clutching a nightgown—a promise of comfort for Fawn. As she neared Jessica's bedroom, she noticed her daughter sitting on the couch, her petite form blending into the canvas of the night. She paused, silhouetted in the doorway.

"It's awfully late, sweetheart. I think it's time for you to go to bed," she suggested, her voice a soft melody of concern echoing through the quiet room.

Jessica nodded, a tired smile tugging at her lips—an attempt to lighten the heaviness of the evening. "I will, Mom. I just want to take a shower first. I feel gross."

Acknowledging this with a warm, understanding smile, Teresa continued to Jessica's room. With careful reverence, she unfolded the nightgown and placed it on the bed. This simple act was her way of offering comfort during this difficult time, a silent reassurance that she and Tom were committed to supporting Fawn through both happy times and family hardships.

As the silence of the house deepened, the sound of the shower shutting off echoed, announcing Fawn's departure from the bathroom. The soft patter of her footsteps, light as summer rain on the windowpanes, signaled her arrival in the sanctity of the bedroom.

With empathetic wisdom, Jessica decided to stay in the living room a little longer, giving Fawn a few precious moments to dry off and slip into her nightgown. When she felt that enough time had passed, she left the solitude of the living room and entered her bedroom.

There, she found Fawn sitting on the bed, wrapped in Teresa's light blue nightgown—a cocoon of warmth and familiarity. Her hair, damp from the shower, lay like a dark curtain against her shoulders. A surge of playful energy pulsed through Jessica, a bubbling well of joy seeking release, causing her to flop down on the bed beside her.

"Hi, Mom," Jessica teased, her eyes twinkling with mischief as they danced in the dim light. Her joke was a lighthearted nod to Fawn wearing one of Teresa's nightgowns, adding a whimsical twist to the evening.

Fawn met Jessica's teasing with a playful retort of her own. "Shut up, you," she laughed, giving Jessica a light shove.

"No, you shut up," Jessica volleyed back, barely holding back her laughter.

"No, you shut up," Fawn shot back, the mock seriousness in her voice belied by the twinkle in her eyes.

"No, you shut up," Jessica replied, chuckling as she exaggerated her seriousness to match Fawn's playful tone.

The cheerful symphony swept through the room, chasing away the lingering shadows of the night and infusing the space with a lightness that lifted their spirits. Jessica was thrilled to see the familiar spark in Fawn's eyes, a beacon of hope amidst life's uncertainties.

After a few more rounds of their playful exchange, Fawn decided to end their banter. With a faux stern expression and a wag of her finger, she scolded, "Hey! That's no way to talk to your mother!"

Jessica burst out laughing, her eyes rolling playfully in response to Fawn's theatrical antics. Their jovial echoes filled the room, reflecting the cherished play of their shared history and deep companionship. This nostalgic dance of camaraderie and love stood as a testament to the resilience of their friendship, always able to revive their spirits and draw their souls closer.

After their laughter faded to a whisper, Jessica stirred from the comforting confines of the bed and walked to her dresser to retrieve her nightwear.

"I'm going to take a shower," she announced, her voice still carrying the sweet cadence of the lingering laughter. "I'll only be a few minutes."

"Okay," Fawn replied, her face illuminated by the tender afterglow of their laughter, a spark of joy still dancing in her eyes.

The shower in the bathroom welcomed Jessica with open arms as she stepped under the warm cascade. Each drop of water felt like a gentle kiss on her skin, washing away the turmoil. She closed her eyes and let the soothing melody of the water envelop her, easing both body and mind. As the tensions ebbed, she surrendered to the comforting serenade, allowing the memories of the evening to drift away like leaves on a gentle stream.

Exhaustion, an uninvited guest that had lingered in the shadows, washed over her in gentle waves, lulling her into the embrace of sleep. After drying off, Jessica slipped into her soft nightclothes, finding comfort in their familiar touch. She then quietly made her way back to the bedroom, the muted silence of the house enveloping her like a beloved childhood blanket.

Upon re-entering the room, Jessica was greeted by the sight of Fawn, a peaceful figure nestled under the soft warmth of the blanket. Sleep had quickly claimed her, her breathing forming a soft, rhythmic melody. She had succumbed to the deep embrace of rest as effortlessly as a leaf drifting onto still water.

With the stealth of a midnight breeze, Jessica found her place on the bed, carefully weaving herself into the inviting comfort without disturbing Fawn's peaceful sleep. She pulled the blanket around her, pulling it up to her chin, its warmth whispering lullabies of comfort. Reaching out, she turned off the bedside lamp, plunging the room into sacred darkness, broken only by the faint glow of streetlights filtering through the curtains.

The dim light lent a surreal charm to the star-shaped stickers adorning the ceiling, their subtle glow mirroring the infinite expanse of the night sky. Amid the soothing symphony of nocturnal whispers and the soothing ballet of shadows, Jessica gave in to the siren song of sleep, drifting into a realm where dreams spun their fanciful tales.

In this land of dreams, life was simpler, stripped of its complexities, untouched by the harsh brushstrokes of reality. Here, Jessica found the solace she sought, cradled in the ethereal embrace of her beloved Ethan, a serene escape from the troubles of the waking world.

As the house settled into a quiet sanctuary, Teresa's footsteps were a soft whisper as she meandered through the dimly lit rooms. Each light she turned off marked the end of a tender chapter, her movements practiced and graceful. The air hummed with gentle nostalgia, memories echoing in the corners and along the well-worn paths of family life.

Arriving at the doorway of Jessica's bedroom, she pushed the door open with the lightest of touches, her heart reaching out to make sure the girls were at peace. The sight that greeted her was a tableau of peace and affection: Fawn and Jessica nestled snugly under the covers, their faces serene, lost in the enchanted realm of dreams. A soft, loving smile bloomed on Teresa's face, her eyes misting with warmth, love, and a hint of wistful longing.

Stepping into the room, Teresa approached Fawn's side of the bed with a dance of maternal grace. Her heart swelled with a deep, all-encompassing love as she gazed upon the young woman before her. A flood of memories washed over her, a river of time carrying images of Fawn growing from a little girl into the extraordinary young woman she was now. With a touch as gentle as a butterfly's wing, Teresa rearranged the blanket, making sure Fawn was tucked in and warm. Her hands traced a loving routine familiar from countless sleepovers past.

Moving to Jessica's side, Teresa repeated those gentle, loving actions, her hands weaving a lullaby of affection as she tucked her daughter in. The soft brush of her lips against Jessica's forehead was a kiss steeped in years of treasured moments.

A pang of bittersweet emotion swept through her, the tenderness tinged with the looming shadow of change. The silent specter of her daughter's impending departure for college hung in the air, compounding Teresa's sense of loss. The thought of missing the sparkle in Jessica's bright blue eyes and the warmth of her infectious laugh unleashed a wave of sadness. Teresa paused, her soul drinking in the sight of the sleeping girls, storing this precious image in the deepest chambers of her heart.

With tiptoe grace, Teresa left the room, the door closing softly behind her, leaving a pang of sadness in its wake. Her heart trembled at the thought of the girls' impending departure, but with a determined inner quiver, she steeled herself against the tide of emotions she wasn't ready to face.

In her bedroom, she found Tom sprawled on the bed, half-submerged in the realm of sleep, his presence a steady beacon in the shifting sands of life. As Teresa settled beside him, a wave of apprehension and uncertainty washed over her like a storm cloud looming on the horizon. She looked into Tom's eyes and whispered, her voice filled with delicate and profound concern. "Tom, we really have to make a decision soon. For the sake of the girls."

Tom met her gaze, his expression a tapestry of concern woven with the weight of their dilemma.

"I know," he murmured, his voice heavy with the gravity of their discussions about selling their home. Each syllable was a stone in a path leading to inevitable changes, changes that would alter the landscape of their family life. In that shared look, they captured a universe of love, worry, responsibility, and the intricate dance of a marriage facing the future with courage and devotion as deep as their souls.

# Chapter 18

-------------------------------------------------------------

In the early hours of Saturday morning, the coastal town of Wavecrest was shrouded in a mist that lent a mystical quality to its familiar streets. Teresa drove through the fog to 501 Oceanside Ave—the house where Fawn and her parents had woven their lives together. A stark "For Sale" sign, planted among cheerful primroses, was a harsh reminder of the purpose of Teresa's visit. A sense of foreboding, uncharacteristic of the festive Fourth of July spirit, clung to her like a shadow.

As she exited her car, Teresa's resolve steadied her as she approached the front door. Her hand trembled slightly, pulsing with her heartbeat as she rang the doorbell.

Anna, dressed in a pink robe and visibly distraught, answered the door. Her hazel eyes reflected turmoil, and her tear-streaked cheeks spoke volumes of her emotional strain. When Teresa saw her friend's tired face, a wave of compassion washed over her. She pulled Anna into a warm hug, the closeness of their embrace reflecting the deep bond between their families, a bond rooted in the enduring friendship of their daughters, Jessica and Fawn.

"Hi, Terri," Anna's voice quivered as she greeted Teresa.

"Hi, Anna. Is Brian here?" Teresa asked, stepping into a home that felt both familiar and alien under the circumstances.

"He's in the living room," Anna replied, her words tinged with anxiety.

As they walked toward the living room, Anna tried to maintain a semblance of normalcy amid the uncertainty. "Can I get you a cup of coffee or tea?" But Teresa's mind was clouded by the weighty discussion that lay ahead, her stomach knotted with apprehension. "No, thank you," she replied, her voice betraying her deep concern.

"Okay," Anna replied, her single word heavy with unspoken emotion. She led Teresa into the living room, each step heavy with the complexities of change and uncertainty.

Teresa took a seat on the embracing leather of the couch, her eyes settling on Brian. He hunched forward, his stocky frame unable to hide the palpable worry creasing his face. The muted light in the room highlighted the sparse strands of his blond hair, and his eyes, visible behind wire-rimmed glasses, were filled with a father's concern. Dressed in a gray t-shirt and green cargo shorts, he tried to put on a casual front, but the tension in his posture betrayed his true feelings.

His voice was a low hum of sorrow as he addressed her. "Hi, Terri. Thanks for coming by. How is Fawn? Is she okay?" Each word carried an undercurrent of dread, the simple question heavy with unspoken fears.

"She's holding up as well as she can under the circumstances. I checked on the girls before I left, and they were still sound asleep," she replied, offering a brief respite from Brian and Anna's worried expressions. But her voice carried a weight of its own as she continued, "But she's also confused, heartbroken, and overwhelmed." Her frankness pierced the brief silence like a shard of glass breaking still water.

Brian and Anna visibly flinched at her words, their heads bowed in silent acknowledgment of their daughter's pain. Anna sat down next to Brian, her movements heavy with maternal anguish. Across from them, Teresa nestled into the soft contours of an armchair, steeling herself for the difficult conversation that would unfold in this room.

Grief clouded Brian's eyes as he met Teresa's gaze, his voice low and burdened. "Terri, this isn't what we wanted. We had no choice but to put the house on the market."

Confusion furrowed Teresa's brow. "What do you mean, you had no choice?"

Taken aback, Brian replied with a hint of surprise. "Haven't you heard? Atlas is closing in September. One hundred and forty-six employees will be laid off, and I'm one of them."

Teresa's breath caught in her throat, disbelief washed over her. "My God, no! We heard some rumors, but we thought that was all they were—just rumors."

"So did we," Brian admitted, bitterness coloring his usual demeanor. "That was until a few months ago when management announced they were closing the plant on the first of September."

Anna's eyes locked on Teresa, who silently confirmed Brian's words with a nod that carried the full weight of their grim reality.

"Fortunately," Brian continued, trying to find a glimmer of hope in the grim situation, "they offered me the same position at their plant in Montana."

As understanding crept into Teresa's expression, her features softened. "Well, that explains a lot."

"We didn't have a choice," Brian insisted, his voice punctuated by restlessness. "It was either accept the offer or face unemployment."

Teresa replied with a sympathetic nod. "My God, guys. We had no idea."

"Believe me," Anna added, her voice thick with emotion, "we're not happy about this at all. We love Wavecrest. But we didn't have another option."

Brian leaned forward, frustration shadowing his features. "After I found out about the plant closing, I tried everything to find another job. I sent out resumes, went on interviews—anything I could think of."

Teresa listened intently, her eyes reflecting deep understanding.

"But it was hopeless," Brian continued, a note of defeat in his voice. "No one would hire me. I was 'too old' or 'overqualified'. They seem to prefer hiring younger, less experienced people to save money. It's a harsh reality, Terri, but it's what I faced."

Teresa reached out and put a comforting hand on Brian's. "I'm so sorry, Brian. That must have been incredibly difficult." She hesitated for a moment before asking another question that lingered in her mind. "But what I don't understand is why you kept this from Fawn?"

Brian nodded, a weight on his face as he thought about their situation. "We didn't tell Fawn because she was still in school. We wanted to shield her from the stress so she could focus on her grades. But after she graduated, reality set in. Despite my best efforts, I couldn't find a job that would pay the salary we needed to maintain our life in Wavecrest. That's when I realized we had no choice but to plan for the move to Montana."

"We thought we were protecting her by not telling her everything right away," Anna added.

"We wanted to wait until the end of the summer," Brian replied, his voice filled with regret. "We didn't want to spoil her last summer here at Wavecrest. Our plan was to tell her before she left for Boston, so she wouldn't have to carry this burden during what should have been a carefree time."

Anna's voice trailed off as she continued, "Had we known in March that Atlas was closing, we might have found other ways to pay for Fawn's tuition or considered a less expensive school."

Brian's voice carried a note of resignation. "We've already spent most of our savings on Fawn's first year of college and art school. I can't afford to be unemployed now."

The room fell into a heavy silence, each person lost in their own thoughts, contemplating the complexities and challenges of the situation they faced.

"Clearly, we handled this all wrong. We should have been open from the beginning," Brian admitted, his voice reflecting a moment of realization.

"We feel like the worst parents right now," Anna added, her voice filled with guilt.

"No, Anna," Teresa reassured her. "You're not bad parents. You've raised an incredible daughter, and you should be proud of her. What you need to do now is sit down with her and explain everything."

Brian and Anna nodded, their expressions somber. "We want to," Brian said, "but I don't think Fawn is ready to listen."

"Give her some time," Teresa advised. " She's getting plenty of love and support at our house. She just needs time to process everything."

"Thank you, Terri," Anna said, her voice filled with gratitude.

"Yes, thank you," Brian echoed. "You and Tom have been incredible friends to us, and we'll always be grateful for the love and care you've shown Fawn."

With emotion still palpable in the room, Teresa finally relented to the earlier offer. "I could really use that cup of coffee now."

The morning sun filtered through Jessica's bedroom curtains, gently coaxing Fawn from the depths of sleep. Her eyelids fluttered open, slowly peeling back the veil of dreams to reveal the crisp clarity of day. The vanity across the room caught her eye, its mirror splintering the sunlight into a playful kaleidoscope. Within these walls, she found herself cradled in a fortress of affection and peace, a stark contrast to the unsettling bustle of strangers that now haunted her home.

Wrapped in the tender embrace of the cozy blanket, Fawn savored the warmth and resisted the inevitable start of the day. Memories of the previous night unfolded in her mind—the emotional turmoil, her mind buckling under its weight, and then being wrapped in the familial warmth of Jessica's parents. Their reassurances from last night echoed in her heart; their home was her home, too, their presence a constant beacon through her stormy seas. Her fondness for Jessica's parents, always deep, was now strengthened by their unwavering support and strength.

With determination running through her mind, Fawn sat up, letting the blanket fall away as she welcomed the day. Her eyes settled on Jessica, who lay wrapped in a nest of pillows and blankets, only strands of her hair fluttering with each soft breath. Fawn's heart swelled with love for her friend; their bond was not just friendship, but kinship—woven from laughter, tears, and an unspoken understanding that words could never fully express.

A pang of sadness tinged Fawn's thoughts as she contemplated the impending separation that college would bring. Jessica, her unwavering pillar of support, would soon be more than a heartbeat away. The prospect of navigating life's complexities without her friend's reassuring presence cast an unfamiliar, intimidating shadow. But she pushed those concerns aside for another time, keeping her feet firmly planted in the present. With careful movements, she swung her legs over the side of the bed and stepped onto the floor, tiptoeing out of the bedroom to freshen up for the day ahead.

After completing her morning routine, Fawn followed the well-worn path to the kitchen, her steps echoing memories of countless shared breakfasts, lazy weekend brunches, and comforting hot chocolates on chilly evenings. The heart of Jessica's home held a magnetic pull, beckoning her with the promise of familiar aromas, warm smiles, and shared stories. Her connection to this place extended beyond its walls; it was woven into the bonds she had forged, the memories she had created, and the love that permeated every corner of her second home.

As Fawn walked down the hallway, she was enveloped in a whirlwind of curiosity and bewilderment. The usually bustling household, typically vibrant with Jessica's parents' animated presence on a Saturday morning, was uncharacteristically quiet. Upon entering the kitchen, Fawn realized her suspicions were correct—the usual familial faces were absent from the room. It seemed as if the house, usually an island of warmth and activity, was now inhabited solely by her and Jessica.

Her eyes swept across the kitchen and settled on a note placed on the table. Intrigue tightened her chest as she reached for it, her heart pounding with anticipation. The hand-scrawled words read: "At Brian and Anna's. Be back soon. Love, Mom." A wave of cautious optimism washed over Fawn, sparking hope that Jessica's mother might persuade her parents to reconsider their decision to sell their beloved home.

The call of hunger grew louder in Fawn's stomach, diverting her thoughts from the quiet house to her need for a comforting breakfast. Memories of her last meal at the boardwalk burger stand lingered in her mind. A sudden craving for the warm taste of eggs ignited within her, and she decided that making an omelet would perfectly satisfy her morning appetite.

She purposefully approached the refrigerator and pulled open the door, letting the cool light spill out. She pulled out a carton of eggs, the sight of them nestled together, bringing a smile to her lips. Seeing that there were enough eggs for two omelets, Fawn felt a quiet joy, ready to extend this morning's kindness to Jessica as well. With renewed energy, Fawn gathered what she needed, moving around the kitchen with the confidence of someone who found joy in the art of cooking.

As the butter hissed against the hot pan, the kitchen filled with the inviting aroma of cooking, promising delicious results. Before she could fully immerse herself in her culinary task, Fawn was drawn to the coffee maker by the prospect of a freshly brewed cup. Lifting the lid, she found the grounds already measured into the filter, a thoughtful preparation by Teresa that touched her deeply. It was another gesture that wove her into the family tapestry, a small act of inclusion that felt like a warm embrace.

With the coffee maker gurgling in the background, Fawn concentrated on preparing breakfast. She whisked the eggs until they blended smoothly, their yellow hues swirling into a creamy consistency. She carefully poured them onto the hot skillet, where they greeted the butter with a satisfying sizzle.

As she tended to both the coffee and the omelet, sounds from the adjoining bathroom signaled Jessica's awakening. The familiar routine of her friend stirring to life brought a smile to Fawn's face; soon, Jessica would join her, completing their duo for the cherished morning symphony, each slipping seamlessly into their role in their shared ritual.

Within minutes, Jessica sauntered into the kitchen, dressed in a vintage pink crop top and loose-fitting sweats that draped comfortably over her figure. The gentle embrace of sleep still lingered at the corners of her bright blue eyes, where the remnants of dreams hadn't quite faded.

At the sight of Fawn standing at the kitchen counter, draped in the silk of Teresa's nightgown, Jessica's eyes lit up with a tenderness that rivaled the whisper of a lullaby. The sight of Fawn, looking more like herself than the fragmented soul of the night before, flooded Jessica with a profound sense of relief. It was like watching dawn break over a restless sea, calming the turbulent waves that had surged through the darkness.

Jessica closed the distance between them with a grace that seemed to defy the morning's sluggishness, watching as Fawn sprinkled cheddar cheese over the sizzling omelet with precision and care. Each flake fell like a golden note, enhancing the melody of their shared morning ritual.

Side by side, they basked in the ease born of years of kinship. A soft smile graced Jessica's lips as she leaned into Fawn with a playful nudge—an instinctive gesture as natural as the rhythm of the waves on the shore.

Fawn turned to her friend, mirroring the spontaneous dance of camaraderie. Even without her usual artistic streaks of eyeliner, Fawn's eyes still danced with a characteristic sparkle of playfulness, though tempered by traces of weariness. Jessica felt a warmth bloom within her at the sight—the resilient spirit she cherished was manifesting in full force.

In a seamless choreography that only true friends could master, Fawn flipped one half of the omelet over the other while Jessica grabbed two coffee cups from the cupboard.

"Would you like an omelet, Jess?" Fawn asked, her voice filled with tenderness.

Jessica paused, savoring the melody of scents that enveloped the kitchen. Her grin widened in silent affirmation, eliciting a laugh from Fawn—a melody as sweet as their morning feast.

"Uh-huh," she finally replied, her voice light with pure satisfaction as she poured rich coffee into both cups.

"This one is yours, then. It's just the way you like it," Fawn declared, her joy evident as she presented her first culinary creation to her dearest friend.

The warmth that coursed through Jessica at that simple gesture was more comforting than any heat from the coffee. As she took her seat, her gaze lingered on Fawn's deft hands as they guided the omelet onto a plate, a sight that deepened her appreciation for their friendship.

With a mixture of pride and humility, Fawn placed the plate in front of Jessica, each movement deliberate and gentle. "I hope you like it," she murmured, her voice carrying the lightness of a hopeful breeze.

Jessica's smile mirrored Fawn's, an exchange as familiar and comforting as their sisterly bond. Confident in Fawn's culinary skills, she looked forward to another treasured breakfast with her best friend.

As she savored the first burst of flavor from her omelet, Jessica's attention shifted to an unattended note left on the table. Recognizing her mother's distinctive handwriting, she felt a surge of curiosity as each word unfolded like a delicate petal, revealing the reason for her absence.

In the quiet kitchen, Fawn's voice cut through the silence, soothing and familiar as the coastal breeze. "So, what's the plan for you and Ethan today?" she asked, her focus momentarily shifting from the eggs she was gently cracking into a bowl.

"We're going to the beach," Jessica replied, her voice full of excitement, but muffled by a mouthful of omelet. Without missing a beat, she added, "And you're coming with us."

Fawn paused, an egg half cracked in her hand, as a wave of reluctance washed over her. The thought of being a third wheel to Jessica and Ethan's blossoming romance weighed heavily.

"No," she murmured, her hesitation seeping into her tone. "You two should have some time alone. I don't want to intrude."

Jessica's reassurance came quickly, her voice bright and comforting. "You're not intruding, Fawn. You're my best friend, and it's important to me that you're here. Besides, after last night, a day at the beach will do wonders for you," she insisted, her tone wrapping around Fawn like a comforting blanket.

Fawn knew the beach was her sanctuary, a place where worries melted away with the rhythmic crash of the waves and the cries of the seagulls. Still, she hesitated, not wanting to intrude on their intimate moments. "Are you sure?" she asked, looking for confirmation.

With an eye roll of playful annoyance and an affectionate toss of her hair, Jessica replied, "Uh, duh!" Her tone was teasing, yet underscored with a sincerity that couldn't be doubted.

Laughter erupted from Fawn, filling the kitchen as she resumed her task and cracked another egg with renewed vigor. In Jessica, Fawn had found more than a friend; she had an unwavering ally, a beacon of support, and a companion who painted vibrant colors on the canvas of her life.

In the soft morning light, Fawn carefully transferred her perfectly cooked omelet to her plate, the aroma of melted cheese and herbs rising to greet her. She took a seat across from Jessica at the table, a humble arena where their life stories often intertwined. As they savored the warmth of their meal in companionable silence, a storm of concern stirred beneath Jessica's calm exterior.

The echo of Fawn's impassioned declaration to forsake her college dreams still reverberated within Jessica's mind. The idea of Fawn abandoning academia—and, with it, her artistic ambitions—sent shivers down her spine. Torn between preserving the peace of their morning and addressing this critical crossroads, Jessica ventured forth with delicate intention.

"You weren't serious about not going to college, were you?" Jessica asked, her voice carrying a soft cadence of concern.

The weighty question hung in the air, thickening the silence, until Fawn finally answered. Keeping her eyes on her plate, she murmured, "I don't want to talk about it," her words tinged with uncertainty.

Respecting Fawn's reluctance, but unwilling to let the matter drop, Jessica tried a different tactic. She threw out a provocative challenge, hoping to provoke some reevaluation in Fawn. "Okay, but if you're not going to college, then I'm not going either," she declared with a hint of defiance.

Fawn's eyes snapped up to meet Jessica's determined gaze. Compelled to protect her friend from the fallout of her own turmoil, she replied with equal determination, "You're going to college, Jess." Her eyebrow arched in a mixture of concern and silent challenge.

With the heavy topic temporarily set aside, Jessica steered their conversation toward more personal matters. As she nibbled on the last bites of her breakfast, she shared a confession that had been weighing on her heart. "You know," she began hesitantly, "if Ethan asked me to go back to Pine Haven with him... I'd drop out of college in a heartbeat."

Fawn took in Jessica's revelation with a mixture of sadness and understanding. She recognized the depth of Jessica's feelings for Ethan and knew the gravity of her words.

"I know you would... and I wouldn't blame you if you did," she replied, her voice a soothing echo of empathy. Reiterating her earlier sentiment, Fawn gently but firmly urged, "That's exactly why you should spend as much time with him as possible—and don't worry about me."

However, Jessica's determination to have Fawn join them on the beach remained unshaken—a testament to the strength of their bond.

"No way," she said firmly. " I want to spend as much time as I can with you, too." Her words were not just a statement of intent, but a pledge to stand together through all of life's changes, affirming the unbreakable nature of their friendship.

The quiet veil of their morning banter was abruptly shattered by the grating creak of the front door swinging open. Both girls turned to face the sound and saw Teresa step into the foyer, a suitcase at her feet.

Hope flashed in Fawn's eyes as she immediately asked, "Did they change their mind about selling the house?"

Treading the path of compassion, Teresa tempered her answer with a mixture of reassurance and regret. "No, honey, they didn't."

Fawn felt the sting of disappointment; the waves of grief threatened to drown her as the harsh reality of abandoning her beloved home resurfaced. She fought to hold on to a fading glimmer of hope that Teresa could somehow influence her parents' decision.

Observing Fawn's desolation, Teresa felt a deep empathy. She understood that revealing the true reasons behind her parents' decision to sell the house might ease some of Fawn's pain. However, she also felt that it wasn't her place to reveal the truths that should rightfully come from Brian and Anna. This was a conversation that needed to happen between Fawn and her parents.

After placing her purse on the kitchen counter, Teresa joined the girls at the table. She looked at Fawn with a gentle gaze and spoke softly, "Fawn, there's more to this situation than you know, and it's important that you talk to your mom and dad."

Fawn's eyes, swirling with confusion and pain, met Teresa's. "What do you mean?" she asked. "What did they tell you?"

Teresa maintained a steady tone, firm yet compassionate. "That's a conversation you need to have with your parents, sweetheart. Believe me, they regret not being open with you sooner."

Fawn's frustration began to mix with curiosity. What could be so important that her parents would keep it from her? Her initial anger gave way to a deeper concern. Teresa then added, "You really need to talk to them. But only when you feel you're ready."

The kitchen fell into a muted silence as Fawn took in Teresa's advice, her heart heavy with an undefined worry. "Okay, Mama. I will," she replied.

Teresa reached out, her affection palpable as she brushed back a stray strand of Fawn's hair. "In the meantime, I brought back some of your clothes and personal items to make you feel more at home here," she cooed, her voice a soothing balm amidst the storm.

"Thank you," Fawn whispered, a grateful smile blooming as she basked in the warmth of her second mother's thoughtfulness.

As Teresa exited, leaving the kitchen to its solemnity, a silent question lingered in the air, weaving itself into the fabric of the room: What was the unspoken truth behind Fawn's parents' decision to sell their home? This unfinished melody hung between Fawn and Jessica, a shared mystery reflected in their exchanged glances.

The kitchen, bathed in the blush of morning light, cradled the girls in its tender embrace as they absorbed the aftermath of Teresa's departure. The unspoken question of Fawn's parents' motives for selling their home lingered with them, an uninvited phantom haunting their quiet breakfast nook.

In this quiet bubble of uncertainty, Jessica allowed a reassuring smile to soften her features. Her hand reached out to cover Fawn's, providing a warm island amidst the cool veneer of the table. That touch acted as a catalyst, gently coaxing words into the ocean of their silence.

"Hey," Jessica murmured, her voice a soothing melody that broke the silence and carried the weight of the morning with effortless elegance. "How about we go to my room? I'll open up one of my drawers for you... you know, for your clothes that Mom brought back."

Fawn's eyes met Jessica's, the suggestion a delicate lifeline that pulled her away from her worries. Her smile unfolded, piercing the darkness of anxiety like the first rays of sunshine through a gathering storm.

"Okay, Jess. That sounds good," she agreed, her voice a soft melody of affirmation.

They left the kitchen table and walked down the hall to Jessica's bedroom. There, they moved into the familiar rhythm of organizing a drawer, each action reinforcing the bonds of their shared life.

As she watched Jessica's methodical movements, Fawn broke the silence with a tremor in her voice. "Jess," she began, fidgeting with her shirt, the fabric twisting under her nervous fingers. "About last night... I hope you won't... I mean, please don't tell Ethan. It's just so embarrassing."

Jessica paused and turned to Fawn with a reassuring grip on her shoulders. " I wasn't going to tell Ethan—or anyone else, for that matter. This stays in the family. It's yours to share if you want to, not mine," she replied, her voice a mixture of understanding and determination.

Fawn's tension visibly eased under Jessica's compassionate touch, and a sigh of relief escaped her. "Thank you, Jess," she exhaled, a small smile of relief appearing on her face.

"You're welcome, girlfriend," Jessica murmured, turning her attention back to the drawer that was becoming more than just storage space; it was a testament to their friendship.

The room hummed with the soft whisper of the fabric shifting, each fold revealing stories captured within. Jessica paused and gave Fawn a reassuring look before excusing herself to the bathroom.

"I'm going to take a shower," she announced, her voice a soothing presence in the thick air. "You can take yours when I'm done."

As the sound of the shower filled the house, Fawn's fingers danced across the fabric of her past. Each garment was like an age-old diary, its folds marking brave strides toward acceptance. She pulled each piece from the suitcase, stirring familiar echoes and coaxing a soft smile onto her lips. Nestled within were her favored blouses and tees, each thread woven with fragments of her past. Deeper in the suitcase, her beloved bikinis hinted at future sun-drenched beach days, whispering tales of laughter and sand-kissed skin.

The familiarity of these clothes provided a comforting rhythm. Amidst the swirl of emotions and an uncertain future, they served as steadfast anchors. Their soft cotton and smooth silk whispered quiet assurances that she was still Fawn—the beach lover, the cherished friend, the young woman standing on the precipice of limitless possibilities.

As Fawn tucked the last of her wardrobe into Jessica's drawer, the symphony of the shower stopped. She pushed the empty suitcase into a quiet corner and sat on the edge of Jessica's bed. The air filled with anticipation as the bathroom door creaked open.

Jessica emerged, her hair a dark river cascading over her shoulders, framing her vibrant bikini. A towel slung over her shoulder added a touch of comic grandeur, like a faux cape. Fawn laughed as she watched Jessica's theatrical attempts to towel dry her hair, her playful expression lighting up the room like dappled sunlight through leaves.

After her lively performance, Jessica dismissed the towel with a graceful flick of her wrist. She strolled to the vanity and paused, her fingers dancing over the round-framed sunglasses before lifting them with theatrical flair. With a smooth motion, she placed them on her nose and turned to face Fawn.

Striking a playful pose, she flashed a mischievous grin. "How do I look?" she asked, her expression inviting a moment of shared amusement.

A delighted laugh sparkled in Fawn's eyes as she shook her head, their camaraderie enriching her response. "You look adorable," she confessed, her voice brimming with affection. Within the welcoming walls of Jessica's room, their shared fears seemed to fade, becoming more bearable by the soft glow of their enduring bond.

Fawn's fingers danced over the neatly folded fabrics, settling on a bikini drenched in soft pinks and lavenders.

"I put a clean towel on the rack for you," Jessica called from across the room as she adjusted the straps of her bikini.

Fawn's response was a gentle smile of gratitude as she slipped into the bathroom, leaving Jessica in the comforting hush of her room.

In this familiar haven, Jessica sat at her vanity, her fingers weaving through the dark waves of her hair with a well-worn brush. The tranquil silence was punctuated by the insistent buzz of her cell phone, which stirred excitement within her. As she reached for the phone, her heart pounded in anticipation, hoping it would be Ethan on the other end.

Joy surged through her when Ethan's name appeared on the screen. She flipped open the message, her pulse quickening with excitement. "I'm on my way, babe. Be there in a few," it read, sending a tremor of delight through her. With his impending arrival whispering excitement into her morning, Jessica resumed her grooming with renewed vigor, the brush gliding effortlessly through the mahogany waves of her hair.

As she drew a smoky path of eyeliner across her deep blue eyes, the bathroom door creaked open to reveal Fawn in her bikini, tousling her hair with a towel. Her eyes caught the beaming smile on Jessica's lips—a dead giveaway—prompting her to tease, "So, what did Ethan have to say?"

Jessica swiveled on her stool to meet Fawn's eyes, her laughter ringing like soft wind chimes in the quiet room. "It's that obvious, huh?" she replied, a mischievous grin spreading across her face. The knowing smile on Fawn's lips needed no words.

"He's on his way. He'll be here soon," Jessica said, her voice tingling with anticipation.

Gripped by a wave of excitement, the girls plunged into the hustle and bustle of beach preparations. Brushes swept through hair, cosmetics were applied with expert finesse, and beach essentials were gathered with eager hands. A day of promise lay ahead, whispers of sun-drenched beach moments filled with laughter and memories waiting to be made.

Time, once dragging, rushed forward as the growl of Ethan's Jeep announced his arrival in the driveway. Jessica's heart beat a lively jig, her steps quick and eager as she rushed to the door, longing for his embrace. He stepped out, his eyes shining with deep affection, and pulled her into his arms. Their world narrowed to just the two of them, the rest fading to a soft blur in the background.

Breaking from their embrace, Ethan looked at her with a gaze filled with love and desire. "You look absolutely beautiful, babe," he whispered, his voice so intimate it brought a blush to Jessica's cheeks.

Overwhelmed by the surge of emotion, all Jessica could manage was a breathy, "Thank you."

As Ethan stepped into the warm ambiance of the house, Teresa greeted him with a beaming smile. "Ethan, it's so nice to see you again. Can I get you something to eat? I was just about to make myself some breakfast," she offered, her voice filled with genuine warmth.

Ethan returned her smile with a charming grin and shook his head politely. "No, thank you, Mrs. Reese. I've already eaten," he assured her, his appreciation evident in his tone. As he glanced around the room, curiosity colored his voice. "Where is Mr. Reese today?" he asked, hoping to catch a glimpse of Jessica's father as well.

Teresa chuckled, her laughter adding a lighthearted note to the conversation. "Oh, he's out on the golf course with his buddies. You know how he enjoys his Saturday mornings," she replied, her eyes twinkling with amusement.

Just then, Fawn appeared, her bright smile lighting up the room. "Hi, Ethan," she greeted him with a cheerful voice that elicited a warm smile in return. As his eyes took in her beach-ready attire, understanding dawned.

"Ah, so you're going with us to the beach... that's awesome," he said, his excitement unmistakable and genuine.

Eager for the day ahead, Jessica and Fawn gathered their beach gear, their steps quickening as they headed for the front door. As they prepared to leave, Jessica called back, "We're leaving now, Mom!"

Teresa's reply floated in from the kitchen, warm and cheerful. "Okay, kids. Have fun."

With the promise of a sun-drenched day unfolding before them, Ethan joined Jessica and Fawn, surfboard in hand. Together, they began their walk to the beach, the ocean breeze beckoning them with whispers of warm sand and waves, hinting at a new chapter of summer just moments away.

# Chapter 19

-----------------------------------------------------------

The Fourth of July weekend infused Wavecrest with an intoxicating sense of anticipation, breathing life into every corner of the town. Jessica, Ethan, and Fawn were caught up in the joyful rhythm that flowed across the bustling boardwalk. At this moment, Wavecrest was at its most charming, drawing a steady stream of visitors with its enchanting seaside allure.

As the day unfolded, the sun wove a golden shimmer over the quaint coastal town. The sandy shoreline was dotted with sun worshippers either soaking under the sun's radiant warmth or plunging into the azure depths of the Pacific.

The beach scene was a colorful mosaic of sun umbrellas, beach blankets, and sunbathers in vivid bikinis and striking trunks. Beach balls and frisbees floated on the breeze, volleyballs flew over nets, and families set up their spots with canopies and blankets.

Children, enchanted by the magic of Wavecrest's summer, played gleefully under the gentle breeze. The boardwalk echoed the vibrant energy of the beach, buzzing with the excitement of the summer crowd. The sound of distant rides mixed with the wind, adding a thrill of anticipation to the festive atmosphere.

Jessica and Fawn, well-acquainted with Wavecrest's charms, took in the scene with a sense of familiarity. For Ethan, however, it was as if he had stepped into another world. Enveloping Jessica in his arms, he gazed at the vibrant scene with wide-eyed wonder.

"This place is incredible," he whispered, awe-struck by the spectacle that surpassed any summer scene he had experienced.

Jessica leaned into Ethan, her eyes shimmering with pride and nostalgia. "I love it here," she murmured, her voice laden with fond memories and a deep affection for her beloved beach town.

After their leisurely stroll along the boardwalk, the trio made their way down a wooden ramp that sloped toward the beach, merging with its lively atmosphere. Upon reaching the sand, Jessica and Fawn kicked off their sandals, letting the warm grains tickle their feet.

Ethan, with his surfboard in tow, led the way with confidence, his footprints marking their path on the smooth beach. The girls trusted his instincts as a seasoned beachgoer to find the perfect spot, and Ethan delivered, selecting a quiet stretch of sand where he planted his surfboard upright, claiming their spot.

As Jessica and Fawn spread out their beach blankets, Ethan was captivated by the rhythmic dance of the Pacific's white-capped waves. Though not ideal for surfing, they were perfect for an afternoon of adventure. He was eager to demonstrate his skills to his attentive audience.

Once the girls laid out the blankets, they stretched out on their stomachs and basked in the sun's warmth. Ethan, ever attentive, retrieved a tube of sunscreen from his bag and knelt beside Jessica, gently applying it to her back. Jessica closed her eyes and relaxed under the soothing rhythm of Ethan's gentle touch.

Watching this tender exchange, Fawn felt a mixture of admiration and longing stir within her. She watched Ethan's gentle affection and hoped to one day find someone who would care for her with the same depth of love.

After finishing with Jessica, Ethan turned to Fawn with a warm smile and said, "Now it's your turn."

As he repeated his careful movements on Fawn's back, Jessica watched with a tender smile. Catching her gaze, Fawn gave her a playful grin and teased, "How sweet of you to lend me your boyfriend, Jess."

Jessica laughed, her eyes loving and playful as she replied, "Only for you, Fawn. Only for you."

With sunscreen glistening on their skin, Ethan stood up, stretching his athletic frame and grabbing his surfboard with determination. He walked to the water's edge, his silhouette stark against the bright beach. The waves were smaller than he preferred, but his resolve was firm, driven by the thrill of performing for an eager audience.

He waded into the shimmering water, the sun casting a glow on his tanned back and strong shoulders. On shore, Jessica and Fawn watched from their sandy perch, their eyes following Ethan as he positioned himself on his board, looking for an opportune wave.

"He really wants to impress us today. Just wait and see," Jessica said with a smile, her voice filled with pride.

Fawn chuckled in response. "When doesn't he? Ethan always aims to impress."

As Ethan spotted a modest swell approaching, he noticed it wasn't very large, but had just the right shape for his intended use. With strong, eager strokes, he paddled towards it, his anticipation building like a tightly wound spring.

Upon meeting the wave, Ethan vaulted upright with practiced ease. He stood defiant against gravity, riding its crest with a surfer's grace. Jessica and Fawn watched intently as he maneuvered with precision, his movements a dance of mastery over the water.

The wave was not formidable, though—it was no fierce beast of the ocean—but Ethan was determined to extract every ounce of potential from it. With a swift motion, he attempted a daring cutback maneuver, eager to carve his mark upon the sea.

But nature had other plans. The wave faltered beneath him; it was too gentle for such bravado. As Ethan's arms windmilled in search of the suddenly elusive balance, his silhouette transformed into a comedic dance with the sea.

Fawn burst into uncontrollable laughter, the sound ringing pure and clear. Jessica quickly joined in, both fully enjoying Ethan's unintended slapstick moment.

"Oh my God," Fawn gasped, still laughing. "Did you see that?"

Wiping tears from her eyes, Jessica nodded amidst her giggles. "I've never seen him wipe out quite like that!"

From the churning white foam of the ocean, Ethan emerged—drenched but undiminished—with a smile as bright as the sun above. Seeing their laughter from afar, he raised a hand to acknowledge his splashy blunder.

"Thank you, thank you! I'll be here all week!" he called out with a theatrical flourish, his laughter joining theirs across the distance between sea and shore. As he paddled back into position for another attempt, a wave of contentment washed over him—a fall well worth it for the shared joy it added to their beach day.

Unperturbed by his earlier mishap, Ethan's spirits were buoyed by the playful teasing from shore and the sea's relentless energy. He turned his attention back to the ocean, where the waves promised a chance for redemption.

With a determined glint in his eye, he vowed to impress Jessica and Fawn with his surfing skills. Spotting a modest wave beginning to swell with potential, he decided to attempt a nose ride—a revered longboard maneuver involving a precise walk to the board's forefront while riding the wave's crest.

"Watch this one!" Ethan shouted to the girls, his energetic gestures signaling his readiness for the approaching wave.

Jessica and Fawn exchanged a conspiratorial glance before focusing back on Ethan. Fawn scooted closer to Jessica and whispered, "This should be good," as she grabbed a handful of popcorn from their beach bag.

Ethan sprang to his feet as the wave lifted him, confidently striding toward the front of his board. The trick, ideal for majestic waves and longboards, was a delicate dance between surfer and sea—a performance requiring precision and poise. As Ethan approached the tip of his board, he felt it slowing beneath him. Edging forward cautiously, he balanced precariously on the board's nose.

From their sandy front-row seats, Jessica and Fawn watched with bated breath as Ethan performed what looked like a daring high-wire act atop his board. His arms flailed for balance one moment, then steadied in concentration the next.

Then, without warning, Ethan's front foot slipped past the nose of the board, disrupting his equilibrium. His other foot soon followed, catapulting him into an impromptu aerial display before he plunged into the ocean below.

The girls burst into peals of laughter as Ethan's comedic descent unfolded—one leg kicked high into the air, and the rest of him vanishing beneath the foam.

"You're killing me!" Jessica gasped between laughs, clutching her sides as she watched Ethan resurface with a sheepish yet spirited expression.

"I meant to do that!" Ethan declared with feigned pride, wiping sea spray from his face, which prompted another round of giggles from Jessica and Fawn.

Ethan's antics might not have showcased surfing finesse, but they were undeniably entertaining. As he paddled back to shore, his heart swelled with the warm realization that today was not about perfecting tricks or conquering waves—it was about creating memories filled with laughter and joy. Ready for more, he steeled himself for another round of playful antics in the ocean's welcoming embrace.

"Brace yourselves for the finale, ladies!" Ethan declared, his grin reflecting unbridled enthusiasm. With a theatrical flourish, he plunged back into the ocean, positioning himself for the incoming surf. This time, he aimed for a feat he had never dared to attempt—a handstand on his trusty surfboard.

Jessica and Fawn watched intently as Ethan positioned himself against the golden-lit horizon, his muscles tensed in determination. Then, in one fluid motion, he hoisted himself up, legs reaching skyward. For a fleeting moment, Ethan achieved the improbable—a perfect handstand on the undulating surface of his board. The sight was as awe-inspiring as it was absurd.

But as quickly as it began, the spectacle unraveled. Ethan's balance faltered, and with cinematic timing, he toppled headfirst into the Pacific. His feet flailed comically above the waterline for a brief moment before disappearing beneath the surface.

On the shore, the girls succumbed to laughter so deep it seemed to imprint joyous echoes on the coastline's memory. "Okay, okay, you win!" Jessica called out between fits of laughter, wiping away tears of mirth.

"You've outdone yourself this time, Ethan," Fawn added through chuckles that seemed to have no end.

From amidst the waves, Ethan gave a playful salute before returning to less dramatic but equally graceful surfing maneuvers. He glided along, moving in harmony with the sea's rhythm, his actions a display of practiced grace.

Watching Ethan's fluid movements, Jessica and Fawn reclined on their blankets. Their laughter slowly subsided into a tranquil silence, yet their smiles remained, radiant like the sun above. They basked in the warmth of the day and the lingering amusement from Ethan's unforgettable antics.

Not long after, Ethan concluded his maritime theatrics and made his way to join the girls on the beach. As he approached, Jessica found herself captivated by his robust, sun-gilded figure and his skin shimmering with seawater. His damp hair, tousled by the wind, added to his charm. Yet, it was the tender look in his sapphire eyes that truly captured her heart, peering into her soul as if they could see right through her.

Filled with tenderness and longing, Jessica watched as Ethan dried himself with a towel. Once done, he settled beside her on the blanket, his warmth melding into hers.

With a jubilant smile playing on her lips and Ethan's aquatic antics fresh in her mind, Jessica teased, "You were quite the character out there." Her wide, guileless blue eyes sparkled with childlike wonder.

Ethan's heart melted at Jessica's enchanting response, his own smile widening. A surge of happiness swelled within him, delighted by the joy his comedic performance had sparked.

Joining the playful exchange, Fawn ribbed, "You should give Jess a surfing lesson."

Jessica turned to Fawn, her laughter erupting at the suggestion. "Seriously? Don't you remember what happened when Kenny Dalton tried to teach us? We were an utter disaster."

Fawn's giggles filled the air as she recalled that sunny, awkward day. "Ah, I remember," she said, her mischievous eyes reflecting the fun of the memory. "Neither of us stayed upright for long, did we?"

Ethan grinned as the girls delved into their shared past, always captivated by stories from Jessica's life. "You just haven't found the right teacher yet," he countered, his eyes twinkling with mischief.

Jessica's cheeks flushed with a mix of bashfulness and uncertainty. "I'm not so sure about that," she replied.

In a bid to soothe her apprehension, Ethan playfully insisted, "Aw, it's not as difficult as you think, babe. Maybe we can give it a go tomorrow. We'll take baby steps."

Jessica met his words with a goofy, nervous smile, sparking laughter from Ethan. She turned to Fawn, nudging her playfully, and retorted, "You're a brat," jestingly reprimanding her friend for the idea.

In return, Fawn stuck out her tongue and giggled along with them. As they settled back on their blankets under Wavecrest's radiant sky, Fawn felt an unexpected serenity wash over her—a precious pause in the relentless march of life.

Several minutes passed before Jessica's eyes were drawn to the horizon, where the Pacific sang its eternal song. The waves, with their ceaseless rhythm, whispered ancient secrets, beckoning her to their crisp embrace. Even now, the enchantment of Wavecrest cradled her, guarding the delicate flame of her innocence against the encroaching tide of adulthood. This allure of the ocean was powerful, kindling a profound yearning deep within her soul.

Beside her, Fawn was equally captivated by the expansive sapphire waters, the ocean's lure mirrored in her mischievous blue eyes. They shared a look that needed no words—the sea was calling them both.

"Let's do it," Fawn suggested, her eyes twinkling with a playful glint that transported them back to the carefree days of their youth.

Caught in a web of spontaneous mirth, Jessica turned to Ethan with a bold declaration, ready to leap off her tongue. "We're going for a swim, babe. You coming?"

Ethan, ensnared in a cocoon of tranquil serenity, replied with relaxed charisma, "No, you girls go. I'll stay here and be your lifeguard."

With a smile brimming with affection, Jessica leaned in and planted a soft kiss on his lips. "Alright then," she breathed out, charged with excitement for their imminent plunge into the ocean.

With spirits high and laughter bubbling up, Jessica and Fawn stood and made their way toward the beckoning waves. The sea welcomed them into its soothing depths as they surrendered to its wet embrace. Their laughter mingled with the coastal symphony—a chorus of joy that resonated along the shoreline.

Ethan remained seated at their sandy outpost, an audience of one to their joyful frolics. Their uninhibited glee painted an enchanting scene that spoke volumes about their bond—two souls intertwined in sisterhood through every trial life might present.

Watching them there—in that moment of pure joy—Ethan felt an overwhelming surge of love for Jessica. Their connection transcended friendship: it was something deeper, something eternal. As he observed their unguarded revelry in the water, he understood that his relationship with Jessica was enriched by the kinship she shared with Fawn—a bond unbreakable by time or tide.

Shortly after their jubilant foray into the ocean's embrace, Jessica and Fawn emerged from the frothy surf, their silhouettes etched against the sprawling canvas of the sunlit beach. They transitioned from the sea's buoyant clutches to the shore's gritty familiarity, where their colorfully patterned blankets awaited. With practiced ease, they each reached into their shared beach bag, pulling out plush towels and wrapping themselves in the comforting ritual of drying off.

Witnessing their camaraderie sparked a yearning in Ethan for a connection just as deep and fulfilling. While he cherished his own friendships, none possessed the same profound intimacy and effortless understanding he saw between Jessica and Fawn. Their friendship, shining as brilliantly as the sunlight on the undulating waves, stood as a testament to the transformative power of human connection—one of life's truest treasures.

Watching Jessica and Fawn dry off, Ethan's curiosity ignited like a flare in the night. "How long have you two known each other?" he asked, his voice filled with both warmth and wonder.

With a playful twinkle in her eye, Fawn turned to Jessica and asked, "Twelve years?"

Jessica smiled in amusement. "Actually, we met in kindergarten. So, it's been more like thirteen years."

Their laughter mingled as Fawn confirmed, "Yeah, on the very first day of kindergarten."

Jessica's expression softened as she recalled, "I was so nervous that morning," she admitted quietly.

"I remember when I saw you for the first time," Fawn murmured, her voice tender. "You were so tiny back then."

A feigned pout crossed Jessica's face amidst her laughter. "I was not tiny!"

"Yes, you were—what were you, like, three feet tall?" Fawn teased, her mischievous grin spreading across her face.

"No! I was three foot two!" Jessica retorted with mock indignation, setting off another round of shared mirth.

Laughing, Ethan looked at Jessica with a mix of amusement and surprise. "Wow, you were little," he said, his voice expressing clear amazement at her small stature back then.

Fawn's affection was evident as she gazed at Jessica. "She still is. That's one of the things I love about her."

Jessica conceded with a slight vulnerability peeking through her humor. "Yeah, I was small for my age... which made me an easy target."

"But that didn't last long, did it?" Fawn declared, her voice infused with defiant loyalty as she recalled being the protective guardian for Jessica whenever someone tried to pick on her.

"Nope. You were my hero from the start," Jessica acknowledged with a grateful smile. "You've always had my back."

"And you've always been there for me," Fawn added, her voice softening. The affectionate glimmer in her eyes conveyed a truth far more profound than words could ever express. As her gaze met Jessica's, their eyes spoke of a timeless promise, a promise to be forever cherished.

The sudden chime of a text alert from Ethan's phone cut through the serene atmosphere like a knife. His hand darted into his bag, and he quickly pulled out the device, his fingers dancing swiftly across the screen. Jessica, nestled comfortably on the beach blanket, watched Ethan with a mix of curiosity and a faint twinge of unease.

After quickly sending a reply, Ethan turned to Jessica, his tone unexpectedly formal against the backdrop of their carefree day. "That was Jake, babe. He was just reminding me about tonight."

Jessica felt a slight pang in her heart at the mention of Ethan's evening plans. She understood the importance of family—the bond between Ethan and his brother Jake was strong, much like her own with Fawn. Yet, she couldn't help but feel a whisper of sadness at the thought of spending the evening without him.

"What do you guys have planned for tonight?" she asked, striving to keep her voice light.

"We're just going out to have a few beers and maybe shoot some pool," Ethan replied with an easy shrug. "Nothing too crazy."

Jessica nodded and offered him a gentle smile, her silent blessing for his night out with his brother. Despite her understanding, her eyes betrayed an undercurrent of longing that she couldn't quite hide.

Ethan picked up on her concealed disappointment and quickly reassured her, "Don't worry, babe. It's just one night." His smile widened as he added, "Remember, we have a surfing date tomorrow."

Jessica feigned shock at the reminder, recalling an earlier disastrous attempt at surfing that had left her tumbling in the waves. She turned to Fawn with mock exasperation, "See what you've started? Thanks a lot!"

Fawn simply laughed in response, her mischievous smile speaking volumes. "You're welcome."

Ethan chuckled along with them, enjoying the easy rapport between the two girls he deeply cared for. As he slipped his phone back into his pocket, he noticed the time displayed on the screen.

"Hey, it's already after four. We should head back," he said with a hint of reluctance.

Jessica and Fawn pouted at the prospect of leaving their seaside haven but acknowledged it was time to pack up and return to Jessica's home, where dinner awaited.

"Are you sure you can't stay for dinner?" Jessica asked Ethan, hope sparkling in her eyes.

"I wish I could," Ethan replied, his voice tinged with regret. "But I promised Jake I'd meet him after we left here."

With all their belongings gathered and the beach pristine once again, they made their way off the sand toward the bustling boardwalk. The sea breeze picked up as they ascended the ramp, wrapping them in its comforting embrace—a gentle reminder from Wavecrest that its spirit would always hold them close.

Bathed in the golden glow of the late afternoon sun, the trio ascended the sandy incline of the beach ramp in harmonious unison. They left behind the rhythmic serenade of the waves, exchanging it for the vibrant energy pulsating along the boardwalk. Leading the way, Jessica guided them through the bustling stretch, embarking on a nostalgic journey toward her seaside home.

After walking a couple of wind-kissed blocks, Jessica's sprawling house came into view, nestled like a treasured memory among its neighbors. Sun-bleached blue shutters flanked windows that gleamed with the reflections of the fading day, while explosions of geraniums danced on the porch, each blooming a vivid brushstroke against the canvas of home.

As they reached the brick path leading to the front door, Fawn peeled off from the couple with an ease born of countless visits. "I'm going to grab a quick shower," she announced, her voice tinged with both fatigue and contentment.

Jessica responded with a smile as warm and welcoming as her home. "Sure thing. Clean towels are in the hall closet," she said, her effortless hospitality speaking volumes about their closeness.

With Fawn retreating into the house's comforting interior, Jessica turned her attention to Ethan. Her smile shifted into something softer and more intimate, reminiscent of a secret whispered between lovers at night.

"I guess this is goodbye for now," Ethan said, his voice carrying a weight that tethered him momentarily to this place and time.

Jessica nodded, feeling a tumult of emotions surge within her like a gathering storm off Wavecrest's coast. She leaned forward, enveloping him in an embrace that sought to bridge any distance that would soon lie between them.

Their lips met in a kiss that was both an anchor and a sail—a connection that grounded them even as it promised journeys yet to come. They lingered in the embrace until reality beckoned them apart, their fingers slowly disentangling, yet still savoring the lingering warmth.

"I'll see you tomorrow, babe," Ethan murmured against her cheek, his touch light and reassuring as he traced the soft line of her face.

"I'm really looking forward to that surfing lesson," Jessica replied, her voice dripping with sarcasm as she rolled her eyes playfully. The jest masked an undercurrent of antici-pation for another day spent in Ethan's company.

With one last touch—a silent vow—they parted ways. Ethan walked to his Jeep while Jessica stood rooted, observing as he drove off. She kept her eyes fixed on him until he turned the corner and disappeared.

Turning back to her house, Jessica let herself be enveloped by its familiarity. Stepping through the front door, she was awash with memories from their day at the beach—the sun's heat on her skin, their laughter mingling with sea breezes, and Ethan's kisses, sweet as saltwater taffy on her lips.

Each memory unfolded before her mind's eye like scenes from a cherished film. With each replay, she became more aware that this summer—woven with tender connections and poignant experiences—would claim its rightful place in the hallowed halls of her heart.

Her feet had barely touched the foyer's floor when the gentle aroma of simmering potatoes greeted her, wafting through the air like a tender embrace from the past. Each breath wove a rich tapestry of warmth and comfort, wrapping her in childhood memories.

She followed the homely scent to the kitchen, where Teresa stood by the stove, stirring a pot with the same love and care that had always been her hallmark. Teresa's eyes, kind and crinkling at the corners, lit up with a smile that seemed to emanate directly from her nurturing soul.

"Hey, sweetheart! How was the beach?" her voice enveloped Jessica in a soft embrace, reminiscent of the soothing sea breeze she'd just left behind.

"It was perfect, Mom," Jessica replied as she hopped onto a stool at the kitchen counter. "The sun was warm, and the waves were just right." Sitting on the stool, she swung her legs freely, just as she had when she was a little girl, a charming echo of her childhood innocence.

Teresa, her eyes filled with concern, looked over. "And how is Fawn doing? Is she feeling any better?"

Jessica's face lit up at the mention of her friend, her smile as bright as the sunlight they had enjoyed. "Today, she was herself again. Ethan tried to impress us with his surfing stunts, but he kept wiping out. We couldn't stop laughing!"

Their laughter filled the kitchen, a cheerful melody lifting the mood. "Aw, poor Ethan," Teresa chuckled. "But I'm glad he brought some laughs."

Jessica nodded, her relief evident in her voice. "She really needed this, Mom—a day just to let go and have fun."

Teresa reached out across the counter, squeezing Jessica's hand. "I'm so happy to hear that," she said, her voice rich with maternal love.

Surrounded by the comforting aromas of dinner and their shared laughter, Jessica felt a brief respite from life's burdens, a moment of light-heartedness she wished could last forever.

Fawn's arrival in the kitchen was heralded by the soft sound of her footsteps, a rhythmic echo that spoke of a day spent by the sea. The delicate fragrance of strawberry-scented shampoo lingered in her wake, gently permeating the cozy space. Jessica stood from her stool, warmth radiating from her as she reached out to touch Fawn's arm—a gesture rich with unspoken affection.

"I'm going to take my shower now," Jessica declared, momentarily pausing the kitchen's cheerful buzz. With a light, relaxed step, she headed toward the bathroom, leaving Fawn in Teresa's warm company.

Fawn took Jessica's place at the counter, her eyes meeting Teresa's with a familiarity born from years spent within these walls.

"Hey, Mama. Dinner smells amazing already," she greeted, her voice imbued with a sense of homecoming.

Teresa beamed at Fawn with a warm smile. "Why thank you, honey," she replied. "Did you have fun at the beach?"

A stream of sunlit memories flooded Fawn's thoughts, and her voice carried the melody of waves as she recounted their day. "I did. It was fun," she said wistfully. "Ethan tried showing off on his surfboard but ended up taking quite a few spills. It was hilarious, as he showed us exactly how not to surf."

The kitchen filled with Fawn's contagious laughter, which blended seamlessly with Teresa's affectionate smile. "Silly boy," Teresa chuckled, sharing in the mirth." I'm glad he made you girls laugh."

Fawn's eyes twinkled with recaptured freedom as she continued, "It was definitely entertaining. And after watching Ethan's demonstration, Jess and I just had to dive into the ocean ourselves. It felt like all my worries just floated away."

Teresa regarded Fawn with tender affection as she patted the girl's hand. "I'm so happy to hear that, Fawn," she said softly. "It sounds like this trip to the beach was exactly what you needed."

Fawn nodded in agreement, her heart resonating with Teresa's sentiment as she basked in the afterglow of their seaside escapade. The worries that had shadowed her seemed to dissipate like mist before the morning sun—a testament to the restorative power of laughter and friendship.

In that kitchen, where the aroma of cooking teased Fawn's nose, the world outside fell away for a spellbinding moment. It was a sanctuary where love and understanding flourished, where true friendship pulsed vibrantly through each shared glance and touch. This was Fawn at her most content, capturing life's simplest yet most profound joys: being surrounded by those who knew your heart best.

Moments later, Jessica emerged from the shower feeling rejuvenated, as if the cascading water had cleansed not just her body, but her spirit as well. Droplets lingered on her skin, reminiscent of dew on the morning grass. Wrapping herself in a large bath towel, she relished its soft embrace. Standing before the full-length mirror, she gazed at her reflection, comforted by the sight of her familiar self.

Her petite stature was complemented by a shapely figure, which she wore with effortless poise. She smiled at her reflection, recognizing the beauty in her form without the need for comparisons or alterations. Her eyes drifted to her breasts, and instead of critique, she felt a surge of self-assurance. They were part of her whole, perfectly suited to her slender frame—a melody of self-acceptance that she embraced wholeheartedly.

Clad in the towel's comforting embrace, Jessica left the bathroom. The cheerful cadence of Teresa and Fawn's conversation beckoned from the kitchen, their voices weaving into a symphony that underscored her life. Hearing them together, their voices harmonizing with familial love, warmed Jessica's heart.

With each step toward her bedroom, Jessica's smile deepened, reflecting the lingering joy of the day. The evening air was filled with promise as she approached her closet, her anticipation akin to an artist choosing a palette. A white dress adorned with delicate florals caught her eye, perfectly reflecting her buoyant spirit. Slipping into it, she felt the fabric caress her body with a softness that harmonized with the gentle euphony of the evening.

After donning the dress, she stood before the mirrored vanity and quickly ran a brush through her damp hair, letting the loose waves cascade gently around her face—each strand contributing to the composition of her relaxed yet elegant appearance.

Satisfied with her reflection, Jessica exited her room and gravitated toward the kitchen, where savory aromas heralded an imminent feast. The scent of grilled steaks tantalized her senses, whetting an appetite sharpened by a day spent by the sea.

As she drew closer, the sounds of laughter and conversation grew louder, wrapping her in the warmth of the moment. This was the essence of summer, captured in a single frame: the laughter, the tender connections, the comfort of home, and the feeling that all was right in her world. It was a moment, simple yet profound, brimming with the nostalgia of countless yesterdays and the promise of countless tomorrows—a heartbeat in the timeless song of family, friendship, and love.

As she stepped back into the kitchen, her eyes were drawn to the heartwarming scene before her. Teresa and Fawn stood shoulder to shoulder at the counter, their movements synchronized in the familiar dance of meal preparation.

Fawn's hands moved with practiced ease, her knife slicing through the boiled potatoes as if they were butter. Beside her, Teresa orchestrated the kitchen like a maestro, each ingredient bending to her will as she crafted her renowned creamy potato salad. This dish was more than a mere side; it was a Wavecrest legend, spoken of in the same reverent tones reserved for Uncle Gary's famous Texas-style baked beans.

As Jessica sidled up to the bustling duo, a swell of affection bloomed within her chest. She nudged Fawn playfully, and a silent exchange passed between them—a glance that spoke volumes of their intertwined lives. Their giggles mingled with the clatter of kitchenware, echoing off the walls and into the annals of their shared history.

"Is there anything I can help with?" Jessica asked, her voice eager to join the culinary chorus.

Teresa glanced up with a smile that radiated years of nurturing love. "Nope, we have everything under control," she assured, her tone light yet firm.

A fleeting shadow of disappointment flickered across Jessica's face—gone almost before it appeared. But Teresa, with her maternal insight, caught it, nonetheless. She offered an alternative with a warmth that seemed to emanate from her soul. "Your dad is outside grilling. Why don't you go see if he needs help with anything?"

"Alright," Jessica agreed gracefully, her smile reflecting Teresa's.

With a gentle pivot on her heel, she glided toward the back door. Stepping out onto the deck, she was welcomed by the evening air, which felt like an old friend. As she approached her father at the grill, the enticing scent of barbecue and the comforting sound of sizzling steaks promised a moment of cherished familial bonding.

The Reese's back deck was a spacious and welcoming area, perfectly designed for summer rituals in Wavecrest. Comfortable chairs, like loyal companions, encircled the space, each paired with a small table standing sentinel for drinks and laughter yet to come. Dominating the center was a large round glass table beneath a vibrant umbrella, providing a cool retreat from the sun's exuberant rays.

At the deck's edge, the grill stood as a monument to the culinary arts—a black steel beast that Tom manned with quiet authority. The air around him was alive with the hiss and aroma of searing meat, each steak an edible testament to the season's joyous bounty.

"Hi, Daddy. Can I help with anything?" she offered, her voice carrying the sweetness of home and history.

Tom turned from his post at the grill, his eyes lighting up at the sight of his daughter. "Hey, baby girl," he greeted her, his affection for her etched into every line on his face. "These steaks are just about done. How about you go ahead and set the table."

With a nod and a smile, Jessica gathered plates and silverware from their resting place beside the grill. She approached the table with an artist's touch, meticulously arranging each setting to create a tableau of familial harmony—a designated place for her mom, dad, herself, and Fawn.

As she finished setting the table, Jessica glanced at her father, who was carefully transferring the steaks from the grill to the platter, their sizzle singing a song of readiness. Tom looked up and caught sight of her handiwork, his smile serving as a silent ovation to her efforts.

"Tell your mom the steaks are ready," he said, his voice tinged with pride that extended beyond the culinary achievements.

Jessica's heart swelled with anticipation as she stepped back into the kitchen. "Dinner's ready," she announced, her enthusiasm rippling through her words. She knew this meal symbolized their shared life—a symphony of flavors and memories that nourished not just their bodies, but also their souls.

In the tender moments that followed, the round glass table on the back deck transformed into a joyous island amidst a sea of love. Jessica, her parents, and Fawn dove into the gastronomic delights spread before them. The grilled steak was tender and juicy, the legendary creamy potato salad was cool and comforting, and the tangy coleslaw added just the right amount of zest. Each bite was a testament to the magic that Teresa's love infused into every dish.

Amid an orchestra of laughter and convivial banter, Jessica and Fawn vividly painted the canvas of their day at the beach with vibrant strokes. Their storytelling, filled with comedic grace, recounted Ethan's surfing antics, sending waves of laughter across the deck. The image of Ethan tumbling off his surfboard, his limbs flailing as chaotically as the waves that toppled him, quickly became a treasured mural on the walls of their hearts.

Tom and Teresa watched the girls with contented smiles gracing their faces. Their hearts were warmed by Fawn's laughter, its sound bright and true as a bell. The twinkle in her mischievous eyes lit up their space like the most radiant star in a clear night sky.

On this summer evening, their dinner table was a sanctuary. Within its bounds, Fawn's emotional maelstrom and any uncertainties lurking on life's horizon were held at bay. Instead, under this roof, Jessica and Fawn basked in the radiant glow of the now—each joyous moment was another precious bead added to their string of shared memories.

Lost in the moment, Tom and Teresa found themselves silently wishing that this enchanted time—a blend of innocence and pure happiness—could stretch on indefinitely. They hoped these moments would add to Jessica and Fawn's treasure chest of precious memories, especially knowing that this might be the girls' last summer together before adulthood swept them onto divergent paths.

The scene at the dinner table was a reminder of the fleeting nature of youth, yet it was also a testament to the enduring strength of their friendship. Tom and Teresa watched with a mix of joy and melancholy, cherishing the present while quietly mourning the inevitable changes the future would bring.

As the evening sun began its slow descent, they savored the last morsels on their plates. Each person at the table was momentarily lost in a comforting silence filled with companionship so content that no words were necessary.

However, as shadows lengthened, painting the world in dusky hues, Jessica and Fawn excused themselves from the table. Their hearts yearned for the privacy and comfort found within the walls of Jessica's bedroom—a place where they could nurture their bond without prying eyes or ears. There, they would relive every blissful moment of today's adventures and cling to these waning moments of youth before the horizon of tomorrow beckoned anew.

# Chapter 20

------------------------------------------------------------

Twilight's tender hues filtered through the curtains of Jessica's bedroom, where she and Fawn settled into the comforting cradle of the plush bed. They sat cross-legged, their knees almost touching, nestled cozily in this cherished retreat. The whimsical lilt of SpongeBob SquarePants coming from the TV filled the air, the familiar notes a comforting undercurrent to the room's warmth and nostalgic charm.

Engrossed in their intimate ritual, Fawn's brush danced across Jessica's slender fingers, each delicate pink stroke a vibrant testament to their profound bond. This exchange was more than an act of grooming; it was a tradition, a sacred dance of femininity, and a testament to their deep friendship.

A soft whisper of melancholy danced its way into Jessica's heart as she watched Fawn's skilled hands, the same hands she would soon yearn for in her solitude.

I am so going to miss this," Jessica confessed, her voice a harmony of longing and sadness as she envisioned her future without Fawn by her side.

"Me too," Fawn whispered back, her voice a soft breeze carrying the weight of imminent separation. A pang of sadness pricked her heart, but Fawn conjured a wellspring of optimism. "But I'm sure you'll find someone to do your nails in Austin."

"No way," Jessica replied, skepticism coloring her words. "No one can make my nails look as pretty as you do."

Fawn's focus momentarily broke from the canvas of Jessica's nails, her eyes meeting hers with a playful twinkle. Her hands were the conductors of an intimate art reserved only for her dearest friend. Still, she persisted with reassurance. "No, you'll see. Before you know it, you'll have so many friends that you'll have no problem finding someone as eager to do your nails as I am." With that, her attention returned to the artistic ballet of painting Jessica's nails.

197

Jessica let her eyes linger on Fawn, savoring the comfort and familiarity of their shared space. With a flourish, Fawn completed the last stroke on Jessica's nails, her artistic gift leaving a tangible mark of their enduring friendship. She looked up, her expression seeking approval.

"So, what do you think?" Fawn asked, her voice tinged with the hopeful anticipation of an artist awaiting a verdict.

"They look great," Jessica beamed, admiration shining in her eyes as she wiggled her fingers playfully. Her nails were a showcase of Fawn's talent, each one adorned with care and precision.

Fawn's heart swelled with pride at the praise, her craft an extension of their connection. Yet, as she stood and made her way to the window, a restlessness stirred within her. The vibrant boardwalk beckoned just beyond the glass, its cheerful chaos a stark contrast to the storm brewing in her thoughts. Before her, the Pacific's expanse unfolded, whispering secrets that remained a mystery to her.

The undercurrent of anxiety that had plagued her since the morning conversation she had with Teresa resurfaced, its tendrils wrapping around her mind. Each looming shadow cast by the impending sale of her home represented change and uncertainty, creating a specter of doubt.

A determination took root amidst the turmoil; it was time for answers. She needed to confront her parents about the forces driving them from Wavecrest—the place that cradled her past and inspired her dreams.

Turning back to Jessica, who was now absorbed in the glow of her phone screen, Fawn cleared her throat. "Hey, Jess," she called out, her voice betraying the weight of what she was about to undertake.

Jessica's attention snapped up, a lighthearted lilt in her response. "Yeah?" she said with an encouraging smile.

Fawn took a steadying breath. "I think I'm going to head over to my house and find out what's really going on," she declared with quiet resolve.

Jessica's expression shifted from playful curiosity to serious concern. "Really?" she asked, sensing the gravity behind Fawn's words.

"Yeah," Fawn confirmed with a heavy heart. "It's something I have to do."

Jessica felt a protective surge at Fawn's admission; she understood all too well what might await her—a shadow of last night's emotional turmoil threatening to rise again.

"Do you want me to go with you?" she offered without hesitation.

Fawn met Jessica's gaze with a deep appreciation for the solidarity and strength found in their friendship. "This is affecting you just as much as it is me," she acknowledged. "So yes, I want you there with me."

Jessica nodded firmly. "Whenever you're ready to go, Fawn, I'll be right beside you."

Encouraged by Jessica's unwavering support, Fawn returned her gaze to the window.

The distant whispers of the sea in her ears gave her the courage and strength to face the night ahead.

Stepping into the gilded embrace of dusk, Jessica and Fawn were greeted by an ethereal ballet in the heavens, where a kaleidoscope of fiery oranges was gradually yielding to the encroaching army of twilight grays. The warmth of the night air enveloped them, a sultry summer caress that was unusual for this time of the year, yet the soft whispers of the ocean breeze delicately offset the heat.

The symphony of the boardwalk echoed around them, a vibrant composition stitched together from laughter, animated chatter, and the irresistible call of distant arcade games. It was a familiar melody, the soundtrack to countless Saturday nights the girls had committed to memory.

Yet, on this Fourth of July weekend, the tourists, eager to drink from the cup of seaside magic, amplified the pulsating life of Wavecrest, turning up the volume before the cruel hand of time snatched them back into the labyrinth of everyday monotony.

In the distance, a constellation of lights shone against the inky backdrop of the night sky, casting an inviting glow over the boardwalk that sang an enticing siren's song of carefree revelry. However, beneath the lure of the lights, a solemn determination resided in the girls' hearts. The quest to unravel the truth about Fawn's house was like an anchor, grounding their youthful spirits and casting a solemn shadow over the prospects of any frivolous diversion.

As Jessica and Fawn looked out toward the vibrant tableau of the boardwalk, a potent mixture of anticipation and apprehension filled their hearts, while their senses focused on their daunting mission. The glow of the lights, the whispers of the breeze, the life-affirming chatter of the crowd, and the intoxicating scent of salty sea air, all became distant echoes drowned out by the deafening silence of the unknown awaiting them.

Their path toward Fawn's house was a slow, deliberate march. Their footsteps echoed with trepidation as they trudged through the unseen fog of dread and uncertainty. What usually was a leisurely five-minute stroll unfolded like a somber procession, stretching for a full ten minutes before they finally stood at the precipice of revelation—the front door of Fawn's home.

Stepping into the eerie calm of the house, Jessica shadowed Fawn, her loyal ally in this silent battlefield. The kitchen materialized before them, a chaotic display of paperwork sprawled like fallen leaves across the table. Anna was at its center, her gaze ensnared by the inky scribbles and figures that danced before her. The light in her eyes sparked as she caught sight of the girls, a fleeting flicker of joy amidst the shadows of distress.

Fawn navigated the space with mechanical precision, reaching into the refrigerator's coolness to retrieve a bottle of water. She turned to Jessica, offering the bottle with a simple, "Want one?"

Jessica's hand fluttered in a gentle refusal. Her inner turmoil left little room for thirst, each wave of emotion churning a sea of discomfort within her.

In an act of maternal grace, Anna drew Fawn into a hug that spoke volumes—a silent symphony of regret, love, and the desperate hope for understanding. Fawn accepted the gesture with an outward stoicism that masked the inner tangle of betrayal and bewilderment. When Anna's arms encircled Jessica next, Jessica welcomed the comfort, allowing her kindness to bridge the gulf of hurt.

A familiar voice cut through the hushed tension as Brian entered the kitchen. His surprised look softened as he noted Fawn and Jessica's presence.

"I'm glad you're here, sweetheart," he uttered, his voice threading through the silence with a quiver of unshed emotions. "If you're ready to hear why we're in this situation, we're ready to tell you."

Fawn anchored her parents with a steely gaze, the weight of their collective sorrow pooling in their eyes. Her words were sharp and swift: "I just want to know why you decided to sell our house without asking me what I thought."

Anna's response was soft, yet heavy with guilt. "We know, baby," she murmured. "We made a mistake. It might be too late for apologies, but if you're willing to hear our side, it might help you understand our decision."

The girls exchanged glances, their emotions fluttering like caught butterflies in their eyes.

"How about we go into the living room so we can talk," Brian proposed with a ray of hope lingering in his words.

Motivated by her parents' readiness to disclose their truths and her hunger for clarity, Fawn relented with a resigned breath. "Okay, Dad. Let's talk."

The atmosphere in the living room was charged with a tense expectancy as they all found their places, the very air seeming to thicken in anticipation of the disclosures that hung heavy on the horizon.

Jessica and Fawn descended onto the cool leather cushions, sinking into its depths as if it could shield them from the impact of the imminent truths. With a measured weariness etched upon his face, Brian eased into his recliner, creating a space of comfort and familiarity. Anna then perched herself on his knee, his arm wrapping around her waist, offering her his reassuring presence.

Anna's voice, tinged with trepidation, broke the silence. "Fawn," she said, her eyes reflecting a storm of emotions. "Atlas Manufacturing, where your father works—the company that's been our financial backbone for years—is shutting down on the first of September."

Jessica and Fawn exchanged a glance, the gravity of Anna's words slowly dawning upon them. It was as if the ground beneath them had shifted; the implications of such a closure reverberated through their cores.

Anna pressed on, her voice threading through her sorrow. "Your dad has poured twenty years of his life into that plant, climbing his way up to management. He's given them everything."

Brian's arm tightened around Anna in a silent pact of mutual support as she continued unraveling the tapestry of their predicament.

"Because of his dedication," Anna's voice quivered just slightly, "the company offered him a position at their Montana facility."

Brian picked up where Anna left off, his voice rich with unspoken strain. "We learned about this back in May," he explained. "You were so deep in studying for your finals and preparing for graduation that we couldn't bring ourselves to burden you with this news then."

Anna's eyes shimmered with empathy as she added, "We were afraid it might throw you off balance and affect your grades right at the finish line."

In that confessional space between parent and child, between lifelong friends sharing in each other's trials, truths unfolded like delicate petals, exposing their cores to the harsh light of reality. Each revelation carried weight, deepening Fawn and Jessica's understanding as they began to grasp the challenges ahead.

With the gravity of their predicament hanging in the air, Jessica and Fawn stayed anchored on the sofa, absorbing the harsh truths that their parents had long hidden. Brian's gaze flickered between his daughter and Jessica as if gauging the depth of their shock before he mustered the courage to continue.

"We had hoped," he said, his voice firm and resolute, "to find a way out, a miracle perhaps. But as days turned into weeks, it became clear that our only option was to accept the transfer to Montana."

Fawn's blue eyes clouded with the weight of this new reality, her lips parted as if to speak, but no words came forth. Beside her, Jessica sat with her hands clasped tightly in her lap, a silent pillar of support.

"It's not just about the job," Anna added, seeking to unveil every layer of their decision. "It's about securing our future—yours included. The cost of living in Montana is significantly lower, and it would allow us to start fresh."

The word 'fresh' lingered in the room like a specter of unwelcome change. Fawn's shoulders tensed as she struggled to reconcile the image of her childhood home with a 'For Sale' sign staked into its heart.

"We're truly sorry," Brian said, his voice strained by the admission. "We never meant to keep you in the dark or make decisions without your input."

Fawn bit her lower lip, battling the swell of emotions that threatened to overflow. She understood the dire nature of their situation now, but it did little to quell the hurt that gnawed at her.

Jessica reached out, placing a comforting hand over Fawn's. Their eyes met in a silent exchange—Jessica's filled with empathy and resolve, while Fawn's were shimmering with tears and vulnerability.

Anna leaned forward, bridging the distance between them. "We've always tried to give you everything we could," she said. "But this... this was beyond our control."

At that moment, amidst the maelstrom of emotions, an unspoken understanding crept into Fawn's heart—a reluctant acceptance that her family was being swept along by an unforgiving current of circumstances. She nodded slowly, keeping her eyes fixed on her parents, who still clung to each other for support. The questions and accusations that had once boiled within her began to simmer into a sad comprehension.

The room settled into a fragile silence as they collectively bore the weight of an uncertain future—a future where change was inevitable, but their bonds remained steadfast.

As Fawn processed her parents' explanation, a fragile understanding began to pierce the fog of her confusion. Her voice, brittle with the frustration of being kept in the dark, broke the silence in the room. "Then why didn't you tell me after graduation?" she asked, the question laced with a plea for transparency.

Anna's heart weighed heavily with regret as she answered, her voice barely above a whisper. "We clung to hope that something would change—that your father might find another job here or that Atlas would reverse their decision. We didn't want your summer to be overshadowed by this... this upheaval."

The soft cadence of Anna's voice rose again, filling the room with a sorrowful melody. "In the meantime, we had to prepare for the worst. That's why we decided to put the house on the market."

Brian interjected, his voice cutting through the thick air with a blend of desperation and resolve. "We prayed for a miracle, Fawn. This is not what we wanted for our family."

The room seemed to shrink under the weight of collective sorrow, each breath more laborious than the last. Brian's eyes, reflecting a father's pain, met Fawn's as he confessed, "We now see we should have told you sooner. Our only wish was for you to enjoy one last summer without burdens."

A single tear escaped Fawn's eye, carving a path down her cheek as she absorbed the full extent of her parents' plight. Her response was tinged with newfound understanding, yet underscored by her need to be acknowledged as more than just their child. "Well, you should've told me from the beginning. I'm not a little girl anymore."

Brian looked at his daughter with tender eyes that held years of love and memories. "You are to us, sweetheart," he said, his voice filled with paternal affection. "You'll always be our little girl."

Jessica tightened her grip on Fawn's hand in solidarity as she witnessed this intimate family moment. The reflection of deep sorrow in Fawn's parents' eyes lit a spark of empathy for their struggle within her.

Seeing Fawn's fading anger, Brian leaned forward with an earnestness that resonated through the stillness of the room. His voice was thick with emotion as he shared his fervent wish. "If there was even a sliver of hope that Atlas would remain here in Wavecrest," he said with conviction, "I'd yank that damn for-sale sign out of the ground right now."

Submerged in a whirlpool of complex emotions, Fawn rose from the sofa's soft hold, embarking on a slow, pensive walk across the room. Her thoughts were turbulent with remorse for the fury she had unleashed on her parents. Now, with the clarity of understanding their mutual pain over losing their cherished home, she found herself grappling with regret.

In a voice tempered by contrition, she let her apology drift through the air. "I'm sorry I lashed out at you last night."

Moved by her daughter's words, Anna pulled away from Brian's embrace and glided toward Fawn, arms open in a gesture of solace. They came together in a warmer embrace this time, charged with mutual forgiveness and a dawning comprehension.

"I'm so sorry, Mom," Fawn murmured into the comfort of her mother's shoulder.

"No, baby. We're the ones who are sorry," Anna whispered back, her eyes reflecting the storm of emotions visible on Fawn's face. "We should have told you everything from the start."

As the emotional exchange continued, Brian stepped forward, expanding their circle of comfort as he wrapped his wife and daughter in his arms. Jessica observed from her place on the sofa, her vision blurred by tears from witnessing such an intimate moment. Her heart was heavy yet hopeful as she watched the family bond over shared sorrows and forgiveness.

As they emerged from beneath the shadow of their emotional tempest, Anna suggested a respite for Fawn from the relentless stress of the house sale. "Why don't you stay at Jessica's until all this is over? It might give you some peace," she said.

Fawn nodded in agreement, her voice steady but soft. "Okay, Mom."

Brian interjected with a note of cautious optimism. "We did receive an offer for the house. If it goes through, there won't be any more showings, and you can come back then."

With each word her parents spoke, Fawn felt her anger dissolve into a sea of newfound understanding and acceptance. Jessica stood up and approached them, adding to the strength of their family unit with her supportive presence.

Brian turned to Jessica and drew her into a loving embrace as well. "We're so sorry, sweetheart," he said warmly. His eyes conveyed a deep appreciation for her steadfast friendship with Fawn. "You're part of our family, too, and we'll get through this together."

As the family made their way into the kitchen, the girls took their seats at the table. The warmth of the room enveloped Fawn like a treasured memory, but there was a spark of desperate hope in her eyes. With her voice quivering with tentative optimism, she offered a solution that dangled on the precipice of possibility.

"If I were not to go to college, you can get your money back, right? That way, you'll have enough money to stay here and find a new job," she proposed, her eyes locked with her parents, seeking a lifeline in their response.

Brian's heart clenched at his daughter's suggestion, her willingness to sacrifice her dreams a testament to her love for family and home. His voice was gentle yet firm as he corrected her misunderstanding. "Unfortunately, honey, that's not how it works. That money is not refundable. So regardless if you go to college or not, that money is spent."

The weight of disappointment descended upon Fawn as she absorbed the stark reality—their departure from Wavecrest was inevitable. A cocktail of fear and resolve stirred within her as she braced herself for the unknowns of Montana.

Amid these swirling emotions, a quiet courage began to form, gently assuring her that she might yet find her way in this uncharted future. Although Wavecrest had become a collage of bygone childhood fantasies, it was time for her to embrace a world filled with both promise and challenge.

As nightfall cloaked Wavecrest in its dark mantle, the town seemed to whisper a plea for retreat. The home that had once been Fawn's sanctuary now felt alien, its rooms heavy with the ghosts of impending farewells. The walls that had shielded her youthful innocence now seemed to reverberate with a somber quiet, a prelude to their eventual goodbye.

"I'm tired, Mom," Fawn finally admitted, allowing vulnerability to lace through the words that connected her with her mother, father, and Jessica. "I think we'll head back to Jessica's house now."

Anna's understanding was immediate, reflected in the soothing timbre of her voice as she conceded to her daughter's need for retreat. "Okay, baby," she said softly, her words offering comfort and steadfast support. "We'll stop by every day to spend some time together."

With this gentle promise sealed between them, Fawn and Jessica rose from their seats—a final shared hug with Anna and Brian imprinting itself upon their hearts. Approaching the threshold of departure, Fawn allowed one last glance back at her parents—a smile touched by melancholy played upon her lips as she murmured a simple yet profound farewell: "See ya." With those words left hanging in the stillness of the kitchen, Fawn stepped out into the embrace of the night air, leaving behind the shell of what once was home.

The balmy night air cradled the girls as they navigated the quiet street back to Jessica's house. Yet, as they walked, a sudden thought ignited within Jessica. She veered off their direct path, her feet carrying her toward the familiar comfort of Fawn's yard. There, shrouded in the shadows beneath the moon's soft glow, was the old white bench swing.

With an intuitive grace, Jessica reached beneath the faded green cushion and retrieved a hidden treasure—Fawn's sketchpad, filled with potential masterpieces yet to be born. As she rejoined Fawn on the sidewalk, a curious look painted Fawn's features.

"What are you doing?" she asked, her eyes locked onto the sketchpad now cradled in Jessica's hands.

In a tender exchange, Jessica handed the pad to its rightful owner. Her gaze was steady and sure, reflecting the faith she held within. "You have an art contest to win, Fawn. You're going to need that prize money for college," she said with quiet conviction.

The corners of Fawn's mouth curled into a smile that radiated gratitude and recognition of Jessica's unshakeable support. Grasping the sketchpad close to her chest, Fawn felt a renewed sense of purpose coursing through her veins. She understood that within those pages lay not only her escape but also her hope for the future.

Their footsteps resumed, now imbued with a shared determination as they moved through the stillness of the night. The remnants of Fourth of July celebrations hung in the air—sporadic bursts of fireworks cast fleeting glimmers against the dark sky while laughter and music drifted from distant backyards.

As they walked, they were cocooned in a tapestry of sensations—the soft glow of streetlights guiding their way, the rhythmic lull of waves whispering promises from afar, and above them, an endless expanse where stars twinkled like distant dreams. This night—filled with revelations and resilience—was etching itself into their hearts.

With each step toward Jessica's home, they were not only leaving behind the echoes of childhood, but also stepping forward into a realm ripe with possibility. The night would end, but its memories would linger—an indelible imprint on their journey from adolescence into the unknown horizons that awaited them both.

# Chapter 21

------------------------------------------------------------

The golden rays of Sunday's dawning sun filtered through the curtains of Jessica's bedroom, casting a warm glow of honey and soft pink over her sanctuary. The light caressed Jessica's face, beckoning her from the depths of slumber. Her sleep had been a brief reprieve from the weighty revelations of the previous night—revelations that had the power to reshape her understanding of the world. As she regained consciousness, the pain of those revelations nestled in her heart like an unread love letter.

The initial numbness parted like a mist, and memories of the grim truths Fawn's parents had shared emerged. They stung, contrasting sharply with the picture-perfect image of Wavecrest—the coastal town she thought she knew. It was as if she had gazed into its reflection on calm waters, only to discover the raging torrents beneath the surface.

Her eyes fluttered open, their deep blue reflecting the calm heart of the ocean on a still day. A remnant of a dream clung to her, slipping away as she sought the familiar comfort of Fawn's presence. But the bed yielded only cool, empty sheets, echoing her absence, though the gentle impression she had left lingered like the final notes of a fading lullaby.

From beyond her door, Jessica heard the cadence of conversations—the deep tones of her parents mingling with Fawn's soft voice. The savory smell of breakfast filled the air—bacon and pancakes, perhaps—calling to her heart as well as her hunger. She stretched, savoring the sensation of life returning to her limbs.

With effortless grace, she swung her legs to the side, her feet meeting the cool touch of the floor. Her eyes landed on the faded pink robe, a relic from her mother's past. Its fabric, softened by time and countless washes, held memories of tender hugs and whispered words of comfort. Wrapping herself in its nostalgic warmth, Jessica felt an unseen embrace, a silent reassurance from days gone by.

Securing the robe, Jessica paused to absorb the symphony of sounds from the kitchen—laughter and conversation in sharp contrast to the emotional upheaval of the previous night. The lighthearted tones suggested a mending, an antidote to yesterday's stormy heartache.

With her curiosity now piqued by the prospect of shared laughter and morning meals, she decided it was time to join the day and embrace the love and understanding that beckoned from the heart of her home.

In the kitchen, the gentle cadence of familial love surrounded Jessica, enveloping her in an atmosphere of comfort and quiet sorrow. Fawn, her form relaxed yet tinged with an undercurrent of restlessness, appeared as if she were a figure etched into the morning's stillness. Her straight blonde hair cascaded down her shoulders, carrying the secrets of the night's dreams, while her blue eyes, bright yet weary, reflected a deep affection for Jessica.

Tom and Teresa, dressed in their Sunday best, greeted Jessica with eyes bright with parental adoration. "Good morning, baby girl," Tom's rich, deep voice greeted her, his eyes sparkling with the same loving light he'd held for her since she was a baby.

Teresa cradled her coffee mug, its steam rising in spirals like wordless hymns to the day. "There's my little sleepyhead," she cooed, her voice dripping with maternal warmth.

Grinning at her welcome, Jessica meandered to the cupboard and lingered for a moment by the dishwasher. Her fingers carefully selected a bowl and spoon, an immaculate set that seemed untouched by time. She poured herself a generous helping of Lucky Charms, bathing the vibrant marshmallows in a cascade of cold milk.

As Jessica settled into her seat at the table, Fawn's lips curled into a mischievous smile. "Aren't you a little old to be eating that?" she joked as Jessica took her first bite.

With milk on her lips and sugar clinging to her smile, Jessica playfully replied between bites, "Nope. It's magically delicious."

Fawn shook her head in mock annoyance at Jessica's humorous retort, her amusement evident in the twinkle in her eye.

But Tom, ever the protective father, saw an opportune moment to wade gently into deeper waters and bring Jessica up to speed in their breakfast conversation. "We've been discussing this whole mess with Atlas shutting down and the situation it has put Fawn's parents in," his voice was tinged with concern.

Jessica's expression darkened as the shadows of last night's revelations flitted across her features. "Isn't there anything you can do, Daddy?" she asked, her voice filled with hope, seeking reassurance from the man who had always been her steadfast protector.

"I already asked, Jess," Fawn interjected, placing a comforting hand on Jessica's arm.

Tom flexed his fingers, as if searching for a tangible solution that was out of reach. "I wish I could, baby girl, but there's nothing I can do," he confessed.

Desperation once again colored Jessica's voice as she pleaded for intervention. "Can't you get him a job where you work?"

With a deep breath that seemed to carry the weight of their collective worries, Tom admitted the hard truth. "Times are tough right now, honey; there are no jobs available. Besides, if Brian leaves Atlas now, he will lose everything: a good paycheck, health insurance, life insurance, and everything else."

The grim realization settled over them like an unwelcome mist—Fawn's home in Wavecrest was slipping from their grasp like sand through outstretched fingers. Vulnerability and strength were intertwined on their youthful faces, marking a delicate balance at the threshold of innocence and a sobering awareness of life's harsh truths. A heavy, unspoken tension filled the room, threatening to consume the morning's serenity.

The anguish etched into Jessica's features struck a chord in Tom's heart, causing him to share a heavy look with Teresa. It was a look that spoke volumes, resonating with the weight of shared concern. He took a deep breath and found within himself the determination to bring their plans to light.

"I think it's time we told the girls about our plan for our house," Tom announced, his voice tinged with cautious optimism.

Teresa, usually the beacon of cheer in their household, nodded solemnly. The simple gesture was heavy with emotion, underscoring the gravity of their discussion.

A shiver ran down Jessica's spine, and Fawn felt a similar chill. Their minds raced with dark possibilities, fear gnawing at them at the thought that Jessica's cherished childhood home might be next. This ghostly apprehension had haunted Jessica's thoughts ever since Fawn's world had begun to crumble.

Tom cleared his throat, his voice soothing as he began to dispel the fear that hung thick in the air. "Your mother and I have been discussing our future here in Wavecrest and whether we should sell or stay," he said, each word deliberate and reassuring. "As you already know, living in Wavecrest has become quite expensive."

Fawn and Jessica exchanged glances that spoke volumes—wordless conversations of treasured memories and shared uncertainties woven through their silent exchange.

Seeking to allay their fears, Tom reached out and took their hands in his, a firm and grounding gesture. "Despite everything, we want you girls to feel safe during this transition in your lives," he continued. "So, we've decided to stay here for at least a couple of years. This will give you time to get comfortable living on your own and know that you still have a home in Wavecrest."

The relief that enveloped Jessica and Fawn was palpable; it washed over them like gentle waves, washing away the remnants of their unease. Jessica let her spoon fall against her bowl with a soft clink as her tense shoulders relaxed.

"Thank you, Daddy," she breathed out, her voice full of gratitude.

Fawn's smile unfolded like a flower touched by sunlight after a storm, its brightness a stark contrast to the shadow of her own familial turmoil. Though their future remained uncertain, Tom's assurance provided an anchor amid turbulent seas.

Time, however, waits for no one, and Tom, attuned to its passage, caught the advance of the clock's hands with a seasoned eye. He stood, his form rising like an ancient oak.

"We better get going, dear," he said to Teresa, his voice carrying the low rumble of distant thunder. "I don't want us to be late for church."

Teresa's eyes flickered with surprise as she glanced at the clock. "Oh, dear. I didn't realize it was that late."

The couple pushed back their chairs with a gentle scratch on the floor, their movements creating long shadows that stretched across the kitchen like silent companions. Their eyes held a ballet of emotions—a twinge of regret at saying goodbye to the girls, yet coupled with the steady rhythm of Sunday routine.

"We're going to spend the day with the Larsons after church," Tom informed them, his tone a mixture of authority and tenderness. "We'll be back later."

As Tom and Teresa made their way to the door, he cast a glance over his shoulder—a playful firmness infusing his words as he reminded them, "You girls behave yourselves now."

Jessica and Fawn responded in unison with a choreographed ease that spoke volumes about their deep-rooted camaraderie. "Yes, Daddy," they chimed, their voices filled with joy and an unspoken promise of youthful adventures to come.

Tom's laughter echoed through the kitchen, a deep sound that seemed to hold all the love and joy of their shared history. It hung in the air like a fond memory as Tom and Teresa stepped out into the day.

The door closed behind them, sealing away the parental presence and leaving Jessica and Fawn enveloped in a cocoon of tranquility. They exchanged glances that sparkled with anticipation—their newfound solitude, an open canvas awaiting the stroke of their day's plans.

In the golden haze of morning, the soft chime of Jessica's spoon dipping back into her Lucky Charms melded with the rhythmic crunch of Fawn enjoying her toast. The kitchen, steeped in memories and comforting traditions, hummed with hope. The upheaval caused by the closing of Atlas Manufacturing had sent ripples through their lives, but the steadfastness of Wavecrest remained a beacon amid the turbulence.

Jessica finished her breakfast and sat back with a satisfied sigh that turned into an unabashed burp, shattering the serene moment. Fawn's eyes danced with amusement as her eyebrows shot up in mock shock. "Jessica!" she scolded playfully. Unimpressed, Jessica's bright eyes flashed back, the picture of playful annoyance.

Thoughts of the upcoming beach adventure with Ethan stirred a mixture of excitement and nerves in Jessica. Memories of her previous fumbling attempts at surfing painted a comical, if not slightly embarrassing, picture. Still, the prospect of Ethan's gentle guidance held a certain appeal.

Fawn rose with grace, gathering the remnants of their meal. Her movements were fluid, a dance that carried her effortlessly to the dishwasher. Jessica broke the comfortable silence that had settled between them. "Are you going with us today?" she asked, her voice filled with hopeful expectation.

The quiet house beckoned Fawn to immerse herself in her art, to channel the day's calm into creative energy. "No, I'm going to stay here and work on my art project," she replied, conveying both reassurance and determination. "You have fun with Ethan." Her eyes brightened, the shadows of worry visibly lifting in the morning light.

The weight of Jessica's morning conversation with her father lingered in the room, wrapping around them like a blanket warmed by the sun. Witnessing Fawn's renewed focus on the art competition filled Jessica with pride for her friend, who had once expressed concern for her future.

"I understand," Jessica said as she got up from the table. "You need to focus on your art project." She walked to the hallway, adding over her shoulder, "I'm going to get ready."

Fawn watched Jessica disappear into the bathroom. She heard the faint whisper of the shower curtain being pulled back and listened to the soothing sound of water streaming down. Taking a deep breath filled with determination and anticipation of creative inspiration, Fawn made her way to Jessica's room, where an atmosphere ripe for artistic endeavor awaited her—a space she hoped would wrap her in its embrace and ignite a masterpiece within her.

In the soft light of early afternoon, Jessica sat on the front steps of her home, her petite figure adorned in a chic black swimsuit that hugged her curves. Sitting next to her, Fawn exuded a relaxed charm, her floral V-neck shirt fluttering in the coastal breeze over classic blue denim shorts. The sounds of Wavecrest enveloped them as they awaited Ethan's arrival. A flicker of anxiety fluttered in Jessica's chest, the weight of concern for her friend not lost amidst her pounding heartbeat.

"Are you sure you're going to be okay?" Jessica asked, a shadow of guilt for leaving Fawn coloring her words.

Fawn looked at her with bright eyes, the sunlight turning them into pools of golden warmth. A smile of reassurance graced her lips as she answered with comforting ease. "I'll be fine," she assured Jessica with a buoyant cadence. "Remember, Ethan is your surfing coach today. You'll need all the concentration you can muster." Her teasing nudge was a gentle reminder of Jessica's upcoming challenge—a challenge Fawn had playfully encouraged.

In return, Jessica offered an affectionate mock glare, silently recalling how this surfing escapade had originated from Fawn's mischievous suggestion to Ethan. Just as the playful banter was about to escalate, the unmistakable rumble of Ethan's Jeep cut through their camaraderie.

As he parked his Jeep in the driveway, Jessica's pulse quickened with anticipation, her excitement transparent in the eager wave she sent his way. Ethan, ever the gentleman, emerged, holding open the passenger door with a broad smile. Fawn rose gracefully beside Jessica, intending to say a quick hello before he and Jessica went on their way.

As Jessica took her seat in the Jeep, Ethan's expression changed to one of slight confusion upon seeing Fawn's intention to stay behind.

"You're not coming with us?" he asked with a gentle furrow of his brow.

Fawn refused with an easy dismissal and a soft voice. "No, I'm going to stay here and work on my art project."

With a nod of understanding, Ethan secured the passenger door and maneuvered himself into the driver's seat. As the Jeep's engine roared to life, he gave Jessica a reassuring look and squeezed her hand. "Don't worry, babe," he said. "Surfing's a breeze. You'll be riding those waves in no time."

Her response was playful, yet laced with genuine nervousness about the challenge ahead. "Yeah, right. We'll see about that," she replied.

The soft hum of the Jeep's engine became part of the afternoon melody as Ethan's chuckle echoed in the cab. As Jessica shot him a mocking glare, the sunlight danced in her eyes—a brilliant blue reminiscent of deep-sea treasures yet to be discovered. Those eyes, so full of innocent apprehension, held a power that Ethan found impossible to resist. A surge of warmth enveloped him, accompanied by a realization as clear as the waves they sought: he was incredibly lucky to have her by his side.

As he stepped on the accelerator, the Jeep hummed beneath them like an old friend telling tales of past adventures. The vehicle jumped forward, as if it understood its role in leading them to the vast sea ahead. With each mile they traveled together, Ethan reaffirmed his commitment—he couldn't wait to share with Jessica the joyous symphony of surf and sea that had long been his blissful escape and source of exhilaration.

As the last hum of the Jeep faded and merged with the distant symphony of waves and seagulls, Fawn retraced her steps into Jessica's bedroom. The room, bathed in soft sunlight streaming through the curtains, seemed to await her return. Hints of Jessica's essence lingered in the air—the delicate scent of her perfume, notes of lavender and jasmine, mingled with memories of whispered secrets and laughter.

Drawn to her sketchpad that lay on Jessica's desk, its pages filled with traces of thoughts and dreams, Fawn grasped it with her fingers. Its familiar weight in her hands felt like an anchor, grounding her in the present moment. She sank into the plush embrace of Jessica's bed, the softness of the linen against her skin carrying an assurance of comfort.

As she nestled against the headboard, Fawn's fingers played along the edges of the sketchpad. Each page whispered tales of previous sketches and imprinted musings, and with a flutter of anticipation, she found herself on an untouched canvas of possibility.

Her eyes, intense yet dreamy, stared at the blank page as if coaxing the shadows of creativity lurking in its corners. Pencil in hand, she was guided by the silent rhythm of her heart, trusting the intuitive dance of graphite and paper to manifest the nebulous vision dancing at the periphery of her mind. Fawn was on a journey, diving deep into the well of her creativity, hoping to retrieve a masterpiece from its depths.

As Jessica and Ethan stood side by side in the embrace of the shallow water, the gentle lullaby of the waves hitting the shore enveloped them, harmonizing with the rhythm of their heartbeats. The surfboard next to Jessica caught the sun's golden rays, casting iridescent reflections that danced like fairy lights, transforming the ordinary fiberglass into something enchanting.

The wrinkles at the corners of Ethan's eyes told the story of countless sunny days on the ocean. He felt the tiny tremors of her excitement mixed with trepidation. "Okay, Jess, first we need to get you used to the feel of the board underneath you. Balance is the key to surfing."

Jessica's expressive eyes, as wide as the ocean in front of her, reflected a swirl of emotions. "It looks a lot easier than it feels," she whispered, her fingers tracing the drops of water on the surface of the board.

A soft laugh escaped him, reminiscent of a fond memory. "It always does. Here, step on the board. I'll hold it for you."

Jessica took a moment to inhale the salty scent of the sea, feeling its timeless energy seep into her. As she carefully placed her feet on the board, the unpredictability of its movement beneath her contrasted with the solid ground to which she was so accustomed. Her arms danced in the air, trying to grasp an invisible wall.

Ethan's voice was a reassuring anchor amid her uncertainty. "Keep your feet shoulder-width apart and bend your knees slightly. It'll help you balance."

She took his words to heart and tried to adjust her body to the temperament of the board. But a playful wave had other ideas. It nudged the board and playfully pushed her into its liquid embrace. Her delightful squeal mingled with the whisper of the ocean.

When she emerged, strands of her hair clung to her face like dark seaweed. The flush on her cheeks rivaled the hues of the horizon. But Ethan's laughter, genuine and free, brought a playful glint in her eyes. "It's not that funny," she retorted, splashing him with her version of oceanic retaliation.

Ethan's eyes, now twinkling with mischief, locked onto hers. "Trust me, everyone has their first fall. It's like an initiation rite." He held out his hand, inviting her back into the dance. "Ready to try again?"

She saw more than encouragement in his looks. It was a silent testament to their journey together, to all the challenges they had faced, and the many more they would overcome.

"Alright, let's do this," she declared, the fire of determination igniting in her eyes.

As the day turned into a symphony of gold and amber, Jessica felt the intimate dialogue between her feet and the board, the delicate balance of give and take. Ethan's closeness, every glance, and subtle touch, whispered secrets into the fabric of the surrounding sea.

"Focus on a point in the distance," he said, his tone softer, more intimate, making her heart flutter.

She did, her gaze fixed on a lone seagull, its wings slicing through the warm embrace of the sunlit sky. And as moments flowed into each other, she and the board became one, dancing to the music only they could hear.

Ethan's voice, rich with pride, brought her back. "Look at you! You're a natural!"

Caught in a playful spirit, Jessica performed an exaggerated bow as they both gave in to laughter, their mirth blending with the timeless melody of the ocean.

With the sensation of damp sand soothing her soles, Jessica met Ethan's gaze, glimpsing in it their intertwined past and the unwritten chapters of their future.

"Thanks, babe," she whispered, her words heavy with emotion. "That was... more fun than I expected."

With a twinkle in his eye, he teased, "Told you. Wait till we hit the real waves. That's when the real fun starts."

The sun draped its golden veil over the shore as Jessica gained confidence in her balancing act. Sensing her budding prowess, Ethan, always the guide on this newfound journey, led her to where the wet sand kissed the dry. The surfboard, once an alien entity, lay on the beach like a steadfast companion, awaiting her return to the sea's embrace.

Ethan's eyes, shimmering with the wisdom of the sea, held a gleam of mischief. "Alright, babe," he said, his voice calm against the symphony of the waves. He wiped a single drop from his forehead, which glistened like a tiny pearl in the sunlight. "Balancing is just the beginning. The real magic happens when you go from lying down to standing in one smooth motion. It's like... going from a mermaid to a land-dweller in a matter of seconds."

Jessica's laughter rang out, mingling with the distant cries of seagulls. "Sounds challenging," she admitted, her tone brimming with an adventurous spirit.

With the grace of someone who had kissed the waves a thousand times, Ethan molded his body to the surfboard, a fluid demonstration of what was to come.

"You start like this," he explained, his voice as soothing as the gentle caress of the waves. In one fluid motion, he demonstrated the transition he had described.

Jessica watched, mesmerized. "It looks so easy when you do it," she murmured, her voice filled with wonder and contemplation.

His laughter, rich and hearty, warmed the air. "Well, let's see your mermaid-to-land-dweller transformation."

Taking a deep breath, filling her lungs with the salty essence of the sea, Jessica tried to mimic his movements. Her first attempt was a chaotic dance of limbs and bursts of sandy laughter. But beneath her carefree exterior, simmered an unyielding determination.

"It's okay, babe. It happens to the best of us! Just focus on getting that front foot forward quickly," Ethan advised, his voice a comforting mix of mirth and encouragement.

Jessica puffed out her cheeks in playful determination. "All right, Mr. Perfect. One more time."

With each successive attempt, she moved closer to mastery. Under Ethan's patient tutelage, her body learned the necessary rhythm—the unity of purpose and action that crystallized with practice. Then, as if by magic, with the sun as her spotlight and the sand as her stage, Jessica executed the dance flawlessly and rose like a phoenix.

Ethan clapped enthusiastically, pride radiating from him like rays from the sun above. "There she is! The land-dweller has risen!"

A flush of victory painted her cheeks as she threw back a spirited retort, "Told you I could do it."

Ethan's chuckle held warmth, the sun's rays encapsulated in his words. "Never doubted you for a second, babe."

Their eyes locked, a universe of shared experiences and silent promises exchanged in that fleeting moment. But then laughter erupted between them, spontaneous as a summer rain, harmonizing with nature's symphony and crystallizing the memory forever in the sands of time.

Amidst the orchestra of waves crashing on the shore and seagulls calling in the distance, Jessica followed Ethan into the vast classroom of the ocean. To her, each wave was a behemoth rising toward the sky, an imposing force that could easily swallow her ambitions whole. But to Ethan, they were mere playful swells, inviting them to dance on their crests.

As Jessica's fear began to run through her veins like cold sea foam, Ethan glanced over his shoulder, his eyes twin beacons of comfort in the vast blue.

"Remember, it's all about timing and positioning," he said, his voice a gentle current in the turbulent waters. "Don't be afraid. I'll be right here to guide you, okay?"

With a deep breath that filled her lungs with salty determination, Jessica steeled herself against the imposing waves. "Okay," she replied, eyeing the towering forms with awe and fear. "It's just... they're big waves."

Ethan's face broke into a heartwarming grin, a mischievous twinkle in his eyes. "They're not that big. Just a little bigger than your board. You got this, babe."

They aligned their board with the incoming set, Ethan's calm presence a grounding force beside her. He demonstrated the paddling technique—a fluid interplay of arms and shoulders in sync with the pulse of the ocean.

"It's all in the arms and shoulders. Paddle hard when I tell you," he instructed. "And when you feel the wave catch you, that's your cue to pop up."

The world around them seemed to dissolve into the rhythm of the sea as they floated on its surface, gently bobbing to its breath. Suddenly, Ethan signaled—the moment had come. "Paddle now! This one's yours!"

Jessica's arms sliced through the water with eager energy as adrenaline coursed through her veins. But as the wave crested and crashed beneath her, it caught her off guard, plunging her into its emerald depths instead of lifting her onto its back.

Bursting from the ocean's clutches as quickly as she had been engulfed, Jessica found Ethan at her side—an unwavering pillar amid the liquid tumult. "Are you okay?" he asked.

She expelled a mouthful of seawater and let out a laugh tinged with chagrin and a newfound reverence for the ocean. "I think I just drank half the ocean."

Ethan's laughter joined hers, echoing over the surface of the water. "It happens to everyone. The first wave is always the hardest." He looked at her with encouraging eyes. "Ready to try again?"

With determination shining in her bright blue eyes like sunlight through the water, Jessica nodded firmly. "Let's do it."

Each wave that followed was a new chapter, a story of falls, perseverance, and sips of salt water. With every challenge and every fall, Ethan was there—a constant support against the shifting tides.

Then came a moment suspended in time when all the elements aligned—Jessica gracefully stood on a cresting wave as it carried her forward in an exhilarating rush of unity with nature.

From his vantage point in the water below, Ethan's voice rose above the din of waves and wind, a triumphant call that echoed across the distance: "I knew you could do it! You're surfing, Jess!"

As the day's canvas blushed with the hues of the afternoon sun, Jessica and Ethan's triumph over the waves crystallized into a memory as enduring as the ocean itself. Jessica, the maiden of the waves, had found her rhythm with the pulse of the ocean, and Ethan, her guiding star, rejoiced in each successful dance she shared with the tide.

With each swell, Jessica harnessed beneath her board, her spirit intertwined more deeply with the boundless sea, her body moving in sync with its rolling cadence. The thrill coursing through her veins was a potent mix of exhilaration and unbridled freedom—a siren's call that spoke to her core.

Yet, for all its beauty and promise of adventure, the ocean was an entity of unfathomable power and caprice. From beyond the idyllic tableau of laughter and light, an unforeseen behemoth rose—a rogue wave that approached with the ferocity of a predator. Its shadow loomed large, a dark omen against the blue sky. Before Jessica could react, it was upon her—a roaring colossus that enveloped surfer and board in its formidable grasp.

Above the tumultuous scene, Ethan's joyous cheer was abruptly cut short by a sharp intake of breath. His eyes scanned the now murky waters where Jessica had disappeared, his heart pounding against his chest with cold fear. Time stretched into an agonizing void as he searched for any sign of her.

Compelled by a visceral urgency that brooked no hesitation, Ethan plunged into the maelstrom. His every thought condensed into a single imperative: find Jessica. The depths enveloped him in their swirling embrace, obscuring vision and direction.

Beneath the turmoil of the surface, Jessica was adrift in an alien realm, where up and down lost meaning amidst spirals of bubbles and relentless currents. The weight of the unyielding and vast ocean bore down on her chest, and darkness crept to the edges of her consciousness.

At that critical moment, when light seemed but a distant memory, Ethan's hands found her—a lifeline amidst the chaos. His face emerged from the darkness—an embodiment of fierce determination—and together, they ascended to salvation.

They broke through into a world reclaimed by sound and sunlight, where Ethan's arms encircled Jessica in an embrace as solid as rock. His powerful strokes carried them back to land—their refuge from the treacherous beauty of the sea.

Her lungs heaving with ragged breaths, Jessica felt Ethan's hands press against her back as his soothing voice enveloped her in warmth and safety. As awareness returned to her senses, she met his gaze—one now filled with stormy relief and exposed vulnerability.

Ethan's touch traced her face—a tactile confirmation of her presence as his voice quivered with barely contained emotion. "Oh my God, Jessica," he murmured hoarsely, "I thought I had lost you."

Her eyes locked with his, gratitude cutting through the shock. "I'm here, babe," she reiterated softly.

Ethan cradled her face in his hands as his breathing stuttered under an emotional weight too heavy to bear in silence. In a fervent outpouring from deep within him came the words that had been longing for release: "I love you, Jessica Reese."

Tears welled in Jessica's eyes—tears that shimmered with happiness to match the magnitude of his declaration. Her heart swelled as she responded with equal passion: "I love you too, Ethan Harris."

Drawn together by an unseen force more powerful than gravity or fear, their lips met in a kiss that reverberated through their very souls—a sealing of their heartfelt confessions on this sacred shoreline. And as they held each other, it was not just two hearts that had found each other amidst the vastness of nature—it was two kindred spirits, forever bound by the unbreakable tide of love.

# Chapter 22

------------------------------------------------------------

The afternoon sun poured through the windows in Jessica's bedroom, enveloping every-thing in a serene, golden embrace. The room, bathed in this amber hue, was a haven of calm, with memories of endless summer days echoing in its corners.

The walls were adorned with photos of Jessica and Fawn, chronicling their adventures from their mischievous childhood exploits to their proud graduation day. Interspersed with these memories were posters of bands, dreamy actors, and inspirational quotes that spoke of teenage dreams and aspirations.

Sprinkled throughout this tapestry were shelves filled with knickknacks Jessica had collected over the years—small mementos of school trips, beach parties, and ordinary days that held special meaning.

In the midst of this warm cocoon, Fawn sat with her back against the plush headboard, cradling a sketchpad that bore the remnants of her artistic struggle. There were half-drawn figures, intertwining patterns, and a myriad of shaded textures, each hinting at the flurry of thoughts that occupied her mind.

But as the hours passed, the dance between her pencil and paper had slowed, the lines had softened, and her eyelids had grown heavy. The rhythmic breathing that accompanied her light sleep was the only sound in the room, the steady heartbeat of a soul at rest.

Startled from her sleep, her eyelids fluttered open, momentarily bathed in the warm glow of sunlight. A soft moan escaped her lips as she sat up, brushing away the strands of hair that had fallen across her face. She glanced at the digital clock on Jessica's nightstand, its red LED display boldly reading 3:15 p.m.

Realization washed over her. "I can't believe I dozed off," she murmured, rubbing the last traces of her brief nap from her eyes.

Fawn's fingers twitched over her sketchpad, the blank page reflecting her current state of inspiration—empty. The anticipation pressed down on her, heavy and unavoidable. Given the uninterrupted hours, she had imagined that an idea would flow naturally onto the paper. Yet it remained stubbornly elusive.

She tilted her head and took a deep breath, the faint scent of frustration mingling with the remnants of her afternoon dream. The edge of hunger gnawed at her, a gentle reminder that she had not eaten since breakfast. Perhaps, she mused, a bite to eat might spark the creative impulse she so desperately sought.

With newfound purpose, she placed the sketchpad on the nightstand, her fingers brushing the surface as if to coax an idea from its depths. Sliding off the bed, the soft carpet welcomed her feet and muffled her footsteps. Each step carried a rhythmic cadence, a dance of determination and hope.

The kitchen was bathed in a soft, quiet light; the sun's rays filtered through the blinds, casting a geometric dance of light and shadow across the terracotta floor. It was silent, except for the low hum of the refrigerator and the faint rustle of leaves from the garden beyond the window.

The room felt still, expectant, as if it, too, was waiting for her arrival. Fawn paused in the doorway, letting the stillness of the room envelop her before she began searching for something to satisfy her hunger.

The kitchen table, polished to a soft sheen, held a centerpiece of nature's bounty—a woven basket containing an assortment of fruit. Oranges sat like little suns next to the rich reds of apples, the deep purples of grapes, and the playful yellow curve of bananas. Drawn to the refreshing simplicity of an apple, Fawn reached out and plucked one, its skin smooth and cool to the touch. She bit into it, enjoying the crisp sound and the burst of sweetness that followed. Its juice was a fleeting balm, soothing more than just her physical hunger.

Chewing thoughtfully, she wandered into the adjoining living room, the apple acting as a tether to ground her amidst the whirlwind of emotions she'd felt. The walls, painted in muted tones, held years of family history in their embrace. Framed photographs captured moments both mundane and momentous—baby's shaky first steps, salt-sprayed grins on summer beaches, and holiday merriment tinged with tinsel and laughter.

Then, a familiar sight caught her eye—a pair of graduation photos proudly displayed side by side. There was Jessica, poised in her graduation robe, cap confidently perched on her head, smile wide and hopeful. But what warmed Fawn's heart even more was the picture next to it. It was her own graduation portrait. The side-by-side arrangement was no accident. Right next to Jessica's, her picture made an undeniable statement: she wasn't a guest here; she was family.

A wave of warmth ran through her, settling deep in her chest. It was a feeling she had known for years—a sense of belonging, an assurance that she held a valued place in this household. But to see it represented visually, to understand that they had chosen to hang her moment next to Jessica's, was a tangible affirmation of the bond she shared with this family. She wasn't just Fawn, the friend. She was Fawn, an irreplaceable thread in their family tapestry.

The soft contours of the living room sofa welcomed her, the familiar fabric brushing against her skin like the pages of an old, beloved book. With each bite of her apple, the sweetness seemed to unleash a cascade of memories, each one a vivid page from the past.

There they were—two young girls huddled together on the couch, a tangle of blankets and limbs, their faces illuminated by the soft glow of the TV screen. Those stolen giggles in the heart of the night, a covert sound in the sanctity of silence, punctuated their many movie marathons. Fawn could almost hear the whisper of "Shh, you'll wake them" from Jessica's lips.

The memory caused a small, nostalgic smile to dance across her lips. Another memory unfolded—Christmas mornings, the room decked out in twinkling lights and festive decorations. She and Jessica would sit side by side, their eager fingers tearing away the wrapping paper to reveal toys and treasures underneath. The anticipation, the joy, and the simple pleasure of those moments sent warmth coursing through Fawn's veins.

Lost in the waltz of yesteryear, a softness enveloped her. With its myriad of memories, this living room had become more than just a room; it was a reservoir of happiness from simpler times that she could always revisit in her heart, especially during those inevitable moments when she'd long for Jessica's presence.

However, as the last bite of the apple disappeared and the real world beckoned, Fawn's reverie abruptly came to an end. She returned to the kitchen, the apple core finding its place in the trash. With her hunger tamed and her heart full, she retraced her steps back to Jessica's room.

Fawn nestled back into the welcoming embrace of Jessica's bed, the familiar contours seeming to hug her in silent encouragement. With a sigh of determination, she leaned back against the mountain of pillows and opened her sketchpad to a blank page. The white expanse before her seemed infinite, a universe brimming with potential that whispered of greatness yet to be born.

The soft scratch of pencil on paper filled the silence as she sketched the familiar lines of Wavecrest's coastline. The curve of the shore and the frothy kiss of the waves on the sand flowed effortlessly from her mind to her hand. Yet, as she drew, a feeling of dissatisfaction gnawed at her. The image was too familiar, too safe—it lacked the spark that could transform it from a mere drawing into art.

Allowing herself a brief pause, Fawn let her eyes wander aimlessly around the room, hoping that somewhere in Jessica's familiar space lay the inspiration she craved. Amidst the vibrant colors, posters, and memorabilia, her eyes fell on a treasured object on the other side of the room. Though it might seem ordinary to others, to Fawn, it was the beacon she had been waiting for. Her heart, briefly held captive by uncertainty, now surged with a rush of inspiration. It was as if she had been reunited with a long-lost friend after years of separation.

A spontaneous exclamation burst from her lips, a jubilant "Yes!" that echoed with genuine enthusiasm. The joy in her voice was palpable, embodying all the pent-up creative energy that had been simmering beneath the surface, waiting for the right spark. For Fawn, this was more than just a competition; it was the reawakening of a dream, of her true self. The realization was profound, and the emotions swelled within her, filling every corner of her being with a renewed sense of purpose.

With eyes aglow with fervor and a smile that shone like the afternoon sun, Fawn was a portrait of pure elation. The once intimidating page now welcomed her with open arms, eager to bear witness to the creation she was destined to uphold. The girl who had once feared she'd lost her artistic touch was now on fire, consumed by the urge to create something extraordinary. With a deep, determined breath, she plunged into her creation, letting the world fade away as her masterpiece began to take shape.

The afternoon sky stretched endlessly above, dotted with cumulus clouds that meandered across, briefly obscuring the sun before allowing its gentle warmth to return. As the holiday weekend came to an end, the ebb and flow of visitors dwindled, and the once crowded sands of Wavecrest's beach were now sparsely populated.

Jessica and Ethan strolled along the shore, their arms wrapped around each other in a tight embrace. The rhythmic sound of the waves served as a backdrop to their heartbeats, which seemed to echo in perfect synchrony. The sand beneath their feet felt cool, a stark contrast to the burning emotions within them—emotions that were still new, raw, and beautifully overwhelming.

A gentle breeze blew in from the ocean, caressing their faces and ruffling their hair. To Ethan, it was more than a breeze—it felt like a tender, ethereal embrace, an invisible being wrapping its arms around him. The sensation was strange, yet comforting. As the wind whispered secrets of the ancient town to him, he felt a connection, not only to Jessica but to Wavecrest itself.

He looked down at Jessica, her face serene, seemingly unaffected by the sensation that stirred something deep within him. To her, this spiritual embrace was as common as the air she breathed, having felt its touch since her earliest days. It was Wavecrest's gentle affirmation, a nod to the deep roots she had in this place.

In the midst of their quiet walk, Ethan paused, his hand tightening around Jessica to hold her still beside him. His shift was abrupt, drawing her attention from the path ahead to the vast expanse of the sea. His eyes, lovingly fixed on her moments before, were now fixed on the horizon. He inhaled deeply, letting the warmth of the summer breeze fill his lungs and touch his very soul. It was as if the wind carried voices, not audible, but words that spoke directly to his heart. An unbidden, radiant smile spread across his face, revealing his wonder.

Stunned by their sudden stop, Jessica scanned the horizon where Ethan's attention had lingered. Her bright blue eyes saw only the vastness of the Pacific—its waves faithfully approaching the land in eternal homage. With her head cocked in confusion and a hint of curiosity in her soft voice, she asked, "What is it, babe?"

The intensity of Ethan's gaze shifted back to Jessica, his eyes now shimmering with awe and a hint of confusion.

"Don't you feel that?" he asked, genuinely surprised.

She looked back at him, her gaze full of love, but now laced with intrigue. "Feel what?"

For a fleeting moment, Ethan wondered if the feeling was his alone, a figment of his overwhelmed heart. He struggled with the idea of sharing this profound experience, afraid of how she might perceive it.

Choosing discretion over revelation, his expression softened into a tender smile. "It's nothing, babe. Never mind." And so, they resumed their leisurely walk, side by side, the waves playfully tickling their toes with each step.

As they continued their walk along Wavecrest's pristine shoreline, a particularly familiar stretch of sand caught Jessica's attention. Her steps slowed, her eyes widened in recognition, an intense excitement coursing through her veins. The unique patterns of the sand, the curvature of the shoreline, and the looming presence of a distinctive rock ahead brought back a fond memory. This wasn't just another part of the beach to her—it was where fate had playfully nudged her toward Ethan only a month ago, leaving an indelible mark on her heart.

"Oh my God! Do you know where we are?" Jessica's voice, filled with wonder, pierced Ethan's contemplation.

He paused, taking in their surroundings, his expression knotted with concentration as he tried to grasp the significance of this location. "No. Where are we?"

Seeing Ethan's genuine confusion, Jessica's face lit up with a smile that reflected the brilliance of the sun. "Seriously?" She gestured to the monolithic rock stationed nearby. "That rock over there, that's where you and I sat... the night of the beach party. Remember?"

Ethan experienced a realization as if a shroud had lifted from his perception. Though the daytime vibrancy of the beach was a stark contrast to the tender, moonlit atmosphere of their first intimate conversation, the same rock stood unchanged—a silent witness to the bond they had begun to forge that very night. Its silhouette against the sparkling sea took him back to that pivotal night—the laughter of partygoers in the distance, the soothing rhythm of the waves, and the feel of Jessica's warmth beside him all came rushing back.

"Come on. Let's sit for a while." Jessica's voice brought him back to the present. Her fingers intertwined with his in an intimate embrace, drawing him to what was now hallowed ground for both of them. There was an unspoken reverence for this rock, a monument to the beginning of their love story.

Surrendering to the poignant gravity of the moment and enchanted by Jessica's spirited enthusiasm, Ethan agreed, his heartbeat finding a rhythm with hers as they approached their treasured spot.

Perched on the gray and time-worn rock, they faced the endless expanse of the Pacific Ocean before them. Side by side on its rough and cool surface, they felt warmth not only from each other but from the profound meaning woven into the simple act of sitting where it all began. They lost themselves in the mesmerizing dance of the waves—a visual symphony before them—and for a moment, time stood still as they gazed at the oceanic horizon where the sea merged seamlessly with the sky.

Ethan's mind drifted back to a few hours ago, the earlier events of the day that played out in his mind like a scene from a movie. Laughter echoed, mingled with the sound of splashing water and the sparkle in Jessica's eyes as she bravely attempted to conquer her first wave. Then, a wave of terror abruptly silenced the laughter as Jessica disappeared beneath the frothy whitecaps. The cold fist of panic had tightened around his heart.

Even now, under the gentle kiss of the late afternoon sun, the memory sent a shiver down his spine. It was as if the universe had cruelly teased him with a glimpse of a world without Jessica, a prospect so bleak that he recoiled inwardly. Instinctively, Ethan pulled her to his side, as if his embrace alone could ward off any future threats to her safety.

"You know," Ethan began, his voice carrying an undercurrent of emotion that had her full attention, "I've never told a girl I loved her before."

Surprise flickered across Jessica's face as she turned to meet his gaze. "Really?" Her voice was a mixture of wonder and affection. His candor touched her deeply; he was sharing not just a story, but a piece of his soul, underscoring the depth and uniqueness of their bond.

He nodded, the words tumbling out with heartfelt gravity. "I've never felt like this before. It's like... you've become a part of me."

Jessica's heart fluttered at his words, reflecting her own emotions. "I've never been in love before, Ethan. You are my first and only love. I think about you all the time," she replied, her voice soft yet filled with intensity.

A tender smile curved Ethan's lips as he contemplated the serendipity of their meeting. "I feel like fate brought you to me that first day we met at the lifeguard stand."

At his mention of fate, a soft chuckle escaped Jessica's lips; she held the playful secret of Fawn's intervention on that fateful day. She vividly remembered Fawn's vibrant encouragement—her friend who had nudged her out of the shadows of shyness and into Ethan's sight.

"Well, you can thank Fawn for that. She's the one who pushed me to talk to you," she revealed with a twinkle in her eye.

Ethan pictured it: a reluctant Jessica, encouraged by Fawn's insistence, making her way to him by the lifeguard stand—a scene that held more significance than he had realized at first glance.

She confessed her natural shyness, and it was then that Ethan realized how meaningful their first interaction had been to Jessica. For someone so reserved, that single act of courage had changed the course of their lives. He squeezed her hand in acknowledgment, grateful for the universe's nudge—or rather, Fawn's nudge—in their direction.

The gentle caress of the ocean breeze couldn't lighten the weight of memories and emotions swirling between Jessica and Ethan. A warm smile graced her lips as Jessica's thoughts turned to Fawn, her lifelong guide and protector. The glow of the sun seemed to frame the many memories of Fawn challenging Jessica to step out of her comfort zone, pushing her to take risks she would never have taken on her own.

"I don't know what I would have done without her," Jessica admitted, her voice a soft whisper of gratitude.

The wind whispered change across the beach, tugging at Jessica's heartstrings as her expression faded, a cloud casting a shadow over her usually radiant features. Her thoughts raced forward, anticipating the inevitable separation between her and Fawn, a prospect as daunting as the endless sea before her.

"I don't know what I'll do when we're not together anymore," she murmured, her voice tinged with the vulnerability of a soul bracing for a storm.

Ethan, who had come to read her emotions with an almost mystical precision, pulled her closer into his protective embrace. He tried to shield her from the wave of anxiety that threatened to overwhelm her.

Jessica's gaze turned inward, wrestling with another painful goodbye—to Ethan himself—as his own departure from Wavecrest loomed on the horizon. The clarity in her eyes now swirled with a storm of sadness and loss.

"I don't know what I'm going to do when you..." but Ethan silenced her with a gentle press of his finger before the wave of fear could escape her lips.

"Let's not go there right now, babe," he whispered, his voice strained with the emotion of wanting to freeze this moment in time. "We still have a lot of tomorrows before that day comes."

To reassure her, he gently stroked her cheek, reiterating the depth of his feelings. "I love you, Jessica. I always will." Their embrace deepened, becoming a refuge from the storms of uncertainty, and for a few moments, everything else fell away.

Their embrace was an oasis in the midst of desolation, each heartbeat a promise to endure whatever might come. Jessica found solace in the comfort of Ethan's arms, allowing herself a fleeting escape from the inexorable march of time.

But as the outside world encroached on their solace, Jessica's thoughts returned to

Fawn—her steadfast confidante who might now feel adrift in loneliness. With reluctance heavy in her heart, she pulled away from Ethan's embrace. Her eyes held an echo of earlier distress as she spoke with a gentle urgency. "I think we should go back to my house and check on Fawn."

Ethan nodded in silent agreement; they were united not only by love but by a shared concern for their friend. Together, they rose from the rock that had witnessed the beginning of their love story and began their journey back hand in hand.

With one last look over their shoulders at the sentinel rock and the whispering waves that swirled around it, they left this place of deep connection. The sounds of the ocean followed them, a chorus bidding them farewell as they stepped forward into the uncertain dance of life.

The soft purr of an engine broke the silence that had settled over Jessica's home, drawing Fawn's attention away from the flickering TV screen. Nestled in the comforting embrace of the couch, she had lost herself in the fantasy of a favorite movie, but now her ears tuned with interest to the sounds of the real world. Peering through the window, a wave of elation washed over her as she recognized the familiar car pulling into the driveway. It was Tom and Teresa, their arrival heralding their return from their day out.

As the car's engine died down, Fawn rose from her cozy nook, a smile lighting up her features. It had been days since she had felt such warmth and excitement. She hurried to greet them at the door and stood in the foyer as sunlight streamed through the windows, casting a warm glow around her.

The front door swung open, revealing the comforting figures of Teresa and Tom. Teresa's gaze met Fawn's, and her eyes instantly softened at the sparkle in the young girl's eyes—a sparkle that had been conspicuously absent in the recent past.

"Hi, sweetheart," Teresa greeted her in a voice as sweet as honey. Her motherly intuition picked up on the change in Fawn's demeanor. "Did you have a nice day?" she asked, her graceful movements carrying her into the kitchen.

Tom followed close behind, his arms laden with groceries. He gave Fawn an affectionate wink before continuing into the kitchen, where he began unpacking with a rustle of paper bags and a clatter of jars.

Fawn's spirits soared as she followed them into the kitchen. "It's been a great day," she beamed, unable to hide her joy.

Teresa turned to Fawn with a warm heart. "Aw, I'm so glad to hear that." The few steps between them disappeared as Teresa wrapped Fawn in a hug that radiated comfort and care.

Watching Tom unload the groceries, Fawn's gratitude swelled. Memories of the comfort he offered during her emotional storm a few nights ago came flooding back. She felt drawn to him like a sunflower to the sun. Without a second thought, she wrapped her arms around him in a tight, loving embrace.

Tom let out a soft chuckle, his muscular frame wrapping around Fawn protectively. "Whoa. What's that about?" he asked, his voice filled with playful surprise and fatherly love.

Looking up at him, Fawn's eyes sparkled with heartfelt sincerity. "Nothing, Papa. I just love you."

Tom's heart swelled, touched by Fawn's open declaration of affection. His reply was gentle yet filled with deep warmth. "Aw, I love you too, sweetheart."

In a room bathed in the soft golden hues of the setting sun, Teresa watched with tender eyes as Fawn and Tom shared a moment of genuine connection. The kitchen seemed to cocoon them, the light casting an ethereal glow over their embrace. It was as if the soft rays were trying to erase the vestiges of Fawn's recent trials, illuminating her with an aura of restored serenity. The sight of their loving embrace brought a deep sense of relief and contentment to Teresa.

She glanced down the hallway, maternal anticipation in her voice as she asked, "Where's Jessica? Has she come home yet?"

Leaning gracefully against the kitchen counter, Fawn replied with an airy note of assurance, "Not yet, but she's with Ethan. They should be here soon."

As if on cue, the distinctive rumble of Ethan's Jeep announced their arrival, punctuating Fawn's words with impeccable timing. "Well, what do you know. Here they are," Teresa remarked with a smile that spread like warmth from a hearth.

The couple emerged, their figures etched against the golden tapestry of early evening, their fingers weaving tales of affection and youthful love in a silent language of intertwined hands. The world seemed to hold its breath as they stepped through the front door, their presence ushering in a gentle breeze that whispered tales of home and familiarity.

As they entered the kitchen, Jessica and Ethan were greeted by bright and welcoming faces. Teresa beamed at them from across the island counter. "Hey, kids! Perfect timing!" she exclaimed, wiping her hands on a nearby towel. "We just got back ourselves. How was your day at the beach?"

"It was amazing," Jessica replied, her voice saturated with the joyful echoes of her day. Beside her, Ethan agreed with a simple nod, his eyes crinkling at the corners as he smiled at his newfound love.

In the dimming embrace of early evening, the room was bathed in a soft golden glow, soft shadows playing on the walls. Against this serene backdrop, Jessica's eyes drifted to Fawn like a butterfly to a radiant flower. There, in her friend's eyes, she noticed a familiar glimmer. It was a glimmer she had missed lately, a sign that Fawn's muse, which had seemingly abandoned her, was stirring again. That mischievous glimmer hinted at a story waiting to be revealed, and Jessica's heart responded, fluttering with relief and elation.

But even as she reveled in the silent stories her friend's eyes told, Fawn returned the observation. She, too, noticed a change—a radiant glow that seemed to emanate from the depths of Jessica's innocent blue eyes. The glow was unfamiliar, and Fawn intuited that it was more than just the afterglow of a day spent in the sun. It was the glow of untold stories, of moments shared with Ethan. An enchanting aura surrounded her friend, and Fawn's instincts, sharpened by years of cherished friendship, hinted that something extraordinary had happened during their seaside adventure.

Breaking their unspoken communion, Jessica's voice danced into the moment, a playful note woven into her words. "All right, enough staring," she scolded with a hint of glee, her smile a bright crescent in the fading light. "What's for dinner?"

Teresa replied, her voice dripping with warmth, like honey on fresh bread. "Your dad's going to grill some chicken. Fawn's favorite," she informed, her tone enveloping them in a comforting embrace.

At that, Fawn's lips curled into a sincere smile, her heart widening with gratitude. To be known, to be loved, to have one's preferences remembered and celebrated—these were the tender gestures that bound souls together. And at that moment, she felt deeply intertwined with the Reese family.

Jessica's attention shifted to Ethan, drawn by an invisible thread of affection, her fingers intertwining with his in a silent language of intimacy.

"Will you be staying for dinner?" she asked, her voice tender, laced with the hope that he would linger in their company.

A shadow of hesitation flitted across Ethan's features, a brief cloud that threatened to obscure the warmth of the gathering. He felt torn between his desire to remain in this cocoon of familial warmth and his fear of overstaying his welcome.

But before the doubt could fully ensnare him, Tom stepped into the spotlight with effortless grace and the authority of a former Marine. His grin was teasing yet welcoming—a bridge over the abyss of Ethan's hesitation.

"You're staying for dinner, son. That's an order," he said in a light-hearted but firm tone, a twinkle in his eye that softened the order into an invitation.

Ethan's lips parted, his earlier apprehension melting away under the warmth of Tom's jest. His eyes, reflecting the amber hues of the setting sun, met Jessica's. In their shared gaze, words were unnecessary.

"Well, I guess that answers that question," he replied, his tone tinged with a delightful mixture of gratitude and amusement, sealing his place at the table.

The room still hummed with the electricity of unspoken stories. Jessica stretched lazily, the weight of the day manifesting itself as a pleasant weariness in her limbs.

"I've got to get out of this bathing suit," she sighed, content but longing for comfort.

As she began her journey down the hallway, the soft patter of Fawn's footsteps followed, a dance they had often performed—a private conversation away from prying eyes. The intimacy of their bond meant no words were needed; the mutual understanding was an unspoken agreement between them.

As they stepped into Jessica's room, the air became thick with anticipation. In a gesture of finality, Fawn closed the door behind them, shielding them from the outside world. Her eyes, now glowing with insatiable curiosity, settled on Jessica.

"So, what happened at the beach that's got you looking so happy?" The soft probe held a warmth that only a true confidant could offer.

A blush crept across Jessica's cheeks as she hesitated, biting her lip in anticipation. "I'll tell you all about it later tonight, after Ethan leaves," she whispered, her voice quivering with suppressed excitement and a hint of shyness. There was a promise in those words—a covenant of shared stories that had been their foundation.

Fawn's lips curled into a knowing smile, her nod conveying understanding. "Fair enough."

But as the seconds ticked by, the roles reversed, and it was now Jessica's turn to wear the mantle of the Inquisitor. Her sapphire eyes, still shimmering with the secrets of the day, rested on Fawn, gently probing, "But what about you? I can tell there's something going on. Spit it out."

Fawn's joy could not be contained as she triumphantly announced, "I finally figured out what I'm going to draw for the Art Contest."

Jessica's reaction was immediate. "Really? That's awesome!" Her words were not mere pleasantries, but genuine joy at her friend's revelation. Leaning forward with curious eyes, she inquired, "What's it going to be?"

With a mischievous twinkle in her eye and a mysterious tilt of her head, Fawn teased back, "That, my friend, is a secret. You'll see when it's done." And with a wink and a grin, she turned gracefully and flitted to the door, leaving a trail of mystery and anticipation in her wake.

For a brief moment, Jessica remained anchored in place, her mind a swirl of the day's events and Fawn's tantalizing secret. The room seemed to pulse with the heartbeat of their shared stories, and a gentle breeze whispered tales of love, art, and youth, resonating with those whose hearts danced to its silent rhythm.

The summer evening enveloped the Reese residence in a soft golden glow as the sun lingered in the sky, casting long shadows and bringing a quiet warmth to the end of the day. Around the glass table on the back deck, the family and Ethan sat comfortably, basking in the evening's soothing light. This soft illumination complemented the tantalizing spread of food before them, enhancing the ambiance of their gathering.

In the serene, magical enclave, time seemed to stand still, inviting each person to embrace the golden moments of their experiences. Fawn savored every bite of her favorite grilled chicken, a culinary creation prepared by Tom with paternal affection. Her joy, unmistakable and pure, sparkled in her mischievous blue eyes. Her laughter, easy and infectious, wove seamlessly into the evening's symphony of soft cutlery chimes and murmured conversation, creating an audible tapestry of her inner happiness.

As the early evening unfolded, conversation flowed like a gentle stream, led primarily by Tom and Teresa. Their exchanges were a comforting background melody, filled with plans and aspirations for the week ahead, subtly reinforcing the stability and love that grounded the family.

Outside, on the back deck decorated with twinkling lights, they each found comfort in the embrace of the darkening sky. A summer breeze flirted with their hair, tangling strands in its playful fingers as it whispered secrets only the night could reveal. Leaning back in his chair, Tom opened up to Ethan, sharing stories and insights from his time as a Marine. Ethan listened intently, his expression shifting through a mosaic of respect and curiosity as he considered his own path, now more intertwined with Jessica's than ever before.

As the moon cast its gentle glow on Jessica's face, highlighting her features with celestial grace, Ethan felt an intense surge of love that threatened to consume him completely. It was a love that made him question the trajectory of his life, beckoning him to reconsider the paths laid out before him.

But time waits for no one—not even for hearts caught in the tender snare of love—and as nine o'clock approached, Ethan felt the subtle nudge of reality. He leaned closer to Jessica, his voice a soft echo against the evening serenade. "I think it's time for me to go back, babe," he whispered reluctantly.

Jessica met his gaze with eyes full of quiet understanding and unspoken vows. Around them, time seemed to stand still; even the rhythm of the sea held its breath for a heartbeat or two.

"I'll see you tomorrow," he promised, his words caressing her soul with the assurance of another day to be painted together on the canvas of life. Jessica nodded silently—their mutual understanding an unspoken language far more eloquent than words could ever be. Under the watchful gaze of the moon, they sealed a promise to continue to weave their destinies into every tomorrow they were granted.

The soft, warm evening had turned into a balmy night, its tranquil aura broken only by the distant laughter and chatter echoing from various backyards as families enjoyed the last night of their Fourth of July weekend celebrations. The dimly lit sidewalk on which Jessica and Fawn walked was bathed in the sporadic glow of streetlights. They were on their way to Fawn's house, a place full of memories now overshadowed by its impending sale. Fawn wanted to spend time with her parents and be in the house she grew up in, even though the thought of selling it weighed heavily on her heart. As they walked, the scent of summer surrounded them, and the gentle whisper of the ocean offered a soothing lullaby to their souls.

"Oh my God!" Fawn suddenly exclaimed, her voice a mixture of shock and remorse. She paused, processing Jessica's confession about her near-drowning experience. Under the glow of a streetlamp that crowned her with light, Fawn's face was a canvas of guilt and regret.

"I'm so sorry, Jess. This is all my fault," she said, her voice heavy with self-blame, echoing the deep-seated responsibility she felt for suggesting the surfing lesson to Ethan.

But Jessica, in her bubbly resilience and the joy of memories that overshadowed the afternoon's terror, laughed it off, her voice filled with a vivacity that made the night seem brighter.

"No, no, no! That doesn't matter!" Her eyes sparkled with a secret she was bursting to reveal. "Ethan told me he loves me! He actually said it, Fawn," she gushed, her hand fluttering to her chest where her heart was pounding with excitement. "He said, 'I love you, Jessica!' Can you believe it?"

A smile spread across Fawn's face as she basked in Jessica's joy. It was a defining moment in her best friend's life, and she was thrilled to be a part of it.

"So, what did you do? What did you say?" she asked, her voice alive with the excitement of her friend's romantic milestone.

Jessica's cheeks flushed with a warmth visible even under the silver glow of the moon—a clear sign of the deep imprint of love. "I told him I loved him, too."

For a moment, the two friends stood still, the gravity of the revelation seeming to stop the world around them. Fawn's eyes softened with affection as she pulled Jessica into a hug. "Aw, Jess, I'm so happy for you," she beamed.

Their journey to Fawn's house became a passage through a world aglow with the magic of a shared secret and the warmth of mutual affection. They walked side by side, their steps in sync, a testament to the years they had walked through life together. The night air, perfumed with the scent of blooming jasmine, seemed to caress them as they walked.

Laughter erupted between them, unbidden and genuine, reflecting an inner joy that required no particular cause. It was as if the night itself conspired to envelop them in its serene magic, honoring the purity of their friendship.

From time to time, they paused to look up at the stars that dotted the velvet sky, a celestial audience for their youthful exuberance. Their eyes sparkled with reflections of the constellations as they talked of memories and dreams, fears and hopes. They shared a knowing glance as their laughter mingled with the distant echoes of celebration, an unspoken acknowledgment that these moments would become the bedrock of their memories for years to come.

The future loomed large and unknown, a vast ocean as mysterious as the depths beyond Wavecrest's sandy shores. But as daunting as adulthood seemed, it held no power over them that night. Under the gentle watch of the moon's silver face, their bond was unshakable—a bond fortified by time and tempered by the trials yet to come.

As they walked on, surrounded by the serene beauty of Wavecrest under the mantle of night, each step was a note in an unwritten symphony of youth. This was their time—a fleeting interlude where love was confessed under the threat of the ocean waves, and friendship proved its strength against the tides of change.

The soft glow from the windows they passed hinted at other lives unfolding in tandem with their own, but tonight belonged to Jessica and Fawn alone. In this moment, there was no grief for days past or fear for what lay ahead; there was only joy for the now—a joy that blazed more brilliantly than any fireworks that had lit up their Fourth of July sky.

And so, on that perfect summer night, as they reached Fawn's doorstep—a threshold between yesterday's innocence and tomorrow's maturity—the essence of their lives at Wavecrest was captured. For Jessica and Fawn, Wavecrest was a place where dreams were as bountiful as the ocean, and every night was an invitation to embrace what lay ahead.

# Chapter 23

-----------------------------------------------------------

*Three years ago, on a hot summer day in July, eighteen-year-old Ethan Harris and his older brother Jake found themselves walking the streets of New Orleans, Louisiana. The two were no strangers to adventure. For the past several summers, the brothers, driven by wanderlust and an insatiable curiosity, had chosen a new destination to immerse themselves in. These annual trips had become a tradition of sorts, days filled with exploration, discovery, and the thrill of bonding with the locals.*

*But the scope of their travels had always been limited to the familiar confines of Pine Haven in Northern California. With Ethan's high school chapter finished and a new college chapter on the horizon, Jake felt it was the perfect time to expand their boundaries. He longed for them to experience the world beyond their home state, to taste the flavors and stories that awaited in distant corners. And so, New Orleans was their chosen destination.*

*Bourbon Street, with its storied history and iconic charm, stretched out before the brothers. Everywhere they looked, there was a vibrant mix of colors, sounds, and smells. Jazz musicians dotted the street corners, their melodies dancing with the ever-present hum of chatter. The aromas of gumbo and jambalaya wafted from nearby eateries, mingling with the sweeter notes of beignets. Amidst it all, tourists and locals moved in a unique New Orleans rhythm that made the city feel alive, like a body with a heartbeat.*

*Ethan, dressed in a light blue short-sleeved shirt and beige shorts, walked with an observant gaze, taking in every detail. His sneakers crunched softly on the worn cobblestones. A cross, a significant relic of his past, swayed across his chest with each step, the intricately crafted pendant catching glimmers of sunlight. It contrasted with the casualness of his clothes, but it felt right, a part of him.*

*Jake, on the other hand, wore a simple white t-shirt, khaki cargo shorts, and comfortable sandals suitable for a day of exploration. His camera hung around his neck, always ready to capture the essence of the vibrant street.*

*As the brothers continued down the street, one building in particular began to stand out from the rest. It stood slightly askew, its timeworn facade possessing a character all its own. Though faded by time and weather, the building's paint bore shades of deep purple and gold, reminiscent of royal tapestries from another era. Intricate ironwork balconies stretched out, draped with hanging moss, and adorned with beads, giving the structure an ethereal, otherworldly feel. It was as if the building had stories that whispered tales of ancient mysticism and folklore.*

*As they approached, a figure appeared on a creaking rocking chair. Sitting there was an African American woman of short stature, her silhouette framed by the unique backdrop of the building. She was dressed in a cascade of wild colors that seemed to dance and shimmer with her every movement, mirroring the vibrant aura around her. Layers of skirts and fabrics draped elegantly around her heavy frame, and her short, curly hair glistened in the sunlight, accentuating her kind brown eyes. Those eyes seemed to possess an ageless wisdom, a deep understanding of the mysteries of the world. Around her neck, countless beads and charms jingled with the rhythm of her sway, each perhaps telling a story of its own. But even as Ethan's eyes met hers, her focus seemed to be elsewhere, directly on the cross that dangled prominently from his neck.*

*The sun blazed overhead, but as Ethan's eyes locked with the woman's, an unexpected chill ran down his spine. Her unyielding focus on his cross felt almost invasive, as if she could decipher the tales it held within. To shake off the unease, Ethan's attention shifted to the sign above the establishment. Elegantly written in faded gold letters, it read: "Madam's Visions: Revelations of the Past, Present, and Future." Below it, an array of mystical symbols and talismans hinted at the services offered within.*

*Brushing off an uneasy feeling, Ethan whispered to Jake, "Probably just another fortune teller trying to make a quick buck." He'd always been skeptical of such things, often dismissing them as mere parlor tricks.*

*As they continued, the distance between them and the woman grew. Just when Ethan thought they'd passed without further incident, her voice, rich and thick with the cadence of the bayou, cut through the ambiance of Bourbon Street.*

*"Young man," she called, attracting the attention of a few passersby, "can you come over here for a minute?"*

*Startled by the unexpected call, Ethan turned on his heels to face her. The backdrop of bustling Bourbon Street seemed to blur as their eyes met, a tunnel of shared intrigue connecting them. With her wise eyes shimmering like still water reflecting moonlight, the woman gestured with a delicate curl of her fingers, beckoning him closer. There was something magnetic about her gesture, an unspoken promise of secrets and ancient tales.*

*Ethan, though a bit cautious, had been raised to show deference to those older than him, believing there was wisdom to be found in age. With a nod to Jake, who wore a slightly more* skeptical expression, they strolled back to the woman. Her gaze was unwavering, fixed on the cross that dangled from his chest. The rhythmic creaking of her rocking chair seemed to be in sync with Ethan's heartbeat.

"I've seen one of these before," she said, her voice filled with awe and nostalgia. "It's a rare piece."

Her fingers brushed the warm air near the cross, but never touched it. "Where did you get it?" she asked, genuine curiosity gleaming in her eyes.

Ethan hesitated for a moment, the constant hum of Bourbon Street fading into the background.

"It was a gift from my grandfather," he began, his voice soft with reverence. "He gave it to me six years ago, just before he died." The words hung heavy in the air, punctuated by the memory of that moment, a moment forever etched in his heart.

The woman, her face clouded with a hint of melancholy, replied, "He must have loved you very much."

The silence that followed was thick, yet comforting. Ethan simply nodded, his eyes drifting downward, lost in the memory of a bond that had been so deep. The cross was more than a piece of jewelry; it was an emblem of protection, a silent promise that his grandfather's love would continue to protect him, even in his absence. It was a poignant reminder that their bond transcended the barriers of life and death.

The woman's fingers, aged with time yet graceful, inched toward the cross, hovering delicately over its gleaming surface. Her intense and unwavering gaze met Ethan's as she asked, "May I?" Nodding, Ethan gave her silent permission, creating a tacit trust between them.

With a gentleness that belied her seemingly frail stature, she cradled the cross between her fingers, the warmth of her touch mingling with its metallic coolness. Her thumb pressed against its intricately etched face, and in an almost transcendent moment, her eyelids lowered, giving way to a serene silence.

Moments later, the corners of her lips curled into a knowing smile, as if she'd unlocked some hidden secret buried deep within the artifact. When her eyes fluttered open, they held a spark of recognition, a hint of a shared memory. She released the cross, letting it sway gently against Ethan's chest.

"Your cross," she began, her voice a mixture of awe and intrigue, "has a story to tell. Come inside, and I'll read it to you."

As they stood on the worn wooden porch, Ethan's eyebrows knit in uncertainty, the weight of the strange woman's words still weighing on him. He glanced sideways at his brother, silently seeking his guidance. Jake, always the protective older sibling, cleared his throat and gave the woman a skeptical look.

"How much is this going to cost?" he asked, a hint of caution in his voice.

The woman, her eyes never leaving Ethan's, replied calmly, "It won't cost you anything.

Consider it a free reading."

Jake shrugged and leaned against a wooden post. "Well, go ahead, bro. We could use a good laugh. I'll wait for you here."

Nodding, the woman stood gracefully, her long dress rustling as she walked toward the entrance of her establishment. With a gentle wave of her hand, she motioned for Ethan to come inside. Hesitating only a moment, Ethan's footsteps faded on the creaky floorboards as he followed her, catching a glimpse of a sign hanging on the door. It read: Madam Cora.

The dim interior of Madam Cora's establishment was in stark contrast to the sunlit streets outside. Antique lanterns hung from the ceiling, casting a soft amber glow over the room. The air was thick with the scent of sandalwood and musk, mingled with hints of something unknown and ancient. Dark wooden shelves lined the walls, filled with jars of dried herbs, crystals of various sizes and hues, and old leather-bound books with faded titles.

Taking in the myriad details, Ethan ventured, "Are you Madam Cora?"

The woman turned, her dark eyes capturing him once more. "I am," she affirmed with a hint of pride.

Nearby, a round table draped in a deep purple cloth waited, intriguing tarot cards and runes scattered around it. Madam Cora gestured to a plush, high-backed chair facing the table.

"Please, take a seat," she invited.

As Ethan sat down, Madam Cora took a seat across from him, her eyes never leaving the cross that hung from his neck, hinting at the source of her impending insights.

As the thick, incense-laden air lingered around them, Madam Cora reached out to the cross once more. "May I?" she asked quietly.

At Ethan's nod, her fingers encircled the artifact and drew it close to her. "Relax, child," she whispered, her tone dripping with warmth and understanding. "All you have to do is listen."

Ethan's chest tightened. It was a mixture of skepticism mixed with an undercurrent of fear. No life experience had prepared him for this mystical moment on Bourbon Street. His eyes were fixed on Madam Cora's face, trying to detect any hint of deception. But as she pressed her thumb to the face of his cross, her expression changed. Her eyelids dropped, obscuring her eyes, and for a lingering moment, there was a profound stillness. The room seemed to pulse with expectation, the walls waiting to hear the story of the cross.

Madam Cora's lips curled into a gentle smile as her fingers delicately explored the tiny perforations that lined the edge of the cross.

"Not only does your cross possess a protective spirit," she began, her voice soft as velvet, "but it also holds echoes of your past and a window to your future."

Ethan's breath caught in his throat. The mention of a protective spirit brought back memories of his grandfather's last words to him about the cross. The precision of her remark was uncanny, and while part of him held onto his skepticism, another part couldn't help but be drawn in by the allure of her words.

*Madam Cora's breathing deepened as she fell silent, her body slackening. She seemed to drift into another realm, the deep energy of the cross drawing her into its embrace and leaving Ethan in palpable suspense.*

*The lines on Madam Cora's face deepened as her eyebrows furrowed, her concentration evident.*

*"I see mountains," she breathed, her voice distant, "huge mountains with snow-capped peaks. I see green meadows dotted with vibrant wildflowers... and forests of evergreen trees so majestic and tall, they seem to touch the sky itself."*

*Ethan's heart skipped a beat as a rush of recognition washed over him. The vivid picture she was painting was none other than Pine Haven, his beloved home, tucked away 3,000 miles from this very spot. Confusion gnawed at him.*

*"That's Pine Haven," he whispered, the words coming out involuntarily. "That's my home."*

*Yet Madam Cora seemed lost to him, sunk deep into another plane of existence, her consciousness adrift and unreachable.*

*After a moment, her expression changed abruptly, her former serenity replaced by a furrowed brow and a hint of unease.*

*"I'm being directed to another window," she said with urgency, a note of trepidation in her voice that had been absent before.*

*Ethan's pulse quickened, a reaction to the sudden change in the old Seer's demeanor. Though a part of him still dismissed her words as mere acting, the genuine concern in her tone sent a shiver down his spine. Moments of tense silence stretched between them, each second heavy with anticipation. Then Madam Cora's features slowly settled back into that mask of deep concentration, her voice steadying as she delved into the emerging vision before her.*

*Suddenly, her body swayed rhythmically, and her expression softened, as if she were recounting a dream. "I see the ocean. The water is so clear and blue... it's like looking through a mirror. There's a beach with sand as white as the snow-capped mountains I saw earlier, and beyond that, a boardwalk, that echoes with the sounds of laughter and life."*

*Ethan, who had been mildly amused, felt a tug of genuine interest. Her words painted a picture of a place foreign to his experiences. However, the subtle change in Madam Cora's demeanor brought him back to the present moment. Though her eyes were closed, they squinted harder, as if trying to bring an elusive image into focus.*

*"There's more," she murmured hesitantly. "I see a soft glow... it surrounds the young souls who live there. It's... protective... like a guardian's shield, preserving a fleeting world of innocence and wonder."*

*Suddenly, Madam Cora's expression softened, her eyes glistening with emotion as she realized its intent. Her voice filled with deep recognition and tenderness as she added, "It wants to protect them from the threatening tides of change."*

*She paused, her eyebrows knitted in concentration. "The ocean... it whispers to them... it* whispers in a voice that only their youthful hearts can hear."

Then suddenly, Madam Cora's face contorted with sudden unease, every line and wrinkle deepening to portray a grave of caution. Her voice, which had danced with intrigue moments before, now held a sharper, more solemn edge. "Beware, child. If you go there and allow it to take hold of you, it will change your life forever."

Despite the surreal nature of the moment, Ethan couldn't help but chuckle. "I guess I better stay away from that place," he remarked, trying to lighten the weight of the moment with humor.

But Madam Cora's abrupt movement stopped him. Her eyes fluttered open, revealing deep, probing irises that seemed to pierce right through him. The intensity of her gaze sent a shiver of unease down his spine. She leaned forward, close enough that he could see the age lines on her face, her expression serious and full of conviction.

"No, Ethan," she whispered, her voice carrying the weight of centuries. "This is the path you are meant to take. It's your destiny."

The whisper took him by surprise. How did she know his name? It wasn't just the revelations that unnerved him, but the simple fact that this stranger seemed to know him intimately.

The weight of Madam Cora's grip on Ethan's cross lightened, and as she released it from her fingers, the chain swayed back to rest against his chest. With an air of finality, she leaned back, her eyes studying him from behind her wizened mask.

"That is all, child. Your path lies before you," she said dismissively.

Though disoriented by the whirlwind of Madam Cora's insights, Ethan brushed them off as mere parlor tricks.

"Thanks," he said, a hint of wry amusement in his voice as he stood. He took one last look around the room, dimly lit by shadows of past and future, before stepping out into the bright daylight.

Jake was outside, engaged in light banter with a local girl, their laughter cutting through the humid air. He spotted Ethan and asked, "So, how'd it go with the mystic?"

Ethan, shaking his head in amusement but still a little unnerved that she knew his name, chuckled. "Let's just say I found out where we don't want to go on our summer adventures."

Jake's brow furrowed in intrigue, but he seemed more inclined to enjoy their day than to probe further. And so, the two brothers delved deeper into the heart of New Orleans, with its rhythmic jazz and tantalizing cuisine. The bizarre encounter with Madam Cora was gradually enveloped by the magic of the city, fading into the recesses of Ethan's mind like an old dream.

The first light of this Monday morning began to paint Wavecrest's sky with shades of gold and pink. As the sun slowly rose from the east, its rays stretched out to touch every nook and cranny of the town. The world was still, save for the occasional chirp of a waking bird, signaling the dawn of a new day.

Ethan stood still in front of the apartment building, his gaze fixed on the distant horizon where he knew the ocean to be. Though the vast expanse of blue could not be seen from his vantage point, the rhythmic lull of waves crashing against the shore reached his ears, a steady and soothing sound. Each gentle gust of wind that brushed against his face carried a hint of salty sea mist and an underlying sensation he couldn't quite place.

As the breeze danced around him, his thoughts inevitably drifted to Jessica—her bright blue eyes, mirrors of her pure and innocent soul, made his heart flutter. Those eyes, deep and inviting, always seemed to ensnare him, forcing him to draw closer, to embrace her and protect her from the harm of the world. But as he stood there, another sensation began to envelop him—familiar yet strange.

It was a feeling that had begun as a faint whisper when he first set foot in Wavecrest and had grown stronger by the day. An enigmatic presence, almost like a gentle embrace from unseen arms, cradled him. The air around him felt alive; every gust of wind seemed to murmur secrets that resonated deep within his soul. It was comforting, but it left him with an unsettling feeling that something was amiss.

Though the origin of this presence eluded him, his instincts drew his gaze once more to the hidden sea beyond. There was a connection, a bond between him, the town, and the ocean—a connection that might have remained dormant were it not for the love he shared with Jessica. While the nature of that bond remained a mystery, one thing was certain: it was intertwined with the very essence of Wavecrest and its young inhabitants. As Ethan pondered these feelings, the dance between the ocean's song and the mystical winds continued, holding him in their gentle embrace.

Ethan's concentration on the distant horizon was so intense, so profound, that the immediate world around him faded into obscurity. The echo of a door above broke the surrounding silence, and the rhythmic sound of footsteps descending the apartment's staircase echoed in the background.

Emerging from the shadows of the balcony above, Jake paused at the base of the stairs, his eyes fixed on his younger brother, who seemed transfixed by the unseen horizon.

"Hey, bro, what's going on?" Jake inquired, noticing Ethan's distant demeanor.

Though his voice was clear, it did not register with Ethan, who seemed to be lost in his own world of thoughts. Concerned by Ethan's unusual detachment, Jake closed the distance between them and placed a reassuring hand on his shoulder. "Are you okay, buddy?"

Ethan didn't answer immediately, but when he finally turned to face Jake, his eyes were filled with a mixture of awe and uncertainty. "Don't you feel that?" he whispered, almost as if sharing a secret.

Puzzled by the question and feeling none of the sensations Ethan seemed to be experiencing, Jake asked with genuine confusion, "Feel what?"

Ethan's mind flashed back to a similar conversation with Jessica. The similarity was uncanny. "I don't know," he replied with a hint of frustration. "I can't explain it."

Ethan's eyes found their way back to the horizon. "There's something out there, man. I don't know what it is, but I can feel it."

Jake glanced toward the ocean for a moment before focusing on Ethan again, trying to ground him in reality. "There's nothing out there, dude. It's just the ocean."

Ethan shook his head violently. "No. It's not just the ocean. It's this whole town. I don't know what it is... I just..." He trailed off, searching for the right words. "There's just something different about this place."

Jake, eyebrows furrowed in concern at Ethan's seemingly unrealistic perception, remarked, "This place is no different from the other places we've visited over the years. Wavecrest is just another town."

A spark of defiance lit up Ethan's eyes. "No, you're wrong. There is something different about Wavecrest."

Recognizing the signs of Ethan's emotional turmoil, Jake wore a knowing grin and nudged his brother teasingly. "Yeah, you're right. Something different is going on here. For the first time, little brother, you're in love. And that's what you feel."

In the gentle embrace of the early morning, the world around Ethan and Jake was silent, save for the distant cries of seagulls and the soothing rhythm of the waves rolling in. Jake's casual mention of Jessica, the implication clear in his voice, stirred a warmth in Ethan's chest. It was true; the deep feelings he felt for Jessica were unlike anything he'd ever experienced before. The depth, the pull—was that the mystery he'd been trying to understand?

"Maybe you're right," Ethan admitted, his voice thoughtful, yielding to Jake's more grounded interpretation.

Jake replied with a steady stare and the confidence of an older brother. "I know I'm right."

The conversation hung in the air for a moment before Jake's attention shifted. The Jeep, a sturdy and familiar presence in their adventures, beckoned. He approached the driver's side, the metallic click of the door breaking the ambient morning sounds.

But before he could fully enter, he paused, a reminder for Ethan playing on his lips. "We need to make some money, dude, if we're going to spend the rest of the summer here. I'm taking the Jeep out this morning to see if I can round up some side jobs."

A silent acknowledgment, a nod, was Ethan's answer. His mind, a swirl of thoughts, was mostly focused on Jessica. The sting of being away from her, even for a day, was heartbreaking, but he understood the necessity. Their past summers, filled with adventure and the occasional hustle for money, had set a precedent, and Wavecrest was no exception.

But as Jake was about to wrap himself in the confines of the Jeep, he hesitated. A heavy thought, dark and deep, pressed upon him. He felt the duty of an older sibling to be the bearer of realities, however harsh they might be.

"You do realize, bro," Jake began, choosing each word carefully as if he were treading on delicate ground. "When it comes time for us to leave Wavecrest, you're going to have to let her go."

The weight of his brother's words washed over Ethan like an unexpected wave, pulling him under its current. The truth in Jake's words was inescapable. The looming end of summer cast a shadow over his blossoming relationship with Jessica. It was a thought he often avoided, burying it deep inside. But faced with this undeniable reality, Ethan's emotions surged. His voice, trembling and filled with raw love, emerged. "I don't think I can do that, Jake."

Jake's brow furrowed in concern. "What are you going to do, Ethan? Are you going to take her back to Pine Haven with us?"

The simple logic of Jake's question was inescapable. With Jessica committed to leaving Wavecrest for Austin at the end of the summer and his own commitment to returning to Pine Haven to complete his final semester, the intricate web of their futures seemed preordained. As the implications sank in, Ethan's response was filled with anguish and uncertainty; he whispered, "I don't know what I'm going to do."

"Listen to me," Jake began, his tone gentle yet firm. "You have to do what's best for Jessica."

Ethan frowned, the raw emotion evident in his eyes. "What do you mean?"

Jake took a deep breath, choosing his words carefully. "You remember all those places we've been to over the summers? The mountains of Colorado? The streets of New Orleans? And the beaches of Florida?"

Ethan nodded, memories of their adventures flashing before his eyes.

"Those weren't just vacations, Ethan," Jake continued, his voice softening. "They were lessons. Lessons about life, about growing up, about understanding the world from different perspectives. They were about learning to be independent, about discovering who we are outside of Pine Haven."

Jake paused and looked Ethan straight in the eye. "Jessica, she's only just begun that journey. She's lived her whole life in this cozy little town. She has yet to experience the vastness of what's out there, the richness of life beyond these shores. She needs to spread her wings, to be on her own, to find herself. If you hold her back now, she may never get that chance."

Ethan's eyes shone with emotion, the weight of Jake's words pressing down on him.

Jake gently squeezed Ethan's shoulder. "I know you love her, man. But love is also about wanting the best for the person you care about. If you don't let her explore the world and discover herself, one day, she might look back with regret. And that regret, my friend, could cast a dark shadow over the love you both share. Do you want that to happen?"

Ethan looked down, struggling with the painful truth in Jake's words. The excitement of their adventures together, the wisdom he had gained from them, and the potential future with Jessica were all tangled up in a complex web of emotions.

"Sometimes," Jake whispered, "letting go is the best way to hold on to someone."

Ethan stood still, the weight of Jake's words pressing heavily on his chest. Each sentiment echoed in his mind, causing the walls he had built around the inevitable future to crumble. His heart was caught in a painful vice of recognition and longing. The thought of leaving Jessica, of watching her venture out into the world on her own, made his heart ache in a way it had never felt before. The truth, hard as it was, remained undeniable.

Sensing the depth of Ethan's turmoil, Jake hesitated for a moment before climbing into the Jeep. The hum of the engine seemed distant and muted, overwhelmed by the profound silence of the moment. He glanced back at Ethan from behind the wheel, noting the unmistakable anguish etched into his brother's features. Jake's heart clenched. Despite the gravity of the conversation, he was certain that he had set Ethan on the right path, even if it was one paved with heartbreak.

"I'm sorry, bro," Jake's voice broke the morning silence, rich with a mixture of sincerity and sadness. "But you know I'm right."

The tires crunched against the gravel as the Jeep pulled out of the parking lot. With each passing distance, the gulf between the brothers seemed to widen, though they remained bound by a bond of love and understanding.

Ethan watched the vehicle grow smaller in the distance, the dust left behind like a fading memory. He felt alone, but not completely abandoned. The ever-present sensation he'd come to recognize—a subtle, comforting embrace—surrounded him, offering solace to his wounded heart. It was a gentle reminder that even in the face of pain, there was still a touch of the mysterious, an unseen force that comforted him.

As the weight of Jake's words settled within him, Ethan felt the familiar weight of the cross around his neck. It was cool to the touch, a stark contrast to the heat of his emotions. Holding it between his fingers, a distant memory began to emerge, blurring the lines between present and past.

A strange woman in New Orleans, her features blurred, but her message was crystal clear. She spoke of visions triggered by his cross, a vast ocean with an enticing beach and boardwalk, and a mystical aura protecting the young people who lived there. She had warned him that if he allowed this place to capture his soul, his life would be changed forever.

The vibrant chaos of New Orleans had made him dismiss her words as mere carnival theatrics. But now, amid the distant murmur of the waves and the lingering scent of the sea carried on the breeze, her prophecies resounded with chilling clarity. As he thought of Jessica, the profound depths of his feelings for her challenged his once carefree aspirations. Perhaps, in some inexplicable way, the woman's foresight had been an omen for the choices he now faced. Choices that would shape his destiny forever.

# Chapter 24

-------------------------------------------------------------------

In the late morning light, Fawn sat on the bed, her knees drawn up as she focused on the task at hand. A bottle of soft pink nail polish rested beside her. With practiced ease, she applied the color to her toes, each stroke giving them a hue reminiscent of cherry blossoms kissed by the morning light. As she worked, occasional rays of sunlight caught her face, casting transient golden highlights. The room, faintly scented with polish, seemed to hold its breath, prolonging the quiet moment, allowing a peaceful pause between yesterday's heartache and tomorrow's uncertainty.

Just as Fawn was putting the finishing touches on her toenails, the door swung open. In walked Jessica, like a spring gust filled with both sunshine and the promise of rain. Her face was a complex tableau of emotion, quivering between joy and sorrow, each feeling vying for dominance but neither quite succeeding. Holding her phone aloft, she raised it as though unveiling a hidden truth. Her voice, tinged with a touch of longing and a note of disappointment, broke the calm. "Ethan just texted. He can't see me today; they're in another town working. That's two days now."

Fawn paused, her nail brush momentarily still, like a painter pausing to absorb the nuance of a fleeting emotion. She looked up, her eyes meeting Jessica's. Today, a stormy sea replaced the usually vibrant pools of summer sky in those bright blue eyes.

"I'm sorry, Jess. It sucks that he can't be with you today, but Ethan needs to work, you know? So he can stay here for the rest of the summer. You'll see him soon enough, I promise."

Jessica let out a sigh, feeling a bit lighter. Fawn had a way of cutting through the confusion, her words acting like a lighthouse that guided Jessica through her swirling emotions.

"I know. You're right," Jessica admitted, her voice tinged with a reluctant acceptance that floated atop an undercurrent of lingering sadness.

Sitting beside Fawn, she rested her head on her shoulder, seeking the silent solace that only a best friend could provide. Even though Fawn's affirmation offered a distant shoreline of comfort, Jessica couldn't shake the ache of Ethan's absence, the emptiness of a day that wouldn't be filled with his presence.

As Fawn capped the bottle of nail polish and admired the last strokes of color on her toes, her thoughts began to shift. As she spoke of Ethan's necessity to work, her mind began filling with thoughts of their looming future. The silence of the room served as a canvas for these impending realities, framed by the golden edges of a summer that was both an end and a beginning. Their time in Wavecrest had always been cushioned by the relative simplicity of part-time summer jobs on the boardwalk. There, the exchange of labor for pay seemed to possess an innocent charm—a job that revolved around funnel cakes, cotton candy, and the laughter of vacationers.

Yet, Fawn knew that those idyllic days of youthful employment, tinged with sea salt and nostalgia, would fade as inevitably as the evening sun sinking into the Pacific. Soon, they'd be navigating the intricate maze of adult life, where summer jobs would yield to the complexities of career paths—places that demanded not just their time and youthful spirit but also fragments of their very souls.

Taking a deep breath, Fawn felt the weight of the approaching reality seep into her very being. It was a sensation mixed with dread and a strange form of excitement—like the feeling they'd get right before the roller coaster plummeted down its steepest incline, an exhilarating blend of thrill and terror that made their hearts race.

Breaking the silence, Fawn shared the thoughts weighing on her mind, pulling Jessica back to the present moment. "You know, we're going to have to get jobs, too. Real jobs. Once we're in college, we can't keep asking our parents for money."

Their eyes met again, this time charged with a sense of recognition of the approaching future. In that room, surrounded by the comfortable relics of their youth, the girls could feel the tinge of adulthood nudging them forward. The unspoken acknowledgment of change hung in the air like the last rays of a setting sun, signaling the end of one chapter and the uncertain beginning of another.

"Yeah, I know," Jessica replied softly, leaning her head on Fawn's shoulder. "Getting a job, growing up—it's all happening so fast. And it's even harder to think about doing all that without you being with me."

Fawn felt the air grow thick with the weight of Jessica's words, each syllable tinged with the bittersweetness of pending separation. "You know, Jess," she began, her hand settling on Jessica's shoulder. "I may not have a home to come back to here in Wavecrest, but that doesn't mean I won't carry this place—and you—with me wherever I go."

She looked into Jessica's eyes, her own reflecting a pool of empathy and reassurance. "Our connection goes further than just here. And believe me, you're not the type to be forgotten—especially by me. We'll stay in touch, and our friendship will survive college, distance, and all the other crap life throws our way."

In that moment, the essence of their friendship seemed to crystallize, as if suspended in the amber light of the room. It was a silent vow—an acknowledgment that despite the changing tides of life and the vast distances that would soon separate them, the core of their friendship would remain unbroken, steadfast as the enduring waves of their coastal hometown.

Jessica lifted her head from Fawn's shoulder, meeting her eyes one last time as if to immortalize the moment. She leaned forward and gave her friend a gentle squeeze.

"I'm going to go take a shower," she said, swinging her legs to the side and stepping off the bed.

As she retreated to the bathroom, Fawn felt the weight of her friend's unspoken sadness. She knew she couldn't lift that weight alone; she needed an ally. Her eyes moved to her phone, a lifeline to the outside world and the friends who filled it.

"Heather," Fawn whispered, as if saying her name could already make it so. The idea formed clearly, a glimmer of hope in the room's silence.

Her fingers flew over the touchscreen with a sense of urgency, crafting a message to Heather. In that small note was a big request: for Heather to bring her signature warmth and help clear the clouds shadowing Jessica's day.

Heather Marino's home was a sprawling estate, an elegant blend of modern and classic architecture, set back from the sandy beaches of Wavecrest. Manicured gardens adorned the grounds, and winding driveways led to well-stocked garages, signaling the family's comfortable affluence.

Inside, the grandeur continued. High ceilings lent an open feel to spacious rooms furnished with a tasteful mix of comfort and luxury. Persian rugs softened the marble floors, and a brilliant chandelier hung in the foyer, its lights scattering like a shower of diamonds.

Heather's room, however, had its own unique charm. It was more personal, capturing her essence in a way the rest of the house couldn't quite manage. The walls were a canvas of memories: framed photos of family and friends, including Jessica and Fawn, intermingled with colorful posters and art prints. In one corner, a vanity filled with makeup and perfumes stood beside a tall mirror that had seen Heather grow from a little girl to the confident young woman she now was.

Amid the palette of eyeshadows and brushes sprawled across her vanity, Heather put the finishing touches on her eyes—a stroke here, a flick there, like an artist finalizing her masterpiece. Her phone, propped against a decorative perfume bottle, buzzed intermittently, alight with messages from Tony Grissom. Their texts danced on the screen, fluttering like electronic butterflies as they made plans for a day trip to Santa Barbara.

Heather's fingers paused mid-air, eyeliner brush in hand, as her phone buzzed again. But this time, the name flashing on the screen wasn't Tony. It was Fawn. A sense of intrigue swelled within her; Fawn seldom texted unless it was something important.

Heather quickly tapped a message back to Tony: "I gotta go. I'll get back to you in a few." Her fingers, which a moment ago had been caressing the curves of her eyes, now hovered over the phone. Her mind shifted, filled with anticipation as the unread text from Fawn awaited her. It seemed the day had taken an unexpected but meaningful turn. She opened the message and read, "Are u busy today?"

A moment of pause. Heather's fingers hovered over the screen as she debated her response. She was preoccupied with plans, but Fawn's text came like an unbidden breeze, stirring the still waters of her day. "Kinda. Wassup?" she texted back.

Almost instantaneously, her phone lit up once more. "I was hopin we could hang today to cheer up Jess," came Fawn's reply.

A pulse of concern radiated through Heather. Jessica in need of cheering up? That was as uncommon as a sunless day in their seaside town. "Wtf is wrong w/ Jess???" she typed, concern punctuating each character.

"She's just feelin down, tho't it'd be cool to hang like old times," Fawn's words appeared on her screen.

As Heather read Fawn's message, memories of their adventures together flooded back like a returning tide. Plans with Tony suddenly seemed less pressing, fading into the background like stars at dawn. "Ur rite, it's been 2 long. Had plans w/ Tony but tbh, this is way more imp," she fired back, her thumbs dancing with conviction.

Fawn's confirmation came a few seconds later: "Ur the best."

Heather grinned at her screen. "Want me 2 call Mich & Kris?" she asked, already anticipating the reunion of their close-knit circle.

"Yaaas, been 4ever since we all chilled," Fawn's words came through, tinged with a nostalgia that Heather had also felt but rarely spoke of.

"U still @ Jess's?" Heather shot back, mentally preparing to shift her day's plans.

"Yeah," Fawn confirmed.

"Bet, on my way," Heather texted, her thumb hitting the heart emoji—a tiny, pixelated symbol that carried more emotion than an ocean of words.

In response, three hearts danced back to her from Fawn's end like a mirrored echo of her own sentiments. It was settled. Heather capped her eyeliner and placed it back on her vanity. Today was no longer an ordinary day, but one woven with threads of friendship, concern, and the unspoken love that only true friends could understand.

As the late morning sunlight poured into the room, an ethereal glow arose, embracing the walls and casting soft shadows. It was as if the universe were trying to cushion Jessica's heart by softening the colors around her. Stepping out from the comforting embrace of a warm shower, she wrapped herself in a sky-blue towel, her skin glistening with residual moisture. Another towel, this one pristine white, drank in the dampness from her long, flowing locks. As she set foot on the carpet in her room, her eyes found Fawn's.

Fawn sat cross-legged on the bed, her phone resting beside her on the quilt, its screen dark, yet imbued with a silent promise of more conversations to come. Seeing Fawn in this intimate setting filled Jessica with a warmth that went beyond gratitude. Here was a slice of normalcy, a vestige of a more carefree time amidst the uncertainty swirling around their lives.

"Who were you talking to?" asked Jessica, her tone a mixture of genuine curiosity and the playful nosiness that friends allow each other.

"Heather," Fawn revealed without hesitation. There was no room for secrets between them. "I asked her to come over and spend the day with us."

Jessica's eyes widened, a flutter of astonishment lifting the cloud of her recent gloom. "And she said yes?"

"Uh-huh," Fawn grinned, her eyes alight with playful mischief, as if she'd managed to coax a star down from the sky just for Jessica.

"I'm surprised," Jessica mused, her eyes widening momentarily. The world Heather had built for herself was sprawling, crowded with new friendships and whirlwind activities. It seemed like a minor miracle that she had found room for them in her ever-expanding life.

"She doesn't seem to have much time for us anymore," Jessica continued, her voice tinged with disappointment. It was a quiet sigh for the days when Heather's schedule wasn't so full, and their friendship fitted more seamlessly into the tapestry of daily existence.

Fawn chuckled, a knowing twinkle in her eye. "Well, you know Heather. She's always been the wild one in our little group. But the moment I mentioned you needed some cheering up, she dropped her plans."

"Aw," Jessica replied, her heart warming at Fawn's thoughtfulness and Heather's undeniable loyalty to their friendship.

She then remembered the Fourth of July night when they all sat under the fireworks-lit sky. Heather, bubbling with a secret yet unwilling to share, had hinted at something 'incredible in the works.' The moment lingered in her mind, as enduring as footprints in wet sand. With her mischievous grin and that memory hanging in the air like an unsolved riddle, she added, "Maybe we can get her to spill the beans on this big mystery she's been keeping from us."

Fawn burst into laughter at the notion. "Good luck with that," she replied, rolling her eyes theatrically.

As Jessica approached her closet, her mind began to ponder what to wear. Fawn sensed it was time to give her friend the private space she needed. Standing, she felt a hollow pang of hunger.

"I'm going to grab a bite to eat while you get dressed," Fawn announced, sensing the emerging appetite that the day's adventures would certainly ignite.

"Okay," Jessica answered, her voice tinged with excitement. "I won't be long."

As Fawn left the room, her heart was alight with anticipation. Today held the promise of a rare gathering with Heather, filled with laughter and shared memories. She could almost feel the contours of the pure joy that awaited them. It was a day designed to rekindle vital and unbreakable bonds, those same magnetic forces that had linked them since the innocent days of their youth.

As she entered the kitchen, the air greeted her with the comforting aroma of coffee mixed with a lingering scent of cinnamon from yesterday's cookies. She made herself a simple breakfast, her movements a comforting ballet of mundane rituals. As she spread almond butter over a slice of whole-grain bread, she found herself lost in thought—thoughts that fluttered between memories and the future, like leaves caught in an autumn wind.

From across the hallway, she heard the soft rustling sounds of Jessica getting dressed. It was a comforting soundtrack, a testament to their deep-seated familiarity with each other's lives. To her, the house was more than wood and walls; it was a repository of memories, of laughter and tears, of secrets whispered and advice doled out. The air seemed imbued with the love and kinship that had bound them for years.

Just then, the soft padding of feet signaled Jessica's arrival from down the hall. She appeared in the doorway, a vision of casual summer elegance. She wore a pair of tailored shorts that captured the season's spirit, paired with an off-the-shoulder blouse that effortlessly blended comfort and style. Her eyes sparkled, softened by a tempered excitement that added depth to her youthful glow.

"You started without me," she teased, sauntering toward the coffee pot with a lighthearted grace.

"And miss your grand entrance? Absolutely not," Fawn replied, her eyes twinkling with mischief as she sought to sprinkle a bit of levity into the air.

Jessica gave Fawn a smirk, her eyes doing a playful roll at Fawn's cheeky remark. A soft giggle escaped her lips, filling the room with its lightness. Today was anything but ordinary; it was a shimmering drop in the ocean of time, about to be adorned with Heather's presence. For a brief moment, they stood together in that understanding, relishing the stillness before the day's adventures truly unfolded. Then, as if led by an invisible thread of curiosity, Jessica's eyes strayed to the fridge.

In the cozy sanctuary of the kitchen, amidst the comforting aroma of coffee and remnants of breakfast, Fawn noticed Jessica's wandering gaze. Both their eyes settled on a photograph affixed to the fridge. Taken last summer, the group selfie had captured a moment of pure, unfiltered joy—there they were with Heather, Michelle, and Krista, each face radiating the unique qualities that made their friendship so unforgettable. Almost a year had passed since they'd all been together like this, and they anticipated the day ahead with a sweet scent of nostalgia.

"Look at us, total squad goals," Jessica mused, her eyes lingering on each face in the photograph, as if tracing an invisible connection that went far beyond the frame.

"Right? Heather's literally mid-dab. Such a show-off," Fawn replied, her laughter bubbling forth, as clear and effervescent as a mountain stream.

Jessica joined in, her laughter blending with Fawn's. "Michelle's face, though. Why does she always look like she's judging us?"

"And Krista, always flashing the peace sign. So on brand for her," Fawn grinned, her eyes twinkling like a sky full of stars, each one a treasured memory with her friends.

As Jessica and Fawn's eyes met, a moment of recognition passed between them. "I love us. I love this," Jessica's voice softened, the unspoken depth of her emotions evident in her eyes. "What would life even be without them? Without all of this?"

Fawn's eyes softened in return, a smile of pure warmth and affection blooming on her face. "I can't even imagine, Jess. And frankly, I don't want to."

In that moment, they stood enveloped in a cocoon of happiness, as if the air around them had thickened, filled with the fragrance of lasting friendships. There was a palpable sense that they were on the verge of something wondrous, a day that would unfold into yet another vibrant chapter in their collective saga.

With a final, lingering glance at the photograph that encapsulated their shared past, Fawn shifted her eyes back to Jessica.

"I better go change," she announced, her voice tinged with a playful urgency. "It's almost noon, and we don't want Heather to waltz in and think we're turning today into some kind of slumber fest."

Jessica chuckled at Fawn's quip, her laughter light yet tinged with a subtle undercurrent of melancholy. "Yeah, we wouldn't want to give her the wrong idea," she agreed. But even as she spoke, a fleeting wistfulness crept into her eyes. It was a muted signal of Ethan's absence, a slight emptiness contrasting with the day's forthcoming joy.

"Go ahead, Fawn. I'm just going to tidy up the kitchen." Though her voice retained its cheerfulness, her eyes—those revealing windows to her soul—hinted at a longing that Fawn, of all people, would recognize.

In the silence that followed Fawn's departure for Jessica's room, the petite brunette found herself alone in the kitchen, her eyes now drawn to the kitchen clock. Its hands moved toward the noon hour, each tick a metronome of her ambivalent emotions.

With a contemplative sigh, she picked up a dish towel and wiped down the countertops. The simple, rhythmic motions provided a therapeutic outlet for the underlying somberness that tempered her anticipation. Ethan's absence still cast a shadow on her thoughts, darkening the bright colors of the upcoming reunion with Heather.

The coffee pot, now emptied of its morning brew, was returned to its resting place with a deliberate care that belied her internal musings. Her eyes wandered to the window, where the sunlight, previously dimmed by clouds, now sparkled on the blades of grass outside, casting a vibrant, golden glow on the lawn. And just as her thoughts began to drift into the what-ifs and the what-could-have-been, the ringing of the doorbell sounded, snapping her back into the immediacy of the present.

Eager footsteps guided her to the front door, which she opened with a flourish to reveal Heather's glowing presence. A whiff of Heather's signature perfume, mingling citrus and floral notes, greeted her senses as if an entire orchard and meadow had conspired to herald her friend's arrival.

"Heather!" Jessica's voice was a jubilant melody, her arms wide open.

With her black, wavy hair framing her face and makeup enhancing her Italian beauty, Heather stepped inside. A warm smile blossomed on her lips as she opened her arms. The embrace that followed was like two stars gravitating towards each other—a quiet testament to the enduring glow of their friendship.

"Oh my God, it feels like forever since the Fourth!" Heather's voice burst forth, infused with a warmth as though the house itself had been waiting for her infectious energy to fill it once more.

"Crazy how time flies, isn't it?" Jessica's voice wove a tapestry of emotion, threads of nostalgia and joy crisscrossing in every syllable.

Her arms enveloped Heather, a tactile testament to a friendship that needed no words for validation. "I've missed you, girlfriend. Come in! Come in!" With the effervescence of their embrace still hanging in the air, she led her friend further into the sanctum of her home.

As Heather stepped through the threshold, her presence seemed to enliven the room like a splash of color on a blank canvas. She was a vision of fearless self-expression, dressed in a breezy, off-the-shoulder top that whispered of endless summers. Her frayed denim shorts clung rebelliously to her hips, each tear a chapter in the chronicle of her adventures.

The ensemble reached its pinnacle with layers of luxurious bohemian jewelry: turquoise and silver necklaces cascading down her neckline, intricate gold bangles encircling her wrists, and delicate, handcrafted earrings that swayed with her every movement. Each crafted piece was a testament to her untamed spirit, yet imbued with an air of sophistication. At that moment, Jessica couldn't help but admire her friend's bold style, a sartorial anthem to living life unapologetically.

"Wow, Heather, you look amazing as always!" Jessica exclaimed, her eyes dancing over her friend's outfit as if trying to absorb every detail. "You're basically a walking fashion statement, you know that?" The compliment spilled from her lips as naturally as sunlight breaking through a dawn sky, heartfelt and warming.

Heather blushed, a light pink tint coloring her cheeks like the first bloom of a cherry blossom in spring. "Aw, thanks. But look at you! That outfit is too cute!"

As Heather's kind words lingered, the sound of footsteps signaled Fawn's approach from down the hall. Emerging from Jessica's room, dressed for whatever the day might bring, she stepped into the kitchen. Her eyes fell on Heather and Jessica, filling her with a quiet sense of contentment.

Dressed in a simple white tank top and black shorts that complemented her lithe frame, Fawn beamed as she approached Heather. The outfit, while uncomplicated, spoke volumes of her penchant for understated elegance.

Heather turned to notice her, their eyes meeting in a familiar warmth that filled the space between them. With a swift, graceful motion, she pulled Fawn into a hug that was warm and comforting. Their embrace silently affirmed the morning's anticipation, weaving it into a moment of shared happiness.

As they pulled apart, Heather's attention shifted toward Jessica, their eyes locking for a moment. In that silent exchange, an unspoken understanding passed between them, a simple glance saying more than words ever could.

"You know, Jess," Heather began, her voice taking on a softer tone. "Ethan might be away today, but you're never alone. We're all here for you, girl, and we got your back."

Heather's words were a gentle touch on a sensitive spot, revealing her knack for soothing both visible and hidden wounds. It was this skill that made her an irreplaceable part of their close-knit circle.

Jessica felt a surge of emotion rise within her, like a tide drawn by the gravitational force of the moon—irresistible, powerful, natural. Her eyes shimmered, not with tears but with the luminosity of gratitude, as if her friends before her had become a lighthouse guiding her through the fog of her feelings.

"I know," she replied softly, her voice rich with sincerity. The words seemed to hang in the air for a moment, as if absorbing the room's warmth before settling back down.

In that quiet affirmation, Jessica found solace. She knew that despite the missing piece in her life, the tapestry of her existence was still rich, colorful, and lovingly woven with the golden threads of friendship.

The moment seemed to flow naturally into the matters of the day, as if guided by an invisible hand that wove the casual and the profound into a seamless narrative. Fawn, the ever-practical orchestrator of plans, shifted her focus toward the unfolding events.

"So, did you get a hold of Michelle and Krista?" Fawn's question broke the moment, nudging aside the emotional atmosphere but leaving a trace of its warmth.

"Ah, yes, the dynamic duo," Heather replied, her voice bouncing back to its usual vivacious tone. "I got through to Michelle. She said she'd rope in Kris. They're planning to meet us at our private beach spot."

The words 'private beach spot' floated in the air like a nostalgic perfume, triggering a kaleidoscope of memories—sunsets and bonfires, flirtatious giggles, and uncontrollable laughter. It was their sacred space, a piece of the world that was unquestionably theirs, an intimate theater where the drama and comedy of their young lives had played out in countless acts.

That familiar spot on the beach settled into Jessica's mind, its significance wrapped around her thoughts like a comforting blanket. As the last words faded into the air, she found her eyes drawn to Fawn. It was as if she could see the invisible threads Fawn had woven to bring this day together, the delicate spider silk of affection and intention, spun solely to cocoon Jessica in a momentary escape from her reality.

Fawn caught her gaze, and in that silent exchange, they spoke volumes. With a simple tilt of her head and a twinkle in her eye, Fawn seemed to say, "This is for you, Jess. For all of us, but especially for you."

Feeling a rare sense of completeness wash over her, Jessica knew they stood on the edge of a luminous day, a bubble in time before they would disperse like dandelion seeds to the wind, each carried away from Wavecrest by the inexorable currents of life's obligations and opportunities.

"But first," Jessica thought, pulling herself back to the present, "we have this day. This glorious, unclaimed day." It was a treasure waiting to be unfurled, much like the vivid colors of the boardwalk they would soon traverse—a stretch of land imbued with the essence of summer and childhood and the heady sense of being alive.

As eyes met, nods were exchanged, and the air seemed to thrum with anticipation. A chapter closed, yet the pages rustled eagerly, restless for the ink of new experiences to mark them forever.

The trio aligned themselves at the threshold of Jessica's house, ready to step out into the sunshine, bound for the boardwalk that served as a vibrant preamble to their secluded beach haven. The door swung open, and as they crossed that invisible line between the known and the hopeful, between the comforting walls of home and the limitless expanse of the world outside, it felt as though they were also crossing the boundaries of their own potential, inching ever closer to becoming the people they were meant to be.

# Chapter 25

------------------------------------------------------------

As the clock ticked past noon, Wavecrest blossomed into a vibrant spectacle, alive with the buzz of summer. Though Wednesday held the promise of routine, it was deftly ignored by the town's youth, who, fueled by the thrill of freedom, pulsed along the boardwalk with a contagious zeal.

The boardwalk itself was nothing short of a riotous festival—a bustling artery that coursed through the heart of Wavecrest. Here, artisans of frosty delights hawked their ice cream to passersby, luring them with promises of sweet respite.

Meanwhile, thrill rides loomed like mechanical titans, clanking and whirring as they lifted brave souls into the sky, only to plunge them back down into the grasp of gravity amidst a chorus of gasps and cheers. The air seemed to dance to a symphony of life's melodies: laughter intermingled with lively conversation, punctuated by the jubilant yelps of children surrendering to the lure of the beach.

Down by the water's edge, the beach stretched out—a masterpiece painted in strokes of emerald green and deep sea blue under the watchful eye of a radiant sun. It was here that families staked their claims on territory made of sand, setting up vibrant enclaves for seaside escapades. Young architects busied themselves with sandy fortresses, destined to be reclaimed by the sea's gentle caress. And there were swimmers, too, welcoming the ocean's playful chase as waves lapped at their toes, a reminder of nature's gentle ebb and flow amidst the day's heat.

As Jessica, Fawn, and Heather ascended the ramp leading to this lively scene, their eyes were immediately drawn to a banner that stretched like a rainbow across the boardwalk's welcoming arch. The fabric seemed to dance in the noon breeze, proclaiming in jubilant lettering: "Wavecrest Summer Dance - Saturday - July 26." The words fluttered and beckoned, echoing youthful freedom and coming-of-age rituals. For a moment, each girl felt the pull of the promise embedded in those words—a promise of a night laced with music and laughter, where memories would be written in the stardust of summer dreams.

As their eyes met, a palpable pause seemed to settle around them. The Wavecrest Summer Dance had always been the grand finale of the season, the crescendo in a symphony of sun-soaked days and moonlit nights. But this time, the words that stretched across the banner held a different resonance—a more intricate melody, tinged with sweetness and sorrow.

Their hearts swelled with anticipation for the dance, yet each beat seemed to echo a silent elegy for their fading days of youth. For all three, this dance would serve as the grand finale of their youthful chapter in Wavecrest before the unwritten pages of adulthood began to turn.

The moment felt bittersweet, like the last golden rays of a day you wish would never end. Yet they moved on, each step filled with the complex beauty of being on the cusp—between the past and the future, adolescence and adulthood, sorrow and joy. And so, they stepped further into the sunlight, determined to live out every remaining drop of this day, this summer, this chapter, before turning the page.

Weaving their way through the crowd on the boardwalk, the trio was captivated by an olfactory melody that rose from a beloved food stand. The aromas were like siren calls, luring them closer with promises of flavors as rich as their memories. The air here was heavy with the aroma of seafood kissed by hot oil and lemonade that held the essence of summer in every drop.

With her usual flair for seizing life's sparkling moments, Heather approached the vendor with an air of ceremony. "Three fish tacos and a pitcher of your best lemonade, if you please!" she announced with a flourish.

The vendor, whose face was carved with lines drawn from years of laughter and salty breezes, responded with a warm chuckle and went to work. The grill sang its sizzling song as he crafted their order—a prelude to the afternoon's unfolding adventures.

As they awaited their seaside feast, Heather couldn't resist injecting her trademark vibrancy into their exchange. "So," she began, curling a lock of her raven hair around her finger, "what are we going to wear for our final dance as Wavecrest's reigning summer queens? I'm planning to dazzle—glitz and glamor all the way!"

Fawn grinned, her eyes twinkling with lighthearted irony. "Oh, you mean the way you normally dress?" Then her tone changed, filled with playful self-assurance. "As for me, I'm thinking of something more elegant, yet kinda daring."

Jessica, lost in thought amid the laughter and chatter, snapped back to the present. Her face broke into a smile, tinged with an elusive shadow of wistfulness. "I think I'll keep it simple and sweet, as always. Something that makes me feel like... well, me."

Heather grinned, handing over plates of succulent fish tacos to her friends as the vendor set a frosted pitcher of lemonade on the counter. "Simple and sweet. Classy and daring.

Glammed up to the max. Here's to us rocking our unique styles!"

They clinked their plastic cups of lemonade, the citrus scent rising in the air as if joining in their toast. For that brief moment, the looming transitions and farewells paused, like waves momentarily halting their endless caress of the shore, allowing the girls to savor the beauty of the now—of friendship, youth, and a summer that would soon become a beloved memory.

Filled with renewed spirits and bonded by laughter that sparkled like sea spray in sunlight, they strolled toward their sacred patch of beach—a place woven into the fabric of countless summers past—each footfall an echo in the symphony of their shared journey.

The girls' approach to the beach's descent was a slow procession, a collective breath drawn in as they neared the sandy threshold that marked the beginning of count-less summers' tales. There, leaning against the sun-warmed railings, Michelle and Krista stood—each a vibrant thread in the tapestry of friendship that adorned the seaside setting.

Michelle's introspective gaze lifted from the last swirl of her ice cream, a dreamy smile blossoming across her face as she recognized the trio's approach. Krista, always spirited, leaned forward with an athlete's casual grace, her laughter already taking flight at the sight of her friends.

"Hey! Took you guys long enough!" Krista's voice cut through the salty air, her arms outstretched in anticipation of an embrace that promised both reunion and respite.

Michelle playfully rolled her eyes. "Seriously, we were about to send a search party! What took you so long?" Her teasing tone was as light as the sea foam, her smile warm like the afternoon sun.

Heather's reply came with a mischievous glint in her eye. "My bad, peeps. I made them stop for lunch." She gestured to Jessica and Fawn with feigned concern. "I mean, look at them. Don't they look malnourished to you?" Her jest danced on the breeze, inviting their laughter to mingle with the rhythm of the waves.

"Malnourished? Really, Heather?" Fawn retorted with an affectionate chuckle, shaking her head at Heather's antics. "You're something else!"

Krista joined in with playful exasperation. "Oh my God, Heather, really? You do know we're within arm's reach of a gazillion food stands, right?" Her tone teased at Heather's penchant for drama.

Heather sighed theatrically in response to their collective skepticism. "Okay, okay. I got hungry. So, sue me!" Her tongue poked out in mock defiance, adding a spark of mischief to their seaside reunion.

As the last ripples of their shared mirth faded away, the girls shared a silent, knowing glance. It was time to claim their spot on the beach—a hallowed ground woven from secrets shared under starlit skies and laughter that resonated above the roar of tides. Here, they stood at summer's threshold once more, each heartbeat echoing a symphony of youthful exuberance and timeless connection.

With their flip-flops and heels clasped in their hands, they let their bare feet touch the weathered wood of the ramp, initiating the transition from the pulsating life of the boardwalk to the serene embrace of the ocean. Each step marked a pilgrimage through time and memory, a shared journey set against the vast blue canvas of the Pacific.

Upon reaching the bottom, they paused to feel the sand sifting between their toes, a grounding touch that had always provided inexplicable comfort. For a moment, the sea breeze seemed to weave through their hair and touch their faces with a little more purpose, like a tender hand that had guided them through joys and sorrows alike. It was as if nature itself had granted them this afternoon, a temporary escape from the encroaching demands of adulthood, allowing them to linger in the illusion that life's responsibilities were as distant as the line where the sky meets the sea.

They continued to their cherished nook, marked not by landmarks but by the invisible threads of friendship that bound them together. Here, atop nothing but sand and under the boundless sky, they found their unity—a unity punctuated by the fleeting impressions their feet made on the sand beneath them.

Settling down on their beach towels, the girls exchanged knowing looks and surrendered to a collective silence. Here, where earth met water, they balanced on the edge of endings and beginnings, confronting a truth as perennial and profound as the ocean's rhythmic advance and retreat.

Krista stretched out her arms, pressing her hands into the sun-baked sand beneath her. She released a contemplative sigh. "You know what's crazy? I can't help but think that this will be our last summer together. Next year, we'll be busy with college stuff or whatever comes next. Our summers will never be like this again. It feels weird to think about that."

Her words hung in the salty air as they all absorbed this impending shift in their reality. Each girl felt the weight of Krista's words, but also a bittersweet resonance. After all, life was calling them to new adventures, yet the familiarity of their shared summers was a hard thing to let go.

Michelle responded with a slow nod, her gaze interlocking with Krista's while she gathered a fistful of sand. She watched it escape through her fingers as if trying to grasp time itself.

"I get it," she murmured. "No more staying up until dawn just because we can, no more sleeping in past noon. No more days like today where we can just be." A shadow crossed her expression—a mix of nostalgia and melancholy as she added, "I know I'm going to miss this place like crazy."

A shared hush fell over them, punctuated only by the distant crash of waves—a silent salute from the sea to their shared feelings. Michelle scanned her circle of friends, each face dear to her heart. Sorrow welled within her at the thought that they, too, would soon scatter like the sand she had let slip through her fingers.

Jessica leaned back, her palms pressing into the warm, giving sand as she gazed up at the sky, its azure vastness stretching out like a promise. For a fleeting moment, she closed her eyes, letting the symphony of seaside life wash over her—a melody made up of her friends' voices and the rhythmic lull of the surf. It was a moment to savor, to capture in the deepest recesses of her memory.

When she opened her eyes again, they met Michelle's introspective gaze and found Krista's animated face. Her voice carried a blend of sadness and wonder. "I know exactly what you mean," she admitted. "Wavecrest is... it's more than just a place. It's the beach, the boardwalk, and all the good times we had. I mean, Fawn and I—oh my God, the crazy adventures we used to have!"

A soft chuckle escaped her lips as she reminisced, her bright blue eyes shining with reflections of days past—each memory sparkling like sunlight on water. "It's hard to imagine next summer without all this. I know it'll still be here when I come back, but it won't be the same without you guys."

In stark contrast to Jessica's gentle nostalgia, Heather flipped her thick black hair back with an air of defiance that cut through the sentimental haze. Her brown eyes sparkled with an untamed spirit as they swept over each friend.

"Well, you guys might miss Wavecrest," she declared boldly, "but not me. I can't wait to get out of here."

Her words fell like a stone in still water, sending ripples through their shared contemplation. The group fell silent, each face reflecting a mixture of emotions—surprise at Heather's candidness and sadness at the thought of separation.

Heather turned her gaze toward the ocean's horizon as if it were a portal to another world—one filled with neon lights and towering ambitions.

"I mean, come on guys. Haven't you ever wanted more? More than this?" Her voice carried an edge that belied a deep-seated yearning for change. "I want to experience everything—the city lights, the skyscrapers... and endless possibilities. I don't want to be some small-town girl my whole life."

In that moment, they glimpsed Heather's innermost desires—the longing for freedom and escape from the invisible constraints that tethered her to Wavecrest. None of them knew the family chains that shackled Heather, but they could sense, at least in that moment, that her eagerness to break free was fueled by more than just youthful restlessness.

Fawn, usually vibrant with creative energy, found herself unusually still, her eyes tracing the horizon where the sea met the sky—a boundary as blurred as her feelings. As she listened, her mind was a labyrinth of its own, haunted by the reality that she had already lost her sanctuary—not just in Wavecrest, but in the very home that had cradled her childhood dreams. She had a place in Boston, a new beginning, but the end of her life here felt like an eraser wiping away her past, tearing her roots out from the soil she had always known.

She glanced at Jessica, whose blue eyes were awash with a nostalgia that mirrored

Fawn's internal turmoil. There was a silent exchange between them, a shared understanding that went beyond words—a mutual recognition of the pain of parting from the familiar embrace of home.

The sense of displacement gnawed at Fawn; she could feel it even now as she sat among her closest friends. Jessica's family had always been a haven of warmth and acceptance for her, but it was not her childhood home. The realization that she would soon inhabit spaces that felt borrowed filled her with an unease she couldn't shake off. She kept her silence, allowing it to grow into a momentary chasm. The physical distance that would soon come between her and her friends became symbolic of the emotional vastness she felt as she realized her path was diverging, permanently changing the course of her life.

Their peaceful gathering on this stretch of beach—so often a stage for their youthful exploits—was tinged with an undercurrent of curiosity as Jessica's eyes settled on Heather. There was something different about Heather today; she seemed to harbor a secret just behind the curtain of her usual exuberance.

"I remember on the Fourth of July," Jessica began, breaking through the silence with a tone colored by curiosity and affection. "You said you had something big in the works. You said it was 'going to be epic,' but you didn't want to jinx it. So, you gonna tell us?"

The group leaned in, drawn by the magnetism of an untold secret—one that promised to add another layer to their intricate web of friendships.

Heather's eyes met Jessica's, then flicked away, as if weighing the merits of disclosure. Her gaze returned, fortified by a decision. "Okay, I'll tell you," she answered, a flicker of vulnerability crossing her features as she gathered her thoughts.

"You guys remember when we were getting our senior pictures taken?" She paused, a reflective smile touching her lips, the memory seemingly distant yet vivid in her mind. "The photographer," she continued, her voice tinged with a mix of surprise and wonder, "said something to me, something I didn't think much of at the time."

Jessica leaned in closer, her full attention on Heather. "Oh? What did he say?"

Heather took a deep breath, her eyes shining with a mixture of excitement and a hint of disbelief.

"He said that I had the potential to become a fashion model." She let the words hang for a moment, letting them soak in. Then, with a growing smile, she added, "So I thought, 'Why not', and talked to my parents about it." Her voice was buoyant, brimming with the thrill of embarking on an unexpected journey, a new dream unfolding right before them.

Fawn's eyes widened, clearly intrigued. "No way! That's crazy. What did your parents say?"

With a confident smile blooming on her lips, Heather replied, "They were all for it. Told me to put together a portfolio and give it a shot. So, I did."

Michelle's soft voice joined the conversation with genuine intrigue. "Wow, Heather, that's a pretty big step."

Heather nodded, her smile tinged with a sense of triumph. "I know, right? So, I sent my portfolio to a few agencies in L.A., not expecting much."

Krista interjected with a playful lilt, "Well, you always had the look and the attitude for it. Did anything come out of it?"

A gleam shone in Heather's eyes as she recounted the unexpected twist in her story. "Two weeks ago, I heard back, but it wasn't from L.A. It was from an agency in New York City. They said they were interested in me."

Jessica's excitement erupted like fireworks against the serene backdrop of waves and sky. "Oh my God, Heather, that's huge! New York City is like the fashion capital of the world!"

Fawn looked at Heather, her eyes filled with happiness for her friend. "Wow, that's amazing. So, what did you do?"

Taking a deep breath filled with anticipation and hope, Heather said, "I emailed them. I told them I'd love to move to New York City. Now, I'm just crossing my fingers and waiting to see what happens."

There was a moment of silence as everyone absorbed the gravity of Heather's revelation. Then, almost in unison, a cascade of congratulations and excited chattering spilled forth, filling the air with a sense of collective joy and anticipation for what lay ahead.

Heather's face was a canvas of contrasting emotions, dappled with relief and streaked with lingering uncertainty. The camaraderie of her friends had always felt like the embrace of a warm summer breeze, providing the comfort and validation she seldom received elsewhere.

"You know, before this modeling thing, I was actually thinking about moving to L.A.," Heather finally spoke, her voice imbued with a touch of wistfulness. "I thought I would try my hand at being a makeup artist, maybe work in a salon or something. But now, with this opportunity, it's like my whole game plan just did a one-eighty, you know? Like, everything just changed—and in the coolest way possible."

Fawn nodded, her eyes shining with the recognition of life's unpredictable nature. "Life is funny that way, isn't it? Just when you think you've got it all figured out, it takes you on a different path."

Jessica beamed at Heather, her enthusiasm echoing the thrumming pulse of their surroundings. "So, are you excited about possibly moving to New York City?"

With a laugh that radiated sheer excitement, Heather replied, "Excited? I'm beyond excited. The thought of living in a city that never sleeps; that's where I feel I'll really come alive."

Michelle leaned back on her beach towel, her eyes wandering to the horizon before settling back on Heather. "Well, wherever you go," she said with conviction, "you're going to shine—just like you always do."

Krista chimed in with unwavering positivity. "Absolutely! Whether it's L.A., New York

City, or anywhere else—the world better get ready for Heather Marino."

Heather's emotions crested as she looked at her friends through grateful eyes—a tear threatening to spill over in response to their heartfelt support. Swiftly brushing it away before it could fall, she smiled through the moisture.

"Thank you, guys," she whispered. "Your faith in me... it's more than I could have asked for."

"So, here we are, talking about our future," Jessica mused, drawing lines in the sand with her fingertip. "We all know where we're heading for college, but what made you decide to go?"

The question floated among them, inviting introspection. A silence fell, thick as the salt in the sea air. Each girl seemed to retreat into a private reverie, pondering the paths ahead. Michelle twirled a lock of auburn hair thoughtfully around her finger. Krista clasped her hands, as if holding onto her dreams before they could take flight. Fawn's eyes wandered out to sea, a silent longing etched across her face. Heather watched them intently; college was not on her horizon, yet she was eager to understand what pulled her friends toward their chosen destinies.

In the lingering pause, it was Krista who broke the silence. The anticipation of the moment seemed to converge upon her, like a river finding its way to the ocean. Her eyes brightened, filled with a flickering flame of passion for all to see.

"You guys know how much I love animals, right?" She began, her voice tinged with a touch of excitement. "That's why I'm going to Colorado State University in Fort Collins. They have an amazing program in animal sciences, and after that," she paused for dramatic effect, "I'm aiming for their vet program."

As Krista spoke of her passion for animals and the future she envisioned for herself—a future spent nurturing and healing—the others couldn't help but be drawn into her excitement. Her enthusiasm was contagious; it spread through them like wildfire.

"I mean," Krista continued, brushing her bright red hair off her face with a gesture as vibrant as her spirit, "Just the thought of being able to help animals, to be able to heal them and give them a better life... That's what drives me."

As Krista's words floated in the air, a palpable awe and admiration knitted around her friends. Their eyes met Krista's, each shimmering with a different hue of pride and affection. It was as if time had paused for a tender moment, allowing their spirits to celebrate the beauty of a calling so pure, so imbued with love.

Krista smiled, a mixture of confidence and earnest anticipation, like a sunflower leaning into the dawn. "So, yeah, Fort Collins will be my new home. I can't wait to be around people who share the same love for animals as I do."

Her eyes scanned the faces of her friends, each expression a testament to their enduring bond. "It's going to be different, being away from all of you. But we'll make it work, right?"

As Krista's question lingered, a hushed pause fell over the group. Their eyes met, each face revealing a mix of hope and uncertainty. It was as if they were all silently asking the same question: Could their friendship withstand the changes ahead? Though no one spoke, their shared silence seemed to acknowledge the unsettling truth—they didn't really know. The question hung in the air, unanswered but deeply felt, like a delicate thread left dangling, waiting to be woven into the fabric of their lives.

With the group awash in a cocktail of emotion, Michelle was on the cusp of sharing. Her eyes, windows to a world full of unwritten stories, met each gaze in turn. Before speaking, she collected her thoughts, as if gathering scattered pearls from the depths of her ambition.

"I'm going to UCSB," Michelle announced, her voice infused with the measured rhythm of a writer choosing her words. "I'm majoring in Journalism." Her declaration was a thread spun from the fabric of her being—a love for storytelling that had blossomed within her since childhood.

"You all know how much I love writing, right?" she continued, her hands moving as if to pluck the right phrases from the air. "I want to use that passion to make a difference. I see myself writing articles, maybe even novels, that shed light on stories that are often left in the dark."

Her words flowed like ink on paper, each sentence more resonant than the last, outlining her dreams as vividly as any article she might one day write. "I want to ask the tough questions, delve into the why and how of things. Make people stop and think."

Like Krista, her hands couldn't stay still; they punctuated her words, etching intangible headlines into the air. "Maybe it's just me, but I believe words have the power to change the world. I want to use that power responsibly."

Her final words hung in the salty air, forming an ethereal sentence that only those who knew her could thoroughly read. Michelle looked at her friends, each in their own boat but all sailing on the same unpredictable sea of life, and sought affirmation.

"It's just a dream for now," she admitted quietly. "But it's mine. What do you guys think?"

Jessica's lips curled into a smile, her eyes twinkling like stars writing their celestial tale. "So, are you going to write a story about Wavecrest someday?" she asked, her tone playful yet layered with genuine curiosity.

Michelle giggled, a sound as light and effervescent as champagne bubbles dancing on the surface of a glass. "Maybe someday," she replied playfully.

But then, her eyes drifted across the faces of her friends—searching, holding, understanding. Her voice softened, imbued with warmth and depth of feeling. "If I ever do write a story about Wavecrest," she paused, her heart in her eyes, "it will be about the incredible friends I was lucky enough to grow up with. It will be about all of you."

Her words, though simple, carried a weight that sank deep into the hearts of her friends. Each syllable was like a drop of ink, indelible and meaningful, outlining the contours of friendships that had flourished under the golden sun and silver moon of their coastal haven. They all sensed that these relationships, these shared experiences, would be the stories most worth telling.

Heather's eyes, so often aglow with vivacity and charisma, softened as they shifted from Krista and Michelle to rest upon Jessica and Fawn. Like heirloom tapestries woven through years of steadfast friendship, Heather not only observed, but also felt the bond between Jessica and Fawn. She had witnessed this extraordinary friendship since their fourth-grade year, a span of time that seemed both like a fleeting moment and a lifetime.

She pondered their upcoming journeys—Jessica to Austin, Fawn to Boston. Each destination felt like an outpost on separate corners of a vast country, both geographically and metaphorically distant from their beloved Wavecrest and, most importantly, from each other.

It wasn't that Heather couldn't comprehend ambition or the yearning for different scenery; it was the "why" that puzzled her. Why would these inseparable souls chart courses so divergent? Michelle was sticking closer to home, enrolling at UCSB, as if she, too, were heeding the siren song of the ocean that framed their lives. But not Jessica and Fawn. It was as if they were willingly untangling their fingers from the intricate latticework of their friendship, loosening a knot that Heather had thought unbreakable.

Capturing the sentimentality of the moment, Heather chose to venture where her heart led her, her voice laced with affectionate curiosity. "I can't help but wonder, you two—why Austin for you, Jess, and Boston for you, Fawn? I mean, why not UCSB? You two could still be near Wavecrest, near each other. After all these years, why this?"

The question hung in the air, like a feather on the edge of a precipice, delicate yet laden with implications. The eyes of their intimate circle turned toward Jessica and Fawn, awaiting the words that would unravel or reaffirm the mystery of their choices.

Jessica and Fawn exchanged a look—a silent conversation that spoke volumes. There was an undeniable hesitance in their eyes, but also an understanding—an acknowledgment that some questions cut deeper than others. They had faced this question before, within themselves and in the quiet spaces they shared, away from prying eyes.

Once upon a time, their dreams had been written in the sand of Wavecrest's beaches, shaped by the footprints of countless barefoot escapades and nurtured by the whispers of the ocean's waves. Santa Barbara had been their mutual choice of destination, a safe haven where they would continue their journey together. But dreams, like tides, were subject to change, swayed by forces beyond their control.

For Fawn, the lure of Boston had been a siren call, one she had resisted until reality—that relentless cartographer—reshaped her map. As an aspiring artist, her talent was a brush that could paint her life in hues more vivid than the summer skies of Wavecrest.

Boston was a vast and empty canvas, full of promise and possibilities. Her art teachers and guidance counselor spoke of this New England city as though it were an undiscovered country, filled with golden opportunities that UCSB couldn't quite match. And when the acceptance letter arrived, sealed with the weight of decision, it was as if Fate had dipped her brush in irrevocable ink. UCSB became the road not taken; Boston became the path that beckoned her with a promise of artistic fulfillment.

Yet, at that juncture, the house that had nurtured her dreams stood unshakably on its foundation—a sanctuary she believed she would return to during her college breaks, its doorway a passageway through which Jessica would forever come and go.

Then there was Jessica—her soul forever etched in the sands and skies of Wavecrest, a spirit as free and yet as bounded as the seagulls that swept over their beloved ocean. Jessica was an open book without a preface, a melody in search of a verse. She lacked Fawn's clear-cut ambitions; her dreams were abstract, not yet translated into the concrete language of 'what to do with one's life.'

Everyone around her seemed to echo the same sentiment: She had to leave her comfort zone; she had to fly. And so, Austin became her chosen horizon, a place far enough away to represent a leap of faith, yet anchored by the comforting presence of family who wouldn't be far away—her aunt, her uncle, her cousins—like buoys in unfamiliar waters.

Fawn's confession emerged, carried on a voice laced with a complex emotion that refused to be neatly categorized. "You know, I always thought we'd go to UCSB. I mean, it's here, it's home." She paused, letting the waves fill the brief silence with their timeless murmur. "But my teachers kept telling me that Boston is like this big hub for artists. More opportunities for me, they said."

Her form shifted atop the sand, her gaze momentarily capturing some distant thought or memory. "When I got the acceptance letter, it just felt right. Back then, I didn't know my parents were going to be selling the house. I thought I'd be back here on breaks, hanging out with Jess like we always do."

Fawn's eyes met Jessica's in a brief but meaningful glance, a silent conversation tinged with the bittersweet reality of change. Releasing a sigh that seemed to lighten her burden, she turned back to Heather.

"But it wasn't just about the art," Fawn's voice rose with conviction. "It was a chance for me to be a part of something new, something different. UCSB would've been cool, but Boston felt like—like a challenge. A scary but exciting challenge."

Heather offered a sympathetic smile in response, her nod an unspoken seal of approval. "That makes a lot of sense, Fawn. Choosing Boston was an act of courage." Her words were a soothing balm to the unease that came with change. "Change is tough, but it's also how we grow, right? You and Jessica have made some brave choices, no joke."

Fawn returned the smile, her eyes glowing with excitement and nervousness. "Exactly. I'm scared, but I also can't wait to see what's out there."

After Fawn's words had settled, filling the space around them like the fading echo of a poignant song, it was Jessica's turn to break the lingering silence. She looked around at her friends, her eyes finally landing on Heather, who seemed so intent on understanding their choices.

"You know, it's kinda funny," Jessica said, her tone tinged with the wavering notes of introspection. "I've always imagined I'd just get married and be a mom. And with Ethan now in my life, that's been like... all I can think about." A smile touched her lips, but it was one that hinted at the complex emotions swirling beneath it—dreams entwined with doubts.

She glanced over at Fawn, the cornerstone of so many of her life's chapters, and felt a mixture of reassurance and sadness, silently acknowledging how their choices had led them on separate paths.

"I mean, I don't have a big career plan like you guys do," Jessica continued, shrugging lightly, as if to shake off the weight of expectations. "I don't even know why I'm going to college, to be honest."

A pause followed as she collected the fragments of her reasoning. "So, when it came to picking a college, Austin felt like a good choice. I'll have family close by, but it's not here. It's not Wavecrest. Maybe being away will help me figure things out; I don't know..." Her words trailed off into the coastal breeze, carrying with them an admission of uncertainty.

Heather offered a nod that cradled Jessica's concerns within its motion. "Jess," she began with heartfelt reassurance, "it's perfectly fine not to have all the answers. College is a place to explore, and you should take full advantage of this opportunity. It may help you find the answers, even if the answers end up being what you've always known."

Jessica smiled, her face glowing with a newfound sense of validation, comforted by the idea that uncertainty, too, had its own value. "Thanks, Heather. It's just... Well, it's a big step," she admitted, glancing at Fawn, who nodded in agreement. "It's a big step for both of us."

Michelle, who had been quietly listening, her eyes alternating between the horizon and her friends, let her voice rise above the sound of the surf. "Listening to you guys talk about your choices is inspiring." She brushed a strand of hair away from her face as her eyes met theirs. "You two have been friends for so long, and now you're making these big decisions. I admire that."

Krista, who had been nodding along with each revelation, shared a look that held a mix of admiration and somber understanding. "Michelle's right," she said, her voice filled with an undercurrent of emotion. "These decisions are hard to make, especially when it means going separate ways."

A hush descended upon the group as they considered the gravity of change and distance. But it was Heather who shattered the contemplative stillness with a smile that seemed to capture the sun's rays in her sparkling eyes.

"Hey, guys? Remember three years ago? Fourth of July, watching the fireworks go off, right here on this spot," she reminisced, inviting them back to a simpler time. "That was the night we claimed this spot as ours!"

The atmosphere transformed as memories took flight like seagulls on an updraft—light and free. The weight of their earlier conversation dissipated as they were transported back to their younger selves—full of giddy energy and untouched by the notion of farewells.

Fawn's grin was radiant, reflecting the sparkle of remembered fireworks. "Oh my God, yes! Running around with sparklers and writing our names in the air!" Her laughter was infectious as she conjured up images of their youthful exuberance.

Jessica joined in, laughter lacing her words. "And let's not forget when Michelle almost set her hair on fire!" The image drew out chuckles from them all.

Michelle groaned in playful embarrassment, yet her eyes laughed. "Thanks for never letting me live that down!"

Krista pitched in with her own vivid recollection. "And the s'mores! Our marshmallows were either perfectly toasted or completely burnt, no in-between!"

Heather erupted into a fit of giggles, the sound a perfect antidote to their earlier solemnity. "You guys, those were the best of times. And you know what? We have the rest of the summer to make this one legendary!"

As Heather's words echoed around their circle, each girl felt a surge of solidarity—a shared determination to make the most of every moment left in their summer together. Bound by history and friendship, they knew that no matter where the currents of life might take them, they would always have Wavecrest—and each other—to anchor their hearts to home.

The emotional terrain of their gathering shifted like the sand beneath them, reshaped by the ceaseless tide of their shared histories. Laughter wafted through the air, a melody that harmonized with the essence of youth and the solidity of lasting bonds.

Their conversation rose and ebbed like the nearby surf, each anecdote cresting, each grin receding, all syncing to a cadence that even the ocean appeared to keep time with. For a fleeting span, time itself seemed to pause its relentless march, allowing them a pause to savor days gone by, even as they teetered on the brink of a future ripe with uncertainty.

With laughter and smiles as their guideposts, the memories flooded back—the hallways of school were no longer corridors of lockers and classrooms; they were galleries where memories hung like artwork. The summers were no longer seasons; they were epochs of personal evolution. The town of Wavecrest, a character in itself, was a silent actor in the theater of their lives.

As the afternoon sun continued its gentle arc through the sky, the girls rose from the sand, their footprints the only trace of the intimate moments they had shared. It was a wordless pact, a mutual understanding that the world beyond the sands of their cherished beach called for their return. The walk to the boardwalk was a brief one, but every step felt like a minor pilgrimage, each footfall echoing with the residual warmth of treasured memories.

Once they reached the bustling boardwalk, the world opened like a carnival—a tapestry of colors, scents, and sounds that beckoned with the allure of simpler joys. Their first stop:

a vendor. Icy drinks were bought and sipped, each a balm to the afternoon heat and a toast to the everlasting now. Suggestions floated in the air—the merry-go-round, perhaps? Or the Ferris wheel, where, for just a few minutes, they could rise above it all, their panoramic view taking in the town that had been the backdrop to so many formative scenes.

It was a pause, a collective breath taken between the chapters of their unfolding lives, a serene afternoon stretched into a tapestry of friendships old and new. Even as the gears of change clicked in the distance, for now, under the late afternoon sun, they were as timeless as the ocean that stretched far beyond their sight.

Seeking to escape the sun's sweltering embrace, they wandered into an arcade, its cool interior contrasting with the heat-soaked boardwalk outside. Their laughter echoed through the pulsating neon wonderland, harmonizing with the cheerful bleeps and bloops of the gaming machines.

As chance would have it, they stumbled upon other faces from their school days—class-mates, teammates, rivals—all glowing with the twilight euphoria of summer freedom. The occasion was especially fortifying for Jessica, who wore an infectious smile that seemed to eclipse the previous shadows of her missing Ethan. Her spirit was revitalized to such an extent that, for those fleeting moments, his absence felt less like a void and more like a space filled with the laughter and love of her dearest friends.

As the girls stepped back onto the boardwalk, Krista glanced at her phone. The dig-ital numbers, impartial and immovable, signaled the impending responsibilities that lay ahead. She and Michelle would soon have to clock in at The Seaside Grill, a restaurant nestled in Wavecrest's bustling tourist hub.

With a sigh that spoke volumes, Krista raised her head, her eyes sweeping over Jessica, Fawn, and Heather. "Looks like Michelle and I have got to bounce," she said, her tone casual but underscored by a hint of reluctance.

Michelle nodded in agreement, her voice echoing Krista's sentiment. "Yeah, duty calls. You know how it is." Her words were an echo of the familiar refrain of adulthood encroach-ing on their cherished freedom.

Amid the chorus of goodbyes, they embraced each other, each hug a silent testament to their friendship, each release a temporary but inevitable letting go.

"Take care, guys. See you later," Krista said with a cheerful and poignant smile. There was an unspoken depth to her goodbye—an acknowledgment of the coming days that would stretch into weeks and months of absence.

"Totally. See ya soon," Michelle added, offering a smile that attempted to preserve the moment like a treasured photograph within her heart.

With waves and backward glances, Krista and Michelle departed, threading their way through the crowd that thronged the boardwalk. They disappeared into the tapestry of faces and laughter, leaving Jessica, Fawn, and Heather to navigate the rest of their day without them.

With years of friendship synchronizing their movements, the trio turned in unison toward Jessica's house. The boardwalk beneath their feet echoed with memories of summers past—of ice creams that melted faster than they could eat them and fireworks that painted the night skies with fleeting artistry.

As they walked, the afternoon sun followed them, its light slanting into the evening and casting longer shadows along their path. But even as daylight began its slow retreat toward dusk, there was something about this golden hour that seemed to stretch out before them with boundless possibility.

As the trio meandered down the street leading to Jessica's house, Heather's car—a sleek embodiment of her affluent lifestyle—rested in the driveway. It was a gleaming testament to Heather's world of luxury and the perpetual motion of living in high gear. Today, however, that polished machine stood idle, a silent testament to Heather's decision to anchor herself in the company of her friends.

The three of them paused in front of the car, the day's residual heat lingering around them like an invisible shroud. Jessica's gaze settled on the vehicle, then lifted to meet Heather's eyes. A surge of gratitude filled her voice as she addressed her friend.

"Thank you, Heather," she said with heartfelt sincerity that seemed to carve itself into the moment. "I know your life is crazy busy, but you being here today... It meant the world to me. Especially today."

Heather stepped forward, her arms open and welcoming as she embraced Jessica. She replied with warmth and an unshakeable certainty. "Jess, you're more to me than a friend; you're like family. You don't have to thank me for being here when you need a lift."

As they parted, Heather turned to Fawn, finding in her eyes a reflection of the collective spirit of the day. "And thank you for reaching out to me this morning," she continued, gratitude shimmering in her tone. "You know, we may be going our separate ways, but we're still connected—and today was proof of that."

Fawn nodded, moved by Heather's words, and pulled her in a hug as well. "Couldn't imagine this day without you, girlfriend."

With a final wave and a blown kiss to each of them, Heather slipped behind the wheel of her car. The engine hummed to life under her touch—a sound that spoke of departures and destinations yet unknown. She pulled out of the driveway with a grace that matched the vehicle's design.

Jessica and Fawn stood side by side, watching Heather carve a path down the street until it became just another detail in the suburban tapestry. In the wake of Heather's departure, they felt a familiar hollowness—an echo of absence left by a departing friend.

After Heather's sports car roared away, Jessica turned to Fawn. Her eyes, pools of gratitude, met hers, and for a moment, they were not two friends on the brink of colossal life changes, but simply Jessica and Fawn—soulmates in friendship, guardians of each other's joy and sorrow.

On the path leading to the welcoming entrance of Jessica's house, Jessica paused and turned to Fawn, her eyes shimmering with unshed tears. "Thank you, Fawn, for always—always—being here, especially when I'm a mess like today." Her voice quivered with the intensity of her gratitude, finding it difficult to put the depth of her feelings into mere words.

Fawn looked at her with a gaze rich with layers of emotion—pride mixed with love and unwavering reassurance. "Jess, there's no one else I'd rather be a mess with," her soft voice imbued the simple statement with profound significance.

With the weight of the day settling into a tender ache, the two girls approached the front door. Fawn reached for the handle, a gesture repeated countless times over the years. As the door swung open, they stepped into the familiar embrace of Jessica's house, and for Fawn, her second home.

Beyond that threshold lay not just a house, but a repository of countless shared moments and precious memories—a tangible monument to their enduring friendship. As they stepped inside, it seemed as though time itself stood still for a heartbeat, granting them a moment of peace amid life's relentless pace.

Behind them, the door closed softly, enveloping them in the comforting cocoon of home. The clamor of the world outside dimmed into silence, leaving only the rich tapestry of their intertwined lives and the boundless horizons of their separate journeys ahead. Although the chapter of this day was closed, their story—filled with hopes, dreams, and indomitable friendship—was far from over.

# Chapter 26

------------------------------------------------------------

In a quaint corner of Wavecrest, where the sky seemed to embrace the ocean in a dance of ever-changing colors, Ethan returned to Jessica's life, filling the void his absence had created. It was as though the universe conspired, rolling back the fog of uncertainty to align their stars once more. When their eyes met, a symphony of unspoken emotions filled the air—each gaze, a musical note building into a harmonious melody only they could hear.

Jessica felt as if her world, which had shifted off its axis in Ethan's absence, had miraculously righted itself. Like a missing puzzle piece, he clicked into the empty space within her, making the picture of her life complete again.

Inside Jessica's home, Fawn immersed herself in a world all her own. With every glide of her charcoal pencil across her sketchbook, she began to see her vision for the Art Contest come alive. The act of creation enveloped her, as if each stroke were a thread weaving the fabric of a universe only she could comprehend.

While Ethan and Jessica basked in their renewed connection and Fawn in her artistic reverie, a palpable sense of completeness enveloped the house as if assuring them that, for this fleeting moment, all was right in their world.

As daylight began to yield to the soft hues of dusk, Jessica and Fawn continued their evening ritual, a practice that had become a comforting cornerstone since Fawn started staying at Jessica's house. Like pilgrims on a sentimental journey, they'd walk the short but meaningful distance to Fawn's still-unsold house, each step tinged with a blend of nostalgia and guarded hope. It had become a sanctuary for both, a place where Fawn could reconnect with her roots, and Jessica could feel the comforting presence of her extended family.

Fawn's emotions rode the ebb and flow of each passing day; the 'For Sale' sign on her lawn wavered between a dreadful omen and a fading threat. Yet, no 'sold' sticker had been slapped onto it, and with each evening visit, that fact alone inflated Fawn's dwindling reservoir of hope. Perhaps, she mused, the universe was offering her a slight reprieve, allowing her the luxury of imagining a future where her childhood home remained an indelible part of her life.

But underneath this thin veneer of hopefulness, a persistent ember of anger and disappointment smoldered. Why did her parents choose a future so far away, so foreign in the vast landscapes of Montana, when they could have explored options closer to home? Why had they discounted the value of this house—this sanctum of memories—not only as a physical space but also as an emotional anchor for her and her friendship with Jessica? With each step toward her childhood home, these questions prickled at the edge of her consciousness, adding a layer of complexity to her already tumultuous emotional landscape.

Uncertainty hung in the air, yet as they approached the familiar front porch, greeted by the reassuring faces of her parents, Fawn couldn't help but feel a small sense of victory. In this liminal space, hovering between the life she knew and an uncertain future, Fawn found a fleeting yet powerful affirmation in these evening visits. They reassured her that, for now, she was still tethered to the home that had shaped her.

And so, on this Monday evening in mid-July, when even the sun seemed reluctant to part ways with the horizon, their ritual continued. As Fawn and Jessica walked down the well-trodden path to Fawn's house, the sun's fading embrace painted their faces with a warm, golden glow. The air, while warm, was rendered comfortable by a breeze that meandered through the streets, caressing their skin and sending playful tendrils through their hair. One by one, the familiar streetlights awoke, casting pools of welcoming light that seemed, if only for a moment, to celebrate the enduring constancy of their friendship and journey.

"So, Miss Mysterious, are you going to tell me what you're drawing for the Art Contest?" Jessica asked, her eyes glinting with curiosity.

Fawn grinned, her eyes twinkling like stars emboldened by the encroaching night. "Nope. I told you, you'll have to wait and see," she replied, her voice laced with a mischievous undertone.

"Still keeping secrets, huh?" Jessica asked, feigning a sigh of exasperation as she narrowed her eyes in a playful challenge.

"Uh-huh. It wouldn't be a surprise otherwise, now, would it?" Fawn replied, her voice carrying a whimsical tone that hinted at deeper layers yet to be revealed. "Let's just say it will be something you won't easily forget."

Jessica shook her head, her laughter light like a summer breeze. "You're so full of surprises, Fawn. One day, you're going to have to share, you know."

Fawn smiled back, her eyes holding a mix of emotions that defied simple categorization. "I know, but not tonight," she said, the complexity of her feelings adding layers to her

voice—like a haunting melody that sang of both happiness and an indescribable wistfulness.

As the girls continued their walk, they approached the cozy house of Mr. and Mrs.
Applegate. The elderly couple sat on their porch, wrapped in the waning light, their faces
creased with lines that told tales of years well lived and wisdom well earned. A gentle
smile graced their faces as they spotted the girls. Over the years, they had become quiet
observers of Jessica and Fawn's growing friendship, their eyes catching fleeting moments
of laughter and the unmistakable bond of sisterhood.

"Evening, girls!" Mr. Applegate greeted, raising his hand in a warm wave. "My, how you
two have grown. It's hard to believe you were just little toddlers running up and down this
street not so long ago."

Mrs. Applegate chimed in, her voice as soft as a lullaby. "It's always a pleasure to see the
two of you passing by. Makes the evening feel complete, doesn't it, Harold?"

"Indeed it does, Martha," Mr. Applegate agreed, his eyes twinkling as if the two girls were
a living testament to the beauty of their neighborhood.

Jessica beamed, her heart swelling with a sense of community and continuity. "Thank
you, Mr. and Mrs. Applegate! Walking by your house always looks... just really cozy and
nice."

Fawn nodded, her eyes briefly meeting those of Applegate's. "Yes, thank you. You have
no idea how much that means to us. Especially now, with everything changing."

For a moment, their eyes met, and in that silent exchange was a mutual understanding.
Time was a river, ever moving and ever changing, but the comfort of familiar faces along
its streets made the journey sweeter. The Applegates' nodded, their smiles etched with a
blend of nostalgia and hopeful anticipation.

"Change is a part of life, dear," Mrs. Applegate said. "But some things—like this little
street of ours—have a way of enduring."

Jessica and Fawn smiled, their hearts absorbing the wisdom offered. With a wave and a
cheerful goodbye, they continued on their way, their spirits lifted by the encounter, grateful
for the constant fixtures in a world of shifting sands.

As they approached Fawn's house, the unwelcome sight of the 'For Sale' sign jolted
them like a dissonant note in an otherwise harmonious symphony. No longer a refuge but
a reminder of familial discord and looming change, the house stood there, its modern and
spacious architecture incongruent with Fawn's turbulent emotions. The concrete steps,
indifferent to her inner turmoil, offered no creaks or sighs—just a steady ascent toward a
home that was increasingly feeling like anything but.

Anna's welcoming smile greeted them as the door opened, yet for Fawn, it was a complex tableau—love mixed with a dose of resentment, comfort clouded by the anticipation
of loss. "Come in, girls," she said, stepping aside to let them enter.

As they crossed the threshold, Fawn couldn't help but feel the unease that had wormed its way into her bones. Her home, once the sanctuary that had nurtured her formative years, was now the setting for an unfolding drama. The walls, adorned with family photos and cherished memories, seemed like a prelude to a play about to change its cast. The air carried the familiar aroma that usually signaled 'home', but today, Fawn and Jessica couldn't ignore the undertone of tension tinged with it.

As they moved further into this comforting yet disconcerting space, Anna's eyes met Fawn's. Those expressive hazel eyes—normally a source of maternal warmth and wisdom—bore a subtle shadow, a hint of worry that Fawn recognized all too well.

"Make yourselves comfortable, girls," Anna said, her voice attempting casual cheerfulness but not quite hitting the mark. She retreated into the kitchen, her short, playful hairstyle doing little to lighten the serious look on her face.

As Fawn and Jessica took their seats on the couch, their eyes turned towards Brian. They noticed him ensconced in his office, a room visible from where they sat. His stocky figure, the epitome of unassuming strength, was in the midst of an evidently serious phone conversation. His wire-framed glasses had slid down the bridge of his nose as he listened intently, nodding occasionally even though the caller couldn't see him. Though his face was obscured by the room's partial wall, the hunch of his shoulders spoke volumes, filling the room with an intangible tension.

Outside, the 'For Sale' sign stood on the lawn, a constant visual reminder that added weight to the atmosphere. The usually inviting room felt different—more like a waiting area, filled with a sense of expectation that no one wanted to acknowledge. This was a room holding its breath, waiting for someone to break the silence and relieve the building tension.

Fawn glanced at Jessica before turning her attention to her mother, who had reappeared from the kitchen holding a tray with cups of coffee. The steaming mugs seemed out of place in the tense atmosphere.

"What's going on, Mom?" Fawn inquired, her voice a blend of concern and burgeoning frustration, like a flame waiting for the right wind to snuff it out or feed it into a blaze.

Anna paused, setting the tray down on the coffee table with a little more care than usual, as if she were laying down fragile pieces of their shared reality.

"Let's wait for your father. He should be done soon," she replied, her voice tinged with a hesitance that made the room feel even smaller.

As she spoke, she moved around the room, busying herself by adjusting the perfectly aligned cushions and flicking imaginary lint from the coffee table. Her hands were busy, but her eyes—those reflective hazel pools—revealed an inner world swirling with thoughts she wasn't yet ready to articulate.

Anna's elegant avoidance made the ticking of the clock on the wall resonate like a drumbeat in the silence, each second stretching as it passed. Jessica felt the weight of the room's atmosphere, an oppressive stillness that challenged her lungs as she breathed. She exchanged another glance with Fawn, her eyes reflecting the growing apprehension she knew they both felt.

Finally, the sound of a phone clicking shut broke the taut quietude, followed by the creak of a swiveling chair and footsteps growing louder as they approached. Brian emerged from the office, his expression unreadable. With his wire-framed glasses perched meticulously back in place, he joined the trio in the living room.

His eyes met Anna's, a fleeting but significant exchange, and for the first time that evening, Fawn felt a trickle of dread knotting in her stomach, as if she were standing on the edge of an abyss that she was about to fall into.

"It's done," he said, locking eyes with Anna. The weight of those two words hung in the air, powerful and laden with unspoken implications.

Fawn looked up, her eyes meeting her father's, then darting to her mother's, her own gaze a puzzle of uncertainty and concern.

"What's done?" she asked, her voice tinged with curiosity and apprehension. The atmosphere thickened, each heartbeat seeming to add to the tension that had quietly built its home in the room.

As Brian's gaze settled on Fawn, a subtle tinge of sadness clouded his usual steadfast eyes. At that moment, he resembled an artist forced to put the final brushstroke on a canvas he'd much rather leave unfinished. Fawn felt her father's regret travel through the invisible thread that had always connected them, a thread now taut with impending change.

"We sold the house, honey," Brian said, the words heavy as if each syllable was a small stone he had to lift off his chest. "I know that's not what you want to hear, but it is what it is."

His eyes shifted to include Jessica in this intimate confession, his expression softening as if trying to cushion the blow he had just dealt. "I'm sorry, girls. I'm truly sorry," he uttered, his voice filled with a sincerity that pierced the room's thick atmosphere.

In that lingering moment, a sense of finality settled over Fawn like a fog rolling in, crystallizing what had been an abstract fear into a tangible reality. Until now, the impending sale of the house had been a distant storm cloud, threatening but not yet here. Suddenly, that storm was upon her, its first raindrops shattering any remaining illusions. Every cherished corner and object in the room seemed to stand out in stark relief, as if urging her to memorize them before they were gone from her life.

For Fawn, the world had become irrevocably smaller. There would be no more hoping against hope, no more praying to the universe to spare her this singular heartache. The house was sold, and with it, a chapter closed that could never be reopened. The definitive tone in her father's voice and the look of resigned sadness in her mother's eyes served as unyielding pillars, marking her passage into an unsettling new normal.

Beside her, Jessica felt the emotional tectonics of the moment shift, her friend's struggle between hope and acceptance suddenly losing its ambiguity. In Fawn's eyes, Jessica saw a flicker of resignation, a painful letting go of illusions, as if she had just been handed an unsolvable puzzle whose missing pieces were fragments of her own heart. It was the look of someone who had crossed a bridge and then watched it crumble behind her, leaving her with no choice but to face what lay ahead.

For a moment, the air in the room seemed to still, as if holding its breath for the fallout that was to come. Fawn's gaze finally lifted from the worn patterns of the carpet to meet her parents' eyes—those eyes that had once been the compass guiding her through life, but now seemed like betrayers of trust. A cold fire burned behind her irises as she spoke.

"Well, you got what you wanted. Congratulations," she said, her voice tinged with a corrosive sarcasm that even she was surprised to hear.

Anna replied softly, her eyes like deep wells of sadness, "It's not what we wanted, sweetheart."

Brian chimed in, wearing his own mask of somber defeat. "No, it's not. It's what we had to do."

Fawn's eyes narrowed, an emotional cauldron brimming just beneath the surface. "That's not true. You could have stayed here and found another job."

As the words escaped her lips, Fawn felt a strange mixture of release and constriction, as if she had unburdened a long-held secret and tightened a noose around her neck. Her anger was a prickly shrub growing in the dry soil of resentment, fed by every unanswered question and nourished by each unmet expectation.

In the strained silence that followed, Fawn realized she had voiced a sentiment, an accusation, that would sear itself into the family's memory like a brand on flesh. It marked an irreversible transition, like passing through a door that shuts and locks behind you. From now on, she knew her relationship with her parents would be overshadowed by this painful moment as she navigated the future.

Brian took a deep breath, his chest rising and falling like a ship in turbulent waters. In the lines etching his face and the gray creeping into his hair, he saw years of decisions and compromises; each choice a stone that had built the life they were all living. He felt the invisible burden of his family's welfare on his shoulders, a weight he had willingly carried, but never heavier than in this moment.

His eyes met Fawn's, young yet filled with an anguish that he would have given the world to spare her from. He opened his mouth, grappling with how to encapsulate a lifetime of responsibilities and fears into words his daughter could understand.

"I wish it were that simple, Fawn," he began, his voice a mix of regret and quiet determination. "Believe me, if I could have found a way to keep us here in this house, I would have taken it without a second thought. But I've been with Atlas for twenty years, and in those years, I've built a safety net that I can't just throw away. A lot of businesses around here are struggling; the chances of me finding another job that offers the same security are slim to none. I had to think about our future—your future."

As Brian spoke, the room seemed to contract, the walls closing in as if absorbing the gravity of his words. His expression was not one of defiance but rather an admission of his own limitations, his own humanity. It was as if he was standing at the edge of a chasm, shouting across it, hoping his words could serve as a bridge to span the emotional distance that had opened up between him and his daughter.

Fawn looked at him, her eyes still harboring the storm of her emotions but also showing the first glimmers of understanding. For the first time, she saw her father not as an infallible figure of authority, but as a man caught in the unforgiving gears of circumstance, making the best choices he could with the cards he had been dealt.

"I get it, Dad," Fawn's voice was softer now, the jagged edge of her earlier words replaced by a weary understanding. "I get that you did what you thought you had to do. But did you ever stop to think what it would do to me? To us?"

As she spoke, Fawn felt as if she were walking along a precipice, each word a step along an unstable ledge. Her anger had not completely dissipated; it hovered in the background like a storm cloud, refusing to be dispelled. She understood, perhaps for the first time, that her parents were not invincible gods but fallible humans. Yet, understanding did not quell her sense of loss, nor did it silence the whispering voice in her mind—a voice that insisted he could have chosen a different path, one that would have kept their family intact in the home she so dearly loved.

"I know I can't relate to all the things you're worried about," she continued, her voice faltering as she navigated the maze of conflicting emotions. "But it feels like you didn't even try to find another way. And now, all the memories, all the love we put into this house—it's like it doesn't even matter."

Her words hung in the air like the last notes of a somber melody, tinged with the sadness and wisdom of a lost innocence. It was an irrevocable shift, a layer of childhood stripped away, leaving her standing in the uneasy terrain of a complex adult world she was not yet ready to fully inhabit but could no longer completely ignore.

Anna's eyes glistened like dew on a morning leaf, revealing a fragility. Beside her, Brian's face was a landscape of emotional turmoil; deep creases of worry that years had carved, now filled with the new sediment of regret.

"You're right, honey," Brian confessed. "We should've talked to you first. And maybe there were other options we could've explored." A sigh escaped him, as if releasing a long-held breath he didn't know he was holding. "But the decision is made, and we can't go back. All we can do is try to move forward. Together."

Anna chimed in, her voice like the soft glow of a candle fighting against the darkness. "We love you, Fawn. We're not the enemy here. Sometimes, life just puts you in situations where there are no easy choices. But we are a family, and we will get through this. We will make a new home and fill it with new memories."

With a deep, silent inhale, Fawn took in their words like one would breathe in the scent of an old, familiar place—recognizing the sweetness, but also the underlying decay. The words did little to resolve the storm within her, but they offered a momentary respite where she could catch her breath before venturing back into the tumult.

Nodding slightly, Fawn broke the lingering gaze between her and her parents. "I need some time alone," she breathed, her voice imbued with a maturity that no one in the room could miss.

As Fawn rose from the couch, Jessica, her silent support throughout this fraught ex-change, met her gaze. For a brief second, their eyes locked, and Jessica felt an ache blossom in her chest—a mingling of loss and understanding. The room they were leaving was more than just a space for Fawn; it had been Jessica's second home, echoing with laughter and brimming with memories. Yet, as she followed Fawn out, Jessica sensed the irreversible march of time, its footsteps invading even this cherished space, crumbling the walls that held their youth and innocence.

Together, they climbed the stairs to a room that had been Fawn's but now felt alien—an intimate cocoon now transformed into a hollow chrysalis, its transformation symbolic of a life left behind and the uncertainty of the one to come. As Jessica followed, her steps grew heavy with the weight of finality, each echoing a whispered goodbye to an era forever closed. The atmosphere carried a gravitational pull, saturated with the undercurrents of nostalgia and a nameless sorrow, as if the very timbers of the house were moaning their farewells.

As the bedroom door creaked open, its sound—once a familiar symphony heralding a realm of refuge—struck a discordant note in the air, devoid of its once comforting warmth. Fawn led Jessica into her room—once a tableau of identity and teenage dreams, but now a strange canvas, distorted and upended. It was as if her room had been dipped in a solution of melancholy and turmoil, preserving a heartbreaking monument to the moment she had left it. On that fateful Fourth of July night, she had seen her room arranged in a way that felt like an invasion of her soul.

Fawn's eyes swept the room, and in that sweeping glance, she felt the emotional weight of every displaced object, every photograph, every nuance of rearranged space pulsating with pain. Her walls were still lined with the bands she loved, the academic accolades, and those sentimental doodles drawn during late-night heart-to-hearts with Jessica. Yet, all these tokens of her past life now felt like ghostly artifacts from a museum that had lost its curator.

"Can you believe it?" The question, laced with a cocktail of disbelief and indignation, escaped Fawn's lips, fluttering like a caged bird longing for open skies. Her eyes found Jessica's, a silent plea for understanding.

Jessica looked around, her eyes widening in amazement and empathy. She had only envisioned the desecration of this once-sacred space through Fawn's vivid descriptions and inconsolable sobs during that tumultuous night of refuge at her home. Now, standing amidst the disarray that marked Fawn's life, Jessica felt as though she was navigating the ruins of a demolished cathedral.

She shook her head slowly, each gesture a wordless sonnet of disbelief and support. She understood now, more than ever, why that night had torn Fawn apart so deeply. Her sanctuary had been desecrated, its soil tilled without consent, its boundaries crossed without reverence.

The silence between them swelled, a tangible response to the stark reality before them. Confronted with the profound disorder of Fawn's bedroom, a space once vibrant and familiar, they found it now unrecognizable. In this moment, Fawn's room was not just a room; it was a crucible of their shared memories. And as they stood there, facing the reality that enveloped them like a haunting fog, they knew that this was yet another threshold they would cross. Not back into the world they had known, but forward into an uncertain landscape fraught with emotional fault lines and the intricate complexities of growing up.

In seamless harmony, Fawn and Jessica set to work, their movements a dance honed through years of shared experiences. They didn't need to speak; their actions were a language forged from the countless days and nights spent in this room. Fawn's hands grasped a misplaced book, her fingers caressing its spine like a long-lost friend before placing it back on its proper shelf.

Knowing the room almost as well as her own, Jessica picked up a dislocated photo frame, its glass face smeared with the grime of neglect. She wiped it clean, almost as if she were erasing the blur of the past weeks, and returned it to its rightful spot.

Bit by bit, the room began to regain its shape, with every placed object serving as a reclaimed fragment of Fawn's life, each contributing to restoring the room to its original composition. For Jessica, each action was an act of reverence, a tribute to a friendship that had anchored her through storms and sunshine alike.

The physical act of rearranging became a cathartic exercise, reclaiming not just space, but identity and history. When Jessica stepped back to survey their work, the room felt once again like an extension of Fawn, an intimate portrait pieced back together. With a sense of gratification and relief, she realized that while rooms could be invaded and per-sonal havens breached, the essence of their friendship was something far more resilient.

After returning the last object to its home, Fawn stepped back, taking in the room like an artist surveying a completed canvas. Every item, every piece of memorabilia, was where it should be, restored to its rightful nook and cranny. Yet, a lingering sense of disquiet hovered in the air, like a haunting melody played on a perfectly tuned instrument.

She turned toward Jessica, her eyes misty with a realization that felt as weighty as it was intangible. "Jess, I can't stay here," she murmured, her voice barely above a whisper. "Everything's back in its place, but it... it just doesn't feel like my room anymore."

Jessica looked at her, the pang in her own chest resonating with the ache in Fawn's words. "I can't even imagine how hard this has to be for you," she said, her voice tender and sincere.

Fawn nodded, her eyes meeting Jessica's in a moment, heavy with unspoken under-standing. Despite the room's familiar facade, an unsettling realization had settled upon her—that while the room remained materially the same, the comfort it once offered was now tinged with the impermanence of an hourglass steadily emptying. The walls, still adorned with echoes of her past, felt like silent witnesses to an ending. It was as if their warmth had dimmed in anticipation of a new family who would soon claim them, erasing her history like footprints on a beach.

"In a strange way, this room isn't mine anymore," Fawn sighed, the timbre of her voice tinged with melancholy. "It's as if it's already waiting for the next person to claim it; like I'm just a fading memory in a space that used to be mine."

Jessica's fingers clasped Fawn's, their touch a living testament to a friendship that time or circumstance could not erode.

"You don't need four walls to call a place home, Fawn," she said, her voice soft yet steady, as if the words were woven from the very threads of their shared history. "You know my house is your house, too, right? Even Mom and Dad told you that. You don't have to stay here if you don't want to."

Amid the quiet disarray of a room losing its soul, Fawn felt a flicker of warmth, a transient glow that, for the first time, felt like the dawn of a new beginning.

"I know, Jess," she whispered, her voice a mixture of gratitude and the dawning accep-tance of her new reality. "Your house has been more of a home to me lately than this could ever be." She paused, her eyes scanning the room one more time, its objects now bearing the weight of a past that was slipping away.

And in that moment, under the gaze of forgotten dreams and reassembled artifacts, both girls realized that their true refuge wasn't within the walls of this room; it had always been found in each other.

Before taking her leave, Fawn cast a final, lingering glance back toward her room. It was as if she were bidding farewell to a cherished friend who had accompanied her through the tumultuous journey of adolescence. The contours of her bed, the colors on the walls, the trophies and pictures—each an intimate confidant that had witnessed her laughter, her tears, and her dreams. The room seemed to look back at her, as if acknowledging the invisible thread of separation that had been cut, the turning of a chapter that neither could undo.

With a soft exhale that mixed resignation with gratitude, Fawn turned away, her gaze fixed on Jessica's supportive eyes. Her friend understood, and that unspoken sympathy was a tender balm that sealed the wound left by her room's alienation.

The girls descended the stairs, each step taking them further from the room that had once been a bastion of Fawn's identity but was now more like a historical site—a place to visit but no longer to inhabit. They rejoined Brian and Anna in the living room, who, despite the lines of concern etched into their faces, smiled with a sense of relief at seeing their daughter return.

Brian broke the silence that followed, his words carefully chosen but tinged with a vulnerability that had become the new undercurrent in their household. "Sweetheart, you can come back now. We won't be showing the house to strangers anymore."

Fawn took in her father's words, and then, looking at Jessica, a small, bittersweet smile escaped her lips. "Thanks, Dad, but I think I'll be staying at Jessica's house. It's what feels right for me now."

Her parents exchanged glances, recognizing the irrevocable shift in the family dynamics. Anna nodded, her eyes shining but holding back the tears. "You do what you feel is best, honey. Just know we're here whenever you need us."

With her parents' blessing hanging in the air, Fawn took Jessica's hand. Together, they walked toward the door, each step an unspoken testament to their journey, their friendship, and the many complexities of growing up. The door closed behind them with a subdued thud, a finality that resonated more within than any spoken farewell.

They stood at the foot of the porch, enveloped in the warm, forgiving embrace of the night air. Here, under the shroud of twilight, far from the curated spaces and shifting sands of their lives, they felt, if only for a fleeting moment, that they had reclaimed something intangible yet crucial. In the chaos of change and the vulnerability of transitions, they had found their footing, and it was on this steady ground that they would continue to forge their paths.

Fawn paused, her eyes drifting toward the old white bench swing that graced the edge of the yard. It stood there as if waiting, a silent keeper of countless secrets and shared moments that had once populated their younger years.

"Hey Jess, let's sit for a while," she said, her voice filled with a sense of yearning that was as palpable as it was indescribable. The words floated in the air, an invitation to revisit a chapter of their lives written in the ink of innocence and the language of unspoken bonds.

Like two ethereal figures against the backdrop of the night, Fawn and Jessica drifted across the lawn, their eyes settling on the old white bench swing that rested under the dappled moonlight. Though time had weathered its paint, its frame stood defiant and resilient—much like the bond the two girls shared.

For Fawn, the swing had always been more than just metal and cushion; it was an emblem of memories imprinted not just on the fabric of the seat, but in the fiber of her soul. It was a piece of a celestial map that navigated her through the labyrinth of childhood, its corners marked with the ink of dreams and tears alike.

With a gentle touch, they lowered themselves onto the swing, the slight groan of the seasoned metal acting as if it were rousing from a long slumber to greet them once again. As they began to sway in that familiar, rhythmic motion, the world around them seemed to soften, fading into hues of nostalgia and serenity. The palm leaves rustled above them, as though they were whispering the lines of an old lullaby, one they had both heard but never fully understood.

Here, they needed no words. The air around them was thick with shared memories, an unspoken language they had created over years of friendship. The mere act of swinging, back and forth, back and forth, seemed to usher them into a forgotten sanctuary—a space still held sacred by whatever powers guided the universe, a space that required no walls or ceilings, just the ever-present beauty of the night and the silent complicity of the wind.

As they swayed to that mysterious rhythm, Fawn turned toward Jessica, their eyes meeting in a wordless communion as intricate and intimate as an unwritten sonnet. Their smiles were silent symphonies, fleeting yet timeless, capturing the essence of years compressed into an instant. And in that moment, they knew—this was their sanctum, a hallowed ground veiled from the rest of the world.

Though other friends had come and gone in Fawn's life, none had ever shared the sacred privilege of that swing, the cradle of their friendship. The swing was their Garden of Eden, unstained by the chaos of the world, a haven where they were free to be nothing more than who they truly were—two souls bound by a love as indefinable as the night sky that enveloped them.

The air around them seemed to hold its breath as Jessica's phone buzzed in her pocket, its vibrations cutting through the gossamer veil of serenity that had enveloped them. With a faint flicker of anticipation, Jessica unlocked her phone to find Ethan's name gleaming on the screen. Her heart, an otherwise steadfast sentinel, fluttered like a caged bird yearning for the sky.

"Hey babe... I fixed the Jeep... u wanna go see a movie or sumthin?" The words unfolded like a melody, their tune so hauntingly familiar that her heart ached with a poignant mix of desire and sadness. Ethan—her touchstone, her love—invited her to step into a world suffused with the warm glow of their shared affection. Each letter in the message felt like a caress, a silent affirmation of the love that had been steadily intensifying since their paths entwined. The fact that Ethan would be leaving Wavecrest at the end of summer made every second with him a gem to be savored, a fleeting moment in an hourglass that was rapidly emptying.

But when she looked at Fawn, whose soul was visibly frayed at the edges, an overwhelming force of loyalty and friendship kept her grounded. It was a conflicting pull of tides within her, one beckoning her to Ethan's arms and the other urging her to stay with her oldest and dearest friend in her hour of need.

Taking a deep breath to steady her trembling hands, her thumbs danced over the phone's screen. "I can't tonight. Something came up." The words were like tiny stones cast into the river of their lives—simple, yet creating ripples that would reach the distant shores of their different worlds.

Ethan's reply flashed almost immediately, a digital whisper laden with concern: "R U OK?" Three simple words, yet each a pulse in the vein of their relationship, a testament to the deeper currents that flowed beneath the surface of their love. His quick response was more than a ping; it was the reverberation of a connected heart, a syncopated rhythm in the silence, as if his soul had sensed the crack in hers and reached out, longing to heal whatever had caused her to waver.

Jessica's thumbs hesitated over the glassy surface of the phone, each potential keystroke an echo of another truth she could convey. A crossroads stretched before her in the pixelated glow: one path cloaked in the comforting mantle of "I'm fine," and the other, a more vulnerable route paved with honesty.

After a pause, she chose the latter. "No, not really. I'll cya tomorrow," she typed, each word carrying a weight far heavier than letters on a screen should.

"OK babe. Cya tomorrow. Love you!" Ethan's reply appeared, each word shimmering with an undercurrent of concern, a love letter compressed into the brevity of a text but no less rich in meaning.

"Love U 2 babe," she typed, her fingers lingering on the screen for a heartbeat, as if infusing each letter with the essence of her love. Then she sent the message off, as if releasing a dove into the digital sky, and returned her phone to its pocket.

"Was that Ethan?" Fawn's voice floated through the air, a delicate question that seemed to tread cautiously on the evening's fragile balance.

"Yeah, that was my baby," Jessica's words unfurled, her voice imbued with a gentle warmth as her face brightened, illuminated by a love-struck smile that flickered like a candle in the dusk.

Fawn smiled, recognizing the flicker of joy that always lit up Jessica's eyes at the mention of Ethan. "What did he want?" she asked, her eyes glowing with curiosity.

Looking down, Jessica considered her words carefully. She knew that revealing Ethan's invitation would cause Fawn to insist that she go, to push her into the arms of romance over the bittersweet tapestry of their friendship. No, tonight was different; tonight was sacred in a way that needed no intrusion.

Lifting her eyes to meet Fawn's, she shook her head and said, "Nothing important. I'll see him tomorrow." In that simple statement, laden with layered meaning, Jessica's love and loyalty to Fawn shone brightly, silently affirming that even the intoxicating allure of romantic love couldn't eclipse the enduring strength of their friendship, especially when faced with life's relentless complexities and setbacks.

Fawn's smile reflected on Jessica's face as both girls leaned back into their seats, allowing the gentle arc of the swing to dissolve the residual tensions of the night. The world around them seemed to sigh in a comforting embrace, as if some ancient, ethereal presence had subtly woven itself into the air, cradling them in unspoken solace.

Unaware of the silent sacrifice her best friend had made, Fawn nestled her head onto

Jessica's shoulder. Jessica looked at her, eyes soft with a love that transcended words, one that spoke volumes in the silence they shared.

For the rest of that warm summer evening, Jessica and Fawn sat on the old white bench swing. They felt wrapped in a quilt sewn from the golden threads of dusk and the silvery strands of moonlight, woven together by a love as transcendent and timeless as the stars. Their hearts—quiet now—were touched, ever so slightly, by an ethereal whisper of comfort that only the children of Wavecrest could hear.

# Chapter 27

-----------------------------------------------------

In the Reese household, morning sunlight streamed through the curtains, casting dappled shadows on the kitchen walls—walls that had been silent witnesses to countless family gatherings, echoing laughter, and homemade meals that nourished both body and soul.

Tom sat at the kitchen table, dressed in a blue shirt and tie, the fabric crisply pressed, revealing the meticulous nature his years in the Military had instilled in him. Across from him was Teresa, dressed in a long pink nightgown, her soft waves of brown hair framing a face with the serenity of a still pond at dawn. The aroma of freshly brewed coffee and the comforting, almost rustic smell of frying bacon scented the room, lending an air of domestic harmony to the scene.

And yet, for all its apparent normalcy, this morning was a dissonant note in the otherwise harmonious symphony of their lives. Usually, the atmosphere in the Reese home was light, buoyed by small talk and future plans, punctuated by the click of the door behind Tom as he left for work. But this morning, a heaviness hung over the room like a gray cloud that refused to be dispelled by the sun. Their words were more subdued, and their pauses were longer and more fraught.

The sale of Fawn's house wasn't just a line item on a real estate contract—it was a tear in the fabric of a community they'd woven together with the neighboring family. The girls' friendship had served as the thread that laced the two households into a single tapestry of warmth, love, and shared history. Fawn and Jessica were not just friends; they were extensions of each family's soul. Thus, the thought of Fawn's imminent departure felt like a part of them was being uprooted, and Tom and Teresa couldn't help but share in the emotional gravity of that loss.

As they sat there, their hands reaching across the table to find comfort in each other's touch, they were both acutely aware that this was not just another morning. It was the morning after a storm, the landscape forever altered, requiring them to navigate the unfamiliar terrain of their emotions as they pondered on how to be the pillars of strength that Jessica and Fawn would undoubtedly need in the difficult days ahead.

Tom's hands clenched briefly, a physical manifestation of the storm of frustration and anger that was raging within him. He shook his head, a small but poignant gesture laden with a weighty despair.

"You know, if Brian had come to me with this back in May, I might have been able to do something," he said, his voice punctuated by the heavy thud of missed opportunities. "I might have been able to get him a job where I work."

Across the table, Teresa's gaze met Tom's, her eyes mirroring his emotional storm and a search for clarity in a situation muddied by inexplicable choices. She, too, wrestled with a knotted bundle of questions, the most perplexing being why Anna, her dearest friend, had kept her in the dark.

"Maybe they just didn't want to burden us with their problems," Teresa suggested, striving to sow a seed of understanding in the harsh soil of the moment. "I mean, they didn't even tell Fawn until it was too late."

Tom's eyes narrowed, the bright blue of his irises turning almost stormy. "I know," he replied, the words etched with an acidic undertone.

His mind flashed back to Jessica and Fawn, the two girls who were like twin stars in the firmament of their lives. The thought of withholding such life-altering news from their own daughter—the girl whom Tom had long since considered an adopted member of the Reese clan—was unfathomable.

"For the life of me, I'll never understand why they did that," he growled, the anger simmering just beneath the surface.

The air between them seemed to thicken in that conversation, as though saturated with the mutual recognition of a painful, irrevocable truth. Their words were an echo of the broader lament, a discordant coda to a song of friendship and community that had sustained them for so long.

Yet amid this landscape of emotional upheaval, Tom and Teresa were anchors, bound not just by love, but by an unspoken commitment to traverse the difficult road ahead, serving as the rocks upon which Jessica and Fawn could still find sure footing.

The symphony of raw emotions that had filled the room only moments ago was interrupted, suspended in a delicate pause by the sound of a bedroom door opening and closing. Tom and Teresa fell silent, their hearts quickening like birds aware of an approaching sunrise. Anticipation swelled between them, like a river held back by a dam, waiting to be released. And then, there she was—Fawn emerging from the hallway.

The sight of her was like the first light of dawn breaking over the horizon, dissolving the remnants of a long, dark night. Dressed in one of Teresa's long blue nightgowns—a garment Fawn had lovingly claimed as her own—she wore the cloth like an extension of herself, as if it were woven from the same fabric that made up the Reese family's love for her. Her long blonde hair, unbound and mussed from sleep, framed her face like the aureole of a halo, while her eyes, though carrying the vestiges of her slumber, still held that quintessential flicker: a mischievous gleam of sunshine that defied the harsh reality of her circumstances.

As Fawn took her seat at the kitchen table, she felt enveloped by the invisible yet palpable warmth emanating from Tom and Teresa—a comfort zone that transcended walls and furnishings. It was a testament to the familial love they extended, which cushioned her like feathers in a nest.

"How are you, honey?" Teresa's voice broke the silence, her words filled with a maternal sweetness that could rival the first light of the morning. "Did you sleep okay?"

Fawn smiled, a radiant burst of emotion that seemed to dispel any lingering shadows. She nodded and then giggled with a lightness as airy as a dandelion's parachute, "Don't tell Jessica, but she snores."

Teresa's laughter danced in the air, harmonizing with Fawn's giggle like the notes of a long-forgotten melody. "Just like her father," she said, glancing playfully at Tom, her eyes shining with a joyful secret.

Caught in the echo of their shared laughter, Tom raised his eyebrows, his face etched with feigned innocence. His eyes met Teresa's, and in that fleeting exchange, they both felt the weight of their worries momentarily lift, replaced by a newfound determination to face the future, whatever it may hold.

"Are you hungry?" she asked, her voice like a warm, nourishing ray of sunshine directed at a fragile bud.

"A little," Fawn admitted, her voice soft as morning mist, as she gently rubbed the sleep from her eyes.

Teresa took this as her cue to assume her well-practiced role in the kitchen. She moved to the counter with the ease of long habit, her hands deftly selecting eggs from their carton and cracking them into a frying pan.

Across the table, Tom studied Fawn with the watchful eyes of a guardian. "So, what plans do you have for the day?" he asked, his words tinged with curiosity and a sense of responsibility.

"I'm thinking about visiting a friend," Fawn replied, her words flavored with the sweetness of anticipation. "I haven't seen him in a while and want to see if he's okay."

At that moment, Fawn's eyebrows arched like the wings of a startled bird, her expression signaling the sudden recollection of something forgotten yet important.

"Oh, that reminds me," she announced, pivoting her gaze toward Teresa. "Mama, would it be okay if I use your car? Mom's working today, so I can't use hers." She knew the rhythms of the household well; Tuesdays, the quiet interlude in the bustle of the week, were Teresa's days off.

"As it turns out, I don't have any plans today," Teresa answered, her voice accompanied by the click of the stove's knob as she lit the flame beneath the pan. "So, of course, you can use the car."

As Fawn mentioned her plans, Tom's mind wandered into unexplored territories. Who was this friend? Could it be someone new, perhaps a flicker of romantic interest sparking in her life? His curiosity, tinged with teasing mischief and underlaid by protective concern, got the better of him.

"So, who is this friend you're going to see?" he asked, his tone lighthearted yet probing.

Sensing the playful undercurrent in his question, Fawn replied with a soft giggle. "He's Felix, Papa. You remember him, right? He was at Jessica's birthday party."

A light of recognition flickered in Tom's eyes. "Ah, the young man who could use a few more home-cooked meals," he mused, recalling the skinny boy from the party.

With a playful roll of her eyes, a retort to Tom's teasing jab, Fawn shook her head. "Yep, that's him."

The mood in the kitchen suddenly became animated by the ripple of a new presence. The soft creak of a door opening and closing signaled a shift in the family dynamic, a prelude to the entrance of another beloved character on this morning stage. When Jessica appeared, the room seemed to rearrange its energies, as though every element was an instrument tuning to a different key.

Jessica's attire was an anthem to casual comfort: a long gray t-shirt and black, loose-fitting sweats. Her hair, resembling a cascading waterfall of brown locks, appeared mussed from the realm of dreams, and her eyes—large, cerulean orbs—still held a fog from the last tendrils of sleep. Yet, in the eyes of Tom and Teresa, she was the epitome of adoration, an affirmation of love's masterpiece in human form. For Fawn, the sight of her best friend was like the comforting glow of a hearth, a source of warmth and solidarity.

"Good morning, everyone," Jessica greeted, her voice tinted with a subdued cheer as she gracefully took her seat at the table.

"Good morning, baby girl," Tom replied, his eyes shining, mirroring the hues of his daughter's eyes.

"Did you have a nice sleep, sweetheart?" Teresa inquired, her voice dipped in maternal sweetness, like honey smoothing over the rough edges of the waking world.

"I think so," Jessica replied, her hands instinctively going to her eyes, rubbing away the last remnants of sleep before smoothing back her disheveled hair.

Sensing an opening in the natural cadence of morning conversations, she turned to Fawn. "Did I hear you say you're going to Felix's today?" Jessica's voice wove a tapestry of curiosity and concern.

"Yeah," Fawn confirmed, her eyes meeting Jessica's. "I thought I'd go see how he's doing. You know, with his dad and all."

Jessica nodded, conveying her understanding. "Do you want me and Ethan to go with you? We wouldn't mind at all," she offered, her words filled with a genuine willingness to share the weight of her friend's concern.

In return, Fawn's smile was like a sunbeam filtering through a canopy of leaves, appreciative of the shelter but content in its own path. "No. You guys do your thing. I'll be okay," she reassured her, gifting her the space for her own narrative, even as they each played vital roles in the other's unfolding stories.

The subtle quiver in Jessica's voice did not escape Tom's seasoned ear. It was as if a delicate note had wavered slightly off-key in a familiar melody, momentarily disrupting the harmonious atmosphere. Sensing an undercurrent of concern that ran deeper than the apparent calm, he fixed his gaze upon Fawn and inquired, "Where does Felix live?"

In that brief pause, the room seemed to inhale collectively, bracing for a shift in the undercurrents of familial concern. Tom's observant eyes settled on Jessica and Fawn, forming a tangible bridge of understanding. It was as if they shared a silent conversation before Fawn, summoning the clarity of a spokesperson, took the initiative.

"He lives about 5 miles from here, on the other side of town. Not far from the bay," she disclosed, each word dropping like a pebble into a still pond.

Tom's eyebrows, the steady horizon to his thoughtful eyes, arched skyward as if pulled by invisible strings of concern. The mention of that part of town did not simply evoke geographical coordinates; it mapped a topography of social disparities, economic hardships, and veiled dangers. Like many towns that had grown organically, Wavecrest had its zones of light and shadow, and Fawn had named a place that was often shrouded in the latter.

"I'm not sure I want you to drive out there by yourself, sweetheart," Tom said, his voice a weighted net of paternal caution. "That's a bad area."

Fawn felt the tide of his apprehensions wash over her the moment he spoke, as strong as an ocean's undertow. In Tom's care, she found an anchorage she had long treasured. Yet, the same tides that once made her feel safe also seemed confining now. She wasn't the fledgling bird tucked safely under paternal wings; she had wings of her own, eager to test their strength against the open sky.

"I'll be fine, Papa. I've been there before," Fawn reassured, her voice carrying the soft undertones of familial love. She wanted him to see her not just as the girl who once needed his guidance, but also as the young woman who had been shaped by it. Pivoting her eyes toward Jessica, she added, "Both of us have."

It was a gentle reminder to Tom and Teresa that their children were growing, blossoming in the complex ecosystems of their lives. And as much as they wanted to keep them in manicured gardens, sometimes they would have to venture into the wilder, untamed parts of the world.

In that fleeting moment, as Tom looked at Fawn and Jessica, his eyes held an ocean of emotion—waves of concern crashing against the rocky shores of acceptance. There was the irrevocable realization that the compass of paternal protection has its limitations; it can point the way, yet it cannot navigate the journey for them. With a quick glance at the wall clock, a silent herald marking the progression of time and the demands of adult responsibility, he realized it was his cue to exit the scene.

"Well, I have to go," he murmured, taking one final sip of his coffee as if savoring the last drops of this morning idyll.

Tom rose, an authoritative pillar in a realm framed by kitchen walls, and navigated toward Teresa. He wrapped her in a tight embrace, as if trying to infuse her with the warmth that would last the day. Their lips met in a brief but meaningful kiss, a silent poem that only they understood.

"Love you, Hun," he whispered, pulling away but leaving the echo of his affection lingering between them.

"Love you, too. Have a nice day," Teresa replied, her voice a soothing counterpoint, smoothing the rough edges of morning anxieties.

As Tom moved past the tableau of his girls seated at the table, his actions transformed into a blessing. He bent down and bestowed a gentle kiss atop each head—soft benedictions laid upon the crowns of two young women growing into their own.

"You be careful, Fawn," he told her, his words a subtle mooring line tossed into the air as he drifted toward the front door.

As the door clicked shut behind him, a hush descended upon the room, as if Tom's departure had briefly muted the household symphony. In this quietude, Teresa became the conductor, calling out the finale of the morning's meal. With graceful movements, she placed plates of eggs, toast, and bacon before Jessica and Fawn.

"Eat up, girls," she said, the corners of her mouth lifting into a comforting smile. "Looks like you both have a busy day ahead."

As they looked up to meet Teresa's eyes—a soft haven reflecting their own—they felt it, both of them. The tangible, nurturing warmth that radiated from this remarkable woman was like a sunbeam breaking through the morning fog. Here, in this humble kitchen, love was their true North, guiding them through the complexities of life's unfolding map.

After breakfast, Jessica and Fawn stepped into the hallway that connected the home's various rooms. As they made their way down the short stretch, they transitioned from the communal atmosphere of shared meals to the privacy of Jessica's room.

Fawn, the first to enter, was drawn to Jessica's vanity like a moth to a flame, captivated by the allure of self-reflection. She picked up the brush, each stroke an act of meditation as she gazed into her own eyes, seeking perhaps the woman she was becoming, hidden behind the girl she once was.

Jessica, on the other hand, meandered toward her drawer, a treasure chest of wearable emotions. She searched for an ensemble that would reflect her inner mood, her fingers sifting through the layers of cotton and linen, lace and silk. When her hand finally rested on a particular fabric, she felt a tingle of rightness. Pulling it out, she held the short-sleeved t-shirt against her chest and turned to Fawn for approval. "What do you think?"

Fawn paused her brushing ritual and shifted her eyes from her own reflection to Jessica's garment. The word "Love" elegantly etched across the fabric was not just a word but a window into Jessica's current feelings.

"That's appropriate. I like it," she affirmed, her smile the unspoken footnote to her words.

"Me too," Jessica beamed back, her spirits high. With that single piece of fabric, she had captured the elusive butterfly of today's emotion, ready to let it take flight in the world beyond her bedroom.

Fawn's eyes returned to the mirror as her brush moved through her hair in fluid strokes. In that reflective plane, it wasn't just her own face she encountered; Jessica was also there, bustling in the background, a flurry of motion as she gathered her clothes and towels for the shower that awaited her.

The sight of Jessica—so casual, so every day—was like the key to a lockbox of memories. It opened the doors to the previous night when they sat side-by-side on the old white bench swing, and when Jessica's phone lit up the dark. A message had buzzed into Jessica's world, courtesy of Ethan. Even though Jessica had casually dismissed its importance, Fawn knew the weight behind those silent words on the screen.

As the memory looped through Fawn's consciousness like a refrain, a surge of emotion rose within her, as if her heart were a vessel brimming with love, so full it threatened to overflow. This was love shaped by time and forged in the crucible of shared experiences—a love that made the ache in her chest feel like the sweetest kind of pain.

With her eyes still transfixed by the mirror's revelations, Fawn's voice dropped to a whisper—a murmur that carried the weight of a hundred unspoken thoughts.

"I know what you did last night, Jess," she breathed, her eyes unwavering on Jessica's reflected presence. "I know what you did... for me."

"What do you mean?" Jessica inquired, her eyes locking onto Fawn's reflection in a tableau of muted curiosity and incipient realization.

"Don't play dumb with me, girl," Fawn replied, the timbre of her voice now resonating like a song, laden with gratitude and profound understanding. "I know when Ethan texted you, it was because he wanted to be with you. And I know you wanted to be with him."

Framed in the rectangle of mirrored glass, Jessica's eyes narrowed slightly, a delicate dance between concealment and disclosure. "I don't know what you're talking about," she deflected, her voice a soft whisper.

"Yes, you do," Fawn replied, her voice filled with certainty. She tilted her head, her lips parting into a teasing smirk. "You forget. After all these years, I can read you like a book. Even when you're trying to lie... which you totally suck at."

Jessica's lips twitched into an involuntary giggle, the light sound floating in the air like a stray note in a symphony. In that laughter was an admission, unspoken yet palpable: Fawn was right. Across the landscapes of years and the geography of their shared world, they'd learned to interpret each other's silences as clearly as spoken words.

Recognizing the futility of any further evasion, Jessica felt an unspoken acknowledgment rise from the depths of her being. It floated up like a bubble in a still pond, shimmering on the surface between reality and reflection. She knew the time for veils and veneers was over; what remained was the unfiltered honesty that could only be spoken in the language of the heart.

"I love you, Fawn," Jessica said, her words filled with sincere affection that could neither be disguised nor diluted. "And I'll always be here for you."

At the altar of Jessica's sincerity, Fawn felt a sacred touch resonate within her core. It dawned on her, like the first rays of sunlight illuminating a misty morning: Jessica had relinquished an evening with Ethan—her sun, her moon, her compass—to be at her side during this time of transition and farewell. Time was a dwindling currency for both of them, yet Jessica had invested one of her diminishing summer nights in the bank of their friendship. That act, that choice, was a treasure more priceless than any gemstone, a gift wrapped in the delicate paper of love and tied with the ribbon of loyalty.

Swallowing a rising tide of emotion and brimming with gratitude so immense it could hardly be contained, Fawn whispered, her voice feather-light but carrying the weight of the world, "I love you too, Jess."

In this quiet chamber of mirrored reflections and unwavering gazes, the boundaries of friendship were neither defined nor limited by words alone. What was spoken seemed to echo not only in the room, but through the corridors of their shared history, weaving its way into the fabric of years woven from joys and sorrows alike.

As Fawn felt her heart swell, filling spaces she hadn't known were empty, and as Jessica caught that emotive glance, an understanding deeper than the ocean passed between them. It was as if the universe had paused, just for a second, to acknowledge the enduring beauty of an unwavering friendship—a friendship so steadfast it needed no map to navigate the complexities of love and life. And so, their souls brushed against each other once more, not in farewell, but in the hope of countless tomorrows yet to be written.

# Chapter 28

----------------------------------------------------------------

Fawn's fingers tapped to the rhythm of a carefree summer tune as she steered Teresa's car through the familiar streets of Wavecrest. The neighborhoods she first passed were mirror images of her own—woven together by the fabric of well-kept lawns, painted picket fences, and houses that exuded an air of coastal charm. Even the sky seemed to conspire in this curated beauty, its blue expanse wistfully caressed by the slender fingers of palm fronds.

As she ventured further from the heart of Wavecrest, the vibrant colors and sunlit serenity gradually ebbed away, as if she were driving into the penumbra of a different world. The lawns grew wild and unkempt; houses wore layers of peeling paint like cracked makeup, revealing the neglected wood beneath. The roads, once smooth and accommodating, turned jarring, as though resentful of any visitor's passage. The sun that had been her companion seemed now distant, its warmth obscured by a dense canopy of overgrown trees, creating pockets of gloom that played tricks on the eyes.

It was as if Fawn was entering a forgotten chapter of a storybook—still part of the narrative but separated by a clear boundary, as vivid as the line that separates the sea from the sand. This uneasy contrast spoke volumes, setting a tone of disquiet that made her grip the steering wheel a little tighter, even as she reminded herself of the purpose of her visit.

And so, amid this landscape of desolation and fading light, Fawn arrived at Felix's house—a dwelling as gloomy as its surroundings, standing like an ancient sentinel observing its slow decay. She parked the car, took a deep breath, and opened the door, stepping out into an atmosphere where hope seemed as scarce as sunlight.

As she stepped out of the car, her eyes settled once more on Felix's house, which stood just as she remembered it—like a wistful stanza in a forgotten poem. The facade was still a ghost of gray, its weary coat of paint curling back from the wood in flaky surrender. There was something hauntingly familiar about its unvarnished vulnerability, as if the house itself wore the pain and discomfort that its inhabitants could not openly show.

The compact structure was further diminished by its sprawling counterparts in the more affluent parts of Wavecrest, yet it bore its modest dimensions with quiet dignity. The screened porch remained the house's solemn sentinel, its concrete steps leading up as if inviting her into a world far removed from her own. The yard was as barren as ever, its grainy, colorless sand, a far cry from the soft golden stretches that graced the beaches she so loved.

Separated from the road by the rusting skeletal remains of a fence, the house seemed almost like a shrine to days long gone, days that were counted but never cherished. A worn path stretched from the bottom of the steps to the corroded gate, which stood askew, ever so slightly, as if undecided whether to let people in or keep them out.

Fawn took it all in, the home's exterior resonating with her own internal landscape—its raw, unfiltered honesty a stark counterpoint to her ongoing struggles. As she faced the trilogy of steps, the world seemed to hold its breath, her heart thrumming a blend of trepidation and resolve. She felt herself crossing an emotional threshold, leaving behind the familiar sunlit charm of Wavecrest.

In the stillness that seemed to have enveloped this corner of her world, Fawn paused before the rusted gate. The air hung heavy, as if the heat had dissolved its liveliness, turning it thick and sluggish. Any semblance of a breeze had surrendered, leaving only the oppressive warmth of the early afternoon to press against her skin.

Her hand reached out tentatively, making contact with the metal, feeling the coarse remnants of paint and years of rust under her fingers. It creaked its own reluctant greeting as she pushed it open, the sound mournful yet oddly satisfying, like the sigh of someone who'd waited long to speak. As she stepped onto the property, the gate swung back behind her with a finality that made her pause.

Making her way to the front porch, Fawn felt the crunch of sand beneath her feet, each step imprinting her presence onto the neglected yard. Just as she was about to ascend the steps, her eyes caught a tall silhouette framed against the faded backdrop of the screened porch door. It wasn't the unassuming form she had come to associate with Felix; this figure exuded a domineering darkness that seemed at odds with the frail structure it inhabited. Felix's father—stood there, an embodiment of that pervasive, uncomfortable silence that she felt upon entering this pocket of the town.

A momentary apprehension gripped her, a recognition not just of the man, but of the air he carried around him—the weight of an unsettling story seldom told. It seemed as though the shadows of the house clung to him, drawn to a darkness that was more than just an absence of light.

In the face of that disquieting tableau, Fawn found her steps weighed down, but resolute. For she hadn't come seeking the easier, sun-drenched narratives she could find elsewhere in Wavecrest; she was here for the subtexts, the raw chapters that people like

Felix were living each day. With her eyes locked onto the shadowy figure behind the screen, Fawn prepared to ascend the steps, her outline merging with the layered complexities that filled the air of this quiet, untamed corner of Wavecrest.

Suddenly, the porch door creaked open with a slow deliberation, jolting Fawn out of her reverie. Felix's father emerged, his hand gripping a worn cane that seemed as much a part of him as his own limbs. The way he clutched it spoke of an uneasy alliance between man and aid—each reluctantly dependent on the other. Fawn's steps stalled, her eyes fixing on the figure that now began its slow descent from the porch.

He wore an old, stained white t-shirt, its original color absorbed by the hue of countless yesterdays. Black baggy pants hung from his frame, a cavernous void filled only by the frail outline of his legs. His feet were encased in work boots that had seen harder days, their wear and tear written into the very fabric of the leather. As he took each step with studied caution, the boots seemed to whisper their own tales of struggle, echoing in quiet solidarity with the scrape of his cane against the concrete steps.

When he reached the bottom of the steps, he paused, his eyes lifting to meet Fawn's. She saw a confluence of pain and meanness in his eyes—a labyrinth of emotions and experiences she could only skirt the edges of. It was as if his eyes were a distillation of life's unkindness; every moment that had carved away at his soul lay bare.

Those eyes weighed heavily on her, yet they imparted a challenge, too. The aura around him felt like a boundary she could either heed or dare to cross. It was the juxtaposition of a frail frame with an indomitable spirit, a tangible manifestation of life's paradoxes.

Here stood the gatekeeper of untold stories, a man sculpted by adversities, both those inflicted upon him and those he may have inflicted upon others. And in that charged moment, their two worlds—a vibrant young artist, and a man worn by life—teetered on the edge of intersection.

"What do you want?" Felix's father growled, his voice filled with bitterness, each word a searing ember. "Are you here to take my boy away from me?"

The hostility in his voice wrapped around Fawn like a vice, constricting her ability to breathe. "No, sir," she replied, her voice laced with an unmistakable tremor. She took a step back, her eyes widening as they absorbed the rage in his.

"Bullshit! I know why you're here! You're here to take my son away!" His volume escalated, each word erupting like a caustic spray.

His eyes turned incendiary, flames dancing in their dark pools. To Fawn, it was a countenance so mean, so filled with antipathy, that it shook her to the core. In her neighborhood, faces wore the patina of kindness; here, she was encountering the disturbing hue of hostility.

Felix's father raised his cane, and for a moment, it became an extension of his anger, an arbiter of threatened violence. "Well, you can't have him, so get out of here! Get out of here, NOW!"

Fawn's heart plummeted as if unmoored, her feet frozen in place. It was as though the air had thickened, each molecule now a shard of palpable menace.

"DAD! STOP!" A desperate voice broke the tension, its urgency like a lifeline thrown into churning waters. Felix burst out of the house, his diminutive frame imbued with a forceful energy. He gripped his father's cane, wrestling it downward. "She's my friend, Dad! Leave her alone!"

Felix's father seemed to deflate, his grip on the cane loosening as if it had drained him of his will. His aura of defiant aggression waned, usurped by a stark, uncomfortable reality: he had failed to impose his narrative on his domain.

"Go back in the house, Dad! Leave us alone!" Felix's words were both a plea and a command, and his father took one lingering, sour look at them both before turning to re-enter the house—a man in retreat, but not defeated.

Felix walked over to Fawn, his eyes awash with relief and regret. "I'm so sorry, Fawn," he said, his voice tinged with a melancholy understanding. "My dad...he isn't well...and that makes him mean sometimes."

As Felix spoke, Fawn looked at him and then back at the house, as if attempting to reconcile the jagged pieces of this unexpected scene. Here, in this tattered landscape of lives frayed by circumstance, Fawn grasped the fragility of humanity. It was a viscerally disturbing realization that momentarily displaced her from the comforting orbit of her own experience. And yet, in that displacement lay the seed of a deeper understanding—one that recognized that kindness and meanness often resided within the same fragile vessels, the balance tipping in mysterious, unfathomable ways.

In the immediate aftermath of his bold intervention, Felix's armor of audacity began to dissolve, like mist succumbing to the sun's scrutiny. His posture subtly reverted, shoulders dropping from their brave height to resume their habitual stoop. Felix was once again Felix—no longer the figure of righteous defiance, but a young man grappling with the awkward symphony of self-doubt and longing.

He stood there, dressed in a buttoned-down, short-sleeved shirt that seemed to almost apologize for its presence, as if aware it wasn't gracing the physique of someone more confident. His baggy blue pants, a flag of some muted rebellion or perhaps just a concession to comfort, hung loosely, contrasting with his dirty sneakers that told tales of an intimacy with roads less traveled. His hair, untamed and disheveled, appeared as though it were a field through which a gentle wind had meandered, leaving traces of its wanderlust upon the strands.

His eyes met Fawn's, and in that gaze was a wellspring of complex emotion. Here was Felix, laid bare, his every vulnerability starkly present but also shaded by an ineffable something—that alchemy of affection and a secret feeling that had propelled him, if briefly, into the realm of heroes.

Though his attire was inconspicuous, even shabby, it was as if Fawn could see through to the fabric of the person within—a tapestry woven of shy threads and embroidered with unspoken dreams. The distance between them in that instant was both physical and metaphorical, filled with the unarticulated complexities of their relationship. Yet, it was also a distance that Felix had momentarily traversed, propelled by an emotion more powerful than his usual reticence.

As he stood there, the tendrils of his earlier courage dissipating into the humid air, Fawn understood that she was in the presence of a mystery: a young man caught in the dance between who he was and who he wished to be. It was a portrait in contradictions, but one that held its own kind of eloquence, a silent narrative of a life yearning for translation.

"Well, that was scary," Fawn said softly, the curl of a smile brushing her lips.

"I know, and I'm sorry," Felix replied, his eyes a wordless echo of apology. "My dad isn't keen on visitors."

As Felix's father retreated into the shadows of the interior, a gentle ease settled over Fawn, her earlier tension dissipating like mist under the morning sun. Felix looked at her, a mixture of relief and curiosity tinting his features. Their last meeting—Jessica's birthday party—loomed in the rearview mirror of his mind, its familiarity now seeming years, not weeks, away.

"I'm surprised to see you," he finally admitted, his voice a small ripple in the air between them.

"You shouldn't be," Fawn's smile deepened, "I said I'd visit, didn't I?"

At hearing Fawn's words, something within Felix glowed softly—a rare warmth in a life often touched more by isolation than camaraderie.

"Yes, you did, but I'm sure you have better things to do than be here," he suggested, his voice betraying a note of self-deprecation.

Fawn's gaze met his, her eyes firming like a sculptor's final touch. "Felix, you are not an obligation. You're my friend."

For Felix, those words were a touchstone, an anchor in the stormy seas of his own insecurities. Though his heart harbored a longing that he knew must remain unspoken, her words were a balm—a confirmation that, in the labyrinth of human connection, they had found at least one unbroken path.

Felix's eyes swept toward the weathered picnic table in the corner of the yard. It was a silent testament to a time when he and his mother sat there, her words hanging in the air, forever promising a better life one day. "Shall we?" he gestured.

Fawn followed his gaze, and her eyes met the timeworn wood with recognition. "Sure," she replied.

So, they walked, each step an unwritten promise, crossing the small expanse of sand as if it were a bridge between the people they had been and the adults they were yet to become. As they reached the picnic table, it was as if they also reached a mutual understanding, undefined yet palpable: that they were no longer mere passersby in the

294

hallways of youth, but fellow travelers on a journey into a realm far more complicated and nuanced—a realm called adulthood.

Felix and Fawn sat down on the old picnic table, their forms illuminated by the dappled sunlight filtering through the leaves overhead. Sitting across from each other, Fawn's eyes wandered, taking in the shadows that seemed to deepen around them, thick as molasses yet elusive as smoke. An uneasiness settled over her, a mix of concern and curiosity, as she felt the weight of the life that Felix had kept hidden during their years together at school.

"Have you lived here all your life?" she ventured, her voice cutting through the quiet that hung between them like a fragile spider web.

Felix's lips curved upwards, a modest smile that carried more weight than a laugh. "Yes, all my life. In this very house, too."

"Is it just you and your dad?" Fawn asked, her voice laced with empathy.

Felix nodded, his gaze dropping for a moment. "Yes, since I was twelve, when my mother died," he responded, a fleeting shadow crossing his face, his words carrying the weight of sorrow and loss.

Fawn's eyes widened, her voice tinged with a heartfelt sadness she hadn't expected to feel. She couldn't help but wonder about the pain Felix must have carried all these years, hidden behind his quiet demeanor. Her heart ached for him. "Oh, wow. I'm so sorry to hear that."

Felix shrugged, his body language betraying the depth of his words. "Yeah, things weren't so bad until that happened. My dad was always mean to us, but after Mom died, he got worse."

"You mean, he's always been this mean?" Fawn asked, her surprise evident in her voice.

"To me and my mom, he was," he confirmed, then paused, as if measuring the weight of his next words. "I think he hates me."

His declaration hung in the air, thick and almost tangible. Fawn shook her head, disbelieving, her voice full of a naivete nurtured by a life of familial warmth. "He's your father, Felix. He doesn't hate you."

Upon hearing Fawn's words, Felix's thoughts drifted like falling leaves to a memory—his presence at Jessica's birthday party, where he had seen up close what love in a family looked like. He had glimpsed the unabashed affection between Jessica and her father and felt a keen sense of absence—a void that had been there all his life.

"I can understand why you think that, Fawn," he murmured. "You lived knowing that your parents loved you. You have no idea how lucky you are."

At that moment, the gravity in Felix's eyes spoke louder than words, filling the space between them with unspoken understanding. Fawn felt a slight shiver of realization; the resentment she'd felt toward her own parents seemed suddenly inconsequential, even frivolous.

"I suppose," she whispered, her voice carrying the weight of a newfound perspective.

Feeling the weight of the conversation shifting into darker territory, Felix searched for a detour—a path that could lead them back to shared interests and lighter heartbeats. It was as if he folded away the darker shades of his life's canvas, focusing instead on the vibrant hues.

"Did you submit your sketch for the contest?" Felix asked, his voice tinged with quiet curiosity. Behind his glasses, his eyes held a glint of recollection, harking back to the day at the high school when Fawn had signed up for the Art Contest.

"No, I'm still working on it," Fawn sighed, her words carrying a subtle sense of exasperation and unspoken thoughts.

Felix lowered his eyes, as if preparing for disappointment. "Well, I know I'm not going to win. Hopefully, you will."

Buoyed by the enduring support of her second family and the resilience of her friendship with Jessica, Fawn offered a glimmer of hope. "You never know, Felix. You have as much of a chance as anyone."

Felix's self-doubt, a constant companion, surfaced again in his words. "It doesn't matter; I'm not going to college, anyway."

"Well, what do you want to do, then?" Fawn asked, her voice imbued with genuine curiosity.

A hesitancy, borne from years of ridicule and rejection, made him hesitant to answer. "You'll laugh if I tell you."

Fawn leaned in, her sincerity almost palpable. "I promise, I won't."

"Promise you won't laugh?" Felix asked, his voice laced with hesitant hope.

Her voice became a soft refuge for his secret dream. "I promise, Felix. I won't laugh."

"I want to be an architect," he finally confessed, as though shedding a weight he had long carried.

Fawn felt her artist's soul resonate with his words. "That would be a great career, Felix."

His voice grew stronger, but a trace of vulnerability lingered. "Ever since I was a little boy, I've been fascinated with big buildings and how they're built."

"Then you should go for it," Fawn spoke not just to Felix, but to herself—two souls on the precipice of change. "It sounds like it would be an exciting career."

"You don't think it's stupid?" Felix asked, his voice tinged with incredulity.

"Why would I? I want to be an artist. Do you think that's stupid?" Her voice challenged him, inviting him to recognize the beauty in both their dreams.

Felix smiled, his eyes meeting hers. "No, I think you're already an artist. And a very good one at that."

Felix's words touched Fawn deeply, a balm for her vulnerable soul. "Thanks. But if I can be an artist, you can be an architect."

Seated at the weathered picnic table in Felix's yard, amidst the remnants of his boyhood and the daunting shadows of an unforgiving town, Felix immersed himself in Fawn's words of encouragement. "Maybe someday," he whispered to himself, a fragile hope taking root within him. "Maybe someday."

The air hung heavy with a sense of stagnation, and the relentless summer sun beat down on Fawn and Felix as they rose from their seats. It had been a heavy conversation, a glimpse into Felix's world of shadows and struggles. With her restless spirit yearning for the respite of a gentle breeze, Fawn decided that a walk might offer just that, a brief escape from the oppressive heat that clung to them like a second skin.

"Let's go for a walk, Felix," she proposed, her voice soft but resolute.

Felix nodded in agreement, his gaze still bearing the weight of the past they had shared. "Okay."

With hesitant steps, they left the worn picnic table behind and ventured toward the rickety gate that marked the boundary of Felix's desolate world. Fawn couldn't help but look back at the porch, her eyes searching for any sign of Felix's imposing father. A sigh of relief escaped her lips when she found the porch vacant, devoid of the looming figure that had cast its shadow over their conversation.

Felix's fingers clasped the gate's rusted frame, and he pushed it open with a creaking protest. They stepped out onto the sun-baked street, leaving the crumbling sanctuary behind. The gate swung shut behind them, a barrier between the world of decay and the uncertain path ahead.

As they began their leisurely walk along the uneven pavement, Fawn couldn't help but take in the details of their surroundings. The houses, their once-vibrant colors faded and peeling, stood as silent witnesses to the passage of time and neglect. Weeds sprouted defiantly from cracks in the sidewalks, reaching for the faint sunlight that filtered through the thick canopy of leaves above. The streets themselves, winding and unpredictable, seemed to lead to destinations known only to the ghosts of this forgotten neighborhood.

Amid this urban decay, Fawn felt a renewed sense of gratitude for her neighborhood's vibrant, well-tended landscapes. The stark contrast between her world and Felix's was a poignant reminder of their disparate lives, and it tugged mercilessly at her heartstrings.

As Fawn and Felix continued their stroll, they passed by a series of houses, each revealing a different facet of the challenging lives that unfolded within. Among them, they walked by a house, similar in size to Felix's dwelling, that bore the weight of neglect like a heavy shroud. Its open porch stood as an eerie testament to abandonment, featuring an old, weathered brown couch surrounded by a haphazard assortment of junk.

Fawn's eyes shifted to the front yard, where the debris extended its reach, casting a dispirited aura over the property. The air was heavy with the cries of a distressed baby emanating from within the house, punctuated by the escalating volume of a couple engaged in a heated argument. She couldn't help but shudder at the discord that seemed to permeate the very walls of the house.

Another house, even smaller than Felix's home, presented a stark tableau of weariness.

Its open porch served as a perch for a middle-aged couple, their faces etched with the lines of time and hardship. The man, dressed in an aging blue shirt and shorts, and the woman, in a faded yellow sundress, regarded Fawn and Felix with unfriendly, mistrusting eyes. Undeterred, Fawn attempted a small, friendly smile, but it fell upon unresponsive hearts, and the couple's eyes remained icily fixed on the passing pair.

Continuing down the street, they came upon a house slightly larger than Felix's house, with a front porch that had transformed into a graveyard for discarded appliances. An old, rusted refrigerator and a washing machine stood as silent witnesses to a life that had seen better days. Yet, amidst the rust and decay, a group of four children, three boys, and a girl, played in worn and tattered clothing that bore the scars of countless adventures. Their innocent laughter seemed out of place against the backdrop of hardship.

As Fawn and Felix walked by, the children's play ended abruptly, their curious eyes locking onto the unfamiliar visitors. Fawn offered them a warm smile and a friendly wave, but the children remained reserved, their gazes unbroken as they watched the couple pass, perhaps longing for a glimpse of the world beyond their porch.

When they reached the end of the road, the metal guardrail loomed before them, marking the boundary between their world and the impenetrable thicket of trees that obscured any view of the distant bay. The air, thick with the pungent scent of swamp gas and decay, clung to Fawn's senses, threatening to turn her stomach.

She turned to Felix, her eyes filled with genuine concern and emotion. "You really need to get out of here, Felix. You don't deserve to live in a place like this."

Felix's eyes fell to the ground, his voice carrying the weight of years of hardship. "My mom hated it here. She'd tell me every night before I went to bed that we were going to move one day. She said she was just waiting for the right time for us to leave."

A mixture of sadness and curiosity filled Fawn's eyes. "What happened to your mom? Did she get sick?"

Felix shook his head slowly, his voice carrying the weight of deep sadness. "I went to wake her up one morning," he admitted with a heavy heart, "but she never woke up."

He paused, the anguish in his eyes reflecting the deep sorrow within. "She left without me," he whispered, the words laden with the pain of a broken promise, his mother's unfulfilled dream of escaping this harsh place, and the loneliness of being left behind.

Fawn's heart ached at the revelation, the depth of Felix's loss cutting through her like a knife.

As the weight of their words hung in the air, Fawn pressed on, her voice filled with compassion. "You can still leave, Felix. Don't you have other family you can go to?"

Felix's eyes met hers, and he shook his head again. "Just my grandmother, but she hates me, too. She only comes here to take care of my dad. We hardly even talk. She's even meaner than him."

Fawn refused to give up, her determination shining through. "Felix, you don't need to stay here. Get a job and save your money. Once you have enough, you can leave. Start a new life. Go to college and be an architect. You don't even have to actually go to college. You can take online courses and get your degree."

Fawn paused, allowing her words to sink in. "Go talk to Mr. Reynolds or even Mr. Morrison. They'll help you with that."

For a fleeting moment, hope flickered in Felix's eyes, but it was quickly extinguished by the weight of his responsibilities.

"I can't do that, Fawn," he replied, his voice tinged with resignation. "I wish I could, but my dad needs me. He got hurt at work a few years ago, you know. I need to stay here and take care of him."

At that moment, Fawn realized her efforts had reached their limits. She understood that Felix's loyalty to his father, no matter how undeserved, ran deep and unshakeable. She accepted defeat, respecting Felix's unwavering commitment to his father, even in the face of a miserable existence. She knew there was nothing more she could say or do to change his mind.

With the weight of their conversation still heavy in the air, Fawn and Felix turned and began the slow walk back toward his house. The shadows of the neighborhood seemed to close in around them, a reminder of the challenges that lay ahead for Felix.

As they reached the familiar yet worn path leading back to Felix's house, Fawn couldn't shake the desire to offer her friend a momentary escape from the heartache that defined his life. She knew that the Summer Dance, the grand finale of a Wavecrest summer, was just around the corner. It was a night when young and old alike would gather on the pavilion for an evening of entertainment and camaraderie. For Fawn and Jessica, it promised a final goodbye to their friends before embarking on their journeys to college.

"Felix," Fawn began, her voice gentle but determined, "I want you to go with me to the Summer Dance in a couple of weeks."

Felix's eyes widened in surprise and uncertainty. The prospect of attending a social event, especially one that involved the very classmates who had bullied him in school, filled him with apprehension.

Sensing his hesitation, Fawn continued with unwavering conviction. "I know it's not easy for you, but I promise no one will bother you there. It's a night for fun and celebration. Besides, Jessica and Ethan will be there."

Felix's eyes perked up at the mention of Ethan, the boy he admired and looked up to. Fawn knew that Ethan's presence would be a strong incentive for him.

"Ethan likes you," she added, her voice warm with reassurance. "And he wouldn't want to see you bullied or unhappy."

Felix's heart swelled with a mix of emotions. He wanted to believe that Fawn was right, that this night could be different, that he could find a sense of belonging and acceptance among his peers. After a moment of contemplation, he finally nodded, his eyes reflecting a glimmer of hope.

"All right, Fawn," he said with a hint of determination. "I'll go to the Summer Dance with you."

Fawn's heart soared at Felix's words, a feeling of happiness and gratitude bubbling inside. She reached out and placed a reassuring hand on his shoulder, her eyes brimming with warmth.

"Thank you, Felix," she replied, her voice filled with sincerity. "You won't regret it. We'll have an amazing time, I promise."

Standing by the gate, Fawn couldn't shake the unsettling sensation of being watched, a phantom presence that sent shivers down her spine. Slowly, she turned her head toward the front porch door, her heart sinking as she met the malevolent gaze of Felix's father. His eyes, filled with a toxic blend of hatred and bitterness, bore into hers like icy daggers, their intensity sending an uncomfortable tremor through her body. It was a look that spoke volumes of a man consumed by anger and resentment.

Catching the shift in Fawn's expression, Felix followed her gaze and locked eyes with his father. At that moment, they shared a silent understanding of the darkness that loomed within his own house.

"I better get back inside," Felix said, his voice tinged with regret, not wanting their all-too-brief time together to end.

Fawn nodded in agreement, her anxiety growing in this gloomy and oppressive place that starkly contrasted with the vibrant world she knew on the other side of town.

"Yeah, I gotta go, too," she replied, her voice tinged with unease.

As they stood by the gate, Fawn closed the distance between them and pulled Felix into a gentle hug. It was a fleeting embrace, but it offered a moment of solace and connection, a balm to soothe the wounds of their encounter.

With a heavy heart, Fawn opened the gate and stepped onto the street. She approached her car, the familiar comfort of her side of town calling out to her. But before getting in, she turned to look at Felix, who stood by the gate.

"Don't forget, Felix," she said, her voice filled with reassurance. "I'll be back on the twenty-sixth to take you to the dance."

Felix met her gaze with a mixture of anxiety and gratitude. The prospect of facing the people who had mistreated him in school weighed heavily on his mind. Still, the knowledge that he would be with her, Jessica, and Ethan brought a measure of comfort.

Fawn climbed into the car, and as she drove away from the shadowy streets of Wavecrest's neglected neighborhood, Felix, the boy who secretly harbored a crush on her, watched her departure, feeling a profound sense of emptiness deep within.

As the cityscape gradually transitioned from decay to vibrancy, Fawn couldn't shake the haunting images of poverty and despair she had witnessed. It was a stark reminder that life, even in the idyllic seaside town of Wavecrest, could take on many shades, some darker and more profound than she had ever imagined.

When she steered the car into Jessica's driveway, a deep sense of relief washed over her. It was as if the familiar sight of Jessica's house brought her back to a world she truly loved, away from the shadows of Wavecrest's neglected streets. The sight of Ethan's Jeep parked nearby only amplified her joy for her best friend.

The moment she stepped out of Teresa's car, the sun's warm embrace enveloped her, filling her with comforting warmth. It was a stark contrast to the gloomy atmosphere she had just left behind.

Inside the house, Fawn found Teresa in the kitchen, her graceful figure poised at the counter as she meticulously iced a freshly baked yellow cake. The gentle clink of the icing spatula against the cake provided a soothing soundtrack to the scene. As Fawn's footsteps echoed in the kitchen, Teresa turned around, her face lighting up with a warm and welcoming smile.

"Hey, sweetheart," she greeted Fawn with a voice as comforting as a familiar lullaby. "Did you have a nice visit with your friend?"

Fawn's heart swelled in response to Teresa's motherly presence, and without hesitation, she crossed the kitchen to wrap her in a warm hug. It was a silent gesture that spoke volumes, conveying the depth of her gratitude for the love and acceptance she received in this home. After glimpsing the loveless life Felix endured, Fawn appreciated this warmth more than ever. When they finally separated, Fawn's eyes sparkled with affection and appreciation for Teresa's unwavering love.

"Oh, my," Teresa said, her voice filled with surprise and affection. "What did I do to deserve this?" Her smile was as radiant as the sun outside.

Fawn returned Teresa's smile with equal brightness, her words spoken from the heart. "I love you, Mama. I love you and Papa so much."

Teresa's heart swelled in response to Fawn's heartfelt declaration. "Aw, we love you too, sweetheart," Teresa replied, her eyes and voice reflecting the deep well of motherly love and affection she held for Fawn.

After another heartfelt embrace, Fawn and Teresa released each other and returned to the rhythm of everyday life. Fawn moved to the end of the kitchen counter and dropped the car keys into a small cup.

Teresa's gentle voice cut through the momentary silence, offering a glimpse of the outside world. "You just missed Jessica and Ethan," she informed Fawn with a warm smile. "They went to the boardwalk. She told me to tell you they'll be at the pavilion."

Fawn nodded, already aware of their plans.

Teresa offered her hospitality once more, a motherly instinct she couldn't suppress. "Would you like me to fix you some lunch?"

Fawn graciously declined, her reply laced with gratitude. "No, thank you. I'll get something to eat on the boardwalk."

With a final hug, Fawn said goodbye to Teresa and approached the front door. As she stepped back into the warm embrace of the sunshine, she heard the distant, rhythmic whispers of the ocean's waves. It seemed to beckon her, its silent invitation offering a momentary escape from the harsh realities that loomed beyond the tranquil shores of Wavecrest.

# Chapter 29

--------------------------------------------------------

As the clock neared two o'clock in the afternoon, the Sandalwood Pavilion served as a seaside haven of sunlight and sociability on Wavecrest's bustling boardwalk. Its quintessential structure, capped with a pointed roof and an ornate weathervane, whispered the tender melodies of nostalgia. Bathed in the golden hues of the afternoon, the pavilion's nameplate shimmered, its gold and crimson lettering a tribute to a timeless invitation.

Beneath its navy-blue awning, patrons found respite, their faces aglow in the uniform sunlight that bathed the boardwalk. Engaged in congenial conversations, their voices mingled with the rhythmic lapping of nearby waves, a chorus underscored by the ocean's timeless refrain. Pots of flourishing flora adorned the surroundings, their vibrant blossoms reflecting the vividness of human emotion, as if each petal were a fleeting yet potent brushstroke on life's ever-changing canvas.

The wooden planks, weathered by the elements yet sturdy in their purpose, led visitors toward this place of collective experience. A lone lamp post waited near the entrance, its unlit frame poised to guide souls into evening reflection, but for now, it stood sentinel over daylight dreams and the shared tapestry of human connection.

With her long, straight blonde hair flowing like a golden stream in the wind, Fawn entered the pavilion and meandered through the labyrinthine arrangement of tables and chairs. A symphony of conversation and laughter, carried by the coastal breeze, filled the air, painting a tableau of lives momentarily intersecting. Her eyes darted, searching for familiar faces as her sandals clicked lightly on the wooden floor, each step leading her toward a haven of friendship amidst the swirling ocean of strangers.

Finally, her eyes caught Jessica and Ethan engrossed in a quiet exchange, seated at a table carved with years of initials and dates, a manuscript of countless intimate moments. The sight swelled Fawn's heart with warmth, and her lips curved into a smile.

As she approached, she noticed Ethan taking a hearty bite of his burger, his attention diverted from Jessica to the plate of golden fries in front of him. Beside him, Jessica's own plate revealed only the last remnants of her fries, each crisp now a memory cradled in the satisfaction of a well-enjoyed meal.

Sliding gracefully into the seat next to Jessica, Fawn's keen eyes met her best friend's, her mischievous blue sparkling in unison with Jessica's own oceanic hues.

"Hey," she said softly, giving Jessica a playful nudge.

Ethan looked up from his half-finished burger, his striking blue eyes meeting Fawn's. "Hey, Fawn," he greeted warmly, the contours of his mouth sketching a welcoming smile.

"Hey," Fawn returned, her own smile a soft echo, reflecting the mutual respect and camaraderie shared in their little circle.

Jessica turned her gaze to Fawn, her bright blue eyes narrowing inquisitively. "So how did it go at Felix's?" she asked, her voice laced with a gentle concern that spoke volumes.

Fawn shook her head, disbelief clouding her animated features. "You have no idea how bad it is for Felix living there. I feel so sorry for him."

"What do you mean?" Jessica asked, her brows arching like two crescents framing a worried moon.

With an air of casual defiance, Fawn reached over to Ethan's plate and grabbed a single French fry. She popped it into her mouth, chewing thoughtfully. Unfazed by the playful pilfering, Ethan grinned, his expression tinged with a kind of silent understanding.

"He's a horrible man, Jess," Fawn said, each word heavy with the burden of her recent experience. Memories of Felix's father flooded back, his hostile demeanor casting a shadow over her thoughts.

Jessica's eyes widened, her unspoken empathy crystallizing at that moment. "You mean Felix's father?"

"Yeah," Fawn answered, her voice tinged with disgust and anger, emotions she could no longer keep at bay. "He's mean as hell."

The atmosphere grew tense for a moment, the three of them enclosed in a bubble of shared concern and disquiet. Even amid the effervescent light and laughter that characterized the Sandalwood Pavilion, their table became a fleeting refuge for the heavier aspects of life, a quiet acknowledgment that even in paradise, harsh realities beckoned.

Jessica and Ethan exchanged looks of disbelief, each pair of eyes speaking a silent language only they understood. They had seen Felix's father before, an almost spectral figure perennially perched on his porch, his demeanor less animated than the wind chimes that occasionally broke the stillness.

Ethan finally broke the silence, his voice tinged with genuine surprise. "You mean he was up and walking around?"

"He sure was," Fawn replied, stretching her hand toward Ethan's plate again to claim a small bounty of three more fries.

Jessica's voice wavered, a fragile mixture of concern and disbelief. "Well, what did he do?"

"He got in my face, for one thing," Fawn's words snapped like brittle twigs underfoot, her anger flaring momentarily. "He accused me of wanting to take Felix away from him."

"Seriously?" Jessica's mouth fell open, her face a vivid canvas of shock.

Ethan shook his head in disbelief. "Unbelievable," he murmured, the usually soft timbre of his voice now edged with a subtle undercurrent of anger.

Fawn nodded in agreement, her head moving in a slow, deliberate motion as she ate the fries one by one. Each chew seemed an attempt to grind away the bitterness she felt, but the taste of injustice lingered, refusing to be easily swallowed.

For a moment, the pavilion changed from a mere shelter to a refuge for lost souls, a place where the bright and dark facets of life came together, acknowledging that even in the idyll of Wavecrest, no one was truly immune to the complexities of the human condition.

Jessica's eyes remained fixed on Fawn, her irises reflecting a swirl of emotion that danced between disbelief and a thirst for the untold. "So, what did you do? What did you say?"

As Fawn weighed her words, she could almost see the chain of events that would unfold if she revealed the whole truth. She pictured Ethan's face hardening, his fists clenching—his protective nature tipping over into that dangerous territory where good intentions meet reckless actions. She knew that if Ethan found out that Felix's father had threatened her with violence, he would not let it go unanswered. He'd confront the man, and in his volatile mix of protectiveness and impulsiveness, she feared an outcome rife with irreversible consequences. So, in that split second, she chose to skirt the darker contours of the story.

"Nothing. Nothing at all. Felix came to the rescue," she said, her words as much a barrier against potential disaster as they were a revelation of partial truths.

The atmosphere in the pavilion shifted subtly, as if touched by an unseen hand. Jessica's and Ethan's eyes widened in tandem, twin mirrors reflecting the shared astonishment that the often reticent Felix had shown some backbone.

Fawn's voice rose, a note of pride threading through her words. "You should've seen him, guys. He actually stood up to him. He told him to go back in the house and leave us alone."

Ethan's lips curved into a grin, his features softening with an inner glow of admiration. He had long known about the cavernous depths of Felix's struggles—tales of schoolyard bullies, familial neglect, and a self-image scarred by life's relentless blows. Now, hearing of this sudden, valiant act, Ethan felt a warm surge of pride for his troubled friend.

"I'm impressed," he said, each syllable infused with a warmth akin to a pat on the back across the miles that separated them from Felix.

Amidst the jovial atmosphere inside the pavilion, a sobering hush fell over the table as

Fawn recounted her visit to Felix's world. Her words wove a tale of sorrow that contrasted sharply with the veneer of lightness and vitality of the surrounding boardwalk. In the telling, even the French fries she plucked from Ethan's plate seemed less like indulgence and more like small comforts against the bleakness she had described.

Jessica and Ethan, their faces shadowed by the weight of Fawn's revelations, shook their heads in shared disbelief and sadness. The table, a repository of their collective experience, now bore the heaviness of untold stories and disturbing truths. For a moment, they sat in a silence that neither the ocean's rhythm nor the boardwalk's cheer could penetrate.

Breaking the silence, Ethan slid his plate toward Fawn, its remaining fries like small offerings in the face of greater difficulties. "You go ahead and eat the rest, Fawn. I'll go get you a burger."

"Oh, no, you don't have to do that," Fawn replied, her voice tinged with gratitude.

Ethan's eyes met hers, his smile breaking like the sun through clouds. "I know, but I want to. Lunch is on me today."

"Okay. If you insist," Fawn replied playfully, her heart swelled, touched by the simple but profound kindness. It was as if Ethan's gesture restored a balance, lending warmth to a scene darkened by the grim realities of Felix's life.

Before standing, Ethan leaned in to plant a tender kiss on Jessica's lips, an affirmation of love amidst the complexities of friendship and the harshness of life's unfairness. He then exited the pavilion, leaving Jessica and Fawn alone, their faces illuminated by the afternoon light as they navigated the delicate terrain between revelation and uncertainty.

As the last echoes of Ethan's footsteps faded, Fawn leaned closer to Jessica, the afternoon sunlight shifting through the navy-blue awning as if sensing the gravity of what was to come. "There's more, Jess, but you have to promise not to tell Ethan or our parents, okay?"

The air between them seemed to thicken, charged with an urgency that made the ambient sounds of the pavilion seem distant and unimportant. "I promise," Jessica whispered, her voice tinged with a somberness that spoke of emotional tension.

"He threatened me, Jess," Fawn's words came forth, each syllable steeped in a disconcerting blend of anger and vulnerability. "That asshole raised his cane and acted like he was going to hit me with it if I didn't leave."

A pallor washed over Jessica's face, as if the sun over the boardwalk had dimmed in response to her shock. "Oh my God," she mouthed, the whisper brimming with disbelief and fear.

"That's when Felix showed up," Fawn continued. "He grabbed his cane and made him put it down."

Jessica clenched her fingers, and her eyes darkened. "That's messed up, man," she said, her voice a low growl. "Don't be going back there, okay?" Her words came out more than a plea than a suggestion, her own fears projecting vivid scenarios she didn't want to contemplate.

Sensing Jessica's growing alarm, Fawn hastened to soften the edges of the portrait she had drawn. "He's a sick man, Jess. I don't think he would have tried to hit me with his cane. I think he just wanted to scare me."

Yet Jessica's gaze remained fixed on Fawn, a medley of emotions dancing in her eyes—concern, skepticism, perhaps even a flicker of indignation. Her lips parted as if to speak, but words failed her. In that lingering silence, both women confronted the gnawing unease that had settled over them, its weight inescapable even amidst the sunlit haven of the seaside oasis.

With the lingering tension almost palpable, Fawn tried to infuse the atmosphere with levity. Her eyes sparkled with a familiar mischief as she revealed her next shocker to Jessica. "I invited Felix to go to the Summer Dance with me, so I'll have to go back again."

"You did what?" Jessica exclaimed, her face a mixture of astonishment and amusement, a reaction so complex that it could not be reduced to a single emotion.

"I had to, Jess," Fawn's voice took on a plaintive quality, an earnestness that almost contradicted her earlier mischief. "The life he's living—it's a never-ending dark tunnel. I just want to be his light, even if it's only for a night."

As she spoke, her words seemed to hang in the air between them, each syllable a visible plea for understanding. Fawn paused, composing her thoughts as if gathering pearls of wisdom on an invisible string.

"Our lives are fantasies next to his grim reality. Just one evening of normalcy—that's all I wish for him. One night, where he can forget."

Jessica looked into Fawn's eyes and saw an irrevocable commitment, an unwavering determination. "I understand, Fawn. But promise me one thing—you won't go there alone."

Fawn tilted her head slightly. "What are you suggesting?"

"I'm suggesting that Ethan and I go with you to pick him up and take him home."

A quizzical eyebrow lifted on Fawn's face. "Do you think Ethan would be up for that?"

It was then that Ethan's voice sliced through their contemplative bubble. "Of course, I'm up for it," he said, his grin unfurling like a flag of unconditional alliance as he placed a burger in front of Fawn.

"Do you even know what you're agreeing to?" Fawn couldn't help but chuckle.

"It doesn't matter," Ethan assured her, expressing a level of loyalty that spoke volumes more than any detailed plan ever could. "If Jessica's up for it, so am I."

In that moment, under the protective embrace of their oceanfront retreat, they found unity in their diverse desires to reach out, to heal, to uplift. Each was committed, in his and her own way, to wading into the hidden sufferings of human experience—each willing to lend a hand in guiding someone else out of their darkness and into the light.

After Fawn finished her burger and sipped the last of Jessica's soft drink, the trio stepped back into the embrace of the sun-drenched boardwalk. Their original plan was to stroll back to Jessica's house, but as fate would have it, a familiar scene caught their eyes. Just below them on the beach, a group of friends from school were engaged in a lively game of volleyball, their laughter rising through the sea air like the notes of a summer symphony. A brief exchange of glances between Jessica and Fawn was all it took; the siren call of camaraderie and play was irresistible.

Jessica relished the opportunity to reintroduce Ethan to her social circle, this time with a hint of proprietary glee in her voice as she announced him as her boyfriend. The words rolled off her tongue with a mixture of pride and affection, forging a subtle yet impactful alteration in the dynamics of her friendships.

Ethan, for his part, wore an easygoing smile, his heart warmed by Jessica's public acknowledgment of him as her boyfriend. Pride flowed through his veins that these people—friends and acquaintances alike—now knew that he belonged to her, and she belonged to him.

For Fawn, the volleying ball and bursts of laughter were more than a game; they were a temporary balm on the raw nerves of her emotional afternoon. With each leap and serve, she carved out a space for lightheartedness, a fleeting but welcome respite from the emotional weight of the day. As the sun began to set, painting the beach in twilight hues, it felt like the world had given her these few hours to be young, free, and momentarily unburdened.

As the golden light began to spread across the sand, signaling the end of the day, the trio returned to Jessica's home, their faces still flushed from the day's adventures. Stepping through the front door, they were met by the rich aroma of roast beef, a savory welcome that beckoned them deeper into the warmth of the home. Teresa greeted them with a smile that radiated the same warmth as the oven.

"Ethan, why don't you stay for dinner? I've got a roast in the oven," she offered, her eyes meeting his as if she already knew his answer.

Ethan glanced at Jessica, and in that brief exchange, an understanding bloomed. "I'd be honored, Mrs. Reese," he replied, touched by the domesticity of the invitation.

Fawn, who had stood silently listening to the exchange, felt the pull of another kind of warmth—the abstract but compelling comfort of her own family home.

"I think I'll have dinner at my house," she said, her voice tinged with a newfound appreciation. "I want to spend some time with my parents tonight."

Jessica met Fawn's eyes, sensing the emotional undercurrents that ebbed beneath her words. After witnessing the stark absence of familial love in Felix's life, it was as if Fawn had glimpsed an alternate reality that she found deeply unsettling. Despite the unresolved bitterness Fawn felt toward her own parents, Jessica understood why she now sought the familiar comfort of home.

"Okay, Fawn," Jessica said, her voice tinged with a knowing softness. "I'll see you later?"

"Absolutely," Fawn assured her. "I'll be back later tonight."

As Fawn made her way to the door, she felt a strange mixture of relief and apprehension, a tightrope stretched taut between her need for familial closeness and realizing how easily it could slip away. With a final wave, she stepped out into the lingering warmth of the late afternoon, leaving Jessica and Ethan in the warm embrace of a home that still knew how to love.

As the evening deepened toward eight o'clock, the boardwalk hummed with magnetic energy, drawing locals and tourists alike into its vibrant embrace. Neon signs flashed over-head, advertising ice cream parlors and surf shops, their lights reflecting off the undulating surface of the ocean. Laughter and chatter floated in the air, melding with the distant serenade of seagulls and the rhythmic crashing of waves.

However, as time unfurled into the night, a subtle shift began to take place. Families with small children drifted away first, their laughter and shouts fading as if swallowed by the evening sea mist. Couples, hand in hand, gradually vacated their seats from ocean-view benches, their faces tinged with the pink and orange remnants of the sunset they had come to witness.

By eleven o'clock, the boardwalk started showing its quieter, introspective side. Street performers packed away their guitars and tip jars, while food stands and restaurants turned their signs from "Open" to "Closed." The ocean, always Wavecrest's faithful com-panion, continued its ceaseless cadence, but now the sound felt more like a whispered lullaby, urging the town to rest.

As midnight approached, only a few souls remained: the late-night joggers, the solitary thinkers, and the starry-eyed wanderers gazing out at the moonlit ocean. They were the guardians of the night, holding space in the tranquil hours when the world seemed to hold its breath.

By this time, Fawn had returned to Jessica's house, slipping silently into her friend's room. As the boardwalk eased into its nightly solitude, Fawn and Jessica lay in bed, side by side, enveloped in a comforting darkness. The soft glow of the streetlights outside seeped through the window, casting a muted glow that caressed their faces.

They looked up at the ceiling where star-shaped decals adorned the plaster, a remnant of childhood dreams and simpler times. The decals seemed to twinkle in the semi-dark-ness, each star a silent witness to the years of friendship, laughter, and unspoken emotions that filled the room. In this intimate setting, under their own private constellation, the girls found themselves on the cusp of conversations that only the sanctity of such a night could properly cradle.

Fawn's finger traced an invisible line through the air, finally settling on a particular star-shaped decal that had always been her favorite. "Look at my star," she said softly, her voice tinged with melancholy. "Its glow isn't as bright as it used to be. It's starting to fade."

Jessica followed the direction Fawn was pointing, her eyes landing on the now dimmed glow of the star. She looked around and noticed that not just one, but many of the celestial stickers had dimmed. Some had even stopped glowing altogether. A wistful sigh escaped her lips.

"Some things don't last forever, I guess," Jessica said, her voice expressing a tender resignation. She thought back to the day her father had applied those decals, his tall frame balanced precariously on a stepladder, as a very young Jessica clapped her hands in delight below him. The room had seemed so magical then, a night sky captured just for her.

And yet, in this moment, as they lay beneath the dimming stars, Fawn understood something profoundly bittersweet. The fading light seemed to mirror their own transitions, the fleeting nature of time that spoke not only of the glowing stickers but of youth and the protected universe she had once believed would last forever. In its imperfections and fading glow, the ceiling told a story of change as compelling as a sky full of stars that refused to disappear.

In that dimly lit room, framed by the muted glow of the streetlights filtering through the window, Fawn and Jessica lay side by side. The star-shaped stickers above them served as a gentle, though fading, tribute to their past—a childhood so seamlessly intertwined that it was hard to tell where one's memories ended and the other's began.

Fawn turned her head, her eyes searching for Jessica's. "Hey, Jess. Don't you find it strange that I'm an only child and you're an only child? I mean, we grew up together like sisters. It just seems weird, don't you think?"

Jessica shifted her gaze to meet Fawn's, her eyes softening. "Well, I know why I'm an only child. I was told that I was a miracle baby because Mom kept having miscarriages."

"That wasn't the case with my parents," Fawn replied, her voice tinged with a reflective note. "Mom had a really rough pregnancy, and I think she was afraid to get pregnant again."

A tender smile crossed Jessica's lips. "Well, maybe it is strange, but I wouldn't trade our childhood for anything."

"Me either, Jess. Me neither." Fawn's voice warmed, echoing the sentiment.

Jessica's curiosity swelled, filling the silent pause. "Have you ever wished you had a brother or sister?"

Fawn grinned at Jessica, her eyes glowing even in the room's dusky light. "Why would I? I have you for a sister."

Jessica's heart expanded in her chest, filled to the brim with the kind of love that only years of friendship could brew. "I feel the same way. You make me feel loved and special every day. I couldn't imagine growing up without you."

As they lay there, looking at the star-shaped decals that had once shined so brightly, Jessica ventured further into the realm of the future. "You know, I want to have a lot of kids someday, and I want them all to have Ethan's beautiful eyes and smile."

Fawn giggled and rolled her eyes playfully. "At this point in my life, I can't even see myself wanting to have kids."

Jessica looked at her, a mixture of surprise and disappointment clouding her features. "You will someday, Fawn. One day, you'll find the love of your life, and you'll want to have his babies."

And there, beneath the fading stars of their childhood, their words hung in the air—a tapestry of dreams, worries, and certainties yet to come. Their bond was like an undying star, defying the transience that seemed to claim the glow of their ceiling constellations.

As they felt the heaviness of sleep slowly take them into a world of dreams, the room seemed to embrace them, its walls a silent witness to their lifelong friendship. It was as if the universe had conspired to bring them together, to bind them in a sisterhood more enduring than time, and more radiant than the most luminous star in the sky.

# Chapter 30

-----------------------------------------------------

The Wednesday morning light filtered through the bedroom curtains, gently coaxing Jessica from the realm of sleep. Warmth and security enveloped her as she opened her eyes to find Fawn just an arm's length away. Their shared space was more than physical; it was a refuge in a sea of change, a testament to unwavering support in the midst of Fawn's emotional upheaval from losing her beloved home.

Jessica's gaze shifted to Fawn, who was already awake and lost in contemplation, her eyes fixed on the ceiling. A sleepy smile formed on Jessica's lips, reflected in Fawn's expression as their eyes met.

"Morning," Jessica's voice was a sleepy rasp, her arms stretching above her.

"Morning," Fawn's reply came with a muffled laugh. "Ready to conquer the day?"

Anticipation lit Jessica's eyes, and her smile widened. The day ahead was filled with personal pursuits—Fawn would be immersing herself in her artistic world, working on her sketch for the art contest at her house. Meanwhile, Jessica was thrilled to have her own house for herself and Ethan, giving them the opportunity to enjoy each other's company without interruption. Though their plans for the day were different, this quiet moment highlighted the underlying strength that anchored them: a friendship that was resilient and deep.

They sat up in unison, bedspreads tumbling down, and began their familiar morning routine. They shared a silent language, punctuated by soft giggles, easy banter, and the ever-present comfort of unwavering camaraderie.

Rubbing the sleep from her eyes, Fawn swung her legs over the side of the bed. "I need to use the bathroom," she announced, a lightheartedness in her tone despite the mundane declaration.

"Race you there!" Jessica replied with a playful grin. Both girls suddenly burst into a flurry of movement, their sleepy sluggishness replaced by the competitive energy of old times.

They made a beeline for the bathroom, laughter trailing behind them, a soundtrack to their morning race. Fawn reached it first, triumphantly claiming her prize, while Jessica waited her turn, feigning impatience with an exaggerated huff.

When they were both finished, they headed to the kitchen, drawn by the enticing aroma of freshly brewed coffee. Teresa, ever the attentive mother, had prepared it for the girls before she left for work, her presence lingering in the comforting details she left behind.

In the kitchen, Jessica and Fawn moved in a familiar rhythm, each filling a mug with coffee. The morning silence was a comfortable canvas for their muted movements and the clinking of ceramic cups.

"What should we have for breakfast?" Jessica asked, rummaging through the refrigerator. "Big day ahead. We should start it right."

"How about an encore of my famous omelet?" Fawn suggested with a playful grin, remembering the morning she'd prepared the same meal. "We've got eggs, tomatoes, and some cheese. A hearty breakfast for an art maestro and," she paused for effect, nodding sagely, "a love-struck heart waiting for her beau."

Jessica laughed, nudging Fawn with her shoulder. "Hey, that omelet was a masterpiece, I'll give you that. And yes, I have a different kind of 'art' to delve into today," she said, her cheeks flushing at the thought of Ethan.

With a giggle, Fawn began gathering the ingredients, expertly dicing the tomatoes as Jessica beat the eggs. "Your 'art,' huh? Make sure you don't tire yourself out too much, or you'll need another omelet by the end of the day!"

Their laughter mingled, filling the kitchen with an atmosphere of warmth and ease. The conversation flowed effortlessly, touching on Fawn's eagerness to work on her sketch and Jessica's deepening romance with Ethan.

"You know," Jessica's voice softened, a tender smile on her lips. "Having you here—it means the world to me. Especially now."

Fawn's knife paused as she looked up, her eyes meeting Jessica's. Emotion swelled, and she returned the smile, her voice steady. "I wouldn't want to be anywhere else, Jess. We've got each other's backs, no matter what. And that," she pointed the knife playfully, "includes making sure you eat a decent breakfast!"

Their laughter filled the kitchen once again, a testament to a bond that was far deeper than shared meals and daily routines. It was a connection that anchored them, providing a sense of stability and understanding amidst the unpredictable whirlwind of life's challenges.

As their breakfast came to a close, the remnants of omelet and toast crumbs remained as evidence of a meal enjoyed. Jessica glanced at the clock and then back to Fawn with a raised eyebrow.

"I suppose we should get moving. Big day for both of us," she said, a playful challenge in her tone.

Fawn nodded in agreement, her eyes sparkling with anticipation for the day's creative endeavors. "You're right. How about I tackle this mess," she gestured to the scattered dishes, "while you get showered and dressed?"

Grateful, Jessica didn't need to be told twice. She rose from her seat, stretching leisurely, and headed to the bathroom. The sound of running water soon echoed through the house, signifying the start of their day's preparations.

Back in the kitchen, Fawn filled the sink with soapy water, the suds swirling around as she washed the dishes. She moved methodically, lost in thought about the sketch that awaited her attention. Every so often, her thoughts drifted to Jessica and Ethan, wondering about the depth of their love and where it might lead. The clatter of dishes being rinsed and placed in the drainer provided a rhythmic soundtrack to her musings.

By the time Jessica reappeared, fresh and rejuvenated, Fawn had restored order to the kitchen. "Your turn," she announced with a smile, her hair damp and a towel draped around her neck to catch the stray droplets.

"Thanks, Jess," Fawn replied, wiping her hands on a dish towel and making her way to the bathroom. The promise of the day, with its creative prospects, buoyed her spirits, and she found herself humming a tune as she stepped into the warm embrace of the shower.

The house settled into a comfortable silence, each girl engrossed in her world of preparation and anticipation. They moved through their routines with the ease of long-standing habit, an unspoken understanding between them that today, like every day they shared in each other's company, was special and held the potential for something remarkable.

By late morning, the house was buzzing with the quiet energy of preparation. Jessica and Fawn, each dressed and imbued with the fresh zeal of the new day, were the very embodiments of eager anticipation. The ping of a text message broke the momentary silence, and Jessica looked down at her phone with a smile.

"It's Ethan. He'll be here in a few minutes," she announced, her voice a mix of excitement and affection.

Fawn nodded, her smile reflecting her friend's happiness. She made her way to Jessica's bedroom and reappeared with her sketchbook clutched to her chest, the pages a secret treasure trove of her artistic visions.

"I guess it's time," Fawn said softly, the sketchbook a tangible reminder of the journey that awaited her.

Jessica approached her, and without hesitation, they embraced in a warm, reassuring hug, a silent promise of support woven into the gesture.

"See you later, Fawn. Good luck with the sketch," Jessica whispered, pulling back but keeping her hands on Fawn's shoulders for a moment longer.

Fawn nodded, her resolve bolstered. "Thanks. Enjoy your day with Ethan. See you later."

And with that, Fawn stepped out, the door closing behind her, leaving Jessica in quiet anticipation of what the day would bring.

The warm morning air was a gentle companion as Fawn made her way to her house, the rhythmic sound of her footsteps a soothing cadence in the quiet neighborhood. The trees swayed gently in the breeze, their leaves whispering secrets, an audience to her thoughts. Fawn's mind was a whirlwind of emotion and determination, her artistic passion a bright flame amidst the uncertainties life had recently presented.

As she approached, her home came into view, its familiar facade a tapestry of memories, each window and door a keeper of stories from years past. But today, something was different, something that sent a small jolt through her heart. The "For Sale" sign, an unwelcome fixture these past weeks, now bore a bold, black "Sold" sticker, its finality stark against the white and yellow background.

Fawn felt her breath catch as the sight hit her unexpectedly, even though she knew this day would come. It wasn't there last night, she thought, realizing that the realtor must have decorated it with its new status in the light of day. Her home, the haven of her happiest memories, was officially awaiting new guardians.

A profound wave of sadness washed over her, dimming the spark of her earlier enthusiasm. The sign stood as a stark reminder of the inexorable march of time, of change, and of the transient nature of the things she held dear. For a fleeting moment, she allowed herself to grieve, mourning the impending loss of her childhood home that would soon be entrusted to strangers.

But Fawn, resilient as she was, knew she couldn't let the melancholy tide pull her under. There was much to be done, dreams to chase, and her art to pour her soul into. She couldn't afford to let the sadness tether her to the ground. The Art Contest was just around the corner, and time, unforgiving as always, was slipping through her fingers.

With a deep, steadying breath, Fawn straightened up, the rough edges of her resolve being smoothed out by her artistic fervor. She afforded the sign one last glance before scurrying past it, her steps quickening as if to outrun the pang in her chest.

Fawn's entrance into the house was a silent crossing into a world of both familiarity and alienation. Her parents' absence, off to their daily jobs, left a void that seemed to echo off the walls themselves. The quiet was not peaceful but poignant, a reminder of the emptiness that often accompanied change. Despite the solitude, Fawn couldn't afford to lose focus. She had a mission—one that demanded her full attention and creativity.

Shaking off the silence that enveloped her, Fawn moved with purpose, her footsteps a solitary rhythm against the stillness of the house. She needed a canvas, a blank slate on which she could spill her imagination and run wild. Her room, where her artistic endeavors had taken root and flourished, was her immediate destination.

As she ascended the stairs, each step was a tread through memories, echoes of laughter, and whispered secrets lingering like a long-forgotten perfume. Upon reaching her room, Fawn hesitated at the doorway. The space before her, though recently restored to its former state, felt foreign. It was her room, but not all at once.

The knowledge that her space would soon embrace a stranger, that her walls would guard different dreams, cast an intangible barrier between her and the room she once claimed as hers. It was a jarring reminder that the tethers were loosening, that the room was slowly detaching from her, ready to begin a new story that she would not write.

But dwelling on the inevitable wouldn't do her any good now, not with the Art Contest's deadline casting its shadow. Pushing the burgeoning sadness to the back of her mind, Fawn stepped forward, her resolve strengthening with each step. Her eyes, bright with determination, scanned the room before settling on the closet. This was where she'd find her tools, the instruments she needed to bring her vision to life.

The door to her closet opened with a familiar creak, revealing shelves filled with the remnants of years of artistic exploration: tubes of paint, frayed brushes, and sketchbooks with curled edges. But today, Fawn's search was unique. She needed the perfect canvas for her pencil sketch, something with a smooth surface to match the soft whisper of graphite.

Her fingers danced over the textures of various canvases, her eyes critically evaluating each potential candidate. They were all echoes of past projects, moments of inspiration that had seen the light of day from within this very closet. Then, her touch paused, recognizing the promise in the feel of one particular canvas. It was an 11 x 14, heavily primed, its surface smooth and unwavering under her fingertips. It was a silent, blank promise, waiting to cradle her creation.

Eager anticipation bubbled inside her as she pulled the canvas out of the closet. As the door clicked shut, Fawn's next destination was her desk—a treasure trove of pencils awaited, each varying in lead and potential. Her hand was already reaching for the familiar handle of the drawer when a sliver of something less familiar caught her eye.

It was a photograph, or at least the corner of one, peeking inconspicuously out from beneath a stack of writing pads. Its presence was an anomaly among the meticulously organized chaos that typically inhabited her desk. Fawn's curiosity was piqued; momentarily forgetting her canvas as she reached for the image and pulled it out into the light of the day.

The photograph was a sunlit memory, captured in time; the colors slightly faded, but the joy radiating from it was as vivid as ever. It portrayed a younger Fawn, Jessica, and their friend, Lily Green, all huddled close together on a playground bench. Their youthful faces were bright with smiles, innocent and unburdened, basking in the glow of a carefree summer day.

Lily sat in the middle, her magnified eyes sparkling with joy behind oversized glasses that seemed almost too big for her small face. Those glasses, Fawn remembered, were a prominent part of Lily's shy, doe-like persona, that made her seem perpetually in awe of the world around her. Lily's quiet demeanor had always complemented her and Jessica's more exuberant natures.

When Fawn's mother took this photo, they were eight years old. It was during one of their many playful afternoons at the park, a day filled with laughter, pretend play, and the kind of pure joy that only children know. Fawn could almost hear the echo of their laughter and the teasing shouts they exchanged, the air around them charged with the electric energy of childhood.

A pang of longing swept through Fawn as she looked at Lily. The Greens had moved away shortly after that photo was taken, pulling Lily away from the woven tapestry of their daily lives. Their departure had left a Lily-shaped void that neither time nor distance had fully managed to heal. Now, as she traced the outline of Lily's face with her finger, the realization dawned on Fawn that soon, she would be the one leaving. She would become a memory, a face in a photograph to be remembered on quiet days.

The edges of the photograph felt fragile under Fawn's touch, much like the delicate nature of human connections. As her finger traced Lily's smiling face, fond memories flooded back, filling her with a deep sense of longing for her friend.

"I hope life is treating you well, Lily," she whispered into the silence of her room, her voice more than a wistful sigh.

For a moment, Fawn allowed the sadness to take hold, letting it wash over her as she mourned the distance, both in miles and years, between that captured moment and her present. But as she set the photograph down, her eyes drifted back to the blank canvas on her desk. It awaited her touch, her emotion, her story. With a deep, calming breath, Fawn let the memories of past friendships, the pain of goodbyes, and the bittersweetness of growth guide her hand. Today, she wasn't just creating art; she was weaving in pieces of her soul, immortalizing connections, and saying silent goodbyes, all with the gentle stroke of pencil on canvas.

Clutching her art supplies, Fawn stepped out of the house and into the warm morning air. Her eyes were immediately drawn to the old white bench swing that stood like a steadfast friend on the edge of the side yard. It was more than just a structure of metal and bolts; it was a symbol, a silent witness to the chronicles of her childhood and the deep bond she shared with Jessica.

The swing had a history, lovingly crafted by Fawn's father when she and Jessica were little girls. Fawn remembered the sense of wonder they felt as they watched her father build it, piece by piece, creating magic before their young, awe-struck eyes. When it was finished, it quickly became more than a plaything—it was their special place. It cradled their secrets, supported their dreams, and swayed with the weight of their uninhibited laughter and boundless imagination.

Now, years later, the swing held a different kind of magic for Fawn. It wasn't just a relic of the past, but a bridge to her inner self. When she sat on it, the world seemed to fall away, leaving her with a chorus of rustling palm leaves and the soft whispers of memories dancing in the dappled sunlight. The swing, with its peeling paint and familiar creaks, connected her to a reservoir of strength she often forgot she had, a silent reassurance that she carried the essence of home within her, no matter where the tides of life might take her.

With a gentle sigh, Fawn made her way to the swing, feeling its familiar presence wrap around her like a comforting embrace. As she settled onto it, the world around her seemed to fall silent in awe of the art that was about to unfold. The canvas rested on her lap, blank and unblemished, eagerly awaiting the story it was about to tell.

Fawn didn't need to close her eyes; she could feel the spirit of the swing, the echoes of her childhood laughter, and the love that went into every piece of metal and bolt. These sensations flowed through her, traveling down her arm and into her hand, which held the pencil poised above the canvas. And then she began. Her hand moved with certainty, guided by memories, emotions, and an intrinsic connection to her surroundings. The lines formed, the image took shape, and her pencil danced across the canvas as if telling a story only she knew, a masterpiece emerging beneath Fawn's deft touch and the swing's silent song.

Back at Jessica's house, Ethan took a moment to absorb the warmth of the living room, his eyes drawn to the framed photographs that adorned the walls. It was like stepping into a visual history of Jessica's life: her birthdays, family gatherings, and holidays. One picture caught his attention—a snapshot of a much younger Jessica standing next to Fawn. They were perhaps five or six years old, but the difference in height was striking even back then. Fawn towered over Jessica, who appeared remarkably petite in comparison.

Smiling, Ethan called out to Jessica, who was busy in the kitchen, preparing a grilled cheese sandwich for the man who had claimed her heart. "Wow, babe, when you were little, you really were tiny."

Jessica couldn't help but giggle at his observation. Once a sore point, her petite frame had long since become a characteristic she embraced. "Yeah, I know," she replied, her voice full of mirth.

The scent of melting cheese and toasting bread filled the air as Ethan made his way into the kitchen. With a sense of playfulness, he slipped his arms around Jessica's waist from behind and pulled her close.

"You know, it made you that much more adorable," he said, nuzzling his face into the crook of her neck.

Jessica's heart swelled with affection, and her earlier giggles turned into a wide smile that made her eyes sparkle. She turned around to face him, her arms now wrapped around his neck. "Oh Ethan, you always make me feel so special and loved. I can never get enough of that. It makes my day when you say things like that to me."

Ethan's eyes met hers, conveying all the sincerity in the world. "And I mean every word, babe."

They sealed their exchange with a tender hug and a loving kiss before Ethan pulled out a chair at the kitchen table and sat down to await the grilled cheese sandwich Jessica had so lovingly prepared for him.

Carefully balancing her attention between the sizzling pan and the conversation, Jessica focused on getting the sandwich just right. With the skill of someone well-versed in the art of sandwich making, she flipped the sandwich over, eyeing the crust until it reached that perfect shade of golden brown. Once satisfied, she slid her culinary creation onto a clean plate with a flourish.

Holding the plate in her hands, she walked over to where Ethan sat and placed it in front of him. "Here you go," she announced, her eyes twinkling with a mixture of pride and modesty.

Ethan looked down, and his eyes met the plate before moving back to hers. "That looks delicious," he said, a genuine note of appreciation in his voice.

"I hope it is," Jessica replied, her voice tinged with nervous anticipation. She wanted this small offering to bring him as much joy as he brought her each day.

Ethan picked up the sandwich and took a hearty bite, his eyes closing as if to savor the simple yet heartfelt meal. Watching Ethan enjoy the food she'd made filled Jessica with an indescribable sense of happiness.

In that fleeting moment, her imagination took flight. She saw herself not only as Jessica Reese, but as Mrs. Ethan Harris, living a life punctuated by these simple, intimate gestures. Unlike her friends, who were busy charting out career paths and contemplating far-off dreams, her deepest aspiration was beautifully uncomplicated. She yearned for the joys of domestic life—of being a loving wife and, someday, a mother.

The thought melted her heart, and she reveled in the dream even as reality beckoned her back. The present moment was its own kind of beautiful, and for now, that was more than enough.

After taking the last bite of his sandwich, Ethan placed the empty plate in the kitchen sink. "That was delicious, babe," he said, grinning at Jessica.

She smiled back, her eyes bright with joy and a hint of relief.

Hand in hand, they made their way to the living room and settled onto the couch. As they curled up together, Ethan's eyes wandered around the room, taking in the many family photos that adorned the walls—snapshots that captured laughter, love, and years of cherished memories.

"I wish my family was more like yours," Ethan said softly, his eyes meeting Jessica's.

"In what way?" she asked, curiosity tinged with concern in her eyes.

Ethan sighed. "Your family just seems so... close, so supportive. Mine is more controlling than anything else. My father already has plans for me and Jake. He wants us to take over the family business someday."

Jessica processed this, her eyes searching his face. "That's not right. Have you talked to your dad about what you want?"

"I've thought about it," Ethan replied. "But he's a stubborn man. That's why I considered joining the Army after college. It felt like a way out, you know? A way to make my own choices."

Jessica felt a sudden knot tighten in her stomach at the mention of the military. "Do you still want to join?" she asked, her voice barely above a whisper.

Ethan looked deep into her eyes, a warmth spreading across his face. "Being here with you, Jess, has changed everything."

Jessica's heart felt like it was going to burst from her chest, so full of emotion it was almost painful. "It's changed everything for me, too," she said, her voice filled with affection.

Unable to resist the magnetic pull between them any longer, Jessica leaned in, and their lips met in a sweet, lingering kiss. In that moment, all thoughts of the future, of family expectations and diverging paths, faded away. All that mattered was the love they had found in each other, a love that had already changed them both in ways they had yet to fully understand.

The atmosphere in the room was palpable, electric with the tension of unspoken desires as Jessica and Ethan held each other tightly. The heat between them had reached a crescendo, leaving both on the edge of a precipice, ready to plunge into new emotional depths.

But just when it felt like they were about to cross an invisible line, Jessica gently pulled away, her face flushed, her eyes filled with a complex mix of longing and uncertainty. "We better stop," she whispered, each word tinged with a sense of reluctance.

Ethan looked into her eyes and saw a reflection of his own feelings—a potent mixture of passion and hesitation. He understood her and knew she was grappling with something internal, something deeply personal.

"It's okay, babe. I can wait," Ethan reassured her, his gaze unwavering.

Jessica's eyes filled with tears, not of sorrow, but of deep gratitude and love. "Are you sure?" she asked, her voice revealing her vulnerability, as if she were baring her soul.

Without a word, Ethan pulled her back into his arms, hugging her tightly as if to anchor her in this moment of emotional tumult.

"I'm absolutely sure," he said, his voice unwavering. "I love you, Jessica. When the time is right for you, for both of us, it will be beautiful."

In that moment, as they held each other, the room around them seemed to exhale, as if to make room for the love that was so obviously blossoming. It became clear that this was not just a youthful dalliance. It was a relationship built on understanding, patience, and a love willing to wait for the right moment. And for Jessica, this realization was the most beautiful gift of all.

Time had a way of slipping through Fawn's fingers when she was immersed in her art, the hours stretching and condensing in a dance that only creative souls understood. It was about three in the afternoon now, the sun casting dappled shadows across her childhood yard, its beams winking through the leaves of the palm trees. The air was infused with the familiar scent of salt and sea, the summer breeze caressing her senses in its own gentle, reassuring manner.

Fawn drew her pencil back and placed it next to the canvas that rested on her lap. Her fingers were stained with graphite, her palms smudged in places where her hand had grazed the canvas. She held it at arm's length, tilting her head and squinting her eyes to scrutinize the lines, the shading, the play of light and dark.

A smile slowly spread across her face. This was it—her masterpiece. She had poured everything into this work of art: her memories, her emotions, and a mystical connection to this very spot. Never before had she poured so much of herself into each stroke of her pencil.

The subject of the sketch? A secret. A sacred, beautiful secret she wasn't ready to share just yet. Even Jessica, her soul sister, wouldn't know what she'd created until the right moment came.

Fawn felt a tinge of melancholy, knowing that this masterpiece, born from this special place and the emotions tethering her to it, was also a form of goodbye. A tribute to a closing chapter. She looked down at the canvas one more time, her eyes tracing over the lines she'd just brought to life. Satisfied, she knew this piece had a purpose far greater than any contest. It was a fragment of her soul, captured in graphite and canvas, a moment forever suspended in time.

Still sitting on the swing, Fawn held her canvas close, her eyes taking in every detail, every line and curve that had flowed from her heart to the pencil and onto the smooth canvas. Even under the afternoon sun, the ancient palm tree that stood guard behind her cast a mottled shade that shielded her from the heat. She felt comfortably cool, and for a brief moment, she was transported back in time. She felt like a little girl again, a sensation she realized had become rare these days.

As she basked in this comforting nostalgia, a soft summer breeze gently caressed her long, blonde hair. Guided more by instinct than thought, she leaned back and raised her eyes to the towering palm leaves above her. They rustled softly, synchronizing with the breeze, casting shifting patterns of light and shadow around her. Their movement was like a silent caress, a touch of intangible love and comfort that seemed to sink past her skin, past her bones, and settle deep within her soul.

She couldn't hear the whispers, but she could feel them—subtle, intimate messages that her heart understood as clearly as any spoken language. They spoke of a quiet sadness, an impending farewell to the innocence and freedom that had once defined her. Yet, within that melancholy was also reassurance—a loving affirmation that change was a part of life, and that she had nothing to fear.

Smiling softly, Fawn closed her eyes and let herself be cradled by the sensations surrounding her. For a few more precious moments, she simply existed there, wrapped in a presence that had been her silent companion since childhood, a presence that she and Jessica had unknowingly shared from their earliest days on this very swing. It felt as if the air, the breeze, and the rustling leaves were imbued with a familiar affection, one that had watched over her for years.

And then, as subtly as it had arrived, it retreated. The leaves fell silent, and the breeze ebbed away, but the serenity it left behind remained. Fawn opened her eyes, the canvas in her hands a testament to that sacred, fleeting moment. The world around her felt a little clearer, as if painted by an artist's loving hand. She took another long look at her masterpiece, knowing that the essence of this place, and of her own past, was captured within it. And for now, that was enough.

Feeling a sense of fulfillment but also a hint of protective secrecy about her artwork, Fawn knew it was time to go back inside. But before stepping off the swing, she took her sketchpad and discreetly slipped it under the green seat cushion. It would be safe there until she decided to retrieve it; that hidden spot had served her well over the years.

Fawn got up from the swing, giving it and the palm tree one last appreciative glance as if thanking them for the comfort and inspiration, and then walked back to her house. The wooden floorboards seemed to welcome her back as she made her way upstairs to her room. She grabbed her backpack from its resting place near her desk and carefully slid the canvas inside.

With her masterpiece safely tucked away, Fawn felt a weight lift off her shoulders. She made her way back downstairs to the living room, where the black leather sofa beckoned. As she settled into its comforting embrace, her thoughts naturally drifted to Jessica and Ethan. They would be spending the day together, alone, in the freedom of Jessica's house. The thought made Fawn chuckle. How wonderful it must be for them to enjoy their own private piece of heaven.

At that moment, a wave of satisfaction washed over her. She had finished her sketch, a work of art that held a special part of her soul, and she was ready to unveil it at the Art Contest. Now, there was nothing left to do but wait for the right moment to share it with the world.

Feeling the pull of a peaceful fatigue, Fawn shifted to a more comfortable position on the sofa. She wasn't quite ready to go back to Jessica's house, not wanting to interrupt their perfect day. Instead, she decided to give in to the sleepiness that had clouded her eyes. Within moments, the soft leather cradled her, her thoughts drifting as she surrendered to a well-deserved rest.

As the sun remained high in the sky, its light warm and inviting on this mid-July afternoon, two souls found themselves unknowingly joined in the intimacy of personal triumphs and unspeakable emotion. While Jessica basked in the burgeoning joys of first love, her heart humming a new tune she'd just begun to understand, Fawn felt the gratification of capturing a lifetime of feelings in a single, unseen sketch. Though they lived only two blocks apart, an invisible thread seemed to connect them—a sense of shared joy that could only be felt, not explained.

On this summer afternoon, the world around them seemed to pause, as if to honor their milestones. As Fawn settled into a comfortable sleep on her black leather sofa, and Jessica lost herself in the embrace of her newfound love, both felt as if they were wrapped in the loving arms of the universe, secure in the knowledge that this day would be one to remember, a jewel in the treasure chest of their youth.

# Chapter 31

The next morning, Jessica and Fawn sat at the kitchen table, each with a bowl of cereal in front of them. With a playful twinkle in her eye, Jessica looked out into the hallway and yelled, "Mom, Fawn won't tell me what her sketch is!"

Teresa walked into the kitchen, shaking her head and smiling, amused by Jessica's antics. "Now, Jessica. We have to respect Fawn's wishes," she replied, struggling to keep a straight face as she glanced at her daughter's exaggerated pout.

Feeling vindicated, Fawn grinned, stuck her tongue out at Jessica, and gloated. "Ha, ha!"

"Brat!" Jessica retorted, feigning annoyance.

Fawn shot her an exaggerated evil glare. "No, you're the brat!"

"You're the brat!" Jessica snapped back, unable to keep the laughter from her voice.

"Am not!" Fawn countered.

Teresa stood there, arms folded, shaking her head and chuckling at the two best friends bickering like they were seven years old again. Pretending to be stern, she intervened, "Okay, girls, that's enough! Don't make me separate you two. You behave yourselves and finish your breakfast!"

Simultaneous bursts of laughter from both Jessica and Fawn punctuated their fake argument, filling the kitchen with a brightness that made Teresa's smile widen even more.

"Okay, Mommy," Jessica surrendered, scooping up another spoonful of cereal.

"Sorry, Mommy," Fawn added, mimicking Jessica's actions.

Teresa felt her heart swell as she swept her eyes over the two girls. It was in moments like these—when the girls slipped into their childhood roles and playfully bickered—that she found pure, unadulterated joy. These precious, fleeting instances would be what she would miss the most when Jessica and Fawn left for college.

With a mixture of happiness and melancholy, Teresa stepped out of the kitchen, contemplating how much she would miss these simple yet precious moments when her girls left the nest. But for now, she cherished them, storing them like keepsakes in the treasure chest of her memory.

In the kitchen, Jessica's expression turned serious as she looked at Fawn. "Seriously though, why don't you want me to see it?"

Fawn met Jessica's gaze with sincerity. "Because it's really special, and I want you to be surprised when you see it at school, displayed with all the other sketches."

Jessica smiled as she murmured, "Okay. " Her curiosity was now tinged with anticipation.

"Besides," Fawn added, her mischievous grin reappearing, "I love torturing you."

"You brat!" Jessica replied, rolling her eyes but grinning all the same.

Savoring the last spoonful of their cereal, Fawn shifted the conversation. "So, what do you and Ethan have planned for the day?"

Jessica's face lit up. "We're going to Santa Barbara. Ethan wants to check out a new surf shop that just opened."

"That sounds like fun," Fawn replied.

"You want to come along?" Jessica asked, looking hopeful.

Fawn shook her head. "Nah, I'm taking my sketch to school today so that I'm officially in the contest."

A proud smile spread across Jessica's face. "You did it, Fawn. I knew you would come through despite everything that's been happening."

Fawn sighed affectionately. "Yeah, you know me better than I know myself."

With that, the two girls carried their empty bowls to the sink, the clinking of porcelain echoing their shared sense of accomplishment and excitement for the day.

Shortly after leaving Jessica's house, Fawn was back at her place and in her bedroom, her heart buzzing with eager anticipation. She picked up her backpack where her hidden sketch lay. With a deep breath to calm her fluttering nerves, she slung the bag over her shoulder and stepped out of her room. The pictures on her walls seemed to wave her on, like a silent choir encouraging her on this momentous day.

As she descended the staircase, the scent of breakfast met her halfway, mingling with the familiar fragrance of her mother's perfume. When she reached the bottom of the stairs, Anna appeared from the kitchen, wiping her hands with a towel. She looked up and caught sight of Fawn, her eyes lighting up with a curious smile.

"Are you going to let me see it?" Anna asked, her voice tinged with excitement.

"Okay," Fawn answered, her voice laced with modesty as she ambled into the living room and placed her backpack on the couch.

The room seemed to hold its breath as Fawn unzipped the backpack and carefully pulled out her sketch. As Anna caught sight of it, her eyes widened in awe. "That is absolutely beautiful, Fawn! You certainly have outdone yourself with this one!"

Fawn felt her cheeks warm at her mother's praise. "Thank you, Mom. I'm happy with it, I guess."

"There's no guessing, honey," Anna reassured her. "You did an amazing job."

Fawn smiled, both relieved and pleased as her mother continued to admire the artwork. Anna seemed to understand, almost instinctively, the depth of emotion Fawn had poured into her sketch. Closing her backpack, Fawn felt a newfound sense of accomplishment.

Anna went back into the kitchen to collect her purse and car keys. "I'm leaving for work now," she said. "Would you like me to drop you off at school?"

Eager to share her work with her peers and teachers, Fawn nodded. "Yeah, would you, please?"

Anna smiled warmly. "Wait until your father sees that. He'll be so impressed."

With that, Fawn picked up her backpack and followed her mother out the door. Once they were in the car, Anna started the engine and steered toward the high school. As they drove away, Fawn's eyes caught the "Sold" sign in their front yard. A twinge of discomfort flickered across her face, but she quickly pushed it aside. Today was not a day for sadness; it was a day for her art to shine.

And so, the car rolled away, each yard increasing the distance from the life Fawn had known but also leading her toward new, uncharted experiences that lay ahead.

As Anna gripped the steering wheel, she noticed Fawn's uneasy glance toward the "Sold" sign. She reached over and took her daughter's hand, her voice tinged with sorrow. "I'm sorry, honey. I know how you feel."

"I doubt it," Fawn said, her voice tinged with bitterness.

Her eyes remained fixed on the window, mulling over what she felt was the ultimate betrayal: her parents' secrecy over the necessity of selling their beloved family home. She couldn't shake the belief that if they had been upfront about their struggles, Jessica's father—her second dad—would have found a way to help.

Anna sighed, her heart aching at her daughter's words. "I know you don't like the idea of us moving to Montana," she said, her voice tinged with an earnest plea. "But please give it a chance, baby. You might even like it there when you come home for Christmas."

Fawn's internal monologue drowned out her mother's hopeful words; she had already decided she despised Montana, sight unseen.

Trying to inject a note of positivity, Anna added, "We may even experience our first white Christmas. Wouldn't that be exciting?"

"Whatever," Fawn muttered, her thoughts drifting to Jessica and the gaping hole her absence would leave during the holidays.

The car finally came to a stop in front of the high school's glass doors, a threshold between youth and impending adulthood. As Fawn prepared to step out, Anna's hand gripped her arm, a tactile punctuation to the conversation.

"I love you, sweetheart," she said, her eyes full of complex emotions, a tableau of love, pain, and regret.

Fawn paused and looked back at her mother. She saw the hurt in her eyes and, despite her own pain, felt a twinge of empathy.

"I know, Mom. I love you too," she replied softly, her words both a balm and an acknowledgment of the distance that had opened between them.

As Anna pulled away from the curb, her emotions rolled inside her like a stormy sea. Gone were the days of lighthearted mother-daughter banter, of heart-to-heart talks that stretched into the wee hours of the night. In their place, stood a wall, built brick by brick from the mortar of mistrust and perceived betrayal. And for that, Anna carried a heavy burden of guilt.

As she drove, her mind teetered between regret and hope. She realized that the upcoming trip to Boston to get Fawn settled could be a chance, however slim, to begin tearing down that wall. It was a fragile hope, but a hope, nonetheless. She understood things would never be quite the same, but perhaps—just perhaps—they could find a new kind of normal, a different but still meaningful mother-daughter connection. With that thought in her heart, she whispered a silent prayer, asking the universe to help her navigate the choppy waters that lay ahead.

Fawn pushed open the glass doors of Wavecrest High School, her footsteps echoing on the polished marble floor as she entered the lobby. Her eyes fell on the eighteen easels scattered throughout the room, each displaying a work of art that captured the essence of youthful talent and ambition. Some canvases showcased intricate ink sketches, while others featured delicate pencil strokes. As an artist, she couldn't help but marvel at the beauty before her, feeling a momentary connection to each individual creator.

Her gaze shifted to the various spectators meandering around the exhibit. People stood in small groups, nodding appreciatively, their eyes moving from one work to another, engaged in quiet conversations about the remarkable artistry on display.

Just as she was about to head toward an empty easel that beckoned in the corner, the sound of her name broke the gentle hum of the lobby.

"Fawn! There you are!" The voice was as familiar as it was warm, tinged with excitement and genuine care.

Turning her head, Fawn saw Mrs. Sprite sitting behind a long table in the far corner, a broad smile adorning her face.

"I was wondering when you would grace us with your presence," Mrs. Sprite called out, her eyes twinkling behind her round, delicate glasses.

Fawn's lips curved into a sincere smile as she approached her beloved art teacher. "Hi, Mrs. Sprite," she began, placing her backpack on the table. "This summer has been... challenging. But here I am, and my sketch is finished."

Mrs. Sprite's eyes shimmered with excitement and curiosity. "Oh, let's have a look then, shall we?"

Unzipping her backpack, Fawn carefully extracted her canvas and unveiled it before Mrs. Sprite, who gasped. "This is nothing short of breathtaking, Fawn," she remarked, captivated by the emotion and detail etched into the piece. "The shading, the lines and curves; it's truly a masterpiece."

Fawn felt her cheeks flush with both pride and humility as Mrs. Sprite's praise enveloped her. "Thank you, Mrs. Sprite. Your approval means a lot to me."

"Then let's not keep the world waiting any longer," Mrs. Sprite exclaimed, rising to her feet with an enthusiasm that belied her years. Taking Fawn's canvas delicately in her hands, they both walked to the empty easel, where a tag bearing Fawn's name awaited. Mrs. Sprite placed it, her fingers gently adjusting its position.

Stepping back, both student and teacher admired the sketch again, this time as part of a collective display of talent.

"Your work has surpassed my wildest expectations, Fawn," Mrs. Sprite broke the silence. "You're a natural, and I can't wait to hear what the judges think. Something tells me they'll be as thrilled as I am."

Fawn felt a surge of gratitude mixed with hope. As she looked at her sketch—now a part of this mosaic of young artistry—she couldn't help but feel that this was only the beginning.

As she ambled through the high school lobby, Fawn's eyes darted from one easel to the next, absorbing the creative expression each sketch offered. Each piece told its own unique story, embodying the spirit and dreams of its creator. But when she reached the end of the row and found herself in front of Felix's sketch, her eyes softened, and her heart swelled with a mixed emotion of pride and sadness.

The sketch was simple, almost childlike in its execution. The lines were hesitant and the shading inconsistent, yet it had a sort of raw honesty that spoke volumes. It may not win any prizes, but Fawn could see that Felix had put his heart into it. She admired that more than she could express. Shaking off a pang of sadness for her friend's unlikely chance of winning, she headed back to the table where Mrs. Sprite was sitting.

"Well, I'll be going now, Mrs. Sprite," Fawn said warmly. "I guess I'll see you on the day of the Art Contest."

Mrs. Sprite glanced up and smiled, her eyes beaming with pride. "Yes, dear, we'll see you then. Good luck to you!"

Fawn returned the smile, then turned and walked away. As she approached the glass doors, her eyes caught sight of her sketch again. A small group of people had gathered around it, their faces displaying unmistakable signs of admiration and intrigue. The sight filled her with an invigorating sense of accomplishment and a newfound sense of confidence.

Feeling her heart swell with a potent mix of hope, pride, and satisfaction, Fawn pressed her palms against the glass doors. They swung open, letting in the warmth of the morning sun, which bathed her face in its golden glow. For a moment, she stood on the precipice between the world she knew and the world she had yet to conquer.

As she stepped outside, she felt as if she was leaving a part of herself behind. That carefully crafted sketch, a distilled essence of her soul and abilities, now stood among the creations of her peers, waiting to be judged, appreciated, and maybe even celebrated.

With a satisfied grin, she walked away from Wavecrest High School, the morning sun at her back. Regardless of the contest outcome, she knew she had already won something invaluable—the affirmation that her art could touch people, that her creativity had value, and above all, that her journey as an artist was just beginning.

The horizon stretched ahead, an unbroken line where the cerulean sky kissed the shimmering sea, and for a fleeting moment, it felt as if time itself had stopped. Jessica and Ethan drove along the Pacific Coast Highway, the top of the Jeep down, its wheels singing to the rhythm of the road. The wind sculpted their hair into wild halos, and laughter floated between them, light and untethered, like the sea foam whipped up by distant waves.

Ethan's blue eyes were mirrors of the ocean, reflecting a genuine kindness that made the world seem less complicated. "So, have you ever thought about what you're going to miss most about Wavecrest?" he asked, his voice tinged with the kind of curious melancholy that only arises when the present is too beautiful to last.

Jessica looked out at the rolling waves as she pondered his question. Her eyes, deep pools of azure, seemed to capture the very essence of the sea—calm yet ever-changing; beautiful, yet mysterious.

"You mean besides the ocean and late-night walks on the boardwalk?" A pause laced her words, a brief suspension in which she revisited her life spent on these shores, and her mind briefly brushed against the silhouettes of people who made her world complete.

"Yeah," Ethan said, seeing a hint of sadness in Jessica's eyes as she gathered her thoughts.

Jessica took a moment before answering. "My friends. I'm going to miss my friends," her voice softened, "Especially Fawn."

Ethan let out a soft sigh, as if trying to capture the weight of her words in the air between them. "I get it, babe. What you and Fawn have is special. That's the kind of friendship you don't see every day."

The tension of impending goodbyes thickened the air as Jessica ventured further into vulnerability. "You know what I'll miss the most, though?"

Ethan glanced at her, his eyes a quick flicker of curiosity before refocusing on the road ahead. "What?"

Tinged with a sadness that she couldn't quite hide, Jessica met his gaze and whispered, "You."

Hearing those simple words, a pang of heartache resonated through Ethan, echoing the looming departure he had been trying to keep at the edge of his own thoughts. For a moment, the Jeep seemed like a fragile vessel suspended between the past and the future.

Not wanting to spoil the day with a feeling of sorrow still lurking, he offered a gentle smile. "Let's not think about that right now. We've still got a beautiful summer ahead of us."

Hearing Ethan's words, a fleeting warmth washed over her, like a comforting hand laid over her troubled heart. For a second, she allowed herself to bask in that comfort. Her eyes locked with his, as if to freeze this moment, this feeling, into permanence.

But reality, ever the relentless companion, reminded them that some goodbyes were as inevitable as the ocean's tides. Still, she nodded, her lips curving into a wistful smile that bore both gratitude and a trace of sorrow.

"You're right," she said, her voice softer now, imbued with a tenderness that danced between hope and resignation. "We do have the rest of this summer, and it's ours to make the most of."

Her eyes drifted toward the endless horizon, where the sky met the sea in a seamless embrace. In that vast expanse, her thoughts found a quiet sanctuary, and she resolved to cherish the time they had left, however fleeting it might be.

As the minutes unfurled like waves beneath them, a sudden glint of sunlight flashed across the Jeep's cabin, catching the iridescent pearl and obsidian-black stones of Ethan's cross. The luminous moment caught Jessica's attention, pulling her eyes toward the artifact that dangled from its woven yak-hair cord around his neck.

"Every time I see your cross, I still can't get over how beautiful it is," Jessica said, her words laced with genuine admiration as she looked at the treasured artifact around Ethan's neck.

Ethan's hand instinctively reached for the cross, his fingers tracing its intricate patterns. "You know, I have never taken it off since the day my grandfather gave it to me," he said, his voice tinged with a depth of emotion that filled the space between them with a weighty resonance.

Jessica felt a sense of awe swell within her as she absorbed the sanctity of his words. She knew how much his grandfather meant to him, how the cross symbolized an enduring connection that transcended earthly boundaries.

"That makes it even more special," she said, her voice conveying an understanding that went beyond words.

Ethan looked at her, his striking blue eyes meeting hers in a moment of shared understanding. "It reminds me every day that he's still with me. Makes me feel protected... safe," he nodded, his words layered with a mix of vulnerability and strength.

Jessica felt her heart swell at his words. This simple piece of metal and stone held stories and emotions far more complex and significant than its physical form could ever suggest. The cross was more than a treasured heirloom; it was a touchstone that linked past and present, earth and ether, in an endless loop of love and memory. And knowing that Ethan felt its importance so deeply only intensified her own feelings for him.

She tilted her head, curiosity illuminating her eyes. "Do you really believe that? I mean, do you think it has the power to protect you and keep you safe?"

Ethan offered her a wry grin, a gleam of mischief flickering in his eyes. "Well, it seems to be working so far, so who knows?"

The atmosphere in the Jeep lightened, each carrying a blend of their own beliefs and the willingness to ponder life's unanswerable questions. The road unfurled before them like a promise, a strip of possibility cutting through the vast, awe-striking landscape.

They rode in a comfortable silence, a cocoon of shared understanding enveloping them. The sun was still high enough to bathe the Pacific Coast Highway with light, each curve revealing another snapshot of the ocean on one side and rugged cliffs on the other. A tranquil sort of magic imbued the air inside the Jeep, as if time had graciously slowed its relentless march to allow them this pocket of serenity.

Just as Ethan's fingers drummed lightly on the steering wheel, as if chasing an elusive melody, he spotted it. The sign for the Surf Shack—a quaint, sun-bleached shop that stood as a tribute to the culture of the coast—emerged on the horizon like an old friend. His eyes lit up, and a palpable sense of eagerness replaced the reflective calm that had settled between them.

"There it is," he announced, as much to himself as to Jessica, who followed his gaze and smiled, understanding his simple joy. The Surf Shack was more than just a shop to him; it was a haven, a tangible piece of a lifestyle he adored, and a community he belonged to.

Ethan steered the Jeep into the gravel parking lot, each crunch under the tires serving as a prelude to another chapter in their unfolding summer. As he turned off the engine, they shared a loving glance, both acutely aware that even amid the tangles of their anxieties and hopes, moments like these—infused with both the unspeakable weight of impending farewells and the irreplaceable thrill of the present—were what made life profoundly beautiful.

Fawn descended the stairs, her feet softly padding each step. The house felt quieter now, each room seeming to hold its breath, as if aware of the transition that enveloped the family. She made her way to the kitchen, its worn countertops and familiar smells offering a momentary refuge from the whirlwind of change swirling around her life.

Pulling open the refrigerator door, Fawn surveyed the landscape of chilled goods. Her eyes landed on a covered dish—leftover chicken legs from last night's dinner. Perfect. She took it out and removed the plastic wrap, placing the dish in the microwave. As she punched in the time and pressed 'start,' the machine hummed to life, its light casting a gentle glow on her thoughtful face.

The muffled chime of her phone broke the spell. She retrieved it from the pocket of her denim shorts and unlocked the screen. Her eyes widened a fraction. A text message from Jerry Cranmer appeared, reading, "u busy?"

Fawn's fingers hovered over the screen as she pondered her reply, finally typing out, "idk, why?"

A moment later, Jerry's text came through: "u wanna hang out?"

She hesitated. Her thumbs hovered over the screen in a moment of indecision. She'd planned on spending the day with friends, strolling the sunlit boardwalk and soaking up the irreplaceable ambiance of a Wavecrest summer. But something in the pit of her stomach nudged her, an intangible inkling that today should be different. After a pause, she typed, "ok."

Jerry didn't miss a beat. "where u at?" appeared on her screen.

Fawn replied, "my house."

Jerry's last message came quickly, "ok on my way."

The exchange was brief, yet it seemed to carry a weight, like the ripples from a stone dropped in a still pond, subtle but far-reaching.

Fawn set the phone down just as the microwave beeped its completion. She took out the heated dish, the steam rising and filling the air with the comforting aroma of seasoned meat. Fork in hand, she sat down at the kitchen table, her mind a swirl of contemplation.

She bit into the chicken, savoring its flavor, but her thoughts were elsewhere. Was it a good idea to hang out with Jerry? After all, their history was a maze of emotions, fraught with the ghosts of their past mistakes and youthful indiscretions.

Yet, as she sat there, the tender meat falling effortlessly from the bone, Fawn felt a subtle undercurrent of anticipation. Maybe, just maybe, the passing of time had seasoned them both, much like the chicken in front of her—infusing depth, fostering tenderness, and transforming raw potential into something worth savoring.

And so, she waited, her heart beating a cautious rhythm of hope and uncertainty, as the seconds on the kitchen clock ticked closer to whatever awaited her and Jerry in the unfolding hours.

Several minutes passed, each one stretching the fabric of time, making the atmosphere in the kitchen heavy with expectation. Then, the distant rumble of an engine permeated the quietude, followed by the crunch of tires on pavement. Fawn stood up and set her fork down beside a half-eaten chicken leg. Her eyes momentarily caught her own reflection in the glass of the patio door. There was a look of quiet intensity there, tinged with a vulnerability she didn't care to examine too closely.

She walked to the front door, opened it, and stepped out into the embrace of the afternoon sun. In her driveway was Jerry's sports car, a crimson Mustang with a gleaming finish that spoke of meticulous care and perhaps a price tag to match. The car's sleek lines and reflective surface seemed to drink in the glow of the sky, making it look almost like a jewel against the backdrop of an ordinary suburban landscape. She approached it, her sandals tapping on the concrete. Leaning against the driver's side door, Fawn met Jerry's gaze through the rolled-down window.

"Where's your sidekick today?" Jerry inquired, his eyes not quite meeting hers. The question hung in the air, fraught with subtext, and even though he didn't say her name, it was clear he was referring to Jessica. After all, Fawn and Jessica were almost inseparable, a perennial duo in the eyes of their community.

"She's with her boyfriend. They'll be back later," Fawn replied, her voice neither warm nor cold, a neutral territory on the emotional landscape.

"She doesn't like me much, does she?" Jerry asked, the weight of the words anchored in his own guilt.

Fawn looked at him, her eyes a deep well that he found difficult to read. She didn't answer, but her silence spoke volumes. It was as if her silence unfurled a banner that read: "Yes, you're right, and you know why."

Jerry's eyes finally met hers, and in that moment, he felt the full brunt of his past actions settle upon him like a yoke. He'd always liked Jessica—her laughter, her openness, her ability to see the goodness in people. Knowing that he'd instilled a sense of animosity in someone like her was its own kind of indictment. It saddened him, another knot in the gnarled rope of regret that he'd been carrying for far too long.

But it was Fawn's eyes that anchored him to the present moment. They weren't condemning, but they weren't forgiving either. They were the eyes of someone who'd been hurt, yet had found the strength to carry on, to remain open to the complicated choreography of human interaction, with all its missteps and occasional grace. Jerry felt an urge to say something, to break the silence with words of remorse or explanation, but he knew some things were better left unsaid—at least for now.

Jerry's eyes shifted from Fawn to the "Sold" sign posted in the front yard, its bold lettering a harbinger of change, a marker of finality.

"The house is sold, huh?" he asked, his voice carrying a faint note of sadness that sounded surprisingly genuine.

Fawn's eyes rolled almost imperceptibly, a succinct dance of eyelashes that said more than words ever could. She didn't bother to answer, but her silence was its own form of communication, and Jerry seemed to understand that.

"Well, I'm glad you decided to hang out with me today," he said, his tone touched with a sincerity that made Fawn pause. "I was worried you would say no."

"So, what do you have in mind?" Fawn asked, her voice a mixture of curiosity and guarded interest.

Jerry's shoulders rose and fell in a slight shrug. "We could go to the beach, take a walk or something."

Fawn studied his face, looking for some hidden agenda in the lines of his expression, but finding none. Their previous encounters, first reaching a sort of truce at the Graduation Party and then spending an unexpected but surprisingly lighthearted Fourth of July together, made his request seem almost plausible. Maybe a walk on the beach wasn't such a bad idea.

"Okay, let's go," she finally said, and walked to the passenger side of the car.

Jerry leaned across the seat and opened the door for her, a small but deliberate gesture. Fawn slid into the passenger seat, her sandals leaving tiny crescents of sand on the car mat—a subtle reminder of beaches past and, perhaps, those yet to come.

With a loud rev of the engine, Jerry maneuvered the Mustang out of the driveway, its wheels carrying them toward the nearby boardwalk. As the car glided through the sun-dappled streets, the atmosphere inside was thick with a cocktail of emotions—regret, hope, uncertainty—all distilled into the quietude of the afternoon.

Each was aware of the delicate balance they were striving to maintain, a dance of sorts, measured not in steps, but in moments of silence and unspoken understanding. The sun was still high enough in the sky, its light filtering through the trees, painting the world in shifting patterns of light and shadow. A quiet symmetry seemed to fall into place, as if the universe had aligned itself just so for this brief span of time.

As Jerry steered his car onto the route leading to the boardwalk, the journey was almost comically short. Fawn's house was so close that they could have reached the boardwalk quicker on foot, but Jerry seemed to relish the drive, however brief. The low growl of the engine seemed to counterpoint to the otherwise quiet afternoon, as if announcing their approach to an environment that had already vibrated with its own kind of energetic hum.

The car coasted into a parking space with the kind of ease that came from familiarity; this wasn't Jerry's first time navigating the popular locale. He shut off the engine, the car's final purrs dissolving into the cacophony of seaside life beyond its confines. For a moment, they both sat in the car, caught in the liminality between the private space they'd just shared and the bustling world awaiting them.

Jerry glanced over at Fawn, his eyes lingering a little longer than necessary, as if asking for a silent affirmation. Fawn sensed this unspoken question and offered a subtle nod, tacitly approving their collective decision to step out and blend into the tapestry of the boardwalk.

Jerry pushed open his door and quickly walked around the car to open hers—a chival-rous act, or maybe a vestige of old habits. As Fawn stepped out and they made their way toward the thrumming heart of the boardwalk, the car sat gleaming in the afternoon sun, a silent yet powerful symbol of Jerry's bravado and the world they'd left behind.

The couple settled into a cozy corner of an outdoor cafe, its decor awash in sun-bleached hues and nautical trinkets. They ordered fries that arrived in little baskets, accompanied by ketchup and small talk that skirted the edges of intimacy—favorite music, college expec-tations, mutual friends. Their laughter rose like sea foam, buoyant and fleeting, blending into the soundscape of distant waves and the delighted screams of children on rides.

As the last fry disappeared and the conversation meandered, Jerry suggested they take a walk. Fawn agreed. They strolled along the boardwalk, their steps synchronized in a rhythm as natural as the ebb and flow of the ocean beside them. They eventually reached the pier, the carnival of it all—flashing lights, mechanical songs, and the centrifugal force of rides whirling in joyous pandemonium.

"Let's go on the Ferris wheel," Jerry suggested, a twinkle in his eyes that looked almost like nostalgia, or perhaps a renewed sense of daring.

The Ferris wheel before them was a towering circle of light and movement, and some-thing about its cyclical journey toward the sky and back appealed to Fawn. "Alright, let's do it," she nodded.

They climbed into the gondola, and as it began its slow ascent, Jerry looked at Fawn. The afternoon sunlight gilded her profile, illuminating the curve of her lips and the glow of her skin. It was as if they were suspended between heaven and earth, and for that brief moment, Jerry's heart felt the pull of a gravity stronger than that of the spinning wheel beneath them. Almost instinctively, he reached for her hand, his fingers intertwining with hers.

Fawn glanced down, noticing the deliberate yet tender touch. A tiny thrill, like the soft caress of a summer breeze, fluttered through her heart. She didn't pull away; instead, her fingers tightened ever so slightly around his. Unspoken, they both plunged into the well of memory—high school football games, midnight movie marathons, shared dreams, and youthful love. It was as if time had looped back, even if just for the duration of a Ferris wheel ride.

They descended back to earth but lingered on that tenuous threshold between what was and what could have been. The wheel stopped, its mechanical groans a grounding call back to the reality of the wooden planks beneath them. As they stepped out, Fawn felt her heart swell, echoing Jerry's silent revelation. Maybe the flame wasn't as extinguished as they had both believed; after all, embers could sometimes be coaxed back into the fire.

Though neither spoke of it, both sensed that this seemingly ordinary afternoon had pivoted into something else—a reassessment, perhaps, or a fragile rekindling. And as they stepped back onto the pier, the sun dipped a little closer to the horizon, casting a warm, golden light that felt, if not like clarity, then like possibility.

As they strolled along the wooden planks, taking in the kaleidoscope of life unfolding around them, they bumped into a pair of familiar faces. Kevin Conroy and Lisa Warwick, friends from high school, stood by a carnival game, clutching oversized stuffed animals as trophies of their victories. Kevin, an easygoing guy who played on the basketball team, was a towering presence, always quick with a joke. Lisa, petite and vivacious, had been a cheerleader, and possessed a smile that could brighten any room.

"Hi Jerry! Hi Fawn! What brings you guys here?" Kevin greeted them, his eyes twinkling behind his ever-present sunglasses.

"Just taking in the scenery," Jerry replied, gesturing to the sea of people and pulsating rides.

"The rides are in full force. You should hang with us!" Lisa chimed in, holding up her stuffed penguin as if it were a medal of honor.

Jerry and Fawn exchanged a quick glance, reading each other's hesitation like an open book, before nodding in agreement. "Sure. Why not?" Fawn said.

The four of them made their way to the roller coaster, its steel framework coiled like a steel dragon, ready to spring into the sky. As the cars clattered up the first incline, anticipation buzzed in the air. Then, with a heart-stopping plunge, they were off, the ride a blur of speed and gravity-defying loops. Each drop made their stomachs churn, and each twist elicited screams of delight from their throats. The wind howled past them, whipping their hair and clothes as if it, too, were caught up in the wild rush of adrenaline, a fellow traveler on this electrifying journey.

As they disembarked, their faces flushed and spirits high, Jerry suggested one last ride. "How about the merry-go-round? For old times' sake?"

Fawn looked at him, her eyes twinkling with a blend of nostalgia and playful skepticism. "Aren't we a little too old for that?"

Jerry grinned. "Come on, it's just a ride," he replied with a laid-back, almost indifferent tone.

And so, they found themselves mounted on the intricately carved horses on the merry-go-round, a relic from an older, simpler time. The ride began to turn, each rotation set to the tune of an old-fashioned organ grinder. Fawn felt a quiet joy settle over her, like the delicate brushstrokes of a fading sunset. Beside her, Jerry seemed to be in a similar state of reverie, his eyes now softer, less guarded.

As they spun in slow, looping circles, surrounded by the laughter of children and the steady creak of the ride, they briefly escaped from the complexities of young adulthood, returning to the innocence of days gone by. Their eyes met, and in that fleeting glance, they both knew that this afternoon was a small yet meaningful step forward, a delicate mending of emotional threads that were frayed, but not broken.

When the merry-go-round came to a gradual stop, Jerry and Fawn hopped off their wooden steeds. They waved goodbye to Kevin and Lisa, who were off to conquer another game booth, their laughter trailing behind them like a youthful echo.

Stepping off the pier and back onto the boardwalk, Jerry turned to Fawn. "Want to go for a walk on the beach?"

Fawn looked out toward the shore, where the sunlight sparkled like a thousand diamonds on the water's surface, making the ocean seem almost endless. "Sure," she said softly.

They made their way down a wooden stairway that led to the sandy expanse below. Once their feet touched the cool grains, Jerry kicked off his shoes, and Fawn followed suit. They walked side by side, close enough for their hands to brush against each other but not quite touching, each lost in their thoughts yet anchored by the other's presence. The ocean whispered its eternal song, a soundtrack that wove itself around them, as if urging them to speak.

Finally, Jerry broke the silence. "It's weird to think we won't be seeing these sights every day, isn't it?"

Fawn nodded. "Yeah. College is going to be a whole new world."

"Do you ever wonder what that's going to be like? You know, being on your own, meeting new people, starting over again?" Jerry asked, his voice tinged with vulnerability.

Fawn looked at him, her eyes reflecting the afternoon light that shimmered on the water. "I do. It's exciting and scary at the same time. It's like standing on the edge of a diving board and looking into a pool you've never swum in before."

Jerry chuckled. "That's a pretty good metaphor." He paused, a knowing smile spreading across his face. "That definitely sounds like Mr. Titus talking," he added, referring to their English teacher, who was known for his penchant for weaving life lessons into literary discussions.

"Well, didn't he tell us that life is a collection of metaphors and that we should use them to help us make sense of things?" Fawn said with a playful tilt of her head, her tone carrying a hint of the lessons they'd picked up from their teacher.

Jerry took a moment, as if letting the resonance of Fawn's words sink in. "Yeah, he did," he answered, his tone thoughtful. "So, how does today make you feel? Being here by the ocean, just you and me?"

Fawn looked out to the horizon, her gaze distant, yet focused. "Today feels like reading a chapter from a book you almost forgot, but realize you still love. It's comforting, even nostalgic, but it also makes me wonder how the story would have been read had it turned out differently."

Jerry felt his heart tighten. He was about to say something, perhaps to add another line to their dialogue of metaphors and memories, when Fawn suddenly stopped walking. She picked up a small, smooth stone and hurled it into the ocean. It skipped twice before sinking into the watery abyss.

"Sometimes, it's better to just let go," she said, her voice tinged with a kind of melancholy wisdom that seemed beyond her years. "Forget about that book and go to the next one."

Jerry nodded, feeling the weight of her words settle in the quiet space between them. They resumed their walk, the ocean continuing its ageless murmur, the sky maintaining its clear afternoon hue. Whatever lay ahead in the unwritten chapters of their lives, at least this page had been a meaningful one.

As they continued their walk along the shoreline, Jerry's eyes fell upon a row of rocks near the water's edge. "How about we sit for a while?" he suggested, his voice tinged with a subtle yearning for stillness, for a pause in the relentless flow of time.

Fawn looked where he was pointing and nodded, her heart acknowledging that some conversations were best had in the sanctuary of seclusion. Together, they veered off their path, walking toward the rocks that stood like sentinels between land and sea.

The rock they chose was worn smooth by the ocean's relentless caresses, a quiet testament to time and tide. They sat side by side, their eyes drawn to the undulating expanse of the Pacific, as if seeking answers in its depths. The sounds of laughter and muffled conversation from the boardwalk behind them seemed miles away.

After a contemplative pause, Jerry spoke, his voice barely above a whisper. "Fawn, I've told you once, and I'll tell you again. I regret what happened between us. I was stupid and immature, and I hurt you. For that, I am truly sorry."

Fawn turned to look at him. His eyes conveyed a sincerity she had not seen in a long time. "I know you're sorry, Jerry," she said softly. "And part of me wishes things could have turned out differently for us."

The air between them was charged with a past that felt both immediate and distant. Jerry broke the silence. "I still love you, Fawn. I don't think I'll ever stop loving you."

Fawn felt a swell of emotion rise within her, filling spaces that had felt empty for an eternity. She wanted to reciprocate his confession, to bridge the emotional divide that choices and circumstances had placed between them. Yet, she hesitated.

The reality of their diverging paths hung in the air, almost palpable. She was leaving Wavecrest, a place that would soon no longer be her home, while he was bound for Pasadena, chasing dreams that didn't include her. Despite the intensity of the moment, she understood that their worlds were pulling them in different directions—directions that made the possibility of "us" increasingly fleeting.

"Jerry," she began, choosing her words carefully. "I'm touched by what you said. Really, I am. But you know as well as I do that we're standing at a crossroads, and our paths are leading us away from each other."

Their eyes met, and for a moment, a wistful sadness flickered between them, each acknowledging the bitter truth in her words. But as they sat there on that rock, staring out at an ocean that stretched far beyond the limits of their vision, there was a shared understanding that the love they had—complicated, lost, but not forgotten—was a chapter in a book that neither would ever truly close.

Summoning the courage that seemed to have eluded him in recent times, Jerry felt a surge of emotion well up within him. It was as if a secret part of his heart had flicked open a latch, allowing a stream of feelings to flow freely. His eyes searched Fawn's, looking for permission, a sign, some unspoken agreement. Sensing an indefinable yet magnetic pull, he leaned in, his lips drawing closer to hers with an ache of both trepidation and desire.

Their kiss was a soft collision of past and present, a mingling of air and intent that seemed to reverberate through layers of emotion. In that moment, there was a sense of reverie, as if they had stepped into a forgotten photograph. Jerry looked into Fawn's eyes, seeing in their depths the reflection of youthful smiles and lingering promises.

Feeling brave, his words almost a whisper, he asked, "Would you go to the Summer Dance with me?"

The question hung in the air, full of implications and memories. Fawn felt a pang of conflict, a tension between old love and new commitments. "I can't. I already promised Felix that I would go with him," she replied, her voice tinged with regret but firm in its resolution.

Jerry's face registered shock, a ripple in his previously serene expression. "Felix Copeland? You're going to the dance with a nerd?"

His words, spoken casually, struck Fawn like a slap. Her eyes narrowed, and a storm seemed to gather behind her gaze.

"Don't you dare call him a nerd!" she spat out, the words tinged with betrayal. "For a moment, I thought you had changed, matured! But it's clear you're still the same high school jerk, ignorant and cruel!"

Her voice quivered with righteous indignation as she added, "His mother died when he was just twelve, and he's been taking care of his sick, abusive father ever since! And through all this hardship, all you and your friends ever did was bully him!"

Jerry looked as if he'd been gut-punched, the weight of his ignorance settling over him like a shroud. "I... I didn't know. I'm sorry, Fawn," he stammered, but his apology was a hollow echo in the air, too late and far too inadequate.

Fawn shook her head, her face a portrait of disappointment and anger. "I don't want to hear your apologies! You should be ashamed of yourself! You and your stupid friends!" She paused, catching her breath as if each word had stolen a bit of her air.

With one last look that seemed to sever the threads of their tangled past and uncertain future, she said, "I think it's time for you to go, Jerry! I don't want to see you anymore!"

Jerry tried to speak, to salvage the ruins of the moment, but Fawn had already turned her back on him. She walked away, her steps a punctuation to their bittersweet reunion. With a heavy heart, he watched her leave, a confluence of regret and sorrow clouding his thoughts as he made his way back to his car.

As Fawn distanced herself, a storm of emotions swirled within her. She felt foolish for even entertaining the notion that Jerry had matured, that he had outgrown the callous indifference of their high school days. His derogatory comment about Felix had shattered that illusion, rekindling old resentments. At that moment, she was angry—not just at him, but at herself for letting her guard down, for letting her heart be swayed by the nostalgia of what was and what could've been.

As Jerry walked back to his crimson sports car, a cauldron of emotions boiled within him—anger, regret, sorrow. Each step seemed to echo in the empty space Fawn had left behind. In a rare moment of raw vulnerability, he kicked an empty soda can, sending it skittering across the asphalt, as if trying to cast away his mistakes. He reached his car but didn't immediately get in, his hand hovering over the door handle. Finally, he slid into the leather seat, but the car's luxury offered no comfort.

He turned the key, the purr of the engine a jarring contrast to his inner turmoil. As he navigated the streets that led him away from Fawn, away from a second chance he had so carelessly squandered, the silence in the car felt oppressive, almost accusatory. The realization that he had just undone whatever fragile progress they had made, clung to him like an anchor, pulling him deeper into a churning sea of regret.

# Chapter 32

----------------------------------------------------------------

For the next five days, Wavecrest pulsated with the fleeting magic of summer. Sunsets melted into the horizon, painting the sky with fleeting shades of orange and pink, while mornings greeted the seaside town with a golden promise. Waves danced with the shore, tracing the boundaries of an ever-changing canvas, each tide embodying the shifting dynamics of life.

During those five days, Jessica and Ethan dedicated their time to exploring the Pacific coast, tracing new latitudes of experience as they delved into the quaint hamlets that dotted the water's edge. Whether it was meandering along cliffside trails or feasting on local delicacies, Jessica found herself enamored not only with the unfolding landscapes, but also with the adventurous spirit that guided her. Ethan's love of uncharted territory resonated with her, and each discovery they made together added depth to their deepening romance.

While Jessica and Ethan charted new terrains, painting horizons with shades of their evolving love, Fawn longed for the comfort of the familiar. With steadfast friends, Michelle and Krista by her side, she navigated the sun-drenched beaches and the bustling boardwalk that had been the backdrop to many a shared story. These havens of nostalgia became pockets of time, where the looming shadow of the future felt momentarily eclipsed.

Amid the laughter and chatter, between the tactile intimacy of sand and beach towels, she reclaimed fragments of her shifting summer, finding snippets of her old self. It was as if the world itself conspired to remind her: Despite life's relentless march forward, some things—friendship and treasured surroundings—remained unyielding.

As dusk settled over Wavecrest, a sacred interval unfolded for Jessica and Fawn—a celestial alignment in their separate lives. With the sweetness of Ethan's parting kiss still imprinted on her lips, Jessica returned to her sanctuary of enduring friendship. Their sisterly hearts reunited in the intimate quietude of the evening, beginning first with a visit to Fawn's house—a place tinged with the heavy resonance of bittersweet memories and shared laughter. As if sensing their complicated emotions, the walls of Fawn's family home stood in silent witness, framing the parents who had also become Jessica's second guardians, yet veiling the discord that tinged their interactions.

Once goodbyes were exchanged and old ties momentarily rekindled, Fawn retreated to Jessica's home. Whether it was the evocative glow of a cherished movie on the screen or the enveloping warmth of a late-night, summer stroll, they found solace in the constancy of each other's company, each night deepening the imprint of their shared history.

As the five days and nights unfurled, each navigated their individual paths while still finding moments of unity—experiences that etched intricate patterns onto the canvas of their last carefree summer. And as the sixth dawn prepared to break, both sensed that the canvas of their lives was about to receive another defining touch.

The late morning light filtered through the curtains of Jessica's kitchen, where the faint scent of brewed coffee and fresh pastries mingled to create a cozy atmosphere. Teresa, off from work on this quiet Tuesday, moved with a grace that only a mother's presence could bring to the familiar space. The clinking of ceramics and the humming of the refrigerator provided a serene backdrop to the comfortable silence.

Jessica, her bright blue eyes reflecting a hint of melancholy, pushed around the fruit on her plate. Her thoughts were on Ethan, who was spending the day working in Malibu. His absence intensified her sadness and made the prospect of not being with him even more poignant. Still, a smile played on her lips, tinged with the anticipation of unfettered hours ahead with Fawn.

In the living room, Fawn stretched out on the sofa, her blonde hair catching the sun in a golden cascade.

"So, Jess," she called out, her voice the spark that started the day, "what do you want to do today?"

Teresa watched as her daughter perked up at the sound of her best friend's voice. Jessica's usual reticence gave way to a gentle enthusiasm. "I don't know," she replied thoughtfully, then brightened. "We could go to the beach if you want."

"Then it's settled!" Fawn declared, leaping up. "A beach day it is! Just like old times, right?"

The decision to embrace the day with the same carefree spirit that had characterized their teenage years was unanimous.

Teresa, leaning against the doorway, her eyes alight with maternal warmth, watched the girls chatter about plans for sunbathing and frolicking. Her heart swelled; these were the moments she cherished, the timeless snapshots of her daughter and Fawn entwined in the purest form of friendship.

In Jessica's bedroom, the two girls sifted through drawers and closets, collecting their beach essentials. Sunscreen, towels, and sunglasses found their way into a cheerful tote bag, each item a promise of the day's light-hearted escapades. The Summer Dance was only four days away, its anticipation hanging in the air like a melody yet to be danced to, sweet and thrilling. But today, they reserved their time for the timeless allure of the shore—the laughter, the splash of waves, and a joyous interlude before the silhouette of adulthood took shape on the horizon of their lives.

The warmth of the sun wrapped them in its embrace as they stepped outside. The familiar path to the beach awaited, as did the cool caress of the ocean. There, with the horizon stretching wide before them, they would shed the weight of impending goodbyes and the mystery of an unwritten future. For now, they were just Jessica and Fawn—inseparable, with the golden sand beneath their feet and the boundless sky above.

As they walked along the boardwalk, the world seemed to blossom with the vigor of youth and summer's touch. Stalls fluttered open like petals to the sun, each offering an array of vibrant beachwear and sweet treats. The scent of salt and sunscreen mingled in the air, a signature perfume of carefree days. Teenagers and young adults eager to claim their piece of summer brought the boardwalk to life, with laughter and chatter filling the air.

The Pacific lay before them, a vast canvas painted in the deepest blues. Its waves rolled in with a rhythm that beckoned one to join in their dance, to become part of the ocean's timeless song.

"Look at that, Jess," Fawn said, nodding toward the horizon. "It's like the ocean's putting on a show just for us."

Jessica smiled, her eyes reflecting the sparkle of the water. "Every time I see it, it's like the first time. It never gets old."

Fawn's lips curled into an affectionate smile as she heard Jessica's excitement. She looked at her friend, recognizing in her eyes the enduring sparkle of the little girls they once were, a timeless reflection of childlike wonder. That pure, unadulterated joy, that innocence that the beach always evoked in Jessica resonated in Fawn, warming her heart like the morning sun.

As they continued their search for the perfect spot, Fawn pointed to an inviting space on the beach. "There, that's the spot. It's got our names written all over it."

They walked down the ramp to the beach, the sand warm and yielding beneath their feet. The girls laid out their blankets, creating a temporary haven amidst the sprawling beach. They pulled chilled bottles of lemonade from their bag, the condensation beading on the glass a testament to the day's warmth.

"Here's to right now, because it doesn't get much better than this," Jessica lifted her bottle with a grin.

Fawn's bottle met Jessica's with a casual clink. "And to beach days with my bestie — a memory we'll carry with us forever."

As they settled onto their blankets, the world seemed to take a breath—a sunlit respite where only the rhythm of the waves kept time. Wrapped in the enduring comfort of their lifelong bond, they lay side by side, kindred spirits under the vast Californian sky.

Time, with its relentless march, seemed to slow, granting Jessica and Fawn an afternoon draped in golden sunbeams and punctuated by the laughter of waves. As the sun made its arc across the sky, its rays unfurling like gentle fingers on their skin, the heat became a playful nudge, urging them toward the ocean's cool embrace.

With the spontaneity that only true friendship can inspire, they dashed toward the water, their footsteps leaving fleeting marks on the wet sand. In they went, the sea welcoming them with its brisk, refreshing touch. Around them, the water was alive with the joyous cacophony of summer shouts and splashes as others took to the waves.

Jessica and Fawn, their spirits untethered, joined a group of kids tossing a beach ball back and forth, its colors a blur against the bright blue of the Pacific. They played with the abandon of youth, strangers yet comrades in this shared euphoria. The ocean around them seemed to laugh, partaking in their carefree revelry.

When their play finally waned, and their new friends became pleasant memories destined to fade, Jessica and Fawn reclaimed their spot on the beach. They wrapped themselves in towels, their skin still tingling from the brisk touch of the waves. Sitting side by side, they watched the world from their vantage point, a world that seemed to consist of broad smiles and the effortless sprawl of a day free from the pull of tomorrow.

Gradually, their laughter faded as they settled back into the familiar rhythm of shared silence, easy and comforting. There, they chatted idly, their conversations ebbing and flowing with the tide, punctuated by sips of cool drinks that beaded with condensation in the warmth. And for a while, they were content to be observers, to let the world spin on while they remained still, a pair of constants in the ever-changing tapestry of Wavecrest.

As the afternoon sun draped the beach in a warm embrace, Jessica and Fawn lounged on their blankets, the salt air mingling with the intermittent laughter and music that bubbled from nearby beachgoers. A familiar tension interrupted their tranquility when a group of five appeared on the horizon. Their silhouettes were sharp against the bright sky, their strides confident and purposeful, a signature walk recognized by any Wavecrest native. It was the group from Coral Heights High School, rivals known for their athletic prowess and the competitive spark that flared whenever the two schools met.

Fawn's curiosity rose with the tide, her sunglasses sliding down the bridge of her nose as she spotted the approaching figures.

"Isn't that Rex Thompson?" she asked, her voice cutting through the quiet sounds of the beach with a hint of surprise. He was Coral Heights' star quarterback, his athletic build unmistakable even from a distance.

Following Fawn's gaze, Jessica squinted behind her shades. The group drew closer, the swagger in Rex's gait confirming his identity as the other figures fell into the supporting roles beside him. The distance between them closed with each purposeful step they took across the sand.

"It sure is," Jessica replied, her voice steady and composed. "And that's definitely Tasha Williams with him." Memories of their final volleyball game flooded back when Tasha had risen like a tidal wave, her arm swinging in a merciless arc to deliver the winning spike that shattered Wavecrest's proud run of victories.

"I wonder what they're doing here?" Fawn's musing carried a note of intrigue as she watched the group navigate through the throng of beach dwellers.

As the group from Coral Heights approached, their presence carried the echoes of past games and the vibrant spirit of school pride. Tasha walked with the grace of an athlete, her rich brown skin glowing in the sunlight, her curls framing her face in a sunlit halo. The confidence in her stride was hard-earned and worn with an ease that spoke of many victories, her laughter rich and sure, a sound that knew the sweetness of triumph.

Beside her, Rex exuded an infectious charm, his broad shoulders relaxed and his step light. His skin, a deep, warm brown, seemed to gleam against the brightness of the beach, and when he laughed, the sound seemed to ripple through the air, drawing grins from even the staunchest Wavecrest supporters.

Close behind them, Carlos Rodriguez's laughter sailed through the air, much like the baseballs he sent flying as a hard hitter for his team. His lean frame doubled over with the infectious joy of his own humor, an ease in his demeanor that marked him as a player of note. His charm wasn't just bold—it was irresistible, causing everyone in its presence to smile without even realizing it.

Sophia Martinez, affectionately known as Sophie to the raucous supporters in the stands, matched Carlos's stride with an energy as vivacious as the seaside town they called home. Her hair captured the golden glow of the midday sun, each strand shimmering in a burnished cascade, a visual foil to her reputation on the volleyball court. There, her skills made her a fierce competitor, spiking balls with a force that struck a blend of fear and admiration into the hearts of her opponents.

Bringing up the rear, Eddie Kim's figure stood out as an island of calm within the boisterous group. His movements were measured, betraying his role as a natural observer, in contrast to his presence on the soccer field, where he was known for his quick reflexes and strategic play for Coral Heights. Yet, despite his composed demeanor, the subtle twitch of his lips hinted at a jest lingering at the edge of his thoughts, an insight shared in hushed tones among close friends who knew the wit and humor beneath his serene surface.

The rivalry between Wavecrest and Coral Heights was not merely a contest of sports. It was an intricate dance of camaraderie and competition, where every serve and touchdown was a thread in the rich tapestry of their collective high school memories. The rivalry brought out the best in them, pushed them to exceed their limits, and forged friendships in the crucible of shared passion for the game.

Yet, as Fawn and Jessica watched them approach, the rivalry seemed to shrink beneath the understanding that life was nudging them all toward new paths—different colleges, careers, and experiences. In that midafternoon light, as past and future merged, the figures walking toward them were not just competitors but kindred spirits marking the end of an era.

The salty breeze tugged at the edges of a fleeting tension as Rex led the group, his steps stopping at the edge of Jessica and Fawn's blankets.

"Well, well, well. Look who we have here. It's the Dynamic Duo of Wavecrest," he announced with a flourish that was Rex all over—a pinch of sarcasm and a wide, disarming grin.

Fawn's reply was immediate, her tone pitched perfectly to match Rex's playful jab. "Shut up, Rex!" Her words, though sharp, were betrayed by the mischievous twinkle in her eyes, revealing the mock severity of their long-standing banter.

Unable to suppress the curve of a smile, Jessica chimed in, her voice rising in playful defiance. "Yeah, why are you even here? Did they finally kick you out of Coral Heights?" The words hung in the air, a shared joke that was woven through their past confrontations and victories, binding them together in a reluctant friendship.

The response from the Coral Heights contingent was a symphony of chuckles, the sound a warm echo under the broad sky. Tasha's laughter was clear, rising above the rest, her amusement in the mock battle evident as she observed the byplay between her boyfriend and the girls.

Rex's laughter was an open challenge as he leaned into the tease. "No, baby," he flirted openly, a rascal's charm about him, as his eyes brazenly admired their shapely forms. "I'm here enjoying the beautiful scenery," he drawled, his voice taking on a half jest, half velvet hue. "And I love what I'm seeing."

The laughter that erupted from Jessica and Fawn was a release, an acknowledgment of the absurdity and the affection wrapped up in their rivalry. Tasha, feigning disapproval, shot Rex a look that was as much a part of their dance as the teasing itself.

Fawn rolled her eyes playfully as she called out Rex's audacity. "You do realize that your girlfriend is standing next to you, right?" Her voice was a mixture of mock annoyance and genuine amusement.

Rex's feigned shock was met with Tasha's smirking retaliation, and the group erupted into laughter.

With a grin that could outshine the sun, Jessica nudged the subject. "Tash?" she asked, her voice laced with humor. "Why do you put up with him? You deserve so much better."

Tasha's smile was a crescent of contentment as she shrugged, her reply warm with affection and seasoned with a touch of resignation. "Nah, I'm used to him making an ass of himself, so it's cool."

The shared chuckle that followed Tasha's quip was a harmonic conclusion to their brief, verbal skirmish. It was a moment suspended between rivalry and respect, a shared history that would linger long after their school days were but a whisper of waves against the shore.

As if driven by an unspoken agreement, the Coral Heights group unfurled their towels and claimed their seats around Jessica and Fawn. The ease with which they settled, a tangle of limbs and laughter, marked the end of an era—a truce formed in the sands that had once been a battlefield.

Carlos, spreading his towel with a flourish, looked over at the Wavecrest pair. "You know, I'm going to miss this—the games, the heat of the competition," he said, a reflective note in his voice.

Sophia, never one to shy away from the heart of things, turned her attention to Jessica and Fawn. "You guys still salty about the last game?" Her voice was teasing, but her eyes were soft, understanding the weight of that final spike.

Jessica exchanged a glance with Fawn before answering, the sting of the loss now just a memory. "It was a good game," she admitted, and there was honesty in her tone, a sportsman's respect. "You guys won it fair and square." It was a concession, a white flag raised not in surrender but in recognition of a worthy opponent.

Tasha leaned back on her elbows, the sun casting a glow on her face that matched her warm smile. "You two were tough out there," she told Jessica and Fawn. "I always had fun playing against you. Made the wins sweeter... and the losses... well, they made us work harder."

Eddie, who had been quietly listening, chimed in with a gentle laugh. "And those wins were rare, thanks to you two," he nodded toward Jessica and Fawn. "You guys kept them on their toes."

As he idly traced patterns in the sand with his finger, Rex paused to look at the group. "You know, maybe it's the sun talking or us not having to wear our colors anymore," he gestured between his Coral Heights shirt and the Wavecrest hues that Jessica and Fawn represented, "but I think we pushed each other to be better. All of us."

The group fell into a contemplative silence, the sound of the waves a gentle backdrop to their thoughts. They were warriors on the court and the field, now laying down their school colors to admit something greater had been forged in the heat of those competitions—respect, camaraderie, and perhaps the faint outlines of friendship.

Sophia nudged Jessica playfully. "Besides, you have to admit, it makes for a pretty good story, right? The whole 'rivals turned pals' thing?"

Jessica grinned, the breeze catching strands of her hair as she gazed at the horizon.

"Yeah," she agreed, her voice carrying the weight of memories and the ease of newfound connections. "It does make for a pretty good story."

As the late afternoon sun began to dip toward the horizon, the Coral Heights group started to pack up their things. Towels were folded, sandals were slipped on, and the idle chatter of departure swirled around Jessica and Fawn.

Fawn watched them, the corners of her mouth lifting into a smile. "Are you guys going to the dance Saturday night?" she asked, her voice carrying the lightness of casual conversation, but her eyes reflecting a deeper desire to hold on to the camaraderie for a little longer.

With that ever-present twinkle in his eye, Rex directed a flirtatious smile at her. "I'll go if you promise to dance with me," he teased, his tone light, hopeful.

A playful giggle escaped Fawn, her cheeks warmed by the sun and his attention. "I already have a date for the Summer Dance," she informed him, the light in her eyes softening the blow of rejection.

Rex's expression shifted to mock desolation; a hand pressed to his heart as he turned to Jessica. "How about you, bright eyes? Will you dance with me if I go?" he asked, the playful lilt in his voice underscored by genuine fondness.

Jessica's laugh was light, her cheeks tinged with a blush. "I would, but I have a boyfriend now," she admitted, her eyes twinkling with the humor of the moment.

"Damn!" Rex exclaimed dramatically, eliciting laughter from the group. His antics were a balm to the bittersweet mood.

Ever the anchor to Rex's buoyant demeanor, Tasha latched onto his arm with feigned exasperation. "Let's go before you make a complete fool of yourself!" she chided, her eyes dancing with mirth.

Eye rolls cascaded through the group, accompanied by the warmth of laughter, as goodbyes came. They each stood, the air between them thick with the unspoken recognition of their shared history and the bittersweet finality of this parting.

With a nod of respect, Carlos was the first to break the silence. "Good luck out there, you two. Life's the real game now."

Jessica nodded, her voice steady but warm. "I'm sure you'll knock it out of the park. You always do."

Sophia's smile was genuine as she echoed the sentiment. "Keep playing hard, okay? And hey, maybe we'll all end up on the same team someday in the real world."

Eddie added with a sincerity that was his trademark, "Thanks for the memories. It was fun watching you girls rule the court."

And Tasha, with a softness in her eyes, conveyed her farewell with a tender strength. "It's been an honor on the court and a pleasure off it. Stay amazing, girls."

As the Coral Heights group walked away, their figures blurred into the canvas of the departing day, leaving a trail of footprints that the tide would soon wash away. Jessica and

Fawn remained, their hearts full of echoes of laughter and the silent promise of a memory that would last long after summer's end.

As the golden hour of the day brushed the sky with a warm palette, its warmth lingered, enveloping the girls in a familiar embrace. The laughter and playful banter with the Coral Heights group had rekindled a spark of youth, a flicker of the days when time seemed as endless as the horizon stretching before them. Gathering their belongings, they shook the sand from their blankets, the grains glittering like tiny jewels in the fading light.

The scent of salt and sand clung to them, a natural perfume that spoke of hours spent in the realm of waves and laughter. With each step they took away from the shoreline, their shadows stretched long on the wooden planks of the boardwalk, like silent, elongated companions joining their retreat.

The promise of Teresa's home-cooked meal seemed to waft across the briny breeze, teasing their senses and hastening their pace. With a playful nudge, Fawn voiced their shared anticipation. "I can almost taste that lasagna from here," she said, her voice carrying the lightness of their spirits.

Jessica laughed, the sound mingling with the soft clatter of the boardwalk underfoot. "Mom's lasagna has that sort of power, doesn't it? Draws you in from miles away."

As they walked, the sun, still high and defiant against the approach of evening, bathed them in its amber light. Its rays were like the final notes of a song, holding on until the very end, reluctant to fade away. Their former rivals' laughter and footsteps had disappeared, but the harmony of their shared histories played on.

"Perfect day," Fawn mused aloud, her voice low but contented.

"The best kind of perfect," Jessica agreed, her heart full. There was a hint of change in the air, a subtle shift as the days of July dwindled, but for now, the embrace of summer was all that mattered.

With the lingering light as their guide, they walked on, their shadows stretching on the boardwalk, two friends moving toward the promise of home-cooked comfort and the tender familiarity of family. The echoes of their carefree laughter mingled with the whispers of the sea, a testament to the day that would soon fold into the treasure chest of their shared past.

With one last glance over their shoulders, Jessica and Fawn bid the beach adieu, stepping over the threshold from the sun-kissed shores of youth into the beckoning warmth of home.

Under the tender gaze of the moon, Jessica and Fawn's evening had unfurled like a wave receding into the sea. They had walked from Fawn's house, where farewells hung heavy in the air, back to Jessica's doorstep, the edge of their shared childhood world. The ocean breeze, a whisper of the day's heat, wrapped around them, a gentle reminder of Wavecrest's nocturnal beauty.

They settled onto Jessica's front step, a stoop worn with the imprints of sun-soaked days and secrets exchanged under the stars. Now a dim constellation of lights and laughter, the boardwalk seemed to sway to the rhythm of the ocean.

A chime broke the calm, a text message from Ethan—a beacon flashing briefly in the night. Jessica's face, illuminated by the glow of her phone, was a canvas of pure joy.

"That was my honey. They're back, but he's beat and going to bed," she shared, her voice a soft melody.

Fawn's response was a nod, as steady and sure as the tide. "Yeah, I bet he is. That's okay, though. You'll see him tomorrow, right?" Her voice carried the weight of understanding, the tacit support that had always woven through their friendship.

"Uh-huh," came Jessica's dreamy confirmation, her mind already wading into the sweet anticipation of a lover's embrace.

Fawn's smile was a silent ode to the love that had blossomed in her best friend's heart, tender and true. But before their reverie could stretch further, the night presented a new intrigue.

A car approached, unfamiliar and sleek, against the backdrop of their small-town tableau. It drove up with a precision that spoke of intent, its headlights a brief glare in the serenity of their vigil. Who could it be at this late hour?

As the passenger door creaked open, Heather Marino stepped out, her presence as striking as a shooting star against the velvet night. Her confident stride spoke of countless such entrances, yet the arrival was a mystery wrapped in the car that the girls did not recognize.

Jessica and Fawn squinted into the darkness, trying to sketch the unknown figure in the car into familiarity. But he remained just beyond the touch of their sight—a man, a shape, a possibility.

As Heather approached, surprise and joy danced in their eyes at their friend's unexpected visit. "Hey, Heather," Fawn greeted with the warmth of long-shared summers. "What brings you here tonight?"

Heather's answer sparked the still night. "New York City, ladies!" Her voice held the tremor of dreams on the cusp of reality.

Jessica stood up, the air around her quickening with shared excitement. "You mean you got the job?" she asked, the words a bridge to their friend's new world.

Side by side, Fawn and Jessica approached Heather, their trio momentarily reunited.

Heather's nod, as vibrant as her smile, announced her new beginning. "Sure did. I'm going to be modeling for some big designers next week. Can you believe it? New York City, here I come!"

"Next week?" The quickening of Fawn's heartbeat was evident in her voice, reflecting the rapid pace of change. "When are you leaving?"

"Tonight," Heather declared, the gleam in her eyes outshining the distant stars. Her gesture toward the waiting car tied the news to the reality of departure. "My friend is driving me to the airport. I wanted to stop by to let you guys know and to say goodbye."

The joy of Heather's success swirled with the sudden pang of imminent farewell, a mixture of bittersweet as the night air itself. Fawn's voice, colored with the hues of dusk and the impending loss, carried her sentiment. "Wow, Heather... congratulations. We're really happy for you."

Jessica's silence was a pool reflecting the depth of their childhood bonds. Heather's impending absence loomed large, a ghostly presence at the upcoming Summer Dance, a tradition as familiar as the boardwalk's timeworn planks.

"I guess that means you won't be going to the dance Saturday night," Jessica murmured, the weight of tradition resting on her words. The realization that one of the stars in their constellation would be missing felt as vast and empty as the ocean at night.

Heather's enthusiasm never wavered, a beacon of her bright future. "No, I won't be there, but don't let that stop you guys from having a good time. Michelle and Kris will still be here."

In the silence that followed, their world felt smaller and infinitely expansive, each girl standing on the threshold of tomorrow, their paths illuminated by the shifting sands of destiny.

Fawn's voice weaved a bittersweet sentiment through the evening air, "It's not going to be the same without you."

Jessica, her heart brimming with memories, nodded, her emotions spilling over as a single tear escaped her eye. "Who's going to keep us laughing and entertained all night?" Her voice barely rose above a whisper.

In the softness of the moment, Heather's presence was both comforting and a reminder of the imminent void. She reached out, her hands a gentle anchor, connecting the three of them.

"Hey girls, don't be sad," she soothed, squeezing their hands. "We'll keep in touch, and who knows, maybe I'll make it back for a visit one day."

Jessica and Fawn tried to let Heather's words of encouragement seep into the crevices of their unsettled hearts, but the weight of reality was a stubborn presence. Fawn's days in Wavecrest were numbered by the looming college calendar, a countdown to when she would surrender her keys to a place that would no longer be hers to call home. Jessica, with her own departure to Texas on the horizon, faced the possible sale of her childhood home, a place that one day may be a memory rather than a destination. The sense of permanence they once felt in Wavecrest was slipping through their fingers like the last grains in an hourglass.

And Heather, with the fire of success and adventure in her eyes, was unlikely to look back, her path diverging sharply from theirs. The trio understood, perhaps without needing to articulate, that farewells were often silent promises of change—unspoken acknowledgments that the thread connecting them now would likely unravel with time and distance.

Jessica's voice was a murmur, a soft undercurrent to the evening's melancholy. "I'm going to miss you, Heather," she admitted, her eyes shimmering pools in the twilight.

Fawn's admission came as a tremor in the night, her own tears not far behind. "Yeah, me too," she echoed.

Heather's reply carried the weight of their shared history, tinged with the inevitable march of time. "I'm going to miss you guys, too. It's been a good ride, hasn't it?" She attempted to lift the mood, a beacon cutting through the fog of sadness.

Fawn's answer was a tapestry of past laughter and adventure, her tone rich with the tones of yesteryear. "It sure was," she agreed, her words painting the essence of their shared childhood. "You made growing up here fun and exciting. We had some amazing times together, didn't we?"

Heather nodded, filling the silence that followed with the resonance of their collective nostalgia, her own heart filled with echoes of the past. With an affectionate gaze, she affirmed softly, "We sure did."

As the moment stretched between them, each lost in their reflections, the night wrapped itself around them like a familiar blanket, its warm embrace acknowledging the end of an era and the dawn of new beginnings.

Jessica's eyes lingered on Heather with the tender reverence one might reserve for a childhood hero, her words spilling out like the contents of a long-held secret. "You know, I've always looked up to you, Heather. For as long as I've known you, I've always wanted to be like you. Bold and adventurous, not caring what people think or say. I always admired that about you."

The raw honesty in Jessica's confession reached Heather in a place she had kept hidden, a place where the light of admiration rarely shone. Heather's eyes, once bright with the thrill of a new beginning, were now dimmed with the gravity of reflection.

"Really?" she asked, a trace of disbelief painting her voice. "You wanted to be like me?"

Jessica offered only a nod, the weight of her confession hanging between them.

Heather seemed to shrink inward in the silence that followed, her outward excitement fading into a vulnerable confession.

"Trust me, Jessica. You don't want to be like me," she said, her voice trembling. "I've done some things I'm not proud of, and I wouldn't wish that on anyone... especially you and Fawn."

The revelation was in stark contrast to the image of Heather that Jessica and Fawn had envisioned. A silence heavy with unasked questions stretched out before them.

"There are things about me you don't know," she continued, her confession painting her excitement with shades of gray. "Things I hope you never find out. Wavecrest hasn't been as kind to me as it's been to you."

Jessica and Fawn received Heather's words like unexpected waves, leaving them adrift in a sea of sudden doubt about the place they had all called home.

Fawn replied with heartfelt sincerity, as if wrapping Heather in a comforting shawl, "I'm so sorry, Heather. We didn't know."

Heather's eyes, now pools of bittersweet memories, acknowledged their sentiment. "I know. It's okay." And just as quickly as the shadow had passed over her, her spirit seemed to lift again, her eyes reigniting with the fiery passion of her impending journey. "But hey, it's New York City, and here I come!" she declared, her enthusiasm a phoenix rising from ashes.

In a spontaneous gesture, Heather opened her arms and, with a step, bridged the space between them. She wrapped Fawn and Jessica in a hug that was both a goodbye and a thank you.

"You girls rock, and I'll never forget you," she said. The sincerity of her words was obvious.

After they parted from the hug, Jessica and Fawn watched in silence as Heather walked back to the car that heralded the start of her new journey. She paused at the door, her look a silent dialogue of appreciation and hope.

"Think of me sometimes, will you?" she implored, the undercurrent of vulnerability unmistakable.

As Heather disappeared into the car and the door closed with a definitive thud, the vehicle rolled away, taking a piece of the summer night with it. Jessica and Fawn stood there, their silence a vessel for the complexity of emotions swirling within them. They watched until the taillights faded into the darkness, and when there was nothing left to see, they turned to each other, their eyes an echo of mutual understanding and the unspoken acknowledgment that some farewells were more than just goodbyes—they were the close of a chapter, with the next page yet to be written.

# Chapter 33

-----------------------------------------------------

In Wavecrest, the last Saturday in July was not just another date on the calendar; it was a symbol of summer's crescendo, a night when the pulsing heart of the seaside town skipped a collective beat—the Summer Dance. A tradition woven into the fabric of the town's identity, this grand finale of Wavecrest summers was a beacon that drew young people from all over, a siren song of rhythm and youthful exuberance. The boardwalk, already alive with the vibrancy of the season, became a tableau of freedom and festivity, as if the spirit of summer itself had manifested to dance among them.

For the town's teenagers, the event was an annual rite, a night to bask in the carefree buzz of music and companionship. The local youth and those from neighboring towns mingled in the camaraderie that only these warm nights could foster. The laughter, the beat of the music, the brush of skin against skin as bodies swayed—these were the threads that embroidered the tapestry of their summer memories.

Yet, for Jessica and Fawn, the night held a different promise, one of a more profound, powerful, and irrevocable transition. This dance was not just another night under the star-filled sky; it was their swan song to the shores of their childhood, the last echoing notes of a symphony that had been their carefree youth. They had twirled through previous summer dances with the innocence of high school days looming ahead, a constant that promised the return of all that was familiar. But this dance was the harbinger of change, an evening awash in the colors of their final carefree summer.

The nostalgia that this night would later evoke was, for now, a silent specter waiting in the wings. For when they stepped onto the boardwalk later that evening, the smiles they would share with friends would be the same, but the air would be charged with the knowledge that these moments were fleeting. The Summer Dance was their threshold between youth and the vast uncertainty of adulthood.

Jessica and Fawn, on the cusp of the evening's jubilee, would soon mingle with their peers on the boardwalk, not with the carelessness of seasons past, but with the deep-seated knowledge that this dance was a farewell to the home they had always known. There would be no casual "see you at school" come fall; instead, they faced the certainty of scattered futures.

And as the evening ended and the last note of music faded into the night, they would find themselves at an inflection point, their hearts full of the night's magic, their goodbyes imbued with the bittersweet tang of growth. At the end of the night, they would bid farewell to their friends with a smile for the past and a quiet hope for all the summers yet to dance in their hearts.

On this Saturday afternoon, in the comfort of Fawn's bedroom, the sunlight played peeka-boo through the curtains, casting a warm, embracing glow over the room. Fawn was in her element, surrounded by a wardrobe of possibilities, each garment a whisper of evenings spent under the stars. With her blonde hair cascading down her back, she stepped into the silken embrace of a party dress, its black fabric contrasting the innocence of the afternoon.

Jessica, perched on the edge of the bed, seemed content as she engaged in a text conversation with Ethan. Her fingers danced across the screen in a rhythm only lovers knew. She looked up as Fawn appeared in a low-cut black dress that seemed to have been spun from the midnight sky.

"How do I look?" Fawn asked, turning from the mirror to Jessica, seeking assurance only a best friend can give.

Jessica's smile was spontaneous, her twinkling eyes reflecting her heart's affection. "You look hot," she said with a sisterly pride that colored her voice.

But then came the caution, a playful lilt in her voice trailing off as she caught the thread of her thought, unsure how to weave it into words without a hint of awkwardness. "But don't forget, you'll be with Felix, and you don't want to make him," she paused, the sentence hanging incomplete, a delicate dance of camaraderie and concern. Choosing the safety of silence, she ended with an uncertain "umm."

Fawn's laughter, light and knowing, filled the space between them. It was a sound Jessica cherished, a reminder of the fearless girl who had painted her life with bold strokes of color.

"Yeah, you're right," she admitted, her intuition confirming Jessica's concern.

Turning back to her closet, Fawn's hands found another dress, its fabric more a whisper of elegance than an announcement. "How about this one?" she asked, holding it against her frame and seeking Jessica's approval once more.

Jessica's eyes lit up, her excitement infectious. "Yes, that one!" she exclaimed, her voice tinged with an unmistakable thrill. "Felix won't be able to take his eyes off you in that dress." She paused, a playful smirk dancing on her lips before continuing in a tone layered with sarcasm and humor, "Just make sure you don't scare him away, okay?"

Fawn answered, the twinkle in her eyes shining through a playful roll of her eyes. "I'll try not to scare him too much," she quipped, her voice dancing with mirth.

As she exchanged the black dress for her summer attire, the room echoed their laughter and the silent understanding that tonight was more than a dance; it was a farewell to their youthful years. Her chosen gown was a statement of the evening's promise, draped over her shoulder like a flag of youthful exuberance. As they descended the stairs, the fabric whispered its secrets of anticipation.

In the Gaddesden home, life's rhythm played out in familiar melodies—the sewing machine purring a gentle staccato beneath Anna's guiding hands, and across the room, Brian settled into the sofa, absorbed in the baseball game that projected its narrative onto the walls, the announcer's voice a comforting backdrop.

Amidst this tapestry of home, Anna paused, the hum of her sewing machine yielding to the moment as she looked up, the soft glow of maternal pride lighting her face as she beheld the prelude to her daughter's night of memories.

She rose from the murmuring chorus of her sewing machine, her smile unfurling with a mother's perennial warmth. "Let's see what we have here," she said with a hint of ceremony.

As Fawn unfolded the dress, the gesture invited a ritual as timeless as their shared history—Anna's fingers tracing the fabric as though reacquainting with an old friend. "I've always loved this dress. It looks perfect on you, honey," Anna affirmed, her voice filled with pride.

"Thanks, Mom. Jessica helped me pick it out," Fawn replied, the connection between mother and daughter shimmering in the air, as tangible as the fabric between them.

Anna's attention then turned to Jessica. "Did you decide what dress you'll be wearing to the dance, sweetheart?" Her words were simple yet steeped in maternal warmth.

Jessica's answer came with a thoughtful tilt of her head. "Not yet. We're going back to my house to look through my closet."

Anna's nod was a silent melody of encouragement. "That sounds like a great idea. Ethan will love whatever you choose." Her affirmation bloomed in the room, settling on Jessica's cheeks in a rosy hue.

"I hope so. He always tells me I look beautiful no matter what I wear." Jessica's reply was a mixture of bashfulness and gratitude, a sonnet of first love.

Anna's affirmation was swift and sure. "And I agree. No matter what you girls wear, you both always look beautiful."

Brian's interjection, his voice the anchor in this sea of gentle emotions, cradled the moment. "That's a fact. Ethan is a lucky boy, Jess." His familiar and reassuring affirmation added a layer of warmth to their exchange.

Fawn and Jessica's hearts swelled under the canopy of parental praise. With a shared look, they wrapped the warmth around them like a blanket. Their laughter and liveliness were not just a celebration of the moment, but also an unspoken pact to set aside the complexities of their lives—for the time being.

"Well, we're going to Jess's house now. I'll see you tomorrow, okay?" Fawn's voice, carrying the lightness of the occasion, was a subtle screen that momentarily veiled the heavier thoughts that lay dormant in the back of her mind.

"Okay, girls. Have fun at the dance," Anna's words fluttered after them like a wish, unwittingly fanning the embers of frustration that Fawn worked to smother with the excitement of the evening.

"And stay with your group," came Brian's reminder, his voice a protective note in the evening's comforting chord—its familiarity a bittersweet touch to Fawn's heart, where old wounds had yet to fully settle.

Giggling at Brian's overprotective comment, Fawn and Jessica acknowledged the cheerful lightness that parental concerns could carry. With a goodbye wave, they turned toward the door, the quiet smile of their shared amusement still on their faces as they faced the hot afternoon air. With the weight of impending changes lurking just beyond the horizon, the familiar path to Jessica's house beckoned, a prelude to an evening etched in the stars.

As the afternoon faded into an amber glow, Jessica's room became a sea of fabrics and colors, exuding a quaint charm. The closet door stood ajar, a sentinel to the chronicles of Jessica's transition from high school frolics to the threshold of her college journey. The two girls, mirrors of eagerness and nostalgia, wove through the closet's offerings, with Fawn's artistic fingers pausing at a dress that seemed to hold the summer sky within its folds.

"This one is perfect for you, Jess," Fawn declared, the dress in her hands a tangible echo of Jessica's bright blue eyes.

"You think?" Doubt laced Jessica's question as she turned the dress over in her hands, its simplicity a canvas for the night's possibilities.

"Well, didn't you tell Heather you were going to wear something simple and sweet?" Fawn's reminder bridged the past and present, a shared day of girlish schemes now touched by a shadow of absence.

"Yeah, I remember," Jessica's answer floated, a melancholy note for the friend now chasing dreams amidst the city lights. The memory painted a wistful brushstroke on the day's joy, but her anticipation for the evening carried an undertow of uncertainty. "Do you think Ethan will like it?"

Fawn's grin was a spark in the dimming light, her confidence as assuring as the sun's daily promise to rise. "Ethan will love anything you wear, so don't worry."

A flush of color painted Jessica's cheeks as she capitulated to the choice, the soft fabric whispering promises against her skin. "Okay, I'll wear this one then." Her voice was the ribbon that bound her decision.

Garbed in the dress, Jessica spun, her form a silent question to Fawn, whose affirmation was the sole compass for Jessica's choices.

"You look beautiful, Jess. Ethan won't be able to keep his eyes off you," Fawn affirmed, her words a gentle balm to any lingering doubt.

With a shared surge of excitement, the air between them became charged with the electricity of the evening ahead. "Put yours on, and we'll show Mom!" Jessica's invitation was a bubble of joy waiting to burst.

"Okay," Fawn agreed, her voice matching Jessica's. Together, they floated out of the realm of youth in their party dresses, seeking the comforting embrace of maternal pride.

The search for Teresa was a dance of its own, a light parade through the quiet corridors of the Reese home. It ended at the threshold of the kitchen's patio door, where the mellow afternoon cradled Teresa amidst her flowerbeds. The scent of petunias mingled with the ocean, a backdrop to a canvas about to be painted with the girls' excitement.

"Mom! What do you think?" Jessica's call fluttered over to where Teresa was nestled with her blossoms, eager to harvest her mother's gaze.

Teresa turned, and in that moment, her world expanded from the roots and petals to the blooming graces of the girls before her. "Oh my! You both look so beautiful," she said, her tone wrapped in warmth, her eyes shining with pride.

Mirth unfurled as the girls, playing to their audience, struck poses that were whimsical mirrors of their inner joy. Their laughter, a duet with Teresa's, made even the flowers seem to sway in appreciation. Such was the scene when Teresa, driven by an urge to capture the memory, called for her husband.

"Tom, come and see our girls in their party dresses," she exclaimed, wanting him to witness this fleeting moment.

From the shed, where tools and solitude were his companions, Tom approached, his steps purposeful yet slowed by the sight that greeted him—his daughter and Fawn, poised in the interlude between girlhood and the cusp of tomorrow. His eyes took in the view, their dresses a testament to the fleeting nature of childhood's end. With a mockingly scandalized tone, he played the part of the protective father.

"Do you think we're going to let you out of the house looking like that?" he jested, turning to his wife with an elaborate plan, "Terri, do we still have those nun costumes the girls wore on Halloween a few years ago?"

His humor evoked rich and sincere laughter from both Jessica and Fawn. "Oh, Dad," Jessica retorted, her voice laden with the exaggerated weariness that only a daughter can fashion toward her father's antics.

Teresa's laughter mingled with the girls' as she shook her head in amused resignation at Tom's charade. But then, the mood shifted as Tom's voice softened, revealing the tender truth behind his jocular facade. "Seriously, you both look absolutely gorgeous, but way too grown up."

Fawn replied with heartfelt warmth, bridging the gap between growing up and remaining forever young in the eyes of her loved ones. "Aw, Papa," her voice carrying the weight of shared years and affection. "We'll always be your little girls." It was a simple truth for them, a promise that this bond would remain unaltered no matter how far life took them.

Then, in an act as timeless as the ocean tides that graced the shores of Wavecrest, Jessica and Fawn approached Tom, giving him a hug and planting a kiss on his cheek—a gesture of gratitude and love that sealed the sweet prelude to their evening's dance.

The late afternoon sun streamed through the windows, bathing Jessica's living room in a golden glow. Outside, Wavecrest's vibrant life buzzed with anticipation for the evening's festivities, but inside, a quiet peace unfolded around the two friends.

As Fawn picked up the nail polish, her hand paused, the brush trembling slightly above Jessica's outstretched fingers. She broke the silence that had settled between them with a gentle concern in her voice. "I hope Felix has a good time tonight."

Jessica's reply was a mirror of warmth and assurance. "Don't worry, we'll make sure he does." The bristles touched Jessica's nails, a peach hue trailing over the curves.

There was a moment of thought before Fawn spoke again, her words carrying the weight of recent memories. "Well, I hope he doesn't get in trouble with his dad."

Jessica's reply was firm, reflecting the protective streak Ethan had inspired in her. "Well, his dad better not start anything while we're there because Ethan likes Felix, and he won't stand for it."

The air tensed as Fawn leaned forward, her voice lowering even though they were alone. "You didn't tell him about his dad threatening me, right?"

Jessica met her eyes, her voice embodying the sanctity of their shared trust. "Oh no," she said, her reassurance as solid as the foundation of their friendship. "That's just between us, but he knows how mean Felix's dad is."

"Yeah, he's a real asshole," Fawn muttered, her contempt for Felix's situation clear as she finished Jessica's nails with a protective coat.

Jessica just nodded, the movement stirring her long brown hair, and sighed, "Poor

Felix." Her eyes spoke volumes of her compassion for their friend, a tender echo of Fawn's worries.

Together, the girls wove a tapestry of comfort and determination in the soft light and in the cocoon of their nest. They were like armorers in a quietude of their making, painting shields on nails, each stroke a reinforcement of camaraderie, preparing their hearts for the evening's promise and its hidden challenges.

The distant rumble of an engine, familiar and eagerly anticipated, broke the lull of the late afternoon hour, sending a ripple of excitement through the house. Jessica's face, reflecting the soft tones of contentment from their girlish bonding, suddenly sparked to life, her eyes gleaming with a thrill only young love could incite.

"Ethan's here!" she announced, her voice tinged with a melody of delight.

Fawn's response was a warm, resonant smile, a silent tribute to the joy that danced in Jessica's eyes. They sprang to their feet, the clatter of nail polish bottles a gentle crescendo to their hurried movements and darted to the front door.

They watched through the screen as Ethan stepped out of his Jeep, the sun casting his silhouette in a halo of light. His light blue shirt, casually unbuttoned at the top, flirted with the breeze, revealing the cross against his chest—a silent testament to the strength within. The denim jeans contoured to his form, prompting an admiring chuckle from Fawn.

"Wow, Ethan looks hot in jeans," she declared, her voice a mix of jest and genuine appreciation as she playfully nudged Jessica.

Wrapped in the glow of Ethan's presence even before he reached the door, Jessica giggled in agreement. "Ethan always looks hot to me," she said, her eyes fixed on the figure approaching the front step.

The moment Ethan's hand touched the door, Jessica flung it open, the coolness of the house spilling out onto the porch. She embraced him with a swift movement born from a hundred such greetings, their shared love imbued in the simple act.

"Hi, babe," she whispered, punctuating it with a kiss, a tradition as timeless as their young love.

Ethan, enveloped by the welcome of Jessica's arms, cradled her face gently, his gaze an ocean of adoration. "Hey, beautiful," he murmured, each word a brushstroke painting his feelings across the canvas of the afternoon.

Acknowledging Fawn with a friendly nod and an easy smile, he greeted her, "Hey, Fawn."

"Hey, Ethan. Thanks for being our chaperone tonight." Her voice was tinted with gratitude and relief; Ethan's presence promised a buffer for the night's uncertainties.

His grin was both an acknowledgment and acceptance of the evening's implied duty. "It's my pleasure," he replied. His words carried the ease of camaraderie and the unspoken promise of solidarity.

Together, they stood at the threshold of an evening that would be filled with more than just the usual festivities—a night where they would quietly fortify the bonds of friendship and affection amidst the backdrop of laughter and dance.

As the sun began its slow descent, bathing the neighborhood in the soft glow of early evening, the warmth of the day lingered, hinting at the summer's reluctance to end. Inside the house, laughter and chatter echoed as Teresa joined the trio in the living room while Tom, the hidden maestro of the grill, presided over sizzling steaks with a watchful eye and a chef's pride.

As time passed, the kitchen became a hub of activity, with Jessica, Ethan, and Fawn assembling a vibrant salad, the greens crisp and fresh, contrasting the day's heat. Baked potatoes wrapped in foil hissed softly in the oven alongside a clay dish cradling a medley of roasted vegetables. With practiced hands and the easy camaraderie of family and close friends, they crafted a feast for the occasion.

Dinner on the deck was a symphony of flavors, the warmth of shared stories, and anticipatory smiles for the night ahead. Plates were piled high, cutlery clanked in rhythm with conversation, and the air filled with the comforting aroma of home-cooked food. Teresa's laughter mingled with the still-bright sky, a melodious accompaniment to the gentle evening air.

After the warm glow of dinner receded, Jessica and Fawn retreated to Jessica's room, the anticipation of the night ahead reflected in their bright eyes. There, the transformation began as dresses unfurled like flowers and accessories clinked like good luck charms.

The change was a dance of fabrics and fastenings as Jessica stepped into her heeled sandals, an act of playful defiance against her petite stature.

"You're wearing your heels tonight, huh?" Fawn humorously inquired as she studied Jessica's determined posture.

"Uh-huh," Jessica replied, her voice wearing the lightness of her sarcasm like a pendant. "I need all the help I can get."

The memory of Jessica's less-than-graceful moment with gravity tugged a giggle from Fawn. "Well, I hope you don't end up falling on your butt like you did the last time you wore them," she jested, with affection lacing her teasing.

Jessica's laughter harmonized with the soft clink of her sandals on the floor, brushing off the jest with a playful glint in her eyes. "Shut up, you!" she retorted, her feigned annoyance as thin as mist.

"No heels for me," Fawn declared as she slipped into her flats. "I'm tall enough. I don't want to be towering over Felix."

"That's a good idea," Jessica agreed, giving a nod of approval at Fawn's choice.

Refreshed and ready, they stepped into the living room, the last rays of the day catching the edges of their dresses, illuminating their excitement. Ethan, anchored on the sofa, became the silent witness to their transformation. His gaze, filled with awe, traveled the length of Jessica's form.

"You look absolutely stunning, babe," he said, the words caressing the air between them.

Her smile was a mirror of his admiration, both wide and unguarded. "Thank you," she uttered, bathing in the warmth of his praise.

Ethan turned to Fawn and extended his praise with equal warmth. "Fawn, you look amazing. Felix is going to be one lucky dude tonight."

The compliment widened Fawn's smile to match Jessica's, a testament to the power of shared affirmation. "Thank you, Ethan," she said, her gratitude as evident as the sparkle in her dress. "That's sweet of you to say."

Ethan's nod sealed the sentiment. "Tonight, I'll be in the company of angels," he declared, his words enveloping the room in the velvet blanket of nightfall's onset. The echo of their laughter and the soft shuffle of preparation filled the house as the evening waited patiently for the joy yet to unfold.

As the clock neared eight o'clock, the home's warmth yielded to the night's allure. The gathering, rich with the day's joy, dispersed with the knowledge that the evening still held its promise. Teresa and Tom stood at the front door, offering hugs and wishes for enjoyment and care, their blessings following the trio as they ventured out.

With Ethan at the wheel, the Jeep cradled Jessica and Fawn in its familiar confines, the rhythmic hum of the engine setting the stage for the adventure ahead. As they set out to pick up Felix, the sun, though inching towards the horizon, still cast a warm, golden glow over the streets of Wavecrest. This lingering sunlight bathed the town in a serene yet vibrant light, painting the ordinary surroundings with an extraordinary hue that hinted at the evening's potential.

In this golden hour, the town seemed to hold its breath in anticipation of the Summer Dance, an event that promised to weave its unique tapestry of memories and experiences. The air was charged with a palpable sense of excitement, a prelude to the laughter and music that would soon fill the evening.

As the Jeep wound through the streets, Jessica and Fawn's hearts pounded with excitement and anticipation. This was not just a simple drive to Felix's house but a journey toward an evening ripe with possibilities, an adventure that could weave new threads into the tapestry of their friendship and youthful explorations. With each turn, the anticipation grew, drawing them closer to a night that promised to be unforgettable, filled with moments of laughter, discovery, and, perhaps, a touch of magic.

# Chapter 34

----------------------------------------------------------------

Ethan steered his Jeep away from the familiar sunlit streets of Wavecrest, and the scenery gradually transformed, signifying their journey to the town's less frequented side. The vibrant hues of the boardwalk, a kaleidoscope of summer bliss, gave way to the subdued, almost eerie landscape that lay beyond. The sun, once a constant companion on their beach-filled days, now struggled to pierce through the dense canopy of wild foliage over-head. Once golden and warm, its rays were reduced to faint spots that barely touched the neglected roads that wound toward Felix's house.

Jessica and Fawn, who are usually so at ease with each other's company, felt a shared sense of trepidation gripping them. They exchanged glances, each pair of eyes reflecting the same unsettled feeling. The Jeep's tires crunched over the uneven road, the sound unnervingly loud in the hushed atmosphere of the area. Houses, standing in various stages of disrepair, loomed on either side. The once cheerful facades now appeared forlorn, echoing the somber mood inside the vehicle.

As they drew closer to Felix's residence, the air seemed to chill, a physical manifestation of the emotional discomfort that seemed to hang between them. The jovial chatter that had filled the Jeep earlier had dwindled to silence, with only the occasional comment about the roughness of the road breaking through. This starkly different part of Wavecrest always unsettled Jessica and Fawn, giving them the heebie-jeebies, a sentiment that hadn't lessened even after a couple of visits.

Ethan slowed the vehicle as they approached Felix's house, the structure standing out in its modesty against the backdrop of its more dilapidated neighbors. With the Jeep parked and the house in view, they steeled themselves for Felix's reception, their hearts a mix of excitement and concern, hopeful that the evening would bring a spark of joy to the solemnity of his existence. And with that hope anchored in their hearts, they remained seated in the Jeep, their eyes fixed on Felix's front door, the weight of unease settling between them, not knowing what lay beyond its weathered frame in the shadowy stillness of the fading day.

With Felix's house looming on the side, Fawn broke the silence that enveloped them. "I think I should go knock. He might not know we're here," she said, her gaze fixed on the uninviting facade of the house.

Jessica, reminded of a troubling secret Fawn had shared, felt a surge of concern. "Fawn, remember what you told me about his dad last time? Maybe it's not a good idea," she cautioned, the memory of Fawn's unsettling encounter with Felix's father casting a shadow over her words.

But Fawn's resolve was firm. "I'll be fine. Felix might just need a little nudge. You know how he is," she replied, her voice blurred with affection and determination.

After quietly observing the exchange, Ethan spoke up, his voice edged with protectiveness. "If you're going up there, I'm coming with you," he stated, his concern for Fawn's safety clear.

Jessica hesitated for a moment before adding, "I'm coming too. We should all go." The bond she shared with Fawn left no room for her to stay behind.

Together, they unbuckled their seatbelts and stepped out of the Jeep. As they walked toward the old iron gate that guarded Felix's home, the still, stagnant air, thick with humidity, enveloped them—a stark contrast to the refreshing breezes of their neighborhood. Fawn reached out, her hand hesitating for a moment before pushing the gate open.

Just as the gate swung open, and they took a step forward, the porch door of Felix's house unexpectedly opened. Felix stood there, his expression of surprise and uncertainty as if he hadn't expected their arrival. The moment hung in the air, a silent intersection of anticipation and the unknown.

He emerged from the porch, his button-down blue short-sleeved shirt hanging loosely over his thin frame, paired with baggy brown shorts and a pair of worn sneakers. His look was casual, yet there was an apparent effort behind it, a tentative step toward something outside his comfort zone.

"Fawn!" Felix exclaimed, his eyes widening in obvious surprise. "I thought you might have forgotten about inviting me to the dance," his words reflected nervousness and disbelief.

Fawn laughed lightly and shook her head. "Felix, you're silly to think that. I would never break a promise," she assured him, her tone warm and sincere.

Felix moved with shy hesitation, every gesture reflecting his uncertainty. He kept glancing back toward his house as if expecting to see his father's figure behind the screened porch windows.

"I'm not sure I should go," he admitted, his eyes flicking back to the house. "My dad might need me."

"C'mon Felix, it's only one night. You deserve a night out on the town," Fawn urged gently, her eyes encouraging.

Jessica chimed in, "C'mon, Felix. It'll be fun. I promise."

Ethan, leaning against the Jeep with an amused grin, unfolded his arms and stepped forward. "Hold up!" he called out, capturing everyone's attention. They all turned to look at him.

"You're going to the dance, and that's final," Ethan declared with a friendly but firm tone. His words carried weight, not just because of his protective nature, but because Felix deeply admired him. Ethan wasn't just an idol for his athletic prowess or relaxed confidence; it was his genuine kindness that Felix respected.

Felix took one last hesitant glance at his house before nodding. "Okay, I'll go with you guys," he said, a faint smile touching his lips as he decided.

Fawn and Jessica applauded Felix's decision, assuring him of the fun that awaited at the Summer Dance. "You're braver than you think, Felix," Fawn said with a smile.

With a newfound determination, they climbed back into the Jeep. Ethan and Jessica took their seats in the front while Fawn and Felix sat in the back. Ethan turned the key, and the engine came to life with a purr. He skillfully maneuvered the vehicle, steering towards the boardwalk and leaving Felix's dim, stagnant neighborhood behind. Inside the Jeep, a sense of anticipation and camaraderie filled the air as they embarked on an evening poised to be unforgettable.

Felix sat upright, his hands awkwardly resting on his thighs, as he nervously peered through the windshield. Fawn and Jessica, observing his tense posture, exchanged knowing glances. They knew Felix rarely ventured out, so they understood the significance of this evening for him.

Seeking to ease his nerves, Fawn leaned toward Felix, her voice a blend of warmth and reassurance. "Relax, Felix. Tonight will be amazing, and you're going to have the best time," she promised, her eyes alight with excitement and encouragement.

Feeling the need to bolster Felix's spirits further, Jessica chimed in with her encouraging words. "We'll go on some rides, play some games, and even eat cotton candy," she said, her voice brimming with cheerfulness.

"Not to mention, dancing until our feet hurt," Fawn added, grinning playfully.

Jessica couldn't help but giggle at Fawn's remark and replied light-heartedly, "Yeah, that too."

Initially brightened by their enthusiasm, Felix's smile faded as a practical concern crossed his mind. "It sounds fun, but I don't have any money," he said, a hint of regret coloring his voice.

Ethan, who had been focusing on the road while listening to their conversation, suddenly spoke up. "You don't worry about the money, dude," he said, flashing his signature grin. "Tonight is on me. You can spend all the tickets and tokens you want." Glancing at

Fawn in the rearview mirror, he added, "That goes for you too, Fawn."

Felix's face lit up with a grateful smile, touched by Ethan's generosity, and Fawn's smile beamed from the back seat. "Aw, that's really sweet of you, Ethan, but I have money. I got this," she replied with an independent sparkle in her eyes.

Touched by Ethan's caring and generous nature, Jessica smiled warmly at him. She moved closer and rested her head on his shoulder in a silent display of affection and gratitude.

Lost in lively conversations about past summer dances, Fawn and Jessica shared laughter and memories, barely noticing the changing scenery around them. The dense, shadowy neighborhood of Felix's home gave way to the open skies and the vibrant atmosphere of their familiar territory.

Felix, however, was acutely aware of the change. Glued to the window, Felix absorbed the expanse of the evening sky and the lively scenes unfolding near the boardwalk. Salty air wafted through the open window, refreshing and invigorating his senses. A smile crept across his face, one of genuine excitement and anticipation. He had been far from the boardwalk and the ocean since Jessica's birthday party a month ago. The memory of that day, still vivid in his mind, added a layer of nostalgia to his current experience.

As Ethan drove along the road that paralleled the boardwalk, Felix's eyes were drawn to the bustling activity. He saw food stands with vendors serving various seaside delicacies, their tantalizing aromas wafting through the air. The game stands buzzed with laughter and the clink of prizes, attracting crowds of eager players. The distant sound of the rides, their mechanical symphony a backdrop to boardwalk's liveliness, added to the intoxicating atmosphere. He could see people strolling, laughing, and enjoying the summer evening.

Felix experienced a long-forgotten sensation—a sense of belonging in this vibrant world. For a moment, the challenges and isolation of his usual life seemed to fade into the background, replaced by the promise of an enjoyable evening among friends.

Finally, Ethan pulled into a small parking lot adjacent to the boardwalk—a spot that held special significance for him and Jessica, as it had been their meeting place during the early days of their blossoming romance. He parked the Jeep and turned off the engine, marking the end of their journey and the beginning of an evening that promised to be filled with fun, camaraderie, and perhaps a touch of magic for Felix.

Eager excitement filled the air as they stepped out of the Jeep, ready to immerse themselves in the boardwalk's festive atmosphere. As they approached the steps leading up to the bustling promenade, Ethan paused and noticed that Felix had fastened the top button of his shirt, making the collar look tight and constricted.

"Hold up," Ethan said, stepping up to Felix. With a mischievous grin, he stood in front of him and unbuttoned the top two buttons of his shirt. "This is how you impress the ladies," he advised, his tone light and playful.

The girls giggled at Ethan's remark. Fawn rolled her eyes and said sarcastically, "Really?"

Ethan responded to Fawn's teasing with a grin and a playful wink.

Amid the light-hearted exchange, Felix's attention shifted to the unique cross dangling from Ethan's neck. "That's a cool looking cross," Felix commented, his curiosity piqued.

Jessica smiled warmly. "It's a magic cross," she said, her voice tinged with affection.

"How so?" he asked, looking at the intricate piece of jewelry.

Jessica turned to Ethan. "Tell him, babe," she urged.

Ethan gently held the cross, his fingers tracing its intricate details. He glanced down at it, a soft expression crossing his face.

"My grandfather gave me this cross before he passed away. He said it would protect me and keep me safe," he explained, his voice carrying a depth of sentiment.

Felix listened intently, clearly impressed by the significance of the cross and its history. Even Fawn, typically playful and spirited, was visibly touched by the emotion in Ethan's voice, her expression softening as she realized the depth of meaning the cross held for him.

Ethan reached out to take Jessica's hand, their fingers intertwining. He led the way up the stairs, setting a pace that balanced excitement with consideration for the group. Fawn and Felix followed close behind, their footsteps echoing on the wooden steps.

When they reached the top and stepped onto the boardwalk, Felix's eyes widened in awe. Before him lay the vast expanse of the ocean, its waves caressing the shore. He hadn't seen this sight since he was ten years old, a cherished yet rare memory from his childhood. Those were the days when his mother, seeking a brief respite from their tumultuous life, would bring him to this very place. Nostalgia washed over him, tinged with joy and sadness, as memories of those fleeting peaceful moments resurfaced.

They walked amongst the crowd, the air filled with laughter, chatter, and distant music. Felix's eyes wandered, taking in the vibrant surroundings that brought back memories of his infrequent visits here as a young boy. Each sight opened doors to his past, reviving long-tucked-away images and emotions.

His heart suddenly warmed when he saw a familiar sign: "Mel's Ice Cream Shack." The small ice cream stand, with its colorful facade and inviting aroma, stood beside a bench overlooking the blue waters of the Pacific. That bench, unassuming yet profoundly significant, represented a poignant chapter in Felix's life. It was there, on that very bench, where he and his mother had sat for what would unknowingly be their last time together on the boardwalk. Memories of that bittersweet and final moment came flooding back, enveloping him in a sea of emotions. Lost in this flood of memories, Felix found the boardwalk's laughter and noise fading into the background, leaving him in a reflective silence.

*Eight years ago, on a cool Saturday afternoon in March, the sky over Wavecrest was a canvas of blue, dotted with large, fluffy clouds drifting across the water. The ocean, calmer that day, whispered softly as its waves caressed the shore in a rhythmic caress.*

*On a bench overlooking this serene scene, ten-year-old Felix and his mother sat close together, their eyes fixed on the horizon. Miles away from the hostility of their home, they shared a rare moment of peace and comfort. With his chocolate ice cream cone now a sweet memory, Felix looked at his mother through his glasses. There was an unmistakable sadness in his eyes.*

*"Why is Dad so mean to us?" he asked, his voice small and uncertain.*

*His mother, a tall, thin woman with long black hair framing her gentle face, turned to face him. Her worn clothes spoke of their family's struggles. As she looked into her son's eyes, her heart broke with silent pain.*

*"I don't know, baby," she answered warmly. "I don't know what changed him."*

*"It was me, Mom," Felix said, a heavy burden in his voice. "It had to be me. I know he hates me."*

*She reached out and took Felix in her arms. "It's not you, sweetheart. Your father loves you. It's me your father doesn't love anymore. Ever since he started drinking," she tried to reassure him, her voice heavy with unspoken grief.*

*"It's not just Dad, Mom," Felix confessed. "Everyone hates me. Especially the kids at school. They pick on me all the time."*

*His mother pulled him closer, her embrace a refuge in their stormy lives. "I know, baby," she said, her voice shaking as she fought back tears. "But soon, I'm going to take you away from here. We'll find a new home, far away from all of this."*

*A wave of excitement flickered in Felix's eyes as his mother spoke. "We're going to have a nice house and a yard for you to play in. And we'll be surrounded by kind and caring people. You're going to have friends—lots of friends who will accept you for who you are," she promised, her words painting a vivid picture of a future filled with hope and happiness.*

*Felix's face broke into a wide, hopeful smile. "You promise, Mom? Do you promise?" he asked, his eyes bright with hope and longing.*

*"I promise, baby," his mother said, hugging him tightly, her eyes shining with determination and love. In their embrace, she silently vowed to make their dream come true, to bring Felix out of the shadows of their life.*

*Then, leaning closer, she whispered in his ear, "I promise you with all my heart," her words not just a reassurance, but a solemn oath, a gentle balm to his wounded spirit.*

*As they sat there, embraced in each other's arms, their eyes returned to the ocean, symbolizing the vast possibilities before them. On that bench, they shared a dream of a better life, a fleeting but powerful escape from their reality.*

Lost in the depths of his memories, Felix stood staring at the bench that held so much of his past, his heart aching with the absence of his mother. The vivid memory of their last visit here, her promises, and their shared dreams clung to him, a poignant reminder of what once was and what could have been.

Fawn's voice, a friendly anchor, suddenly broke his reverie, drawing him back to the present. "C'mon, Felix," she called out, her voice filled with warmth and camaraderie.

As Felix turned to Fawn, he was greeted with her mischievous grin, a sight that never failed to melt his heart. Every time he saw that smile, it reaffirmed the deep, unvoiced crush he had always held for her. Fawn's hand reached out to his, an inviting gesture that spoke volumes of her support and understanding. Behind her stood Jessica and Ethan, their expressions cheerful, unaware of the memory that had just engulfed him or of the quiet yearning that lingered within him.

With Fawn's encouragement, Felix allowed himself to be drawn back into the here and now, leaving the echoes of the past on the bench behind him. Together, they moved forward, side by side, each step taking them further into the welcoming embrace of the world around them. For Felix, however, it was more than just a walk on the boardwalk; it was a step toward new memories, healing, and perhaps the fulfillment of those long-ago dreams whispered on a bench by the ocean.

Ethan's voice cut through the bustling noise of the boardwalk. "Who's hungry?"

"I could eat," Jessica replied with a smile.

"Me too," Fawn chimed in, her eyes scanning the food stands around them.

Felix's stomach growled, but his shyness made him hesitate to voice his hunger. However, Fawn's perceptive gaze fell on him.

"What about you, Felix? Are you hungry?" she asked.

Felix nodded nervously. "A little," he admitted, his voice barely above a whisper.

As they strolled along the boardwalk, they passed by various food stands, each with its enticing aroma. Eventually, they found a burger stand that was surprisingly not swamped with customers.

Spotting the opportunity, Ethan turned to the group with a decisive tone. "Let's grab some burgers." After a brief pause, Ethan asked Fawn and Felix, "Why don't you guys grab a table? Jess and I will order the food."

Fawn and Felix wandered off and spotted an empty round metal table with four seats. It was a cozy spot, away from the hustle and bustle of the boardwalk. Settling down, Fawn looked around at the lively scene surrounding them.

"So, Felix, what do you think of the boardwalk so far?" Fawn asked, her tone casual yet welcoming.

"It's... different. It's a lot livelier than I remember," Felix replied, scanning the vibrant scene around them.

Fawn grinned. "Wait till you see it all lit up at night. It's like a whole other world."

Soon, Ethan and Jessica returned, balancing a tray of juicy hamburgers, golden French fries, and four cups of lemonade. The aroma was mouthwatering, and Felix felt his appetite surge.

As they settled into their seats and ate, the atmosphere around them buzzed with energy. The laughter of passersby, the distant music from the rides, and the occasional shout from a vendor created a backdrop to their meal. The sun began to set, casting a warm glow over their table.

"This is really good," Felix commented, surprising himself at how relaxed he felt in their company.

"Nothing beats boardwalk burgers," Ethan declared, grinning and taking a big bite.

They ate, talked, and laughed, enjoying the simple pleasure of their meal and each other's company. While the world around them buzzed with energy and life, their little table became a haven of belonging and ease.

As they finished their food, thoughts of what to do next lingered. The boardwalk awaited them with its myriad of rides and attractions, promising more adventures as the evening wore on. However, they stayed seated at their table, content in the moment.

With childlike excitement sparkling in her eyes, Jessica suggested, "We should go on a few of the rides before the dance starts."

Always ready for a thrill, Fawn looked at Jessica with a hint of caution. This was different from their casual summer days, when they wore simple clothes. Tonight, they were dressed in elegant party gowns—Fawn, in her sleek black silk dress, and Jessica, in her flowing blue party dress, seemed ill-suited for the boardwalk's adventurous rides.

"You think that's a good idea, Jess?" Fawn asked, her eyes wandering over their dresses.

Realization dawned on Jessica, her face transforming into a comical expression of shock, her eyes widening and her mouth forming an 'O' as she realized the impracticality of their dresses for the rides.

Ethan, unable to contain his amusement, chuckled at their predicament. Mirth filled his eyes as he watched the girls weigh the pros and cons of their adventurous proposal.

Meanwhile, Felix remained silent, unsure about the rides they were discussing. His childhood memories were of riding the Merry-Go-Round with his mother, a far cry from the thrilling attractions of the boardwalk.

Sensing the hesitation, Ethan decided to up the ante. "We should at least go on the rollercoaster," he chimed in, his enthusiasm contagious. "It's a must-do boardwalk experience."

He turned to Felix with an encouraging grin. "You in, bro?"

Felix's eyes widened, fear and nervousness flickering across his face. The mere thought of a rollercoaster ride sent shivers through him.

"Um, I don't know," he stuttered, his hesitation clearly visible on his face.

Understanding Felix's sheltered life, Ethan saw an opportunity. He wanted to offer Felix a slice of the teenage experiences he had missed.

"You can do it, dude. I have faith in you," he encouraged, giving Felix a light, playful punch on the shoulder. "Besides, Fawn and Jess won't be able to survive it on their own."

Jessica and Fawn burst into laughter at Ethan's teasing. "Shut up, Ethan," Jessica retorted playfully. "We're a lot tougher than you!"

"Prove it," Ethan shot back, his grin widening.

The girls exchanged glances, and, in a moment of silent agreement, Fawn turned to Ethan, who was already on his feet. "If Felix will ride the rollercoaster, then so will we," she declared, sticking her tongue out at him.

Fawn's unexpected proposal caught Felix off guard, sending a wave of shock and surprise through him. "What?"

Ethan laughed, pleased with the unfolding plan. He pulled Jessica to his side. "Then it's settled. Rollercoaster, here we come."

And so, united in their pact, they rose from the table, ready to face the legendary rollercoaster, marking the beginning of an unforgettable part of their evening.

Their walk to the ride brimmed with a mix of anticipation and excitement. The towering structure loomed ahead, its tracks weaving an intricate pattern against the sky. Felix's steps were hesitant, his heart racing with nervousness and excitement.

As they joined the line, the chatter and laughter of the crowd enveloped them. "You're going to love it, Felix," Jessica said with a grin.

"Yeah, there's nothing like the rush of a rollercoaster," Ethan added, his eyes shining with excitement.

Fawn looked back at Felix with an encouraging expression. "Just wait for the first drop. That's the best part," she said, her voice tinged with excitement.

Felix swallowed hard, trying to calm his racing heart. "I can't believe I'm actually doing this," he muttered, mostly to himself.

Slowly but surely, the line moved forward, and before long, it was their turn. As the rollercoaster came to a stop, it released its riders. In the middle of the train, the group arranged themselves in a four-seat car, with Jessica and Ethan occupying the front seats and Fawn and Felix in the back.

The ride began with a slow, suspenseful climb, each click of the coaster building anticipation. At its peak, Felix's breath hitched in his throat. Then, with a sudden rush, the coaster plunged down the first drop, sending a wave of exhilaration through them all. Felix's nervousness transformed into sheer thrill as they zoomed through the dips and sharp turns, the wind whipping their faces.

The train twisted and turned, each new movement bringing a chorus of screams and laughter from the four friends. Felix, experiencing his first-ever rollercoaster ride, felt a rush unlike anything he'd ever known. The world spun around him in a blur of speed and excitement.

As the ride ended and the coaster came to a slow stop, they disembarked, their faces beaming with joy. Felix stepped off, grinning ear to ear, radiating newfound confidence. His initial nervousness had completely faded away.

"So, how was it, Felix?" Fawn asked, her eyes sparkling with curiosity.

Ethan and Jessica turned to him, eager to hear his answer.

Still buzzing from the experience, Felix replied enthusiastically, "It was incredible! I never knew it could be so much fun. I'm so glad I did it!"

His words elicited cheers and pats on the back as everyone basked in his newfound courage. Beyond its role as an amusement ride, the roller coaster symbolized Felix's personal growth and the thrill of venturing beyond his comfort zone.

As the night sky draped itself over Wavecrest, the boardwalk, already buzzing with activity, swelled with an influx of teenagers and young adults. The atmosphere was reminiscent of the vibrancy seen during the Fourth of July weekend, yet tonight, the attire was markedly different. Bikinis and summer shorts gave way to elegant dresses and trendy outfits, with everyone dressed in their best for the highly anticipated Summer Dance.

Overhead, the boardwalk lights twinkled like stars, casting a magical glow over the scene. The pulsating music from the Sandalwood Pavilion added to the enchantment, setting a rhythm that resonated with the heartbeats of those gathered.

As they walked alongside Ethan and Felix, Jessica and Fawn encountered familiar faces. Each encounter ignited warm hugs, hearty handshakes, and an easy camaraderie forged through years of shared experiences. Old friends and schoolmates shared laughs and cherished memories tempered by the bittersweet reality of parting ways. A palpable sense of an era ending enveloped them, with each goodbye reminding them that their paths might not cross again after this night.

In the midst of these exchanges, Felix found himself in a novel situation. The people who approached them, classmates and friends of Jessica and Fawn, were strangers to him. Yet, to his surprise, these peers, once mere acquaintances from school, greeted him with the same warmth and kindness they showed the girls. There were no labels here, no traces of the teasing or exclusion he had endured in school. Instead, he was greeted with friendly smiles and sincere wishes for his future.

For the first time, Felix felt a true sense of belonging, a recognition that he, too, was part of the journey into adulthood. This acceptance, this unspoken inclusion, was a new and heartwarming experience that left him with a sense of hope and a feeling of being part of something larger than himself.

As the group neared the pavilion, the sudden screeching sound of a PA system echoed through the air, startling them momentarily. The abrupt noise prompted surprised laughs and quick glances from the crowd. The boardwalk, already alive with the buzz of conversation and laughter, quieted down in anticipation.

"Hey, boys and girls, and children of ALL ages, this is Smiley Bob here, and I'll be your DJ for the night," the voice boomed over the speakers, full of energy and excitement. The voice belonged to the well-known local DJ, whose nickname reflected his ever-cheerful persona.

A wave of laughter and applause rolled through the crowd on the pier, reaching the foursome as they continued their way toward the festivities. The DJ's voice carried over the boardwalk, adding an extra spark of anticipation to the night.

"Wavecrest, are you ready to kick off the most epic Summer Dance of the year?" Smiley Bob continued, his voice echoing against the backdrop of the ocean. The crowd erupted in cheers and whistles, their excitement palpable.

"Tonight, we celebrate the grand finale of our summer season, a night to remember for all our awesome youth! Let's make this a night of unforgettable memories, fantastic music, and the best dance moves you've got. So come on down to Sandalwood Pavilion and let the fun begin!"

The crowd's enthusiasm surged as the first beats of a popular summer hit filled the air. The boardwalk lights danced in time with the music, creating a festive and vibrant atmosphere. Jessica, Ethan, Fawn, and Felix joined the crowd, moving in sync with the rhythm, their hearts beating in unison with the excitement of the night.

As nine o'clock struck, marking the official start of the Summer Dance, the youth of Wavecrest gathered under the stars, ready to embrace the joy and freedom of the moment, a fitting tribute to the end of a beautiful season.

# Chapter 35

--------------------------------------------------------------

Standing at the entrance to Sandalwood Pavilion, the quartet was enveloped by the pulsating rhythm of The Weeknd's "Blinding Lights." The song's catchy beat reverberated through the transformed boardwalk, now a vibrant dance floor under festive strings of lights. The atmosphere was electric, the air thick with excitement.

Jessica and Fawn swayed to the music, their faces alight with joy, sharing a look of mutual readiness to dive into the dance. Ethan, standing next to Jessica, took in the scene, the rhythm resonating with him and bringing a subtle smile to his face.

Standing next to Fawn, Felix watched with wide eyes. Amidst the lively crowd, his first experience of such a spirited gathering was both awe-inspiring and overwhelming, causing a nervous flutter in his heart. The music, lights, and dancing crowd opened a vibrant world he had only ever observed from afar.

Together, they stood within the festive tapestry of sound, light, and movement, each friend absorbing the moment's essence—a vivid snapshot of youth and exuberance at the heart of Wavecrest's Summer Dance.

Jessica felt a tap on her shoulder as the group passed through the entrance. Turning around, she was greeted by Krista. Her vibrant red hair was a fiery contrast against the night, and her face lit up with a broad smile.

"Hey, girlfriend!" Krista shouted over the music, her voice full of excitement.

Standing next to Krista was her boyfriend, Donny Richardson. He had his arm wrapped around her waist, a comfortable and familiar gesture.

Jessica's face lit up. "Hey, Kris! Hey, Donny!" she shouted back. "I'm glad you guys could make it tonight!"

Krista's grin widened. "Are you kidding me? We wouldn't miss this for the world," she replied, her enthusiasm infectious.

Donny just smiled and bobbed his head in time to the pulsating beat of the music.

A mischievous sparkle lit Krista's eyes as she turned to Fawn and Felix. "I didn't know you and Felix were dating," she teased loud enough to be heard over the music.

Fawn played along, her voice loud and playful. "Yep, he's my date for tonight," she said, giving Felix a friendly nudge.

Slightly taken aback by the teasing, Felix managed a shy smile, his cheeks colored with a bashful flush.

Watching the exchange, Ethan chuckled, amused by the playful dynamics within their group.

Jessica, her attention shifting, asked Krista, "Is Michelle still coming?"

Krista nodded and shouted back, "Yeah, she'll be here! She gets off work at nine, so she should be here soon!"

Feeling the irresistible pull of the dance floor, Jessica and Fawn started getting antsy. As if on cue, Smiley Bob segued to "Wake Me Up," by Avicii, the song's upbeat rhythm filling the air.

Jessica turned to Ethan, her voice raised to cut through the music. "You want to dance, babe?"

Ethan grinned, his eyes crinkling with amusement. "Nah, not right now," he replied, his voice warm over the music. "You girls, go ahead. Felix and I will grab some drinks and watch you from the sideline."

After giving Ethan a quick kiss, Jessica followed Fawn and Krista into the lively crowd. They began to dance, their bodies moving in sync with the pulsating rhythm, blending into the sea of dancers under the neon lights of the summer night.

Ethan turned to Donny with a polite nod, mindful that they were still strangers. "You coming, bro?" he asked, extending a friendly gesture.

Donny, his eyes lingering on Krista's dancing form, shook his head. "Nah, I'm good," he replied, his contented voice reflecting the pleasure of watching his girlfriend at the moment.

Ethan and Felix strolled away from the pavilion, their steps leading them to a nearby lemonade stand. The night air felt cooler, a welcome respite from the heat of the crowd. Ethan bought two cups of lemonade, and they walked a little farther to a quieter spot, where the music was just a distant throb. They leaned against the railing, sipping their drinks and gazing out at the vast ocean.

Ethan broke the silence. "Are you having a good time, Felix?" he asked, sipping his lemonade.

Felix turned to Ethan, a small smile on his lips. "Yes, I'm having a wonderful time. I never experienced anything like this," he admitted, his voice carrying a tone of genuine amazement.

Ethan gave him a reassuring pat on the shoulder. "You deserve to have a good time, buddy."

Felix shifted, his face reflecting deep gratitude. "You guys will never know how much I appreciate the kindness you showed me."

Ethan replied with a mixture of encouragement and frankness. "Felix, you're a good dude, and it's time you start believing in yourself."

Those words resonated deeply with Felix. He looked out over the ocean with a thoughtful expression on his face. "You know what? For the first time, I feel like I am starting to believe in myself."

"That's good," Ethan replied with a hint of pride in his voice.

A shared silence fell between them, both absorbing the moonlight shimmering over the vast expanse of the ocean. It was a contemplative pause, a quiet interlude in the excitement of the night.

Finally, after emptying their cups, they turned back toward the pavilion, a renewed sense of camaraderie guiding them back into the beating heart of the Summer Dance.

As they approached the entrance, Ethan and Felix were greeted by familiar voices weaving through the air. Amidst the lively crowd of dancers, they spotted Jessica and Fawn talking with Michelle, who had just arrived. Clad in a simple yet elegant black party dress, Michelle exuded a quiet sophistication that reflected her reserved grace.

Upon their approach, Michelle turned and greeted them with a bright, welcoming smile. "Hey, guys," she called out over the music, her voice carrying a warm welcome.

Ethan, always appreciating Michelle's calm demeanor, returned her warm smile. Still struggling with his social awkwardness, Felix managed a shy nod in response. As perceptive as ever, Fawn wrapped her arm around Felix's, conveying both support and inclusion. Felix's shoulders relaxed, comforted by her closeness.

With her characteristic perceptiveness, Michelle turned to Felix, her tone warm and understanding. "Remember me? From Jessica's birthday party?" she asked.

A sheepish yet genuine grin lit up Felix's face. "I remember," he said, his voice hinting at newfound confidence.

Michelle continued, her tone friendly and inviting. "I'm glad you came tonight, Felix. This is a big night for all of us," she said, reassuring and encouraging.

Felix felt a sense of belonging, his nervousness ebbing away under Michelle's kind eyes. Like Fawn and the others, it was clear that she saw beyond the surface and offered a connection based on genuine kindness.

Their conversation was suddenly interrupted by the opening bars of Dua Lipa's "Levitating" playing over the speakers. "Oh my God, I love this song!" Jessica exclaimed, her excitement evident.

Ethan, recognizing the familiar tune, grinned at Jessica. Michelle and Fawn exchanged glances, understanding the unspoken excitement between them.

Without hesitation, Jessica grabbed Ethan's arm and pulled him toward the dance floor, her eagerness undeniable. Ethan, caught up in the moment, laughed and followed her lead.

"C'mon, Felix," Fawn urged, her voice filled with playful determination as she took his hand.

Felix, though surprised, found himself being led onto the dance floor, his heart racing with a mix of nervousness and excitement.

Graceful and poised, Michelle followed suit, her steps revealing a hidden passion for dancing. Krista and Donny, sharing a look of amusement and joy, joined their friends, their laughter and moves blending into the vibrant atmosphere of the summer night.

The dance floor thrummed with the group's energy as they swayed and moved with the music, their laughter rising above the pulsating beats. The girls, especially Jessica and Fawn, danced with an infectious energy, their bodies moving fluidly and effortlessly to the beat. Their arms waved in the air, their laughter uninhibited, as if embracing the essence of youth and freedom.

Embodying a more relaxed style, Ethan swayed to the music with laid-back ease. His enjoyment was evident in his smile as he watched Jessica dance with such fervor. There was a contentment in his eyes, a pleasure in seeing her so happy and free.

Felix, on the other hand, seemed timid on the dance floor, his movements hesitant and slightly out of sync with the rhythm. Fawn, ever supportive, noticed his discomfort and stepped in. Smiling, she took his hands and gently guided him, demonstrating how to move in harmony with the music. With the patience of a saint, she slowly coaxed Felix out of his shell.

Krista and Donny echoed the girls' enthusiasm, dancing with energetic and synchronized movements. Michelle, too, found her rhythm, dancing with a guy she met on the floor.

Seizing the opportunity to add to the fun, Ethan decided to put on a little show. His exaggerated steps and humorous gestures drew peals of laughter from the girls. Even Felix couldn't help but chuckle, feeling more at ease thanks to Ethan's antics.

As the last notes of the song faded into the night, Jessica and Fawn paused, their faces flushed from the vigorous dancing. Slightly breathless, their laughter mingled with the fading notes of music.

"Wow, that was intense!" Fawn exclaimed, fanning herself with her hand. "I think we need a little break."

Still catching her breath, Jessica nodded in agreement. "Definitely. A little fresh air sounds perfect right now," she said, her voice showing her exhilaration.

Krista, bubbling with energy, laughed. "Can't handle one more song, huh?" she teased playfully.

With his arm wrapped around Krista's shoulder, Donny looked around and suggested, "How about we take a break near one of the benches? It's cooler and not too far from here."

With a collective nod, they left the pavilion, away from the pulsating energy of the dance floor. Stepping onto the boardwalk, they immediately felt a change in the atmosphere. The open space welcomed them with its more relaxed ambiance, offering a soothing contrast to the heated intensity inside the pavilion. The gentle sea breeze, mingling with the sounds of the boardwalk, brushed against their skin, offering a welcome relief.

As the group walked, Ethan approached a nearby beverage stand to make a purchase. He cheerfully bought a bottle of cold water for each of them.

Jessica watched him with a grin. "You're being generous tonight," she said, her eyes sparkling with gratitude.

Ethan shrugged, his grin matching hers. "Eh, it's only money," he replied, his tone light and carefree.

They opened their bottles one by one, the sound of the caps twisting off, punctuating the brief silence. In unison, they took long, refreshing gulps, the cool liquid a welcome relief that seemed to rejuvenate them instantly.

As they enjoyed their brief respite, Lila, a familiar and friendly face from their school days, approached. Her presence brought a warmth and camaraderie they had always appreciated.

"Hey, girls. It's great to see you all here, but isn't someone missing from your usual crew?" she asked, her observation sharp yet delivered with a gentle curiosity.

Krista felt a pang at the question. "Yeah, we're missing one. Heather moved to New York City," she replied, her voice tinged with pride for their friend's new chapter and a sense of loss at her absence.

The mention of their missing friend stirred a wave of nostalgia in Jessica, Fawn, and Michelle. The void that Heather left in their tight-knit circle felt more profound.

Jessica, quick to lift the spirits, chimed in with her characteristic optimism. "Hey guys, let's take a selfie and send it to Heather; show her what she's missing," she suggested, her tone bright and upbeat.

The girls quickly huddled together, the vibrant backdrop of the pavilion's activities framing them perfectly. Jessica stretched out her arm, phone in hand, ready for the perfect group shot. Their faces broke into wide, genuine smiles, the kind only shared among the closest of friends. With a click, Jessica's phone captured the moment—a snapshot of their enduring bond, a memory to bridge the gap between them and Heather.

Jessica quickly sent the picture, creating a digital bridge across the miles and ensuring that her friend became part of a night where her presence was missed. It was a small gesture, but one filled with love and the unspoken message that no matter how far apart they were, their friendship remained as strong as ever.

As the evening progressed, the group remained near the pavilion, surrounded by the festive atmosphere of the boardwalk. Throughout the night, the girls and Donny were either greeted by old friends from school or called out to acquaintances as they walked by.

Each encounter sparked lively conversations—reminiscing about the past, laughing over favorite memories, and discussing their hopes and dreams for the future.

The mood changed, however, when the first chords of Savage Garden's "I Knew I Loved You" blared over the speakers. The song's tender lyrics and melody resonated deeply with Ethan, echoing his deep feelings for Jessica. To him, the song reflected his heart, a musical embodiment of his love for Jessica.

Ethan took her hand, his eyes offering an unspoken invitation. "Now it's my turn to ask you for a dance," he said, his voice filled with affection.

Jessica's smile was radiant, her eyes reflecting her love for him. Allowing Ethan to lead the way, Jessica stepped back into the pavilion, her heart fluttering with emotion. As he embraced her, their bodies came together in a tender, slow dance. Their eyes locked, full of love and admiration, speaking volumes more than words ever could. Jessica felt overwhelmed by the song's lyrics, as if Ethan himself was serenading her, her heart swelling with each verse.

Nearby, Fawn saw an opportunity to get Felix back onto the dance floor. "C'mon, Felix. Let's have one more dance to finish the evening," she said, her voice encouraging. She held out her hand, a gentle invitation.

Buoyed by his newfound confidence, Felix allowed Fawn to lead him onto the dance floor. Their dance was more tentative, with Felix's inexperience evident, but Fawn led with patience. She maintained a friendly distance, mindful of their budding friendship, as they moved to the music.

As Ethan and Jessica swayed gracefully on the dance floor, their love was palpable, creating a moment of pure, emotional beauty amidst the gentle rhythm of the music. Nearby, Krista and Michelle stood together, their attention drawn to the couple. Both were visibly touched by the depth of affection evident between their friends.

Emotion softened Krista's eyes as she murmured to Michelle, "They look so perfect together," her voice tinged with happiness and awe. "I've never seen Jess so happy."

Michelle nodded in agreement, her eyes also fixed on the couple. "It's wonderful to see," she added, a gentle smile on her lips.

At that moment, Donny approached Krista, affection written across his face. "Want to join them for a dance?" he asked, nodding towards Jessica and Ethan.

Krista glanced at Donny and then back at the couple. "No, I just want to watch for now," she replied. "It's their moment."

Understanding her sentiment, Donny nodded and remained by her side, observing the touching scene.

Their attention briefly shifted to Fawn and Felix, attempting a slow dance. "Look at them," Michelle pointed out. "She's really helping him come out of his shell tonight."

A warm smile graced Krista's face, touched by Fawn's kindness. "She's always been amazing like that," she remarked with admiration in her voice.

The group remained in quiet observation, immersed in the emotional richness of the scene. The song's tender melody captured the essence of the night—love, friendship, and unforgettable moments, marking the Summer Dance as a poignant farewell to their youth and a threshold to new beginnings.

Jessica and Ethan were lost in their own world, each moment of their dance becoming a precious memory in the making. Every word of the song felt like a personal message from him, filling her heart with love.

For Fawn and Felix, their dance was a sweet, if tentative, step closer in their friendship. A profound sense of gratitude enveloped Felix, filling him with a triumphant feeling of accomplishment and connection.

As the song neared its end, the emotional depth of the moment was palpable. Jessica and Ethan, lost in each other's embrace, savored the final notes of the song. Their dance became a beautiful testament to the depth of their love and connection.

As the music faded, the magic of the moment remained in the air. Ethan and Jessica walked away from the pavilion, their arms wrapped around each other's waists, their bond stronger than ever. Behind them, Fawn and Felix followed, both smiling, their evening together ending on a note of warm friendship.

As the hour approached eleven o'clock, Fawn checked her phone, her expression reflecting surprise at how quickly the time had passed.

"Hey guys," she announced with a hint of regret. "It's getting kinda late, and I think we should start heading back." Turning to Felix, her expression softened with concern. "Felix needs to get back to his father."

Felix sighed as Fawn's words brought him back to the less pleasant realities of his life. "Yeah, I guess it's time," he said, his tone a mixture of disappointment and reluctance.

Jessica, Ethan, and Fawn's expressions mirrored Felix's disappointment, reflecting the sadness they shared. They all knew about Felix's situation and the necessity of his early departure.

Ethan was the first to break the silence. "Hey man, we totally get it. You gotta do what you gotta do," he said, patting Felix on the back.

In a gentle voice, Jessica added, "But we had a great night, right?"

As the group strolled along the boardwalk, the lively atmosphere of the Summer Dance fading behind them, they approached the bumper car ride. Ethan's eyes lit up at the sight.

"I haven't been on this ride in years," he exclaimed, grinning at the group. "Are you guys in?"

The group responded immediately, their enthusiasm palpable. Jessica playfully nudged Ethan. "Oh, you're on. I'm gonna kick your butt, babe," she declared with a laugh.

Fawn chimed in, her eyes gleaming with mischief. "Just don't mess with me, or you'll be sorry!" she replied with mock severity.

Joining in the playful banter, Donny laughed, "Oh, you don't scare me, Fawn. Bring it on!"

Feeling emboldened from the night's experiences, Felix added, "I'll give it a try."

Michelle and Krista laughed as they watched their friends exchange playful threats and challenges, the camaraderie of the group shining through.

Ethan purchased the tickets, and then everyone boarded the ride, each one settling into their colorful bumper cars. Excitement and laughter filled the air as they prepared for one more adventure together, making it a perfect end to an unforgettable evening.

The bumper car arena became a whirlwind of laughter as the friends took to the wheel. With a mischievous twinkle in his eyes, Ethan playfully took aim at the girls' cars, with Jessica as his primary target. Each time he crashed into her car, he'd shout, "Gotcha!"

Unleashing her wild spirit, Fawn zipped across the floor, crashing into everyone with gleeful abandon. Her laughter was contagious and echoed through the arena.

"Watch out, here I come!" she yelled, hurtling her toward her unsuspecting friends.

Jessica, intent on getting back at Ethan, maneuvered her car with determined focus. But whenever she got close, someone else bumped into her, eliciting a playful scream.

"You brat!" she'd shout, followed by "Leave me alone!" as she tried to navigate through the chaos.

Krista, Donny, and Michelle were in their element, driving around and bumping into whoever crossed their paths. Their laughter mingled with the others, creating a joyous chaos.

Felix, who was cautious at first, soon got caught up in the excitement. He darted around, trying to avoid collisions. Emboldened, he joined the fray, crashing into Ethan and the others with newfound gusto. However, when it came to Fawn, his actions were more hesitant. On the rare occasion when he bumped into her car, it was a gentle, almost tender nudge, silently conveying his hidden feelings.

The arena was a blur of laughter, playful yells, and the thrill of the chase. Even Felix, who was experiencing the bumper cars for the first time, got caught up in the fun and forgot about his earlier shyness in the joy of the moment.

As the ride came to an end, the friends slowed their cars, their laughter echoing as they came to a stop. They exited the ride, still chuckling and teasing each other about their driving antics.

"That was awesome!" Ethan exclaimed as he high-fived Felix.

"Yeah, but next time, you better watch out!" Jessica warned, her eyes sparkling with amusement.

As the group continued their leisurely walk along the boardwalk, they approached a building that housed the restrooms. Feeling the call of nature, Ethan turned to the group.

"Hey, I gotta use the bathroom, man. I'll be right back," he said, excusing himself from his friends.

In Ethan's absence, Krista glanced between Donny and the others. "We're thinking of heading back to the pavilion," she suggested. "There's still a bit of the night left to enjoy."

Michelle, standing next to Krista, nodded in agreement. "I think I'll join you guys."

Jessica and Fawn shared a knowing look, empathizing with their friends' wish to savor the rest of the evening. They each exchanged warm hugs, feeling the significance of the moment.

Jessica spoke up, her voice filled with warmth and urgency. "We definitely need to see each other again before we all go off to college."

Krista and Michelle returned the smile, a hint of regret in their eyes. "Our jobs keep us busy, but we promise to make time. One last get-together before the summer ends," Krista assured them.

With the promise of another get-together, Krista, Donny, and Michelle returned to the bustling scene.

As they left, Fawn spotted a familiar face working at a game stand across the boardwalk. "Hey, Felix, we're going to go say hi to a friend," she told him, pointing toward the game stand. "I'll be over here if you need me."

Felix gave her a warm, understanding smile. "Sure, take your time," he said, his voice tinged with newfound confidence.

As Fawn and Jessica walked toward the game stand, Felix leaned against the railing, his eyes wandering to the ocean's dark expanse. The sound of the waves provided a soothing backdrop as he stood alone, lost in thought, the energy of the boardwalk a distant hum behind him.

Then, out of nowhere, an unsettling feeling shattered Felix's moment of solitude, a premonition that something was amiss. Pulling away from the railing, he turned, his heart sinking as he recognized the approaching figures. With two of his friends at his side, Jerry Cranmer was coming straight for him. Memories of mockery and humiliation flooded his mind, echoes of a painful school experience.

A tense silence hung in the air as Jerry came face-to-face with Felix. He braced himself for the familiar barrage of insults. But to his surprise, Jerry's expression shifted from its usual indifference to something more remorseful.

"Hey, Felix," Jerry said, surprising Felix with a tone that was gentle and free of malice.

Felix, taken aback, managed a nervous reply. "Hi, Jerry."

Jerry looked earnestly at Felix. "I know it's too little and too late, but I owe you an apology," he began, his voice filled with sincerity. "I just want to tell you that I'm sorry for being such a jerk to you in school."

A mix of disbelief and relief washed over Felix as he listened to Jerry's continued apology.

"I'm an asshole, Felix. I admit it. And I'm truly sorry for all the pain I've caused you," Jerry said, gesturing to his friends who echoed his sentiment. "We're all sorry, Felix. We hope you can forgive us someday."

Across the way, Fawn and Jessica were deep in conversation at the game stand when Fawn glanced back at Felix. Seeing Jerry and his friends facing Felix sparked a protective fire in her, but it was quickly doused as she watched the scene unfold. Seeing Jerry extend his hand in a gesture of peace and Felix accepting it with a shy smile eased her concern. Jerry's friends followed suit, each offering a handshake to Felix, who responded with a growing sense of ease.

During this unexpected reconciliation, Jerry's gaze found Fawn's. Their eyes locked, and in that brief exchange, Fawn saw a glimmer of the old Jerry she had fallen in love with. The pain and sorrow in his eyes were unmistakable, stirring old feelings within her. Yet, there was an unspoken understanding between them; their story was a chapter ended by time and circumstance.

As Jerry and his friends turned to leave, Jerry gave Fawn one last look. She acknowledged him with a nod and a smile, sharing a moment of mutual understanding. But his returning smile did little to hide the sadness in his eyes. It was their silent farewell to what once was and what could never be again.

Ethan emerged from his visit to the restroom, and his return did not go unnoticed. Seeing him, Jessica gave Fawn a quick nudge before eagerly approaching him. Smiling at her friend's eagerness, Fawn followed suit, and soon, the four friends were reunited.

As they resumed their walk along the boardwalk, the bright lights and lingering sounds of laughter and music accompanied them. The atmosphere was still lively, with people enjoying the end of the evening. They sauntered toward the parking lot, where Ethan's Jeep was waiting.

Approaching Mel's Ice Cream Shack, Jessica and Fawn spotted a few friends chatting nearby. "Hey, babe," Jessica said, turning to him, "Fawn and I are going to talk to our friends for a few minutes. Do you mind?"

Ethan replied with a relaxed smile. "Sure. Felix and I will wait here," he gestured toward the railing.

As the girls made their way to their friends, Ethan and Felix leaned against the railing and looked out over the ocean. The expanse of water stretched before them, its surface reflecting the myriad lights of the boardwalk and the stars above.

Suddenly, an inexplicable pull drew Felix's attention to a nearby bench where he and his mother had sat together for the last time. A wave of sadness washed over him, intensifying his longing for her. Without a word, Felix walked toward the spot, his feet moving almost on their own.

When he reached the bench, Felix sat down, his eyes fixed on the vast ocean. As he sat there, memories of his mother filled his mind, silencing the sounds of the boardwalk around him. The world seemed to fade away, leaving only Felix, an empty boardwalk and beach, and the ocean before him.

A gentle breeze caressed his face, bringing with it an unexpected comfort. He closed his eyes for a moment, savoring this newfound serenity. When he opened them again, his eyes landed on a figure emerging from the shoreline, a woman in a flowing white dress that seemed to dance with the ocean's breeze.

Felix squinted through his glasses as the figure drew nearer, trying to make out her features. His heart skipped a beat as he realized, in disbelief, that the approaching woman bore an uncanny resemblance to his mother. She looked just as she had in his last memories of her, but now there was no sign of exhaustion or illness. Instead, she radiated happiness and an effervescent energy.

"Mom?" Felix called out, his voice trembling with hope and confusion. He couldn't take his eyes off her.

The woman, standing near the railing, didn't answer. Instead, she fixed her gaze on him, her eyes brimming with love and tenderness. She looked at him as if absorbing every detail, her expression a beautiful tapestry of pride, love, and joy. Her smile was radiant, lighting up her entire being.

A single tear trickled down Felix's cheek, but he barely noticed. He was overwhelmed by the sight before him, gripped by the feeling that his mother had returned to him, fulfilling her promise in a way he never thought possible.

As he sat on the bench, the ocean breeze seemed to carry his mother's voice to his ears, her words gently riding the wind and resonating within his heart. When their eyes met, he felt her words vibrate within him, deepening their heartfelt connection.

"Don't be sad, my son, for I have never left you," his heart echoed her words.

A warm wave of comfort washed over him, as though his mother's presence were embracing him. Overwhelmed by both grief and love, tears welled up in his eyes as he realized she had always been with him, silently witnessing his life.

"I've watched you grow into the wonderful young man you are today, and I'm so proud of you. You have a kind and loving heart, Felix. Let no one take that away from you."

As these words of pride and love resonated through him, Felix was overwhelmed with emotion. His mother's deep admiration and belief in him transcended all barriers, affirming his worth and fortifying his spirit.

"Stay true to yourself and your dreams, and you will succeed in life." Her final advice resonated deeply in Felix's heart, filling him with renewed strength and determination. His mother's unwavering faith reignited an inner flame that had been dimmed by life's challenges.

Tears streamed down Felix's cheeks as he absorbed his mother's comforting and encouraging words. He longed to reach out, to feel her embrace once more, but he remained rooted to the spot, unable to move, as her words continued to fill his heart.

Then, as if being carried away by the very breeze that had brought her to him, his mother began to fade, her form dissolving into the night air.

"No, Mom. Please don't go," Felix cried out, his voice choked with emotion.

But as she drifted back toward the ocean, her smile grew, emanating a more profound love and warmth. From his heart, Felix heard her departing words.

"I love you, my beautiful boy. Remember, I'm always with you, even when you feel you are alone. You are never alone, my angel."

And then she was gone. The world around Felix slowly returned to normal. The sounds of the boardwalk, the distant laughter, and the rhythmic crashing of the waves crept back into his awareness. He sat on the bench, holding his glasses in one hand while wiping away his tears with the other.

The bench, the boardwalk, and the ocean remained unchanged, but for Felix, everything had changed in those precious moments. He took a deep breath, feeling a new sense of strength and comfort, knowing that his mother's love and presence would always be a part of him.

Standing just a few feet away from Felix, Ethan found his eyes drawn to the same spot on the beach where Felix's intense gaze was fixed. A look of disbelief and bewilderment crossed his face, for in that very spot, Ethan saw a figure he immediately recognized as his grandfather. But this wasn't the old, sickly man he remembered; instead, his grandfather appeared as he had when Ethan was just a boy, exuding health and vitality.

Transfixed, Ethan watched as his grandfather's eyes, initially on Felix, gradually shifted to meet his. He found himself rooted to the spot on the boardwalk, his mind struggling to process the sight of his youthful grandfather standing before him. As he watched, his grandfather's smile gradually widened as he absorbed the presence of his grandson. The smile was familiar and warm, igniting a feeling of love and warmth in Ethan's heart—emotions he hadn't felt so strongly since his grandfather's passing.

Ethan instinctively moved his hand to his cross and gently grasped it between his fingers. He looked down at it, sensing a subtle, mysterious connection between its presence and the apparition of his grandfather. A familiar warmth from the cross against his fingertips came with a tingling sensation that surged through him.

Lifting his head to look at his grandfather, their eyes met again. His grandfather's smile widened, and he nodded, conveying an unspoken message of recognition and connection. At that moment, the breeze along the boardwalk picked up, and the figure of Ethan's grandfather began to fade into the night, slowly dissolving into the air.

Ethan stood still as he watched the figure disappear, his face etched with confusion and contemplation. He looked back down at the cross, his mind racing with questions. He wondered if this extraordinary encounter had anything to do with the cross his grandfather had given him. And was there even a deeper connection to the strange presence that he had felt since his arrival in town?

These questions lingered in Ethan's mind, leaving him to ponder the mystical and the unexplained as he stood on the boardwalk, the night air swirling around him.

Felix rose to his feet, his emotions still raw from his encounter. He looked over at Ethan, who met his gaze. Unaware of each other's profound experiences, they stood in silence, each lost in his own thoughts.

At that moment, Jessica and Fawn returned from their brief meeting with their friends, their faces radiant with joy and beaming smiles. They approached the boys, breaking the quiet spell.

When Jessica saw Ethan, she knew something was wrong. She enveloped him in a loving embrace, feeling his tension and noting his shocked, bewildered expression.

"What happened, babe? You look like you just saw a ghost," she asked, her voice laced with concern.

Ethan chuckled awkwardly, meeting her gaze but choosing to keep the encounter to himself, unsure of how to explain it.

"It's nothing, just a weird moment," he said, attempting to brush it off.

Meanwhile, Fawn approached a solemn-looking Felix, despite his attempt at a smile. "Are you okay, Felix?" she asked, her eyes searching for any sign of distress.

Felix nodded and gave Fawn a forced, but reassuring smile. "Yeah, I'm okay. Thank you," he replied, trying to mask the emotional turmoil he had just undergone.

Ethan glanced around the boardwalk as if to confirm his reality, then took Jessica's hand. "Let's take Felix home," he suggested, the weight of his encounter with his grandfather's spirit still lingering in his voice.

As they began their walk toward the steps leading to the parking lot, Jessica hugged Ethan's arm, sensing his need for comfort. Ethan welcomed her support, the warmth of her embrace grounding him. Fawn and Felix followed, walking side by side, each couple wrapped in their own world of thoughts and emotions.

The night had been filled with unexpected revelations and emotional encounters for Ethan and Felix. As they walked toward the parking lot, each was lost in their thoughts, reflecting on the profound experiences that had just taken place under the mystical canopy of Wavecrest's night sky.

Parked in front of Felix's house, the Jeep's engine was silent, blending into the stillness of the night. Felix stood by the iron gate, a somber figure under the night sky, with Fawn standing beside him. Jessica and Ethan leaned casually against the side of the Jeep, their presence contrasting the surrounding darkness.

In this part of Wavecrest, the night air was thick and warm, a noticeable stillness devoid of any comforting breeze. Darkness enveloped the neighborhood, punctuated only by faint orange glows from a few distant houses. In stark contrast, Felix's house sat in total darkness, its windows devoid of light, giving it an almost lifeless appearance.

An eerie silence hung over the area, a stark reminder of the isolation that characterized this part of the neighborhood. It was a silence so profound that even the occasional distant bark of a dog seemed to underscore the solitude rather than disrupt it.

This was the world Felix lived in—a stark contrast to the vibrant, lively parts of Wavecrest. It was a place where the joy and light of the boardwalk felt like a distant memory, where the chill of loneliness and neglect seemed to seep from the ground. As Felix stood there, the stark reality of this part of town became palpable, casting a shadow over the group's earlier experiences of the night.

In the dim light of the quiet street, Felix felt a poignant heaviness in his heart. He realized that this might be the last time he'd see these friends who had become an unexpected part of his life. The approaching days of August signaled more than just the end of summer; they marked the impending departure of his friends to begin new chapters of their lives far from the shores of Wavecrest.

Feeling the weight of impending goodbyes, Felix gathered his composure and tried to hide his sadness. He took a slow, deliberate step toward Jessica, taking a deep breath to steady himself.

"Thank you, Jessica, for being my friend," he began, his voice tinged with heartfelt sincerity. "Thank you for inviting me to your birthday party and allowing me to go with you guys to the dance."

Jessica responded with a warmth that was both comforting and genuine. Her smile was radiant, and her bright blue eyes sparkled with affection.

"You don't have to thank me, Felix. I enjoyed being with you. You're a cool guy to hang out with," she said, her sincerity matching the warmth in her eyes.

A swell of gratitude lightened Felix's heart, breaking through the somber mood. Emboldened, he ventured a request, his voice taking on a pleading tone. "Would you do something for me when you get to Texas?" he asked.

Curiosity flickered in Jessica's eyes as she nodded, "Sure."

Felix spoke in a shy tone, his usual nervousness resurfacing. "When you see Emily, will you tell her I said, 'Hi'?" His question was simple, but it held significant meaning for him.

Jessica's smile widened with understanding. "I will," she promised.

Felix then turned to Ethan with a mixture of admiration and sadness. In the short time they had spent together, Ethan had become more than just a friend to him; he had become a role model, an example of what he aspired to be. Ethan's consistent kindness and respect was a stark contrast to the harshness he had endured from others, notably the jocks at school. For Felix, Ethan was like the big brother he never had, symbolizing the respect and acceptance he had always craved. This made saying goodbye especially difficult for him.

"I want to thank you too, Ethan, for being a good friend. You taught me a lot and made me feel like I belong, that I am somebody," Felix said, his voice overflowing with genuine gratitude.

"You are somebody, Felix, and you deserve to be treated well," Ethan replied, his tone earnest and reassuring. "Don't let anyone make you feel less than who you are, okay buddy?"

A moment of genuine camaraderie followed as Ethan extended his hand for a handshake. Felix reached out, expecting the usual gesture, but Ethan surprised him with the 'bro' handshake he had taught him at Jessica's birthday party. The handshake was a symbol of their bond, a mutual understanding and respect. Ethan was visibly pleased that Felix remembered how to do it.

Jessica and Fawn observed the exchange, their faces smiling at the sight of the heartfelt connection.

After completing their unique handshake, Ethan took Felix's hand in both of his, a gesture that conveyed a deeper connection.

"You go out there and kick ass, bro. Don't be afraid to go after what you want," Ethan encouraged, his words filled with belief in Felix's potential.

Felix nodded, deeply moved by Ethan's support and belief in him. The moment was a poignant one, marking not only a farewell but also a lasting impact on Felix's journey to self-confidence and acceptance.

Finally, Felix turned to Fawn, who had welcomed him into their tight-knit circle. It was Fawn who had included him in Jessica's birthday party and the Summer Dance, opening a world he had never thought he'd be part of. As he faced her, Felix felt his eyes swell with tears, the emotion of the moment catching up with him.

Noticing the sadness in Felix's eyes, Fawn quickly moved to reassure him. "Felix, next month is going to be a busy month for me," she said gently. "But I promise I'll stop by before I leave for Boston." Her words were a balm to Felix's anxious heart, offering him the comfort of one more meeting before their paths diverged.

Mustering his courage, Felix managed a smile and said with genuine hope and sincerity, "I hope you win the Art Contest, Fawn. I really do."

Fawn's face lit up with a warm smile. "Aw, thanks," she replied. "Are you going to be there? You might be the one who wins, you know."

Felix shrugged modestly. "Nah, I don't stand a chance," he admitted. "I'm nowhere near as good as you guys."

Fawn, always encouraging, replied, "You never know. Art is about passion and heart, not just skill. Don't count yourself out just yet."

Her words elicited a smile and a chuckle from Felix. "If you say so, Fawn."

Fawn gave Felix a somber smile. "Well, we gotta go now. It's getting really late."

Felix felt a pang of sadness as he realized that this was indeed their last goodbye. Yet, he masked it with a brave face, wishing his friends a cheerful farewell.

Ethan opened the passenger door and tilted the seat forward, letting Fawn slide into the back seat. But before climbing in, Fawn gave Felix one last smile. "See you in a few weeks."

Once Fawn was settled, Ethan adjusted the seat back into position for Jessica. "Good-bye, Felix. You take care of yourself, okay?" Jessica said, her smile warm yet tinged with the sadness of parting.

Jessica settled into the seat as Ethan closed her door, then walked around to the driver's side. As he opened his door, he turned to Felix for a final word. "So long, Felix," he said, waving his hand before climbing into the driver's seat.

In the silence of the night, the sound of the Jeep's engine roared to life under Ethan's command. Felix stood and watched as the Jeep turned and headed back toward the heart of Wavecrest, the vehicle gradually disappearing into the evening's shadow.

Alone in the darkness, Felix remained at the gate, feeling a whirlwind of emotions—sadness at their parting, gratitude for the memories they had given him, and hope for the future. This summer had been unlike any other, transformed by the unexpected friendships with Fawn, Jessica, and Ethan, marking a chapter in his life that he would always cherish.

# Chapter 36

-------------------------------------------------------

As the calendar turned its page from the vibrancy of July to the waning days of August, Wavecrest's once bustling boardwalk began to quiet. The lingering echoes of the Summer Dance still hung in the air, a sweet reminder of the season's finale, but now a subtle change was palpable. Once a vibrant tapestry of laughter and youthful exuberance, the crowds thinned as teenagers turned their attention to the upcoming school year. The beach, too, felt the change; its sands were less trodden as the end of summer approached.

As August unfolded, Wavecrest took on a more reflective mood. In just a few short weeks, it would be a time of goodbyes—for some, a routine farewell to their summer break as they prepared to return to college or embark on new careers. But for others, particularly the young souls standing on the cusp of adulthood, these farewells would carry a more profound significance. It would be a farewell to the innocence and freedom of youth, a step into a world where the realities of life awaited to consume their carefree spirits.

In the early hours of Saturday, the quietude of the morning blanketed Jessica's house. Inside, Teresa and Anna sat at the kitchen table, their conversation a soft hum over the steaming cups of coffee. The aroma filled the room, a gentle reminder of the day's slow start.

Down the hallway, Jessica and Fawn were still nestled in the comforting embrace of sleep, unaware of the day's significance that awaited them. Today was not just another day; it was August 9th, the day of the Art Contest, an event that could mark a turning point in Fawn's artistic journey. As the sun began its ascent, painting the sky with soft hues of dawn, the day held promise and potential, a canvas awaiting the brushstrokes of fate.

Anna sighed, staring into her coffee cup. "Fawn's been so distant with us. I don't know if she'll ever forgive us for not telling her sooner about Atlas and our move." She looked up, her eyes holding a mixture of regret and sadness. "We really screwed this up, Terri. We should've told her from the start."

Teresa reached across the table, offering a comforting hand. "Give her time, Anna. She's still processing all of this. And who knows, maybe your trip to Boston with her will help bridge the gap. She might see things differently once she settles into her new life there."

Anna nodded slowly, but her concern was obvious. "I hope so. But right now, it feels like we've just turned her world upside down. Jessica's, too."

Teresa's voice was gentle but firm. "Anna, they're young. Kids their age... they don't fully understand some of the hard decisions we parents have to make. Sometimes, there are no easy choices."

Anna nodded, though her expression remained troubled. "Brian insisted that we keep it from her. He didn't want to ruin her last summer here or make her feel guilty because we used our savings to pay for her Art School." She paused briefly, her gaze drifting away as if lost in thought. Then, with a hint of a deeper insight, she added, "But I think it was more than that."

Teresa leaned in, her eyes reflecting a blend of curiosity and concern. "What do you mean?"

"He didn't want anyone to know, especially Tom. It's his ego, you know? He didn't want anyone to pity us for our financial troubles." Anna's voice was a mix of disappointment and resignation. "I wanted to tell you guys. I really did. But Brian... he just wouldn't budge."

Teresa's expression changed to one of understanding. "Men can be stubborn about these things. I wish you had come to us, though. Maybe Tom could've helped Brian find a job here."

Anna chuckled ruefully. "I know. Brian just didn't want help. I disagreed, but he was adamant."

The conversation shifted as Anna reflected on the passage of time. "Seems like only yesterday our girls were starting kindergarten," she mused, her voice soft with nostalgia.

Teresa nodded, her eyes distant. "That's how we met, remember? Our daughters brought us together. And now, look at them... all grown up."

Anna's voice cracked with emotion, and her eyes filled with tears. "You know, I'm not just losing my daughter to college, Terri. I'm losing my home, and my best friend." Her voice trailed off as tears finally escaped. "I don't want to leave Wavecrest, but I have no choice. And knowing how much our girls are hurting just breaks my heart."

Tears welled up in Teresa's eyes as she reached across the table and gently squeezed Anna's hand. "We're all feeling it, Anna. It's hard letting go. But today's Fawn's big day. We need to be there for her."

Anna wiped away her tears and gave a weak smile. "Right, the Art Contest. I need to pull myself together."

Trying to lighten the mood, Teresa quipped with a small, tearful smile, "Maybe we should swap our coffee for something a bit stronger, huh?"

Anna let out a small chuckle, the corners of her mouth lifting slightly. "Maybe that's what we need right now," she replied with a weary smile.

As the conversation dwindled, an eerie silence filled the kitchen. The two mothers, bound by years of shared experiences and mutual affection, sat together in silent contemplation. Their hands remained entwined atop the kitchen table, showing their enduring support for one another.

The world outside continued to awaken, but at that moment, inside the Reese home, time seemed to pause. These were two women grappling with the reality of change, of letting go and embracing the new chapters in their families. With a final sip of their coffee, they acknowledged the day ahead—a day marked by pride, hope, and a lingering nostalgia for the years that had passed all too quickly.

As the late morning sun cast a soft glow over the town, Jessica and Fawn emerged from the bedroom, still clad in their nightgowns, their hair tousled, and sleep lingering in their eyes. The soft sunlight gave the house a serene atmosphere, signaling the beginning of a new day. As they walked past the living room on their way to the kitchen, they saw Teresa and Anna sitting on the sofa, engrossed in a scrapbook, their laughter and the rustling of pages creating a backdrop of warm memories.

Noticing the girls, Teresa and Anna set the scrapbook aside and moved to the kitchen, their faces lighting up with affectionate smiles.

"Good morning, girls," Teresa greeted them, her voice warm with maternal love as she enveloped Jessica in a quick, tender hug.

"Good morning, sweetie," Anna echoed, wrapping Fawn in a loving embrace and holding her for a moment longer. She then turned to Jessica and gave her the same heartfelt warmth.

As Teresa's arms wrapped around Fawn, she couldn't help but share her excitement for the day. "Today's the big day. Are you excited, honey?" she asked, her eyes sparkling with anticipation.

Still shaking off the remnants of sleep, Fawn managed a sleepy smile. "A little," she replied, her restrained response belying her excitement.

Teresa looked at Anna knowingly, both mothers recognizing their daughters' understated excitement. "Yep, she's excited, alright," Teresa grinned.

Anna chuckled and then announced, "How about you girls take a seat? I'll whip up some breakfast."

Teresa quickly interjected. "No, Anna, let me handle breakfast. You sit and relax with the girls."

But Anna insisted, a soft determination in her voice. "Please, Terri. I haven't made breakfast for our girls in a while. Let me do this."

Teresa relented, her expression softening. "Okay, then. At least let me help." She then turned to Jessica and Fawn. "Why don't you girls go get dressed, and by the time you come back, breakfast will be ready."

With nods of agreement, Jessica and Fawn returned to the bedroom to get ready for the day. In the kitchen, Teresa and Anna moved in unison, their shared task of preparing pancakes and toast, a harmonious dance of friendship and motherhood. The aroma of breakfast soon filled the house, a tangible symbol of the care and love that bound these two families together.

The morning routine at Jessica's home took an unexpected turn when the front door opened and closed, announcing Tom's arrival. He entered the kitchen carrying a white box of freshly baked donuts from the bakery. When he saw Teresa and Anna busy with breakfast preparations, he quipped, "Oh, you're cooking breakfast. I got donuts."

Tom set the box of donuts on the kitchen table and opened it, revealing an array of glazed temptations.

While fixing a fresh pot of coffee, Teresa glanced at him with a playful eye. "Well, our breakfast is more nutritious," she informed him.

Unfazed, Tom picked a glazed donut and teased back. "Fine. That's more for me," and then took a satisfying bite.

Teresa smirked at her husband's comment. "You men can carry donuts better than us women," she replied.

Tom chuckled, enjoying his donut. "Well, one donut won't hurt," he said with a shrug.

"Tell my thighs that," Teresa retorted, eliciting a laugh from Tom.

Always the affectionate husband, he strolled over to Teresa and playfully patted her on the butt, saying with a grin, "I love your thighs."

Their playful banter came to an end as Jessica and Fawn entered the kitchen, dressed and ready for the day. Fawn's sundress fluttered at the hem, its ruffles adding a whimsical touch. Jessica's ensemble, a tailored black and white outfit, seamlessly blended modern chic with classic elegance.

Anna's and Teresa's faces lit up with smiles at the sight of their daughters. "Aw, you girls look adorable," Anna exclaimed, flipping a pancake before turning to greet them.

Teresa echoed the sentiment as she managed the toaster. "Yes, you both look absolutely beautiful," she said with motherly pride.

Glowing with appreciation, the girls returned the compliment with radiant smiles and took their seats at the kitchen table, ready to enjoy the breakfast their mothers had lovingly prepared.

As they settled into their breakfast, Jessica's excitement bubbled over. "I'm so excited. I finally get to see the big secret Fawn kept from me," she exclaimed, her eyes sparkling with anticipation.

Fawn couldn't help but giggle, barely containing her excitement at the thought of Jessica seeing her artwork.

"I'm excited, too," Teresa chimed in as she buttered the toast. She looked at Fawn with a curious smile. "I haven't seen it either."

Anna, sliding pancakes onto Jessica and Fawn's plates, couldn't help but playfully boast, "I did. I know what it is." She wore a teasing smile.

As Teresa brought the plate of toast to the table, she grinned at Anna. "Oh, that's cold," she chided playfully.

Jessica, her mouth open in mock shock at Anna's bragging, chimed in, "Yeah, really." Then, putting on a playful pout, she added, "Don't tease me, Mama."

Always softened by Jessica's playful pout, Anna smiled as she set the plates on the table. She wrapped her arm around Jessica's head and planted a big kiss on it. "Aw, but I love teasing you, sweetheart."

The girls smiled warmly, indulging in the teasing as they ate their breakfast. Tom strolled over to Teresa and put his arm around her, both watching the girls with affectionate eyes.

When breakfast was over, Anna stood up, ready to leave. "Well, I better get back. I have things to do before we go to the Art Contest."

Tom, ever the helpful friend, offered, "Do you need help with anything, Anna?"

"No, but thanks anyway," she replied graciously. Then she turned to the girls. "Are you riding with us to the school?"

Fawn turned to Jessica, her eyes seeking guidance, leaving the decision to her friend.

"Well, Ethan's working today, so he won't be able to make it," Jessica replied. "So, why don't we ride with Mama and Papa?"

"Okay, we can do that," Fawn nodded, agreeing with Jessica's plan.

Jessica turned to her mother with a hint of concern in her eyes and asked, "Is that okay with you?" She didn't want to inadvertently hurt her feelings by choosing to ride with Fawn and her parents.

"Yeah, that's fine," Teresa replied with a nod of understanding, recognizing the importance of Jessica being with Fawn on this special day. "We'll meet up in the parking lot a little before two."

"Sounds perfect," Anna replied with a warm smile that reflected her happiness with the arrangement.

After giving Teresa and Tom a warm hug, Anna walked over to the table and kissed the girls on the top of their heads. "Okay, we'll see you later," she said as she opened the front door and walked out, closing it behind her.

The sound of Anna's car pulling out of the driveway and fading into the distance marked a shift in the atmosphere of the kitchen, settling it into hopeful anticipation. Teresa and Tom stood side by side, their expressions a blend of pride and excitement. The hum of the morning's activities gave way to a quieter, more reflective mood, each considering the significance of the day ahead.

The girls remained seated at the table, their plates now empty, but their faces illuminated with the thrill of what was to come. The Art Contest was not just another event; it was a milestone, a moment that could define the beginning of Fawn's journey in the art world.

Teresa broke the silence, her voice laced with optimism. "I have a good feeling about today," she mused, glancing towards Fawn with a mother's pride.

Tom nodded in agreement, his eyes twinkling. "Fawn has talent. No doubt she'll impress them."

Jessica leaned toward Fawn, her excitement barely contained. "Your sketch is going to be amazing, Fawn. I just know it," she said, her confidence in her friend unwavering.

Feeling nervous and excited, Fawn gave a shy but hopeful smile. "Thanks, guys. I just hope the judges like it," she replied, her modesty shining through.

Teresa moved closer and placed a reassuring hand on Fawn's shoulder. "Honey, no matter what happens, we're all so proud of you. You've already won in our eyes," she said, her voice brimming with sincerity.

Tom chimed in, his tone upbeat and encouraging. "Absolutely! Today's about celebrating your talent, Fawn. Winning would just be the icing on the cake."

As Jessica and Fawn cleared the table, their movements were playful, each nudging the other in a light-hearted dance of excitement. Today was more than just an art contest; it was about celebrating Fawn's passion, hard work, and future potential. The thought that she could win only added an extra layer of excitement, making the day feel charged with possibility.

With each dish washed and the countertop wiped, the kitchen gradually returned to its normal state, but the anticipation for the afternoon remained. In that kitchen, the ordinary routine of breakfast had become a prelude to something extraordinary. The day held the promise of new beginnings and, perhaps, a memorable victory. But most of all, it was a day to cherish the bonds of friendship and family, a day when hope and art would intertwine under the warm August sun.

# Chapter 37

----------------------------------------------------------------

In the busy parking lot of Wavecrest High School, a distinct sense of anticipation hung in the air. It was a beautiful Saturday afternoon, the kind that felt like a gentle embrace, with its clear blue sky and the sun casting a warm, golden glow. The parking lot, unusually full for so early in the month, was buzzing with the arrival of young, aspiring artists and their families, drawn to the Art Contest that had become a focal point in this small coastal town.

Jessica, her excitement palpable, walked in small, restless circles, her hands buried in the pockets of her light summer jacket. Her bright blue eyes scanned the area, a mixture of eagerness and impatience dancing in them. She had been waiting for what felt like forever to see Fawn's secretive sketch, a piece of art that her best friend had guarded with fervent dedication.

Next to her, Fawn paced in front of their parked car, the picture of nervous energy. The sunlight caught in her blonde hair, creating a halo effect that contrasted with the storm of emotions in her expressive eyes. The sketch, her labor of love and artistic expression, weighed heavily on her mind. How would it be received? Would the judges understand the depth and emotion she had poured into it?

Meanwhile, Brian and Anna leaned against the side of the car, embodying quiet patience. They kept a watchful eye on the entrance to the parking lot, awaiting Tom and Teresa's arrival. The atmosphere was a blend of nervousness and anticipation, mirroring the emotions of the young artists around them.

Finally, they spotted the familiar car as it pulled into the school parking lot. Jessica joined Fawn at her side, and they both watched Tom navigate the car into an empty space. When they exited the vehicle, the girls anxiously walked over to them, with Brian and Anna following closely behind.

Once the two families were together, Anna greeted Teresa with a warm hug, her happiness evident in being in the company of her best friend on such a special day. Tom and Brian exchanged a handshake, but the warmth in Tom's gesture was noticeably absent. He still harbored discontent with Brian's decision to sell the house and move to Montana—a decision Tom believed could have been avoided if Brian had confided in him back in May. In Tom's mind, he believed he could have found Brian a new job, which would have prevented the need for their families' lives from being so drastically disrupted.

"How have you been, Tom? I haven't seen you in a while," Brian ventured, attempting to bridge the gap.

Tom's reply was quick, his tone stiff. "Fine, Brian. I'm doing just fine."

Brian immediately sensed Tom's coldness and decided to drop the small talk. He knew Tom was not one who easily forgave and forgot. So, he simply nodded and shifted his focus to Fawn and Jessica, who were leading the way, their anxiety and excitement palpable.

"C'mon, guys," Jessica called out, her voice tinged with impatience as she turned to see her parents lagging behind. She grabbed Fawn's hand and jogged toward the entrance.

Tom and Teresa laughed at Jessica's impatience, a moment of lightness breaking through the tension. Brian and Anna couldn't help but smile at the youthful exuberance that the girls always seemed to inspire in each other.

Following at a more leisurely pace, the parents made their way to the entrance, eager to witness Fawn's moment to shine with her artwork. Though shadowed by complex emotions and impending changes, the day held a promise of celebration and recognition for Fawn's artistic passion.

As Jessica and Fawn pushed open the glass doors, they stepped into the high school lobby, which had been transformed into a vibrant gallery of creativity and talent. The room was bustling with people, showing the excitement surrounding the Art Contest. Seventeen of Fawn's competitors stood proudly in front of their art exhibits, each surrounded by supportive family members. The sketches, arrayed in their full glory on easels, showcased diverse artistic skills and visions, turning the lobby into a monochrome mosaic of lines and shadows, each piece a silent testament to its creator's expression.

In the far-right corner of the room stood a podium with a small microphone attached to it, waiting for the event to officially begin. The atmosphere was electric, the voices of the crowd blending into a symphony of excitement and anticipation. The girls were awed by seeing their high school transformed into an epicenter of artistic expression.

Jessica, who had no idea what Fawn's sketch looked like, turned to her friend with wide, inquisitive eyes. "Where's your sketch?" she asked eagerly, her curiosity palpable.

Being tall, Fawn scanned over the heads of the crowd. Her eyes searched meticulously until they landed on her piece.

"There it is. Right over there," she said, pointing toward her artwork.

She glanced back to ensure that both their families were with them. Seeing they were, she took Jessica's hand and said, "Follow me!" Her voice was a mixture of excitement and nervousness as she led Jessica through the crowd, weaving their way toward her creation.

The journey through the crowd was a sensory experience, as snippets of conversation, laughter, and the occasional gasp of admiration at the works on display filled the air. Each step brought them closer to Fawn's creation, a piece that represented more than just artistic skill. It embodied her emotions, her life experiences, and her deep connection to Jessica. The air crackled with anticipation, each breath carrying the weight of a moment that would be engraved in their memories for years to come.

As Fawn led Jessica through the throng of people, the sketch finally came into view, and Jessica's breath caught in her throat. On the easel was a stunningly detailed portrait of the two of them sitting on their treasured white bench swing in Fawn's side yard.

On the left, the portrait depicted Jessica with her deep brown hair cascading around her shoulders, framing her large, bright eyes that seemed to sparkle with a life of their own. The detail was so precise that Jessica could almost feel the gentle gaze emanating from her own sketched eyes, reflecting a sweetness and vulnerability that Fawn had always understood.

On the right, Fawn's portrait was every bit of her vibrant self. Her long, blonde hair flowed freely, and her eyes glowed with the spark of her free-spirited nature. The sketch captured her essence perfectly, the mischievous twinkle in her eyes that Jessica knew so well, the kind that often led to their adventures together.

Though drawn in black and white, the bench swing seemed to exude the warmth and joy of their childhood. It was rendered with such care that it looked as if it had been plucked from the past, on the day it was built, new and full of promise. The ropes of the swing were shaded with such attention to texture that Jessica could almost hear them creak as they swayed back and forth.

This was no mere sketch; it was a testament to their friendship, a moment captured in time, immortalized by an artist who knew them better than they knew themselves. As Jessica looked at the image of them together, gently swinging, suspended in a moment between laughter and serenity, she felt a surge of gratitude for the bond Fawn had so beautifully captured on the blank canvas of possibility.

The sheer skill and emotion Fawn had poured into the drawing left Jessica speechless. The shading was impeccable, the lines fluid, and the way the light seemed to dance across their faces was nothing short of masterful. In Jessica's eyes, it was the pinnacle of Fawn's talent. Seeing them together on the swing, not as the little girls they once were, but as the young women they had become, stirred something deep within her. A tear trickled down her cheek, a silent testament to the storm of emotions swirling in her chest.

With her eyes fixed on the sketch, Jessica could only nod, her voice a whisper of awe, "Oh my God, Fawn. This is amazing." Her words were few, but they held a universe of meaning—recognition, love, and a shared past that would always bind them, no matter where life's paths took them.

Anna approached the easel with a familiarity tempered by awe. She'd seen the sketch before, but the hum of admiration from the gathering crowd gave it a new reverence.

"It's even more beautiful than I remembered," she murmured, her voice tinged with pride. Her eyes, reflecting the artistry of her daughter's work, beamed with joy and a mother's love.

Standing next to her, Brian was the picture of paternal admiration. His chest swelled as he examined the piece, his eyes tracing the careful details of the sketch. "Honey, you've outdone yourself," he said, his voice resonant and warm. He reached out and placed a supportive hand on Fawn's shoulder, a silent testament to his deep satisfaction in her abilities.

Meanwhile, Teresa's hand flew to her heart as she took in the portrait. "Oh my God, the detail here is extraordinary," she exclaimed as her eyes scanned the realistic touches Fawn had applied to their faces. "You've captured Jessica and yourself in form and spirit."

Tom, who had been quiet, stepped forward for a closer look. His gaze locked onto the sketch, and his eyes mirrored Teresa's amazement. "I've seen a lot of your art," he finally spoke, his voice carrying a note of respect and wonder, "but what you've done here, it almost looks like a photograph." He gave a slight, appreciative shake of his head. "Truly remarkable work, sweetheart."

Overwhelmed by the warmth emanating from her loved ones, Fawn felt her emotions rise, a flood that could not be held back. This moment eclipsed all her ambitions for the contest. The approval and affection of her family, who had been her anchor and guiding stars, meant more to her than any accolade the judges could offer.

With a voice full of emotion, Fawn addressed them all. "Thank you, guys. Your support... It means the world to me. More than winning, more than anything." Her words were simple, but they resonated with sincerity and a humility that was quintessentially Fawn.

Moved by the scene and the strength of their bond, Jessica stepped closer to Fawn. She wrapped her arm around her best friend, pulling her into a side hug that was both comforting and celebratory.

"I love you so much, Fawn," she whispered, a sentiment that carried the weight of years of friendship.

Fawn felt the warmth of Jessica's embrace envelop her, a balm to the whirlwind of emotions swirling inside. She leaned into her, her arm rising to return the gesture, holding Jessica close.

"I love you, too, Jess," she said softly, her voice rich with emotion.

Amid this tender moment, a flurry of activity near the podium caught their attention. Heads turned, and the murmur of the crowd shifted to a hush of anticipation. Jessica and Fawn's eyes followed the collective gaze to see Mrs. Sprite, their beloved art teacher, making her way to the podium. The realization that the announcement of the contest winner was imminent sent a flutter of nerves through their stomachs. Their hearts sank, not from fear of the outcome but from the sudden reminder that this moment marked an end, regardless of who would win. The name to be called out next would close this chapter of their lives, sealing the memory of this day with a bittersweet edge.

Mrs. Sprite stood poised behind the podium, her eyes sweeping over the crowd with a smile that crinkled the corners of her eyes. She wore a colorful sundress that seemed to capture the essence of summer itself—vibrant, warm, and full of life, much like the art surrounding her. She cleared her throat, the simple action drawing the room to a hushed anticipation.

"Good afternoon, everyone," Mrs. Sprite began, her voice carrying a melodic quality that effortlessly commanded attention. "My name is Gwendolyn Sprite, and for the past fourteen years, I've had the pleasure of teaching Arts and Crafts here at Wavecrest High School. Today is a very special occasion for us all."

As Mrs. Sprite spoke, the audience, a mosaic of hopeful artists and their families, gave her their undivided attention. Fawn and Jessica stood side by side, their hands clasped tightly, their eyes locked on Mrs. Sprite.

"I'm thrilled to see such a wonderful turnout for Wavecrest's inaugural Art Contest," Mrs. Sprite continued, her eyes twinkling with excitement. "It is heartening to see students from Coral Heights and Cherry Springs among our entrants. Eighteen budding artists have graced us with their talent, and one of you will soon hold a trophy and a check for two thousand dollars."

A wave of eager murmurs swept through the crowd. Fawn's grip on Jessica's hand tightened, a silent communication of hope and shared nerves.

Mrs. Sprite continued, "The contest was open to all high school students and this year's graduates in our district, challenging them to express their vision through ink or pencil sketches. The theme allowed for an amazing array of creativity and skill, which you all see here today."

As Mrs. Sprite expressed her gratitude to the sponsors, her eyes shone with sincerity. "None of this would be possible without Cranmer Industries, The Ink Spot on Water Street, and Well's Shopping Center. And a special thanks to Principal Morrison and Assistant Principal Pennington for their cooperation and support of the arts in our school."

The audience applauded, some nodding in appreciation of the sponsors mentioned. Jessica and Fawn exchanged a brief, supportive smile, a silent acknowledgment of the efforts that had made this day possible.

"And of course," Mrs. Sprite continued, "we are incredibly grateful to the three esteemed art professors from the University of California in Santa Barbara, who volunteered their time to judge today's contest. It is they who will declare the winner of this year's competition."

The room seemed to hold its collective breath, the tension of the competition palpable in the air. Fawn's eyes shimmered, reflecting every emotion she had poured into her sketch.

Finally, Mrs. Sprite offered a concluding smile. "So, without further ado, I present to you, Professor Martin Hayes."

Applause erupted as a figure made his way toward the podium. Fawn and Jessica's hearts raced in unison, their journey together symbolized in that sketch on the easel, awaiting its crowning moment.

Professor Hayes, a distinguished figure with silver hair that spoke of wisdom and experience, stood behind the podium. His suit and tie exuded an air of professionalism and respect for the occasion. As he scanned the audience, his keen eyes reflected a deep appreciation for the artists before him.

"First and foremost, I would like to extend my gratitude to Mrs. Sprite for her unwavering dedication to the arts and for sharing her vast knowledge with her students," Professor Hayes began, his voice steady and reassuring.

He then turned to introduce his colleagues, gesturing to Professor Angela Rivera and Professor Leonard Wu. Professor Rivera, vibrant in her colorful attire and expressive manner, radiated warmth and enthusiasm. Beside her, the young Asian Professor Wu stood, his modern style evident in his tailored suit, embodying a blend of contemporary artistry and academic rigor.

"It has been an honor to be surrounded by such talented, aspiring artists," Professor Hayes continued, his eyes sweeping across the crowd. "The quality of work we've seen today is a testament to your passion and skill. It was a challenging task to select just one winner among so many incredible entries."

Fawn and Jessica hung on every word, their hands clasped together, their hearts beating in unison. The tension and excitement between them were almost palpable.

"Art is not just about creating a visually pleasing image," Professor Hayes explained. "It's about the emotions, the feelings that are woven into the creation. It's about an artist's ability to put their passion into their work, and that's what we, as judges, sought to find in these pieces."

He emphasized that their judgment was unbiased, free from any preconceived notions about the artists or their backgrounds. "Our focus was on the art itself to ensure a fair evaluation."

Noticing the audience's mounting anticipation, Professor Hayes smiled, "It's a beautiful day outside, and I'm sure you're all anxious to get back. So, are you ready to hear who the winner of this year's Art Contest is?"

A wave of eager nods and murmurs swept through the crowd. Anna placed her hands on Fawn's shoulders, a silent show of support and shared excitement. The moment stretched, every second feeling like an eternity.

With a dramatic flourish, Professor Hayes retrieved an envelope from his inside pocket and carefully opened it. The action unfolded in slow motion, adding to the suspense.

Fawn and Jessica's hearts pounded, their breaths held in anticipation.

He pulled out the paper, his smile widening as he read the name. Turning back to the audience, he paused, savoring the moment.

"I am pleased to announce that this year's winner of Wavecrest High School's Art Contest is…" He let the suspense linger for a moment longer before finally announcing, "Fawn Gaddesden."

A wave of disbelief washed over Fawn at the sound of her name being announced as the winner. Professor Hayes's voice echoed in her mind, repeating her name like a mantra that slowly anchored her back to reality. She, Fawn Gaddesden, and her heartfelt sketch had triumphed over seventeen other talented artists. Frozen in a moment of sheer astonishment, her thoughts raced between disbelief and elation.

Then, almost instinctively, her arms rose, her hands covering her mouth as a rush of emotions cascaded through her. Happiness, excitement, gratitude—they all swirled within her, so intense that her eyes brimmed with tears of joy.

Next to her, Jessica's reaction was one of shock and overwhelming delight. Her jaw dropped, her eyes wide with astonishment. She couldn't contain her excitement as she wrapped Fawn in a tight, heartfelt hug.

"Oh my God, Fawn! You won!" she exclaimed, her voice a vibrant mix of joy and pride. Holding Fawn close, she added, "I'm so proud of you. " Her words were slightly muffled but charged with the depth of their shared journey.

In their bubble of emotion, Fawn and Jessica were oblivious to the thunderous applause that erupted around them. It wasn't just a clap of hands; it was an outpouring of admiration, respect, and joy from everyone in the room.

As the applause continued, Jessica released Fawn, allowing space for others to offer their congratulations. Fawn's parents were the first to reach her. Anna wrapped her arms around her daughter, her embrace conveying a mother's deep love and pride.

"You did it, sweetheart," she whispered, tears of joy glistening in her eyes.

Beaming with fatherly pride, Brian joined the embrace, his eyes reflecting the same admiration that shone in Anna's. His hug was strong and protective, a silent message of his unwavering support and belief in his daughter's talent.

Then came Jessica's parents. Teresa approached Fawn, her arms wide open, and pulled her into a warm, maternal hug.

"We're so proud of you, honey," she said, her voice trembling with emotion.

Tom's embrace was equally heartfelt. His hug was a solid and reassuring presence, his admiration for Fawn's accomplishment evident in his firm pat on her back.

"Well done, sweetheart. Truly well done," he said, his words simple but meaningful.

The room was a whirlwind of emotions, each hug and congratulation adding to the crescendo of joy and admiration that enveloped Fawn. Amidst the applause and tears, the moment was etched into the hearts of everyone in the room, a celebration of talent, hard work, and the unbreakable bond of friendship.

Mrs. Sprite, her hands clapping in time with the applause, beamed as she scanned the audience for Fawn. Her eyes, full of affection and pride, finally settled on the young artist standing with her family.

"Fawn, will you and your family please come up here?" she called out, her voice echoing through the room.

Fawn's face lit up with a radiant smile as she turned toward Mrs. Sprite. Jessica, ever the supportive friend, gave her a gentle nudge, her face aglow with excitement. Together, they began to make their way through the crowd toward the podium, their families in tow.

The path to the front was like the parting of the sea, the audience stepping aside to create a clear passage for Fawn and her entourage. The applause continued, a soundtrack to this momentous walk.

Unaccustomed to being the center of attention, Fawn felt a mixture of nervousness and awe. The many eyes on her, all smiling and celebratory, were both exhilarating and overwhelming. She glanced at Jessica, a shy grin coupled with a look of embarrassment on her face.

"I'm so nervous," she whispered, her voice barely audible over the applause.

Jessica's response was a light, affectionate giggle. She was enjoying the attention, not for herself, but for Fawn. In her eyes, Fawn more than deserved this moment of glory.

"Don't worry, Fawn. I'm here with you," she assured, her words meant to offer comfort and strength. Jessica's presence, a constant in Fawn's life, was her anchor in that sea of applause and admiration.

Together, they reached the podium and stood before Mrs. Sprite and the esteemed judges. The journey, short in distance but significant in meaning, was a testament to Fawn's talent and the collective support of those who cherished her.

As Fawn and her parents stood before the podium, Tom and Teresa gracefully stepped aside, allowing Anna and Brian to bask in the limelight with their daughter. Mrs. Sprite, visibly moved by the success of her prized student, stepped forward and gave Fawn a heartfelt hug.

"Congratulations, Fawn. I had a feeling you were going to win. Your sketch is beautiful," she whispered, her voice tinged with admiration and affection.

Touched by her teacher's words, Fawn could only look at Mrs. Sprite through tear-filled eyes. The surge of emotions was almost too much to bear—happiness, accomplishment, and a sense of fulfillment she had never experienced before.

After releasing Fawn, Mrs. Sprite turned to Jessica and offered her a warm and affectionate smile. She had always admired the close bond between the two girls. Feeling the weight of the moment, Jessica returned the smile and wrapped Fawn in a loving side hug.

Mrs. Sprite then turned to Anna and Brian and extended her hand in a warm gesture of acknowledgment. "Congratulations, Mr. and Mrs. Gaddesden. You've raised a beautiful and talented young lady," she commended them, her handshake firm and meaningful.

Gathered around Fawn and her parents, the three judges—Professor Hayes, Professor Rivera, and Professor Wu—wore expressions of admiration and respect.

Professor Hayes approached Fawn and placed his hand on her shoulder. "Ms. Gaddesden, your talent is evident in every line and shade on your sketch. We were unanimous in our decision, and I speak for all three of us when I say that you deserve this win." His voice, rich with authority and wisdom, conveyed the depth of their judgment.

With her characteristic enthusiasm, Professor Rivera added, "Your sketch is a masterpiece. It's so alive, so full of emotion. Congratulations!" Her words danced with genuine affection and admiration.

More reserved but equally impressed, Professor Wu smiled as he spoke. "Fawn, your sketch stood out as a remarkable piece. You've showcased a raw talent and an understanding of art that most people spend years honing. Well done."

Overwhelmed with humility and gratitude, Fawn replied in a soft, trembling voice, "Thank you all so much. I can't believe I won." Her response reflected her heartfelt emotions, a sincere expression of how much this recognition meant to her—a defining moment in her young artistic journey.

Mrs. Sprite returned to the podium, her smile unwavering as she faced the audience. The applause began to die down, and a hush fell over the room, every pair of eyes fixed on her in anticipation.

With a warm, proud smile, she addressed the room. "I can't tell you how thrilled I am to have one of my students receive this honor," she said, her voice brimming with excitement. "Having been Fawn's art teacher for the past four years, I've seen firsthand her immense talent—not only in her drawings, but in all forms of artistic expression."

Fawn's heart pounded with nervous anticipation as she stood next to Jessica. She felt her hand squeeze hers in support as Mrs. Sprite continued.

"Fawn's relationship with her best friend Jessica was beautifully captured in her sketch," Mrs. Sprite explained. "It's a relationship that embodies the essence of their life's journey, expressed through the art that Fawn skillfully created."

Reaching into the podium's shelf, Mrs. Sprite pulled out the trophy with a flourish. As she turned to Fawn, the young artist's body trembled with overwhelming emotion.

"Fawn, on behalf of Wavecrest High School and all the judges, we would like to present you with this trophy and a check for two thousand dollars. Congratulations, honey."

The trophy that Mrs. Sprite presented to Fawn was a magnificent sight. Its design was elegant and symbolic, featuring the figure of a muse holding a brush and palette, wings outstretched behind her, all cast in a shimmering gold that caught the room's light. The base, a sleek black marble, bore a plaque proclaiming Fawn Gaddesden as the winner of this year's Wavecrest High School Art Contest.

With trembling hands, Fawn took hold of the trophy, feeling its weight and the coolness of the metal. Tears of joy spilled over her cheeks as she gazed at it, taking in every detail, from the graceful lines of the wings to the intricate details of the muse's expression.

Beside her, Jessica couldn't hold back her tears as she witnessed the joy and fulfillment that washed over her best friend. Their parents stood back, their faces glowing with pride, their emotions palpable as they took in the scene before them.

As Fawn clutched the trophy to her chest, the audience applauded again, a standing ovation for the young artist who had touched their hearts with her talent. The sound filled the room, a chorus of admiration and celebration for Fawn's well-deserved moment of triumph.

Leaning close, Mrs. Sprite whispered to Fawn, "Would you like to say a few words?"

Amid the whirlwind of emotions, Fawn found herself at the edge of laughter and tears, a perfect reflection of the joyous chaos within her heart. With a nod and clutching her trophy, she approached the microphone.

The crowd fell silent in anticipation. Fawn looked out, her eyes sparkling, a tender smile playing on her lips as a nervous chuckle escaped through her tears. Her voice was a melodic quiver when she spoke.

"Thank you," she began, the simple words imbued with a depth of gratitude that echoed throughout the room. "Thank you so much," she continued, her voice cracking under the weight of her emotions.

Even Mrs. Sprite, who had seen countless students grow and evolve, found her eyes welling up, touched by Fawn's genuine humility and deep appreciation for the award.

As the ceremony drew to a close, Fawn and Jessica were soon enveloped in the warm embrace of their parents. The six came together in a group hug that embodied their love and shared history.

Mrs. Sprite addressed the audience once more, her voice strong yet warm. "This year's Art Contest has been a remarkable journey for all of us," she announced. "Thank you to all the students who took part and to all of you who came out to support these young artists and our school's commitment to nurturing their talents. I look forward to next year's contest and the incredible artistry I am sure it will bring. Let's continue to encourage our children to explore and express their artistic potential."

As her words settled over the crowd, the attendees began to stir, a gentle rustle of movement that filled the room. Artists and their families gathered their sketches, each piece carefully removed from its easel. The sounds of congratulations and goodbyes mingled with the shuffling of feet as the lobby slowly emptied. The artists carried not just their sketches, but the memories of a day that celebrated art, friendship, and the promise of tomorrow.

A young man with the polished look of a professional made his way through the dispersing crowd toward Fawn. He wore a blue dress shirt and black pants and had a camera slung over his shoulder. He introduced himself with friendly ease.

"Hi, I'm Tyler, a reporter for the 'Wavecrest Weekly'," he said, flashing a press badge.

"Could I get a picture of you with your sketch?"

Fawn blinked, taken aback by the unexpected request. The idea that their local newspaper would be interested in the school art contest hadn't occurred to her.

"Oh, wow," she murmured, a flush of honor mixing with her lingering embarrassment from the unexpected attention. She hastily dabbed at the remaining tears on her cheeks. "Okay," she agreed, her voice tinged with nervous excitement.

As Tyler prepared his camera, Mrs. Sprite came over, her expression soft with affection. She wrapped Fawn in a heartfelt hug that said more than words ever could.

"I am so proud of you," she whispered, pulling back just enough to look into Fawn's eyes. "In these four years, I've grown very fond of you. Your energy, your creativity—it's been a highlight of my teaching career. I'm going to miss you dearly."

She paused, her voice thickening with emotion. "Good luck in Boston, Fawn. I hope you'll come back to visit someday."

Releasing Fawn, Mrs. Sprite turned to Jessica, who had watched the farewell with a soft, wistful expression. With a gentle touch on Jessica's cheek, Mrs. Sprite offered a warm smile.

"Good luck, Jessica. You will be missed, too." Her words were simple but laden with the sentiment of a teacher who had seen her students grow and blossom, acknowledging Jessica's part in Fawn's story and her unique journey ahead.

The room seemed to hold its breath, honoring the intimacy of the goodbyes. The emotional exchange, a poignant capstone to the day's excitement, was a testament to a teacher's impact and the indelible marks of friendship and achievement.

As Tyler readied his camera, Anna nodded to the girls, indicating that she and the rest of the family would give them the space and meet them outside. Feeling the shift toward the day's end, Jessica turned to her parents.

"I'll be going back to Fawn's house and hanging out there for a while," she informed them.

With the same warmth and understanding that always characterized her, Teresa replied, "Okay, sweetheart. We'll see you back at the house."

Tyler approached with an easy smile. "Are you ready?" he asked, his professional demeanor mixed with a hint of the celebratory spirit of the day.

Fawn's response was a nervous giggle, betraying the mix of excitement and slight trepidation. "Okay, let's get this over with," she said, the laughter in her voice easing the tension of the moment.

The girls, still basking in the glow of their shared triumph, giggled their way across the room to Fawn's exhibit. When they reached the easel holding the winning sketch, Tyler gestured for Fawn to stand beside it.

But before Tyler could raise his camera, Fawn reached for Jessica, insistently. "C'mon, Jess. This is your moment, too. Get over here."

Jessica hesitated; the spotlight was never her preferred place, but seeing the earnest look in Fawn's eyes, she couldn't refuse.

Recognizing the faces from the sketch and the living counterparts in front of him, Tyler couldn't help but agree. "Yes, that will be a perfect picture." He positioned Jessica on the left side of the easel and Fawn on the right, creating a real-life reflection of the art between them.

"Perfect," he said, a satisfied tone in his voice. He snapped the photo, capturing the moment for posterity.

Peering at the camera's digital screen, Tyler showed them the result. The photograph revealed Jessica and Fawn, their smiles bright and genuine, standing proudly beside the sketch that had so beautifully immortalized their friendship. The image captured more than just their physical likeness; it was a snapshot of their journey, their joy, and the culmination of Fawn's dedication to her art.

The girls leaned in together, admiring the picture. It was a perfect representation of the day, a keepsake that would no doubt be treasured for years to come. Their eyes lit up, their smiles widened, seeing themselves through Tyler's lens had a magical way of making the day feel even more real.

Tyler offered them one last smile, filled with the unspoken promise of future success.

"Thank you, girls. I wish you the best," he said, then turned and walked away, leaving the girls amidst the lingering echoes of applause and the soft shuffling of the quiet bustle of the departing crowd.

"I guess we better get going, huh?" Fawn said, her voice still tinged with the excitement of the day's events.

Absorbed in her phone, Jessica quickly raised her hand. "Hold up," she said, her fingers flying across the screen. "I just told Ethan you won the Art Contest, and he says congratulations."

"Aw, tell him thanks," Fawn replied, her affection for Ethan evident in her warm smile.

"Ethan says he'll be over later and that we're all going out to celebrate," Jessica beamed.

The news sent a wave of excitement through Fawn. "Awesome!" she exclaimed, the joy of celebrating with her friends lighting up her face.

As Fawn and Jessica were chatting about the evening's plans, Professor Hayes approached, a thoughtful expression on his face. Fawn noticed him coming and turned to face him, her curiosity piqued by his intent gaze.

"Ms. Gaddesden, do you have a minute?" he asked, with an air of sincerity that immediately captured her attention.

She nodded, her eyes locking onto his with interest. "Of course, Professor Hayes," Fawn replied.

"I heard that you're going to college in Boston," he began, adjusting his glasses as he spoke. His voice held a note of genuine interest, and it was clear that he had something important on his mind.

Fawn confirmed with a soft smile, pride lacing her words. "Yes, I am."

Professor Hayes nodded approvingly before continuing. "While I have no doubt that the schools in Boston are very good, I believe UCSB can offer you the same learning opportunities as Boston." He spoke with conviction, hoping to sway her consideration.

Fawn listened intently but felt a pang of loyalty to her parents' sacrifice. "I appreciate that, Professor Hayes, but my parents have already paid for my first year in Boston," she explained, her voice tinged with respect and a hint of finality.

Understanding her position yet undeterred, Professor Hayes leaned in slightly. "I understand your situation," he said with empathy. "However, if you change your mind about Boston, I think I might be able to get you a full scholarship here at UCSB."

Fawn hesitated before responding. She respected Professor Hayes, but felt the weight of her parents' investment.

"It's very kind of you to offer," she said. "But if I were to change my mind now, my parents would lose the money they've spent on my tuition."

Professor Hayes gave her a reassuring nod as he slipped his hand into his inside pocket and pulled out a business card.

"Well, if you change your mind and you want to go to UCSB," he said while handing her the card, "call me. I'll arrange the transfer, and I might even be able to get your parents their money back."

Fawn took the card between her fingers and met his gaze once more. The offer was generous and unexpected—a possibility she hadn't considered before.

After a brief pause filled with unspoken thoughts and potential decisions, Professor Hayes offered Fawn an encouraging smile.

"Just think about it," he urged before turning away and walked toward the exit.

Fawn and Jessica exchanged a look of surprise, the weight of Professor Hayes' unexpected offer hanging between them. With the professor's words still echoing in her mind, Fawn carefully detached her sketch from the easel, handling it with a tenderness that spoke of its importance.

As the girls prepared to leave and ride back with Fawn's parents to her house, Fawn's eyes inadvertently fell upon a solitary sketch still resting on its easel. It stood there, a lone piece among the empty easels, an image seemingly lost in the quiet aftermath of the event. With its lingering presence, the sketch seemed almost forlorn in the now vacant lobby, where excitement and applause had filled the air just minutes ago.

It was Felix's sketch, the depiction of Lipton Manor he had so eagerly described. The realization brought a poignant clarity to the scene. His was the only sketch left unclaimed, a silent testament to his efforts and aspirations, now overshadowed by the day's events.

As Fawn gazed at the lone sketch left on an easel, her thoughts drifted back to the day she had signed up for the Art Contest. That was when she had unexpectedly run into him, who was proudly but nervously showing off his sketch of Lipton Manor. She vividly recalled his earnest expression as he presented his work, a raw demonstration of his passion. She had instinctively encouraged him, recognizing his effort yet unaware of his deeper aspirations.

Now, seeing his sketch standing alone in the quiet lobby, Fawn felt a poignant mix of her own joy and deep sadness. She understood Felix's hardships and realized that these challenges would make it nearly impossible for him to pursue his dream of becoming an architect. This somber thought cast a shadow over her victory, adding a layer of empathy and reflection to her emotions.

Noticing the change in Fawn's expression, Jessica voiced her concern. "What's the matter?"

Fawn's face, a canvas of mixed emotions, turned toward Jessica, her expression settling into a soft pout. Following Fawn's gaze, Jessica's eyes landed on Felix's sketch. Understanding dawned on her, and a sympathetic sadness touched her features.

Taking Fawn's hand in hers, Jessica murmured, "I know, Fawn. I know."

Together, they walked toward the glass doors of the high school. With each step, memories of their time there played in their minds like a silent movie—moments of laughter, growth, challenges, and triumphs. As they passed through the doors, it was more than just a physical departure; it marked the end of an era. They were leaving their high school for the last time and stepping into a future filled with new dreams, challenges, and the unbreakable bond of their friendship.

Beneath the ancient palm tree in Fawn's yard, the old white bench swing swayed gently, carrying Fawn and Jessica in its familiar embrace. Despite the typical heat of an August afternoon, they sat comfortably in the shade of the palm's sprawling fronds. The late afternoon sun, still bright in the sky, cast a warm, golden glow around them, highlighting the tranquility of the moment.

Holding Fawn's sketch, Jessica looked at it with unabated awe. The details Fawn had put into the artwork continued to amaze her. Curious about the inspiration behind such a personal piece, she turned to Fawn. "So, what inspired you to draw us sitting on our bench swing?"

Fawn's smile, as bright as the sun above, still seemed to float in the joy of winning the Art Contest. She turned to Jessica, a mischievous grin playing on her lips. "You know that gift I gave you for your birthday?"

Jessica's smile mirrored Fawn's as she recalled the gift. "Yeah, that cute little replica you made of us sitting on the bench swing. What about it?"

"Well," Fawn began, her voice laced with a hint of amusement. "I was sitting on your bed that day, trying so hard to think of something to draw, and then I saw it sitting on your shelf."

"Really?" Jessica replied, her expression a mix of surprise and delight.

"Yep," Fawn giggled, her laughter light and carefree. "After all that time of struggling for inspiration, it was right there in front of me."

"Aw," Jessica cooed, her heart warmed by the revelation. "I love your birthday gift. It makes me smile every time I look at it."

Hearing Jessica's affection in her voice, Fawn's smile grew even warmer. Knowing that her gift brought such joy to Jessica filled her with a deep sense of satisfaction. That gift, a symbol of their friendship, held more meaning now than ever.

Jessica looked back at the sketch. "And I so love your drawing, Fawn. I can't tell you how happy I am that you won."

Fawn's eyes sparkled, her smile unwavering. She gave Jessica a gentle nudge. "Thanks, Jess. Having you there with me made it even more special."

On that swing, under the protective canopy of the palm tree, the two friends shared a moment of mutual admiration and love. It was a testament to their journey together, a journey beautifully captured in Fawn's sketch and the miniature replica—symbols of their enduring friendship and the memories they cherished.

As the girls relaxed on the swing, they noticed Anna making her way across the yard toward them. The gentle rocking of the swing and their laughter added a timeless quality to the scene, reminiscent of countless similar days. The late afternoon sun cast long, warm shadows across the yard, highlighting Anna's path, each step bringing her closer to the pair.

As Anna approached the girls, memories flooded her heart. She saw Fawn and Jessica as they were now, and as the little girls who had spent countless hours on that swing, their laughter and playful banter echoing through the years. Seeing them together, still so close, brought a pang of nostalgia and a warm smile to her face.

"You girls look so adorable sitting there," Anna said, her voice rich with the warmth of a mother's love.

Fawn and Jessica, unable to resist, giggled at her comment. "We're not little girls any-more, Mom," Fawn replied, her grin a mix of affection and mild embarrassment.

Anna's smile broadened, her eyes reflecting a mother's timeless perspective. "You'll always be little girls in my eyes," she replied

Laying the sketch beside her, Jessica leaned into Fawn and affectionately held her arm. Looking up at Anna, her blue eyes sparkling with sweetness, she said, "I don't mind, Mama. I like being a little girl."

Fawn turned to Jessica, her laughter light and full of affection. "Silly girl," she teased, giving her a playful nudge.

Still smiling, Anna turned her attention to the sketch. "We should put that in a safe place where it won't get dirty or damaged," she suggested.

The girls nodded in agreement, recognizing the importance of preserving the artwork.

"I have the perfect box where we can store it until we get it framed. I just have to find it," Anna mused aloud. "How about we keep it in your hope chest for now? It will be safe there."

"Okay, Mom," Fawn agreed, her tone reflecting her trust in her mother's care.

Jessica carefully picked up the canvas, treating it with the reverence it deserved, and handed it to Anna. The sketch, a symbol of their friendship and Fawn's talent, was now in safe hands.

Anna's maternal instincts were ever-present as she inquired about the money's where-abouts. "Where did you put the check, Fawn?" she asked, her tone mixing curiosity with a hint of motherly concern.

Still dazed by the day's events, Fawn replied, "It's on the desk in my bedroom."

Anna nodded, her approach always practical. "I'll go to the bank on Monday and cash it for you," she offered, planning to take care of the formalities so Fawn wouldn't have to worry.

Appreciating the gesture, Fawn replied with a heartfelt, "Thanks, Mom."

Anna gave the girls another warm smile. "You two have a good time tonight with Ethan," she said before returning to the house, leaving them to their thoughts and the gentle sway of the swing.

In the silence that followed, Jessica's curiosity piqued. She looked at Fawn, a smile playing on her lips. "So, what are you going to do with all that money?"

Fawn shrugged nonchalantly. "I don't know," she answered honestly.

While the prize money was a significant bonus, it wasn't her primary motivation. The recognition for her art and the validation of her talent had been the real prize. The two thousand dollars was, as she saw it, just icing on the cake.

Ever the brainstormer, Jessica offered a few suggestions. "Maybe you can get that new computer you've been wanting. Or a new phone," she mused. After a brief pause, another idea came to her. "Or, just put it towards a car. You might need a car in Boston."

The mention of Boston seemed to cast a shadow over Fawn's expression. "Maybe," she replied, her voice tinged with the bittersweet realization of the changes to come. Boston meant a new chapter, a life away from Wavecrest, away from the familiarity and comfort of home, and most importantly, away from Jessica.

Jessica also felt the weight of that reality, especially after mentioning Boston. The dread of their impending departures—Fawn to Boston, herself to Texas—suddenly became more palpable. Though Jessica knew she would have a home in Wavecrest to return to, the thought of being separated from her best friend was daunting. And with Ethan returning to Pine Haven in a few weeks, she would also have to face the anguish of being separated from the love of her life.

The last carefree days of summer were slipping away, and with them, the comfort of their familiar life in Wavecrest. They both knew this day would come, but as it drew closer, the inevitability of their separation became more poignant and real.

The air around the old white bench swing had subtly changed, taking on a melancholic hue as the late afternoon sun cast long shadows across the yard. Jessica turned to Fawn, a heavy sadness in her eyes.

"Are you taking your sketch with you?" she asked, her voice tinged with concern.

Surprised by the question, Fawn looked back at Jessica curiously. "I don't know. Why?"

Jessica's answer was firm, yet filled with an underlying emotion. "I think you should, Fawn. I really think you should take it with you."

The seriousness in Jessica's expression prompted Fawn to probe further. "Why? Why is it so important that I take it with me?"

Jessica's vulnerability surfaced as she struggled to articulate her deepest fear.

"Because if you take it with you and look at it every day..." She paused, her voice faltering as tears welled in her eyes, "You won't forget about me."

Fawn's heart ached at the sight of her best friend's distress, her own emotions swelling in response. "I'm not going to forget about you, Jess. Never," she reassured her, her smile tender and comforting.

"I know," Jessica replied, attempting to regain her composure. As she wiped her eyes and took a deep breath, a forced smile crossed her face. "You should take it with you, anyway. Just in case."

Fawn chuckled softly at Jessica's suggestion, her affection for her friend evident in her gaze. "Silly girl. I don't need that sketch or anything else to remind me how much I love you."

Then, with gentle firmness, Fawn took hold of Jessica's shoulders, ensuring she had her full attention. "We're besties, right? We'll always be besties, Jess. Forever and ever."

Jessica met Fawn's gaze, her eyes conveying affection and gratitude. "Forever and ever," she whispered in return.

When Jessica's smile returned, Fawn hoped her words had brought some comfort. "C'mon, let's get out of here," Fawn said enthusiastically, ready to embrace the moment.

Together, they stepped off the swing, leaving behind the place that had witnessed so many of their shared memories. They began their familiar walk back to Jessica's house, where Ethan would join them later that evening. The plan for the night was simple: celebrate Fawn's victory and, for a little while, set aside thoughts of the future. It was a night for laughter, celebration, and cherishing the present moment—a perfect end to an unforgettable day.

# Chapter 38

----------------------------------------------------------

The Sunday morning light streamed through the curtains of Jessica's bedroom, casting a soft glow across the space that had become a refuge for two soul sisters. Turning her head, Jessica found Fawn's side of the bed empty, the sheets cool and untouched since her friend had risen. A frown creased her brow as she glanced at the clock on her nightstand—9:45. The house was already awake without her.

With a languid stretch that chased the remnants of sleep from her limbs, Jessica slid out of bed, her feet touching the floor with a soft thud. The house, usually quiet at this hour, hummed with the murmur of distant voices. Curiosity piqued, she padded out of her room; the voices growing more profound with each step toward the kitchen.

The familiar cadence of conversation, woven with an undercurrent of seriousness, drew her forward. Krista's unexpected yet unmistakable voice cut through the morning haze, igniting a flare of surprise in Jessica's heart. What brought her here so early and with such urgency in her tone?

Crossing the threshold into the kitchen, Jessica found Fawn, Krista, and Teresa gathered around the table. The smiles that usually greeted her were absent today, replaced by a serious undertone that made her pulse quicken with concern.

"Good morning," Jessica greeted them, her voice laced with hesitant cheerfulness.

"Good morning, sweetheart," Teresa replied, her smile a warm welcome, yet tinged with the gravity of the moment.

Jessica's eyes flickered from her mother to Fawn before landing on Krista. The vibrant redhead, usually a whirlwind of energy, now sat deflated, her hands wrapped around a mug of coffee. It was clear that something had punctured their usual ease.

"What's going on?" Jessica asked, her voice heavy with concern as she pulled out a chair and sat down next to Fawn.

Krista let out a breath that seemed to carry more weight than air. "Donny and I broke up," she announced, her voice calm, but the hurt unmistakable.

The words hung heavy in the air like a thick fog rolling in from the sea. Jessica's eyes widened, unable to hide her shock at Krista's announcement. Donny and Krista were inseparable—their relationship had always seemed as steadfast as the waves crashing against Wavecrest's shores.

"What?" Disbelief laced her one-word question, a mirror to the shock that rippled through her.

"Yep." Krista forced out a brittle laugh devoid of humor. "I guess Donny couldn't handle me going off to Colorado in a few weeks, so he broke up with me."

Jessica absorbed this new information like a blow to the chest; it echoed inside her like an unexpected ending to a familiar story. She reached out and placed her hand over Krista's—an anchor amidst stormy emotions.

"I'm so sorry, Kris," Jessica said softly, giving Krista's hand a reassuring squeeze.

Krista offered a small smile, but remained silent for a moment before speaking again.

"I just... I didn't see it coming," she admitted. "We had all these plans—to see each other during our breaks... but he said he couldn't do the long-distance thing."

"But you guys were so good together," Jessica murmured, trying to wrap her head around this unexpected turn in Krista's life.

"I thought so, too," she said, staring down into the dark liquid in her cup as if it might hold answers. "But he said that it'd be better for us to end things now rather than wait for it to fall apart later."

Teresa rose from her seat and moved around the kitchen with practiced grace, pulling out plates and setting them on the counter—a distraction from the tension coiling tight in their midst.

Fawn spoke for the first time since Jessica had entered the room. "We were just talking about how things are changing so fast," she said. "It feels like we're all going in different directions and... I don't know... it's like we're trying to hold on to the sand, but it keeps slipping through our fingers."

The analogy wasn't lost on any of them; Wavecrest had been their sandbox—a place where they built dreams and castles—but high tide was approaching, ready to wash away what they knew and force them to rebuild elsewhere.

Jessica nodded; this was what change felt like—raw and disconcerting—like watching pieces of your world rearrange themselves without your consent. She squeezed Krista's hand tighter, wanting to offer comfort but finding herself equally adrift in this sea of new beginnings and endings.

Teresa placed a plate of eggs in front of each girl before retaking her seat. "Life is full of surprises," she began in an attempt at reassurance. "Some good, some not so good... But you girls are strong—you'll get through this."

Their breakfast, a simple offering laid out before them, was a reminder that life, with all its unexpected twists and turns, goes on. It was in this shared moment, in the quiet strength of their companionship, that the girls found a semblance of peace. Though their paths were branching off in different directions, they knew that the roots of their friendship, deep and enduring, would anchor them to the shores of Wavecrest, holding them steady no matter where life's journey might lead.

The unexpected ring of the doorbell sliced through the somber mood of the kitchen, a sharp reminder of the world beyond their cocoon of shared sorrows. Jessica, with a last glance at her nearly finished breakfast, rose and moved toward the door, her voice a gentle echo in the quiet room, "I'll get it."

Teresa, poised to answer the door herself, redirected her steps toward her bedroom, leaving Jessica to greet their unexpected visitor.

When Jessica opened the front door, there stood Michelle, her face etched with worry and concern. Her eyes, usually brimming with a dreamy quality, were clouded over like a sky threatening rain.

"Hey, Jess. Is Krista here?" Michelle's voice trembled slightly, betraying the urgency behind her visit.

"Yeah, she's in the kitchen," Jessica replied, stepping aside to let Michelle into the foyer. After closing the door, she followed Michelle's hurried steps into the kitchen.

The moment Michelle's eyes met Krista's, the air shifted, charged with the raw intensity of unspoken emotions. Krista stood as if drawn by a magnetic pull, her movements bridging the distance between them until Michelle's arms wrapped around her in a warm embrace. It was a hug that spoke volumes, a mixture of comfort and shared understanding that only deepened as Krista's tears flowed freely.

"Oh, Krista," Michelle murmured, tears filling her eyes. The sorrow in her voice resonated through the room like a chord struck on a piano—full of empathy and shared heartache.

Holding Krista in her arms, Michelle's tears flowed from her eyes as she tried to find words that would help ease the pain in Krista's heart—a task both immense and intimate. There were no perfect words for moments like these—only presence, only touch.

Jessica, moved by the depth of their connection and the raw display of vulnerability, stepped forward, tears blurring her vision as she wrapped her arms around both Michelle and Krista. It was an instinctive gesture, a physical manifestation of the support and unity that had always defined their friendship.

Witnessing the scene unfold, Fawn felt a surge of empathy and sorrow wash over her. The tears that had been threatening to spill finally broke free, tracing paths down her cheeks as she rose from the table to join the embrace. It was a powerful, heartfelt moment—a group hug that enveloped Krista in a sea of support, each friend sharing in the weight of her sadness, reinforcing the unspoken promise that no matter what trials they faced, they would face them together.

In that moment, time itself seemed to slow as they remained locked in a hug that was both a shelter and a testament to their bond. The air around them felt charged with the heaviness of change; the upheaval in Krista's life was just one of the many changes they were all navigating, a poignant symbol of the broader transformations that awaited them all.

When they finally parted, their eyes met in silent conversation, a shared understanding that while the fabric of their reality was fraying at the edges, the core of their connection remained intact, unyielding. The physical space between them was minimal, a mere breath, yet it was enough to allow them to look at each other with a depth of feeling that words could scarcely convey.

Michelle, her voice a whisper marred by sniffles, broke the silence with her news of Donny, adding another layer to the complex tapestry of their emotions. "I saw Donny this morning at the 7-Eleven. He looked just as miserable." Her words, meant to offer solace, hung in the air, a bitter reminder of the reality of the situation.

Krista's response was a whisper of resilience amidst the storm of her feelings. "Maybe he is," she conceded, her voice betraying the effort it took to maintain her composure. "But it doesn't change anything." Her words, though faint, echoed with a strength that spoke of acceptance and the painful process of moving forward.

"You're right," Fawn said softly, reaching out to brush away a tear from Krista's cheek with gentle fingers. "It doesn't change how much we love you or how much we're here for you." It was a reaffirmation of their unwavering support, a promise that transcended the trials they faced.

The room filled with quiet sobs and murmurs of comfort as they clung to one another—a circle unbroken by grief but instead strengthened by it. Each friend held space for Krista's hurt while grappling with their own sense of loss—of relationships ending and uncertainty of the future.

This was not how any of them had envisioned their summer—their last carefree celebration before college carried them away. But as they stood together in Jessica's kitchen—a room where they'd shared countless meals and laughter—they were reminded that their friendship was not confined by geography or circumstance; it was woven through their very being—as unyielding and steadfast like the ocean waves that defined their beloved hometown.

Jessica separated herself from her friends and walked to the kitchen table, where her phone lay next to a bowl of fruit. Her fingers hovered over the screen, the weight of her friends' grief pressing against her resolve. The message to Ethan, half-typed, was a testament to the conflict raging within her—a battle between loyalty and love, each demanding its due.

Fawn's question, tinged with curiosity and concern, broke Jessica's contemplation. "What are you doing?" she asked, her gaze piercing, as if she could sense the conflict stirring inside her.

Jessica looked up, her blue eyes a mirror to the turmoil in her heart. "I'm canceling my plans with Ethan so I can be with you guys today." The words, though softly spoken, carried the weight of her commitment to their friendship, a bond she valued above all else.

The confession pulled Krista and Michelle out of their reverie, their eyes shifting to Jessica, expressions of protest forming on their faces.

Krista's reaction was swift and firm, a reflection of her selfless nature. "Jess—No! You are not canceling your plans with Ethan today!"

"But I want to," Jessica insisted, her thumb hovering over the 'send' button. "We all need to be together today."

Krista shook her head, her red hair catching the light, like flickering flames of determination. "No, Jess. You need to spend as much time with Ethan as you can. There's not that much summer left."

"I know," Jessica murmured, biting her lip as she considered Krista's words. "But you guys were here for me when I was acting like a baby, and this is way more serious."

Fawn, ever the mediator, stepped in, her presence reassuring as she placed a comforting hand on Jessica's shoulder.

"Jess," she began in a soothing tone, "Michelle and I, we got this. We're going to spend the day with Krista, and you're going to spend the day with Ethan." Her words, gentle yet firm, echoed the collective sentiment of the group.

Michelle's support further cemented the decision. "That's right. We all know how much you were looking forward to going on a picnic with Ethan. We don't want you to miss out on that." Her heartfelt and sincere encouragement left little room for Jessica to argue.

"But..." Jessica tried to interject, only to be cut off by Fawn's gentle firmness. "No buts about it," she declared. "You're going on that picnic, and that's final!"

Krista walked over to Jessica and embraced her in a hug that seemed to strengthen her resolve.

"I'll be fine, Jess," she reassured. "You have a wonderful day with Ethan. You deserve it." Her words were a balm to Jessica's guilt, a reminder of the strength and independence they each possessed.

A cloud of guilt still hung over Jessica as she set down her phone on the table. "Okay," she conceded, her voice threaded with lingering doubt. "But I'm going to feel guilty leaving you all."

"Don't," Krista said as she pulled away from their hug. "Michelle and Fawn will take good care of me. Now go get ready for your picnic date!"

Jessica turned to look at Fawn and Michelle again, as if seeking confirmation of what seemed an impossible decision—to enjoy herself while her friends dealt with heartache.

"Are you sure, guys?" she asked hesitantly.

In unison, and with lightheartedness twinkling in their eyes like stars in the evening sky, they replied, "We're sure! Go!"

"Okay," she relented with a laugh born from their assurance. "But I owe you guys big time."

Krista waved off Jessica's sense of indebtedness with a breezy gesture. "No, you don't," she insisted. "Just enjoy your day with Ethan."

With one last round of hugs, Jessica made her way to her bedroom, her heart heavy yet buoyed by the love and support of her friends. They had given her a gift—the freedom to embrace the day with Ethan without the shadow of guilt. In that moment, the depth of their friendship was crystal clear; it was a bond not easily broken, despite the distance or the changes that lay ahead.

In the solitude of her bedroom, Jessica stood in front of her open closet, running her fingers over her clothes before deciding on the perfect outfit for the picnic with Ethan. She chose a summer dress, the fabric flowing and light, as if someone had spun it from the very essence of the season itself.

As she slipped into the dress, she felt it caress her skin, a delicate embrace. The dress was a kaleidoscope of vibrant hues—a rich mosaic of warm corals and cool teals, mimicking the palette of the seaside haven that was Wavecrest. Intricate patterns, reminiscent of exotic tapestries and wild ocean waves, adorned the fabric, while an embellished neckline of ornate beading added a touch of bohemian elegance. The hem flirted just above her knees, playful and carefree, much like the spirit of the day that awaited her.

With each movement, the dress seemed to capture the light and colors of the summer day, a perfect complement to her long brown hair and the bright blue eyes that held the depth of the ocean itself. As Jessica turned to the mirror, the dress twirled around her, a reflection of the joy and anticipation she felt at the prospect of the day ahead.

Jessica made her way over to the vanity, where she took her seat and reached for her favorite hairbrush. She brushed her hair in gentle strokes, each movement was a meditation, her thoughts drifting like leaves on a slow-moving stream.

As the brush glided through her hair, Jessica's reflection seemed to blur, the glass becoming a window to her uncertainties. If Krista and Donny's two-year romance had crumbled under the pressure of impending separation, she thought, what then of her and Ethan? A silent fear crept within her, that the miles between her and Ethan might extend far beyond the physical. Could their budding love weather the same storm that had capsized Krista and Donny's long-standing bond?

She set the brush down, her fingers tracing the edges of the vanity, her heart reaching for the assurance she so desperately needed. The thought of Ethan's warm smile and gentle eyes brought a flutter to her chest, a counterpoint to her fears. Yet, the question remained, unspoken but heavy in her heart—would the love that had blossomed under the summer sun wither in the face of autumn's inevitable arrival? It was a possibility that Jessica knew she would have to face, the answer to which lay hidden in the unknown tapestry of time.

The bedroom door creaked open, a subtle sound that snapped Jessica from her thoughts. She turned, her eyes meeting Fawn's as she stepped into the room. Despite the warmth of Jessica's smile, Fawn's intuition, honed through years of friendship, detected the shadow of concern lurking in Jessica's eyes.

"Are you okay?" Fawn asked as she stepped closer.

"No, not really," Jessica admitted, the facade of her smile faltering as the truth of her emotions surfaced.

"What's the matter?" Fawn probed further, sensing Jessica's distress like a storm on the horizon.

Jessica's worries spilled out, her voice a soft echo of vulnerability. "I'm worried about Ethan and me." The admission hung in the air, raw and real.

"Why?" Fawn's question was a prompt, an invitation for Jessica to voice the fears that lay heavy on her heart.

"Because Krista and Donny are proof that long-distance relationships don't work out." The words were spoken with a conviction born of fear, a reflection of the uncertainty that had been quietly gnawing at her.

Fawn's heart felt the weight of Jessica's words, empathy blooming within her. She knew how much Jessica had fallen for Ethan and how much their relationship meant to her. She walked over to Jessica and put a hand on her shoulder.

"Just because Krista and Donny's relationship didn't work out, doesn't mean yours and Ethan's won't," Fawn countered, expressing her unwavering faith in the unique bond that Jessica and Ethan shared.

"But what if it doesn't? What if Ethan decides to break up with me?" The questions tumbled from Jessica's lips, her fears painting scenarios she couldn't bear to face.

Jessica paused as she absorbed her own words, sadness etched across her face. "I don't want to lose him, Fawn," she confided, her eyes pleading, seeking solace in the eyes of her dearest friend.

Fawn felt moved by Jessica's vulnerability. It was rare for her to reveal such raw emotion. She knew what she had to do—offer comfort and assurance as only a best friend could. It was their unspoken ritual—a dance they had performed countless times throughout their friendship.

Reaching for the hairbrush on the vanity table, Fawn picked it up and gently resumed brushing Jessica's hair. "You can't compare your relationship to Donny and Krista's. What you and Ethan have is very special. It's nothing like what Donny and Krista had."

Jessica looked at Fawn through their reflections in the mirror. "What do you mean?"

"I see how Ethan looks at you and how you look at him," Fawn continued as she brushed through each strand of brown hair. "What you two have is real love—the kind of love that will withstand any obstacle that comes your way."

Jessica listened intently, drawing strength from Fawn's words, which flowed over her like a soothing balm.

"I hope you're right," Jessica said after a moment, feeling some of her worries melt away under Fawn's care. "Because I can't imagine my life without him."

Fawn met Jessica's eyes in their mirrored reflections with an unwavering look of certainty. "I'm always right. Trust me," she reassured with an affectionate smile that brought comfort beyond words.

A soft chuckle escaped Jessica's lips as the tension around them eased—a testament to their friendship that never wavered, even in moments of doubt or fear.

"Thank you, Fawn," Jessica said warmly as Fawn set aside the brush. "You always know how to make me feel better."

They shared another smile, a silent promise that whatever may come, they would always have each other. Then, with a deep breath that seemed to gather the strength of their years of friendship, Jessica rose from her seat, and together, they stepped out of the bedroom, their hearts fortified for the day's adventures that lay ahead.

Upon entering the kitchen, Jessica and Fawn were greeted by the familiar sight of Jessica's father standing tall and commanding in front of them. Dressed in his Sunday attire, a crisp purple dress shirt neatly tucked into dark slacks, he exuded the dignified grace of a military man accustomed to standing at the helm of life's unexpected storms.

"Hello, girls," he greeted them, his voice laced with a hint of concern that belied his jovial demeanor. There was an innate authority in his posture, a byproduct of years spent in uniform, yet his eyes held the softness that only family could inspire.

Tom motioned to the kitchen table with a broad sweep of his hand. "I brought back fresh pastries from the bakery. Help yourself." His smile was inviting, encouraging them to partake in the simple pleasures of a Sunday morning.

Jessica and Fawn's eyes gazed at the white box sitting on the table; its lid opened, revealing an assortment of sweet and savory delights that filled the room with a tantalizing aroma. They also noticed that Krista and Michelle had already dipped their fingers into the treats, each girl with a smear of frosting on their lips—a telltale sign of indulgence.

As Jessica and Fawn squeezed by Tom to make their way to the table, they felt the playful tug at the back of their hair from Tom's teasing fingers. It was a familiar gesture, one that reminded them of countless Sundays spent in this very kitchen.

Settling into their chairs at the table, Jessica and Fawn reached for the pastries. Their fingers brushed against flaky croissants and delicate fruit tarts, each bite a comforting reminder of home.

Meanwhile, Tom walked over to Krista and placed his hands on her shoulders with a gentle firmness that seemed to offer support without words.

"How are you holding up, honey?" he asked, genuine concern written all over his face. His question was simple, yet filled with empathy for Krista's recent heartbreak.

"I'm okay, Mr. Reese. Thanks for asking," Krista answered, her voice steady despite the storm she had weathered—a testament to her resilience. She offered him a small smile that expressed both gratitude and determination.

Just then, Teresa stepped into the kitchen, dressed in a sophisticated black lace dress that hugged her contours with an understated elegance. The dress was trimmed with sleek satin bands that accentuated her waist, while the sheer overlay of lace created a delicate interplay of shadow and texture. Her outfit was complemented by classic black heels that added an air of grace to her every step.

Michelle looked up at Teresa in awe as she entered. "Wow, Mrs. Reese, you look so pretty."

Teresa smiled as she grabbed her purse from the counter. "Aw, thank you, Michelle." Her voice was as warm as her smile.

Turning to Tom, who stood by Krista's side, Teresa asked, "Are you ready?"

Tom nodded as he gave Krista's shoulders another squeeze before turning to Jessica and Fawn, who were enjoying their pastries.

"Okay, girls," he announced with fatherly affection in his tone. "We're going to church. See you later!"

As Tom and Teresa left the kitchen and walked toward the front door, Teresa paused and turned around to face the four girls. Her eyes swept over them with maternal warmth as she offered one last piece of advice: "You girls have fun today. Remember, the ocean isn't going anywhere, and neither are we. So don't worry too much!"

With those parting words of reassurance and love, Tom and Teresa left the house through the front door—leaving behind an echo of parental care.

Their absence made the room seem larger as the four girls were left alone in the kitchen. Krista looked around at her friends—Jessica savoring a chocolate croissant, Fawn nibbling on a cheese Danish, and Michelle finishing off an apple turnover—and smiled despite herself.

Deep down, she knew that Donny breaking up with her was just one ripple in the vast ocean they were all navigating—the beginning of challenges that lay ahead: college life, filled with new people and experiences far from home. But sitting in Jessica's kitchen among friends who had become family in all but blood, Krista felt something shift within her—a seedling of courage taking root in the midst of uncertainty.

And though she didn't voice it aloud just yet, she felt grateful for Jessica's steadfast presence, for Fawn's empathetic heart, for Michelle's unwavering support; they were beacons on her horizon, promising that no matter what lay ahead—they would face it together.

As the girls finished the last bites of their pastries, Jessica's eyes lingered on her friends, each one a thread woven into the fabric of her life. She felt a surge of gratitude for their presence, yet a whisper of guilt tugged at her for planning to spend the day with Ethan.

"So, what are you guys going to do today?" Jessica asked, her curiosity peaking as she pushed aside the pang of remorse.

Licking the sweetness from her fingers, Fawn replied with a satisfied smile, "We're going to my house first. Michelle and Krista want to see the sketch I made and the trophy I won in the Art Contest."

Jessica's face lit up with pride as she beamed at Fawn. "Awesome. Wait till you see it, girls. It's going to blow you away."

A giggle escaped Fawn at Jessica's unbridled enthusiasm. "Thanks, Jess," she said warmly. "After that, I think we'll head to the mall and hang out there for a while."

Michelle chimed in, her hazel eyes gleaming with anticipation. "Yeah, and maybe we'll go get our nails done. We haven't done that in, like, forever!"

"That sounds like fun," Jessica replied, nodding enthusiastically.

Michelle leaned forward, her eyes sparkling with determination. "Today is about pampering Krista and making her feel better. We're going to show her a good time and make her forget all about Donny!"

Krista's expression softened into a grateful smile as she acknowledged their support. "Aw, you guys are the best. Thank you for being here for me."

Fawn reached across the table to give Krista's hand a reassuring squeeze. "Of course, Kris. That's what friends are for."

Jessica's eyes lingered on her friends, her heart echoing Fawn's sentiment. "Absolutely," she agreed wholeheartedly. "I just wish I could be in two places at once. I would love to join you guys."

Michelle waved off Jessica's regret with an understanding smile. "Don't worry about it, Jess. You've got Ethan waiting for you. Just enjoy your day with him."

With a sheepish smile tugging at her lips, Jessica replied, "Okay, I will. I hope you all have fun today! Let me know how it goes."

"Oh, don't worry about that, Jess," Fawn assured her as she rose from her seat with a stretch. "I'll tell you all about it when I see you later."

With that, Fawn turned to Krista and Michelle. "You guys ready to go?"

Michelle and Krista exchanged knowing looks and stood up in unison. "Yeah, let's go," Krista agreed.

The trio gathered their purses and made their way to the front door, with Jessica trailing behind them. Fawn opened the door to a world bathed in sunlight as they stepped outside.

"You got your brother's car today, huh?" Jessica observed as they stepped outside, eyeing Michelle's car parked in the driveway.

Michelle grinned as she twirled the keys around her finger in triumph. "Yep! He does let me borrow it sometimes."

Krista shook her head playfully at Michelle's good fortune. "Lucky you. I wish I had a car of my own."

"We all do, Krista," Fawn chimed in, a knowing grin spreading across her face.

Together, they strolled across the yard toward Michelle's car—four girls on the brink of adulthood yet still clinging to the remnants of their youth.

Before getting into the car, each girl gave Jessica a heartfelt hug—a final touchstone before parting ways for the day.

"Don't worry about me, Jess," Krista said affectionately after hugging her close. "You have a good time with your boyfriend."

"Have fun, Jess," Michelle cheerfully added as she hugged her next. "Enjoy your day!"

Fawn's hug came last, warm and lingering as she looked sincerely into Jessica's eyes. "See you later. Text me if you need anything."

Once inside the car, they buckled up as Jessica waved them off from the sidewalk. She watched until the car disappeared around the corner—out of sight but never out of mind or heart—and then turned back toward home, where she'd wait for Ethan's arrival.

Jessica re-entered her house where silence greeted her—an echo chamber of moments just passed and those still waiting to be discovered—and though part of her longed to be with them on their day out, another part couldn't wait for what lay ahead with Ethan, a balance struck between friendship and love that would carry her through whatever came next on this August summer day.

# Chapter 39

As noon approached, heralded by the sun climbing to its peak, a warm glow bathed the kitchen. Here, Jessica busied herself with the final touches of a carefully planned picnic. She placed two cold-cut sandwiches, each wrapped in parchment, alongside two pieces of leftover chicken legs, into a small cooler. She then added two bottles of flavored water to keep her, and Ethan hydrated.

As she secured the lid on the cooler, the familiar rumble of Ethan's Jeep broke the quiet, sending a wave of excitement through her. Her heart, like a compass pointing toward Ethan, fluttered with anticipation. She wiped her hands on a kitchen towel and hurried to the front door. The moment she swung it open, the bright light of day greeted her. As she stepped out onto the steps, her eyes found Ethan, and the world, with all its worries and wonders, seemed to pause in quiet acknowledgment of their young love.

She watched as Ethan emerged from the Jeep, the summer sun casting a golden hue over his figure. He was the embodiment of casual elegance, his navy blue button-up shirt speckled with white dots hugging his chest just enough to hint at the strength underneath. The shirt was unbuttoned at the top, revealing Ethan's cross with his tan skin. His shorts were a soft cream that contrasted against his darkened legs. He moved with an easy confidence that drew her in, the kind of allure that was understated yet undeniable.

As Ethan walked toward her, his sunglasses perched atop his head, his eyes locked onto hers, igniting a familiar warmth that spread through her chest. The world seemed to fall away as he reached her, his arms pulling her into a hug that spoke volumes of the longing they'd felt in their brief separation. Jessica melted into his embrace, her senses filled with his familiar scent, the touch of his skin, the feel of his body close to hers.

Their embrace deepened, and as they pulled back slightly, their eyes met in silent conversation. Without a word, their lips met in a kiss that was both a greeting and a proclamation—a seamless continuation of their unspoken dialogue. It was long and passionate, a kiss that carried the taste of their shared history and the promise of moments yet to come.

Reluctantly, they ended their kiss, but their arms remained wrapped around each other—not wanting to break the physical connection. With smiles that echoed joy from their reunion, they turned hand in hand and entered the house—ready to embark on their day's adventure.

In the kitchen, Jessica and Ethan stood together at the counter, her hands skimming over the cooler as she showcased the picnic lunch she had lovingly prepared. Her bright blue eyes sparkled with excitement as she lifted the lid to reveal the neatly wrapped sandwiches and chilled bottles of water.

"You've outdone yourself, babe," Ethan said, his eyes twinkling with a smile as he watched her enthusiasm. Her excitement, so genuine and pure, never failed to warm his heart.

Jessica beamed with pride at his compliment, but couldn't quite shake a lingering shadow from her expression. Ethan, attuned to the subtle shifts in her mood, caught the flicker of concern. His smile softened into a look of tender inquisition.

"You okay, babe?" he asked, reaching for her hand across the counter.

Jessica glanced up, her bright blue eyes clouded with worry and sadness tinting her voice. "It's Krista. Donny broke up with her. She's pretty torn up about it."

Ethan's expression grew serious as he took in the news. "That's tough, man. I don't know her that well, but I know she means a lot to you."

"Yeah, she does," Jessica said, her voice full of affection. "Fawn and Michelle are going to spend the day with her, so hopefully, that will help."

"It's good she's not alone," Ethan replied. He remembered Donny from the Summer Dance—a tall guy with an air of arrogance that had rubbed him the wrong way. "Can't say I'm a fan of that dude, especially now after hearing this."

Jessica nodded, her agreement laced with an undertone of personal concern. "It was totally out of the blue. Makes you think about... well, about everything, you know?"

Her eyes drifted for a moment, a reflective shadow passing over her features. In that brief look, Ethan saw not just empathy for her friend's situation but a mirror of her own fears—fears of distance and change that threatened the very essence of their relationship.

Ethan squeezed her hand, his touch offering gentle reassurance as his thumb moved over her skin. He paused, his gaze catching hers, recognizing the vulnerability reflected in her eyes.

"Hey, we're good, Jess", he began, the warmth in his voice meant to envelop her doubts. After a brief pause, his voice steady with determination, he continued, "What we have... I mean..." He took a deep breath, and then, with a conviction that resonated from the depths of his heart, he affirmed, "I love you. You know that, right?"

Her heart lifted at his words, and although the cloud of unease didn't completely dissipate, it broke just enough to allow a smile to reclaim her features.

"I do," she affirmed. "And I'm really looking forward to our day together," she added with renewed vigor.

Ethan's smile returned in full force, dispelling any lingering doubts that had crept into their morning.

"Me too, babe. Today is about us, and it's going to be great." With a gentle tug on her hand, he pulled her close until they were side by side—her head against his shoulder—a perfect fit.

Their shared anticipation for the day ahead created an intimate bubble around them—a reminder that despite life's inevitable changes and challenges, their connection remained a constant source of joy and strength.

With everything packed and ready for their seaside picnic adventure, the promise of laughter and cherished moments awaited them just beyond the comfort of Jessica's home.

A few minutes later, they emerged from the house, greeted by the embrace of the day's warmth as they approached the Jeep. Parked in the driveway, it sat quietly, almost as if it, too, anticipated the journey ahead. They climbed in, the familiarity of the seats a testament to the adventures they'd already shared.

In the stillness of the driveway, Ethan turned to Jessica, his expression a mixture of openness and expectancy, his smile hinting at the day's potential.

"So, where are we going for our picnic? Let's find a place where we can be alone. Just the two of us," he suggested.

Jessica's thoughts danced from one potential spot to another, searching for the perfect setting. It wasn't until the serene image of her favorite cove came to mind that her heart settled. Secluded and peaceful, it was a place where the hustle and bustle of the world seemed to fade into the background, replaced by the melody of nature and the soothing whispers of an unseen presence that had always felt like an integral part of Wavecrest.

With enthusiasm lighting up her face, Jessica turned to Ethan. "How about we head over to the secret coves? Let's go to my favorite one," she suggested, her voice ringing with a mix of excitement and nostalgia.

Ethan's memory flickered back to that day in June, their first real outing together after meeting at the beach party the night before. Their journey to the secret coves, especially to Jessica's favorite, marked the beginning of something special between them. It was there, amidst the tranquility of her cherished hideaway, that he was struck by its beauty—a beauty that seemed to envelop them in a world apart from the rest.

"I remember that cove," he reflected, warmth spreading through his voice as he recalled the serene beauty that had enveloped them. "I remember feeling like we were the only two people in the world, like we were in our own secluded paradise."

He paused, his eyes meeting hers with a warmth that mirrored his words. "Going back there for our picnic, just the two of us, sounds perfect. I can't think of a better place to spend our day together."

The spark of excitement between them was palpable. This outing was more than just a picnic; it was a return to where their story had taken root, in the tranquil embrace of the cove that had witnessed the early blossoming of their love.

"Then, let's do it," Jessica said with determination, her anticipation for the day growing. "It's quiet, it's beautiful, and it's ours."

With a sense of purpose, Ethan started the Jeep, the engine purring to life as they backed out of the driveway. Ahead of them lay the cove, ready to welcome them back to its secluded beauty and to be part of their continuing story.

And so, they set off together into another golden California day—unaware that these very moments would one day become treasured memories of youthful summers spent under the vast expanse of cerulean skies.

The Cherry Springs Mall revealed itself in a cascade of bright lights and the inviting hum of activity, a sprawling temple to commerce and leisure that attracted people from all walks of life. As Fawn, Krista, and Michelle meandered through its wide, polished corridors, the atmosphere enveloped them with a bustling and comforting vibe. The mall's high glass ceiling bathed the interior in soft, natural light, making the plants that dotted the walkways appear lush and vibrant, and casting soft shadows that danced across the floor as clouds passed overhead.

Storefronts, each more enticing than the last, lined their path, showcasing the latest in fashion, technology, and home decor. The girls paused outside a clothing store, its windows adorned with mannequins clad in the season's trends—flowing dresses, sharp casuals, and accessories that promised to add just the right touch of flair to any outfit. Inside, racks of clothing in a kaleidoscope of colors and textures beckoned. For a moment, they allowed themselves to be drawn into the world of fabrics and designs, sharing opinions and laughing over daring fashion choices.

Continuing their stroll, they passed by a bustling food court, where the air was rich with the mingling scents of a dozen cuisines—from the spicy tang of Asian dishes to the hearty warmth of Italian pasta and the comforting simplicity of American fast food. The buzz of conversation and clattering trays created a backdrop of sound that was as much a part of the mall experience as the shopping itself.

The mall was more than just a collection of stores and restaurants; it was a community hub, a place where people came not just to shop but to meet, relax, and be entertained. Digital displays flashed with advertisements for upcoming events—a local band's performance, a charity fashion show, a children's art contest—each promising to bring a new wave of excitement to Cherry Springs.

As they walked, the girls basked in the mall's vibrant energy, their laughter blending with the surrounding chorus of voices and music. It was a day like any other at Cherry Springs Mall, yet for Fawn, Krista, and Michelle, it was a backdrop for friendship, for healing, and for making memories that would linger long after they stepped back into the sunlight beyond the mall's glass doors.

As they continued their leisurely stroll, the sight of 'Back to School Sale' signs hanging in the windows of nearly every store caught their attention. Bright banners and posters of cheerful students clutching books and wearing trendy backpacks, seemed to adorn every corner. In years past, these signs had heralded a familiar ritual—picking out new outfits, gathering supplies, and the bubbling anticipation of returning to school, surrounded by friends in the comfortable, well-trodden halls of Wavecrest High.

But this year, the colorful displays stirred a different emotion in the hearts of Fawn, Krista, and Michelle. The signs, once symbols of eternal youth and routine, now marked the end of an era. They were reminders that soon, the trio would be scattered to the winds, each to a new school, far from the sandy shores of their hometown and the faces that had populated their world since childhood.

For a moment, they paused, caught in the tide of memories—the laughter that echoed through the hallways, the secrets whispered next to lockers, and the collective groan that rose at the end of summer break. It was a shared history, a tapestry of moments that had seemed as enduring as the ocean itself, now giving way to an unknown future.

"It's weird, isn't it?" Krista broke the silence, her voice tinged with nostalgia. "Seeing all these back-to-school signs and knowing we won't be going back to Wavecrest High in a few weeks."

"Yeah," Fawn agreed, a soft sigh escaping her lips. "It feels weird knowing we're not going back there. Moving to Boston is a big step for me. I'm excited, but..." her voice trailed off, the weight of her next words hanging in the air. "I'm going to miss this—us—being together, more than anything."

Michelle's expression softened, reflecting the mix of sadness and resolve in Fawn's words.

"I know it's going to be hard," she said, her voice tinged with both assurance and a hint of melancholy. "But we're going to make new memories, Fawn. No matter where we are, we'll stay in touch and support each other."

The girls nodded in mutual understanding, taking a moment to absorb the weight of their promise. Then, with a sense of camaraderie, they moved past the displays, the bittersweet moment lingering like the last rays of a sunset. As they walked, a silent resolve between them grew stronger—a vow that no matter where life's journey took them, the bonds forged in the halls of Wavecrest High would remain unbreakable, a constant in the midst of change.

As they rounded a corner, their lighthearted chatter was abruptly interrupted by the sound of distressed yipping. The girls' steps slowed, their attention drawn to a small, frantic crowd gathered near the food court. Their curiosity piqued, they edged closer, only to discover the source of the commotion: a tiny puppy, its coat a mix of brown and white, darting fearfully between the legs of concerned shoppers.

The puppy, with wide, bewildered eyes, seemed lost, its tiny form quivering as it evaded the grasping hands of well-meaning bystanders. Krista's heart immediately went out to the frightened animal. Her worries momentarily forgotten, she knelt and extended a gentle hand, her voice soft and coaxing. "Hey there, little one," she murmured, trying to calm the frightened pup.

Fawn and Michelle watched, holding their breath as the puppy hesitated. Then, drawn by Krista's kindness, the puppy slowly approached her. With cautious movements, Krista scooped the trembling puppy into her arms, where it instantly calmed and nestled into her embrace.

The girls looked at each other, a new resolve forming. "We should try to find its owner," Michelle suggested, her previous sadness replaced with determination. Fawn nodded in agreement, her eyes scanning the mall for anyone who looked like they might be searching for the tiny runaway.

Armed with newfound purpose, the girls set out on their mission, the lost puppy safely cradled in Krista's arms. This unexpected adventure not only distracted them from their sorrows but also brought them closer together, united in their effort to reunite the puppy with its owner.

As they stepped away from the crowd, Krista examined the puppy, checking for any sign of injury before determining its gender.

"It's a girl," she announced, a smile spreading across her face as the puppy licked her hand. "Don't worry, little girl, we'll find where you belong."

Michelle and Fawn leaned in, cooing over the puppy, their earlier concerns temporarily forgotten in the face of such innocence and vulnerability.

"She's adorable," Fawn murmured, her fingers gently stroking the puppy's head.

"Yeah, and brave, too, wandering around this big place all by herself," Michelle added, her tone a mix of admiration and concern.

With the puppy's gender known, the girls began their mission with renewed vigor, asking shopkeepers and mall-goers if they recognized the little wanderer or knew of anyone who had lost a puppy. Krista held the puppy, her actions reflecting her nurturing instincts and perhaps foreshadowing the compassionate veterinarian she was destined to become.

With no immediate success in locating the puppy's owner, the girls decided to take a short break in their search. They settled down in a quieter corner of the mall's spacious atrium, dotted with comfortable seating and planters. The area offered a respite from their mission and a chance for the puppy to rest.

As they sat, the little puppy, now seemingly at ease in Krista's lap, began to show her playful side. She nuzzled Krista's hand with her nose before playfully nibbling on her fingers, eliciting gentle laughter from the girls. Krista, in turn, rolled a small, soft ball they'd found at one of the stores towards the puppy and watched as she chased it with clumsy enthusiasm, her tail wagging furiously.

The sight of the puppy's antics brought a lightness to their hearts, a moment of pure joy amidst the uncertainty of the day. Michelle brought a small cup of water for the puppy, who eagerly lapped it up and then bounded back to Krista, her eyes shining with what could only be described as gratitude and affection.

"It's like she knows we're trying to help her," Fawn observed, watching as the puppy settled back into Krista's arms, snuggling close and letting out a contented sigh.

Krista stroked the puppy's soft fur, feeling an unexpected bond forming between them. "She's so trusting," she whispered, feeling the puppy's warmth against her comforting weight. "It's going to be hard to let her go."

For a while, they simply enjoyed the puppy's company, their laughter and playful exchanges with the little dog creating a bubble of happiness around them. It was a welcome distraction, a reminder of the simple pleasures that could be found even in the most unexpected circumstances.

Rejuvenated by the puppy's antics, they regrouped to continue their search. With renewed determination, they moved through the mall, the puppy now an honorary member of their group, a symbol of their shared adventure.

# Chapter 40

-------------------------------------------------------------

Ethan and Jessica's hearts raced with excitement as they approached a secluded stretch of Wavecrest's coastline. Here, the landscape harbored hidden coves nestled between a mystical forest and the rhythmic whispers of the Pacific. Ethan skillfully navigated the Jeep to a convenient spot near the trailhead, ensuring a short walk to the treasured cove Jessica held dear.

Upon reaching the cove's entrance, Ethan and Jessica paused for a moment to take in the natural arch formed by intertwining branches that marked the entrance to this secret haven. As they stepped inside, the world around them seemed to change, the ambient noise of the outside world fading into a serene silence, punctuated only by the gentle sounds of nature.

The cove unfurled before them like a scene from a dream. Sunlight streamed through the canopy, casting a soft glow that illuminated the vibrant greens of the forest and the myriad colors of the wildflowers that dotted the landscape. The air was alive with the scent of the sea, mingled with the earthy aroma of the forest floor, creating an atmosphere that was at once exhilarating and comforting.

In a burst of elation, Jessica spun around with her arms outstretched, her dress dancing around her in joyous spirals. The intricate details of her gown caught the light, embodying the spirit of the cove's natural beauty. The environment enveloped her in its familiar, comforting embrace, much like the hug of an old friend, as if to welcome her back.

Ethan watched her, a smile spreading across his face as he was touched by the tranquility of the cove and the pure joy in her eyes. He felt that same inexplicable allure he had felt on their last visit—the sense that the cove recognized him, its mysterious guardianship even stronger now. Though it was an unfamiliar sensation, he willingly surrendered to it, basking in the shared peace that Jessica found here.

Together, in that moment, they shared a connection not only with each other, but with the very essence of the cove itself. For Jessica, it was a return to a place of deep, personal significance. For Ethan, it was an embrace of the unknown, a step toward understanding the mystical bond Jessica had with this place. Surrounded by the cove's enchanting beauty and the subtle, protective presence that lingered in the air, they stood hand in hand, ready to explore the depths of their connection and the secrets the cove held.

As Ethan and Jessica ventured deeper, the memories of their last visit danced around them like the light filtering through the leaves. Ethan, with the cooler in hand, followed Jessica's lead, her eyes searching for the ideal spot to lay their blanket. It wasn't long before a smile of recognition lit up her face—there, just ahead, was the log they had sat on during their first visit, a simple piece of the cove's tapestry that had witnessed the beginning of their journey together.

With a shared glance that spoke volumes of their fond memories, they walked past the log, allowing the memory to guide them to a new spot, one that felt like it was waiting just for them. In a secluded nook embraced by nature's natural beauty, they found it—a rectangular patch of grass that seemed to be made just for their blanket. The grass was unlike any other, soft and smooth underfoot, a natural carpet that invited them to sit and stay a while.

With a gentle flourish, Jessica spread the blanket over the lush turf, transforming the spot into their own private haven. They settled in, with Ethan positioning the cooler within easy reach. Around them, the area thrummed with life, the gentle murmur of the stream, the whisper of the leaves, and the distant call of seabirds weaving a symphony of natural harmony.

Here, in the middle of the cove, on a bed of grass as inviting as any room of their own making, they found a moment of perfect peace. The world outside the cove's embrace seemed miles away, leaving Ethan and Jessica in a bubble of contentment, surrounded by an unseen but deeply felt presence that seemed to bless their union and deepen their bond without a word spoken.

Ethan's eyes swept over the serene expanse, the beauty of the cove casting its spell around him. With every rustle of leaves and the distant lapping of waves against the shore, he felt it more strongly—a sensation that was both unfamiliar and comforting. It was a presence, ethereal and subtle, yet undeniably there, embracing him in its invisible arms. He turned to Jessica, his expression a mix of bewilderment and curiosity, as if he were seeing the cove, and perhaps even the world, in a new light.

"You know, Jess, I don't think we're alone here," Ethan spoke softly, making sure his voice was just a whisper meant only for her.

There was a pause, a moment of hesitation as he searched for the right words. He wasn't afraid, but the depth of what he felt was so strange to him, that articulating it felt like navigating uncharted waters. He didn't want to alarm her or seem irrational in the serene stillness that surrounded them.

"There's something here. I can feel it," he continued after a breath, his words weighed down by the gravity of his admission. His voice, soft and thoughtful, carried a mixture of wonder as he struggled to describe the elusive sensation. "And it's not just here, in the cove. I feel it when we're on the beach or walking along the boardwalk. There's this strange calmness, a presence..."

Ethan trailed off for a moment, lost in thought, before regaining his composure. His eyes met Jessica's, seeking not only her attention but also her understanding. "It's hard to explain. But this presence, it's like it's always around me. Do you feel it, too?"

Jessica's face showed a blend of gentle confusion and curiosity as she considered his question. Her smile, tinged with amusement, invited him to share more.

"A presence?" she echoed, tilting her head with a light laugh that underscored her bemusement. "What do you mean?"

Ethan mulled over his own words, a flicker of doubt crossing his face as he pondered the adequacy of his description. Finally, he nodded, seemingly reconciled with his choice of words.

"Yeah, I guess that's the best way to describe it," Ethan began, pausing as he gathered his thoughts. "It's like there's something... or someone... near me. Like it's holding me, protecting me." There was a moment of reflection in his voice, a sense of wonder weaving through his words.

"I can feel it now, more than ever... right here in this cove," he continued, his voice imbued with a newfound certainty. His words lingered in the air between them, an intimate revelation shared in this secluded slice of paradise.

Jessica's expression softened, a soft glow of recognition illuminating her eyes. It was a look that spoke volumes, bridging the gap between Ethan's newfound sensations and her lifelong experiences.

"I know that feeling," Jessica replied, her voice carrying a warmth of understanding. "I've always felt like there's someone watching over me, like a guardian angel."

She let the words hang in the air for a moment, allowing the depth of that acknowledgment to settle between them. Then, with a tone rich in contemplation, she continued, "But it's more than that. Sometimes I feel like the town itself wraps its arms around me... like it's guiding me somehow."

Jessica paused, her eyes drifting across the cove, as if seeing it anew through Ethan's eyes.

"But this cove," she mused, her voice softening, "feels like it was made just for me. And that feeling you're talking about? It's with me all the time... reminding me I'm never really alone."

Her words wove a tapestry of understanding, offering Ethan a glimpse into the depth of connection she felt—not just with the cove, but with Wavecrest itself. It was a moment of profound connection, one that transcended the physical beauty of their surroundings to touch on something deeply spiritual and communal.

Ethan's eyes swept over the quiet expanse of the cove, his senses caressed by the peace that seemed to permeate the air. When he turned back to Jessica, his eyes were pensive, reflecting the thoughts that had been percolating in his mind since he'd arrived in Wavecrest.

"You know, since I've been hanging around Wavecrest, I've picked up on something," he started, his tone casual yet tinged with genuine intrigue. "The people here are just... different... in a good way. Like, everyone's genuinely nice, and I haven't seen anyone being outright mean. It's like there's this vibe of mutual respect or something, no matter what."

Ethan paused as he gathered his thoughts, allowing the weight of his observation to sink in. Then, with a contemplative air, he added, "There's this sense of security here that I haven't seen anywhere else. Like, people are out walking around, even late at night, and they're just chill. Everyone seems so at ease, like they don't have a care in the world."

He looked at Jessica, his eyes reflecting mild wonder, as if he were seeing Wavecrest's uniqueness in a whole new light.

Jessica's smile widened as she absorbed Ethan's observations. "You know, it's kinda funny. Hearing you talk about Wavecrest like that makes me realize how special it really is." Her voice warmed with affection and a hint of surprise. "I mean, deep down, I've always known it, but I never really thought about it. You're right, though. There is a sense of community. People do look out for each other. It's like there's this harmony, you know? Makes you feel connected, even when you don't realize it."

Her eyes drifted across the cove, seeking and finding confirmation in the natural beauty that cradled them.

"Maybe there is something about Wavecrest that ties us all together. I've always felt safe and protected." She shrugged, a thoughtful smile playing on her lips. "It's been like that all my life, like there's always been this invisible net to catch me if I fall."

Their conversation, deep and revealing, unfolded against the backdrop of the cove's serene beauty. It was a moment of shared insights and mutual understanding, a bridge between Ethan's fresh perspective and Jessica's lifelong experience. Together, they uncovered the essence of Wavecrest—not just a place of scenic beauty, but a community bound by a profound, ever-present force that made everyone feel safe, loved, and part of something larger than themselves.

Ethan's voice softened, blending seamlessly with the whispers of the cove around them. "You know," he began, his eyes lingering on the natural beauty that surrounded them. "Wavecrest would be the perfect place to raise a family."

He then turned to face Jessica, reaching out to take her hands in his. His eyes, intense and revealing a vulnerability he rarely showed, locked with hers.

"Our family, Jess," he whispered, the words a soft yet profound vow, laden with dreams of a future together. The simplicity of his declaration belied the depth of its meaning, encapsulating not just a desire but a vision—a life intertwined with love, shared in the very essence of Wavecrest.

In that instant, Jessica's world stilled. Ethan's earnest words resonated within her, unleashing a tide of warmth and promise that overwhelmed her. The sudden realization of his commitment and the clarity of his vision for their future together filled her with wonder and a deep sense of security. Ethan's declaration was more than mere words; it was a vow—a beacon of hope that cut through the fog of her uncertainties, dissipating the weight of worries that had loomed large in her mind.

She looked into Ethan's eyes and found the reflection of her own emotions in them—hope, love, and a shared vision for the future. His declaration wasn't just about a hypothetical family; it was a vow of commitment, a testament to his willingness to face the challenges of distance together. For Jessica, it was the assurance she had silently longed for, the answer to the unspoken questions that had lingered in her heart.

Overwhelmed by the intensity of her feelings, Jessica acted on impulse, letting her heart guide her actions. She leaned forward, closing the distance between them, and pulled Ethan close. Their lips met in a kiss that was both a seal of their promises to each other and a celebration of the love that bound them. It was a gentle yet profound kiss, one that spoke volumes, conveying their emotions more eloquently than words ever could.

Their kiss grew more passionate as Jessica felt her inhibitions melt away like the morning mist. Ethan, too, felt the flames of desire flicker within him and responded to her passion with equal intensity.

As the tide of their passion rose, the gentle sounds of the cove seemed to swell around them, nature bearing witness to their love. Jessica, her heart pounding with a mixture of anticipation and exhilaration, found courage in her desire. With a delicate touch, she guided Ethan to the blanket beneath them and pulled him down with her. The soft fabric cradled their entwined bodies as they lost themselves in each other, their hearts beating in sync like the rhythm of the ocean waves.

Ethan's gentle touch sent shivers of pleasure down Jessica's spine, igniting a fire within her. Her soft moans of ecstasy echoed through the cove, blending with the natural symphony of the wind whispering through the leaves and the distant lullaby of the waves. Jessica's breath hitched as his hands traced the contours of her body, each touch sending a jolt of electricity through her.

His heart raced as he responded to Jessica's touch, his body burning with desire. It was a moment of pure bliss, a fusion of their hearts and bodies, a celebration of their shared destiny. He felt the connection between them deepen, as if the universe itself had conspired to bind them together.

Suddenly, without a moment's hesitation, Jessica reached down and grasped the fabric of her dress. With her eyes full of lust, she locked her eyes onto Ethan's and pulled it over her head, casting it aside. The cool air of the cove caressed her bare skin, sending a shiver down her spine. Ethan's eyes widened in awe, his breath catching in his throat as he took in her natural beauty.

"Oh my God, Jessica," Ethan whispered, his voice filled with awe. "You are so beautiful."

Jessica smiled, encouraged by Ethan's admiration. She leaned forward and kissed him with renewed fervor, her tongue dancing with his in a sensual duet. As she pressed her body against him, she felt his hardness against her, an affirmation of his desire.

As their passion brought them to the point of no return, Ethan carefully rolled over, taking Jessica with him. In that moment, he knew they were at a crossroads. Though they had shared intimacy before, this moment carried a deeper meaning, a transition to something new and profound. He knew Jessica was a virgin, and he wanted her first time to be special. But he wanted to be sure she was ready, so he paused, searching her eyes for any hesitation or doubt.

"Are you sure about this, babe?" he asked, wanting to ensure she was ready for what they were about to share.

Jessica's mind raced with thoughts and emotions, but one thing remained clear: her love for Ethan. She knew that she wanted to give herself completely to him, to share this intimate moment that would bind them together in a way that nothing else could. She felt a deep sense of trust, knowing that he would cherish and protect her. She also felt a sense of empowerment, knowing that she was making this choice for herself, not out of pressure or expectation, but out of love and desire.

Her eyes glistened with tears as she looked up at Ethan, her voice thick with emotion. "I've never been more sure of anything in my life," she replied, her words revealing the depth of her feelings. She reached up and cupped Ethan's face in her hands, pulling him down for another passionate kiss.

With that affirmation, Ethan slowly eased himself into her, his movements gentle and deliberate. The tenderness in his touch spoke volumes, reflecting the depth of his love for her. He moaned out loud as he felt the overwhelming sensation of their bodies merging, becoming one. It was a connection that transcended the physical, a profound bond that seemed to stitch their souls together.

Jessica gasped, her breath catching in her throat as the sensation of Ethan filling her overwhelmed her. It was a blend of pleasure and pain, a delicate dance that transcended the physical realm. Her eyes fluttered shut, her body reacting to the exquisite sensations that washed over her. In that moment, she felt as if she was being reborn, her spirit soaring as Ethan's tender touch ignited a fire within her.

Emboldened by her love for Ethan, Jessica allowed herself to surrender to the moment. She wrapped her legs around him, pulling him deeper, her body responding with an intensity that left her breathless. As they moved together, lost in the throes of ecstasy, they found themselves transported to a place beyond words, a sacred space that was theirs alone.

In the midst of their embrace, the cove itself seemed to respond, as if it, too, recognized the significance of their union. The birds, nestled in the protective arms of ancient trees, took flight in a graceful arc, their departure a silent blessing. The rustle of their wings whispered through the air, a delicate symphony that seemed to echo the beating of their hearts.

High above, the seagulls, those watchful guardians of the shoreline, perched at the entrance to the cove, their watchful eyes fixed on the sea. It was as if they were standing guard, protecting this moment of pure connection from any intrusion. Their silence seemed to cast a spell over the cove, a hallowed quiet that encircled Jessica and Ethan, cocooning them in a bubble of love and reverence.

And then, as if the very air of Wavecrest were humming with a heavenly melody, the natural world around them seemed to sing—a chorus of unseen angels, their voices weaving through the rustle of the leaves and the gentle lapping of distant waves. It was a song of love, timeless and ethereal, a melody that seemed to resonate within their very souls. The notes danced around them, a delicate harmony that seemed to wrap their union in a blanket of pure, unadulterated joy.

In that moment, the cove became more than just a place; it transformed into a sacred space where two hearts declared their devotion not only to each other, but to a future they would build together. Their connection was palpable—a living, breathing entity that seemed to pulse with its own heartbeat.

Their movements grew more urgent, their bodies intertwined in a dance of love and passion. As they climbed higher and higher, their hearts racing, their breaths mingling, they felt the presence around them, guiding them, protecting them, loving them. And as they reached the peak of their ecstasy, their bodies trembling with the power of their release, they knew that they were truly one, bound together by love, by destiny, and by the eternal Spirit of Wavecrest.

An hour had woven its way through the afternoon, leaving the hustle and bustle of Cherry Springs Mall unchanged in its wake. Yet, for Krista, Fawn, and Michelle, that span of time had transformed their day from a mission of comfort to one of unexpected joy. During the interlude, Krista, with a newfound sense of purpose, had purchased a puppy leash and an assortment of toys—a colorful ball, a bone-shaped squeaker, and a soft, stuffed animal. Each purchase was made with a smile, her affection for the little lost puppy growing with each passing moment.

The puppy, now adorned with a bright new leash and surrounded by her toys, became the center of their world. Her playful antics and bursts of energy as she chased the ball or tugged at the squeaky toy brought peals of laughter from the girls. Even shoppers passing by couldn't help but pause, drawn in by the infectious joy radiating from their small circle.

Krista, in particular, was buoyed by the puppy's presence. The weight of her breakup with Donny, which had loomed so large at the beginning of the day, seemed to melt away with each wag of the puppy's tail. Surrounded by her friends and this bundle of joy, she felt a lightness she hadn't known she needed.

"I can't believe how much she's cheered me up," Krista confessed as she watched the puppy strut around triumphantly with the stuffed animal in her mouth. "It's like she knew we needed her as much as she needed us."

Fawn and Michelle exchanged knowing glances, their hearts warmed by Krista's recovery. "She's a little miracle," Fawn remarked, reaching out to gently ruffle the puppy's fur.

"Yeah, and she's got the best temporary mom," Michelle added, nudging Krista with a smile. "Who knew our day would turn out like this?"

As the puppy curled up on Krista's lap, exhausted from her play, the girls took a moment to bask in the simple contentment of their company. The challenges ahead—of distance, of change—seemed less daunting with the bond they shared, a bond now strengthened by the smallest of guardians.

Their laughter and chatter resumed, the puppy's soft snores a gentle accompaniment as they began to plan the rest of their day. Though they hadn't yet found the puppy's owner, they were united in their determination to do so, their spirits lifted by the unexpected detour their day had taken.

Just as they were settling into this newfound peace, a sudden commotion at the other end of the mall's atrium shattered their tranquility. A mall security guard, looking slightly frazzled, was making his way through the crowd, his eyes scanning the area intently.

Trailing behind him was an elderly woman, her silver hair tied back into a neat bun, the lines on her face etched with concern and urgency. Dressed in a light cardigan, she clutched a small handbag to her chest as if it were a lifeline, her eyes scanning the crowd for something—or someone.

The girls' curiosity was piqued, and they watched as the duo approached. Eventually, the security guard's eyes settled on them—or, more specifically, on the puppy in Krista's lap. On seeing the puppy, the woman's face transformed, relief and joy chasing away the worry lines as she quickened her pace towards them.

"Ruby!" she exclaimed, her voice carrying the gentle rasp that spoke of many years lived. "I've been looking all over for you!"

The girls exchanged glances, the realization dawning that their time with the puppy was coming to an end. Krista felt a pang in her heart; the prospect of saying goodbye to the puppy was suddenly real and imminent. Yet, the relief and happiness on the old woman's face were undeniable, a reminder of the purpose behind their day's mission.

The woman, now slowly kneeling with a slight tremor of effort to embrace Ruby, looked up at the girls with watery eyes, her aged face softening into a tableau of relief and gratitude.

"She's all I have," she explained, her voice trembling, not just from age but from the swell of emotions. "When I lost sight of her, it felt as though I was losing a part of my family all over again."

Moved by the woman's heartfelt words, Krista lowered herself to Ruby's level, mindful of the elderly woman's careful movements. As she stroked the puppy's head, her voice carried a mix of reassurance and empathy. "We're just glad we could keep her safe until you found her," she said, her own emotions surfacing.

The security guard, having observed the tender exchange, offered a small, respectful smile. "You girls did a great job. It's not every day we see a happy ending like that around here."

The woman, still holding Ruby, paused as if struck by a thought. "Would you... could you maybe join me for a cup of coffee?" she asked, looking at each of the girls in turn. "It's the least I can do to thank you. And Ruby seems to have taken quite a liking to you all."

The invitation took the girls by surprise. Fawn and Michelle quickly turned to Krista, waiting to see how she would react.

Krista hesitated, torn between wanting to spend more time with Ruby and knowing her friends wanted to pamper her in her time of need. Still, the opportunity to make sure Ruby was really okay, and perhaps help ease the transition for both the puppy and herself, was hard to resist.

After a moment of deliberation, Krista nodded. "We'd like that," she agreed, a small smile forming. "It would be nice to sit down and chat for a bit."

As the girls accepted her invitation and started walking toward the mall's quaint little cafe, the elderly woman's steps seemed lighter with Ruby content in her arms.

"Oh, where are my manners?" she exclaimed, looking at the girls with a grateful smile. "I'm Sally Kellett, but please, call me Sally."

The girls introduced themselves in turn, the exchange breaking the ice and deepening their sense of connection. Krista couldn't help but feel a pang of sadness at the thought of parting ways with Ruby soon, but the warmth of the budding friendship with Sally offered a comforting balm.

As they settled into the cafe's welcoming embrace, each with a drink in hand, Ruby found her place back in Krista's lap, seemingly content and at ease. Sally, her eyes twinkling with affection, began to recount Ruby's little adventures.

"You wouldn't believe the mischief this one gets into," Sally chuckled, sipping her coffee. "Just last week, she managed to unlock the backyard gate. I found her two doors down, hosting what I can only describe as a neighborhood dog meet-and-greet."

The girls laughed as they imagined the scene. Krista chimed in, "She was quite the adventurer today as well. We found her exploring the mall like she owned the place."

Sally's laughter joined theirs, a sound rich with joy. "That sounds just like Ruby. Always curious, always exploring."

Michelle leaned forward, her curiosity piqued. "What's the funniest thing Ruby's ever done?" she asked, eager to hear more.

Sally pondered for a moment before replying, "Oh, there are so many... but the cake incident takes the prize. Imagine a freshly baked chocolate cake left to cool, and a very quiet, very sneaky Ruby. The chaos that followed was... let's just say, memorable."

Their conversation flowed effortlessly; stories of Ruby's antics interspersed with tales of the day's unexpected journey. The laughter and shared stories wove a tapestry of connection, the clinking of cups a gentle accompaniment to their budding friendship. In that moment, the girls realized that their encounter with Ruby and Sally was more than just a diversion; it was a reminder of the unpredictability of life and the beauty of unexpected friendships.

As their time together neared its end, the cafe's atmosphere, still bathed in the soft light of the afternoon, took on a poignant quality. Ruby, ever perceptive, seemed to understand the special moment at hand. She gave each of the girls gentle licks, her small way of thanking them for the warmth and care they'd given her.

Krista held Ruby close, her eyes glistening with tears. "I didn't expect saying goodbye to be this hard," she whispered, her voice betraying her emotions. "Looking after Ruby, even for a little while, it's like she filled a space in my heart that I didn't know was empty."

Sally, with a gentle understanding in her eyes, reached out to touch Krista's arm. "You girls have done something wonderful today, not just for Ruby, but for me as well," she said warmly. "This kind of compassion from people we've just met... it's a beautiful reminder of the good in the world."

Their final farewell was tender. Each girl took a moment to cuddle Ruby, whispering their goodbyes and hopes for her happiness. Ruby responded with affectionate nuzzles, her way of saying she would not forget them.

As the girls walked away, the bittersweet feeling of parting was balanced by a sense of lightness and reflection. The experience with Ruby had opened their eyes in unexpected ways, teaching them about the depth of connection that can be found, not only with each other, but also with those they had just met. It was a brief encounter that would leave a lasting impression, a reminder of life's fleeting yet profoundly touching moments of friendship.

As Jessica and Ethan nestled on the blanket, their bodies entwined in a cocoon of serene bliss, the silent spectacle of nature unfolded around them. In this moment of quiet intimacy, Jessica held Ethan's cross in her hands, her fingers gently exploring its intricate design. The metal radiated a gentle warmth, reflecting the heat of their recent closeness, sending ripples of comfort and a sense of deep connection through her. This simple piece of metal, steeped in memories and meaning, became a tangible link between them, a silent testament to the invisible threads of affection that bound their hearts.

In the aftermath of their intimacy, clarity settled over Jessica, sharpening the edges of her desires and fears. The thought of college, once a distant concern, now felt like an insurmountable barrier between her and the future she longed for—a future with Ethan. With the knowledge of his impending departure from Wavecrest hanging over them—a mere twelve days away—the prospect of separation clawed at her with visceral pain. The ticking clock of reality shadowed the joy of their unity, each second a reminder of the countdown to their separation.

Gathering the courage that love both demands and bestows, Jessica lifted her gaze to Ethan, her eyes brimming with a mix of hope and vulnerability. The warmth of the cross in her hand seemed to embolden her, lending weight to her words as she voiced the plea that had been haunting the corners of her mind.

"Ethan, when it's time for you to go back to Pine Haven," she paused, the weight of her request hanging in the air. Gathering her breath, she added softly but with undeniable seriousness, "please take me with you."

Ethan looked up at Jessica, a storm of emotions swirling in his eyes. The soft light of the cove illuminated his features, casting shadows that danced with the conflict within him. His desire to keep her close, to say yes and shield her from any pain, battled with the knowledge of what was truly right for her. He reached for her hand, intertwining his fingers with hers, seeking a tangible connection in this moment of intangible choices.

"I want to, Jess. I really want to," he confessed, his voice heavy with the weight of his longing and the complexity of their situation.

But Ethan's mind flashed back to his conversation with Jake. The stark contrast between his brother's logic and his own fervent desires stood out as he mulled over Jessica's heartfelt plea. Jake's words, emphasizing the importance of Jessica's personal growth and exploration, echoed in his mind: "I know you love her, man. But love is also about wanting the best for the person you care about. If you don't let her explore the world and discover herself, one day she might look back with regret."

Though Ethan found this perspective difficult to accept, its truth was undeniable. He realized that Jessica's path to self-discovery, to truly find herself, required her own journey—a journey that, for now, will have to be made without him by her side.

Ethan looked into Jessica's eyes, a tumult of emotions swirling within him as he contemplated their future. He took a deep breath, the weight of his decision weighing heavily on him.

"But there's a whole new world waiting for you to discover," he began, the depth of his love and concern for her evident in his voice. He paused, gathering his thoughts and emotions before continuing. "It's a beautiful world out there, Jess. There are so many wonderful things to see and experience," he said, his tone tinged with nostalgia, reflecting on his own adventures with Jake as he encouraged her to explore.

Jessica's response came softly, her head shaking in denial as tears filled her eyes. "You are my world, Ethan," she whispered, her voice breaking with emotion as she imagined a future apart from him. "Can't you see that?"

Ethan's eyes softened, the conflict evident in the lines of his face as he searched for the words to convey the turmoil in his heart.

"Jess, believe me, nothing would make me happier than having you by my side. But I keep thinking about what Jake told me," he said, his voice low and earnest. "He reminded me that love isn't just about being together; it's about wanting what's truly best for each other."

He took her hand and squeezed it gently, a physical affirmation of the emotional connection they shared. "Jake made me realize that part of loving someone is giving them the space to grow, to explore, and to find their own path. And as much as it hurts to even think about us being apart, I know he's right. You have so much to see, so much to experience."

He paused, the weight of his next words hanging between them. "Your journey is just beginning, and it's a journey you need to take on your own, to discover who you are outside of Wavecrest... outside of us."

Ethan's voice was thick with emotion, his gaze unwavering as he held Jessica's. "And I'll be waiting for you, babe, supporting you every step of the way. Because that's what it means to truly love someone."

Jessica took a moment to absorb Ethan's words, each one landing with the weight of a profound truth. She looked into his eyes, seeing not just the man she loved, but also a partner who truly wanted the best for her, even if it meant enduring a separation.

"Listening to you, knowing how much you care... it makes this even harder," Jessica began, her voice a whisper against the backdrop of their secluded sanctuary.

She paused, searching Ethan's eyes for understanding. "But I understand what you're saying. I've always known there's a big world out there. I've just been afraid to face it alone."

Her admission hung in the air, exposing the depth of her vulnerability. But as Ethan listened, offering silent support, Jessica found a glimmer of courage.

"But knowing that you believe in me, that you think I'm strong enough to do this on my own... that means everything." The words tumbled out, each one punctuated by the weight of realization and gratitude.

Jessica took a deep breath, summoning all the strength her love for him gave her. "I love you, Ethan. And because I love you, I'll try. I'll try to be brave, for both of us." Her declaration, filled with love and newfound resolve, echoed the promise of their bond, resilient even in the face of impending separation.

In that moment, Jessica's journey from fear to determination was laid bare, her words weaving a poignant tale of the power of love to inspire courage and change.

As the silence of the cove enveloped them, Ethan offered Jessica a warm, reassuring smile, a beacon of comfort in the midst of their emotional storm. With a tenderness that spoke volumes, he cupped her face in his hands, drawing her eyes to meet his.

"This is not the end for us, Jessica. I love you. And one day, we'll be together again, stronger than ever," he said, his voice thick with emotion and conviction. It was a promise, not just of hope, but of an unwavering belief in their future together.

Ethan's assurance was like a balm to Jessica's aching heart, a reminder of the depth of their connection. He leaned in, closing the distance between them, and with a gentle caress that spoke of love and longing, he sealed his vow with a tender kiss. It was a moment suspended in time, a kiss that lingered long after their lips parted, leaving an imprint on their souls.

As the afternoon light began to fade, casting a golden glow over the secluded cove, Jessica and Ethan remained entwined, a silent vow hanging in the air between them. Each moment was a treasure, a poignant reminder of the fleeting nature of their current bliss. They shared whispered words, soft laughter, and tender touches, each gesture deepening the connection they had nurtured. In the sanctuary of the cove, with the gentle sound of the waves and the rustle of leaves as their only witness, they pledged to cherish these precious hours.

Their connection, both physical and emotional, was a balm to the pain of impending separation. With every look and every touch, they conveyed a multitude of unspoken promises and shared dreams. It was a time of profound intimacy, not just of bodies but of souls, as they sought to memorize every detail of each other to carry with them over the coming distance.

As the day waned, they lay together, watching the sky transition from the brilliant blues of day to the soft pinks and golds that heralded the approach of early evening. It was a moment suspended outside of time, a bubble of perfect peace in a world that would soon demand their return. They understood, with a clarity born of their shared experience, that though the future was uncertain, their love was a constant—a beacon that would guide them back to each other, no matter how many miles lay between them.

As the early evening colors painted the sky over Cherry Springs Mall, the atmosphere inside buzzed with the dwindling energy of the day. Shoppers, their numbers thinning as the day wore on, moved about at a leisurely pace. The mall, a bustling hub of activity and laughter throughout the day, now echoed with the serene lull of the evening, marking the end of another vibrant day.

Fawn, Krista, and Michelle meandered through its corridors, their steps slow, reluctant to end the day. Their laughter echoed, a reflection of the joy and camaraderie they shared.

"I can still see the look on your face, Kris, when that stylist at the salon suggested that bold new haircut," Fawn teased, her eyes alight with mischief. "I thought you were going to jump out of your chair!"

Krista rolled her eyes, a smile playing on her lips. "I know, right? Like I'd ever let anyone chop my hair like that," she said, her tone light and teasing. Then, her expression softened as she added, "But I do love my manicure and pedicure. Thanks, guys."

Fawn and Michelle exchanged a glance, their smiles rich with satisfaction and warmth, silently communicating their happiness at having given Krista a day of pampering and care.

Then Michelle chimed in, her voice warm with affection. "I wonder how Ruby is doing. I loved how she snuggled right into your lap... as if she knew you needed that little bit of happiness."

Krista's expression softened, her eyes taking on a distant, thoughtful glow as she remembered those moments. "She was a little sweetheart, wasn't she?"

They paused, a silence settling over them, not one of awkwardness but of thoughtful appreciation. The mall's ambient music provided a soft backdrop to their shared memories, a soothing rhythm to their collective reflection.

"It's been quite a day," Michelle mused, looking at her friends. "From finding Ruby to pampering ourselves a bit. I wouldn't change a thing."

"Yeah," Fawn agreed, her eyes lingering on the fading daylight outside the mall windows. "It's been a great day. I just wish Jessica could have been here with us."

Krista nodded, her earlier concerns momentarily forgotten in the warmth of friendship. "I know. But I'm sure her day was just as good as ours, if not better."

As they walked on, each step carried the laughter and lightness of the day's experiences. Inside the mall, with its stores and bright lights, it felt like a cocoon, wrapping up their experience in a warm embrace, a final salute to a day well spent.

As they made their way to the glass doors marking the mall's exit, Fawn broke the comfortable silence with a light-hearted remark: "I don't know about you guys, but I'm getting hungry." Her words were met with nods of agreement, the shared sentiment sparking a decision to head home.

Krista, her spirits visibly lifted by the day's events, chimed in, "Me too. I guess we should head back."

Michelle, always the enthusiastic one, added, "Agreed. We're having lamb chops for dinner tonight. My favorite." Her anticipation for the meal reflected her appreciation for the small joys in life.

Fawn's thoughts turned to the Sunday dinner that was waiting for her at Jessica's house, a tradition that held more meaning than just the food. "Sunday dinners at Jess's house are always the best. I can't wait!" she exclaimed, her excitement contagious.

Krista reflected on the day, a soft smile touching her lips. "You know what? I think this has been the perfect way to end the weekend. It's been such a fun day, and I can't thank you guys enough." Her sincere and heartfelt words resonated with her friends.

Feeling a surge of affection, Michelle shared her sentiment. "Yes, it has. And I'm so grateful to have you guys as my besties." Her voice carried the weight of genuine gratitude.

Moved by the moment, Fawn expressed her own feelings. "Aw, thanks, Michelle. You guys are the best, too. Love you both."

"Group hug!" Krista exclaimed, her voice bubbling with enthusiasm. The three girls embraced, their arms wrapped around each other in a moment of tenderness and gratitude. The warmth of their hug encapsulated the day's joy, laughter, and shared experiences, a poignant reminder of their enduring friendship.

As they parted from their embrace, they knew that while their day at Cherry Springs Mall had come to an end, the memories they had created would remain, a beacon of light in the days to come. With smiles on their faces and warmth in their hearts, they made their way out of the mall, ready to face the new week with the strength of their friendship to guide them.

The soft hum of Michelle's car engine filled the air as the girls settled into their seats, Michelle and Krista in the front and Fawn nestled in the back. As they pulled out of the parking lot, the golden hues of the early evening sun painted a serene backdrop, a fitting end to their day of camaraderie and unexpected adventures. The road to Wavecrest unfolded before them, each mile bringing them closer to the familiar comfort of home.

The quaint streets of Wavecrest welcomed them back, the cozy atmosphere of the town a stark contrast to the bustling energy of the mall. Michelle's car wound through the streets of the neighborhood, each turn taking them deeper into the heart of their memories. Finally, they arrived at Jessica's house, the destination that had become a second home to Fawn.

As the car came to a gentle stop, the moment of parting had arrived. After stepping out of the car, Fawn turned to face Krista and Michelle. The warmth of the day's shared laughter and the strength of their bond lingered in the air between them.

"Thanks for everything, Fawn. It meant a lot," Krista said, her voice imbued with genuine gratitude. Her words reflected the comfort and joy her friends had given her at a time when she needed it most.

Fawn offered a bright, reassuring smile, her eyes reflecting the depth of their friendship. "Anytime, Kris. You know we're always here for you," she replied, her voice steady and sincere.

With a final round of goodbyes and a promise to see each other soon, Fawn watched as Michelle's car drove away, leaving behind a trail of laughter and plans for their final gathering.

With that, Fawn made her way to the front door of Jessica's house, the familiarity of the steps and the anticipation of Sunday dinner enveloping her in a sense of belonging. As she stepped inside, she carried the memories of the day with her, a poignant reminder of the strength and beauty of friendship, cherishing these moments as treasures for the uncertain roads ahead.

# Chapter 41

-------------------------------------------------------------

The Reese family kitchen, a room filled with warm aromas and familial love, was winding down from the day's events. The hands of the clock nudged toward eleven as night claimed the vibrant town of Wavecrest. In this space, laughter and earnest words had often danced among the terracotta tiles and wooden cabinetry, but tonight, the atmosphere held a quieter, more reflective mood.

Fawn sat at the kitchen table, her legs curled beneath her on the chair. The pink t-shirt she wore was soft and worn, a stark contrast to the sleek elegance of Teresa's long black nightgown, which whispered with every movement she made. Across from Fawn, Teresa rested her chin in her hand, her eyes fixed thoughtfully on the young woman before her.

Tom stood at a distance, his posture relaxed against the surface of the kitchen counter. He idly rolled a bottle of beer between his palms, his eyes occasionally drifting to the two women engaged in conversation. His gray t-shirt hung loosely on his frame, and his tan shorts were a sign of the day spent in leisure.

The conversation that wove through the air was tender, tinged with excitement and a hint of paternal concern. It was about Jessica and Ethan—two young hearts who had found each other amidst summer kisses and sandy embraces.

Fawn's voice broke through, rich with the affection only a best friend could harbor. "I'm so happy for Jessica and Ethan! They're such a beautiful couple," she exclaimed with genuine warmth, her mischievous blue eyes shining.

Teresa smiled in agreement. "I agree! They really do complement each other." Her voice carried a softness that often came with thinking about her daughter's happiness.

Tom took a sip from his beer before setting it down with a muted clink. "Well, I don't know about Ethan. He's a little wild and reckless for my liking." His brows furrowed slightly as he spoke, revealing an undercurrent of protective concern that had always been part of his nature.

Teresa turned to look at him, a playful yet understanding glint in her eyes. "Oh, come on, Tom. He's a good kid. Jessica could use someone like him in her life. He brings out her adventurous side."

"Hmph." Tom's lips formed a tight line for a moment before relaxing. "I just don't want her to get hurt."

Fawn nodded sympathetically but quickly chimed in with conviction. "Jessica knows what she's doing. She's smart, you guys. And Ethan is crazy about her!" Her voice carried confidence in her friend's judgment—a belief forged through years of friendship.

Teresa leaned back in her chair, crossing one leg over the other as she considered Fawn's words. "I know, honey. And Jessica feels the same way about Ethan. It's so cute to see them together."

The kitchen brimmed with an unspoken acknowledgment of change—of children growing up and stepping into their own stories—yet a subtle note of resilience permeated the atmosphere; they were family, after all.

Tom picked up his beer again but didn't drink from it this time; instead, he allowed himself to absorb Fawn's optimism and Teresa's faith in their daughter's choices.

"Well," he said after a brief pause, "all I'm saying is that he better treat her right."

His words weren't heavy with threat but laden with the hope that every father harbors for his child—to find happiness without the sting of heartache. Fawn smiled at him, recognizing that no matter how old they got or where life took them, some things remained steadfast—the love and care within these walls would always be one of them.

As Sunday night deepened its grip on Wavecrest, and the stars peppered the sky outside the kitchen window, three people—a mother, a father, and their daughter's closest friend—found solace in their shared concern for two young hearts navigating love's unpredictable waters.

The sound of the front door opening and closing sliced through their conversation like a knife, announcing the arrival of someone familiar. Moments later, Jessica breezed into the kitchen, her presence like a burst of energy that shifted the atmosphere. Windswept hair framed her face, her cheeks kissed by the last embers of the setting sun, and her smile—oh, that smile—was radiant and infectious as she greeted her parents and Fawn.

"Hi, everyone!" she exclaimed, breathless from excitement, or perhaps the sprint from the door to the kitchen. Without ceremony, she plopped down onto the chair beside Fawn. "Sorry, I'm late. Ethan and I went for a drive along the coast." A brief pause for air did little to dampen her enthusiasm. "It was so beautiful! We stopped to watch the sunset, and then we parked on the beach to talk and listen to music." Her eyes sparkled with an elation that was almost palpable.

Teresa's motherly gaze softened as she watched her daughter recount the evening. "Sounds wonderful, sweetheart. I'm glad you had fun."

She then turned to Tom with a look that spoke volumes—a mixture of I-told-you-so and gentle teasing. "See? Ethan isn't so bad."

Though gruff in his protective instincts, Tom couldn't resist the warmth in Teresa's eyes or the joy in his daughter's voice. His lips curled into a smile as Jessica recounted more of her night's escapades.

Fawn absorbed every word with rapt attention. But beyond Jessica's stories, it was the transformation in her friend that captivated her most—the permanent smile etched on Jessica's lips, the light in her eyes like never before. It was clear to Fawn that something had happened to make Jessica's world more vibrant.

"Sounds like you guys had quite a day," Fawn commented with a mixture of awe and excitement after Jessica wrapped up her tale. She leaned forward, mischief twinkling in her eyes, and quipped, "So, when's the wedding?"

The kitchen erupted with Jessica's laughter—clear and joyful, like chimes in a gentle breeze.

"Oh, stop it! Ethan and I aren't even engaged yet." As she spoke those words, a delicate blush flushed across her cheeks. The way her eyes darted away for just a moment didn't escape Fawn's notice; it was clear Jessica harbored dreams where Ethan played a leading role.

Tom chimed in after a moment of observing his daughter's reactions. "That's probably a good thing. Marriage is a serious commitment, and you two are still so young."

Jessica nodded at her father's words; she knew well his concerns were born from love and care.

"I know, Dad. Don't worry. Ethan and I aren't rushing into anything." Her smile was steady—a bridge between youthful enthusiasm for love and understanding of its gravity.

Teresa reached across the table and patted Jessica's hand—a silent acknowledgment of both Jessica's maturity and their shared confidence in her judgment.

Despite the waves of joy from her day with Ethan, Jessica's thoughts drifted back to Krista, who had been navigating the stormy aftermath of a breakup.

"How's Krista doing?" Jessica asked, turning to Fawn. "Is she feeling any better?" The concern in her voice washed over the quiet kitchen like a soothing tide.

Fawn's eyes met Jessica's, a glimmer of reassurance in their depths. "Yes, she seems to be okay. I think our trip to the mall helped take her mind off things," she replied, her voice a soft melody in the night.

"That's good," Jessica murmured, a small smile gracing her lips. "I want to hear all about it, but first, I need to get a shower."

Tom took his last swig of beer and tossed the empty bottle into the recycling bin with practiced ease.

"Well, I'm going to bed," he announced. "Monday mornings seem to come early these days."

He paused by Teresa and planted a tender kiss on her lips before leaving the kitchen. His footsteps were measured and familiar as he walked over to each of the girls, giving them a gentle kiss on their head before bidding them goodnight with loving finality.

Teresa rose from her chair, smoothing out her nightgown. A smile bloomed across her face—a garden of love and maternal warmth as she looked at Jessica and Fawn. "Goodnight, girls. Sweet dreams."

With that, she, too, retired for the night, her presence lingering like a comforting embrace even as she left the kitchen.

In the silence that followed, Jessica and Fawn exchanged a look of mutual understanding—a silent conversation that spoke volumes about their shared history and uncertain future. Their carefree days of youthful innocence were being chased away by life's relentless march toward change and growth. Yet amidst this landscape of unknowns, one thing was certain—the impending separation from their friends and each other was inevitable.

"You know," Fawn broke the silence, her voice tinged with sadness, "Krista will be leaving for Colorado next Sunday."

Jessica's eyes widened in surprise. "Next Sunday?"

"Yeah," Fawn nodded solemnly. "She wants us to have one last get-together before she leaves."

"Of course," Jessica replied. "Let's make it count!"

"Definitely!" Fawn said with conviction. "Next Saturday night, at our spot on the beach. Just the four of us."

"Sounds perfect," Jessica agreed with a smile that didn't quite reach her eyes. It was a bittersweet thought—they would be getting together at that cherished spot on the beach where so many memories had been etched into their hearts.

"Yeah," Fawn echoed wistfully. "Lots of good memories there."

For a moment, they were lost in thoughts of past summers—their sacred spot on the beach had witnessed their laughter under firework-lit skies, intimate conversations around crackling campfires, and shared dreams under an endless canopy of stars.

Jessica sighed softly as she rose from her chair—a ship setting sail from port. "Well, I'm going to go get my shower," she announced while stretching lazily.

"Okay," Fawn replied as she stood up as well.

She reached out to turn off the light in the kitchen—a gesture marking an end but also acknowledging tomorrow's light—and followed Jessica through the darkened house.

Once inside her bedroom, Jessica gathered her sleeping clothes and headed for the bathroom, while Fawn sat on the edge of the bed. Her mind wandered through the day's events—the joyous highs and poignant lows—and wondered how these fleeting moments would shape their tomorrows.

The bathroom door clicked shut behind Jessica as water cascaded down like spring rain—washing away remnants of saltwater and sand—while Fawn remained seated in contemplation amidst the shadows cast by the moonlight filtering through the curtains.

As the midnight hour approached, Jessica emerged from the bathroom, her hair still damp and her skin flushed pink from the heat of the shower. Droplets of water clung to the ends of her honey-colored strands as she walked across the bedroom to where her hairbrush lay.

Fawn watched her friend, noticing how she seemed to glow from within. Her lips curled into a soft smile as Jessica took a seat beside her and playfully nudged her shoulder.

"So, tell me about your day at the mall," Jessica said, her voice bubbling with curiosity. She turned her body to face Fawn and gave her full attention.

Fawn's eyes sparkled with mischief. "Well, it started out like any other trip to the mall," she began, "until we came across this little lost puppy near the food court."

Jessica listened intently as Fawn recounted the day's adventures—how they had found Ruby the puppy and helped reunite her with her owner, Mrs. Kellett. She then told her all about Krista's surprise manicure and pedicure that she and Michelle had paid for.

When she finished, Jessica shook her head in amazement. "Wow, sounds like you guys had quite an adventure!"

Fawn nodded, a note of pride in her voice as she replied, "We sure did!"

The room became silent, a space for contemplation as the events of the day sank in. Jessica placed her hands on her lap and gazed down at the floor. The smile of unfiltered joy returned to her face as she reflected on her day with Ethan.

Noticing the change in Jessica's demeanor, Fawn studied her friend's features. There was something new there—a glow, a lightness—a blissful radiance that spoke of an untold story.

Fawn couldn't help but smile as she looked at Jessica curiously. "Something happened today, didn't it?" she asked, her voice a whisper in the night.

Jessica's head snapped up, her cheeks flushing pink. "What do you mean?" she asked, feigning innocence.

Fawn raised her eyebrows, a smirk playing on her lips. "Don't play coy with me. I've never seen you look so... happy. Something did happen today, didn't it?"

Jessica looked away for a moment before meeting Fawn's gaze again. She nodded slowly, a shy smile tugging at the corners of her mouth as she whispered, "I did it."

"You did what?" Fawn asked, her curiosity piqued.

Jessica giggled nervously, fiddling with the hem of her shirt. "You know... That!"

Fawn's eyes widened as realization dawned upon her. She leaned forward and grabbed Jessica's hand excitedly. "Oh my god! You mean...?"

Jessica's cheeks reddened even more as she nodded sheepishly.

The sudden realization of what Jessica had cryptically confessed hit Fawn like a bolt of lightning. She gasped as she exclaimed, "Jessica, you lost your virginity?" There was an edge of disbelief in her voice, as if she couldn't quite believe that her best friend had finally crossed that threshold.

Jessica laughed nervously again, her cheeks still blushing. "Uh-huh," she confirmed, her voice barely above a whisper.

Fawn squealed with delight, pulling Jessica into a tight hug. "Oh my God, Jess. I'm so happy for you."

Jessica hugged her back, giggling slightly as she pulled away from Fawn's warm embrace.

The room fell silent again as Fawn absorbed what Jessica had revealed. She looked at her in awe as she asked, "So, how was it? Was it everything you hoped it would be?"

Jessica's eyes sparkled as those intimate moments with Ethan flashed through her mind.

"It was beautiful," she breathed, a smile lingering on her lips. "It was everything I hoped for and more."

Fawn beamed at her friend, ecstatic for Jessica's happiness and the new intimacy discovered between two intertwined hearts.

"Aw, Jess, I'm so happy to hear that," Fawn murmured in heartfelt tones. "Ethan must be quite the guy to have made your first time so special," she added with warmth enveloping each word.

In the quiet room, as time seemed to pause, Fawn noticed Jessica stifling a yawn behind her delicate fingers.

"Come on, Jess," Fawn said gently as she sat up and reached over to turn off the bedside lamp. "You should get some sleep."

Jessica nodded and rolled onto her side of the bed, her exhaustion evident as the whirlwind of emotions from the day finally began to settle.

Fawn lay down on her side of the bed and pulled the covers over them. As they settled on their pillows, their eyes gazed at the ceiling, where the dimming glow of stars looked down upon them.

Lying in bed, Fawn's eyes fixed on the celestial gathering above her, her attention drawn inexorably to her favorite star. With a tender gesture, she reached out, her finger tracing its unique outline in the air, an invisible caress to her cherished companion in the night sky.

Tracing the air with her finger, Fawn whispered to the dimly lit star, "Aw, you poor baby," her voice filled with sadness at its fading light.

"What's the matter?" Jessica asked, turning to Fawn with concern.

Fawn turned to Jessica, a sad smile on her lips as she replied, "My favorite star. Its glow is getting weaker every night. It makes me so sad to see it go."

Jessica's eyes softened as she reached out and squeezed Fawn's hand. "I'm sorry, Fawn. I know how much you love that star."

Returning her gaze to the ceiling, Jessica found herself lost in the memory of her day with Ethan. The passion, the tenderness, the exhilaration—it all came flooding back in vivid detail. It was all new to her. She had never felt this way before. This was beyond love. This was something more profound—a connection that transcended beyond the physical and into the depths of her soul.

Turning back to face Fawn, she asked, "Can I ask you something?"

Fawn turned to face Jessica, her voice soft as she replied, "Of course you can."

Jessica paused as she collected her thoughts, trying to find the right words to articulate what she was feeling. "How was your first time? You know, you and Jerry."

Fawn smiled melancholically, remembering the tenderness and awkwardness of that night. "It was okay," she admitted.

"Just, okay?" Jessica asked, surprised by Fawn's answer.

Fawn shrugged and sighed as she replied, "Yeah, it was nice enough, but it wasn't magical or anything."

Jessica paused for a moment as she considered Fawn's words. Then she asked, "Did Jerry ever make you feel the way Ethan makes me feel?"

Fawn shook her head, a slight frown creasing her forehead. "You can't compare what you have with Ethan to what Jerry and I had, Jess. It's totally different."

She paused for a second before adding, "What you and Ethan have is real. It's the kind of love that lasts forever."

She paused again as she took a moment to reflect on her time with Jerry. "What Jerry and I had, well, it wasn't like that."

Jessica nodded, understanding Fawn's words. "I think I understand what you're saying. I guess what Ethan and I have is just a little more intense, more meaningful."

Fawn nodded in agreement. "Exactly. And that's a good thing. It means you guys have something truly special."

As their conversation faded into silence and their thoughts settled back into their own realms of reflection—Jessica on her newfound connection with Ethan and Fawn on the delicate intricacies of love—they both lay still under Jessica's star-filled ceiling.

Outside Jessica's window, where the soft murmur of Wavecrest's nocturnal symphony played—a dog barking in the distance and an occasional passing car—the two girls lay awake, their minds swirling with the complexities and beauty of life's mysteries.

After a while, Fawn turned to Jessica, a mischievous glint in her eyes. "Hey, Jess," she whispered, a hint of playfulness in her voice.

"Yeah?" Jessica replied, turning to face Fawn.

"You know what I'm thinking about doing when I get to Boston?" Fawn asked, her voice low and conspiratorial.

Jessica raised an eyebrow, her curiosity piqued. "What?" she asked.

With a mischievous grin, Fawn replied, "I think I'm going to get my tongue pierced."

Jessica's eyes widened in shock. "Really?" she asked incredulously.

"Yeah, I saw this piercing place at the mall today, and I think it'll look so cool!" Fawn exclaimed.

Jessica's face twisted into a grimace. "Ouch! There's no way I would let someone put a hole in my tongue," she laughed.

Fawn burst out in laughter at Jessica's reaction. "Why not?" she asked between her giggles. "Ethan might like that, you know."

Jessica laughed as she rolled her eyes, a blush creeping across her cheeks. "I don't know about that. Besides, I'm afraid of needles."

When the laughter died down, Fawn finally confessed. "Nah, I'm just kidding," she said with a grin. "I'm not going to get my tongue pierced."

"Whew," Jessica breathed, relieved that Fawn was only joking.

The playful atmosphere in Jessica's bedroom grew as she stuck out her tongue, pretending to examine it for a piercing. Her face contorted into a series of exaggerated, humorous expressions, each more comical than the last.

Unable to resist joining in, Fawn mirrored Jessica's antics, sticking out her tongue and twisting her features into ridiculous faces, trying to outdo Jessica's comedic performance.

"Look at me, Jess! I think I see it!" Fawn declared through stifled laughter, pretending to find the perfect spot on her tongue for a piercing.

Their raucous laughter filled the room as they continued their playful charade. Each girl strived to make the silliest face possible—eyes crossed, tongues lolling to one side or the other—eliciting peals of laughter from each other.

When they finally caught their breath after their fits of giggles subsided, they settled back down on the bed. Jessica glanced over at Fawn with fond amusement dancing in her eyes.

"You're crazy," she said with an affectionate shake of her head.

Fawn grinned at her best friend. "Takes one to know one," she cheerfully quipped back.

The bond between them was undeniable—built over years of countless moments like these, where they could be themselves without fear of judgment.

Fawn leaned back against the pillows and sighed. "I can't believe how fast time is flying by," she murmured after a moment of quiet reflection.

Jessica nodded in agreement as she lay back next to Fawn. A heavy feeling hung in the air between them—the knowledge that their time together was precious and fleeting.

"I know," Jessica replied quietly. "But no matter what happens or where we go... I'll never forget nights like this."

Fawn smiled at the thought—a smile filled with warmth and gratitude for the friendship they shared. "Yeah," she murmured as she reached over to squeeze Jessica's hand. "Me neither."

Under the faint glow of the stars above them, and amidst the bursts of laughter that had filled the room only moments before, there was comfort in knowing that some things—like their friendship—would endure beyond distance and change.

In the sanctity of Tom and Teresa's bedroom, the dim glow from a streetlight cast a soft light across the room. Teresa lay beside Tom, her eyes fixed on the ceiling, listening intently to the laughter and giggles emanating from Jessica's room down the hall. Normally, since this was a work night and Tom had to get up early, she would have marched down the hall and told the girls it was time to go to sleep. But not tonight. Tonight was different.

In just a few short weeks, Jessica and Fawn would embark on new chapters of their lives, away from the protective walls of home. The sounds of joyous laughter and youthful exuberance that floated into Teresa's ears were music to her soul. It transported her back to countless sleepovers past, where Jessica and Fawn had filled the house with their boundless energy and innocent joy. Every giggle was a tender reminder of those precious moments of childhood that were now ebbing away all too quickly.

As she lay there listening, Teresa's mind wandered through a vibrant mosaic of memories, each one more vivid than the last.

The day Jessica was born was forever etched in her memory—a day when her heart overflowed with joy as she held her baby girl for the first time. She could still recall the tiny weight in her arms, the little bundle looking up at her with bright, trusting eyes.

Over the years, the sound of Jessica's laughter had filled the house, bringing light to even the darkest corners. She could vividly picture her little girl tearing open Christmas presents each year, her bright blue eyes wide with wonder and excitement.

And then there was Fawn—always by Jessica's side since they first met in kindergarten. Her protective nature and caring heart had endeared her to Tom and Teresa as if she were their own daughter. Fawn had effortlessly woven herself into the tapestry of their family, a constant presence who shared every high and comforted every low.

Teresa smiled at these reflections, feeling a lone tear escape and make its way down her cheek. It was remarkable how these moments—the ones that sometimes felt so routine—had stitched themselves together into years that had slipped by way too fast.

She thought about how Jessica and Fawn would soon be packing up their rooms and leaving for places unknown to them. There would be no more impromptu dance parties in the living room or late-night baking sessions that left flour dust on every surface of the kitchen.

Teresa sighed, another tear running down her cheek as she realized that these moments, these precious years, had passed too quickly. Turning to Tom, she nudged his shoulder, waking him from his slumber.

"Hey, Hun?" she whispered, her voice barely louder than the distant murmur of laughter from Jessica's room.

Tom turned to face Teresa, his eyes slowly adjusting to the dim light. "Yeah?" he replied, his voice groggy with sleep.

Teresa's breath caught in her throat as she struggled to articulate a whimsical thought. "Let's lock the girls in their room so they can't leave," she said, half-joking and half-serious.

Seeing the tears in Teresa's eyes, Tom's expression softened. "Aw, honey, we knew this day would come," he whispered.

"I know. I know." Teresa's voice trembled as the dam of her emotions broke, and she began to cry. "But she's my baby, Tom—my little girl. And I'm not ready to let her go," Teresa confessed through the tears that rolled down her cheek.

Tom sighed as he felt Teresa's pain echo within him. "Neither am I, honey, but we have to. We can't keep her here forever," he said with gentle finality.

"I know. I'm just going to miss seeing her smile every morning when she comes into the kitchen—and hearing her laughter. This house is going to feel so empty without her," Teresa said through her tears.

Tom nodded silently, knowing exactly what Teresa meant. They lay there for a moment, wrapped in each other's arms, sharing a silent grief for the loss of their daughter's childhood—a time that had seemed infinite and yet had slipped through their fingers like grains of sand.

"And there's Fawn," Teresa continued after catching her breath, "always looking out for her like a sister, always encouraging her to try something new."

Another memory flashed through her mind—those random moments when Fawn would give her a hug and say, "I love you, Mama." It was those spontaneous expressions of affection that had woven Fawn into the fabric of their family as if she had always belonged.

Tom reached up and wiped away Teresa's tears with his thumb. "I know, sweetheart. It's going to be hard for both of us, but we'll get through this," he assured her.

Teresa tried to regain control of her emotions as she considered what lay ahead. "It's just going to be so hard to say goodbye. I wish she would have allowed me to fly with her to Texas."

"She wanted to do this on her own. You know Jessica. She can be stubborn as a mule when she wants to be," Tom said with an attempt at lightheartedness.

Teresa chuckled softly—her daughter's stubbornness was indeed something familiar—and gave Tom a knowing smirk. "Yeah, and I wonder where she got that from?"

Tom couldn't help but grin at Teresa's remark; it was well known that Jessica had inherited some of his own tenacity.

"She'll be fine, Terri," Tom reassured again, with conviction in his voice. "She's a smart girl, and Gary and Veronica will be waiting for her at the airport."

Teresa nodded, taking comfort in the knowledge that Jessica would not be alone when she arrived; her family would be there to greet her.

"Besides," Tom continued as he stroked Teresa's back in comforting circles, "you'll be there a few days later to help her get settled."

He paused for a moment before continuing: "And you know we'll be there for Thanksgiving. And before you know it, she'll be back home for Christmas."

Teresa let out a long sigh as she wiped away the last of her tears and snuggled closer into Tom's embrace—her safe haven in moments like these—resting her head on his chest.

"You're right," she finally admitted, feeling the steady rhythm of his heartbeat beneath her ear. "She's going to be okay."

Tom held his wife tightly against him; no words were needed between them now—only shared strength as they faced this new chapter together. The house might soon grow quieter without Jessica's footsteps echoing down the hall or Fawn's laughter mingling with hers—but their love would remain loud and unyielding, echoing through every room, nonetheless.

As the house darkened and the laughter and giggles from Jessica's bedroom finally ceased, an enveloping silence settled over the Reese household. The lively energy that had filled the air just minutes ago now gave way to a profound stillness, marking the end of another day in the life of a family on the cusp of significant change.

In their bedroom, Teresa lay beside Tom, her mind adrift in a sea of emotions. She visualized Jessica and Fawn, now quiet and snuggled together under the covers, their sleep peaceful and deep. The image brought her a bittersweet comfort, a reminder of the countless nights just like this one, yet tinged with the painful knowledge that these moments were fleeting.

With each passing day, the reality that the next two weeks would be a challenge to overcome grew more pronounced. Teresa closed her eyes, the silence of the house a stark contrast to the cacophony of memories running through her mind. In the quiet, she grappled with the duality of her emotions—pride in her daughter's impending journey into adulthood and a deep, unyielding sadness for the childhood that was slowly slipping through her fingers.

Feeling Teresa's restless shifting beside him, Tom reached out and placed his hand over hers. They lay there in silence for several minutes, two hearts beating in sync in an ocean of unspoken understanding. It was not just Jessica's bedroom that had gone silent; it was as if every corner of their home whispered with echoes of days gone by.

The living room, where toys once lay scattered and abandoned after hours of play, now held neat piles of college brochures and moving boxes, a testament to the transition that lay ahead. The kitchen, instead of buzzing with early morning preparations for school, bore witness to late-night discussions about campus life and future aspirations.

Tom broke the silence with a voice softened by emotion. "We did good, Terri," he whispered. "She's ready."

Teresa opened her eyes to meet Tom's gaze in the dim light filtering through the curtains. "But are we?" she asked.

The question hung between them—a palpable presence in the room—as they both considered what Jessica's departure would mean for them as parents.

"We have to be," Tom replied after a moment of reflection. "It's our job to let her go."

Teresa sighed, feeling every inch of their bed like an island in a vast expanse—a sanctuary where they could momentarily shield themselves from the tides of change that threatened to sweep them away.

"It doesn't make it any easier," she whispered back.

Tom squeezed her hand tighter in acknowledgment. "No," he agreed. "It doesn't."

They remained silent again—comfortable yet heavy-hearted—each lost in their reverie until Teresa spoke up once more.

"I keep thinking about all those firsts we've experienced with her," she murmured. "Her first steps... her first day of school... and now this."

"Yeah," Tom said with a nod. "But there will be new firsts—firsts we can't even imagine yet."

His words were as much for himself as they were for Teresa—an attempt to paint hope on the canvas of uncertainty that lay before them.

Teresa rolled over to face him, seeking solace in his familiar features—the lines etched by laughter and worry.

"I just wish time would slow down," she said softly.

Tom reached out and brushed away a stray tear that had escaped down Teresa's cheek.

"Me too, baby," he replied before adding with a gentle smile, "But you know what? We've been blessed with a beautiful daughter who has brought so much joy into our lives."

Teresa smiled back, feeling Tom's words resonate within her. "Yes, we have," she agreed. "And I wouldn't trade a single moment with her for anything."

As sleep finally began to take hold of them both—its tendrils tugging at their eyelids like a lullaby, Teresa nestled herself deeper into Tom's embrace. With memories of Jessica's laughter still lingering in the air, she found a measure of peace in knowing that no matter how far away she went, Jessica would always carry a piece of their home in her heart. And with that knowledge, she finally allowed sleep to claim her—drifting off into dreams filled with echoes of childhood laughter and hopes for tomorrow's smiles.

# Chapter 42

----------------------------------------------------------------

As the heart of August pulsed under the waning summer sun, Wavecrest found itself in a seasonal transition. The once bustling boardwalk and sun-kissed beaches, a testament to youthful exuberance and freedom, now echoed with a quieter melody. The joviality of early summer, with its endless days of surf and sand, had subtly shifted to a more introspective mood. Teenagers, who mere weeks before frolicked without a care in the world, now navigated the aisles of local malls, their thoughts as much on the future as on the fit of their new clothes or the latest school supplies cradled in their arms.

For the seniors at Wavecrest High, the approaching school year carried the weight of futures yet unwritten. College applications, once a distant thought amidst summer adventures, now demanded attention with a sense of urgency. Acceptance letters, those harbingers of new beginnings, will be received with a mix of exhilaration and apprehension, each envelope a step toward an uncharted journey beyond the familiar confines of Wavecrest.

For the town's recent graduates, including Jessica and Fawn, this period of preparation took on a more personal significance. Jessica faced the task of packing with a pragmatic approach, selecting the essentials she would need for her freshman year in Austin. Her suitcase, once filled with beachwear and novels for leisurely reading, will soon contain the essentials of collegiate life: toiletries, clothes, and textbooks.

Fawn's preparations, however, delved deeper than the physical act of packing. Her imminent departure to Boston was shadowed by the knowledge that Wavecrest, the backdrop of her childhood and teenage years, would no longer be her home to return to during holiday and summer breaks. The rooms that held memories of laughter, dreams, and occasional tears would soon be emptied, and her possessions shipped to a new home in Montana. Unlike Jessica, Fawn faced not only the transition to college life but also the emotional task of saying goodbye to the town that shaped her.

In these final weeks of August, anticipation and nostalgia threaded the fabric of life in Wavecrest. As the town's youth stood on the cusp of change, the fading days of summer became a poignant reminder of the inevitable passage of time and the transformative journey of growing up.

The morning light filtered through the windows of The Reese's kitchen, casting a warm glow on the scene inside. Jessica and Fawn sat at the table immersed in the comfort of routine—their breakfast bowls nearly empty, save for the milk-soaked remnants of their cereal.

Teresa, her motherly instincts never far from the surface, affectionately ran her fingers through Fawn's hair as she stepped back into the kitchen and moved toward the counter. The gentle touch was a silent testament to the bond they shared, one that had only deepened with time and circumstance.

"You need to start thinking about what you're going to want to take with you to Austin," Teresa said to Jessica, her voice laced with a mix of excitement and the inevitable sadness of an impending farewell.

Jessica sighed, not out of annoyance but from the weight of anticipation that lay before her.

"I know, Mom," she replied, her words tinged with reluctance. The task ahead seemed monumental—a physical and emotional packing of eighteen years.

Teresa understood her daughter's hesitation. "I know it might seem overwhelming, but it's important to make sure you have everything you need before you go."

"Yeah, I just don't know where to start," Jessica confessed, her eyes fixed on the patterns her spoon was making in the leftover milk.

"Well, how about starting with clothes? Pack a few outfits to wear for when you go to class and some comfortable ones for when you're lounging around the dorm," Teresa suggested.

"I'm also going to need my makeup and toiletries, too," Jessica added, trying to envision her new life in a different city.

"You might want to take something warmer with you, like a sweater or a light jacket, for when it gets colder. We'll go shopping while I'm there, okay?" Teresa suggested, knowing that Jessica's closet was still filled with summer clothes.

"Okay, Mom. That sounds good." Jessica smiled, appreciative but still intimidated.

After a brief pause, Teresa resumed her guidance. "Make sure to double check your syllabus and maybe talk to your roommate about what else you might need."

"Oh yeah," Jessica pondered aloud. "I forgot about her! I hope we get along."

"I'm sure you will, honey." Teresa's encouraging voice continued, "And we'll definitely have to get you some pillows and sheets. Maybe some cute decorations for your side of the room?"

The idea of decorating her new space ignited a spark of excitement in Jessica. "Yes! I've already seen some cool stuff online!"

"Well," Teresa suggested as she poured herself another cup of coffee from the pot on the counter, "go ahead and order them and have it shipped to your aunt and uncle's house. That way, it will be there when you arrive."

"Okay, Mom. That sounds like a good plan," Jessica nodded, a newfound determination in her voice as she envisioned her journey to Austin, supported and guided by her mother's love and wisdom.

As Fawn turned to face Jessica, her eyes burdened with the weight of her upcoming task, she couldn't help but compare their situations.

"Looks like you got the easy job. I have a whole room to pack," she remarked, a note of regret in her voice tempered by the camaraderie that had always existed between them.

Jessica's reply was immediate, her voice rich with sympathy. "I know. It sucks, but I'll help you as much as I can," she promised.

Fawn managed a smile, her gratitude evident. "Thanks, Jess. I appreciate it," she said, the simplicity of her words belying the complexity of her emotions.

Teresa, always the maternal figure to both girls, placed her hand on Fawn's shoulder as she took her seat at the table. "I know it's going to be hard to leave, sweetheart, but you're going to make so many new memories and friends in Boston. And you'll always have us here."

Fawn looked up at Teresa, the woman who had become a second mother to her, her voice carrying a mix of sorrow and hope. "I know. Just promise you'll come to visit me?" she asked, seeking assurance.

"Of course we will," Teresa said, squeezing Fawn's shoulder. "We'll come as often as we can."

Jessica, moved by the exchange, reached out to take Fawn's hand, her voice thick with emotion. "Don't worry, Fawn. Ethan and I will help you pack. You're not going to do this alone," she assured her, her commitment unwavering.

"I know, Jess. You've always been there for me," Fawn replied, her smile now tinged with gratitude.

Reaching across the table to place her other hand on Jessica's, Teresa added, "You two have been inseparable since kindergarten. I don't see that ever changing."

The emotional weight of the moment was palpable, with Jessica tearing up as she absorbed the reality of their situation.

"I know. This is just so hard," she confessed, her vulnerability exposed.

"Yeah," Fawn agreed, dabbing at a tear that escaped down her cheek. "Change is hard, but I guess we have to be brave, right?"

With a nod and a look of resolve in her bright blue eyes, Jessica replied firmly, "Yeah, but we can do this. Together."

Teresa squeezed both girls' hands reassuringly and offered a last piece of wisdom that resonated with them both. "You girls will be fine. Just remember, change can be exciting, too. Think of all the new experiences you're going to have. Both of you."

She knew that despite the challenges ahead, they would adapt to the changes with time and perspective. And as Jessica and Fawn navigated the journey into adulthood, their friendship would remain a constant, a source of strength and comfort, no matter the distance between them.

With breakfast out of the way, Jessica and Fawn headed to Jessica's bedroom to begin the daunting task of packing. Clothes were strewn across the bed, and hangers clattered as Jessica sorted through her closet, trying to decide what would make the cut for her new college life.

Fawn sat on the edge of the bed, her gaze distant, her mind wandering to Boston and the unknown that awaited her. She pulled out her phone, swiped through her gallery, and opened a photo of the house in Montana. With a grimace, she held the phone out to Jessica.

"This is what I have to look forward to at Christmas time," Fawn said, the look of disgust clear on her face.

Jessica took Fawn's phone and looked at the photo of Fawn's new home. The image displayed a modest single-story structure with weathered gray paint and black shutters framing the windows. It lacked the ornate gardens and sprawling porches common in Wavecrest. Instead, a small porch with white railings offered a humble welcome. The front yard was simple and bare, reflective of Montana's harsh winters.

Jessica couldn't help but notice the stark contrast between Fawn's new home and the vibrant, beachside houses they grew up around in Wavecrest. The house in Montana was much smaller and simpler, lacking the bright, airy feel of their coastal homes. She felt a pang of sympathy for Fawn, but tried to keep her expression neutral.

"It looks like a cute little house. It could be worse, right?" Jessica said, attempting to infuse some positivity into the situation.

Fawn rolled her eyes as she reclaimed her phone. "It's not even our house, Jess. It belongs to Atlas."

Jessica took a seat next to Fawn and gently touched her shoulder. "I get it, Fawn. It's not ideal, and it's not what you're used to. But think of it this way—maybe it's just temporary. Once you're in Boston, you won't be spending much time there, anyway. And who knows? It might have some hidden charm."

"It's Montana, Jess. There are more cows than people. How charming can it be?" Fawn replied with a hint of sarcasm.

Despite the circumstances, Jessica couldn't help but smile at her friend's comment. "I know it's a huge change. But maybe it'll surprise you. You're good at finding the bright side of things, even if it's hidden behind a herd of cows."

At that moment, Fawn couldn't help but giggle at Jessica's attempt to lighten the mood, feeling a little lighter despite everything.

"You know, I'm not even looking forward to Christmas this year. It just won't be the same without us being together," Fawn confessed, her voice carrying the weight of a thousand unspoken emotions.

The room fell silent as both girls drifted into their memories, wrapped in a blanket of shared nostalgia.

"You know how we always decorate our Christmas trees together?" Jessica mused, her voice soft with longing.

"Yeah," Fawn murmured, a bittersweet smile tugging at her lips. "Your mom always had the best ornaments." Her mind wandered back to the scent of pine in the air, their laughter blending with the soft hum of holiday carols.

"And opening our presents together on Christmas morning," Jessica added, a faint twinkle in her eye. "That started when we were, what, eight? I always loved how both our families made it a tradition."

Fawn nodded, her heart full of the memories they both held dear.

The warmth of those memories—the love, laughter, and comfort of being surrounded by family—was a treasure neither could bear to part with. Now, the thought of spending Christmas apart felt like another change they weren't ready for.

Breaking through the silence, Fawn's voice quivered with melancholy. "I can't believe it's going to be so different this year. No more decorating trees together, no more opening presents with you on Christmas morning. It just feels so wrong."

Jessica nodded, her heart heavy at the thought. "Yeah, it's hard to think about. But maybe we can find a way to keep some of our traditions alive, even if we're apart."

"Like how?" Fawn asked, a glimmer of hope flickering in her eyes.

After a thoughtful pause, Jessica's face brightened with an idea. "We could FaceTime during Christmas Eve dinner. That way, we can still eat together, even if we're far apart."

Fawn's face lit up at the suggestion. "That's a great idea! We could also FaceTime throughout Christmas and open presents together over video chat."

Jessica's eyes shone with determination to maintain their bond despite the miles that would soon separate them. "You know what, though?"

Fawn's curiosity piqued as she leaned closer. "What?"

Jessica took a deep breath before confessing her own plans for the holidays. "I don't think I want to come back here for Christmas. I think I'm going to stay at Uncle Gary and Aunt Veronica's house over the break."

"Yeah?" Fawn replied, trying to hide her disappointment behind a supportive smile.

"Yeah," Jessica affirmed softly. "It'll be too hard being here without you. At least I'll have my cousins to hang out with."

"That's probably a good idea, Jess," Fawn conceded, her tone understanding. "You also won't have to worry about making a long trip again."

"I guess," Jessica sighed, her voice heavy with emotion.

The room fell silent once more as they grappled with the reality of their separation—a reality that was coming all too soon. They both knew that being apart would be one of the hardest things they had ever faced. The thought of not being able to share everyday moments, let alone special occasions like Christmas, was almost unbearable.

Feeling the need to lighten the mood, Jessica decided to change the subject. She stood up and walked over to her closet, turning to Fawn with a playful smile.

"Alright, enough of the heavy stuff. Help me pick out some outfits. I need your expert fashion advice," she said, a hint of excitement in her voice.

Fawn smiled back, appreciating Jessica's effort to change the subject. She got up from the bed and joined her by the closet.

"Alright, let's see what you've got. We need to make sure you're the most stylish Texan on campus," Fawn grinned as she started sifting through the clothes, sliding hangers aside as she examined each piece.

She pulled out a bright, summery top and held it up, inspecting it with a critical eye. She then moved on to a pair of denim shorts, lifting them out and holding them up to Jessica to gauge the fit.

"Here's one. You'll look adorable in this outfit," Fawn said with a smile.

With a thoughtful expression, she continued to pull out a few more items, occasionally glancing at Jessica for her reaction before placing them on a pile of potential outfits.

As she sorted through the clothes, Fawn's mind drifted back to what Jessica had said earlier about helping her pack for the move to Montana. She appreciated Jessica's thoughtfulness and support, but she also knew that Ethan's days in Wavecrest were numbered.

"Jess, I've been thinking about what you said earlier about helping me pack," Fawn said gently, her voice tinged with resolve.

Jessica looked up curiously from the pile of clothes. "Yeah? What about it?"

Fawn paused, gathering her thoughts before continuing. "I don't want you to worry about me. Ethan's leaving in a week, and you should spend as much time with him as possible before he goes."

Jessica felt a wave of conflicting emotions wash over her. She desperately wanted to spend these last precious days with Ethan, but she couldn't bear the thought of neglecting her best friend.

"I want to spend time with you too, Fawn. We've been through so much together, and I don't want you to feel left out."

Fawn gave Jessica a reassuring smile. "I know, but you and Ethan are in love, and you only have a week left together. I don't want to take that time away from you."

Jessica let out a breath she hadn't realized she was holding and gave Fawn a tearful smile. "But you're my best friend, Fawn. I want..."

Fawn cut her off firmly yet lovingly. "You're my best friend, too, and that's why I want you two to make the most of it."

The air was thick with emotion as both girls navigated their complex feelings—grappling with change but bound by an unbreakable friendship. They returned to their task, while words were left unspoken. Together, they continued sorting through clothes—a simple act that brought comfort amidst the sea of change that enveloped them.

Teresa's knock was gentle, the rhythm familiar. The door to Jessica's bedroom creaked open as she entered, a warm smile lighting her face. In her hands, she carried an empty box, which she carefully placed on the bed.

"Hey, girls, I thought you might need this," Teresa said, her voice soft but clear. "Jessica, you can put the clothes you want to take to Austin in here. We'll ship it to Aunt Veronica and Uncle Gary's house, so it'll be there when you get there."

Jessica looked up from the pile of clothes scattered around her, offering a nod of gratitude for her mother's thoughtful gesture.

"Okay, Mom," she replied, her mind already sorting out which items would make the journey with her.

Fawn chuckled as she picked up another pair of denim shorts from the pile and playfully tossed them into the box.

"Just make sure you take these shorts. You're going to need them when it gets to be a hundred degrees there!" she teased.

In the midst of their packing efforts, Jessica's phone buzzed with a message that drew her attention away. She couldn't help but smile at the screen.

Fawn's curiosity piqued as she glanced over. "Is that Ethan?" she asked, leaning in slightly.

Jessica felt a blush rise to her cheeks as she nodded. "Yeah, he's asking if I'm free this afternoon. We were thinking of hanging out on the boardwalk today."

The excitement was evident in Jessica's eyes, but so was a tinge of guilt; time with Ethan was precious, yet she couldn't shake off the feeling that she was abandoning Fawn.

"You should go," Fawn said with a reassuring smile that reached her eyes. "We've done enough packing for now. Besides, I have to go to my house and help Mom pack."

"Then Ethan and I will come with you and help," Jessica said, her voice filled with determination.

Fawn shook her head gently, but firmly. "No, Jess. You and Ethan should stick to your plans. I've got this, and if I need any help, I'll text you."

"Okay," Jessica relented with a sigh, but smiled in return. "But you have to promise to call me if you need anything."

"Don't worry, I will," Fawn grinned back.

As if on cue, Teresa reappeared in the doorway, dressed in her beautician smock—her signal that it was almost time for work.

"Hey, girls, I'm going to Brenda's shop now. But first, I'm going to stop by your house to visit with your mom and see if she needs anything." Teresa announced as she saw Fawn getting ready to leave. "I heard you're going there, too. Want to ride with me? Save yourself the walk."

Fawn beamed at the offer. "Okay, Mama. Thanks!"

With that settled, Fawn gathered her belongings, her movements purposeful yet unhurried. She stepped forward and wrapped her arms around Jessica in a brief but firm hug, conveying strength and support in their silent embrace.

"See you later, Fawn," Jessica said with determination softened by affection as she squeezed Fawn's hand. "Don't forget to call me if you need anything."

"I won't," Fawn replied before nodding in affirmation. "Have fun on the boardwalk with Ethan!"

As Teresa and Fawn left together, Jessica watched them go, feeling the tension ease from her shoulders. She noticed her mother's arm draped over Fawn's shoulder, a gesture of comfort and solidarity. The sight brought a small, satisfied smile to her lips.

She turned back to her room, the cluttered space now seeming a bit more organized, much like her thoughts. Her fingers danced over her belongings, gathering the essentials for a day on the boardwalk. Her heart fluttered with an array of emotions as she tucked her phone and keys into her purse. The roar of Ethan's Jeep grew louder, signaling his arrival and offering a brief escape from the whirlwind of change.

As she flung open the front door, there he was, Ethan, stepping out of his Jeep, his casual grace accentuated by the bright California sun. His smile was the beacon that always seemed to guide her through any storm. Jessica's steps quickened as she walked toward him, and within moments, Ethan's arms enveloped her, pulling her into the safe harbor of his embrace.

"Hey, you ready to go?" Ethan's voice was a melody that soothed Jessica's anxious heart.

"Yeah, I'm ready," she replied, her voice revealing a hint of anxiety she couldn't quite hide.

Ethan's eyes searched hers, a frown creasing his brow as he picked up on the unspoken tension.

"Is everything okay?" he asked, his concern wrapping around her like a warm blanket.

Jessica mustered an affectionate smile and leaned into him. "It is now," she whispered, allowing herself to bask in the comfort his presence brought.

Hand in hand, they began their stroll down the street that led to the boardwalk. The sun hung high above them, casting a golden glow on the sidewalk. Jessica's eyes drifted toward Fawn's house. The sight tugged at her heartstrings; it was painful not to be there with her. But Fawn had insisted—she wanted Jessica to enjoy these last days with Ethan.

As they approached the vibrancy of the boardwalk—where music mingled with laughter, and the scent of saltwater filled the air, Jessica allowed herself to be drawn into the present moment. The upcoming Saturday loomed in her mind—a day set for one last get-together with Krista and Michelle before their worlds transformed and distance wedged itself between them.

For now, though, Jessica clung to this moment with Ethan at her side—the boardwalk stretched out before them like an invitation to hold on to youth just a little longer. She soaked in the feeling of Ethan's hand in hers and let out a contented sigh.

"This is perfect," Jessica said softly as they reached their destination.

Ethan squeezed her hand in response, his gaze holding hers with an intensity that spoke volumes. "As long as I'm with you, my life is perfect," he replied earnestly.

The rest of the world seemed to fade away as they stood on the threshold of change—two hearts intertwined amidst an ocean of possibilities. They stepped onto the boardwalk together, a symbol of their journey and the precious memories they had created. As they ventured forward into laughter and lightheartedness, Jessica took comfort in knowing that no matter where life took them next, these moments would forever be woven into the fabric of their shared history.

# Chapter 43

-------------------------------------------------------------------

Jessica stood in the midst of Fawn's bedroom, a room now littered with open boxes and scattered belongings. It was a landscape of memories, each object a portal to a time when life was simpler, their worries no more significant than school projects and childhood games. She lifted a framed photograph from the dresser—a snapshot of herself and Fawn, sun-kissed and smiling on the beach. A wave of nostalgia washed over her as she placed it in a box.

Ethan watched from the doorway, his presence a quiet support. He marveled at the depth of their friendship, understanding now why Jessica had been so insistent on staying by Fawn's side through this. He moved into the room, picking up a small porcelain figurine—a horse, chipped but cherished.

"This one was my grandmother's," Fawn explained from where she sat cross-legged on the floor, wrapping another figurine in bubble wrap. "She gave it to me when I was ten."

Ethan turned the horse over in his hands, its imperfections telling of its age and the love it had received. "It's beautiful," he said sincerely.

Fawn looked up with a smile that didn't quite reach her eyes. "Thanks," she murmured before returning her gaze to her task.

Jessica knelt beside her friend, reaching out to squeeze her shoulder reassuringly. They had spent hours sorting through Fawn's childhood keepsakes—dolls, drawings, countless trinkets—all telling stories that Jessica knew by heart. It was bittersweet work; with each item packed away, they sealed away pieces of their past.

Ethan had listened intently as they shared anecdotes—about late-night sleepovers with their friends and the times they were called into Mr. Morrison's office for a prank they played on their teachers—each tale weaving an intricate tapestry of their bond. He felt privileged to be let into this intimate space, witnessing firsthand the love and history that bound these two souls together.

He helped where he could, carrying boxes or fetching tape, but mostly, he just took in the scene before him: two girls who had grown into young women without losing the essence of their friendship. It was clear that this bond was unbreakable; not even distance could erode what they had built over countless summers and school years.

As Saturday afternoon faded into evening, Ethan realized that his affection for both Jessica and Fawn had only deepened. Watching them laugh through their tears and cling to each other through this transition, touched something in him he hadn't known was there.

He smiled to himself as he taped up another box. He might have come into this weekend thinking he was just lending a helping hand, but he'll be leaving with so much more—a profound respect for the friendship that helped shape the girl he fell in love with.

"C'mon kids, pizza is here," Brian's voice echoed up the staircase, slicing through the quietude of Fawn's bedroom. The scent of melted cheese and spicy wings wafted up from the kitchen, tugging at their appetites.

Fawn, Jessica, and Ethan emerged from the room, descending the stairs into the warmth of the kitchen. The table held boxes of pizza, their lids ajar, releasing plumes of steam into the air. Ethan's stomach growled in response, and he couldn't help but smile as he took his seat beside Jessica.

Brian leaned against the counter, arms folded, a contented look on his face as he watched the young adults settle in.

"Ethan, I can't thank you enough for coming over and helping out today," he said, his voice carrying a sincere gratitude.

Ethan glanced up from a slice of pepperoni pizza he had just lifted onto his plate. "It's my pleasure, sir," he replied with a respectful nod. He meant it; helping Fawn felt like the right thing to do—it was what anyone would do for family.

Anna breezed into the room, her hands occupied with cold bottles of water, which she distributed to each of them.

"So, what do you girls have planned for the evening?" she asked as she took her seat at the table.

Fawn took a long sip from her bottle before answering. "Jessica and I are going to hang out with Krista and Michelle tonight." She paused for a moment before continuing, "It's going to be our last get-together because Krista is leaving for Colorado in the morning, and Michelle will be moving to her dorm in Santa Barbara on Monday."

A heavy silence followed her words—a silence filled with unspoken emotions and a shared understanding of what these farewells meant. Jessica met Fawn's gaze across the table; there was a hint of sadness in Fawn's eyes that mirrored her own. The realization that this was indeed their last evening together with their friends hung in the air between them.

Jessica turned to face Ethan, her eyes bright with the possibility of shared laughter and camaraderie. "You can come with us, you know." Then, swiveling to Fawn, she added, "Right? Michelle and Krista wouldn't mind."

Fawn's smile spread across her face as she answered with unmistakable enthusiasm. "Absolutely!" Her eyes shifted to Ethan, inviting him into their circle. "You're gonna chill with us tonight, right?"

Ethan, clearly moved by Fawn's eagerness for him to join their last get-together with the friends who had been integral to their lives, nodded with an appreciative smile. His heart swelled at the thought of being included in such a momentous evening.

As much as he wanted to spend the evening wrapped in the warmth of Jessica's company and be a part of their gathering, he recognized the significance of this night for the girls—a final celebration of their shared history before embarking on separate journeys.

"No, that's okay," Ethan said. "You girls enjoy your time together." His voice was calm but full of respect for the moment they were facing—a moment that belonged to them.

Then, as he turned back to Jessica, his eyes softened. "I'll just hang out with Jake tonight; maybe go out and shoot some pool." His voice carried a note of sacrifice masked by casualness.

Jessica's lips curved into a small smile, her expression a mixture of gratitude and disappointment. She would have loved nothing more than to have Ethan by her side as they reminisced and laughed with her friends one last time. Yet she understood his gesture for what it was—an act of love and respect for the bond she shared with Fawn and their friends.

"Thanks, babe," Jessica said softly, her hand finding his for a brief squeeze. She admired his thoughtfulness in stepping back so that she could step forward into this precious sliver of time with her friends.

Laughter and the clatter of plates punctuated the small talk that floated around the kitchen table. Fawn, Jessica, and Ethan dove into the pizza and wings with gusto, relishing the comfort food as much as the comfort of each other's company. Anna and Brian, sensing the need for privacy among the trio, quietly retreated to the living room, leaving behind a subtle buzz of conversation.

As they ate, conversations meandered from reminiscing about high school shenanigans to speculating about their futures. Ethan's stories about his surfing mishaps had both girls giggling, while Jessica's recounting of a high school prank gone wrong had Ethan shaking his head in amused disbelief. Fawn chimed in with anecdotes of her own, her mischievous sparkling eyes lighting up with each memory she shared. Jessica, while amused, couldn't help but feel a pang of sadness, knowing that these simple moments would soon become memories.

As they finished their meal, Ethan glanced at his phone and noticed the time. "It's almost seven, guess I better be going," he said with a hint of reluctance, locking eyes with Jessica.

Her face fell at his words, mirroring his sentiment. The sadness in her eyes spoke volumes; it was an acknowledgment of the inevitable goodbye that loomed on the horizon.

They rose to their feet, and before Ethan could walk away, Fawn wrapped him in a warm hug.

"Thank you for your help, Ethan," she murmured into his shoulder.

Ethan returned her hug with the same warmth. Pulling back just enough to look at her, he gave her a warm and affectionate smile.

"Anytime, Fawn. I'm always here for you," he assured her sincerely.

Jessica watched them with a swell of gratitude in her heart for both her best friend and the boy who had become so much more to her.

"I'll be right back," she told Fawn, reaching out to grasp Ethan's hand.

Fawn nodded, understanding that this was a moment for just Jessica and Ethan. She watched as they walked out the front door together—a picture of young love in its most tender form. As the door closed behind them, a sense of gratitude overcame her. She not only appreciated Jessica's unwavering friendship, but also the love that had blossomed between her best friend and Ethan. She had watched this love grow under her watchful eye, and now it promised to endure whatever changes lay ahead.

Standing in the driveway beside his Jeep, Ethan pulled Jessica close, and they shared a long and lingering kiss—an expression of their love and a silent plea for time to halt its relentless march. Their lips moved with a passion that conveyed more than words ever could, speaking volumes of their profound connection and shared desires. As the kiss ended and their arms hesitantly parted, Ethan climbed into the driver's seat, the weight of the moment settling heavily between them.

He rolled down the window, his gaze soft yet filled with an intensity that mirrored Jessica's own. "Have a good time with Michelle and Krista," he said, his voice low and steady. "Tell them goodbye from me and that I wish them good luck."

Jessica, feeling the sting of tears threatening to spill over, managed a nod. "I will," she whispered, her voice barely audible over the growing lump in her throat.

Ethan studied her face, the emotion brimming in her eyes tugging at his heartstrings. He reached out through the open window and squeezed her hand.

"I'll see you tomorrow, okay?" His words were an attempt to bridge the distance that would soon separate them, to reassure her despite the uncertainty that lay ahead.

She nodded again, forcing a smile through the emotional haze. "I'll see you tomorrow," Jessica replied with as much conviction as she could muster.

With a look that lingered like the last rays of a sunset, Ethan started the Jeep and slowly pulled out of the driveway. Jessica stood there, watching him disappear into the approaching night. She watched until the red taillights were no longer visible, aware that in less than a week's time, they would be facing a more daunting farewell—one without the promise of seeing each other tomorrow.

Under the shifting canvas of the evening sky, Jessica and Fawn made their way to Arnold's Arcade. The sun had begun its descent, casting a warm, golden glow that transformed the boardwalk into a spectacle of light and shadow. The ocean mirrored the changing hues of the sky, its waves glinting with reflections of pink and orange.

As they strolled along the boardwalk, the fading sounds of summer echoed around them. The Ferris wheel, a familiar landmark against the skyline, turned lazily in the gentle evening breeze. Its colorful cabins were mostly empty now, the laughter and excited screams of riders replaced by a calm silence that spoke volumes about the fleeting nature of time.

Nearby, the beach lay in a quiet lull. Once a bustling hub of activity with beachgoers basking in the sun and enjoying evening bonfires, it was now largely deserted. Only a handful of people lingered on the sandy shore, savoring the last vestiges of summer.

The change was not unusual for this time of year; Wavecrest's summer charm had always ebbed away with August. Yet this time, Jessica and Fawn felt it more acutely. They walked side by side in comfortable silence, each acutely aware that this would be their last shared summer before life took them on separate paths.

As they approached Arnold's Arcade, they could see their friends Krista and Michelle waiting outside. The bright neon sign above bathed them in an array of colors that flickered in sync with their laughter.

"There you two are!" Krista called out as they got closer. Her vibrant red hair seemed muted without the sun igniting its fiery hues.

Michelle offered a gentle smile that reached her hazel eyes. "We were starting to think you'd ditch us for one last moonlit swim," she teased.

Fawn laughed and shook her head. "Not tonight," she said. "Tonight is for us—just us girls."

They all exchanged knowing looks; no words were needed to convey what they all felt. This night was an unspoken farewell to their shared summers, an acknowledgment that their lives were about to change forever.

Together, they entered Arnold's Arcade—the sound of electronic beeps and chimes welcoming them into its familiar embrace—and for a moment, they allowed themselves to forget about tomorrow.

Krista turned to her friends, her eyes sparkling with mischief. "How about a game of Skee-Ball, ladies?" she suggested, gesturing toward the row of arcade games that lined the far wall.

Never one to back down from a challenge, Jessica flashed a teasing grin. "Sure, if you don't mind getting your butts kicked," she replied.

Krista rolled her eyes dramatically. "Oh please, Jessica. You're not the only one who's spent countless summers perfecting her throw."

Michelle chimed in, her voice filled with humor. "Yeah, Jess. Remember last time when I was just one point away from beating you?"

Even Fawn joined in on the banter. "And don't forget about me. I've been practicing too, you know."

Jessica's eyes danced with amusement as she replied, "Let's go, then. I'll show you who is the Queen of Skee-Ball here."

And so, the friendly competition began. The girls huddled around the Skee-Ball lanes, their laughter echoing through the arcade as they took turns rolling balls up the sloping lane and into the scoring holes.

Despite their efforts and the occasional lucky shot, Jessica remained undefeated. Her throws were precise and consistent—evidence of years spent mastering the game.

As she landed her final ball into the hundred-point hole, she raised her arms in victory and triumphantly declared, "Yep, I still got it."

The girls erupted into laughter at her antics; Jessica always had a flair for the dramatics.

Fawn wrapped an arm around her shoulder and leaned in close. "You'll always be the Queen of Skee-Ball, Jess." Her voice was soft but filled with the warmth of years of shared history and unspoken affection.

They all knew that no matter where life took them, they would always have moments like these to remember—their laughter echoing through the arcade, their hearts light and carefree.

Immersed in their own world of joy and laughter, the girls found themselves lost in the magic of the arcade. Michelle was captivated by the Claw Crane game, feeding it token after token in a relentless quest to win a stuffed teddy bear for her little brother. Despite her failed attempts, she laughed it off and shrugged, a testament to her carefree spirit.

Fawn and Krista gravitated toward the Foosball table, their friendly rivalry evident in the way they manipulated their team of miniature players with focused precision. Their playful taunts and triumphant cheers filled the air, adding to the lively atmosphere of Arnold's Arcade.

Meanwhile, Jessica was engaged in a battle of reflexes with Whack-A-Mole. Her friends watched in amusement as she swung the mallet with animated frustration each time a mole evaded her strike. The sight of Jessica—normally so poised—wielding a mallet with such comedic fervor brought peals of laughter from her friends.

As they reveled in their games, time slipped away unnoticed. It was not until they stepped outside that they realized how late it had become. The sky had faded to an inky black canvas studded with stars, and the cool ocean breeze signaled the arrival of night.

They made a quick stop at the cotton candy stand, where Jessica had spent her past summers spinning pink clouds of sugar, before heading to the funnel cake stand—Fawn's old summer gig. With their hands full of sweet treats and memories, they found a bench facing the ocean, settling down to savor both the snacks and the moment.

"So, what do you wanna do now?" Michelle asked, licking powdered sugar off her fingers.

Jessica pondered for a moment before suggesting, "Let's go to our special spot on the beach and hang out there for the rest of the night."

The girls' faces lit up at Jessica's suggestion. Their special spot had been a haven for them since they'd claimed it four years ago. It had witnessed their youthful shenanigans, their Fourth of July fireworks, and countless quiet evenings when they just wanted to be together. Now, it seemed like the perfect place to spend their last night together before they went their separate ways.

"That's a great idea," Krista agreed, standing up. "I'll go find someone to build us a fire. You guys go ahead."

With that, the girls made their way toward their special spot on the beach, their hearts heavy with the bittersweet realization that this was their last night together before they embarked on their separate journeys. But for now, they had the night and each other's company to hold on to, one last summer memory in the making.

The familiar silhouette of the distinct-looking rock jutted out from the sand, standing in stark contrast to the smooth, uniform shapes scattered along the beach. It was their beacon—a marker to a world they had created together. A world that resonated with laughter, friendship, and countless memories etched into the sands of time.

At the sight of the rock, Jessica's mind was yanked back to the Fourth of July night when she and Ethan had sat on that very spot, their eyes wide with awe as the sky lit up with a kaleidoscope of fireworks. The memory surged through her, sparking a swirl of emotion—the elation of having Ethan by her side, his hand in hers, mixed with a melancholic undercurrent. The uncertainty loomed like an unwelcome shadow: would they still be together when the next Fourth of July rolled around?

Settling down on the sand, Fawn cast a sideways glance at Jessica. Even in the fading light, she noticed a glimmer of sadness clouding Jessica's usually vibrant eyes.

Fawn expressed concern in her voice as she asked, "Are you okay, Jess?"

Jessica mustered a smile that didn't quite reach her eyes. "Yep, I'm good," she said, her voice steadier than she felt.

Michelle plopped down next to them, brushing off sand grains clinging to her legs. "I wish we'd brought our blankets," she murmured, more to herself than anyone else.

Before anyone could respond, their attention was drawn toward Krista approaching with a burly man in tow. He carried a bucket filled with sticks and wood—fuel for their beach bonfire.

When they arrived, Krista sank down next to Michelle while the girls watched the man build their fire. He arranged the sticks and wood with an ease that came from years of experience, and soon, a small flame sprang to life, its flickering light painting their faces with a warm glow.

"Thanks a lot, Mr. Harrington," Krista voiced their collective gratitude, her smile bright in the firelight.

Mr. Harrington, his eyes twinkling with affection, replied, "You're welcome. Just make sure you put out the fire before you leave, okay?"

They all nodded in agreement, and with a final wave, Mr. Harrington made his way back to the boardwalk, leaving the girls to enjoy their night together. The fire flickered before them, casting dancing shadows on the sand and setting the stage for a night of cherished memories.

As the girls sat around the fire, its warmth provided a comforting presence against the cooling night air. The rhythmic sound of the crashing waves and the scent of the salty air filled their senses, evoking a familiar tranquility that only their special spot could provide. But amidst the comfort of the familiar, there was an unfamiliar absence—a void in their circle where Heather should have been.

Heather's absence was a silent acknowledgment of the changes they were all facing. It was a harsh reminder that their carefree high school days were behind them, and their tight-knit group would never be quite the same. The memory of Heather's abrupt departure lingered in their minds, an unfinished chapter in their shared history.

Krista's voice broke the silence that hung in the air. "Have you guys heard from Heather?" she asked, her voice tinged with a mixture of sadness and curiosity.

Fawn and Jessica exchanged a glance before turning back to Krista and Michelle.

"No," Fawn replied, her voice a little more than a whisper. "The last time we saw or heard from her was when she came to Jess's house to say goodbye."

Jessica nodded in agreement. "Yeah, she was on her way to the airport."

Michelle let out a sigh of disappointment. "Well, at least you got to see her before she left," she said, a hint of annoyance in her voice. "All we got was a text saying goodbye and that she was on her way to New York City."

Jessica and Fawn looked at their friends with sympathetic eyes. They knew how hurtful Heather's abrupt departure had been for them.

"I never heard back from her after I sent that picture of us at the Summer Dance," Jessica confessed, her voice carrying a hint of sadness.

Krista added to Jessica's confession, "I've texted her several times and never got a response."

"Me neither. I think she got a new phone. A different number," Michelle said, her voice a faint murmur against the sound of the waves.

A somber silence fell over the group as they each processed the reality of Heather's departure and its impact on their friendship. Their eyes remained fixed on the flickering flames, lost in a swirl of emotions—sadness, frustration, grief, and reflection. The fire crackled in response, its warmth offering a silent comfort as the sound of waves filled the silence.

Jessica swallowed hard, her throat tight with unshed tears. The reality of Heather's absence had settled in like a heavy fog, clouding her thoughts and amplifying her fears. Heather had been her idol, the one she'd always looked up to. She had been a pillar of strength and inspiration to her, and their friendship had always been a source of comfort.

But now, Heather was gone, her presence reduced to a void that echoed with memories and unanswered questions. Jessica felt the sting of abandonment, a wound fresh and raw. Eight years of friendship, laughter, shared secrets, and dreams seemed to have faded into nothingness for Heather. Did their friendship mean nothing to her?

A chill ran down Jessica's spine as she pondered these questions. The fire in front of her flickered and crackled, but its warmth did little to dispel the icy fear that crept into her heart. Her eyes moved from the dancing flames to her friends sitting next to her. Krista and Michelle appeared lost in their thoughts, their expressions mirroring the same pain she felt.

Jessica's heart clenched at the sight of them. Would they, too, forget about her once they left Wavecrest? Would their shared history become nothing more than distant memories as they embarked on their new journeys? The thought was too much to bear.

Her eyes then landed on Fawn, who sat silently next to her, staring into the fire with a distant look in her eyes. Fawn was not just her best friend; she was a part of her, a reflection of her soul. They had stood by each other through thick and thin, their bond stronger than any storm they had faced together. But what will happen when Fawn leaves for Boston? Will she, too, drift away from her?

Jessica felt a lump form in her throat as she struggled with these unsettling thoughts. The reality of their impending separation and the fear of being forgotten was overwhelming. It felt like she was standing on the edge of a precipice, staring into an abyss of uncertainty.

She looked at her friends again, their faces illuminated by the firelight. They had been her constants, her anchors in the turbulent sea of adolescence. The thought of losing them, of their friendship fading into oblivion like Heather's had, filled her with a profound sense of dread.

"I can't stop thinking about Heather. How can someone who was such a big part of our lives just forget about us like that?" Jessica's voice was low, the words tumbling out into the night. She looked around at her friends, her eyes filled with deep-rooted fear. "Is that going to happen to us? Are you guys going to forget about me, too?"

The sudden question caught them off guard. Krista, Michelle, and Fawn all turned to look at Jessica, their eyes wide with surprise.

"That's what's going to happen, right?" Jessica continued, her voice rising with emotion. "We're all going to get so busy with school and working a full-time job that there will be no time to keep in touch with each other. And then, one day, we'll wake up and realize that we haven't talked to each other in months, maybe even years."

The flickering light from the fire pit reflected in Jessica's blue eyes as she spoke. Her vulnerability was tangible, and Fawn felt a tug at her heartstrings.

She reached over and gently squeezed Jessica's arm. "That's not going to happen, Jess," she assured her. Her eyes met Jessica's, filled with affection and sincerity. "We're not going to forget about you. We're not going to forget about anyone."

Jessica looked at Fawn, her expression fraught with worry. "Heather did," she countered, her voice tense. "If she had no problem forgetting about us, why should you guys be any different?"

Krista shook her head, her expression firm. "We're not Heather, Jessica," she said with conviction. "She's not like us. Heather has always been... well, Heather. She's always been selfish and self-centered."

Michelle nodded in agreement with Krista's words. "Yeah," she chimed in. "Heather was always about Heather. But we're different. We care about each other. We're not going to forget about you."

Jessica studied the faces of her friends, their words seeping into her, a balm to the fear that had taken root. She wanted to believe them, to hold on to the promise that their friendship would withstand the trials of distance and time. Yet, the gnawing uncertainty still lingered.

Michelle, always the logical one among them, broke the silence. "Let's make a pact," she proposed, her voice steady and clear. Her hazel eyes shimmered in the firelight, radiating an intensity that commanded attention. Her suggestion hung in the air, prompting Jessica, Fawn, and Krista to look at her with rapt attention.

"Let's promise to stay in touch and keep our friendships alive, no matter how far apart we are," she continued, her words cutting through the tension like a beacon of hope.

A murmur of agreement rippled through the group. Michelle was known for her thoughtfulness, and this suggestion was just another example of her ability to find solutions when they seemed elusive.

"Let's set aside a day and a time when we'll all get on FaceTime and catch up about what's happening in our lives," she suggested further. "We'll do it every week so that we always know what's going on with each other."

Krista nodded in approval, her face glowing in the flickering firelight. "That's a great idea, Michelle," she agreed wholeheartedly. "Once we're all settled and know our schedules, we can pick a day that works for all of us."

Fawn chimed in, her voice brimming with optimism. "Yeah, that way, we have something to look forward to every week." She turned toward Jessica then, seeking affirmation. "How does that sound to you, Jess?"

A slow smile spread across Jessica's face at Fawn's question. She was touched by their earnest efforts to reassure her. Their commitment to staying connected was comforting, easing some of the tension that had been coiling in her chest.

"It sounds like a plan," she replied, her words ringing in the night air.

Her smile broadened into a grin, a silent thank you to her friends for their unwavering support and the lifeline they had thrown her way. It wasn't a foolproof plan, and it didn't extinguish her fears. But it was a start—a beacon of hope in the face of impending change.

Fawn glanced around the circle, her eyes darting from one friend to another. The conversation had left a heavy silence in its wake, a cloud of uncertainty that needed to be dispelled. A glimmer of an idea sparked in her mind, and she leaned forward, her blue eyes twinkling with excitement.

"Hey," she began, her voice instantly brightening the mood. "Why don't we play a game? Something fun to lighten the mood."

Krista's eyes lit up at the suggestion. She sat up straighter, a grin spreading across her face.

"How about 'Truth or Dare'?" she suggested. "It's been a while since we played that."

Fawn's grin mirrored Krista's. She nodded enthusiastically. "Great idea! I'll go first." She turned to face her, mischief dancing in her eyes. "Krista, truth or dare?"

A playful smirk spread across Krista's face as she contemplated her options. After a moment, she confidently announced, "Dare."

Fawn's grin widened at the answer. Her eyes shifted to the dark expanse of water shimmering under the moonlight before returning to Krista.

"Okay," she said, her voice filled with playful anticipation. "I dare you to run down to the water and dip your toes in. It's probably freezing by now!"

Laughter erupted from the group as Krista shot up from her seat, accepting the challenge with glee. "Challenge accepted!" she declared before sprinting towards the shoreline.

The girls watched in amusement as Krista's shrieks of surprise echoed back to them when the chilly waves lapped at her feet. When she jogged back to their circle, shivering but laughing, they clapped and cheered.

Wiping away tears of laughter, Krista pointed to Jessica. "Your turn, Jess," she announced. "Truth or dare?"

Jessica, ever the cautious one, opted for truth. She knew better than to risk a dare from Krista. "Truth," she replied, a giggle escaping her lips.

Krista pondered for a moment before asking, "What's the most embarrassing thing that's happened to you this summer?"

A blush crept across Jessica's cheeks as she recalled a particularly embarrassing incident.

"Oh my God! Okay, so there was this time when I was at the boardwalk with Ethan," she started, her voice trembling with suppressed laughter. "And I tripped over a loose board and fell right into a street performer's act. Everyone was staring, and I was mortified!"

The circle erupted in laughter once more, the tension from their earlier conversation dissolving in the wake of their shared amusement. As they continued their game into the night, the beach filled with their laughter and camaraderie—a testament to their enduring friendship amidst life's inevitable changes.

As the night wore on, their laughter faded into the sea breeze, replaced by the soothing rhythm of the ocean waves and the soft crackling of the dying fire. Their faces, bathed in the warm glow of the embers, turned to watch the shoreline as if the lapping waves had the answers to their looming questions.

Michelle broke their reverie, her voice cutting through their silence like a beacon. "Do you guys want to hear about something weird that happened to me two days ago?" she asked, leaning back on her elbows.

With their interest piqued, the girls sat up straighter, their eyes fixed on Michelle. Fawn, ever curious and adventurous, was the first to answer. "Sure, what happened?"

Michelle took a deep breath, her eyes reflecting the memory. "So, two days ago, I went out onto the porch to get the mail. You know, the usual stuff. But then I saw a letter from UCSB addressed to me. I was nervous but opened it, anyway."

"Oh, no. What did they want?" Jessica interjected, her voice full of curiosity.

"Nothing. It was a tuition statement," Michelle replied. "Detailing all the upcoming fees and costs. It just hit me, you know? The realization that I'll have to handle all these financial responsibilities on my own."

Jessica offered a sympathetic nod while Fawn admitted that she had received a similar letter. But it was Michelle's next revelation that brought an unexpected chill to their beach-side gathering.

"That's when things got really weird," she continued. "I looked up and saw an old man standing on the edge of my front yard. He was just... standing there, smiling at me."

"Really? Did he talk to you?" Fawn asked, her eyebrows furrowing in confusion.

"No," Michelle shook her head. "But there was something about him. He looked familiar... like I knew who he was."

Krista leaned forward, her brow furrowed with curiosity as she asked, "What did he look like?"

Michelle tilted her head in thought before answering, "He looked old. Very old. He looked frail and hunched over. He was wearing a baggy white shirt with black slacks and a black bow tie."

She paused for a moment, her expression deep in thought, as if trying to pull a piece of her memory from the depths of her mind. "You know what was weird? Even though he was smiling at me, his eyes looked so sad."

The girls listened in rapt silence as Michelle described her unusual encounter. They were all too familiar with the faces in Wavecrest, but this old man seemed different. There was a certain mystery about him that tugged at their curiosity.

"He gave me a little nod, like a farewell gesture, and then he walked away," Michelle finished her tale, her voice barely above a whisper. "It was like he was saying goodbye to me."

Fawn tilted her head in thought, mulling over Michelle's strange encounter. "That's so strange," she murmured. "Do you think he was just a random passerby?"

Michelle shrugged, her eyes lost in the embers of the fire. "I don't know. Maybe. But I think he was more than that."

She looked up at her friends, her eyes glistening with unshed tears. "It was like I knew him, and he knew me. I feel like he's been with me since I was little... watching over me... protecting me. It's hard to explain, but I haven't been able to stop thinking about it since."

Krista turned to Michelle, her eyes wide with astonishment. "You know what?" she began, her voice unsteady. "The same thing happened to me six days ago, when I got home from our trip to the Mall."

Fawn looked at Krista, her eyebrows raised in surprise. "You saw the old man, too?"

Krista nodded, her hands nervously twisting the hem of her shirt.

"Yeah," she confirmed. "When Michelle dropped me off at my house. I was just standing there in the driveway, thinking about Donny, when I noticed an old man standing on the edge of my front yard." Her voice trailed off, a bitter edge creeping into her tone as she mentioned Donny.

Jessica reached over and gave Krista's hand a quick squeeze of sympathy before asking, "How did you know he was the same old man Michelle saw?"

"Well," Krista hesitated, her eyes shifting to the dying embers of the fire. "From what Michelle just said. The man I saw also looked frail and hunchbacked. He was wearing the same clothes: a baggy white shirt, black pants, and a black bow tie."

She looked up at them again, a distant look in her eyes. "His face looked really old. He was smiling, but his eyes... I saw so much sadness in them."

Michelle's eyes widened as Krista described her encounter. "Yep," she excitedly agreed. "That's exactly what I saw!"

Krista continued, the unease evident in her voice. "The thing is, I felt like I knew him too, even though I'd never seen him before."

She paused, then confessed, almost as an afterthought. "You know, I always felt this presence around me, like there were these invisible arms holding me. It made me feel loved and safe."

Jessica nodded in understanding. "I know that feeling. I feel it all the time. I never really thought about it before."

Fawn's voice broke the silence that had fallen over them. "Me too," she confessed, a sadness seeping into her voice. "But I don't feel it much anymore."

Michelle turned back to Krista, her curiosity piqued. "Wow, Kris. Did he say anything to you?"

Krista shook her head, her eyes downcast. "No. He just nodded his head, like he was saying goodbye." Her voice wavered as she added, "And then, as he walked away, I felt those invisible arms release me." She looked up at her friends, her eyes filled with a profound sadness. "It was so strange. It made me feel really sad."

Fawn looked at each of her friends thoughtfully. "Do you think it means something?" she asked.

Krista gave a nonchalant shrug, her gaze returning to the fire. "I don't know," she admitted quietly. "But hearing what Michelle experienced makes me wonder now."

After a long period of silence, Michelle, who had been lost in thought, raised her head and scanned her eyes over her friends. Her lips parted, words hovering on the edge of being spoken.

"I think I know who he is," she finally confessed.

Fawn's eyes widened in surprise at Michelle's statement. "Who is he, Michelle? Is he someone we know?" she asked, her curiosity piqued.

Michelle nodded slowly, her gaze steady. "You know him. We all know him. But he's not an old man. Not really," she began, pausing to gather her thoughts. "I think he's a spirit."

Krista's eyebrows shot up at the revelation. "A spirit? You mean like a ghost?" she questioned skeptically.

"No, not a ghost," Michelle quickly clarified. "I think he's a spirit that lives here in Wavecrest."

Fawn frowned at Michelle's explanation, trying to make sense of it all. "Well, that sounds weird," she remarked, unable to hide her confusion. "What makes you think that?"

Michelle leaned back on the log they were sitting on and looked up at the starlit sky.

"Think about it," she began. "Remember all those times when we were kids, and we felt like someone, or something was watching over us? I think it was the spirit."

She turned back to face her friends, her expression earnest. "I think the spirit attaches itself to all the children that live here. It wants to protect and guide us." Her voice dropped to a whisper as she continued, "It's like he's always been there for us, through the good times and the bad."

Krista chewed on her lower lip as she considered Michelle's words. "But why would he appear to us now, as an old man?" she asked. "And why is he saying goodbye?"

Michelle fell silent for a moment, her eyes dropping to the sand beneath their feet. When she finally spoke, sadness tinged her voice.

"Because we grew up," she said simply. "We're transitioning into adulthood, and the spirit has to let us go."

She looked up at her friends, her eyes filled with understanding. "He knows we have to face adult responsibilities and challenges on our own now," she explained. "That's why he's saying goodbye, not to our physical part, but to our childhood spirit."

Jessica looked at Michelle, her mind spinning with the implications of her friend's theory. "So, he's been with us all along, like a guardian?" she asked in wonder.

Michelle nodded in agreement. "I think so," she confirmed. "He's releasing us because he understands that we need to move on, that we have to find our own way."

She paused before adding, "But he's still here, a part of Wavecrest, nurturing the next generation of children."

Fawn nodded thoughtfully at Michelle's explanation. "That actually makes sense," she admitted after a moment of silence. "I always felt that there was something special about this place."

Michelle shrugged modestly at Fawn's words. "Well, that's what I think anyway," she admitted with a small smile. "But what do I know."

Jessica chuckled at Michelle's modesty. "You have a great imagination, Michelle," she complimented warmly. "You're going to be a great writer someday."

Michelle blushed at Jessica's praise but managed to flash her a grateful smile. "Aw, thanks, Jess. I hope so," she replied with a hint of embarrassment.

After Michelle's revelation, the girls sat in silence, each lost in thought as they absorbed the idea of a guardian spirit watching over them. The dying embers of the fire flickered in their eyes, casting long shadows that danced in rhythm with the gentle sea breeze.

A glance toward the boardwalk, previously alive with energy and life, now revealed a quiet, almost desolate scene. Gone were the small crowds of people strolling along its planks, replaced by an eerie calm that whispered of the approaching midnight hour.

The once bustling food and drink vendors, whose enticing aromas had filled the air just hours before, now stood closed. The few that remained were in the process of packing up, their owners weary yet satisfied after a long day's work. The Ferris wheel, once a spinning kaleidoscope of lights and laughter, now stood still and silent against the night sky.

The vibrant glow that had once illuminated the boardwalk had dimmed considerably. The colorful lights that adorned the shops and attractions gradually extinguished one by one, leaving only a soft glow from scattered lamp posts. The beating heart of Wavecrest had fallen into a peaceful slumber.

The girls took in the sight before them. Their beachside retreat felt removed from time itself; but as they gazed at the tranquil boardwalk, reality seeped back in. The night had unfurled faster than they realized.

Jessica broke the silence first. "Wow. I guess it's later than we thought.".

Fawn nodded, pushing herself up from where she sat on the sand. "Yeah," she agreed. "Time flies when you're having fun."

Krista glanced at her phone and winced at the late hour displayed. "We should probably head back. I have an early flight to catch," she suggested.

Michelle stood up as well, brushing sand off her jeans. "Yeah," she agreed with a sigh. "I guess it's time."

Reluctantly, they left their special spot on the beach, their footprints fading behind them as they trudged toward the boardwalk. As they ascended the wooden steps, each girl carried with her not just the lingering scent of salt and bonfire smoke but also the memories of a night spent laughing and sharing stories.

As they reached the top of the steps, they paused to take one last look at their special spot on the beach. The sadness was palpable; it washed over them like an incoming tide. Tonight, their goodbyes would not be like those of summers past. There would be no more saying, "See you tomorrow," or "Catch you later." This time, they would be saying farewell not only to each other but also to an era of innocence that had shaped them into who they were.

Jessica and Fawn stood side by side on the worn boards of the boardwalk, their eyes meeting Michelle's and Krista's. Silence settled around them, their hearts heavy, knowing that this was not just another summer farewell. It was the end of countless shared sunsets, quiet confessions, and laughter that seemed as endless as the ocean before them.

Michelle took a tentative step forward, her arms reaching out to pull Jessica into a hug.

"I'm going to miss you, Jess. You've always been like a sister to me," she managed to say, her voice betraying the turmoil inside.

Jessica returned the hug just as fiercely. "I'll miss you too, Michelle. Thank you for always being there for me," she replied, her own voice thick with emotion.

When Michelle stepped back, Krista filled the space she left. She wrapped Jessica in a hug that was both tight and tender.

"Take care of yourself, Jess. You're stronger than you think, and I know you'll do great things," she whispered in her ear.

Jessica's response was muffled against Krista's shoulder. "You too, Kris. Keep being your amazing self and don't let anything hold you back."

Krista nodded as she stepped away, wiping her eyes. Fawn watched the exchanges with a bittersweet ache in her chest. Unlike Jessica, who would leave Wavecrest but still have a home to return to during breaks and holidays, Fawn faced an additional layer of finality. Her family's move meant there was no home in Wavecrest to return to. It wasn't just college she was leaving for; she was leaving for a whole new life.

She gathered Michelle and Krista into a group hug that spoke volumes more than words could express. "I love you guys so much. You'll always be my besties," she said, her voice breaking with emotion.

"I love you too, Fawn. I'm going to miss you so much," Michelle replied, tears streaming down her face.

Krista added with determination, her sniffling voice filled with resolve. "Me too. We're going to keep in touch, right? Just like we talked about."

Fawn could only nod against the tight knot in her throat as they held each other close.

When they finally broke their embrace, Krista wiped away her tears and made a suggestion that brought a semblance of cheer to their somber mood. "Hey, before we go, let's take one last selfie. Something to remember this night by."

"Yeah, that sounds perfect," Michelle agreed with a watery smile.

Fawn fished out her phone from her pocket while still trying to steady her shaky hands. "Okay, everyone, huddle up."

They huddled together once more—this time for the camera—arms entwined and smiles flickering through their tears. The flash captured more than just their faces; it froze a moment of love and friendship that would outlast any distance between them.

"We've had some great times together, haven't we," Jessica said as they lingered close together after the flash faded. Her voice trembled with each word, making it seem all too real. "You guys are the best, and... I hope we'll always find our way back to each other, no matter where life takes us."

Nods and silent agreements came from Michelle and Krista—they knew the value of what they shared and the pain of letting it go. The idea of not knowing when or if they would ever see each other again weighed heavily on their hearts.

As they embraced one last time under the soft glow of the boardwalk lights, they held on a little longer than necessary—neither wanting to be the first to let go—a silent promise hanging in the air that no matter what changes came their way, their bond would remain unbroken.

Jessica and Fawn stood in silence as they watched Michelle and Krista make their way down the boardwalk. The soft glow of the lampposts cast long shadows behind their departing friends, stretching across the weathered wooden planks like fingers reaching for what was slipping away.

Jessica's mind became filled with memories of their times together. She saw flashes of high school volleyball games, the four of them cheering each other on the court. Late-night study sessions in Jessica's room came to mind, textbooks sprawled across the floor and laughter punctuating their attempts to cram for exams. Campfires on the beach danced in her memory, the crackling flames reflecting the warmth of their friendship. She recalled Heather's spontaneous road trips, windows down and music blaring as they chased adventure along the coast. Those moments felt like lifelines now, binding them together in a way words could never fully capture.

Next to her, Fawn was lost in her own thoughts. Her brow furrowed slightly as she worried about what the future held, not just for herself but for all of them, especially Jessica. She clung to the belief that this was not an end but a new chapter in their lives. She held onto the hope that someday, they would all find their way back to each other. Despite her fears and uncertainties, however, Fawn felt a profound gratitude for the friendship they shared—a bond that had shaped their lives and would hopefully continue to do so, no matter where life took them.

As Michelle and Krista's figures faded into the night, Fawn turned to Jessica, her once mischievous eyes now darkened with sadness.

"I guess it's just you and me now, Jess," she said, wrapping her arm around her in a comforting embrace.

Jessica looked back at Fawn with the same sadness but didn't say a word. Instead, she leaned into Fawn's embrace and tried to focus on the moment they were in. She knew it wouldn't be long before Fawn was gone, too, and the thought of facing the future without her closest friend by her side filled her with an overwhelming sense of loneliness.

With an unspoken understanding, Jessica and Fawn began their walk back to Jessica's house. It was a slow walk, each step taking them further from cherished memories and the friends they had to leave behind. The boardwalk seemed longer than usual as they trudged along in silence, their hearts heavy but united by a bond that distance could never break.

The cool night air brushed against their skin as they moved closer to home, each step a bittersweet reminder of the changes ahead. Jessica glanced at Fawn, finding solace in her presence amidst the deepening night. In the quiet of their shared journey, every glance and silent step spoke volumes of their enduring friendship. For now, having each other was enough—a fragile but precious comfort in the face of an uncertain future.

# Chapter 44

----------------------------------------------------------------

Monday morning arrived with a bittersweet clarity in Wavecrest, California. The sun rose over the town, casting its golden rays across the Pacific waters, illuminating the last week of summer freedom for its youth. For Jessica and Fawn, this was not just another week—it was the final stretch before life, as they knew it would change forever.

The beach, once teeming with spontaneous volleyball tournaments and carefree paddle boarding sessions, now seemed to hold a quieter, almost reflective air. The boardwalk that had been alive with music and laughter would soon be just a memory of evenings spent in youthful revelry. The weight of these impending changes pressed heavily on Jessica's heart as she lay in bed, staring at the ceiling adorned with glow-in-the-dark stars—a comforting relic of her childhood.

She could feel the knot in her stomach tighten as she thought about Friday, the day she would have to say goodbye to Ethan. He would be returning to Pine Haven to finish his college journey, leaving her behind in Wavecrest. The thought of not seeing his smile or hearing his laugh every day filled her with a sense of dread. Each moment spent with him now felt like it was slipping through her fingers, an hourglass running out of sand.

Jessica rolled over to see her packed suitcase sitting by the door, a constant reminder that she would be moving to Austin next Monday. The uncertainty of starting college was overshadowed by the sadness of leaving everything she had ever known behind. Her heart ached with the realization that Fawn would no longer be just a short walk away; they were both entering new chapters of their lives, miles apart.

For Fawn, the emotions were just as heavy, if not more so. Standing in her nearly empty bedroom, she gazed at the walls that had witnessed her growth from a child into a young woman. The room felt foreign now, stripped of its personality and warmth, much like how she felt inside. Knowing that her family home had been sold added another layer of sorrow—there was no home in Wavecrest for her to return to during holidays or breaks.

Packing for Boston should have been an exciting task, filled with the anticipation of a new beginning. Instead, it felt like preparing for an end. But what weighed most on Fawn's heart was saying goodbye to Jessica—the friend who had been more like a sister all these years. This week would be their final moments together in Wavecrest—a week filled with memories they would cling to as they stepped into their separate futures.

Fawn sat at her desk, the last bastion of familiarity in a room that had once been a vibrant canvas of her life. The stark white walls now loomed around her, stripped of the posters and paintings that once proclaimed her artistic spirit. Only one wall defied the blankness: a mural of Wavecrest's shoreline. Painted with love and painstaking detail, it was a tribute to the countless sunsets she had shared with Jessica and their friends over the years.

The shelves that once overflowed with art books and supplies now stood barren, their contents meticulously stored in cardboard boxes and plastic totes stacked neatly along the carpeted floor. The carpet itself, once a patchwork of paint splatters chronicling Fawn's creative journey, was hidden beneath the weight of her packed belongings. Each droplet of paint had been a footnote in her story, now obscured by the inevitability of change.

Against one wall stood her mirrored vanity, a silent witness to countless mornings and evenings spent transforming herself into visions of beauty and confidence. The surface, once cluttered with makeup palettes, jewelry boxes, and hair care products, was now bare. The drawers yawned empty, devoid of the treasures they had once guarded.

Fawn's eyes wandered around the room, taking in the emptiness that had replaced her sanctuary. Her heart ached with each bare spot on the walls, each cleared surface on her furniture. This room had been more than just a bedroom; it had been a gallery of her dreams and her growth. Now, it was reduced to mere architecture, awaiting its new occupants who would never know its history.

Turning her attention back to the desk in front of her, Fawn focused on the notepad and envelope lying on its surface. They seemed out of place in the stripped-down room, but were perhaps the most important items left unpacked. She picked up her pen, ready to write the words that carried so much meaning. The surrounding emptiness pressed in as she wrote, each word a small act of defiance against the void swallowing up her past.

Fawn's hand hovered for a moment before letting the pen fall back onto the desk with a soft clink. She exhaled, a sense of finality settling in her chest as she tore the paper from the notepad. The edges were clean and precise, mirroring the deliberate intention behind her words. She took a moment to read over what she had written, her eyes tracing each word, each curve of ink that bled her thoughts onto the page.

A small smile tugged at the corners of her mouth, a rare visitor amidst the chaos of packing and goodbyes. It was a smile of satisfaction, born of the knowledge that she had articulated everything she needed to say. The paper crinkled as she folded it in half, a crisp sound in the quiet room that had once thrummed with life and creativity.

With gentle fingers, Fawn tucked the folded letter into the envelope. The taste of glue lingered on her tongue as she sealed it closed, a mundane act that somehow felt significant—a physical seal on her emotions. She placed the envelope on the desk and picked up the pen once more.

She wrote "Felix" on the front of the envelope in flowing script, each letter a silent testament to their friendship. With a nod of approval at her handiwork, Fawn rose from the desk and walked over to her bed where her purse lay waiting—a faithful companion ready for new adventures.

She slid the envelope into its depths, ensuring its safety among her belongings. The soft leather of the purse felt reassuring under her touch as she slung it over her shoulder, ready to face what lay ahead.

With her hand gripping her purse firmly, she approached the doorway, but hesitated before descending the stairs. Turning back to survey her once vibrant room, now hollowed out and echoing with memories, her eyes found their way to the mural on the wall.

The mural stood as a testament to countless summers spent on the beaches of Wavecrest, each brushstroke a word in the visual diary she had kept throughout her teenage years. Now, as she took in every detail—the way the painted light seemed to dance on the waves, how each color blended seamlessly into the next—her heart swelled with an affection for what would soon be left behind.

A pang of sadness clenched at her heart, a heavy cloud dimming the light in her eyes. She knew that this piece of art would likely meet its end under a fresh coat of paint, its vibrancy and meaning obscured as new owners made their mark. It was not just a mural that would be covered; it was an era of her life that would be quietly painted over.

With one last lingering look at what had been her world, Fawn turned away from the mural and made her way downstairs, each step away from her room a step closer to an uncertain but inevitable future.

The morning light spilled into the kitchen, casting a soft glow on Anna as she carefully wiped a piece of porcelain and nestled it in a box. Fawn watched from the doorway, her heart torn by the sadness in her mother's eyes. Anna was not just packing away their fine china, she was packing away years of memories held within the walls of this house.

She cleared her throat as she stepped into the room. "Are you okay, Mom?"

Anna glanced up, offering a weak smile that didn't quite reach her eyes. She picked up another plate, her fingers tracing the delicate pattern etched on its surface.

"I'm fine," she replied, her voice barely above a whisper. "Just trying to get our good china safely packed away."

Fawn crossed the room to stand beside her mother. The sight of packing boxes scattered around the kitchen was a stark reminder of their impending move.

"I know this is hard for you, too, Mom," Fawn said softly. "Is there anything I can do to help?"

Anna shook her head, her attention still focused on the plate in her hands. "No, honey, you go ahead with your plans for the day. You don't need to worry about me."

There was a silence between them, punctuated only by the sound of paper rustling as Anna wrapped another plate. Fawn knew that beneath her mother's brave front was an ocean of emotions—regret for having to leave behind their home and sadness at having to part ways with her closest friend, Teresa, Jessica's mother.

"I'm just going to stop by Felix's house for a bit," Fawn said, breaking the silence as she looked at her mother. "I promised I would visit him before I leave for Boston."

Anna nodded, pausing to give Fawn a thoughtful look. "That's nice of you, honey. Felix seems like such a sweet boy. I hope he finds his own happiness and friends someday."

Fawn sighed at the thought of Felix's difficult life, "Yeah, me too."

After a moment of silence, Fawn spoke again. "Is it okay if I use your car? I won't be gone that long."

"Sure. I'm not going anywhere right now," Anna said, putting down the china and walking over to the counter where her purse sat. She rummaged through it, pulled out a set of keys, and handed them to Fawn. "Here you go, dear. Have fun and be careful!"

"Thanks, Mom," Fawn said, clutching the keys in her hand. "I'll be back soon."

With that, she turned and left the kitchen, leaving Anna alone with her thoughts and the box of china. The hum of the car echoed faintly as Fawn drove away from her home—a home that would soon belong to someone else.

As she drove toward the darker side of Wavecrest, Fawn braced herself not only for the journey but also for what it represented—a final goodbye to a friend she knew she would never see again.

The chirp of Jessica's phone sliced through the silence, a beacon in the morning light streaming through her bedroom curtains. She jolted upright, a mix of nerves and anticipation propelling her hand toward the nightstand. Her thumb hovered, then pressed down, revealing Ethan's message on the screen. "I'm on my way, babe. Be there in a few." A spontaneous grin blossomed across her face, her anxiety melting into a bubbling thrill.

She tossed aside the covers and swung her legs over the side of the bed, her movements brisk with urgency. She crossed the room to her dresser and pulled out a pink halter top from its drawer. Slipping it on, she felt its lightness drape over her skin, a perfect choice for the balmy day ahead. Next came the blue shorts, hugging her hips just right as she buttoned them up.

She moved to the vanity, catching a glimpse of herself in the mirror. Her hair was a tousled wave from sleep, but there wasn't much time to fuss. Grabbing a brush, she ran it through her locks with efficient strokes, taming them into submission. A few quick sweeps, and she appraised herself with a nod of approval.

With no more moments to spare, Jessica stepped out of her sanctuary of memories and into the hallway that led to the rest of the house. Her footsteps were light on the carpet as she made her way toward the kitchen, where another day in Wavecrest awaited her.

Teresa, dressed in her beautician smock, hummed softly as she tended to a vase brimming with vibrant flowers. The kitchen was her realm of comfort and nurturing—a place where she started each day by infusing life into every bloom with a gentle sprinkle of water.

The sound of footsteps drew her attention, and she glanced up, her eyes widening into a warm smile at the sight of her daughter. "Good morning, sweetheart. I was just about to get you up."

Jessica padded into the kitchen, rubbing sleep from her eyes. "Morning, Mommy," she mumbled, her voice still thick with the remnants of dreams.

She approached the cupboard and swung its doors wide, surveying the contents before deciding on a breakfast that matched her cheerful mood. Lucky Charms it was. She pulled out the box and an empty bowl left clean in the dishwasher, setting them on the counter with a soft clink.

As Jessica filled her bowl with the colorful cereal, Teresa returned to pruning a particularly stubborn stem. The silence between them was companionable until Jessica broke it with a question as she walked to the refrigerator. "Did Fawn leave already?"

"Yep. You just missed her. She left about fifteen minutes ago," Teresa replied without turning, focused on trimming a wilting leaf.

Jessica's eyebrows knitted together briefly in mild disappointment. "Oh, okay. I'll text her later, then. She's going back to her house to help Mama after she visits Felix."

Milk cascaded over the cereal as Jessica poured it from the carton, watching the marshmallows bob to the surface like tiny buoys in a milky sea. She took her seat at the table, her spoon diving into the bowl with an eagerness that wasn't just for the sugary breakfast.

Teresa watched her daughter eat, noting the hurried pace of her spoon. "Slow down, Jessica. You don't want to choke on your breakfast."

Jessica looked up from her bowl with an apologetic smile. "I just want to hurry because Ethan is on his way."

The corners of Teresa's mouth lifted in an understanding smile—she knew all too well that fluttering pulse of young love.

"You don't need to rush. You two have the whole day ahead of you," Teresa reassured.

"I know," Jessica admitted between bites. "I just want to be ready when he gets here."

A last look of maternal affection passed between them before Teresa turned away from her daughter's anxious heart and eager eyes—eyes that mirrored those of a young Teresa who had once waited for Tom with equal impatience.

As the kitchen clock approached eleven, Teresa grabbed her purse from the counter and walked toward Jessica. "Well, I have to go now," she said as she leaned down to plant a kiss atop Jessica's head—a kiss that held all the tenderness of their years together.

"Okay, Mommy." The childlike tone that slipped from Jessica tugged at Teresa's heart-strings—a melody she hoped would play on through all seasons of life.

She stood in the foyer for a moment, savoring this snapshot of home life before stepping toward the door.

"Say hi to Ethan for me. And don't forget to lock the door before you leave," she called out as she opened it.

With that parting reminder echoing behind her, Teresa stepped out into another bustling day as Jessica sat at the table finishing her cereal—the ticking clock now a drum-beat counting down to Ethan's arrival.

Jessica barely had time to place her empty cereal bowl in the dishwasher before the fa-miliar rumble of Ethan's Jeep echoed through the quiet neighborhood. Her heart skipped as she dashed to the doorway, flinging it open just as Ethan swung his legs out of the driver's seat. His lopsided smile greeted her, a smile that never failed to send her heart into a flutter.

He sauntered across the yard, and upon reaching the porch, Jessica pulled him into a fervent embrace. Words were unnecessary; their lips met in a kiss that spoke volumes, an expression of their enduring love.

Ethan's arms wrapped around Jessica's waist, pulling her closer as their kiss intensified. It was a moment of pure passion and longing, a connection that left them both breathless and eager for more.

As the intensity of their kiss subsided, Jessica and Ethan clung to each other, their breaths mingling in the quiet of the open doorway. The world outside seemed to pause, giving them a moment of solitude in the midst of an emotional day. Ethan's hand found Jessica's, their fingers intertwining with a familiarity that spoke of countless shared mo-ments.

Stepping inside Jessica's house, Ethan scanned the surroundings for another familiar face. His eyes settled on Jessica, still catching her breath from their greeting.

"Where's Fawn? I thought she was going to hang out with us today," he asked, a hint of disappointment lacing his voice.

Jessica leaned against the doorframe. "She wanted to go visit Felix today. You know, to say goodbye."

Ethan frowned slightly. "Aw, I wish she had waited. We could have gone with her."

"I told her," Jessica said with a shrug. "But she said that she wanted to do this alone. You know Fawn."

"Yeah, I get it," Ethan sighed, accepting Fawn's decision.

They moved to the couch, the soft cushions enveloping them as they sat down. Jessica nestled into the crook of Ethan's arm, her head resting peacefully on his shoulder. The rhythm of his breathing and the steady beat of his heart beneath her ear were comforting constants amidst the whirlwind of change.

"So, what do you want to do today?" she asked, her voice a soft murmur against the fabric of his shirt.

Ethan's fingers idly traced patterns on her arm as he pondered. "I have an idea. Jake wants to use the Jeep this afternoon, so why don't we hang out at my apartment?"

Jessica lifted her head to meet his gaze. A playful glint sparkled in her eyes. "Your apartment, huh?"

A smile played on Ethan's lips as he reached out to tuck an errant strand of hair behind her ear. "Yeah. It will just be the two of us. No interruptions or distractions."

The unspoken promise in his words hung in the air between them, charging the atmosphere with a heady mix of excitement and nervous anticipation. The fluttering in Jessica's stomach intensified as she considered his words—no distractions could only mean one thing.

She took a moment to reflect on what Ethan said, her mind racing with the implications. The corners of her lips curled up into a coy smile as she asked, "No distractions, huh?"

Ethan's grin widened, his gaze holding hers with an intensity that left no room for doubt. "No distractions."

In that moment, words became superfluous. Jessica's response came in the form of another kiss—a tender affirmation of her feelings for him. It was a kiss that spoke of trust, of a love nurtured by the salty breeze of Wavecrest and the golden warmth of shared sunsets.

As their embrace deepened, Jessica felt the world around her fade into the background, leaving only the two of them in a bubble of their own making. The intensity of their kiss grew, fueling the fire of their desire for one another. At that moment, she knew, without a shadow of a doubt, that this day would carve out a new chapter in their story—one that would hold a special place in their memories for years to come.

The drive through Wavecrest's contrasting landscape was always unsettling for Fawn. As she drove away from the sunlit streets of her neighborhood, the vibrancy of her beloved beach town gave way to an eerie stillness. A thick canopy of untamed foliage cast long shadows on the road, a stark departure from the sun-kissed beaches she was accustomed to.

Pulling up alongside a house cloaked in faded gray, Fawn felt an icy shiver crawl up her spine. This was Felix's home, a structure that bore witness to time's relentless march, its flaking paint and decaying fence speaking volumes about its neglect.

She sat in her car for a moment, staring at the front porch through the passenger window. Her last visit here had been far from pleasant—Felix's father had been anything but welcoming. She didn't relish the thought of another encounter with him.

After a moment's hesitation, she turned off the engine and grabbed her purse. Taking one last look at the porch and seeing no sign of Felix's father, she cautiously stepped out of her car.

The crunch of gravel under her feet seemed louder than usual as she approached the rusty gate. She paused when she spotted Felix at the side of his house. He was kneeling next to his bicycle, diligently pumping air into its rear tire. The sight tugged at her heartstrings—his bicycle was as weathered as his house, yet he treated it with such care.

As if sensing her presence, Felix glanced up from his task. His eyes widened when he saw Fawn standing by the gate, lines of surprise etched into his forehead. His hand froze on the pump handle as he gifted her a shy smile.

He rose to his feet, abandoning his bicycle against the wall as he walked toward Fawn. His heart pounded against his ribs with every step he took—Felix had harbored a secret crush on Fawn for years, and her unexpected presence was both exciting and overwhelming.

Fawn watched him approach, a smile tugging at the corners of her mouth. He stopped on the other side of the gate, his eyes meeting hers with an earnest gaze.

"Hi, Fawn," he greeted her, his voice a mix of surprise and happiness.

"You look surprised to see me," Fawn giggled. "I told you I would stop by before I left for college."

"I know you did," Felix admitted, his eyes dropping to his feet.

"I would have come sooner, but with moving and all," she continued.

"You didn't have to come, Fawn. I would have understood," he assured her, his eyes meeting hers once more.

"I made a promise, right? I don't like to break my promises," she replied with a gentle shrug.

"I know you don't. You've always kept your promises to me," Felix replied, a smile tugging at his lips.

"That's because you're my friend, and I don't break promises with my friends," she stated firmly.

They stood in comfortable silence for a moment, letting the weight of their words settle in the air.

Fawn's eyes drifted toward the bicycle leaning against the side of the house. It was a relic of past decades, its frame marred by rust that crept like ivy along the once vibrant paint. The handlebars were wrapped in frayed tape, and the seat, patched with duct tape, bore the imprint of countless journeys under the relentless California sun.

Yet, there was a nobility to it—the tires, worn thin from miles of pavement, whispered tales of resilience—of every trip to school, every errand run, and every escape from the confines of a home that felt more like a prison. The bike was a testament to perseverance, much like Felix himself.

Turning back to Felix with a slight smile, Fawn asked, "That's your transportation, huh?"

Felix looked at his beloved bicycle. He sighed, a mix of affection and resignation in his voice. "It's old, but it still gets me around. I can't afford to buy a car. I don't even have my driver's license."

Fawn's smile faded, replaced by a deep swell of understanding and empathy. She felt a surge of respect for Felix's determination to make do with what he had, a silent sadness threading through her admiration.

Felix opened the rusty gate, its hinges protesting with a metallic groan. "Come in," he beckoned Fawn into the yard, a space that felt both familiar and foreign to her.

Before crossing the threshold, Fawn glanced over to the front porch. She half expected to see the frail figure of Felix's father silhouetted against the doorframe. The porch, however, was vacant.

"Where's your dad?" she asked, with a hint of nervousness.

Felix's face softened, the sadness in his eyes briefly betraying the exhaustion of his double life as a caregiver. "He's sleeping," he answered. "He had a bad night."

"Oh, I'm sorry to hear that," Fawn said sympathetically as she passed through the opening of the gate.

Felix dismissed her concern with a shake of his head, as if he, too, could shake off the weight of his worries. He was quick to change the subject, eager to distract them both from the grim realities that lay just beyond the door of his home.

"So, who won the art contest?" Felix asked, his voice tinged with genuine interest.

Fawn's cheeks turned a modest shade, her voice softening. "I did."

"That's awesome, Fawn," Felix's face brightened with a wide smile. "I knew you would. You're a really good artist."

A blush deepened on Fawn's face as she ducked her head slightly. "Thanks," she murmured.

"Can I ask..." Felix hesitated, his curiosity piqued, "What did you draw?"

"I drew a sketch of Jessica and me sitting on our bench swing," Fawn replied, her voice filled with pride.

Felix furrowed his brow, a confused look on his face. "Really? I don't remember seeing a swing in Jessica's yard at her birthday party."

Fawn shook her head, a lock of hair slipping from behind her ear. "No. The swing is in my yard. My dad built it when I was a little girl."

Felix nodded. "Oh, okay."

"Yeah. That swing has been our special place ever since we were little. It's where we would go to talk and just be together." Fawn's eyes shimmered with nostalgia as she spoke.

"We have so many memories of sitting on that swing, and that's what I tried to put into my sketch."

Felix looked at her, his eyes revealing a sense of longing. "You and Jessica have been friends for a long time, huh?"

Fawn paused, allowing herself a moment to reflect before answering with a faint smile. "Yeah, long time."

"You're lucky, Fawn." Felix's voice held a note of wistfulness. "I wish I had a friend like that."

Her smile shifted, taking on a reassuring warmth. "You will, Felix. You will."

In the quiet space between them, there was a sense of unwavering certainty that in their friendship, Felix had found a connection that mirrored the loyalty and depth of what she shared with Jessica.

The weight of the moment settled over Felix like a shroud. The vibrancy of summer was ebbing away, and with it, Fawn's comforting presence. He swallowed the lump forming in his throat and ventured the question that had been lingering in his mind: "So, when are you leaving for Boston?"

Fawn turned away, her gaze lost to the horizon for a moment. The realization that she would be leaving in just a week stirred up a melancholy she wasn't prepared to face. Excitement about attending school in Boston was tinged with the sorrow of leaving behind her childhood home—a home that would soon belong to someone else.

With a heavy heart, she looked back at Felix and answered softly, "Next Monday."

Felix's eyes clouded with a mix of sadness and envy. He had always looked up to Fawn for her spirited nature and artistic talent. How he wished he could embrace life with the same zest, to step out into the world with such fearless ambition.

"Are you nervous? Scared?" he asked, his voice soft and concerned. "I know I would be. Boston is… it's so far away."

Fawn paused, allowing herself to consider his words. She thought of the bustling streets of Boston, so different from the familiar embrace of Wavecrest—the only home she'd ever known.

"I am," she admitted, her voice steady despite the turmoil within. "But it's something new, something different."

She let her eyes wander once more, taking in the entirety of her surroundings—the town that cradled all her memories from youth. "I want to see what it's like beyond Wavecrest. Beyond California."

When her eyes met Felix's again, they were resolute. "I think Boston will give me the opportunity to grow, to find myself, and become a better person."

Felix listened intently to Fawn's aspirations, admiration blooming in his chest even as a shadow crossed his face at her last words. In his heart, he believed Fawn was already one of the best people he knew—kind-hearted and genuine—and he wanted her to see that truth within herself.

"You are a good person, Fawn," Felix said earnestly, his eyes reflecting sincerity.

The simplicity of his compliment warmed Fawn more than she expected, causing a soft blush to spread across her cheeks. With a smile that lit up her face and made her eyes sparkle even brighter than usual, she replied sincerely, "Aw, thanks."

For the next fifteen minutes, Fawn and Felix stood by the gate, their conversation weaving through dreams and realities. Fawn spoke with a fervor that belied the uncertainty of her future, painting pictures of Boston's autumn leaves and the art scene she longed to join. Felix listened, his face a canvas of quiet attention, a smile occasionally breaking through as Fawn's words stirred a sense of wonder within him.

Felix's contributions were modest murmurs of affirmation, his aspirations muted by the boundaries of his existence. He shared no grand plans, only vague notions of escaping the life that confined him. Fawn's words were a balm to his spirit, yet they also served as a reminder of the chasm between their worlds.

As Fawn detailed the steps she would take to achieve her dreams, Felix couldn't help but smile. Her enthusiasm was a beacon in his otherwise bleak outlook. But when the conversation circled back to her moving, Fawn's expression changed. Guilt gnawed at her for leaving her mother to deal with the upheaval alone.

Fawn's face softened with concern, a hint of worry flickering in her eyes. "Well, I have to get going, Felix. I need to get back and help my mom," she said gently, her voice laced with regret.

Felix's smile faded. He understood her need to leave, but felt an acute sense of loss at her departure. The look in his eyes spoke volumes of the loneliness that awaited him.

Seeing the sadness in Felix's eyes, Fawn felt a tug at her heartstrings. She knew all too well the shadows that hung over his life. Reaching for her purse, she pulled out the envelope. Knowing this would be her last visit with Felix, Fawn wanted to give him something more than just memories to hold on to—she wanted to give him a gift of hope.

"This is for you, Felix. Take it," she said as she handed him the envelope.

Felix's hands hesitated as he accepted the envelope. "What's this?" he asked, his fingers tracing the sealed edge.

"Just something. You can open it after I leave," she replied with solemn sincerity.

He nodded silently, feeling the weight of the moment settle on them both—a farewell that was final in more ways than one.

"I'm never going to see you again, am I?" he asked, his voice low but full of emotion.

The question hung heavy in the air as Fawn moved closer to wrap Felix in a comforting hug—a silent acknowledgment of their parting. They held onto each other tightly, their embrace filled with the poignant knowledge that this would be their last moment together.

Pulling back slightly, Fawn looked into Felix's eyes and mustered a hopeful smile. "I hope you find a good life, Felix. I really do."

Tears blurred Felix's vision as he replied with a choked voice, "I hope you do, too, Fawn."

With finality etched into their final exchange, Fawn stepped through the gate and walked to her car. She glanced back at Felix one last time before starting the engine and driving away from everything they had known together.

Alone in the silence of his yard, Felix clutched the envelope tighter. A solitary tear ran down his cheek as he watched her car disappear into the distance—the last physical tether to Fawn now severed by time and circumstance.

He stood motionless, the weight of the envelope in his hands grounding him at the moment. His thumb, still trembling, slipped under the sealed flap, and he pulled it across, breaking the paper's resistance. Peering inside, the first thing that caught his eye was a bundle of green bills tucked neatly in a row. Confusion furrowed his brow as he carefully withdrew the money.

One by one, Felix counted the bills, his fingers quivering as if they were afraid to disturb the quiet order of the currency. He counted once and then again to confirm what his eyes were seeing—twenty bills, each worth one hundred dollars. Two thousand dollars in all—a small fortune that seemed to expand, filling the space around him with its significance.

A surge of emotion welled up inside Felix as he realized that this was Fawn's prize money from the Art Contest. She had given it all to him. The realization of her sacrifice and generosity crashed over him like a wave, leaving his heart pounding against his chest in a rhythm that sang of gratitude and disbelief.

Tears blurred Felix's vision as he placed the money back into the envelope. It was then that he noticed a small piece of paper, folded neatly at the bottom—a secret hidden in the depths of the envelope. Curiosity piqued, he pulled out the note and unfolded it.

He removed his glasses to wipe away the tears that threatened to overflow. As he replaced them on his nose, his eyes fell on Fawn's elegant handwriting dancing across the paper. The note was brief, but it contained three simple words that struck him with their potency: "Be an architect!"

In those three words was every hope Fawn had for him—every ounce of belief she held in his dreams. They were a directive, a wish, and a vote of confidence all at once.

Overwhelmed by the magnitude of Fawn's gesture, Felix felt a swell of emotions too vast to contain. Gratitude for her kindness filled every corner of his being, accompanied by awe at her selflessness and a deep appreciation for her belief in him.

For Felix, Fawn's gift was more than monetary—it was permission to dream without restraint, to reach for something beyond the confines of his current existence. It was also an acknowledgment of their shared summer moments—moments when he had been more than just a background character in someone else's story. He thought back to Jessica's birthday party and the Summer Dance—memories now cherished treasures in his heart. Those moments of joy and acceptance were priceless gifts from Fawn, experiences un-tainted by ridicule or shame.

As Felix stood before the rusted gate, tears streamed down his cheeks. Yet these tears were not born from sorrow or grief; they were tears of happiness—happiness rooted in having known a true friend who saw beyond his quiet exterior and believed in his dreams.

He glanced down the empty street one last time, where the girl he had secretly crushed on vanished from sight but not from memory. With gratitude radiating from his every pore, Felix whispered into the silence left in her wake.

"Thank you, Fawn. I will never forget you."

In the Reese family living room, the flickering lights from the television danced across Tom's face as he sat back in his recliner, absorbed in the eleven o'clock nightly news. The anchors discussed the latest updates, their voices a steady hum that filled the room with a sense of normalcy.

In the warm embrace of the kitchen, Teresa and Fawn occupied their usual spots at the table. The soft light from the pendant above bathed them in a comforting glow. A jar filled with tips from Teresa's day at the salon sat between them, its contents carefully counted by her meticulous hands. Across from her, Fawn glued her eyes to the screen of her phone, aimlessly scrolling with her thumb. She looked up occasionally to exchange small talk with Teresa, but her weary eyes betrayed the exhaustion of an emotionally draining day.

Teresa glanced at Fawn over her reading glasses, noting the weariness etched into her daughter's best friend's eyes.

"You look tired, sweetheart. Why don't you go to bed," she suggested, her voice carrying the tender warmth of a mother.

Fawn lifted her eyes to meet Teresa's concerned gaze. "I will, Mama. I'm just waiting for Jessica to get home," she replied, a faint smile touching her lips.

A few minutes later, the distant rumble of Ethan's Jeep approached, growing louder until it came to a stop outside. Teresa and Fawn turned their heads toward the sound, anticipation lighting their faces.

As the sound of the engine faded into the night, the front door swung open, and Jessica's cheerful voice rang out through the house. "I'm home!" Her words brought a smile to Teresa's and Fawn's faces.

Peeking into the living room, Jessica caught sight of her father in his usual spot. "Hi, Daddy," she greeted him warmly.

Tom returned her greeting with an affectionate smile that crinkled the corners of his eyes.

Jessica then made her way into the kitchen and took her seat at the table next to Fawn. The homely scent of freshly baked cookies lingered in the air—a small comfort after a day filled with farewells and promises.

"How was your day with Ethan?" Teresa asked as she put away her tip jar and gave Jessica her full attention.

"It was great," Jessica beamed, recalling their drive along the Pacific coast with fondness. "We just got back from cruising along the coastline. Ethan knows all these cool spots that are just... amazing."

Turning to Fawn, who had been quietly listening, Jessica asked with genuine curiosity, "How did your visit with Felix go?"

Fawn paused for a moment before answering. "It was okay," she said quietly, choosing not to divulge the emotional weight of their parting or mention the envelope of the prize money she had left him. That gesture was something deeply personal—a silent pact between herself and Felix—and for now, she wanted to keep it that way.

The glow of the TV faded, plunging the living room into darkness as Tom clicked the remote. He pushed himself out of the recliner, his joints protesting quietly. The room seemed to hold its breath in the sudden silence, the echoes of the day lingering in the corners.

He walked into the kitchen, where the light spilled out like a warm invitation. Teresa, Jessica, and Fawn sat at the table, a small island of life amid the quiet house. Tom's gaze softened as he looked at them, his girls.

"I'm going to bed," he announced, his voice carrying a gentle finality that marked the end of the day. Leaning down, he planted a kiss on top of Jessica's head, then Fawn's—a nightly ritual that felt more poignant with each passing day.

Teresa smiled up at him. "I'll be there shortly," she assured him, her hand reaching out to squeeze his for a moment—a silent exchange of understanding and shared sentiment.

Turning to Jessica and Fawn, she echoed Tom's sentiment with maternal firmness tinged with tenderness. "You girls should do the same. You both had a busy day, and you need your sleep."

Jessica nodded, a softness in her eyes reflecting the love and respect she held for her mother. "Okay, Mommy. Goodnight," she replied, her voice carrying a hint of the child she once was.

Fawn echoed her sentiment with equal warmth. "Goodnight, Mama," she said, offering a smile that conveyed both gratitude and sadness for the approaching changes.

The girls rose to their feet in unison and headed down the hallway toward Jessica's room, their steps in sync as if choreographed by years of friendship. Teresa watched them go, her heart swelling with love and contracting with impending loss.

Next week at this time, these halls would echo with absence—the absence of laughter that had filled every corner, of mischief that had breathed life into still afternoons. Teresa could almost hear it already—the silence that would stretch through the rooms like an unwelcome guest.

She let out a deep sigh that seemed to carry all her unspoken thoughts and emotions—a mother's lament for time's relentless march. With one last glance at the empty chairs where Jessica and Fawn had sat moments before, Teresa reached out to turn off the lights.

As the house settled into its nightly slumber, Teresa made her way to join Tom in their bedroom—two pillars standing strong amidst the shifting sands of family life.

In Jessica's bedroom, the two girls, now changed into their sleepwear, moved through their nightly routines. Fawn, dressed in a soft nightshirt, climbed into her side of the bed and pulled the blanket up to her chin. She turned on her side, facing the window, where moonlight spilled in, casting a gentle glow.

Across the room, Jessica stood at her vanity, brushing her long hair as she gazed at her reflection. Her face, lit by the lamp's warm light, bore traces of the day's emotions—a blend of joy for Fawn's art contest win and sadness for the inevitable farewells. Putting down her brush, she walked over to her side of the bed and slipped under the covers.

With a contented sigh, she reached out and flicked off the bedside lamp. Darkness enveloped the room, wrapping around them like a shroud. The silence was thick, only broken by their soft breathing and the distant sound of waves crashing against the shore.

As Jessica turned away from Fawn to find comfort in sleep's embrace, a sudden exclamation shattered the quiet.

"Oh, no," Fawn cried out, her voice quivering with distress.

Jessica quickly turned to face her friend. "What's the matter?" she asked, concern lacing her words.

Fawn pointed upward with a shaky hand. "My star. It stopped glowing," she said, her eyes filled with sadness.

Jessica followed Fawn's gaze to the ceiling, where countless stars had once shone like a promise of dreams and nighttime adventures. But now, only darkness stared back at them — Fawn's favorite star no longer glowed with its unique imperfection.

A wave of sadness washed over Jessica as she, too, observed that many of their luminescent companions had faded away. "It looks like almost all of them stopped glowing," she murmured.

Fawn nodded slowly, her eyes lingering on the dim shapes above them. "I guess it's just another sign that our time here is coming to an end," she whispered.

The two lay there in silence for a moment longer, enveloped in memories and facing the reality that their childhood was slipping from their grasp like sand through their fingers. The glow-in-the-dark stars on Jessica's ceiling had been more than decorations; they were guardians of dreams and secrets shared between two souls who had grown up side by side. Now, as the stars dimmed one by one, so did their days together, each one fading like the soft glow above them.

Under the veil of night, Jessica and Fawn lay in the darkness. The void where Fawn's favorite star once glimmered was now a silent reminder of their fleeting youth. They faced each other, the moonlight casting a gentle glow on their faces, a soft illumination that seemed to hold them in a tender embrace.

"Goodnight, Fawn," Jessica whispered, her voice tinged with the warmth of years spent in laughter and companionship. It was a simple goodnight, yet it carried the weight of all the unspoken emotions churning within her—the love, the gratitude, and the sorrow of imminent parting.

"Goodnight, Jess," Fawn replied, her words echoing Jessica's affection. She turned away to face her side of the bed, her heart brimming with similar sentiments. Each syllable was a gentle brushstroke on the canvas of their shared history.

As silence reclaimed the room, sleep began to weave its tranquil spell over them. The world outside faded away, leaving only the sacred space of their intertwined lives. Their breathing slowed, deepened, and synchronized—a silent duet that spoke volumes of their bond.

In the sanctuary of slumber, Jessica and Fawn drifted back to a time when life was an endless horizon of possibilities—back to when they were younger, and their tomorrows were certain. Their worries were nonexistent then; each challenge was merely a detour on the grand adventure that was growing up.

As their sleep deepened, they found themselves once again as children under the bright sun of Wavecrest's summers past, running through sprinklers that cast rainbows in the air, building sandcastles destined to be claimed by the tide, and whispering secrets under starry skies. In this dream world, they were invincible—queens of their domain with crowns woven from wildflowers and seashells.

Their laughter echoed through their dreamscape—a sound as pure and vibrant as the first day they met. It was their brief escape to a simpler time, when every moment brimmed with magic, and each day was an adventure waiting to happen.

# Chapter 45

---

Over the next three days, Jessica, Ethan, and Fawn tried to savor every moment together before the inevitable goodbyes. They clung to the present, seeking out the places along the Pacific coast that had once felt like extensions of their carefree summers.

On Tuesday, they set out early in Ethan's Jeep, winding along the coastal highway. The trio stopped at historical landmarks where they posed for photos, their smiles a temporary shield against the impending changes. They shared stories and laughter, a camaraderie that seemed to defy time itself. The day was a colorful blur of sightseeing—old missions with their bell towers reaching toward the sky, grand vistas overlooking the ocean, and sleepy little towns that seemed untouched by time.

As the sun began its descent toward the horizon, they found themselves on a secluded beach. There, with a picnic blanket spread beneath them and a feast of their favorite snacks laid out, they watched as the sky painted itself in hues of orange and pink. Words were unnecessary as they sat side by side, letting the beauty of the sunset wash over them.

Wednesday brought a different tempo as Fawn's grandmother, Anna's mother, arrived from Malibu with her suitcase and opinions in tow. At Fawn's house, Grace Ellington's presence filled the rooms with energy and an undercurrent of tension. She made no effort to conceal her disapproval of the family's move to Montana or Fawn's decision to attend college in Boston. Her outspokenness hung heavy in the air, causing Brian to bristle and Anna to cast worried glances toward Fawn.

Jessica and Ethan helped where they could, wrapping dishes and boxing up memories. The house was becoming emptier by the hour, a hollow shell echoing with past laughter. In between Grandma Ellington's sharp remarks and commands, there were moments of tender nostalgia—a photo found behind a dresser and a forgotten toy under a bed—each discovery a bittersweet reminder of what was being left behind.

On Thursday, Jessica refused to let Fawn spend another day consumed by packing boxes and family tension. Together with Ethan, they returned to the boardwalk, where arcade games awaited challengers. The clangs and electronic cheers filled the air as they jumped from one game to another—Ethan scoring at basketball hoops, Jessica hitting high scores on Skee-Ball, and Fawn mastering dance steps on a flashing floor.

Later, as the sky began its evening performance, they found themselves back on the beach where they had watched so many sunsets together. They sat close on the sand as they gazed out at the deepening colors of twilight. Each sunset now felt like a count-down—a reminder that time was slipping away from them.

With each passing day, a sense of dread settled deeper in their hearts. They knew these were their last moments together before Ethan returned to Pine Haven and before Jessica and Fawn ventured off to colleges in different cities. It was as if they could feel pieces of their world quietly fracturing away with each tick of the clock—an ache inside that reminded them just how much they'd miss one another when they parted ways.

Friday morning arrived in Wavecrest, casting a soft golden glow over the town. At the Reese house, however, the light seemed to touch everything but the hearts of those inside. A somber air permeated the room, a prelude to Ethan's impending departure. It was a contrast that seemed to mirror the emotional storm brewing inside, where every heartbeat was a mixture of anticipation and dread.

In Jessica's bedroom, soft light filtered through the curtains, casting a warm glow on Fawn as she slept. A slight movement on the bed disturbed the stillness of the scene, causing Fawn to stir. Lifting her head, she saw Jessica sitting on the edge of the bed, carefully pulling on a pair of sweats.

The digital clock on the nightstand read 8:25, its red numbers bold against the morning silence. Fawn's eyes flicked from the clock back to Jessica and remarked groggily, "You're up early."

Jessica glanced over her shoulder, a hint of apology in her tone. "Did I wake you? I'm sorry."

Fawn sat up, letting the blanket gather around her waist as she rubbed the remnants of sleep from her eyes.

"It's okay. It's just not like you to be up this early," she observed.

Jessica stood and tugged at her pants to straighten them. "I'm meeting Ethan on the boardwalk at nine," she explained.

A hint of disappointment colored Fawn's voice as she asked, "He's not coming here this morning?"

Jessica shook her head. "No. Jake's dropping Ethan off in the parking lot, so I'm going to meet him there."

The parking lot that had been their meeting place in the early days of their blossoming relationship now took on a different meaning.

The realization that these would be their last moments together before Ethan returned to Pine Haven settled heavily on Fawn. Trying to offer some comfort, she said brightly, "Well, at least you'll have some alone time together before he leaves."

But Jessica's eyes betrayed her deepest fear—a fear that felt permanent. "What if this is the last time I ever see him?" she whispered.

Fawn's brow furrowed in confusion and worry. "What do you mean?"

Jessica's voice trembled with vulnerability as she explained, "You know how these things end. Look what happened to Krista and Donny."

Moved by an impulse to comfort her friend, Fawn positioned herself next to Jessica on the bed and wrapped an arm around her shoulder. "Jess, stop it. This isn't going to happen to you and Ethan."

Jessica's eyes glistened with unshed tears as she expressed her uncertainty. "How do you know that? You can't be sure of these things. No one can."

Fawn held Jessica's gaze and spoke with conviction. "I know because I see the way Ethan looks at you. He loves you, Jessica. He really does. He's not going to let that happen. Trust me."

Jessica turned to Fawn, desperate for faith in her words—faith that would anchor her through the storm of goodbye.

"Have I ever lied to you?" Fawn asked.

In a voice as fragile as glass, Jessica answered simply and truthfully. "No."

Fawn wrapped Jessica in a warm hug, her words wrapping around her friend like a protective shawl.

"You guys are going to make it. Ethan adores you, and he's not going to let you go." Her voice carried the certainty of the sun's rise, a surety that Ethan's feelings for Jessica were as deep as the ocean that bordered their town. She believed, without a shadow of a doubt, that Ethan would move mountains to keep their love alive across the miles that would soon separate them.

Jessica's anxious heartbeat slowed against Fawn's chest. She pulled away and met her friend's eyes. Her face showed worry but softened as she found comfort in Fawn's presence.

"I hope you're right, Fawn. I don't know what I would do if I lost Ethan. He means so much to me, and I don't want to lose him. But I guess we just have to take it one day at a time, right?"

The corners of Fawn's mouth lifted into a tender smile as she nodded. "Yeah, that's all we can do, Jess. Take each day as it comes. Just remember how lucky you are to have found someone who cares so much about you. It's rare to find love like that."

A heavy sigh escaped Jessica as she leaned into Fawn for another hug. "Thank you for always being here for me, Fawn. I don't know what I would do without you."

With a soft chuckle, Fawn nuzzled Jessica back, urging her toward the door with an affectionate smile. "Okay, now. Go see Ethan. I'm going back to sleep for a while."

Jessica nodded, her resolve strengthened by Fawn's support. With one last look at her friend snuggling back into bed, she quietly left the room.

As the door closed behind Jessica, Fawn snuggled back into the cozy bed and pulled the blanket up to her chin. She lay there for a moment, eyes open, thinking about Jessica and Ethan's future. The uncertainty was palpable, yet there was hope in their bond that felt unbreakable. As Jessica's footsteps faded down the hallway, Fawn allowed herself to drift back into the embrace of sleep, carrying with her wishes for enduring love against all odds.

Jessica entered the kitchen, where the aroma of freshly brewed coffee mingled with the early morning light streaming through the windows. Teresa, dressed in a pink nightgown, sat at the table with a cup of coffee cradled in her hands. She looked up and greeted her daughter with a smile that was both warm and tinged with concern. "Good morning, sweetheart. You're up early."

"I'm meeting Ethan on the boardwalk at nine," Jessica replied as she took a seat opposite her mother.

Teresa's expression softened as she recognized the anguish etched in Jessica's eyes. She knew today would be challenging for her daughter. With a sympathetic look, she asked, "Can I fix you some breakfast?"

Jessica shook her head, her thoughts too scattered for food. "No, thanks. I'll grab a muffin or something later."

With motherly intuition, Teresa reached across the table and gently squeezed Jessica's hand. "Honey, please don't be sad. You and Ethan have a special connection. This isn't the end for you two. I truly believe that."

The corners of Jessica's mouth lifted in a feeble attempt at a smile as she bit her lip and nodded. She wanted to cling to her mother's faith in her relationship with Ethan, but the fear of losing him seemed to cloud every silver lining.

Glancing around, Jessica turned in her seat to look into the living room, where she expected to see her suitcase, but found nothing.

"Where's my suitcase?" she asked with a hint of panic in her voice.

Teresa glanced in the same direction before her gaze returned to meet Jessica's eyes. "Your father took it. He shipped it to your aunt and uncle's house on his way to work this morning. We want it to be there when you arrive on Monday."

Jessica rested her elbows on the table and cupped her chin with her hands as a sense of finality washed over her. "I wish I wasn't going to college. I wish Fawn and I were staying here."

Teresa looked at Jessica with eyes full of empathy, aware of how difficult this transition was for her daughter.

"I know, baby," she replied softly. "To be honest, I wish you girls weren't going either. It's going to be hard for all of us, but we'll manage. I know you and Fawn are going to make the most of your time in college. You'll meet new people, learn new things, and discover who you really are. "

"I already know who I am and what I want," Jessica retorted, the frustration evident in her voice. "I don't need college to tell me that."

Standing abruptly, she grabbed her purse from the back of the chair. "I'm going to go now," she announced, heading for the foyer.

Teresa watched her daughter move across the room with a heart full of maternal concern. As Jessica reached for the door handle, Teresa called out, "Put on a light jacket, sweetheart. It's a chilly morning."

"Okay, Mommy," Jessica replied with a voice tinged with vulnerability—a reminder of the little girl she once was. She reached for a light blue windbreaker hanging on the coat rack and slipped it over her shoulders.

With one last deep breath that carried more than just the cool morning air, Jessica opened the front door and stepped into the day—a day fraught with goodbyes and silent promises of new beginnings etched in every step away from home.

The morning air held a briskness that spoke of summer's end as Jessica walked the two blocks to the boardwalk. Her footsteps, rhythmic against the pavement, echoed the conflicted drumbeat of her heart—each step a bittersweet march toward a future filled with uncertainty.

As she passed the familiar houses lining her street, neighbors emerged, starting their day with the same routines that had woven the fabric of this tight-knit community. Mr. Johansson, watering his meticulously kept roses, looked up and offered a warm smile.

"Off to see Ethan?" he called out, his voice carrying across the dew-laden grass.

Jessica nodded, returning his smile with one that didn't quite reach her eyes. "Yes, he's leaving today," she replied, her voice tinged with sadness.

Further down the street, Mrs. Henley stepped onto her porch, cradling a steaming mug of coffee. The soft clink of her spoon against the ceramic was a familiar morning chime. She waved to Jessica.

"You have yourself a good day now," she said, her gaze lingering with a hint of maternal concern.

"Thank you, Mrs. Henley," Jessica replied, grateful for the simple kindness that seemed to cushion her heart against the day's looming goodbyes.

Reaching the boardwalk's entrance, Jessica climbed the wooden ramp leading up to its planked expanse. The normally bustling path was now subdued, populated only by a few early strollers and joggers taking advantage of the quiet hour. The laughter and shouts of summer's past seemed to echo like ghosts among the empty concession stands and shuttered souvenir shops.

She paused for a moment at the top of the ramp, taking in the sight of the deserted boardwalk stretching out before her. It was as if Wavecrest itself was holding its breath, bracing for change just as she was. The absence of familiar faces and summer tourists made it all too clear—this season was coming to an end.

With each step toward the parking lot where Ethan would be waiting, Jessica felt an acute awareness of endings—the end of summer, the end of childhood adventures on this very boardwalk, and perhaps even an end to what she and Ethan had found together under its sunlit skies.

She reached for the phone in her purse, tempted to call Ethan and hear his voice, assuring her that everything would be alright. But she resisted; she wanted to see him face-to-face without any prelude—a direct connection without wires or waves.

Jessica continued her solitary walk through this familiar yet strangely transformed place—a tableau of their shared memories now quieted by time and circumstance. She pressed forward through the morning chill that whispered promises of autumn—a season of change that seemed intent on arriving too soon.

Descending the ramp to the parking lot, Jessica's pulse quickened as she caught sight of Ethan. He stood under the familiar canopy of the old palm tree, wearing a black muscle shirt and shorts that accentuated his tanned skin. Around his neck dangled the cross his grandfather had given him, a small but profound reminder of the love and protection that was always with him. His casual stance, with feet clad in sandals, was a stark contrast to the tension in Jessica's heart. As he turned and their eyes met, time seemed to stand still.

With a few strides, Ethan closed the distance between them, his approach filled with eager anticipation—a reflection of his desire to cherish each remaining moment with Jessica. When they finally met on the asphalt that had witnessed the early days of their courtship, Ethan wrapped her in an embrace that spoke volumes.

Jessica melted into him, feeling every bit of love and emotion Ethan exuded. She rested her head on his chest, a perfect fit, as if made to belong there. They clung to each other, their silence a shared language of love and the knowledge that this was their last day together.

In the comfort of Ethan's arms, Jessica felt a poignant ache in her chest—a mix of gratitude for this moment and sorrow for all the moments they would miss in each other's absence. They remained locked together, reluctant to acknowledge the impending good-bye that loomed over them like an unwelcome shadow.

The parking lot around them faded into insignificance as they stood there, holding onto one another as if trying to fuse their souls together against the tide of change. This place, where their romance had blossomed amidst shy glances and tentative conversations, now witnessed the moment they had long dreaded.

After minutes that felt both eternal and fleeting, they finally allowed space between them. Jessica lifted her head to look at Ethan, her eyes glistening with unshed tears.

"How much time do we have?" she asked, her voice laced with a vulnerability she couldn't hide.

Ethan swallowed hard before answering. "I have to be back here at three," he said with a tinge of dread. "That's when Jake is coming to get me."

Jessica absorbed his words, each one landing like a stone in her stomach. Three o'clock—the hour that would mark the end of their summer together and usher in an undefined future apart.

They embraced once more in the parking lot—their sacred space where each hello had been bright with promise, and now each second ticked toward an inevitable goodbye.

Time seemed to pause as they held each other, neither one eager to be the first to let go. But eventually, they reluctantly allowed distance to return between them. With the warmth of Ethan's arms still lingering around her, Jessica brushed a loose strand of hair from her face, her blue eyes reflecting a mix of emotions.

"So, what do you want to do?" she asked, her voice steady but laced with a sadness she couldn't conceal.

Ethan glanced down at her, his hand finding hers, their fingers intertwining as naturally as the waves meeting the shore.

"I haven't eaten yet, so let's go see if we can find a place on the boardwalk that's open," he suggested, trying to maintain a semblance of normalcy despite the heavy air between them.

Hand in hand, they walked up the ramp to the boardwalk. The planks creaked beneath their steps, echoing in the quiet morning. They passed closed shops with chairs stacked and signs that read: "See you next summer," a stark reminder of the season's end.

The rich and inviting scent of buttered rolls ensnared Ethan's senses, drawing him irresistibly toward a familiar stand nestled among the sleepy storefronts. His stomach rumbled in agreement as they approached.

"Isn't that the same stand we went to back in June?" Ethan asked, looking at Jessica with a surprised look that matched his nostalgic tone.

Jessica took a moment to study the stand and realized it was indeed the same food stand they had visited during their first date. A smile spread across her face as she remembered that day—the excitement of new love and the promise of summer unfolding before them.

"Yes, it is," she confirmed with a giggle. "It was the day after the beach party. It was our first real date. You were hungry that morning."

Ethan grinned as he acknowledged the memory. "Well, you know what? I can never resist buttered rolls. Do you want one?"

"No, thanks," Jessica replied with a smile. "I'll get something later." After a moment of thought, she added, "But a bottle of water would be great."

They approached the vendor, and Jessica took a seat at a nearby table—a replica of that early summer day when they sat together, making plans for adventure. Unlike their previous visit to this vendor, where Ethan had to wait in line to be served, there was no one else in line this time. In a few short minutes, Ethan joined Jessica at their table with a buttered roll and a bottle of water in hand.

For the next few minutes, Jessica watched Ethan relish his buttered roll—the simple pleasure pushing aside their worries. Each bite he took brought back memories of that day at this very stand, where they had made plans to visit hidden coves for the first time—a chapter now bookmarked in their shared history.

As she sat there with Ethan, his contentment momentarily filling the space between them, Jessica couldn't help but wish she could turn back time and start their summer all over again.

After Ethan finished his buttered roll, he wiped his hands on a napkin and stood up, offering his hand to Jessica. With no particular destination in mind, they began a leisurely stroll along the boardwalk, absorbing the sights and sounds around them. The rhythmic crash of waves provided a soothing soundtrack to their walk. The few people they encountered—a couple jogging past and an old man sweeping the sand with a metal detector—were met with a friendly wave from the pair.

Jessica's eyes wandered to the empty beach—a canvas of sand stretched out before them, another reminder that summer was coming to an end. Then, amidst the vast emptiness, she spotted a solitary object that sent her heart fluttering. It was the lifeguard stand where she first saw Ethan, standing tall and proud against the sky. Memories flooded her mind—Ethan standing next to it, dressed in a white muscle shirt and colorful shorts, his eyes hidden behind dark sunglasses.

Without thinking, Jessica grabbed Ethan's hand and pulled him toward the steps that led down to the deserted beach. "C'mon. I want to show you something," she said with an excitement that belied the bittersweet nostalgia swirling inside her.

Ethan let Jessica lead the way, his curiosity piqued by her sudden excitement. They descended the steps together, her grip firm around his hand as she navigated them around the beach until they reached a particular spot on the sand—the very spot where she and Fawn had spent their first beach day after graduating from high school.

Jessica paused and looked toward the distant lifeguard stand before turning back to Ethan. "This is where I was when I first saw you by that lifeguard stand," she said, with a hint of awe in her voice.

Ethan's face lit up with surprise, and a broad grin stretched across his face. "You saw me from way over here?"

"Uh-huh," Jessica replied with a nod. "You were like a magnet. I couldn't take my eyes off you."

He turned his gaze back to the lifeguard stand, smiling at the memory. "I remember that day," Ethan said warmly. "The first time I saw you, I felt an instant connection. You looked so beautiful—like an angel."

Jessica's cheeks blushed at his words, and she glanced down shyly before looking back up at him. "Me too," she confessed. "I never felt that with anyone before."

"Neither have I, Jess," Ethan replied earnestly. "Neither have I."

As they continued sharing memories of their early days together, they wrapped their arms around each other and made their way back to the boardwalk. With each step along its length, they held on to each other and to the precious moments they still had left.

The weathered planks beneath their feet creaked rhythmically, echoing the familiar cadence of their summer spent together. The sun, climbing higher in the sky, cast a warm glow over Sandalwood Pavilion, lighting up the very spot where they had danced at Wavecrest's annual Summer Dance just a month ago.

The pavilion stood nearly empty now, save for a lone fisherman casting his line into the shimmering sea. The absence of music and laughter made the scene feel like a different world to Jessica—one devoid of the vibrant energy that had defined their night under the stars. For Ethan, the memory of that evening was overshadowed by an apparition that had appeared to him—an image of his grandfather that had haunted him since.

Jessica's thoughts were abruptly brought back to the present as a sweet aroma wafted through the air, teasing her senses. Down the boardwalk, a food vendor was selling freshly fried dough, its surface dusted with powdered sugar. The scent pulled at her appetite, and she nudged Ethan toward the stand.

"Smells too good to pass up," she said with a smile, her voice brightening at the prospect of indulging in one of her favorite treats.

Ethan grinned in agreement, and they joined the short line at the vendor's cart. Moments later, they walked away with paper plates in hand, each bearing a warm, sugary confection that promised a momentary escape from their looming farewells.

With their sweet cravings satisfied and their fingers dusted with powdered sugar, they continued their stroll down the boardwalk until they reached its end. There, spread out before them like a canvas painted with memories, was Callahan Cove—the site of that fateful beach party where everything began.

The cove beckoned them with waves lapping at its shore and golden sand reflecting the morning light. Jessica felt a lump form in her throat as she recalled how they had first seen each other across this very stretch of beach. Their eyes met, sharing an unspoken understanding—they needed to visit this landmark one more time.

Hand in hand, they descended from the wooden structure onto the sandy expanse of Callahan Cove. Each step took them closer to where it all started—a place full of laughter, music, and the first steps toward new love. It was here they would pause and savor their journey together before reality beckoned them onto separate paths.

With a shared determination, they walked to the water's edge, their footprints marking the wet sand as they traversed the shoreline. The ocean air carried the scent of salt and freedom, a stark contrast to the gravity of their hearts. In the distance, they spotted the monolithic rock, its familiar silhouette a beacon amidst the ebb and flow of the tide.

Picking up their pace, Jessica and Ethan made their way to their treasured spot. As they approached, the memories of that night—the night of the beach party—flooded back with vivid clarity. It was here that their paths had converged under a canopy of stars and possibilities.

Arriving at the rock, they took their seats on its time-worn surface. Side by side, they faced the endless expanse of the Pacific Ocean, allowing its vastness to envelop them in a comforting embrace. The rock was cool against their skin, but the warmth between them filled any void left by the sea breeze.

They sat in silence, each lost in thought yet acutely aware of the other's presence. No words were needed; their shared view of the horizon spoke volumes. It was as if time itself had slowed to allow them this moment—a pause in the inevitable march toward their separate futures.

Jessica leaned against Ethan, resting her head on his shoulder as a wave of contentment washed over her. Here on this hallowed ground where it all began, she found peace in knowing that this was where they would spend the rest of their time together. It was a sacred space that held both joy and sorrow, cradling them as it witnessed the beginning and now the end of their summer love story.

As they gazed out to the horizon, there was an unspoken recognition between them—this place would forever hold a piece of their hearts. It was here that their paths had crossed for one brief, beautiful summer. And though their journey together would come to a pause with the setting sun, the memories etched on this rock would endure long after they left its steadfast presence.

The midday sun was high in the sky, its light streaming through the windows of Fawn's house, casting a warm glow over the cardboard boxes that now contained the essence of a family's life. Inside, Brian, Anna, and Anna's mother, moved with quiet efficiency, their motions punctuated by the sound of tape sealing cardboard flaps. The air was thick with dust motes dancing in the sunbeams and nostalgia.

Each item had been wrapped with care, a testament to their life in Wavecrest. The walls, once adorned with photographs and paintings, were now bare, echoing with the memories of laughter and conversations that once filled the rooms. The house felt different—emptier—as they awaited the arrival of the moving truck that would carry away their physical ties to this place.

Outside, Fawn sat on the old white bench swing, her legs dangling listlessly as she moved back and forth with a half-hearted push of her toes against the ground. Her sketchpad lay open on her lap, a pencil in hand poised above a blank page. But she was not seeking inspiration for her art; she was trying to escape from what was happening inside.

She sketched aimlessly, lines and curves spilling across the page without intention. Normally, the gentle sway of the swing and the rustling of leaves would soothe her, but today, there was an unsettling stillness in the air. The palm leaves were motionless despite the sea breeze that usually danced through them. The whispering voices that once spoke to her heart were now absent.

Fawn paused, her pencil hovering over the paper. She lifted her eyes to the palm tree above her—and searched for some sign of comfort.

"Where are you?" she whispered to it, half-expecting it to respond as it always had. But no whisper came from its leaves; no reassuring rustle comforted her. It stood stoic and indifferent against the clear blue sky.

Her eyes fell back to her sketchpad, where only faint lines marred the surface—lines that failed to convey what she felt inside. With a sigh, Fawn closed the pad and hugged it to her chest. The swing creaked beneath her—a sound that normally would have been soothing—but now it seemed like a goodbye.

The low rumble of an engine pulled Fawn from her thoughts. She lifted her gaze just as a white box truck rolled to a stop, the engine's growl ceasing as it stopped in front of her house. The side of the vehicle bore the 'Atlas Manufacturing' logo, its starkness a reminder of her father's workplace and the catalyst for their move. As two men hopped out and headed toward the front door, a weighty realization settled over her. The life she knew in Wavecrest was truly coming to an end.

Fawn carefully tucked her sketchpad and pencil under the swing's faded green cushion—a gesture so familiar, yet now tinged with finality. Her fingers lingered on the fabric, tracing the patterns woven into its weathered threads. But before she could rise, a feeling washed over her—an inexplicable pull that drew her eyes to the street.

She turned her head and saw an old man standing there, his eyes locked onto hers. His attire was simple—a baggy white shirt paired with black slacks—and a black bow tie hung loosely around his neck. His face bore the marks of many years, etched with lines that told stories of joy and sorrow. Despite never having seen him before, Fawn felt an undeniable familiarity in his gaze, one that seemed to stretch back to her earliest memories.

"Who are you?" she whispered into the space between them, her voice filled with a mixture of curiosity and recognition.

The old man's eyes brimmed with warmth and wisdom, yet a veil of sadness shadowed them. He seemed to hear Fawn's quiet plea, and in response, he offered a gentle tilt of his head, accompanied by an attempt at a smile that didn't quite reach his eyes. Despite this, the gesture conveyed a clear message—it was a goodbye from someone who had been watching over her for longer than she had realized.

Fawn watched, transfixed, as he nodded farewell—a silent acknowledgment that spoke volumes. Then he turned and walked away, his movements slow and deliberate. She followed his retreat with her eyes until he faded from view behind tall bushes, disappearing as if he had never been there at all.

In that fleeting interaction, Fawn felt a profound sense of loss, but also gratitude—for whatever role this spirit had played in her life here in Wavecrest. She sat still for a moment on the swing that had held so many dreams and silent wishes under the watchful eye of the palm tree. Then, gathering herself, she stood up to face what lay ahead.

With the old man's departure still casting a shadow in her heart, Fawn walked across the yard toward the front of her house. The crunch of dried grass underfoot was a stark contrast to the softness of the grass she had just left behind. Her eyes were drawn to the small group in the driveway: her mother, father, and grandmother, engaged in what was clearly an intense conversation.

Fawn couldn't hear their words, but the tension in their postures spoke volumes. Grandma Ellington spoke with animated hands, her gestures sharp and emphatic. Brian's jaw was set, his stance firm against the barrage of her disapproval. Anna stood between them, a mediator whose presence did little to soften the edges of their exchange.

As Fawn drew closer, Anna caught sight of her daughter and immediately straightened up. Her voice carried across the driveway as she addressed Fawn's grandmother, "Alright, Mother, that's enough."

The confrontation paused abruptly. Grandma Ellington turned to face Fawn, her expression softening into a mixture of concern and determination. Without missing a beat, she declared, "I'm taking my granddaughter out to lunch."

Brian and Anna exchanged a glance—there was no arguing with Grandma Ellington when she made up her mind. With a protective arm wrapped around Fawn's shoulder, Grandma Ellington steered her toward the car parked at the curb. "C'mon, honey. Let's go get some lunch," she said with a comforting firmness.

Fawn offered a small smile—a gesture that acknowledged her grandmother's intentions. "Okay, Nana," she replied quietly.

As they approached the car, Grandma Ellington opened the passenger door for Fawn and ensured she was settled before sliding into the driver's seat herself. With a final look back at Brian and Anna, who stood watching their departure with mixed emotions painted on their faces, she started the car. The engine hummed to life, breaking through the silence that had settled over them.

As they slowly pulled out of the driveway, Fawn looked out the window at her parents. Brian lifted his hand in a solemn wave while Anna placed a hand over her heart—a silent message of love and reassurance to her daughter.

The car turned onto the street, carrying Fawn and Grandma Ellington away from what had once been home, leaving Brian and Anna in a cloud of exhaust and dust—a symbol of all that was changing and all they were leaving behind.

Once they were out of sight, Anna turned sharply to Brian. Her eyes blazed with a mix of anger and concern as she said, "I hope this is all worth it." Without waiting for a response, she spun on her heel and walked back to the house.

Brian remained where he was, alone in the driveway as the dust settled from his mother-in law and Fawn's departure. He stared after them until they were long gone before he finally allowed himself to move—his expression one of a man burdened by decisions made and those yet to come.

The afternoon sun dipped toward the horizon, casting long shadows on the boardwalk as it approached three o'clock. The smell of saltwater mingled with the scent of fried food from nearby stands. Seagulls cawed overhead, riding the gentle sea breeze that fluttered through the vibrant banners of the arcade. Families and couples strolled by, enjoying the final moments of their summer bliss, oblivious to the bittersweet farewell unfolding amidst them.

Jessica and Ethan walked together toward the parking lot, arms wrapped around each other's waists, their steps measured and heavy with unspoken emotions. Each footfall on the weathered planks was a silent countdown to their imminent separation. The noise of the boardwalk faded into a distant hum against the quiet turmoil that was building inside them.

Ethan's grip tightened as he felt Jessica lean into him, her head resting against his shoulder. He could sense her fear, as tangible as the weight of her body against his. The fear wasn't just about when they would reunite, but was laced with the terrifying possibility of an eternal goodbye. Jessica's heart ached at the thought of a future where Ethan might walk beside another, where her place by his side would be just a memory swallowed by time and distance.

They paused for a moment at the edge of the boardwalk, where the wooden ramp gave way to asphalt. The parking lot lay ahead, an unassuming field of faded lines and sun-bleached tarmac that had become an arena for their unspoken dread.

Hand in hand, Jessica and Ethan descended the ramp and walked toward the patch of grass that was shaded by the old palm tree. The rustle of the fronds whispered of the countless moments they had shared beneath its canopy, a quiet reminder of the love that had blossomed between them.

When they reached the spot, they stood face to face, the world around them fading into the background as they found themselves enveloped in the shadow of the palm. The air was thick with emotion, a tangible presence that weighed heavily upon them. With tears in her eyes, Jessica searched Ethan's face for reassurance, for something to anchor her to the hope that this was not their final chapter.

"I don't want to lose you," she whispered, her voice nearly swallowed by the sounds of the nearby ocean.

Ethan's heart clenched at her words. He reached out and gently cupped her cheek in his hand.

"You won't," he said, his tone steady and sure, though doubt gnawed at the edges of his confidence. The future was a vast, uncharted expanse that threatened to pull them apart.

Jessica's voice trembled as she voiced her deepest fear. "You don't know that. You could meet a girl at college and fall in love with her."

The very thought pierced Ethan's soul. "That's not going to happen, Jess. I love you. You're my girl." His declaration was fierce, a protective barrier against the uncertainties that lay ahead.

Tears began to trickle down Jessica's cheeks, each one a reflection of her vulnerability. "Yeah, right now. But what about next week? Or the week after? Are you still going to love me one year from now?" Her words were a plea for reassurance, a lifeline cast into the churning waters of the future.

Ethan pulled Jessica into his arms, holding her close as if to shield her from the world.

"Jessica, listen to me. I have never felt this way about anyone before, and I never will. I love you with all my heart. You're my soulmate, and I know we can make it work." His voice was a deep rumble against her ear, a solemn vow that echoed in the space between them.

Jessica tilted her head back to meet his gaze, her eyes shining with love and fragile hope. "I love you, too. I'm just scared." Her admission was a soft murmur, a confession of the fears that haunted her dreams.

With the pad of his thumb, Ethan wiped away the tears that stained her cheeks. "Don't be. We'll talk on the phone every day. We'll even video chat. And as soon as I finish school and work things out with my family, we'll be together again." His words were a promise, a beacon of hope amidst the uncertainty ahead.

For a moment, Jessica allowed herself to bask in the warmth of his love. Looking up at him, her innocent blue eyes shimmering with tears, she whispered, "Forever and ever?"

The look on Jessica's face ignited a tender warmth in Ethan's heart, and a gentle smile spread across his lips. "Forever and ever," he replied, his voice steady yet imbued with a deep conviction.

With that promise hanging in the air between them, Ethan pulled Jessica into another embrace. They held each other tight in the shade of the palm tree—two souls clinging to the belief that love could bridge any distance.

Encased in each other's arms, they stood under the old palm tree, their hearts beating in sync with the rhythm of the nearby waves. The world around them seemed to have paused, allowing them this final moment of solace before their lives took them down separate paths.

Ethan's hand tenderly stroked Jessica's hair as she rested her head against his chest, listening to the steady drum of his heart. The symphony of the ocean and the rustling palm fronds above wove a cocoon of peace around them, a brief respite from the turmoil that awaited.

The serenity was suddenly shattered by the unmistakable sound of Ethan's Jeep approaching. They both turned and watched Jake maneuver the vehicle into a parking space, bringing the stark reality of Ethan's looming departure. The moment they had both been dreading, the one that had cast a shadow over their entire summer, had finally arrived, ushering in a wave of profound sadness that threatened to overwhelm them.

Jessica's breath hitched in her throat as she fought back the tears that threatened to spill. She looked up at Ethan, her eyes pleading with him, begging him to stay. But she knew that no amount of wishing or hoping could alter the course they were on. This was a reality they had to face, a separation they had to endure.

Ethan's eyes glistened with unshed tears as he held Jessica's gaze. He could see the silent struggle she was waging against her emotions, which mirrored his own inner turmoil. With a strength that belied the pain in his heart, he pulled her close once more, enveloping her in the warmth of his embrace, a final attempt to shield her from the inevitable farewell.

They stood there, locked in an embrace that seemed to defy time itself. But the world would not stop spinning, and the relentless march of time would not be denied. Reluctantly, Ethan loosened his hold on Jessica and took a step back. His hands trembled slightly as he reached behind his neck, his fingers deftly unfastening the cross that had been his constant companion for years.

The cross, a gift from his grandfather and a symbol of his family's legacy, held more than just sentimental value; it was a talisman that had seen him through the most difficult moments of his life. It was this very symbol of protection and faith that Ethan now chose to entrust to Jessica.

With the cross resting in the palm of his hand, Ethan reached out to Jessica and carefully placed it around her neck. His fingers lingered a moment to make sure the cross was securely fastened before he withdrew.

Jessica's eyes widened in surprise as she beheld the sacred object, a silent question forming in her mind. "What are you doing?" she asked.

Ethan's voice was barely above a whisper as he spoke, his words carrying the weight of his love and devotion. "Keep this with you, Jess. It will keep you safe."

Jessica's hand instinctively reached for the cross, her fingers brushing against the cool metal. She looked down at the necklace that now hung around her neck, the significance of Ethan's gesture settling over her like a comforting blanket. It was more than just a piece of jewelry; it was a tangible reminder of their love, a connection that would transcend the miles that would soon separate them.

Overwhelmed by the depth of his love for her, Jessica's eyes met Ethan's in a silent vow to treasure the cross and all it represented. She clutched the pendant tightly, a lifeline in the tumultuous days ahead.

With a heavy heart, Ethan turned toward the Jeep, each step away from Jessica, a painful reminder of the distance that was about to come between them. He opened the passenger door, the metallic click echoing in the afternoon's stillness. Before stepping inside, he cast one last glance over his shoulder at Jessica, his face a mask of sorrow and longing.

Jessica stood rooted to the spot, her eyes never leaving Ethan's face. She wanted him to stay, to turn back toward her, but she knew that it was a futile wish. All she could do was stand there and watch the man she loved prepare to leave her world.

As Ethan climbed into the Jeep, he kept his eyes on Jessica. Their silent exchange said more than words ever could. There was no need for a dramatic goodbye, no need for empty promises that the winds of change might sweep away. Instead, they had made a pact to let the moment pass and allow time to decide their fate.

The engine roared to life, its familiar sound a painful reminder of the countless adventures they had shared. As Jake pulled out of the parking lot, Ethan's eyes remained locked on Jessica's, drinking in the sight of her one last time. A single tear escaped from the corner of his eye, a silent testament to the depth of his emotions, as the Jeep slowly disappeared.

Jessica's world, once vibrant and filled with the promise of endless summers, crumbled around her as Ethan's Jeep faded into the distance. A deep, hollow emptiness settled in her chest, and she could no longer hold back the flood of emotions that surged within her. Tears streamed down her face, unrestrained and unending. She sank to the ground, her back against the rough bark of the palm tree that had witnessed the blossoming of their love.

With her knees drawn up, Jessica buried her head in her arms, each sob a tremor that shook her slender frame. Her mind was a whirlwind of memories—the sparkle of laughter in Ethan's eyes, the warmth of his hand in hers, and the electric sensation of his lips meeting hers. The recollection of their shared adventures—each joke, each tender moment—was like a sharp knife twisting in her heart.

The scent of his cologne lingered on her clothes, a cruel reminder of the distance that now separated them. It was as if a vital chapter of her life had been ripped away, leaving behind only echoes and shadows.

As she wept beneath the palm tree, Jessica felt a gentle touch on her shoulder. She lifted her tear-streaked face to find Fawn kneeling beside her, eyes filled with empathy and grief. The sight of her best friend—a pillar in her storm-tossed sea—brought a fresh wave of tears.

"Oh, Fawn," Jessica sobbed, her voice breaking as she reached out for her best friend, the one who had been her confidante through all the seasons of life.

Fawn wrapped her arms around Jessica and pulled her close. "I know, Jess," she whispered, her voice thick with emotion. "I know."

As Fawn held Jessica tight against her chest, she felt the raw pain pouring from her shattered heart. Their bond was palpable at this moment—two souls bound by an unbreakable thread woven through years of friendship.

Tears began to spill from Fawn's eyes—not just for Jessica's heartache, but also for the miles that would soon separate them. Her heart ached to know that she wouldn't be there to wipe away Jessica's tears or offer comfort when she needed it most.

Under the old palm tree that had stood sentinel over so many of their memories, Jessica and Fawn clung to each other. Their embrace was not only an offering of solace but also a silent pledge to cherish every second they had together before life pulled them apart.

# Chapter 46

-------------------------------------------------------------

On this Saturday morning in late August, Wavecrest found itself caught in the liminal space between the carefree exuberance of summer and the creeping melancholy of autumn. The once bustling boardwalk, a vibrant tapestry of laughter and the salty tang of the ocean, now wore a forlorn look as the game and food stands began their annual hibernation. One by one, the shutters came down, the lights were turned off, and the rides stood silent, their vibrant colors muted under the graying sky.

Labor Day, the symbolic end of summer, loomed on the horizon, a mere week away. The beaches, once crowded with sun-kissed revelers, now lay empty, the sands littered with the remnants of countless memories. Only the occasional jogger and dog walker traversed the stretch of shoreline, their footprints a temporary etching on the canvas of the beach. The wind carried a new chill, a gentle reminder of the change in seasons to come.

This poignant transition echoed in the lives of Jessica and Fawn, whose last weekend together unfolded in the shadow of their impending departure. For Fawn, Monday morning marked more than just a trip to Boston and the beginning of her college career; it signified the severing of a lifeline—her childhood home in Wavecrest. The walls that once echoed with the laughter of youth would no longer be her home to return to.

For Jessica, the ache of absence was already a palpable presence; Ethan, the boy whose love had become as vital as the air she breathed, had returned to his home in Pine Haven. The void left by his departure was immense, and the three thousand miles that would soon separate her from Fawn only deepened that emptiness. The thought of navigating the vast, uncharted waters of adulthood without the comfort of her best friend's presence by her side was a prospect that filled her with a profound sense of dread.

As the Saturday morning sun cast a golden glow over Wavecrest, the Reese family home stood as a silent witness to the emotional undercurrents of their last weekend together.

519

Once a beacon of joy and laughter, the house now held a quiet solemnity, its rooms filled with the echoes of memories that would all too soon become part of the past.

The weight of the girls' shared sadness hung heavy in the air, a tangible presence that permeated the walls of the home that had been the backdrop for so much of their lives. Yet, amidst the sorrow, there was a sense of reflection—a quiet acknowledgment of the passage of time and the transformative journey that lay ahead for each of them.

In the stillness of this late summer morning, the Reese household stood as a testament to the enduring bond of friendship and the profound impact of change. As the sun continued its ascent into the sky, it heralded the beginning of a weekend that would forever be etched in the hearts of Jessica and Fawn—a weekend of quiet introspection, shared glances and unspoken words.

Jessica's house embraced the morning with a comfortable familiarity, the kitchen filled with the scents of brewed coffee and toasted bread. Fawn, her hair tousled from sleep, sat at the table, her focus on the phone screen, as she munched on a piece of toast. Tom sat across from her, engrossed in the Wavecrest Weekly, the paper softly rustling with each turn of the page. His casual Saturday attire, a stark contrast to his usual work uniform, spoke of a day free from the regimented schedule of the week.

Teresa, clad in a long, pink nightgown that swished as she moved, entered the kitchen. The soft morning light cast a warm glow on her face as she glanced at the empty seat where Jessica usually sat.

"Jessica isn't up yet, huh?" she asked, her voice carrying a maternal mix of concern and understanding.

Fawn looked up from her phone, the glow of the screen illuminating her face in the quiet kitchen. "No, she was up until one o'clock in the morning talking to Ethan," she replied, her voice tinged with empathy for her friend's late-night heartache.

Tom set down his newspaper, his attention shifting from the local news to the conversation at hand. "Well, it's not easy saying goodbye to someone you care about," he said, his voice reflecting the weight of experience. "I remember how hard it was when I had to leave Teresa for my deployment to Iraq."

He turned to his wife, their shared history unspoken but powerfully present between them. "It was tough for both of us, right, hun?"

Teresa nodded, her mind traveling back to those days filled with worry and longing. The memory of counting the days until Tom's return, the sleepless nights spent praying for his safety, came flooding back.

"I remember," she said, her voice soft but steady. "It takes time to adjust, but she'll get through it."

She then turned to Fawn, her gaze warm and reassuring. "Just encourage her to talk about how she's feeling—sometimes that helps more than anything else."

Meeting Teresa's eyes, Fawn placed her phone down, her full attention now on the conversation.

"I will, Mama. I plan to stay by her side all weekend." Her words were a solemn vow, a promise to be the steadfast friend Jessica needed in these tumultuous times.

Teresa's smile was a silent thank you, a mother's gratitude for the young woman's loyalty and the depth of her friendship with Jessica.

Just then, the sound of footsteps echoed from the hallway, followed by the soft creak of the bedroom door. Jessica, her eyes a little puffy from the previous night's tears, stepped into the kitchen, phone in hand. She was wearing an oversized hoodie that draped over her petite frame, the sleeves a little too long, and her hair tousled as if she had just rolled out of bed.

As she stumbled into the kitchen, her bright blue eyes squinted in the morning light. Her eyes found Fawn's, and in that shared look, an unspoken understanding passed between them—this was their last weekend together at Wavecrest, the final chapter in the story of their youth.

As Jessica took her seat next to Fawn, Teresa cheerfully greeted her, "Good morning, sleepy head."

Tom looked up from his paper, a father's concern etched into his features. "Good morning, baby girl," he said, his voice a soothing baritone.

Fawn turned to Jessica with an affectionate smile, the bond between them visible in the softness of her gaze.

Once settled, Jessica tapped her phone, her face lighting up with a grin. "Look what Ethan just sent me," she said, handing the phone to Fawn.

Fawn looked at the photo, her smile widening. "Aw, how sweet," she murmured, the warmth in her voice matching the tender moment captured on the screen.

Teresa leaned in, her curiosity piqued. "Let me see," she insisted, reaching for the phone. Her eyes danced with delight as she took in the image.

Tom, ever the patriarch, held out his hand. "Let me see that," he commanded with a playful twinkle in his eye. He took Jessica's phone and examined the selfie. Ethan's familiar face drew a nod of recognition, but his eyes lingered on the large white house in the background.

"Is that Ethan's house back there?" he asked, his interest piqued.

Jessica nodded, her eyes following the line of Tom's gaze to the building behind Ethan. "Yeah, that's his family's home."

Tom whistled softly, impressed by the scale and grandeur of the property. "They must be quite wealthy," he commented, an undercurrent of surprise in his tone. He looked back at Jessica, his curiosity unsated. "What does his father do for a living?"

Jessica hesitated, her shoulders lifting in a slight shrug. "I'm not really sure," she admitted. "Ethan doesn't like to talk about it much."

She took a deep breath, her expression becoming thoughtful. "All I know is that there's a family business that Ethan's father wants him to take over someday. But Ethan wants no part of it."

Tom's features softened with understanding, his fatherly instincts kicking in. He handed the phone back to Jessica, his eyes meeting hers with a look of sympathy. It was clear he disapproved of the pressure Ethan's father was putting on him, and that unspoken message was evident in his compassionate gaze.

"Would you like for me to make you some eggs?" Teresa asked, her voice pulling Jessica back from the image of Ethan's house.

"No, thank you. I'll just eat the rest of Fawn's toast," Jessica replied as she plucked a slice from Fawn's plate.

"Hey," Fawn protested playfully, her eyes wide with mock indignation. "You brat!"

Jessica grinned, the warmth of humor brightening her somber mood. "You snooze, you lose!" she quipped between chews, her laughter filling the kitchen as Fawn huffed in playful annoyance.

Teresa couldn't help but smile at the girls' playful banter, her maternal heart swelling with affection. She loved these morning rituals, the little, everyday moments that stitched together the fabric of their family life.

"It's okay, Fawn. I'll make you some more toast," she assured her, reaching for the bread.

In response, Jessica stuck her tongue out at Fawn, who laughed and rolled her eyes at the silly gesture.

Tom, smiling at the exchange between 'his girls', raised his cup to take a last sip of his coffee. The rich aroma of the brew filled his senses, a comforting ritual that marked the start of his day. After placing the cup back on the table, he stood up and stretched his back with a slight groan.

"Well, I promised Steve Donovan that I would fix his generator today, so I'm off to Lenny's shop to pick up some parts," he announced, already mentally preparing for the task ahead.

Teresa gently reminded Tom, her voice tinged with concern. "Don't forget. Brian and Anna are leaving for Malibu as soon as the movers finish loading the truck."

Hearing Teresa's words, Tom's demeanor changed. The mention of Brian's name cast a shadow over his usual warmth. He still hadn't come to terms with Brian's decision to move without coming to him first. It was a matter of pride, of friendship, and it stung.

"Yeah, I know," Tom replied, his voice betraying a low rumble of anger he couldn't quite hide. "I'll make sure to see them before they leave."

As Tom made his way to the front door, he kissed Teresa, a soft peck that held years of love and shared understanding. Then he turned to Jessica and Fawn and planted a kiss on their heads as well. With an effort to hide his anger, he teased them, "You two behave yourselves."

Teresa and the girls watched Tom leave the house, the door closing behind him with a soft click. Despite the familiar teasing, they could sense Tom's deep-seated resentment towards Brian for not coming to him first before making such a drastic decision. The air seemed to hold his lingering frustration, a silent echo of the conversations they all had over the summer.

The silence left by Tom's departure hung in the kitchen for a moment before Teresa broke it with her gentle voice. "So, what are your plans for today?" she asked, her eyes moving between Jessica and Fawn.

Fawn looked up, a thoughtful expression on her face. "We're just going to hang out at my house until my parents and Nana leave for Malibu," she explained, her fingers tracing the rim of her coffee cup. "They'll be staying at Nana's house over the weekend."

Jessica paused, her hand hovering in the air with a slice of toast halfway to her mouth. She hadn't quite processed the finality of Fawn's words until that moment.

Fawn continued, unaware of the growing lump in Jessica's throat. "They'll be back on Monday morning at eight to take me to the airport." Her voice was calm, but there was a slight tremor in her hand as she set down her cup.

Jessica let her toast slip from her fingers onto the table, her appetite forgotten. Monday morning—the moment she had been dreading—loomed suddenly before her. Her heart sank at the thought of saying goodbye to Fawn, the person who had been her rock throughout all the highs and lows of their childhood.

Fawn noticed the change in Jessica's demeanor and saw the sad look that had settled over her friend's face. In an instant, Fawn's heart mirrored the feeling. She, too, had been dreading the moment when she would have to say goodbye. Suddenly, the room felt smaller, the air heavier, as the reality of their situation settled over them like a thick blanket.

They sat there for a heartbeat, two best friends caught in a silent exchange of unspoken fears and unshed tears. Their look on their faces spoke volumes, conveying the painful awareness that each moment now brought them one step closer to separation.

Teresa watched the exchange, her heart aching for the girls. She remembered the lingering sting of her own past goodbyes, and how their impact remained long after the words were spoken.

"You girls have been through so much together," she said gently. "But remember, this isn't the end. It's just the start of a new chapter."

Fawn and Jessica remained silent, the weight of the moment pressing down on them. They both knew that no matter the miles or the changes that lay ahead, the bond they shared could not be easily broken. But that knowledge did little to ease the ache of the impending parting.

The clock on the wall ticked on, marking the passage of time, as if urging them to cherish these last moments together in Wavecrest. With each tick, the reality of Monday morning loomed larger, a silent specter at the table with them.

The afternoon sun filtered through the clouds, casting a soft, diffused light over the Reese family's backyard. A warm breeze carried the salty scent of the ocean, rustling the leaves of the palm trees that bordered the property. In the far corner, Tom's work shed stood, its door ajar, revealing a space cluttered with the organized chaos of a man's sanctuary.

Inside, Tom hunched over his workbench, his broad shoulders casting a large shadow on the small generator spread out before him. Various tools lay scattered around the engine, a testament to the work in progress. The rhythmic sound of metal tapping against metal echoed through the shed as Tom methodically tinkered with the generator's innards.

As he worked, his mind wandered to the impending changes in his household. The thought of Jessica leaving for college had been gnawing at him, stirring a mixture of pride and melancholy. The shed had witnessed countless projects and father-daughter moments, from building birdhouses to repairing bikes. Each memory was a treasure he held close, especially now.

"Hey," a voice called from behind him, its familiarity cutting through the steady rhythm of Tom's work.

He turned, squinting slightly as his eyes adjusted to the figure framed in the doorway of his shed. Brian stood there, an awkward silhouette against the bright light of the waning afternoon.

"Hey," Tom replied, his voice colder than the steel he was working on. The air between them grew thick with unspoken tension.

Brian shifted his weight from one foot to the other, the discomfort clear in his posture. He knew the root of it all too well—Tom's disapproval of his decision to sell the house and move his family to Montana.

"I just came by to drop off the weed whacker and the tools you lent me. I put them in your garage," Brian said, attempting to navigate the awkward silence.

"Okay." The word was sharp, a dismissal hanging in the air as Tom turned back to the generator and picked up a wrench, signaling his intention to end the conversation there.

But Brian wasn't ready to leave things as they were. "You're still mad at me for selling the house and moving, aren't you," he ventured, his voice a mix of concern and defiance.

Tom paused, setting the wrench down with deliberate slowness, as he turned to face Brian. His eyes bored into Brian's, a storm brewing in their depths.

"You really want to go there right now?" he asked, the note of anger in his voice now unmistakable.

Brian knew he was treading on thin ice, but the weight of their unspoken conflict was too much to bear in silence.

"Yes, I do. We haven't talked about it since you found out about us moving. I know you're upset, but I think we should at least try to understand each other's perspective before we leave." His voice softened, trying to bridge the gap that had formed between them. After a moment of silence, he added, "After all, Tom, we've been friends for a long time."

Tom's jaw clenched as he stared at Brian, his voice rising with each word. "Friends, you say? Well, I thought we were friends, Brian." His hands gripped the edge of the workbench. "But friends don't just sell their homes and move away without a word."

Brian stood rooted to the spot, his face paling under Tom's scrutiny. The shed felt smaller, the walls closing in as the weight of Tom's anger filled the space.

"And friends don't keep secrets," he continued, his voice heavy with accusation. He shook his head, disbelief etched into the furrows of his brow. "When you first found out that Atlas was closing, you should have told me."

Brian's shoulders slumped, the weight of Tom's accusations bearing down on him. He looked down at his feet, unable to meet Tom's piercing eyes.

"But instead, you took it upon yourself to make this decision without even consulting any of us first—as if our feelings didn't matter."

A pained expression crossed Brian's face, the burden of his decisions manifesting in his defeated posture.

"If you had just told me in May that Atlas was shutting down, I would have rallied our friends, and we would have helped you find a better solution." Tom shook his head, his voice softening, but the disappointment remained. "There was no need to take such a drastic move without letting us step in to help. That's what friends do, Brian."

Brian's eyes flickered with regret, his lips parting as if to speak, but no words came out.

"But no. You panicked, and you let your fear, or maybe your ego, drive your choices. You didn't have to take that job in Montana. You had other options."

Brian's hands fidgeted, his fingers intertwining and then spreading in a nervous dance.

"What options?" he asked, his voice shaky and tinged with desperation as he grappled with the reality of Tom's accusations.

"Atlas was going to give you six months' severance pay if you didn't take the Montana offer, right?" Tom's voice softened, but the edge remained.

A slight nod was Brian's only response, a silent concession to the truth in Tom's words.

"That would've given you ample time to search for something else. And in the unlikely event that you didn't find a job by then, we would have made sure you and your family were taken care of until you did. That's what friends do, Brian. That's what families do."

Brian's jaw tightened, the reality of Tom's words hitting him like a physical blow.

"Our families have always been connected because of our girls." Tom's gaze turned steely again. "Do you think your wife is happy about moving to Montana? What about your daughter—do you think she's excited about leaving Jessica and everything she's ever known behind?"

Brian's eyes filled with tears, the mention of his daughter's pain cutting through him.

"Here's a wake-up call, Brian: they're not!" Tom's voice was a hammer, each word a blow. "For the life of me, I can't wrap my head around why you'd make such a hasty decision without talking to us first."

The silence that followed was thick, broken only by the distant sound of the ocean. Brian swallowed hard, his voice barely audible as he confessed, "You're right. I screwed up." He took a deep breath, trying to steady his voice. "I should have told you right from the start."

Tom's anger subsided slightly, replaced by a hint of understanding as he watched Brian grapple with his regrets.

"But to be honest, I thought I could handle it on my own." Brian's admission was a quiet confession, his eyes downcast. "I did go looking for a new job. I didn't say anything at that time because I didn't want to worry everyone, especially Fawn and Jessica."

Tom's expression softened, the rigid lines of his face relaxing as he considered Brian's struggle.

"But by the time I realized there were no jobs around that would pay me the kind of salary I needed to take care of my family, it was too late." Brian's voice quavered, the weight of his decisions pressing down on him. "I had no choice but to accept the job offer in Montana."

He paused to reflect on his choices, the weight of the moment pressing down on him as he knew how deeply his decision had affected their families.

"I regret making that decision now." Brian's shoulders slumped, a physical manifestation of his remorse. "If I could go back knowing what I know now, I would have handled it differently. I would have stuck it out here and kept looking for a new job."

He paused, reflecting on his choices, the weight of the moment pressing down on him. He exhaled slowly, realizing that staying in Wavecrest would have been the better choice for his family.

"But I guess it's too late for that now." Brian's voice was resigned, accepting the finality of his actions. "It is what it is, and there's nothing I can do about it now."

A heavy silence descended upon the shed once again, as the air grew thick with the weight of what had been said. Brian took a moment to gather his emotions, his face a mixture of sorrow and resolve as he looked up at Tom.

"I'm sorry, Tom. I'm sorry for everything." His apology was heartfelt, a plea for forgiveness. "I just hope we can still be friends."

Tom's features softened for a moment, a glimpse of the camaraderie they once shared.

"I'm still your friend, Brian." His voice was low, tinged with lingering anger. "I'm just not feeling very friendly right now."

Brian gave Tom one last look, his eyes conveying the depth of his regret. "Fair enough," he said, his voice a quiet acceptance of Tom's feelings.

With that, Brian turned and walked away from the shed, leaving Tom alone with his thoughts. The tinge of anger still simmered inside him, but the conversation had brought some closure. He picked up the wrench once more and turned back to the generator, the task at hand a welcome distraction from the emotional turmoil of the day.

The late afternoon sky above 501 Oceanside Ave had turned a brooding shade of gray, and a chill had crept into the air, signaling the approach of evening. The once vibrant hues of a California summer were now subdued, echoing the mood of the scene unfolding in front of the Gaddesden home. The white box truck emblazoned with the Atlas Manufacturing logo stood stark against the drab backdrop, its back doors swung wide open as two movers carried the last of the household items and secured them inside.

Anna's silver Toyota Prius, hitched to the back of the truck, seemed equally ready for the trip to Montana. Its once shiny finish was now dulled by the grayness of the day, the vehicle appearing as if it were bracing itself for the long road ahead.

At the edge of the side yard, sat the old white bench swing. It had always been a beacon of childhood innocence and joy, but now it offered a quiet refuge for Fawn and Jessica, who sat close together, sharing the swing's gentle sway. Jessica's head rested on Fawn's shoulder, her eyes lifting occasionally to watch the movers. The sight of the truck and Fawn's mother's car was a harsh reminder of the reality they faced.

Despite the somber atmosphere that enveloped them, a burst of soft laughter punctuated the quiet as they engaged in one of their favorite childhood games. Fawn's hand moved deftly over the page, the pencil sketching the first lines of a new creation.

"A pumpkin?" Jessica guessed, her voice tinged with a playful challenge as she glanced at the emerging lines on the sketchpad.

Fawn chuckled and shook her head. "No! You can't tell what it is yet. I just started." Her laughter was a warm sound in the cool air, a reminder of the countless afternoons they'd spent just like this, lost in their imaginations.

Jessica watched intently as Fawn's pencil danced across the page, adding layers and curves to the drawing.

"An apple?" she ventured, a hint of mischief in her voice, knowing well that the guess was likely off the mark.

Fawn's grin was infectious as she replied, "It's not a fruit!" The swing creaked under their weight, a familiar and comforting sound amidst the changes around them.

Undeterred, Jessica focused on the sketchpad as Fawn's hand moved with confident strokes, the image slowly taking shape.

"A mouse." Jessica suggested, the absurdity of the guess coaxing a giggle from her lips.

Fawn's laughter joined Jessica's, the sound floating across the yard and briefly overshadowing the drone of the movers' work.

"Nope!" she said, amusement sparkling in her eyes as she continued to draw.

The game on the sketchpad came to an abrupt halt as the metallic clang of the truck's back doors echoed through the quiet neighborhood. Jessica and Fawn turned in unison toward the sound, their eyes landing on the white box truck that had become a symbol of finality. It stood ready, a behemoth poised to transport a life's worth of belongings to a place far from the ocean's embrace.

The engine roared to life, its growl shattering the remnants of their childhood bubble. The girls watched, their hearts sinking, as the truck began its slow departure from the curb. It moved with a certainty that neither of them felt, carrying away the tangible pieces of a past that could now only be revisited in memory.

The scent of exhaust hung in the air, a bitter reminder of the truck's purpose. Jessica's hand found Fawn's, a silent gesture of support that needed no words. The two watched, eyes wide and hearts sinking, as the truck made its way down the street. The void it left behind was palpable, a physical representation of the space that Fawn's absence would soon create in Jessica's life.

As the truck turned the corner and disappeared, a quiet hush fell over the yard. The girls' breaths were shallow, their chests tight with emotion. They sat enveloped in the lingering scent of the truck's passage, a bitter reminder of the reality they now faced.

The house, once a vessel of warmth and love, stood desolate across the neatly trimmed lawn. Its walls, which had echoed with laughter and witnessed countless dreams, now seemed to hold their breath, waiting for a new family.

Fawn's gaze wandered to the side of the house, her eyes lifting to the window of the room that had once been her sanctuary. It was no longer filled with her presence, her art, or her spirit—for it was no longer her bedroom.

Tears welled in Fawn's eyes as she allowed herself to truly see the empty shell that her home had become. It was a tangible loss, the severing of a tie that had anchored her to this place, to these memories, to a version of herself that she would have to leave behind.

In the silence that followed, Jessica and Fawn remained on the old white bench swing, a relic from a time that felt both distant and painfully close. The silence between them was heavy with words yet to be spoken and with goodbyes that loomed on the horizon. The swing, once a symbol of carefree youth, now bore the weight of their shared sorrow, cradling them as they faced the unwelcome embrace of change.

As the last echoes of the moving truck faded into the distance, Anna, Brian, Anna's mother, and Tom and Teresa emerged from the house, their faces etched with the bitter-sweet pain of parting.

Teresa and Anna, whose lives had been intertwined through their daughters' friendship, moved toward each other with open arms. They embraced, a testament to the bond they shared, mothers of children who had grown too quickly. Tears flowed freely, glistening in the light, each drop a memory, a shared laugh, a moment of solace through the years. Now, as their daughters stood on the cusp of adulthood, they faced a future where those shared moments would be few and far between.

With his earlier frustrations with Brian seemingly dissolved in the gravity of the moment, Tom stepped forward. He held out his hand, and Brian took it, their grip firm, the shake lingering. It was more than a gesture of farewell; it was an acknowledgment of the journey they had traveled together as fathers, as friends, as men who had found common ground in the joys and trials of raising their daughters.

On the swing, Jessica and Fawn exchanged a look that needed no words—their sanctuary of youth was now a memory to be cherished. With a quiet resolve, Fawn slipped her sketchpad and pencil under the swing's faded green cushion, an instinctive act born out of years of hiding her drawings from prying eyes. They stood, their movements synchronized in the dance of long-standing friendship, and walked toward their families.

Grandma Ellington, her face a mosaic of pride and sorrow, waved to the girls. "Come here, girls, and give your grandmother a hug goodbye."

Fawn wrapped her arms around her grandmother, feeling the strength and love that had always been a constant in her life.

"Your poppy and I are proud of you, dear. You do well in your new school, and remember, we will always be there for you. You can always come home to us," her grandmother said, her voice a steady anchor.

Fawn managed a small smile through her tears. "Okay, Nana," she replied, her voice thick with emotion.

Jessica stepped into Grandma Ellington's waiting embrace, comforted by the warmth that had always enveloped her in this second home. "That goes for you too, Jessica. Our house is your house. Your poppy and I hope you'll come to visit us someday."

"I will, Nana. Tell Poppy I love him," Jessica promised, the simplicity of her words carrying the weight of her gratitude.

With a final look, Grandma Ellington made her way to Brian's SUV, her departure another thread pulling the fabric of the day to its close.

Anna and Brian approached the girls, their eyes brimming with the pain of goodbye. Anna enfolded Jessica in her arms, her hug a fortress against the uncertainty of the days ahead.

"Have a safe trip, sweetheart. Stay in touch with us, okay?" Anna's voice quivered as she held back her sobs.

Tears streamed down Jessica's cheeks, her voice barely a whisper. "I will, Mama."

Brian's turn came, and he wrapped Jessica in a hug that spoke volumes of his love and pride. "We're going to miss you, Jessica. We love you so much. Keep doing well in school, and always remember... we're only a phone call away."

Jessica clung to Brian, her words muffled against his shoulder. "Thank you, Papa. I love you, too."

Anna's eyes, still glistening from the tears she'd fought to control, searched Fawn's face as she pulled her into a gentle embrace.

"We'll be back on Monday at eight o'clock. Make sure you're ready to go so that we can be at the airport by ten," she said, her voice steady but soft. "Even though our flight leaves at eleven, that will give us plenty of time to get our luggage checked and grab some breakfast."

Fawn nodded against her mother's shoulder, her voice a soft echo, "Okay, Mom."

As they parted, Anna's maternal instincts kicked in, her need to make sure everything was ready for their trip to Boston. "Your suitcase is in the car, right?"

"Yes, Mom, it's in the car," Fawn confirmed, her voice betraying a hint of impatience she couldn't quite hide.

"And you have your backpack, right? We don't want to forget that," Anna continued, her eyes scanning her daughter's eyes.

With a hint of annoyance now coloring her words, Fawn reassured her, "Yes, Mom. I have my backpack." She met her mother's gaze, hoping to convey her readiness without further questioning.

Anna seemed to understand, and with a soft kiss on Fawn's forehead, she turned and joined her mother by the SUV.

Brian stepped forward and wrapped his arms around Fawn in a hug that was meant to convey all the love and regret he felt. Her arms hung loosely at her sides; the warmth she once felt was chilled by the resentment that had wedged itself between them. As they parted, Brian's eyes lingered on his daughter, aware of the coldness that had seeped into her embrace.

"Okay, honey. We'll see you on Monday. Enjoy the rest of your weekend," he said, hoping to bridge the gap just a little.

He turned and walked to the SUV, his shoulders heavy with the weight of his daughter's unspoken words.

As the vehicle came to life, Tom and Teresa stepped closer to the girls. Tom's hand found Fawn's shoulder, pulling her in with a squeeze meant to comfort her. Teresa mirrored the gesture with Jessica, her arms wrapping around her daughter from behind as she planted a kiss atop her head.

They stood together, a silent quartet, as the SUV pulled out of the driveway and onto the street, its departure leaving a palpable void in its wake.

As the engine's sound faded to a distant hum, Tom's voice, thick with emotion, broke the silence. "We'll see you back at the house."

Teresa, her smile forced against the tide of sadness, took Tom's hand, and together, they started the walk back to their home, leaving the girls with their thoughts.

Fawn and Jessica lingered in the driveway, their eyes tracing the outline of the house that had been a home to them both. The pain in their hearts was a mirror to the empty windows staring back at them.

"Goodbye, house," Fawn murmured, the words heavy on her tongue.

Jessica could only nod, her own heart tight with sympathy for her friend's loss.

"Let's get out of here," Fawn said, her voice carrying a finality that echoed the closing of a chapter.

They stepped off the property, the weight of years pressing down on them with each step away from the house that no longer belonged to Fawn. The familiar path to Jessica's house was a path they'd walked a thousand times, yet now it felt different—like a bridge between past and future.

Halfway through their journey, Jessica stopped short, a sudden realization dawning on her. "Hey, Fawn. You forgot your sketchpad. Want me to go get it?"

Fawn paused, her mind racing back to the swing where she'd left it. After a moment, she shook her head. "No, that's okay. I'll get it later." Her voice was quiet, surrendering to the emotion of the moment.

With a shared understanding that some things were best left for another time, the girls continued on their way. The familiar path to Jessica's house offered no comfort, for each step taken was a reminder of the growing distance between their present and their future.

# Chapter 47

-------------------------------------------------------------

The Sunday morning sunlight streamed through the kitchen window, spilling over the breakfast table where Jessica and Fawn sat, a laptop open in front of them. The smell of freshly brewed coffee filled the air, mingling with the aroma of buttered toast and scrambled eggs. Ethan's face appeared on the screen, his smile bridging the distance between Pine Haven and Wavecrest.

"Morning, you two," Ethan's voice was clear, his image a comforting presence.

Jessica leaned in, her reply a soft murmur of affection. "Hey, baby."

Feeling playful, Fawn nudged Jessica aside with a grin, her voice teasing as she chimed in, "Move over. I want to say hi, too!"

Ethan laughed as the screen swayed, the girls' banter a momentary reprieve from the sadness of the impending goodbyes. They exchanged stories and updates, Ethan's eyes holding a gentle concern as he took in their somber expressions. But as the conversation ended, the screen went black, and reality settled back over the kitchen like a blanket.

Tom and Teresa bustled around the kitchen, the familiar rhythm of Sunday morning preparations filling the room. Teresa paused, her suggestion carrying an air of tradition. "Why don't you girls come to church with us this morning? Pastor Bob wants to say goodbye before you leave."

Jessica hesitated, her eyes drifting from the laptop screen to her mother. They hadn't set foot in church all summer, but the thought of seeing Pastor Bob, who had watched them grow up, held a certain appeal.

"I think I'd like that," Jessica finally said, a small smile tugging at her lips. "I have a couple of things I want to ask God about while I'm there."

Fawn nodded in agreement, the idea of church as a distraction from their emotional turmoil a welcome one. "Let's do it," she said, her voice stronger than she felt.

The ride to the church was quiet, each lost in their thoughts. As they entered, the familiar faces of the congregation greeted them, their warmth a stark contrast to the girls' inner turmoil.

While sitting in the pews, Jessica and Fawn tried to immerse themselves in the sermon, but their minds were elsewhere. It wasn't until they slipped into their roles as Sunday school teachers that they found a welcome distraction. Surrounded by eager children, their laughter and innocence pulled Jessica and Fawn away from their concerns, if only for a moment. They let themselves be silly, acting out Bible stories with gusto, drawing giggles and cheers from their young audience.

Pastor Bob's words were a balm, his goodbye a poignant reminder of the new chapters that awaited them. As the service concluded, the girls found themselves surrounded by well-wishers, the support of their community a steadying force amidst the waves of change.

The afternoon stretched out before them, the hours passing in the quiet comfort of Jessica's home. They lounged in the back and front yards, their conversations meandering and punctuated by long silences. The laughter and voices of neighborhood friends drifted over as they stopped by, each goodbye a gentle tug at their hearts.

Dinner time approached, and Teresa, with her innate sense of nurturing, prepared a feast fit for a send-off. The table was set with care, each dish a testament to the countless meals shared in this house. Jessica and Fawn picked at their food, their minds preoccupied with the farewells that were fast approaching.

As the evening shadows grew long, the girls retreated to the solitude of the porch, the world around them quieting as they prepared to face their last night together in Wavecrest.

As the sun began its slow descent over the ocean's horizon, casting a golden glow that seemed to bid farewell to the carefree days of summer, Jessica and Fawn decided to take their last walk on the boardwalk together. The wooden planks beneath their feet were familiar and comforting. The boardwalk stood empty, a silent witness to the changing season, the laughter and footsteps of tourists now a summer memory.

The only sound was the rhythmic lapping of the waves against the shore, a natural symphony that had always been the backdrop to their lives. For the moment, the boardwalk was theirs alone, a private stage for their final duet as children of Wavecrest.

Their footsteps took them to their sacred place, a secluded rock on the beach, where they had shared dreams, secrets, and hopes for years. The rock, warmed by the day's sun, offered a solid foundation beneath them as they took their seats. It was as if the rock itself remembered their last visit in June, the evening Fawn broke the news of her family's impending move.

Now, with the house standing empty and their departure for college mere hours away, the finality of the moment weighed heavily on them. Together, they faced the ocean, the sun's glow now a fiery line on the edge of the world.

Fawn's eyes lingered on the spectacle before them, her voice soft with a tinge of sorrow. "I'm going to miss watching this. It looks so beautiful."

She paused, a quiet sigh escaping her lips. "You know, I've always taken moments like these for granted. But now, knowing that there will be no more sunsets like this for me to see, makes me realize I should have appreciated them more."

Jessica nodded, her heart heavy with her own thoughts. The looming reality of leaving for Austin, of facing a new school without the comfort of familiar faces, tied knots in her stomach. And the distance from Ethan only deepened the pain.

She turned to Fawn, her eyes pleading. "Why don't we just forget about going to college this semester? Let's just stay here instead. We can get a job, save our money, and go to college in Santa Barbara like we originally planned."

Fawn turned to Jessica, her eyes reflecting the desperate hope in her friend's. The suggestion was tempting, a fleeting fantasy that promised to keep their world intact. But the weight of reality pressed down on her, understanding what was at stake.

"You know our parents would kill us if we suddenly changed our mind about going to college," Fawn said with a forced smile. "I mean, look at all the money they spent so that we could go to college."

She looked back at the sun, now just a sliver of light on the edge of the horizon, and collected her thoughts. A heavy weight of sadness laced her words, but determination carried her forward.

"Besides, I want to go to Boston. I want to see what it's like, to see a part of the world I've only seen in pictures." Fawn's eyes wandered, imagining the autumn leaves and the winter snow. "I'm anxious to see what Autumn is really like, to see the leaves change their colors and fall to the ground. And I want to see snow, Jess. I've always wondered what it would be like to throw a snowball and build a snowman."

Jessica listened, her imagination ignited by Fawn's words, allowing herself a moment to picture the wonders of seasons they had never known. Finally, she nodded, understanding and acceptance warming her voice. "I understand, Fawn. I just wish I could go with you."

Fawn reached for Jessica's hand and squeezed it gently. "Me, too, Jess. Me, too."

Together, they turned back toward the horizon, where the sun had almost completely disappeared, surrendering to the embrace of the approaching night. Jessica rested her head on Fawn's shoulder, and they watched in silence as the last light of day dipped below the water, their last sunset in Wavecrest coming to a close.

Night had fallen like a soft shroud over the Reese house, casting long shadows through the windows and muting the vibrant colors of the day. Inside, Jessica and Fawn, fueled by a mix of adrenaline and the bittersweet taste of their last night together, made a pact to stay awake. They would not let sleep steal any of their precious remaining hours before they left for college in the morning.

For the next few hours, they sank into the comfort of the living room couch, surrounded by blankets and pillows that served as their makeshift fortress against the night. The glow from the TV screen flickered across their faces as they watched a couple of their favorite movies, each frame and line infused with memories of sleepovers past.

When Angelina Jolie appeared on screen in "Maleficent," Jessica couldn't help but admire her. "I love Angelina Jolie. She's so beautiful," she said, passing a bowl of popcorn to Fawn.

"Yeah, she has this elegance about her that's just... wow," Fawn agreed, taking a handful of popcorn.

They giggled and quoted lines from the movie, immersing themselves in its fantasy world where good triumphs over evil—a comforting thought on this threshold between their known past and uncertain future.

Later, while watching "Shrek," Fawn couldn't contain her frustration at the grumpy ogre's behavior toward his lovable sidekick.

"Dude, stop being so mean to Donkey!" she scolded the TV. Jessica laughed at her friend's empathy for animated characters—it was classic Fawn, always rooting for friendship and kindness.

As the clock's hands inched toward two a.m., Jessica reached for the remote and clicked off the television. The abrupt darkness seemed to solidify the lateness of the hour; even their whispers seemed too loud in the quiet that followed. With heavy eyelids and yawns they couldn't suppress, they decided to move to Jessica's room—a haven adorned with memories and secrets only best friends share.

Dragging themselves away from the couch's embrace, they stumbled into the room. Jessica flicked on a lamp by her vanity table, casting a warm, comforting glow around her sanctuary of youthful dreams and memories.

"Let me do your hair," Jessica offered with a yawn she tried to hide behind her hand.

Fawn nodded and took her seat at the vanity table. As she watched Jessica's reflection in the mirror braid her hair into an elegant French plait, she couldn't help but admire her friend's skill. "You know, you're really good at this. You should be a hairstylist, like Mama."

Jessica caught Fawn's eyes in the mirror and chuckled softly. "You think so?"

"Yeah, I really do," Fawn said with conviction.

Jessica considered this as she continued to weave strands of Fawn's hair with practiced ease. "Well, I did learn a lot from watching Mom, so maybe."

Fawn watched as Jessica's fingers danced through her hair—so confident and sure. "No maybe, Jess. I'm serious. You're really good at this."

Jessica finished the braid with a flourish and gave Fawn's tail a playful tug—a silent thank you for her faith.

Determined to resist the lure of sleep, Jessica and Fawn decided to make some coffee. They slipped out of the bedroom, their footsteps light on the floor as they followed the familiar path to the kitchen.

As they made their way down the hallway, each step was a whisper against the carpet, a delicate dance designed not to disturb the gentle rhythm of Tom and Teresa's slumber. Their eyes, still heavy with the remnants of drowsiness they fought to banish, remained fixed ahead as they reached the kitchen door.

Fawn reached for the light switch, her fingers hesitating for a fraction of a second before flipping it on. The sudden brightness assaulted their eyes, causing them to squint and shield their faces with raised hands.

With a slight smile warming her features, Fawn turned to Jessica. "Would you like me to do your nails?" she asked, the offer hanging between them like a cherished ritual.

Jessica's smile mirrored Fawn's as she nodded eagerly. "Can you paint butterflies on them?" she asked, hope threading her words.

Fawn's grin broadened at Jessica's request; she knew how much her friend cherished those delicate touches of art on her nails, and she loved painting them.

"Of course," Fawn replied, excitement tinging her voice. "You go ahead and get the coffee started, and I'll go get my brushes and polish."

As Fawn retraced her steps back down the hallway to Jessica's room, Jessica busied herself with measuring out coffee grounds and filling the coffee pot with water. The familiar movements were comforting, even in their current state of limbo between yesterday's childhood and tomorrow's adulthood.

Back in Jessica's bedroom, Fawn crouched down to retrieve her backpack from its resting place on the floor. She hoisted it onto the bed and unzipped it with practiced ease. Her fingers found their way to a thin, rectangular white box neatly tied with a ribbon. Holding it gently with both hands, she allowed herself a momentary smile—a secret nestled within its cardboard walls.

After making sure that Jessica was still busy in the kitchen, Fawn approached Jessica's backpack perched atop the dresser. Her movements were deliberate yet swift as she listened for any sign of disturbance. Satisfied by the continued silence, she unzipped Jessica's bag. Inside were only a laptop and two books—a sign that there was room for whatever Fawn had planned.

With a tenderness that belied her urgency, Fawn slid the mystery box into Jessica's backpack before zipping it shut. She hoped Jessica would discover this parting gift only after they had said their goodbyes.

Returning to her backpack, Fawn retrieved several bottles of colored polish and two fine brushes—the tools of her craft—and made her way back toward the kitchen.

Before leaving the room, Fawn paused for a heartbeat to look back at Jessica's backpack, which now held more than just belongings—it held a piece of Fawn's heart. Her eyes lingered on it, an expression of longing etched onto her face—an unspoken wish for this token to bridge the distance that would soon separate them.

Fawn returned from Jessica's room with her small arsenal of nail polishes and brushes. The aroma of freshly brewed coffee filled the air, a lifeline for the two girls determined to stave off sleep on their last night together.

Jessica sat at the kitchen table, cradling a steaming mug between her hands, watching as the dark liquid swirled within. Fawn set down her artistic arsenal beside her cup and took a seat opposite her friend.

"Ready for your early morning manicure?" Fawn teased, a hint of laughter in her voice as she selected a delicate brush.

Jessica extended her hands across the table, offering her nails as a canvas. "Ready as I'll ever be."

As Fawn painted tiny butterflies on Jessica's nails, a thoughtful expression clouded her features. She broke the comfortable silence that had settled between them.

"You know, I've been thinking about a lot of things lately," Fawn murmured, her focus never wavering from the task at hand.

Jessica tilted her head curiously. "Like what?"

Fawn dipped the brush into a pastel polish, contemplating her next words. "Like, I've been thinking about how I might have overreacted when Jerry called Felix a dork." Her tone carried a weight of introspection. "I know he got mad because he wanted to take me to the dance, but still, I came down on him pretty hard."

Jessica's eyes narrowed slightly, protective instincts flaring for her friend. "That was no reason for him to get mad. You guys aren't even together anymore. He was just being a jerk, as usual. So yeah, he deserved it."

Fawn sighed softly as she finished another butterfly wing with an almost imperceptible shake of her hand. "I know. But I still feel bad about it."

She paused to examine Jessica's nails before continuing. "I mean, up to that point, it felt like we were reconnecting. You should have seen us at the boardwalk, laughing, talking like old times. It almost felt like we were a couple again." A nostalgic smile tugged at her lips despite the confusion in her heart.

"It was nice, Jess," she admitted with vulnerability. "For a little while, it felt like our past just melted away, and we had this chance to start all over again."

Fawn paused, taking a moment to collect her emotions, her brush hovering in the air.

"But when I saw how he reacted when I told him I was going to the dance with Felix... that old arrogance, the way he looked down on Felix... it all came rushing back."

She resumed painting with renewed focus, as if each stroke could help organize her tangled thoughts.

"It's ironic, really. There I was, defending someone who used to be just another face in the crowd to me, and yet, I suddenly felt this surge of—I don't know—protectiveness, I guess." Her voice grew tighter with each word. "And anger. A lot of anger."

Jessica reached across the table and squeezed Fawn's hand reassuringly. "You stood up for Felix because it was the right thing to do," she said firmly. "Jerry needs to grow up. You can't keep making excuses for him, Fawn."

A moment passed before Fawn slowly nodded, acceptance flickering in her eyes as she absorbed Jessica's words.

"I know," Fawn admitted. "But it's hard, Jess." She locked eyes with her—a silent plea for understanding shining through them. "Despite everything, there were these brief moments where I thought maybe Jerry and I..." she trailed off before swallowing hard and admitting in barely more than a whisper, "I thought perhaps there might be a future for us."

Jessica watched Fawn wrestle with feelings she herself couldn't fully understand—a testament to how complex matters of the heart could be.

"You're still in love with him, aren't you," Jessica asked knowingly.

Fawn put down her brush and let out an exhausted sigh that seemed to carry more weight than any confession could hold.

"I don't think I ever stopped loving him," she confessed under the hum of silence that had once again fallen between them—a silence heavy with unspoken feelings and lingering affection. "I don't think I ever will."

Jessica took a moment to absorb Fawn's confession, her own emotions mirroring the melancholy that had settled over the kitchen. She offered Fawn a sympathetic look, her blue eyes reflecting an understanding that only years of friendship could provide.

"I'm so sorry, Fawn. I didn't know you still had feelings for him," Jessica said softly, her voice tinged with sympathy.

Fawn just shrugged her shoulders, a sad smile tugging at the corners of her lips. "Don't be. It's for the best. With Mom and Dad moving to Montana and me going to Boston, it's not like anything could have come of it, anyway." There was a sense of resignation in her words—a mature acknowledgment of their separate paths.

With that, Fawn resumed painting Jessica's nails. Despite the late hour, the kitchen around them felt cozy. Jessica watched affectionately, her heart aching for Fawn's heartbreak but also filled with admiration for her friend's strength and resilience.

And so, in that kitchen, with painted nails and hearts heavy with the gravity of parting ways, they found solace in each other's presence. Each butterfly that emerged on Jessica's nails became a testament to their journey into adulthood—a journey woven with laughter and tears, love lost, love found, and a friendship that endured. These butterflies were more than just delicate creatures adorning Jessica's nails; they were memories crystallized in vibrant colors, a tribute to every challenge they faced and every dream they dared to chase.

In the silence of Jessica's bedroom, where shadows played on the walls and the faint light of a streetlamp filtered through the window, Fawn and Jessica lay side by side, their eyes wide open in the darkness, fixed upon the ceiling where a galaxy of adhesive stars had once glowed.

Fawn's eyes lingered on her favorite star, a beacon that had shone through countless nights, guiding her through sleepovers and heart-to-hearts. But tonight, its glow was gone, just like all the others around it, leaving the ceiling in darkness. Her heart clenched at the sight—each unlit star seemed to mark the end of an era. Their luminosity, like their childhood, had been stolen by the hands of time.

Her eyes moved to the clock on the nightstand—4:15 a.m. The digits glowed red, marking the relentless march toward dawn and her departure. In less than four hours, she would begin her journey to Boston, leaving behind her hometown, her family, and Jessica. The weight of this realization pressed heavily on her heart, a burden she could not shake off.

Her eyes then moved to Jessica's dresser, where Jessica's backpack sat, ready for the trip to Austin. Inside was a white box—a secret addition Fawn had placed there earlier. It was a parting gift, a piece of her heart she hoped would provide solace to Jessica in the days to come.

As Fawn turned her gaze back to the lifeless stars above, her thoughts turned to Felix—and to his life, which seemed so devoid of the warmth and affection she and Jessica had always known. She thought of his father's harshness, his grandmother's cold demeanor, and how, at twelve years old, Felix had lost his mother—the only beacon of love in his turbulent sea. A deep sense of gratitude welled up inside Fawn as she considered her own good fortune.

"You know what, Jess?" she whispered into the quiet room, her voice full of emotion. "We're pretty lucky, you and me. Not only do we have our parents who love us, but we actually have two sets of parents who have always been there for us."

She turned slightly toward Jessica, ensuring each word carried weight. "I know without a shadow of a doubt that Mama and Papa love me like a daughter," she continued. "And I know Mom and Dad love you like a daughter."

A tear escaped down Fawn's cheek as she poured out her heart. "And I'm thankful for that. I'm grateful for having two families who love and support me, and I'm thankful to have a best friend like you who has always been by my side, no matter what."

But as Fawn spoke those heartfelt words, she noticed that Jessica's response was absent—an unusual silence from someone who was always ready with words of comfort or a playful rebuttal. Turning toward Jessica with concern creasing her brow, Fawn found her friend deep in slumber; her eyelids peacefully closed against dreams unknown.

A tender smile graced Fawn's face at the sight—a smile woven from every cherished memory they had shared. No matter how determined Jessica was to stay awake during their many sleepovers, she was always the first to succumb to sleep's embrace, even as their friends remained awake. It was just one of the many traits that endeared Jessica to Fawn's heart, another thread in the fabric of their friendship.

With that affectionate smile still lingering on her lips, Fawn settled back against her pillow. She watched over Jessica now—as much a guardian as a friend—in these final hours before dawn would bring departure and new beginnings.

The quiet hum of the night was Fawn's only company as she lay there, her eyes still fixed on the ceiling where the stars had lost their shine. A sudden sensation startled her, a light pressure landing directly on her chest. She tensed, her mind racing with images of nocturnal critters that might have found their way into Jessica's room. With a swift motion, her hand darted to her chest, her fingers instinctively curling around the unexpected visitor. Holding her breath, she brought her hand closer to her face, afraid of what she might find within the confines of her trembling grasp.

The silence of the room seemed to thicken with anticipation as Fawn cautiously unfurled her fingers. The dim light from the streetlamp outside cast a faint glow over her palm, revealing not the legs of a bug, but a single, silver star. It was an escapee from the constellation above them—a fallen celestial body that had once shimmered alongside its companions on Jessica's ceiling.

A wave of relief washed over her as she realized there was no cause for alarm. She peered at the star nestled in her hand and recognized it immediately—it was her favorite one, the star with the slightly deformed point that had always stood out to her. It felt almost like a message or a sign from the universe itself.

As Fawn delicately traced the contours of the tiny star with her fingertip, she contemplated its journey from the ceiling to her hand. Could it be that this little beacon of light had chosen to accompany her on her journey? It seemed to possess an understanding beyond its inanimate nature—a recognition of Fawn's affection for it despite its imperfection.

Determined to keep the star close to her heart, Fawn rose from the bed and tiptoed over to where her backpack lay on the floor. Crouching down, she opened the pouch and, with a reverence befitting the moment, gently placed the star inside. A smile tugged at the corners of her mouth as she secured it within—this star would travel with her as a treasured keepsake and a reminder of her childhood, a time that had passed by all too quickly.

Rising to her feet, Fawn glanced at Jessica's peaceful form before walking to the window. She looked out into the darkness that stretched beyond the glass—a darkness that would soon give way to dawn's first light.

"What are you doing?" Jessica's voice cut through the silence of the room.

Fawn turned to find Jessica sitting up on the edge of the bed, sleepiness giving way to curiosity in her bright blue eyes.

"Nothing. Go back to sleep," she replied, her voice a gentle whisper.

But Jessica was already shaking off any remnants of sleep as she claimed with mock annoyance, "I wasn't sleeping."

With a playful grin tugging at her lips, Fawn teased back, "Sure, whatever you say, silly girl."

Jessica peeled herself from the comfort of the bed, drawn to the window where Fawn stood. A silhouette against the encroaching dawn, she moved with a grace that belied the heaviness in her heart. Joining Fawn, she reached for the latch with a familiarity born from countless summer nights spent seeking the solace of the ocean's whispers.

With a gentle push, the window swung open, and the cool ocean breeze rushed in to kiss their faces, carrying with it the distant, soothing sound of the Pacific's waves—a lullaby that had cradled them through the years. The early morning mist, a soft veil over the world, seemed to hold the promise of unseen horizons as it caressed their skin.

Fawn wrapped her arm around Jessica, pulling her close. Their shoulders touched, a shared warmth in the cool air, as they gazed out into the misty expanse. The intimacy of the embrace spoke volumes, a silent acknowledgment of the bond that had carried them through every high and low of their young lives.

With heavy hearts, Jessica and Fawn stood together, waiting not only for the dawning of a new day but for the dawning of a whole new world—a world filled with promise, adventure, and change.

# Chapter 48

--------------------------------------------------------

On this morning thirteen years ago, five-year-old Jessica Reese, a tiny, petite figure standing just a little over three feet tall, clung to her mother's hand as they stood at the threshold of the kindergarten classroom. The air was thick with a mixture of anticipation and anxiety, as it was the first day of school for all these children.

With her long, wavy brown hair cascading down her back, Jessica hesitated in the doorway. Her bright blue eyes, shimmering with a blend of wonder and trepidation, flitted from child to child, many of them equally nervous. Every so often, she'd glance back at her mother, her gaze pleading for the comfort of familiarity. Her small stature, combined with those expressive eyes, radiated a poignant sweetness that could melt the heart of any observer.

With the weight of the unfamiliar world pressing down on her, Jessica's eyes began to glisten with tears. Lifting her face to Teresa, her small voice quivered, "Mommy, please don't leave me here."

The raw vulnerability in her plea made Teresa's heart clench in her chest. Every instinct screamed for her to scoop up her daughter and shield her from any distress, but deep down, she understood the importance of this milestone. Swallowing hard, she mustered all her strength to calm her own rising emotions. She crouched down to Jessica's level and gently cupped her face, determined to instill a sense of courage and assurance in her little girl.

"Sweetheart, you have nothing to worry about. I'll be back later to take you home," Teresa said gently, her eyes radiating warmth and love.

The soft and comforting words from Teresa seemed to bring some solace, but Jessica's grip on her mother's hand still remained firm. Drawing Jessica's attention, she pointed towards the children playing, talking, and fidgeting in the classroom.

"See all those kids? This is their first day, too. They're just as nervous as you are. You're going to make a lot of new friends here, I promise."

Jessica blinked a few times, processing her mother's words, and looked back into the classroom. The scene before her took on a different hue as she noticed a boy nervously twirling his hair and a girl clutching a stuffed animal, perhaps seeking comfort. They were, in a sense, all in the same boat.

Just as Jessica was soaking in this realization, a shadow fell over her. Mrs. Engstrom, her new teacher, was approaching them. With soft wrinkles outlining her eyes and a warm, motherly smile, Mrs. Engstrom exuded kindness. But to Jessica, she was still an unfamiliar face, a symbol of the unknown she was about to step into. A pang of fear made her heart race, and she instinctively moved closer to her mother, as if seeking refuge from the uncertainties that lay ahead.

With the kindness that came naturally to her, Mrs. Engstrom leaned down and lowered herself closer to Jessica's level. Her smile radiated a warmth that seemed to penetrate even the thickest of apprehensions.

"You must be Jessica," she remarked, her voice filled with enthusiasm that suggested she had been looking forward to this introduction. "I've been so anxious to meet you." She paused, letting her words sink in, then added, "We're going to have so much fun together and learn lots of new things."

Mrs. Engstrom's words, combined with her gentle demeanor, seemed to chip away at the towering wall of Jessica's fear. The little girl found herself momentarily entranced by the sincere eyes of her new teacher.

Encouraged by this connection, Mrs. Engstrom continued, "Your mommy will be gone for a little while, but before you know it, she'll be back. How about we go inside together and find you a seat next to some new friends?"

Feeling the weight of the impending separation, Jessica turned to her mother. Teresa, sensing her daughter's need for reassurance, enveloped her in a warm, comforting embrace. "Remember, sweetheart, I'll be back later. Enjoy your day, and know that Mrs. Engstrom will take good care of you."

With a gentle confidence, Mrs. Engstrom held out her hand, and Jessica, albeit hesitantly, placed her tiny hand in it. The two began to walk towards the beckoning adventures of the classroom.

Teresa lingered for a moment longer, watching until her precious daughter was no longer in sight. The weight of the moment hit her then, tears spilling from her eyes in a silent testament to the bittersweet pain of watching one's child grow up. With a heavy heart, she left the premises of Wavecrest Elementary School, already counting down the hours until she could hold her baby girl again.

Inside the cheerful, colorful classroom, Mrs. Engstrom carefully assessed the surroundings to find the most comforting spot for Jessica. Her eyes wandered until they settled on a group of four little girls huddled around a large round table near the back of the room.

Hoping this would be an ideal setting for Jessica to gradually warm up, Mrs. Engstrom said cheerfully, "Here we go," her voice imbued with encouraging warmth.

As she led Jessica over, she noticed the lively sparkle in the eyes of the four girls as they took in the newcomer.

"Jessica," Mrs. Engstrom began, her tone tender, trying to ease the palpable nervous energy emanating from the small child beside her. She gestured toward a bright-eyed girl with a freckled face and soft red hair. "This is Allison."

Moving her hand slightly, she introduced the next girl, a mousy-looking child with over-sized glasses that seemed almost too big for her delicate features. "And this is Lily."

She then pointed her finger to a vibrant young girl with short, bouncy brown hair and prominent dimples that flashed whenever she smiled, adding a touch of cheerfulness to the scene. "And here we have Kayla."

Last, her hand rested in the direction of a blonde-haired girl, her playful blue eyes twinkling with mischief. "And this is Fawn."

Throughout the introduction, Jessica remained still, her shyness forming a barrier that kept words of greeting at bay. Her small form seemed to shrink further, a clear sign of her overwhelming nervousness. Recognizing her silence, Mrs. Engstrom gestured towards the only empty chair at the table.

"And girls, this is Jessica," her voice carried a gentle encouragement, nudging Jessica to take the step that marked the beginning of her school journey.

Jessica took her seat, a knot of apprehension tightening in her stomach, her eyes focused on the smooth surface of the table as she tried to escape the curious glances directed at her.

The other girls continued to observe her with a mixture of shyness and curiosity reflected in their innocent eyes. Amid the mutual curiosity, Lily, with her large glasses, broke the silence with a soft, "Hi, Jessica," to which Jessica managed a timid, almost whispery, "Hi" in return.

In the background, Fawn was engrossed in her own thoughts, a spark of empathy kindling in her as she noticed the petite newcomer. Something about Jessica's small frame and bright blue eyes reminded her of her cherished baby dolls, a familiarity that tugged at her childish heart.

Before long, Mrs. Engstrom gathered the children's attention to introduce them to their cubbyholes. "Okay, children. It's time to pick out your cubbyhole. Remember to take the name tag off your shirt and place it above your chosen space," she instructed. Signaling Jessica's table and another occupied by three boys, she continued, "We'll start with these two tables."

Standing in front of the array of cubbyholes, Jessica naturally gravitated toward a lower one. As she positioned her name tag, a sneering voice interrupted, "Hey, teeny-weeny, I want that one!"

Before she could react, a hand shoved her aside. The bratty voice belonged to one boy from the neighboring table. The sudden aggression left Jessica paralyzed with fear, so she backed away.

But before the tears could well up in her eyes, Fawn materialized beside her, a tall figure *of defiance against the boy's aggression.*

*"That's hers! She chose it first!" she asserted, her voice, though small, rang with an unexpected authority.*

*"And her name is Jessica!" Fawn declared firmly, punctuating each word clearly and decisively, her voice brimming with compassion for her new friend.*

*The room held its breath, the tension palpable, until the boy stepped back, startled by Fawn's unexpected aggression. Her firm stance had flustered him, causing him to shrink away in uncertainty.*

*With her name tag in place, Jessica gave Fawn a small nod of appreciation, a simple acknowledgment of her kind act. Fawn, in return, gave a brief smile before continuing with her own tasks, choosing a cubbyhole right next to Jessica's and placing her name tag above it. It was just a fleeting moment in a day filled with new experiences, but it was clear that this event would leave an indelible mark on both their memories.*

*As the morning unfolded, Jessica began to settle into her new surroundings. The company of the four girls, with their shared activities of coloring and puzzle-solving, brought a semblance of comfort that buffered her initial apprehensions.*

*Mrs. Engstrom orchestrated intermittent breaks from their table activities to acquaint the children with the various niches within the classroom. Jessica's eyes widened with childlike wonder when she saw the make-believe kitchen, its array of pretend appliances, inviting her to step into a world of imaginative play.*

*Fawn, on the other hand, was enchanted when the group reached the art center. The shelves brimming with crayons, colored pencils, and an assortment of other art supplies seemed like a rainbow of opportunities, beckoning her to craft her fantasies into tangible forms. The sight ignited a latent spark within her, laying the foundation for a lifelong love for art.*

*Lunchtime brought a welcome break, and soon, the children were enjoying a meal of cheese pizza, fresh salad, and slices of vibrant oranges. They gathered around their familiar table, the atmosphere light and filled with the curious observations and questions typical of their age.*

*Allison, with a hint of innocent curiosity, turned to Jessica with a question that had been lingering in her mind, "Why are you so little?"*

*Jessica felt a blush creep across her cheeks, the directness of the question catching her off guard. Gathering herself, she echoed the explanation her mother had once given her. "Because God made me this way," she murmured, her voice tinged with shyness.*

*Before the conversation could deepen, Fawn, ever the protector, quickly intervened. "Why do you have freckles?" she countered, addressing Allison.*

*This diversion elicited a chorus of giggles from Lily and Kayla. Caught off guard, Allison lowered her head, a little flustered, and murmured, "I don't know."*

*Fawn's intervention earned her a thankful smile from Jessica, who felt protected by her* new friend's aura. Turning to Jessica, Fawn said simply, "You're lucky. I wish I was shorter."

"You do?" Jessica tilted her head, her tiny voice piping with innocent wonder. "How come?"

Fawn looked shyly down at the floor. "Because I'm taller than most kids my age. It makes me feel different sometimes," she mumbled, her cheeks turning pink.

Eager to reassure her new friend, Jessica said, "But that's okay! God made you that way, too."

A small smile curled Fawn's lips as she considered Jessica's words. "Yeah, you're right," she agreed. "God made us all special."

The mutual exchange of understanding and acceptance was clear, as both girls recognized and celebrated the beauty of their individualities.

In that small circle, amidst giggles and shared slices of oranges, a beautiful friendship blossomed. With smiles exchanged and an unspoken pledge of mutual respect, Jessica and Fawn laid the very first, and most significant brick in the foundation of a friendship that promised to stand the test of time. It was a bond that would only deepen, weaving them together in a tapestry of shared experiences and mutual affection—a thread connecting two souls who saw beyond appearances into the beautiful core of each other's being.

As lunch ended and the clatter of trays subsided, Mrs. Engstrom's cheerful voice echoed through the room, heralding the transition to the next activity. "Okay, children. Let's go outside and get some fresh air," she announced, her voice tinged with an encouraging lilt.

The children, buoyed by her enthusiasm, quickly formed a line as they were led to the playground, where the early afternoon sun lavished the area with a warm glow, and the late August breeze playfully flirted with their hair.

At first, Jessica remained a silent sentinel, her petite figure set slightly apart from the chaotic swirl of activity as her classmates descended upon the playground equipment with unbridled glee. Her big blue eyes watched, a mix of longing and apprehension dancing within them.

Lily, her spirit as fluttery as the swing she had been on, caught sight of Jessica's solitude. Seeing the girl standing alone, she felt sorry for her and wanted to offer comfort. The swing's motion slowly stopped, its final arc punctuated by a soft thud as Lily's feet hit the ground. With a heartfelt compassion shining in her eyes, she made her way to the quiet girl.

She took a moment to gauge Jessica's mood before suggesting, "Come swing with us."

Jessica responded with a reluctant shake of her head, her shyness holding her back from the beckoning play.

Reading the situation with a tender heart, Lily declared with determination and kindness, "Then I'll stay here with you." Her words, sincere and gentle, wrapped around Jessica, providing a comforting embrace without the need for any physical touch.

Not long after, Kayla's curiosity guided her to where Jessica and Lily were standing. "What's the matter?" she asked.

Lily, her voice gentle and sweet, replied, "Nothing. I just want to be here with Jessica."

Sensing the solidarity between the two, Kayla nodded and said, "Okay, I'll stay here, too." Their conversation was quiet, filled with the undertones of a blossoming friendship.

As they talked, Fawn was busy demonstrating her adventurous nature by hanging upside down on the monkey bars. From her inverted position, she noticed Jessica standing with Lily and Kayla. Sensing a moment to assert her protective side, she agilely dropped to her feet and made a purposeful beeline toward the trio, her protective instincts already homing in on Jessica's timidity.

Fawn's hand found its way into Jessica's, their fingers intertwining in a warm embrace that seemed to transfer courage and camaraderie with a simple touch. "Come on, Jessica. Let's play on the swing," Fawn suggested, her voice a soothing melody that calmed the smaller girl's tumultuous sea of nerves.

The hesitant look that clouded Jessica's features slowly lifted as she met Fawn's eyes. "I won't push you too high," Fawn promised, seeing the uncertainty in Jessica's eyes. That promise, combined with Fawn's reassuring presence, replaced Jessica's hesitance with a tentative sparkle of trust.

As Jessica settled onto the swing, a newfound excitement stirred within her. Fawn's hands gently pushed the swing, coaxing Jessica into the rhythm of the motion.

"Higher," Jessica said, her voice barely rising above the playground's symphony of laughter and playful shouts.

Fawn responded with another gentle push, careful to not go too far. With the wind caressing her face and Fawn's presence behind her, Jessica's apprehension began to melt away.

"Higher," she requested again, her voice more confident this time. Each upward swing seemed to peel away her layers of fear, revealing the joyous spirit within. Fawn giggled, pushing her newfound friend with increased vigor, their bond echoing with each laughter-filled moment.

Their laughter mingled with the summer breeze, becoming a harmonious duet that sang of friendship and newfound freedom. But as all beautiful moments tend to do, it came to an end with Mrs. Engstrom's call, pulling them back to the structure of the classroom. Yet, as they walked hand in hand toward the building, their shared smiles were a silent promise, a vow of a friendship that had only just begun to bloom, painting a beautiful tableau of innocence and camaraderie in the golden hues of the warm summer afternoon.

The classroom buzzed with activity as the children returned from the playground, their faces flushed from their outdoor adventures. Mrs. Engstrom, a pillar of calm amidst the swirl of energy, raised her voice gently yet authoritatively.

"It's time to rest, children," she announced. She then gestured toward a small bookcase in the reading area, its shelves lined with a variety of books. "Go find a comfortable spot to relax, take a nap, or read a book," she continued. The purpose was clear: this was to be their quiet time, a chance for her students to recharge.

*The classroom became a flurry of movement as the children scattered, each seeking their ideal rest spot. Among them, Fawn reached out and intertwined her fingers with Jessica's. The two girls headed purposefully toward the coat closet. There, they each pulled out a small green mat, their shared mission evident in their synchronized movements.*

*With mats in hand, they scouted the room for the perfect location. They settled on an unoccupied spot toward the back of the classroom, away from the soft hum of the others. Side by side, they laid down, the cool mats beneath them a stark contrast to the sun-warmed playground outside. Their eyes drifted upward to the expanse of the ceiling.*

*The rest of the room began to melt away, the noises dimming as the two girls entered their shared bubble of peace. A mischievous twinkle flickered in Fawn's eyes as she looked at Jessica. Suppressing a giggle, she whispered, "Shh."*

*Catching onto Fawn's playful mood, Jessica responded with a giggle of her own. Their shared secret? Neither had any intention of taking a nap.*

*Moments flowed into one another as the two friends lay there, staring at the ceiling. Then Jessica turned her face towards Fawn, a hint of pride evident in her whisper. "There are stars on my ceiling," she shared, her voice filled with wonder.*

*Fawn's eyes widened in amazement, her head pivoting to meet Jessica's gaze. "Really?" she breathed out, the single word heavy with curiosity.*

*Jessica's nod was accompanied by another whisper. "Uh-huh. My daddy put them there."*

*Lost in the magic of the moment and imagining a night sky in her own room, Fawn could only muster a hushed, "Wow."*

*Time seemed to stand still as the two girls lay there, their whispers painting vivid daydreams that floated up to join the imagined stars on Jessica's bedroom ceiling.*

*Minutes passed as the children rested, allowing the hum of activity in the room to fade. When their brief respite ended, Mrs. Engstrom's voice beckoned them to gather for Circle Time. Their colorful sanctuary, the large rug, seemed all the more vibrant as they took their positions, the patterns reflecting the diversity of their personalities. Amidst the gentle chaos, Jessica deliberately placed herself next to Fawn.*

*With practiced ease, Mrs. Engstrom's fingers selected a book from the shelf, its cover attracting many curious eyes. She paused, allowing a moment of suspense before posing her question: "Has anyone here seen snow?"*

*Her raised hand was both an example and a testament to her own snowy escapades. The question was met with a sea of blank expressions, particularly notable between Jessica and Fawn. Reveling in their curiosity, Mrs. Engstrom declared, "Well, today we're going to learn about snow," as she revealed her selection, "The Snowy Day by Ezra Jack Keats."*

*Wavecrest's Mediterranean air had never embraced snow, making this reading even more enchanting. As the story of Peter's winter adventures unfolded, Jessica and Fawn, sitting side by side, became increasingly engrossed. Jessica imagined how magical it would feel to catch falling snow on her tongue, while Fawn envisioned herself sledding faster than any of the* neighborhood kids. Their reality, a stark contrast to the illustrations, led to playful whispers. "He looks like a spaceman!" Fawn remarked upon seeing Peter in his snowsuit, drawing a suppressed giggle from Jessica.

Each of Peter's snowy exploits made Jessica and Fawn feel like they were right there with him. The thrill of his sled ride, the heartache of his melted snowball—they lived it all. The classroom atmosphere, already thick with anticipation, grew even more intense as Peter's tale unfolded.

As Mrs. Engstrom brought the narrative journey to a close, the soft rustle of the book closing seemed to echo in the hushed room. Jessica met Fawn's eager eyes, and together, they sighed, a harmonious sound that encapsulated their longings and dreams. In that moment, they were transported into a world where they could feel the crunch of snow underfoot, their laughter echoing as they built snowmen together, leaving playful tracks in a pristine blanket of snow.

With an almost reverential tone, Jessica leaned in close to Fawn, her bright blue eyes pooling with a shimmering hope as she whispered, "I wish with all my heart that it would snow here." It was a wish pulled from the very depths of her youthful spirit, saturated with the longing to experience the magical wonders of snow.

Fawn responded in kind, her voice brimming with fervency, her face blossoming into a warm hue that mirrored her excitement.

"Me too!" she echoed, the sincerity in her voice resonating deeply within Jessica. There was a palpable connection, a shared yearning that seemed to bind them together in that singular moment of heartfelt desire.

The burgeoning atmosphere of hope seemed to infuse Jessica with a newfound determination. "Let's close our eyes and wish really, really hard for snow," she suggested, her voice tinged with hope and a hint of magic.

Fawn quickly embraced the idea, her spirit soaring with anticipation. "Yes, let's pretend it's snowing right now!" she exclaimed, her eyes already squeezed shut, her face a canvas of eager concentration and hopeful wishing. The two of them sat there, a picture of youthful optimism, their brows furrowed in intense concentration, hands clenched as if holding onto their wish, willing it into existence.

Their fervent display did not go unnoticed. Mrs. Engstrom observed them with a gentle, knowing smile. The air seemed charged with a kind of magic as she gently inquired, "Fawn, Jessica, what are you up to over there?" Her voice was soft, filled with affection and curiosity.

Caught in the act, Jessica's eyes fluttered open, her face momentarily marred with worry, fearing that they might have done something wrong. But Fawn, buoyed by their shared wish, confidently revealed, "We're wishing for snow!" The declaration seemed to reverberate, vibrating with a powerful mix of hope and longing.

Jessica's initial nervousness melted away as quickly as it had appeared. Her face changed, taking on an angelic smile that seemed to light up her face, reflecting the glowing ember of hope that resided within her. A hopeful nod followed, as if to underscore the weight of their shared wish.

Their innocent wish seemed to magnetize Mrs. Engstrom, who grinned widely, her heart touched by their genuine longing.

"Fawn and Jessica want it to snow here in Wavecrest," she announced, her voice adopting a conspiratorial tone that seemed to echo their wishes. "Who else wants to see snow?"

The question ignited a flurry of activity as a sea of tiny hands shot up, their voices overlapping in a chorus of agreement. "Me!" "And me!" "I do!" The room transformed into a haven of bouncing bodies and beaming faces, each child infused with a feverish anticipation at the prospect of a snow-filled wonderland in Wavecrest.

Embracing the infectious energy, Mrs. Engstrom rallied her troops, her voice tinged with a playful seriousness. "Alright, let's all wish for that special icy magic together."

As if on cue, a synchronized movement of scrunching eyes filled the room, with each child pouring their very being into the wish, a fervent hope that seemed to transcend reality and unite them in a common dream.

In the midst of this beautiful display, even Mrs. Engstrom succumbed, her eyes closing as she joined her students in their wish, her heart heavy with a touch of sadness, knowing the reality of their Mediterranean climate. Yet, in that magical moment, she allowed herself to dream with them, to believe in the beauty of their innocent wishes, even if it was just for a fleeting moment in time.

The late afternoon sun bathed the school's hallway in a soft amber glow. Parents buzzed around with a mixture of anxiety and anticipation as they looked for their little ones, all eager to hear stories of their child's first day of kindergarten. The air filled with the murmur of conversation and the distant sounds of children laughing and talking.

Teresa, though part of this atmosphere, felt slightly distanced from it all. The weight of the morning's emotional goodbye to Jessica was still fresh. Every step she took on the polished floor felt heavy, echoing her anxiety. Each classroom she passed filled her with both hope and apprehension; would Jessica be happy? Did she make friends? Is she okay?

The vibrant colors of the kindergarten classroom spilled into the hallway, capturing Teresa's attention as she neared. The walls adorned with children's art, the tiny chairs around small round tables, and the array of crayons and papers scattered about suggested an eventful day. But what really eased Teresa's worries was the sight of her daughter, Jessica, with her dark hair falling gently over her face, deeply engrossed in her drawing. Right next to her sat another child, her golden locks shimmering in the room's light, both of them lost in a world of colors.

While Teresa was lost in this sight, someone else stood nearby, also peering into the classroom. A woman, slightly taller than Teresa, with soft dark blonde waves that touched her shoulders, seemed equally transfixed by the scene inside. Her features lit up with the gentle pride that only a mother could wear.

*"Look at that little girl,"* she said fondly, pointing to Jessica. *"Isn't she adorable?"*

Teresa couldn't help but smile as she heard the woman complimenting her daughter. With a hint of pride in her voice, she proudly proclaimed, *"Aw, thank you. That's my Jessica."*

Raising her eyebrows in surprise, the woman replied, *"Really?"* And then, with the same enthusiastic voice, she announced, *"That's my Fawn sitting next to her."*

With that said, both women turned their attention back to their daughters and watched them color. As they watched the girls exchange smiles and giggles as they worked their crayons, Teresa's eyes sparkled with relief. *"They seem to be getting along well. I was so worried this morning."* Her voice trailed off as she remembered the morning's anxiety.

The woman nodded, her eyes softening. *"I know exactly what you mean. First days can be so tough."* She shot a quick glance at the two girls, adding, *"But it looks like they've found a friend in each other."*

With a deep breath and a satisfied sigh, she turned to Fawn's mother with a bright smile. *"By the way, I'm Teresa."*

The woman's face broke into a warm, inviting grin. *"It's a pleasure, Teresa. I'm Anna."*

Teresa's head tilted, curiosity in her eyes. *"It's nice to meet you, Anna. Do you live nearby?"*

Anna chuckled, a playful twinkle in her eyes. *"Oh, not too far. We live on Oceanside Avenue."*

Recognition flashed across Teresa's face, her surprise obvious. *"Really? We're on Driftwood Drive."*

Anna's brows rose in delighted astonishment, her lips parting in a cheerful exclamation. *"Seriously? That's just around the corner! Looks like we're practically neighbors!"*

Their conversation flowed naturally, much like the relaxed waves that caressed the shores of their neighboring streets. It was clear from their exchange that destiny had intertwined their paths. The day that started with anxiety for Teresa ended with the promise of a new friendship.

The end of the day bell punctuated the classroom atmosphere, echoing the frenzied energy that only the culmination of a school day can induce. As the children erupted into chatter, Mrs. Engstrom directed them toward the bus line, ensuring an orderly dismissal. Yet, amidst the buzz, two pairs of bright eyes fixed upon the doorway, where two mothers awaited their little ones.

Jessica and Fawn's faces instantly lit up when they saw them. The sheer joy in their eyes made the trepidation of the early morning a distant memory. Jessica's enthusiasm bubbled over as she exclaimed, *"Mommy! Mommy!"* Grabbing Fawn's hand, they sprinted toward the door, their little feet pounding on the classroom floor.

Teresa and Anna stood side by side, their hearts warmed by the sight of their daughters racing towards them. The innocence and joy of the moment were not lost on either mother.

Pausing for a moment, Jessica introduced her new friend. *"This is Fawn! She's my friend!"* Her voice carried the unmistakable pride and excitement of someone who had just made her *very first friend.*

*In a similar burst of excitement, Fawn affirmed, "She's my friend too, Mommy!"*

*Both mothers exchanged knowing glances, their smiles mirroring each other's. "We can see that," Teresa replied, her pride evident.*

*Sensing the waning sunlight and the ticking clock, Anna gently reminded her daughter, "We have to go home now, baby. Daddy will be home soon, and he'll want to hear all about your first day of school."*

*As if on cue, Fawn and Jessica's jubilation gave way to a quiet disappointment. Their faces, once brimming with smiles, now sported adorable pouts. "Oh, do we have to?" Fawn's voice echoed the sentiment shared by both.*

*Jessica, employing her best persuasive voice, chimed in. "Please? Please? Please, Mommy? Can we stay a little longer?"*

*Teresa, ever the loving mother, smoothed Jessica's hair, her fingers dancing over her daughter's delicate strands. "We have to go too, sweetheart. But don't worry, you'll see Fawn tomorrow," she assured her.*

*Anna nodded in agreement and murmured, "Say goodbye, Fawn. You'll see Jessica at school tomorrow."*

*Accepting the inevitable, Jessica and Fawn stepped closer, their small arms wrapping around each other in a tender hug. The sight of their little heads nestled against each other's shoulders, their eyes closed in the warmth of the moment, was a pure depiction of childhood innocence and affection. The sight was so touching, it seemed to slow time itself. Both Teresa and Anna found themselves momentarily captivated, their hearts swelling with emotion, as they appreciated the profound bond their daughters were beginning to build.*

*Leading their girls by hand, Teresa and Anna exited the school, their footsteps echoing in the quiet hallway. Once outside, their paths diverged, each heading toward their respective cars. As they drove off, Jessica caught a glimpse of Fawn through the window. Their eyes locked for the last time that day, holding the promise of countless adventures yet to come. In that fleeting moment, the beauty of a new friendship shone brightly between them.*

On this morning, the sky over Jessica's house wore a gloomy white shroud, with patches of dark gray clouds scattered like blemishes across its expanse. A cool, strong breeze rolled off the ocean, bringing with it a chill that seeped into the morning air. It was a little before eight o'clock, and the world seemed to hold its breath in silence before the day truly began.

Fawn sat on the front step, crouched with her knees pulled up to her chest. Her pink hoodie and ripped jeans were a stark contrast to the somber mood. She crossed her arms over her knees and rested her head on them, her posture resembling a sculpture of contemplation. Her blue eyes, usually vibrant with life, now bore the weight of sleeplessness and the sting of tears shed during the tearful goodbye she had shared with Teresa and Tom just minutes ago.

Sitting next to Fawn, Jessica was equally exhausted. She wore a blue windbreaker that fluttered in the breeze and black sweatpants gathered at her ankles. Unlike Fawn, Jessica sat upright, her eyes wide as they wandered over the landscape before her. The houses, the streets, and the very air around them seemed to echo with the memories of summers past.

The mood between them was thick with dread and anxiety. They knew that in a few short minutes, Fawn's parents would arrive to take Fawn to the airport. The inevitability of their parting loomed over them like the heavy clouds above—dark and oppressive. It was a moment suspended in time, their shared history as palpable as the salt in the air but as intangible as the wind that whipped around them.

Jessica's mind, a whirlpool of sorrow and nostalgia, clung desperately to the slivers of light that memories provided. Her gaze was distant, lost in the past as she recalled a conversation they had at Fawn's house just two days after their high school graduation. In the golden light of a summer afternoon, they sat in Fawn's living room, laughing and painting nails as they confronted the bittersweet reality of their separate paths ahead. It was there, amid their shared history, that Fawn's words had offered a beacon of hope:

*"And next summer? We'll be right back here after finishing our first year in college, just like always."*

Those words had given Jessica enough courage to face the uncertainty of their new journeys, a poignant reminder of the bond that promised to endure the trials of time and distance. She turned to face Fawn, a glimmer of hope in her eyes.

"You're coming back here next summer, right?" Jessica asked, clinging to the memory as if it were a lifeline. "Remember when you said that we'll both be back here next summer after finishing our first year in college?"

Fawn lifted her head, her braided blonde hair stirring slightly in the morning breeze. The memory was clear as day—a snapshot of a time when their biggest worry was which beach to choose for their next adventure. The world of Wavecrest had seemed unbreakable then, an unyielding fortress against the tides of change. On that day, she had been blissfully unaware of the impending sale of her family home, or of the upheaval that lay ahead.

But now reality stretched before her like an uncharted map. Her ties to Wavecrest were severed; Montana beckoned with unfamiliarity, and Boston promised nothing but hard work and canvases yet to be filled. The thought of next summer was a mirage on a horizon clouded by responsibilities and adulthood's relentless march.

With Jessica's hopeful words hanging between them, Fawn's mind raced. She searched for the words that would soften the blow, words that would not betray the truth of her uncertainty. She had always been honest with Jessica, and she would not abandon that truth now, even if it meant revealing the harsh reality that next summer was a horizon too distant to see.

But before she could speak, the sound of an approaching car pierced the quiet morning. Both girls turned toward the noise, watching as Brian's SUV rolled into view. The moment they had both dreaded had arrived—their final goodbye was upon them. They looked at each other once more, their eyes glistening with tears that mirrored the pain in their hearts.

The SUV rolled to a stop in front of Jessica's house, its presence an unwelcome signal of finality. Fawn hesitated, the weight of the moment anchoring her to the step. She glanced at Jessica, her blue eyes swimming with unshed tears, then at the vehicle that would take her away from everything familiar. With a deep breath that did little to steady her trembling hands, Fawn grabbed her backpack and rose to her feet.

Jessica followed suit and stood as Fawn began her walk to the SUV. She followed her friend, a silent sentinel, until she reached the end of the sidewalk. She watched as Fawn, with a movement that spoke of reluctant acceptance, opened the back door and tossed her backpack inside. She lingered for a second, her back to Jessica, as if gathering the strength to face her friend one last time.

Turning around, Fawn walked over to Jessica, and for a long moment, they faced each other. No words were spoken; none were needed. It was as if they were engraving the image of each other into their memories, a mental photograph for the days when they longed to be in each other's company. Their faces, marked by trails of dried tears and the pallor of sorrow, betrayed the pain they both felt yet tried to conceal.

They had made a pact, promising each other that there would be no tears, no crying. They would be strong, brave—unyielding in the face of this separation.

As Fawn struggled to maintain her composure, she found her voice, though it trembled with the effort of restraint. "I'll call you when I get settled in. You do the same, okay?"

Jessica's face contorted as she tried to hold back a fresh wave of tears. She had vowed not to cry in front of Fawn, to remain stoic, a pillar of strength. But her emotions were churning inside her like a storm within her, threatening to break through her carefully constructed dam.

Unable to trust her voice, she replied with a firm nod, the gesture sharp against the tension of her clenched jaw. Words were beyond her, each one a potential trigger for the tears she fought so hard to contain.

Time seemed to stretch and contract as they stood there, wrapped in a silence heavy with unspoken words. Finally, Fawn pulled Jessica into an embrace—a hug that carried with it the weight of shared childhoods, whispered secrets under starry skies, and dreams nurtured side by side. They held each other close, hearts beating in tandem, reluctant to let go.

When they finally separated, tears began to stream down both their faces. The flood-gates had breached despite their resolve. Fawn placed her hands on Jessica's shoulders, her grip a lifeline as she mustered the strength to speak the words that had always been a source of encouragement. "You got this, Jess," she whispered with an assurance that belied her trembling lips.

Jessica's face creased again, her battle with her emotions almost lost. She could only nod, her eyes swimming with tears that blurred her vision.

With one last attempt at a smile, Fawn turned and stepped into the SUV, the click of the closing door resonating like a period at the end of a significant chapter. When the vehicle pulled away, Jessica and Fawn's eyes locked, holding a silent conversation of love and longing—until the turn on the street tore their gaze apart.

Jessica stood alone on the sidewalk at the edge of the street, her eyes locked on where Fawn had disappeared from sight. The world seemed to stand still, the wind holding its breath, the ocean's whisper falling silent. It was then that she allowed herself to cry—the sobs coming hard and fast—as an emptiness engulfed her like never before.

For the first time in her life, Jessica felt truly alone and abandoned. The pain was so deep, so all-consuming, that it clawed at her chest, taking her breath away. She stood there, tears streaming down her cheeks, grappling with a loneliness that felt as vast as the ocean itself.

# Chapter 49

--------------------------------------------------------

Time ticked away in the Reese kitchen, the low hum of the refrigerator the only companion to Jessica's loneliness. She sat at the kitchen table, her fingers tracing the grain of the wood, her mind adrift in a sea of tumultuous emotions. Two hours had passed since Fawn's departure, but the weight of her absence pressed down on Jessica like hours of relentless waves.

Her eyes, still puffy from tears, scanned the room where countless memories danced in the muted light streaming through the window. This kitchen had been a sanctuary of laughter, silly banter over steaming cups of cocoa, and plans for a future that seemed so certain just a couple of months ago. Now, it felt like an echo chamber for her swirling thoughts.

Jessica's heart ached for Ethan, whose recent absence left a void no phone call could fill. Their connection was now stretched across miles, and the cold screen of her phone was a poor substitute for his warm embrace. With each passing day, the silence grew louder, and she couldn't help but wonder if their love would withstand the test of distance and time.

The room around her was a stark reminder of the disbanding of her circle of friends, the people who had been her anchors. They had ventured out to forge their paths, leaving Jessica to face the impending journey to Austin—a path she had chosen but now questioned. The fear of navigating it alone overshadowed the thrill of independence that college promised.

Her fingers paused on a scratch on the table, a battle scar from one of Fawn's art projects, when she accidentally gouged the wood with a pair of scissors. It was a testament to the carefree days of her youth, a time when her biggest worry was convincing her parents to extend her curfew. How she longed for that simplicity now, as the complexities of adulthood loomed before her.

Jessica exhaled, her breath fogging the surface of the table, and she watched as it slowly dissipated—much like the presence of her friends in Wavecrest. The nostalgia for those bygone days mingled with trepidation for what lay ahead. Could she truly leave behind the crashing waves and sandy shores that were as much a part of her as her heartbeat?

She rose from the table and moved to the window, pressing her forehead against the cool glass. Outside, the palm trees swayed, indifferent to her inner turmoil. Jessica closed her eyes, summoning the courage that Fawn had always inspired in her. But even as she tried to steady her resolve, the whispering doubts returned, and she couldn't help but wonder if she was making the right decision.

Was Austin really where she was meant to be, or was she simply chasing a dream that might not even be her own? The uncertainty was a heavy shroud, and Jessica felt its weight as she returned to her seat, contemplating the precipice of her new life.

Tom and Teresa walked into the kitchen, their faces etched with concern as they took in the sight of their daughter, lost in thought at the kitchen table. Teresa approached her, her voice gentle. "Honey, would you like something to eat?"

Jessica looked up, her gaze hollow, and shook her head. "No, thanks, Mom. I'm not really hungry." She slumped back into the chair, her eyes returning to the wood grain that had captivated her attention all morning.

Teresa pulled out a chair and sat down across from her daughter. "We've been watching you all morning, sweetheart. You haven't moved from that spot. Talk to me. What's going through your mind?" Her voice was soft, inviting a confession.

Jessica's fingers stilled, and she took a deep breath, her chest tight with unspoken fears. "It's just... this house feels so empty without Fawn. And I can't stop thinking about Austin. I'm scared, Mom. What if I don't fit in? What if I'm not smart enough for college?" The words spilled out, revealing the depth of her insecurities.

Teresa's heart clenched at the sight of her daughter's distress. "It's perfectly normal to feel scared, Jess. Starting somewhere new is a big change. But you've faced difficult challenges before, and you've always risen to the occasion."

Jessica let out a weary sigh. "Not without Fawn, though. She's always been there for me, pushing me, and now she's gone." Her voice wavered, a testament to the void left by her best friend's departure.

Tom, who had been standing by the doorway, finally spoke up. "Jessica, you are a strong and capable young lady. You've just got to have a little faith in yourself." His words were firm, but Jessica's doubtful expression remained unchanged.

Teresa leaned forward, a new idea brightening her features. "I've been thinking. How about we cancel your flight and book another one so that we can go together? That way, you won't have to fly alone." She turned to Tom, seeking affirmation. "We can do that, right?"

"Absolutely," Tom replied without hesitation, his agreement immediate and unwavering.

But Jessica was quick to dismiss the offer. "No, that's okay, Mom. There's no point in doing that. I know you'll be there on Thursday." Her words were an attempt to reassure them, to alleviate the burden she felt she was placing on their shoulders.

Sensing his daughter's resolve but wanting to comfort her, Tom offered another alternative: "You know, baby girl, no one is forcing you to go to college. If you don't want to go, that's okay, too."

Jessica's eyes met Tom's, her decision clear. "I know, Daddy. But honestly, I want to go. Wavecrest doesn't feel the same to me anymore. Everywhere I look, it reminds me of Fawn, Ethan, and all my friends who aren't here anymore. I think I just need to find my own way, even if it scares me."

Teresa and Tom exchanged a glance, realizing there was nothing more they could say. They knew all they could do was to be there for her and support her as she faced the next chapter of her life.

Teresa reached across the table and took hold of Jessica's hands. They didn't need words; their touch conveyed everything—their love, their support, and a shared strength for whatever lay ahead.

Jessica's hand hesitated on the doorknob before she pushed open the door to her bedroom. The room was dim, the clouds outside casting a somber light that matched the turmoil in her heart. She took a seat on the edge of her bed, her eyes falling on the crumpled covers—a stark reminder of the previous night when she and Fawn had lain there, their eyes tracing the constellations of stars that once glowed on the ceiling.

A pang of longing twisted inside her as she inhaled; the air was still heavy with the sweet scent of Fawn's perfume, amplifying her sense of loss. The room felt different now, hollowed out by Fawn's absence, and the silence only deepened Jessica's ache.

She glanced at the digital clock on her nightstand. It was 11:10 a.m. Her mind painted a vivid picture: Fawn and Anna, seated side by side on a plane, soaring through the morning sky toward Boston. Every minute that ticked by was a minute that took Fawn farther away from the small coastal town they both called home.

Reaching into the pocket of her windbreaker, Jessica pulled out her phone, her thumb hovering over the screen with a mix of hope and resignation. She tapped the screen to bring it to life, but the absence of new messages from Ethan was like a silent echo in the quiet room. Disappointment settled in her chest, though it was tempered with understanding. Ethan had returned to his college life, his days now filled with the bustle of classes and the clamor of campus.

Yet the longing for his comforting presence persisted. She opened their last conversation and reread his morning text. "Love you babe. Call me when you get there," it read. The simple words were a balm, and warmth spread through her as she pictured Ethan's smile, the way his eyes crinkled in the corners when he laughed.

Jessica held the phone close, the glow of the screen a faint light in the dim room. She closed her eyes for a moment, allowing herself to bask in the feeling of love that still bound her to Ethan despite the miles between them.

With the clock ticking towards noon, Jessica felt the urgency to double-check her backpack. Rising from the bed, she walked over to the dresser and retrieved the bag, its weight a reminder of the imminent journey.

Sitting back on the bed, Jessica unzipped the smaller compartment first. Inside, she had neatly tucked away her essentials—a phone charger, earbuds, scrunchies, and a small box of tissues. She nodded, satisfied that all was in order. Next, she turned her attention to the larger compartment, pulling the zipper with a smooth motion that revealed the contents she had carefully packed.

Among the familiar items—a laptop snug in its sleeve and two books for the flight—was an unexpected addition: a thin, white, rectangular box nestled between her electronics and literature. It was a mystery, its presence unexplained. Jessica's brows furrowed in confusion. Had her mom or dad slipped it in there as a surprise? She couldn't recall placing it there herself.

With gentle fingers, Jessica eased the box from its cradle of items and sat back against her pillows, resting it on her lap. The sight of the ribbon neatly tied around the box made her heart skip a beat. She knew that precision, the care with which it was done—there was only one person who would package something so meticulously.

She confirmed her suspicions when she saw her own name written in an elegant script on the lid. The handwriting was unmistakably Fawn's. A rush of warmth surged through Jessica, mixed with a wave of sadness. It was just like Fawn to do something so thoughtful, so perfectly in secret.

Taking a deep breath to steady her trembling hands, Jessica untied the ribbon. She lifted the lid with reverence, as if opening a treasure chest. And there it was—Fawn's sketch, the very piece that had won her the Art Contest. It was a beautiful portrayal of them side by side on their cherished white bench swing, framed against the backdrop of their beloved town. But what struck Jessica even harder was the word "Sisters" Fawn had written across the bottom, its "I" dotted with a tiny heart—a small, personal touch that felt like Fawn's final message to her. The realization that Fawn had left this for her, this piece of herself, hit Jessica like a bolt of lightning.

The sketch, once a mere image on paper, now held the weight of their entire friendship. It was Fawn's world on canvas, and she had given it to Jessica as a keepsake. Jessica's throat tightened, her eyes glistening as she carefully lifted the drawing. Each line, each shade on the canvas, brought back the sound of their laughter, the whispers of their dreams, and the strength of their friendship.

Memories cascaded through her mind—the laughter, the late-night confessions, the silent promises. Tears streamed down her cheeks, and she let them fall, a release for the tightness that had built in her chest.

Despite the pain of Fawn's absence, Jessica felt a profound sense of gratitude. This sketch was Fawn's way of saying she would always be with her, no matter where life took them. It was a promise that their friendship would withstand the distance, a bridge between their two worlds.

Holding the sketch for a moment longer, Jessica allowed herself to bask in the comfort it brought. It was a piece of Fawn's soul, a reminder that their bond was unbreakable. With tender care, she placed the sketch back in its box, retying the ribbon just as Fawn had done.

She carefully slid the box back into her backpack, ensuring it was safely tucked between her laptop and books. Zipping the compartment closed, she pulled the backpack into her embrace, clutching it to her chest as if it could fill the void left by Fawn's departure.

Turning her head toward her knick-knack shelf, Jessica's teary eyes fell on the miniature white bench swing Fawn had given her on her birthday. The tiny replica of their cherished spot brought back memories of that evening they had sat on the old white bench swing.

With the whisper of Fawn's name on her lips, Jessica closed her eyes and let the wave of emotion wash over her once again. "I miss you, Fawn," she murmured, her voice barely audible, a testament to the depth of their friendship and the pain of parting.

Tom strode into the kitchen from the living room, holding his phone in front of him with a quizzical look creasing his forehead. Teresa, standing by the counter as she wrapped a sandwich for Jessica's flight, glanced up at him, noticing the concern on his face.

"Give me your phone, will you?" Tom asked, his voice urgent.

Teresa set the sandwich down and turned toward her purse on the counter. "What's the matter?" she asked, her brows knitting together in worry as she retrieved her phone.

"I've been trying to call the airport to check if Jessica's flight is still on schedule, but I can't seem to get through," Tom explained, his eyes still glued to his device. "Every time I try, there's this weird noise—like a loud hum. I even tried to call Brian, but I couldn't get through."

With a frown, Teresa reached into her purse, retrieved her phone, and handed it to Tom. At that moment, Jessica emerged from her bedroom, catching the tail end of their conversation. The confusion in her parents' eyes was unmistakable.

"What's going on, Mom?" Jessica asked, her voice tinged with concern.

"Shh," Teresa replied with a finger to her lips, her eyes following Tom as he attempted another call.

Tom dialed again, this time using Teresa's phone, and placed it to his ear. A few tense moments passed before he lowered the phone, a look of bafflement washing over his face.

"I can't get through on your phone, either," he said as he handed the device back to his wife. "If I didn't know any better, I'd say our phone is being jammed."

Tom turned to Jessica, his expression serious. "Baby girl, can I use your phone?"

Without hesitation, Jessica pulled her phone from her pocket and handed it to her father. Tom repeated the process, attempting to make a call, only to be met with the same result.

Handing the phone back to Jessica, Tom met Teresa's gaze, his puzzlement now mingling with concern. "What the hell is going on here?" he muttered.

Teresa, ever the voice of reason, suggested, "Maybe one of the cell phone towers is down?"

"Maybe," Tom conceded, though the crease in his brow suggested he wasn't entirely convinced.

Jessica clutched her phone, her mind racing with thoughts of Ethan and Fawn. The fact that she couldn't reach out to them, especially today, made her feel an isolation she wasn't prepared for.

She walked to the foyer, her hand trailing along the wall until she reached the window that looked out toward the ocean. Outside, the boardwalk lay beneath a heavy blanket of clouds that hung low, as if weighed down by the world's collective sighs. The dark and dreary clouds loomed idle across the horizon, and a dull light filtered through, casting a monochrome hue over the seascape.

On days like this, the gray sky seemed to mirror the melancholy in Jessica's heart, each dreary day making her feel as though a part of her was missing. It was unusual for her to venture to the boardwalk under such gloomy skies, but today, she felt an inexplicable pull tugging at her core. It was as if the boardwalk and ocean were calling, beckoning her to find solace in their embrace.

With her mind set, Jessica called out to her parents, "I'm going to take a walk on the boardwalk!"

From the kitchen, Teresa's voice carried a note of maternal caution. "Keep an eye on the time, sweetheart! Remember, we're leaving for the airport at noon."

Jessica nodded, though she knew her mother couldn't see it. "I will," she promised.

She opened the front door and stepped out into the damp air. A chill swept over her, prompting her to zip up her windbreaker with a quick, determined motion. She began her walk to the boardwalk, the route as familiar to her as the rhythm of her heartbeat.

Arriving at the corner of Driftwood Drive and Long Point Avenue, Jessica turned left and began the two block walk to the boardwalk. It was the same path she and Fawn had walked countless times, their laughter a familiar echo along the streets of their neighborhood.

Jessica's mind drifted back to those days with Fawn—their playful races, the banter, and the unspoken promise that they would always have moments like this. But Fawn wasn't with her now, and her absence only amplified Jessica's loneliness and sadness.

Halfway to the boardwalk, Jessica passed the house of her fourth-grade teacher, Mr. Fitzpatrick. The man stood in his front yard, a familiar figure beneath the vibrant flowers cascading from his front porch.

"Good morning, Jessica," Mr. Fitzpatrick called out, a warm smile creasing his face. "Leaving for college today?"

Under normal circumstances, Jessica would have paused, maybe even shared a moment of excitement about her future. But today, her heart was too heavy for pleasantries. She felt her steps slow, but she didn't stop.

"I guess," Jessica replied, her voice laden with a sadness that seemed to seep into the very air around her. Her words faintly drifted to Mr. Fitzpatrick's ears as she continued her way, not looking back, her eyes fixed on the gray expanse before her.

Jessica arrived at the boardwalk, her sneakers making soft thuds on the ramp leading up to the weathered wooden planks. She paused, her eyes sweeping over the familiar sights—the benches where she and Fawn shared ice cream, the railing where they'd leaned and watched the surfers, the stands now shuttered. It was all there, yet it felt empty without the vibrant energy of people and the laughter that usually accompanied the summer months.

The sun hid behind dark, brooding clouds, casting the world in a pall of gray that seemed to mirror Jessica's internal storm. She missed the warmth of the sun on her face, the light that usually danced across the ocean's surface, turning the water into a glittering expanse. Today, the ocean looked dark and foreboding, its waves rising like wild horses, white foam cresting their tips before crashing against the shore with a relentless rhythm.

Jessica found an empty bench, its paint peeling and wood splintered, a testament to the countless seasons it had weathered. She took her seat, pulling her knees up and wrapping her arms around them as she looked out at the ocean. It was empty, too—no surfers braved the tumultuous waves today.

She imagined Ethan sitting next to her, his eyes gleaming at the sight of the turbulent sea. She could almost hear his voice, filled with excitement and that touch of awe he reserved for the ocean's raw power. "Look at those swells," he would say, the surfer in him itching to grab his board and paddle out into the chaos.

Jessica reached up to touch the cross hanging around her neck, Ethan's cross, feeling its familiar weight against her chest. The metal was cool against her skin, but as she pressed her thumb against its face, a warm vibration pulsed through her fingertips, a sensation so unexpected that it made her gasp.

The warmth spread, radiating up her arm and into her heart, and with it came a flood of memories. She saw herself again in the water, on the day Ethan taught her how to surf, panic gripping her as the ocean threatened to swallow her whole. And then he was there, his strong arms pulling her to safety, his voice a soothing force against the roar of the waves.

But it wasn't the fear she dwelled on, nor the cold bite of the water. It was what came after—the two of them sitting on the sand, hearts pounding, when Ethan had looked into her eyes and said those five words that had changed everything. "I love you, Jessica Reese," he had said. She had seen the truth of it in his eyes, as clear and deep as the ocean before them.

Holding on to the cross, Jessica closed her eyes and let the memory wash over her. It was a moment of pure connection, a beacon in the storm of her emotions. And as she sat there, the sound of the waves crashing on the shore seemed to echo the rhythm of her heart—one that ached with love and longing for the boy who had become her anchor in an ever-changing sea.

When Jessica's eyelids fluttered open, she was met with the overcast sky pressing down on the ocean, casting a muted gray over the boardwalk. As her eyes adjusted to the dim light, she noticed a figure approaching—a Black woman of voluptuous build, swathed in layers of colorful fabrics that flowed around her like the petals of a blooming flower. Her dark skin, rich and deep, contrasted beautifully with the vibrant patterns she wore, evoking the warmth of the South. She walked with the aid of a cane, each step measured and deliberate, yet there was a grace to her movements that belied her need for support.

The woman's silver curls framed her face like a crown, and her kind eyes peeked out from beneath a wide-brimmed hat, decorated with beads and charms that jingled softly with each step. Her presence felt as timeless and comforting as the sea itself, an inseparable part of the boardwalk.

"Would you mind if an old lady takes a seat next to you?" the woman asked, her voice carrying the rich timbre of the deep south. "These legs of mine aren't what they used to be."

Taken aback by the woman's sudden appearance, Jessica nodded shyly. "Okay," she replied, her voice barely above a whisper.

The woman lowered herself onto the bench with a grateful sigh, leaning her cane against its side. She turned to Jessica, her face softening at the sight of the young girl's obvious sorrow. "What is your name, little angel?" she asked, her tone gentle and inviting.

"Jessica," she replied, her voice quivering.

"Aw, what a beautiful name," the woman said, her smile revealing lines of a life rich with stories. "People know me as Madam Cora, but you can call me Cora if you like."

Jessica managed a small nod, trying to muster a smile in return.

For a few silent minutes, they both stared out at the ocean, lost in their thoughts. Jessica's heart ached to speak, to fill the void with words that might ease the heaviness within her, but she found herself unable to articulate her pain.

Eventually, Madam Cora's eyes drifted to the cross in Jessica's hand. "I've seen one of those before. It's a rare piece," she commented, her eyes reflecting genuine interest. After a pause, she continued, "May I ask where you got that?"

Jessica looked at the cross, the symbol of her connection to Ethan, before answering. "My boyfriend gave it to me before he left for college. He said it will protect me and keep me safe until we are together again, whenever that will be."

Madam Cora nodded, understanding the depth of Jessica's sadness. "He must love you very much," she said, her voice tinged with sympathy. She reached out, her fingers inching toward the cross. "May I?"

With a nod, Jessica granted her permission.

Madam Cora held the cross delicately, her thumb pressing against its surface. Her eyelids fluttered shut, and for a moment, it was as if she were communing with the cross, her expression serene and knowing. When she opened her eyes, she looked at Jessica with a gaze that seemed to pierce her very soul.

"You're going to receive a gift," Madam Cora whispered, her voice filled with conviction. "Cherish it, little angel, for this gift is only given once in a lifetime,"

Jessica's features were etched with confusion. "What do you mean? I don't understand," she said, seeking clarification.

There was a hint of mystery in Madam Cora's smile as she replied, "You will. So don't you fret none. Everything is going to work out in the end."

Jessica embraced Madam Cora's words, wanting to believe in the promise of a future where she and Ethan would be reunited. But doubt clouded her heart, causing her to ask, "How do you know that?"

Madam Cora leaned closer and rested her hand on Jessica's thigh. "It's your destiny, child. It's your destiny," she answered, her voice imbued with a certainty that was both comforting and enigmatic.

With a gentle pat, Madam Cora rose from the bench and retrieved her cane. She offered no further explanation as she walked away, leaving Jessica to ponder the cryptic message. She watched the retreating figure, her mind swirling with questions and the faintest glimmer of hope.

Her gaze returned to the ocean, her eyes fixed on a dark cloud that hovered ominously on the horizon. It seemed out of place amid the vast expanse of gray, a sentinel in the otherwise uniform sky. Within its dark mass, a speck of light caught her eye, a tiny beacon defying the gloom. The light expanded, growing until it transformed into a brilliant beam that pierced the cloud and shot directly toward her.

The world around Jessica stilled. The wind, once playful and cool against her skin, ceased. The rhythmic crashing of the waves fell silent. It was as if time itself had paused, holding its breath. The boardwalk, the beach, even the murmur of the sea—all faded away, leaving Jessica enveloped in silence and surrounded by a white light that now filled her world.

She found herself in an endless void, a place devoid of horizon or boundary, where the light was not blinding but soothing, wrapping around her in a comforting embrace. It penetrated her, filling her with an overwhelming sense of love and protection.

Jessica's ears caught the distant echoes of children's laughter, emerging from within the light. She recognized the sound instantly—it was the voices of the childhood friends she had grown up with. A flicker of realization stirred inside her. Could it really be them? The thought was impossible, and yet, the laughter seemed to belong to a place where their childhood spirits still existed—untouched by time, forever playing in a world beyond her reach.

From the heart of the light, a figure emerged, walking towards her with a grace that seemed to transcend the very fabric of the surrounding space. The figure's form was both ethereal and distinct, a tall, elegant silhouette draped in flowing robes of immaculate white. Patterns on the fabric seemed to shift and dance, catching the light in a display of quiet beauty. His face was serene, his eyes pools of tranquility that promised understanding and compassion.

As the figure approached, his eyes fixed on Jessica with such profound love that it stirred her soul. She felt as if she truly knew him, as though the connection between them transcended words or gestures. It was as though every moment of joy, every scrape of pain she had ever experienced, was reflected in his eyes.

Jessica looked up at him through tear-filled eyes, recognition dawning within her. This figure was the Spirit of Wavecrest, the guardian of her childhood, the unseen protector who had silently guided her through life's trials and joys. With a touch as tender as a whisper, the Spirit brushed away her tears and placed a comforting hand on her shoulder. He squinted, peering through the luminescence that surrounded them, and then returned his eyes to Jessica with a knowing smile. His voice, laced with playful secrecy, spoke words that stirred her heart. "There's someone looking for you."

Jessica's eyes widened, a plea shimmering within them. "What? Who?" she asked, the urgency in her voice echoing in the stillness.

The Spirit did not answer. Instead, he stepped back, his smile unwavering, his eyes never leaving Jessica's. She watched as the white light began to recede, pulling back like the tide from the shore. As it faded, the Spirit's form began to change, his ethereal presence transforming in harmony with the diminishing glow.

Slowly, the boardwalk came back into focus; the benches, the railings, the closed stands—all returned to their place. And where the Spirit had stood, an old man now occupied the space. His attire was simple: a baggy white shirt and black slacks, his bow tie a stark contrast to the muted colors of the beach. His face bore lines that told of a life rich with experience. His eyes, though aged, sparkled with the same warmth and wisdom that Jessica had seen in the Spirit.

The old man stepped forward and placed his hand on Jessica's shoulder. A single tear traced its way down his weathered cheek as he looked into her eyes with palpable sadness.

"Goodbye, Jessica," he said, his voice carrying the weight of a final farewell.

Jessica could only watch, her heart heavy, as the old man turned and made his way toward the steps leading down to the beach. With each step he took, his form grew fainter, until he reached the sand and faded into the air, leaving behind only the echo of his parting words and the profound sense of loss that now enveloped her.

She remained seated on the bench, her body immobilized by the shock of the vanishing figure. The wind, once a comforting whisper of her past, now seemed to chill her to the bone. It whispered through the empty boardwalk, carrying with it a loneliness that settled deep within her.

Her mind, a whirlpool of confusion and wonder, replayed the encounter with the old man. She couldn't deny the reality of his touch, the warmth of his hand on her shoulder, or the sadness in his eyes. The logical part of her, the part that demanded explanations and evidence, grappled with the surreal nature of what she had witnessed. It was as if Wavecrest itself had conjured up a ghost from her past to say goodbye.

But why? Why now, when the threads of her life were unraveling, when Fawn was soaring high above the clouds on her way to Boston, and Ethan was miles away in Pine Haven? The timing felt cruel, leaving her with more questions than answers, more shadows than light.

As Jessica's thoughts spiraled, her eyes drifted to the ocean, its vastness mirroring her own uncertainty. The waves rolled in relentlessly, each one a heartbeat, reminding her of the constant motion of life, of time slipping through her fingers like the sand on the beach. Fawn's absence was a void, a silence where once there was laughter and shared adventures. Jessica ached to reach out, to tell her about the old man, the Spirit, the feeling of an invisible thread that tied them to this place.

The boardwalk lay empty, a skeleton of summer's past joys, and Jessica felt the sting of isolation. The presence of the Spirit, or the old man who bore his face, seemed like a final acknowledgment of the end of an era—a sign that it was time to let go of the innocence and shelter of childhood.

But just as the weight of her loneliness pressed down upon her, the gray canvas above her began to dissolve. Streaks of blue tore through the monochrome sky, the sun's rays piercing the gloom, casting a golden glow over the world. The transformation was slow but deliberate, as if the heavens themselves were wiping away the tears of the morning.

Jessica lifted her face to the sky, the warmth of the sun caressing her cheeks, drying the remnants of her tears. It was as though the light was answering her silent pleas for clarity, for warmth, amid the cold winds of change. She closed her eyes, letting the sunlight filter through her eyelids, painting her world in hues of red and orange.

When she opened her eyes again, the boardwalk was bathed in a new light. The sun's reflection danced across the ocean's surface, turning the water into a shimmering expanse that stretched to the horizon. The warmth seeped into her heart, rekindling the embers of hope that had dimmed in the face of her uncertainties.

In this moment of transformation, Jessica found a semblance of peace. The Spirit's parting words echoed in her mind, a gentle reminder that she was not alone, that the love and bonds she cherished would endure the distances and the changes. With a deep breath, she rose from the bench, her heart lighter, ready to face the world anew.

Jessica's steps faltered as she walked back toward the ramp that led to the street back to her house. Her mind was still swirling with the encounter, trying to make sense of the spectral visit and the old man's goodbye. But then, a voice pierced the quiet—a voice that shouldn't have been there, a voice she knew as well as her own. "There you are!"

Jessica froze mid-step, her heart skipping a beat. Slowly, she turned, her breath hitching in her throat, and there—at the foot of the ramp—stood Fawn. Her eyes widened in disbelief, her mind struggling to process the sight before her. A flood of emotions surged through her—shock, disbelief, and a joy so intense it nearly knocked the breath from her lungs. Just moments ago, she carried a heavy burden of sorrow in her heart, but now it pounded with an exhilarating rush of relief, as if someone had removed an unbearable weight from her chest.

She hurried down the ramp toward Fawn, her voice overflowing with excitement and disbelief. "Oh my God! You came back!"

Fawn smiled as she met Jessica halfway up the ramp, her voice full of excitement as well. "Yep, I'm back!"

Without hesitation, Jessica pulled Fawn into her arms, hugging her as tight as she could, and Fawn returned the hug with equal fervor. Jessica began to sob, tears streaming down her cheeks—tears of happiness, overwhelmed by the return of her best friend.

As they embraced, time seemed to stand still around them. Jessica clung to Fawn as if letting go would make her disappear all over again, and Fawn's arms wrapped around Jessica's shoulders just as tightly. Their connection, once severed by the cruel reality of distance, was now mended in that single moment.

This wasn't just a hug; it was a reunion of two souls, a shared heartbeat of relief and belonging. For a long moment, they held each other, hearts full, tears flowing, as if the world beyond them ceased to exist.

When the girls finally separated from their emotional embrace, each attempted to regain her composure. Jessica wiped the happy tears from her face, a shaky laugh escaping her as she looked at Fawn with a mixture of disbelief and overwhelming joy.

"What made you come back?" she asked, her voice still trembling from the unexpected turn of events.

Fawn's eyes sparkled with the same tears that had been streaming down Jessica's cheeks. "You know, all the way to the airport, all I could think about was you in Austin, me in Boston, and how hard it was going to be for you being so far away from Ethan."

She paused, taking a shaky breath, as if the weight of her realization had only just settled. "And then, as we got closer, it just hit me. I was like, 'What am I doing? I can't leave my little sister. Not now.' That's when I realized... I can't go to Boston. So, I told Dad to turn around, that I'm not getting on the plane."

Jessica sniffed, a breathy laugh slipping from her lips. "You... you really told him to turn around? Just like that?" She blinked in disbelief, her voice trembling with joy.

Fawn nodded emphatically. "I did. And you'll never guess what happened next!"

Jessica's heart pounded in her chest, barely able to contain her excitement. "What? What happened?"

"We hadn't even gotten that far when Dad got a call from the realtor. It turns out that the people who bought our house had to back out. Apparently, something went wrong with their bank loan, and they can't buy the house now."

Jessica's jaw dropped on hearing the news. "So, Mama and Papa aren't moving to Montana?"

Fawn's smile widened, and her voice filled with excitement. "Nope. Dad says we're staying in Wavecrest and that he's going to look for a new job."

Jessica's eyes filled with another wave of happy tears. "Oh my God! You're not moving?"

Fawn's eyes lit up as she replied, her voice bubbling with excitement, "Nope! And that's not all of it, Jess! Do you remember Professor Hayes, one of the judges at the Art Contest?"

Jessica nodded her head, anxiously waiting to hear what Fawn had to say next.

"I remembered him telling me to call if I ever changed my mind about Boston and wanted to go to UCSB instead. So, I did! I called him, Jess, and he's getting my classes transferred to UCSB!"

Jessica's eyes widened in shock, her hands flying to her mouth. "Wait—what?! Are you serious? You're going to UCSB?"

Fawn nodded enthusiastically. "Yes, and guess what! When I left your house, Papa was on the phone with Professor Hayes and someone at the University of Texas, getting your classes transferred to UCSB!"

Jessica's heart skipped a beat, stunned. "No... no way! You mean I'm going to UCSB too?"

Fawn grabbed Jessica's hands, her eyes lighting up as she bounced with excitement. "Yes! We're going to Santa Barbara, Jess! Just like we talked about!" Her voice bubbled over with joy, their hands clasped tightly as the reality of their shared future sank in.

Jessica's voice broke as tears of joy filled her eyes again. "Oh my God, Fawn! This is everything we dreamed of! I can't believe this is happening!"

"And you know what's even better?" Fawn paused, taking a moment to catch her breath, giddy with the overwhelming news she was about to share. Her eyes sparkled with anticipation as she continued, "Since it's too late for us to get into a dorm, our parents are getting us an apartment. Our very own apartment, Jess! Can you believe it?"

Jessica stood there in shock, overwhelmed with emotion as she absorbed everything her best friend had just revealed.

Fawn beamed with excitement, practically bouncing on her toes as she tugged on Jessica's arm. "We're going to Santa Barbara, Jess! Come on! They're waiting for us!" Her impatience was palpable, her energy infectious as she urged Jessica forward.

With her hand clasped in Jessica's, Fawn led her down the ramp, their quickening steps driven by the excitement propelling them forward. Their voices, bubbling with joy, faded into the distance, carried by the ocean breeze as they left the boardwalk behind. Their laughter echoed in the air, blending with the rhythmic murmur of the ocean, while the anticipation of Santa Barbara and their future shimmered on their new horizon.

Madam Cora stood at the top of the ramp, her eyes locked on Jessica and Fawn as they made their way toward Jessica's house. As she watched, the two young women seemed to blur, as if time were folding in on itself. Instead of seeing two eighteen-year-old girls, she saw two little girls—one, a tiny, petite girl with long brown hair that shimmered in the sunlight as she ran, and the other, a little taller, with long blonde hair, her steadfast companion. Their hands were clasped, their laughter ringing clear as they rushed down Long Point Avenue with the carefree exuberance of childhood.

The sight of these little girls, so full of life and untamed joy, stirred a deep sense of contentment in Madam Cora's heart. She understood that their childhood spirits—their innocence and boundless hope—were still very much a part of them. They carried within them the essence of their younger selves, a treasured time that neither the passage of years nor the distance between them could diminish.

As she watched the little girls turn the corner on Driftwood Drive and disappear, Madam Cora allowed herself a small, knowing smile. Her thoughts wandered to the Spirit of Wavecrest, that gentle guardian who had watched over them, guiding them through the trials and triumphs of their young lives. She felt a profound gratitude for the Spirit's gift—the invisible threads that had woven Jessica and Fawn's lives together and now, once again, brought them back to each other.

In a quiet, reverent motion, Madam Cora reached inside her blouse and felt for the cross concealed there. It was a beautiful piece, identical to the one Ethan had cherished, and now the one Jessica wore close to her heart. Her fingers closed around it, feeling the intricate details and the smoothness of the stones set within it.

Holding the cross tightly between her fingers, Madam Cora brought it to her lips. "Thank you for giving me the opportunity to guide them and help them find their way back to each other. Please continue to bless and protect them," she murmured, her words barely audible above the sound of the waves, but they carried the weight of her heartfelt intention.

After giving the cross a tender kiss, she tucked it back under her blouse, its presence a comforting weight against her skin. Madam Cora took one last look at the space where the girls had been, her eyes sparkling with the knowledge of the magic she had been a part of—a magic that intertwined destinies and forged unbreakable bonds.

With a last glance at the boardwalk, Madam Cora turned and walked away. Each step was measured, carrying with it the grace and wisdom of her years. She left behind the sights and sounds of Wavecrest, the place where two souls had found each other once again. It was a moment that she would always hold dear, a testament to the enduring power of love and friendship.

# Chapter 50

------------------------------------------------------------

The golden California sun cast a warm glow through the windows of Teresa's car as it cruised north along U.S. 101. Teresa's hands were steady on the wheel, a relaxed grip that matched her eased state of mind. After the emotional turmoil of the morning, this serene drive to Santa Barbara felt like a gift—a chance to start anew with a clear horizon ahead.

Anna, her phone now resting in her lap, turned to Teresa, her voice tinged with relief. "Brian finally got ahold of the movers, and they're on their way back. They should arrive sometime tomorrow, most likely late afternoon or early evening."

"That's good. The sooner they get back, the sooner we can get your house back in order," Teresa replied, her voice calm as she navigated the car around a slow-moving vehicle, its driver seemingly lost in thought.

Anna glanced out the window, her eyes following the landscape as it changed from rugged cliffs to rolling hills dotted with the occasional farmhouse. "Isn't it strange how we couldn't get through to you guys this morning? I was trying to call you all morning, and Fawn was trying to call Jessica, but we just kept getting this weird noise. But we had no problem calling anyone outside of Wavecrest."

"I know. The same thing happened when Tom tried to call the airport to check on Jessica's flight," Teresa said, a hint of wonder in her voice as she passed an empty school bus, its yellow paint bright against the backdrop of the road.

"Maybe there was some kind of interference. Sunspots, maybe? I've heard they can mess with phones," Anna mused, her gaze drifting to a car that sped past them, its occupants a blur of laughter and motion.

"Maybe. Whatever it was, our phones seem to be working now," Teresa replied, slowing down as they approached a gentle curve in the road.

Anna sighed, shaking her head in disbelief. "I'll tell you what, Terri, this whole day has been strange. We started the morning driving to the airport, thinking we were saying goodbye for good. We were almost there when Fawn told us to turn around. She was so insistent... wouldn't let up at all. She just kept saying she wasn't getting on the plane."

"That sounds just like Fawn," Teresa said with a grin, understanding the girl's stubborn streak, which matched her own daughter's.

Anna smiled slightly, still in awe of how everything unfolded. "And then, the minute we turned around, Brian got that call from the realtor. Just like that, the buyers had a problem with their mortgage, and they couldn't go through with the deal."

She paused, letting the weight of those words sink in before continuing. "It felt like the universe was telling us we weren't supposed to leave. That's when Brian said we're staying and that he'll just look for a new job here instead."

"It's amazing how everything worked out in the end," Teresa remarked, the hint of a smile playing on her lips.

"It really is, Terri. And Fawn... oh, she didn't waste any time, either. She called Professor Hayes right away, and can you believe it? He got her transferred to Santa Barbara! I swear... that man is a godsend."

"I know," Teresa agreed. "He played a big part in getting Jessica transferred, too. It all just fell into place."

"It did. I mean, what are the chances?" Anna said, her voice filled with amazement.

She shook her head, still processing the events. "Everything just turned completely around after Fawn insisted we turn back. I don't know how, but it feels like things were meant to work out this way."

"It really does feel that way, doesn't it? Like everything just fell into place once Brian made that decision," Teresa mused, her voice soft with wonder. "I guess sometimes life has a way of steering us exactly where we need to be,"

As they continued their journey, a silence settled between them, filled with the weight of their thoughts. Anna gazed out the window, watching the scenery pass by—the fields and orchards giving way to the occasional shopping center or roadside diner. A feeling of gratitude washed over her as she considered the extraordinary turn of events that had led them here. But then, a shadow of worry crossed her features.

"It's just there's so much to do. Getting everything moved back in, trying to settle in again. It almost feels like we're starting over," Anna confessed, her voice tinged with fatigue.

"Don't even think about it, Anna. I told Brenda I'm taking the rest of the week off, and Tom's doing the same," Teresa assured her, her voice strong and confident. "And you know how their buddies are—they'll be taking a couple of days off to help us get your house back in shape."

Anna managed to smile, her spirits lifting slightly at the thought of their friends' support. "You guys are lifesavers, seriously."

"Oh, that's not all. Some people from our church family will be coming over to pitch in, too," Teresa said, her smile widening as she pictured the community coming together. "So, don't worry. By the end of the week, you won't even be able to tell your house was even empty. Everything will be right back where it belongs,"

Anna's smile mirrored Teresa's as she let out a sigh of relief. The prospect of having their friends and church family rally around them made the overwhelming task ahead seem much more manageable. The reassurance warmed her heart, and she settled back into her seat, comforted by the knowledge that they wouldn't be facing the challenge alone.

The car moved smoothly along the highway, the rhythmic hum of the tires on the asphalt a soothing soundtrack to their thoughts. As they approached the sign that read "80 miles to Santa Barbara," the future seemed a little less daunting, a little more hopeful. Their daughters' new adventure was just ahead, and for the first time in a long while, the road ahead felt bright and full of promise.

Teresa found it unusual that Jessica and Fawn, typically as vibrant and chatty as a pair of sparrows, hadn't uttered a word since they left the familiar streets of their hometown. Glancing in the rearview mirror, Teresa's maternal instincts flared with concern, but the sight that greeted her turned concern into warmth. She tapped Anna's leg, a silent gesture to draw her attention to the backseat.

Anna turned around, and the sight that met her eyes caused her heart to swell with a tenderness she couldn't contain. There was Jessica, her head nestled against Fawn's shoulder, and Fawn, in turn, resting her head atop Jessica's, both girls sound asleep. It was a scene that spoke volumes of their deep connection, the kind of friendship that was as rare as it was precious.

With a smile blooming across her face, one that crinkled the corners of her eyes, Anna whispered to Teresa, "Aw, that's our girls."

Teresa, still wearing the smile that had settled on her lips, glanced at the girls again through the rearview mirror. "Our babies," she echoed, the simple phrase encapsulating the ocean of love she felt for them.

Anna settled back into her seat, her eyes lingering on Jessica and Fawn's sleeping forms. "Yeah, our babies," she echoed softly, her voice barely above a murmur.

As the car hummed along the highway, the two women shared a quiet understanding. They were witnessing the end of one chapter and the beginning of another for their daughters. Jessica and Fawn had begun their journey in kindergarten, a time filled with the innocent joys of childhood. They had grown up together, side by side, experiencing the wonders of Wavecrest, the strength of their bond reflected in the endless summer days and moonlit nights.

Now, as they embarked on the untraveled road of adulthood, they would do so together, facing the challenges of growing up and becoming independent adults. The road ahead would be new, filled with lessons and experiences that would shape them further. Yet, their connection, forged in the magic of their youth, would endure. And though their paths will diverge one day, one thing is certain: their childhood spirits will forever be bound to each other... and to the mystical town of Wavecrest.

This book is dedicated to all the Jessicas and Fawns out there.

Enjoy the ride while it lasts.
(Childhood is fleeting—cherish every moment.)

Made in the USA
Monee, IL
19 April 2025

16079065R00340